FYODOR DOSTOYEVSKY, the 19th-century Russian writer, was considered by Gide to be "the greatest of all novelists," and Freud gave him a place in literature second only to Shakespeare.

For mastery of the psychological novel, and particularly for insight into abnormal states of mind, Dostoyevsky has no equal in fiction. Like his protagonists, he knew the height of human aspiration and the abyss of criminality, derangement and despair. The extremes of man's nature, his spiritual duality, the conflict between moral sense and primal urge lay at the core of all Dostoyevsky's major works.

Among these works is *NOTES FROM UNDERGROUND,* the revolutionary short novel which probably has had a more profound effect upon literature than any other of Dostoyevsky's writings. It is presented here with two quite varied short novels, a trio of works which shows the remarkable range of the author's genius.

The introduction which appears in this volume was written for *The Laurel Dostoyevsky* series by Ernest J. Simmons, distinguished critic and formerly Professor of Russian Literature at Columbia University.

Notes from Underground
Poor People
The Friend of the Family

3 Short Novels

by Fyodor Dostoyevsky

Translated by Constance Garnett

With a general introduction by

ERNEST J. SIMMONS

The Laurel   Dostoyevsky

Published by
Dell Publishing Co., Inc.
750 Third Avenue
New York 17, N.Y.

Designed and produced by
Western Printing and Lithographing Company

Cover design by Push Pin Studios

ACKNOWLEDGMENTS:
Notes from Underground, from WHITE NIGHTS; *The Friend
of the Family,* from the volume of the same name; and
Poor People, from THE GAMBLER, translated by Constance
Garnett, reprinted by permission of The Macmillan Com-
pany, New York.

First printing—March, 1960
Second printing—April, 1961
Third printing—December, 1963
Fourth printing—January, 1965
Fifth printing—February, 1966
Sixth printing—June, 1967
Seventh printing—November, 1967

Printed in U.S.A.

Contents

Introduction

by Ernest J. Simmons

At seventeen Fyodor Mikhailovich Dostoyevsky (1821-1881) was sent to a military engineering school in St. Petersburg. Coming from an insecure middle-class family, he lacked the breeding and culture that informed the youthful years of Turgenev and Tolstoy. In fact, Dostoyevsky's background strongly influenced his intellectual and literary interests and the subjects he selected for his novels, which were so different from those of his two great rivals. At the engineering school he compensated for deficiencies in formal education by extensive reading. He began there his life-long habit of sitting up half the night poring over books by candlelight and taking endless notes. In addition to the literary classics of Russia and Western Europe, he also read at this time the lurid fiction of Ann Radcliffe, "Monk" Lewis, Hoffmann, and Eugène Sue. This youthful reading encouraged his taste for the melodramatic and no doubt suggested plots of adventure and crime to which he added his highly original characters and their philosophical dialogue.

By the time Dostoyevsky had graduated from engineering school, he had already decided upon literature as a career. It was a bold step for he could count on little financial support from home. He finished his first story, *Poor Folk*, in 1845, and the happy accident that brought about its publication is one of the best-known pages in the annals of Russian literature: the author had entrusted the manuscript to two young literary friends who sat up half the night reading it; in rapture they stormed Dostoyevsky's room at four in the morning to tell him that his story was "superior to sleep!"; the next day the manuscript was taken to the celebrated critic Vissarion Belinsky, who read it and summoned the author; in a torrent of words Belinsky acclaimed the bewildered but ecstatic Dostoyevsky as a writer who valued truth in art: "The truth has been revealed and announced to you as an artist, it has been brought as a gift; value this gift and remain faithful to it, and you will be a great writer!"

It is difficult for the modern reader to share Belinsky's enthusiasm for this story of a copying clerk's strange affection for a persecuted heroine. In one important respect, however, Belinsky was right. Although influences, especially Gogol's, can be detected, *Poor Folk* opened up a new vein in Russian fiction. The cocky young author wrote his brother: "They [Belinsky and others] find in me a new and original spirit in that I proceed by analysis and not by synthesis, i.e., I plunge into the depths, and while analyzing every atom, I search out the whole: Gogol takes a direct path and hence is not so profound as I. Read and see for yourself. Brother, I have a most brilliant future before me!"

True enough, Dostoyevsky concentrated upon an analysis of the hero's dualistic feelings of humility and the hope and pride that at times inflate his crushed ego. This method of psychological analysis, of preoccupation with the internal world of men and women, was the method Dostoyevsky developed in all his succeeding works; and in the character of the hero he projected the first of a long series of "Doubles," the split-personality type.

From 1846 to 1849, when prison put an end to his artistic career for years, Dostoyevsky wrote twelve more pieces. One of them "The Double," is a masterly study of the split personality, in which the hero's ambivalence is pushed to pathological extremes. "A Faint Heart" is again the story of a poor copying clerk, this time one who not only fails to protest against his miserable condition but actually seeks self-destruction as something he deserves. He is the first representative of another group of characters often designated as the "Meek type. The moral force of meekness and humility became a major factor in Dostoyevsky's theorizing and its importance in his later novels is reflected in such characters as Sonia Marmeladov, Prince Myshkin, and Alyosha Karamazov.

The wretched clerks and poor students of these early tales are preliminary studies of the great characters. From them emerge the two well-defined types—the Double and the Meek characters. Though literary influences and Dostoyevsky's observations of life contributed to the creation of these dreamy, unpractical, and suffering people, it is quite certain that something of his own emotional and spiritual dualism was projected into these creatures of his imagination.

The early tales also anticipate Dostoyevsky's characteristic narrative method, which he developed and refined in later works. The method is essentially dramatic. He likes to begin with the action, avoiding long, careful build-ups. Little attention is paid to chronology or logical sequence. Incidents are described before the conditions governing them, and relations between people are explained before the characters themselves are introduced. The action develops swiftly and often in an atmosphere of mystery.

II

In 1849 Dostoyevsky's arrest and sentence to four years at hard labor in Siberia for participating in the activities of the Petrashevsky Circle, a liberal group that met to discuss political, social, and literary questions, was an event of his life that haunted his memory and the pages of his novels. He served his term like any of the common thieves and murderers among whom he lived in his prison at Omsk. His experiences there played an important part in his future development. The teachings of Christ and the spirituality of the Russian Orthodox Church took on a deeper meaning for him, and in the doctrine of salvation by suffering he learned to rationalize his own misfortunes. His youthful liberalism gave way to a respect for the established order of things and to a new faith in the messianic mission of the Russian masses. Creatively, prison life provided him with rich material for further study of the insulted and injured, the suffering individuals who had interested him at the beginning of his writing career.

Ten years after Dostoyevsky set out for Siberia in chains he was permitted to return to St. Petersburg. For following his prison term he had to serve in the army, in the garrison town of Semipalatinsk. There he married (1857)—unhappily it turned out—a consumptive widow. Now he wished to get the feel of the pen again, for various designs crowded his brain as he built upon ideas for stories that he had thought out in prison. Pressing financial needs that came with his new domestic responsibilities made it essential that he publish.

The planning went slowly as Dostoyevsky struggled with several significant themes which might enable him to reassert the leading position he had held as a writer before his arrest. It is rather curious then that his first published piece after years of enforced silence was a comic short story, "Uncle's Dream" (1859), quite unrelated in subject and treatment to his earlier writing. This was followed by *The Village of Stepanchikova* (also published in 1859), a novelette which he set great store by, but it was coldly received by the critics. In it he picked up again the thread of his youthful tales, and from this point on he never relinquished it. For in the unusual character of Opiskin, Dostoyevsky adds another portrait to his gallery of split personalities. However, the painting is more subtle, the colors stronger, and the image more lifelike than the earlier figures in this group. Opiskin is the first solid evidence of Dostoyevsky's maturing artistic skill and developing psychological powers after his release from prison.

The House of the Dead would have been the ideal work to re-introduce Dostoyevsky to the public. Apparently he was aware of this fact, for it was one of the first projects he undertook after his release from prison and it is clear that he was convinced of its striking literary possibilities. For some unaccountable reason he put it aside until 1859. Because of censorship and other difficulties, the work did not appear in complete form until 1862, and then in his own magazine, *Time*, which he had successfully launched the year before on a platform designed to reconcile the conflicting views of the Westernizers and the Slavophiles, the two ideologically opposed camps in Russian intellectual life.

Although *The House of the Dead* is largely an account of Dostoyevsky's prison experiences, he represents the work as the memoirs of a man condemned to ten years of penal servitude for murdering his wife. The device favors an objective, impersonal narrative, and to this end Dostoyevsky rarely indulges in preaching or moralizing. He is not concerned with a crusade for prison reforms or with eliciting sympathy for his years in chains at hard labor amid filth, lice, and the hatred of low-born fellow convicts. He regarded the work as the artistic re-creation of a terrible experience that crushes the human dignity of man while regenerating him spiritually.

Nevertheless, critics often fail to see in *The House of the Dead* anything of Dostoyevsky the artist, the creator of the fascinating characters of the great novels. Rather it is appraised as a piece of superb reporting and nothing more. Tolstoy, on the other hand, valued it as the best of Dostoyevsky's works perhaps because he recognized in it the objectivity, unity of purpose, and unerring selection of realistic details which he demanded from great literature. The talent of a consummate artist, and not mere reportorial skill, is in evidence in such effective scenes as the convicts in the communal bath and the brilliantly described theatrical performance, and Dostoyevsky achieves an artistic unity of purpose by sustaining the conviction throughout the book that many of these convicts were "perhaps the strongest, and, in one way or another, the most gifted of our people."

However, it is the inmates of this prison and not the scenes and situations that captivate the artist's eye. Though these thieves and murderers rejected Dostoyevsky as an educated man and made him feel like an outcast in a world of outcasts, they never destroyed his optimistic faith in them as human beings. And those he singles out for special treatment he imaginatively apprehends and psychologically analyzes so that they emerge as memorable characters. This is particularly true of the convicts Orlov and Petrov.

In his early tales Dostoyevsky had evinced a fugitive interest in the criminal type. His prison experience deepened this interest, which is reflected in *The House of the Dead,* with important consequences for his later works. Orlov, writes Dostoyevsky, is a "brilliant example of the victory of spirit over matter." Proud and contemptuous of the weaker convicts, he possesses an indomitable force of will that can drive him on to murder in cold blood. Petrov resembles him in that he too is beyond the power of reason; his actions are dictated by force of will. Ordinarily quiet and reserved, for some unaccountable reason he will instantly kill.

This criminal type that acts on impulse, by sheer will rather than by reason, psychologically fascinated Dostoyevsky. He emphasized the same traits in his analysis of other convicts in *The House of the Dead.* The type obviously led him to see a connection between criminality and the dominance of self-will in human nature. He peers into the souls of these convicts and tries to discover what they think, why they committed crime, and how they react to their punishment. Some of the great characters of the novels, especially the "Self-Willed" type, were inspired by that extraordinary mixture of human derelicts who lived in "The House of the Dead."

III

The next four years (1862-66) were among the most troubled but also among the most emotionally and creatively enriching in Dostoyevsky's life. In 1862 he visited several countries of Western Europe. The published account of this trip, "Winter Notes on Summer Impressions," reveals his further drift in the direction of Slavophilism and his hostility to what he considered the destructive influence of European thought in Russia.

Time was suppressed in 1863 because of an unfortunate

article on the Polish rebellion. Although in financial difficulties, Dostoyevsky borrowed money to go to Western Europe again. The ostensible reason was to secure treatment for his epilepsy; actually he wished to try his luck at the gaming tables of Wiesbaden and to keep a rendezvous with Polina Suslova, a young devotee of the new type of emancipated Russian woman, with whom he had already become intimate in St. Petersburg. His luck with both was execrable. But Dostoyevsky's prolonged experience with this strange woman and the mixed feeling of love and hate which she had for him contributed to his conception of the female Doubles, the so-called "infernal woman" of his novels.

Upon his return to Russia a small legacy enabled Dostoyevsky, in 1864, to start another magazine, *The Epoch*. That same year his consumptive wife died and some four months later his favorite brother, Mikhail. Shortly thereafter, as a final blow, his magazine failed. He felt responsible for the support of his stepson and the children of his brother's widow and her numerous relatives. In these adverse circumstances Dostoyevsky's only resource was his pen, and during this period he wrote two long novels and a shorter piece of fiction of exceptional merit besides a considerable amount of journalism.

The Insulted and Injured, Dostoyevsky's first completed long novel, which appeared serially in *Time* (1861-62), is not much favored by the critics, but in it one senses the authentic atmosphere of the great novels. The heroine Natasha, whose emotional dualism compels her to suffer and to make her beloved suffer, expresses this famous Dostoyevskian doctrine for the first time in his fiction: "We shall have to work out our future happiness somehow by suffering; pay for it somehow by fresh miseries. Everything is purified by suffering."

In 1864 *The Epoch* published a remarkable work of about a hundred pages, *Notes from the Underground,* which is a kind of prologue to the five great novels to come and a superb example of Dostoyevsky's concentrated powers of psychological analysis. It also marks an abrupt change in his method of characterization, for the nameless hero, thoroughly aware of his distorted personality, is a profound analyst of his own feelings and those of others. Though he finally realizes that the fundamental opposition of his nature is one between will and reason, he cannot resolve the contradition and thus retreats into himself and stores up spite and venom for all. His conviction of the irrationality of man and his rejection of the reasoned panaceas of the socialists for the ills of society had already become Dostoyevsky's own position. As a piece of self-revelation *Notes from the Underground* is one of the most powerful in literature and its hero is cast in the same mold that would soon produce such thought-tormented, ambivalent characters as Raskolnikov and Ivan Karamazov.

The masterpiece of the period, however, is *Crime and Punishment*, which appeared serially over 1866. It won instant success and is Dostoyevsky's most popular novel abroad. One detects in it a broadening of the base of experience which he now desired to reflect in fiction, for the accumulated happenings of the previous twenty years of his life had thrust upon him the central problem of human thought—the relation of man to the world. Further, the care he expended upon the writing offers some correction to the notion that he was a slipshod author. His notebooks, containing preliminary drafts of chapters, outlines of characters, notes on the plot, trial attempts in methods of narration and much other material bearing on *Crime and Punishment*, print up to over two hundred pages and provide eloquent testimony to his concern for the discipline of great art.

In the planning stages of the novel Dostoyevsky wrote the prospective publisher to explain that it was a psychological account of a certain crime: a poor student, expelled from the university and filled with "strange incomplete ideas," decides to murder and rob an old pawnbroker and with the money aid his mother and sister, complete his education and for the rest of his life fulfil his debt to society, and thus "expiate his crime." At the end of the letter Dostoyevsky adds that "legal punishment inflicted for a crime intimidates a criminal infinitely less than the law-makers think, partly because *he himself morally demands it*. . . . I should like to show this particularly in the case of a well-developed person of the new generation in order that the idea may be seen more clearly and tangibly."

At the opening of the novel, however, Raskolnikov is introduced at the moment of the birth of a terribly destructive idea which is the fruit of his intellectual rebellion against society. In an article he divides mankind into the mass of submissive, ordinary people and the few extraordinary Napoleons who wade through seas of blood, if need be, in order to achieve their ends. Raskolnikov plans to take his place among the leaders by committing a murder. After the crime he attempts to rationalize his deed, and his endless fluctuating between the arrogant pride and humble submissiveness of his dualistic nature causes him to lose all faith in himself and to seek expiation for his offense against society. The account of his regeneration, in the Epilogue, under the influence of the Christian humility and love of Sonia, is neither artistically acceptable nor psychologically sound. In the notes Dostoyevsky contemplated a variant ending—Raskolnikov's suicide.

In Dostoyevsky's eye Raskolnikov had been infected by the rationalistic nihilism of the young revolutionary-minded generation. This is the central idea of the novel, Raskolnikov had substituted reason for life, and only by living life and accepting its suffering would he achieve salvation and atone for his crime.

The secondary characters, unlike those in Dostoyevsky's earlier fiction, play important roles and in nearly all cases are brilliantly portrayed. Sonia, one of the best examples of the Meek type, is inimitably characterized as a living universal symbol of crushed and suffering humanity; the wonderfully drawn chronic drunkard Marmeladov experiences every feeling of degradation in an unequal struggle to preserve his human dignity; and the mysterious, gripping, self-willed Svidrigailov, whose instinctive actions represent a criminal force directed against society, fulfils his development in the only possible way by killing himself. If Dostoyevsky scorns any character in the novel it is Luzhin, the suitor of Dounia, Raskolnikov's sister. For Luzhin has nothing of the intense passion, generosity, and impulsiveness which Dostoyevsky obviously admired in real men and women, as well as in his imaginary creatures, such as in the large-souled Razumihin and in the lovable, wise, but strong-willed Dounia. Much of Dostoyevsky himself may be found in the subtle psychologizing of the police inspector, Porfiry, and especially in his opinion on Raskolnikov's crime and his moral need to atone for it.

All the mature art of Dostoyevsky is everywhere in evidence in *Crime and Punishment:* the nervous tension of the dialogue and the incomparable manner in which he employs it in the art of individualization; the enormous vitality he imparts to his characters, as he does in all the novels about ideas, in which the ideas are literally "felt" rather than rationally or philosophically developed; the creation of realistic scenes of tremendous dramatic power, such as Raskolnikov's murder of the pawnbroker, or scenes pregnant with dream symbolism like the horrifying beating of the horse and Svidrigailov's shocking visions. Finally, there is the characteristic spiritual glow that radiates through all the action of the novel and illuminates the darkest recesses of the minds of these tormented and suffering men and women.

IV

While working on the last part of *Crime and Punishment* Dostoyevsky suddenly awoke to the fact that in three months he owed a novel to an unscrupulous publisher from whom he had taken an advance. Failure to fulfil the agreement meant that the publisher had the right to print everything Dostoyevsky might produce in the next nine years without paying him. With great effort and the aid of a young stenographer, he produced a short novel on time, *The Gambler* (1866), a lesser work which is plainly an outgrowth of his own passion for gambling and his unhappy emotional experiences with Polina Suslova. The next year he married the young stenographer and the couple set off for Europe.

Almost three years passed before Dostoyevsky produced his next novel. He began *The Idiot* in the autumn of 1867 and finished it in January, 1869. Illness, the birth and death of his first child, and financial worries account for part of the delay. At this dark time his young wife was his sole comfort; although she had married a sick, nervous, irritable man nearly twice her age, her endless devotion was equal to the task.

However, there was another reason for the delay. During the critical period of planning the novel, its central idea evaded formulation because of Dostoyevsky's inability to grasp the complete image of his hero (all his masterpieces are novels about ideas which are embodied in the main characters). The many manuscript drafts reveal strikingly the intricate pattern of his lengthy efforts before he arrived at a clear conception of the total personality of Prince Myshkin. The formulation of the central idea quickly followed. Dostoyevsky explained it in a letter to his niece: "The chief idea of the novel is to portray the positively good man. There is nothing in the world more difficult to do, and especially now. All writers, and not only ours, but even all Europeans, who have tried to portray the positively good man have always failed. . . . The good is an ideal, but this ideal, both ours and that of civilized Europe, is still far from having been worked out. There is only one positively good man in the world—Christ."

Myshkin's external appearance, his moral nature, and his actions leave no doubt that the conception of the character was inspired by the figure of Christ. However, Dostoyevsky realized that perfection did not exist in real life, and in order to make Myshkin more credible, he introduced flaws in the otherwise perfect marble radiance of his hero's moral beauty—it is marred by the afflictions of epilepsy and idiocy. For the first time in Dostoyevsky's works a Meek character becomes the hero of a novel. And the idea of the entirely good man which Myshkin embodies is worked out by bringing his Christ-like character into contact with a world of greedy, sinning people. His influence is exercised through the spiritual perfection of his life, by his humility and patient submission to suffering.

Myshkin's political, social, and religious views resemble those which Dostoyevsky advocated in his journalistic writings. He sees a fatal division between the Russian masses and those educated people who, influenced by European radicalism, preach an authoritarian doctrine designed to achieve social equality by oppression and force. To this, Myshkin opposes his philosophy of service, which seeks social harmony through mutual submission of one to another. He identifies this doctrine with Christ and the Russian Orthodox faith. Despite his efforts, Myshkin is doomed to fail in a world of little faith where things of the spirit are consumed in the flame of reality. Nearly all the people he influences are eventually rendered unhappy and he himself lapses into idiocy.

The active story of *The Idiot* is the love of Nastasya and Aglaia for Myshkin. Nastasya is an immense creation of the infernal woman type; her relations with Rogozhin and Myshkin alternate between love and hate. Seduced as a young girl, she suffers from the social degradation of a fallen woman while her spiritual and moral being is dominated by an idea of chastity. Aglaia's passionate and proud nature is not unlike her rival's, and though virtuous and socially superior, she is humbled by Nastasya in that amazing scene where the two women meet in their duel over Myshkin's love. And it is characteristic of Myshkin's meek, sexless nature that he cannot understand why he should not love both women.

Among the many secondary figures some are highly successful but a few fall short of this. In his mysterious and melodramatic behavior, Rogozhin strikes one as a literary device necessary to sustain the action and to provide suspense. Young Terentyev is an early sketch of Kirillov in *The Possessed*. His rebellion against God, which grows out of a struggle between pride and submissiveness in his nature, involves a preliminary formulation of a philosophical problem that profoundly concerned Dostoyevsky in his later fiction. Though Ganya is a pale creation, his father, that "poet of lying," the drunken and humorous General Ivolgin, and his bottle-companion, the amateur philosopher Lebedyev, are excellently drawn, as is the forthright and amusing Madame Epanchin.

After the wonderfully executed first part of *The Idiot*, confusion in the plot and other technical drawbacks mar the artistic achievement. The later parts give the impression of a series of loosely connected and often vaguely motivated dramatic scenes, though these are nearly always powerfully and brilliantly realized. And the conclusion leaves one with a sense of frustration: a magnificent spiritual idea has been refuted in the end by evil forces. Nevertheless, Dostoyevsky's partiality for *The Idiot* among his works rests upon his belief that the spiritual idea had been convincingly embodied in the unforgettable personality of Myshkin, certainly one of the most successfully portrayed "positively good" characters in fiction.

V

While still abroad, in 1869, and desperately in need of funds, Dostoyevsky sent his publisher a novelette, *The Eternal Husband*. This work reveals no particular advance in his creative art, but it does contain a subtle psychological analysis of the complex impulses and motivation behind the thought and actions of a betrayed husband who seeks to revenge himself on his wife's seducer.

Meanwhile, Dostoyevsky's lively imagination was haunted by the expanding design of a huge novel, his *magnum opus*, for in it he hoped to express the full measure of his search for God. The hero of the "Life of a Great Sinner"—so he entitled the projected work—would be guilty of the most heinous crimes, but in his spiritual pilgrimage through the world he would redeem himself and achieve salvation. Dostoyevsky never lived to write this work, but he pilfered from its design ideas, scenes, and characters for his last three novels. One of these was his next work, *The Possessed*.

Dostoyevsky began the novel that turned out to be *The Possessed* in the shadow of "The Life of a Great Sinner." In financial need again, he borrowed certain ideas and the rough sketch of Stavrogin from the design of his *magnum opus* as the basis for a story he could write in a hurry. While he worked away he was suddenly electrified to read in the press of the murder of a young student in Moscow. S. G. Nechayev, leader of a small revolutionary cell to which the student belonged, had ordered the slaying because the group feared betrayal by the victim. The press was full of the details of the crime and the celebrated trial that followed.

Dostoyevsky put aside what he was doing and seized upon this theme of political conspiracy for a short satirical piece on the revolutionists which would bring him the quick financial return he needed. The work expanded, however, and soon attracted into its orbit the novel he had previously been writing. Upon the Nechayev affair he built a huge superstructure which enabled him to connect Stavrogin of the earlier plan with the revolutionary conspiracy. Change followed change and large quantities of draft material were destroyed as he repeatedly started out afresh. No work, he wrote to a friend, had ever cost him so much effort. The first two chapters of *The Possessed* did not appear in the *Russian Messenger* until January, 1871. Desperately homesick and loathing Europe, he insisted that he could not continue the novel abroad. The publisher finally provided him with the money to return to Russia and there *The Possessed* was finished in the autumn of 1872.

The purely human and comic traits of Stepan Verhovensky, the idealized old Westernizer with whom *The Possessed* begins, at once win the reader's sympathy for this amiable creation who imagines himself endowed with profound wisdom. In the fine scene at the end of his life we learn that the religion of the masses, which he had scorned, has vanquished his ancient liberalism.

It is Stavrogin, however, who dominates the novel and yet Dostoyevsky makes an artistic virtue of ambiguity in this characterization—his notes indicate that he deliberately sought to clothe Stavrogin in a cloak of mystery. Though Stavrogin's influence on many of the characters is decisive, he appears neither to understand his actions nor to offer any reasons for them. He is capable of the worst crimes and vilest debauchery and, as Shatov declares, he has lost the distinction between good and evil because he has ceased to know his own people.

The revolutionary conspiracy absorbs the romantic aspects of the novel over which Stavrogin presides, and the characters connected with this stratum, especially Pyotr Verhovensky, Shatov, Kirillov, and Karmazinov, a satiric portrait of Turgenev as a Westernizer, reflect both negatively and positively Dostoyevsky's thinking on social, political, and religious questions. For in many respects the novel is a violent attack on the revolutionists of 1870. Shatov, the reformed radical, presents Dostoyevsky's own ideological answer to the revolutionists. It amounts to an expression of nationalistic faith in the world destiny of Russia which has meaning only as a part of one's faith in the Christ of Russian Orthodoxy. Pyotr Verhovensky, inspired by Nechayev, is the center of the conspiracy, but he and his fellow-conspirators are really caricatures of Russian revolutionists of the time. Young Verhovensky is a criminal and a scoundrel, and the system of Shigalov which he advocates, while amazingly prophetic of the worst excesses of the Soviet revolution some fifty years later, betrays Dostoyevsky's lack of understanding of the revolutionary movement of his own day.

Despite Dostoyevsky's manifest didactic intention, the work is saved from becoming an inflated satirical purpose-novel by the magnificent force of his art. No work of his is richer than *The Possessed* in those essential units of his fiction—his characters. Finally, in no other novel of his is the combination of the ideological and purely sensational elements handled with such literary skill.

The success of *The Possessed* and its attack on radicalism aided Dostoyevsky's appointment, in 1872, as editor of the conservative magazine, *The Citizen,* but this publication proved to be too reactionary even for him and he resigned after a year. However, a weekly piece he contributed to it, "The Diary of a Writer," he later continued as a separate publication, and it has become one of the main sources for our knowledge of his views. Now Dostoyevsky's financial circumstances improved, for his wife undertook the publication of his works and managed the business profitably. In fact, in this last period of his life, the uncertainties of his former troubled existence returned no more. Happy in the circle of his growing family and nationally recognized as a famous author, he continued to apply himself to fiction, the next major fruit of which was *A Raw Youth* (1875).

Of the last five full-length novels, *A Raw Youth* is accorded the least esteem. It lacks Dostoyevsky's special quality of inwardness, and the customary concern of his characters with great moral and ethical problems never really penetrates to the core of their relations to life. The promising theme with which the novel begins, the efforts of the raw youth, an illegitimate son, to win a place in the heart of his father, Versilov, who has cruelly neglected him, is handled with an appealing freshness which Dostoyevsky always seemed capable of invoking in his treatment of childhood and youth. But this theme is soon lost in several others. Dostoyevsky told his wife that there were at least four novels in *A Raw Youth.* This is the principal trouble; the plot is almost strangled by excessive motivation and a profusion of characters, very few of whom are memorable. However, the novel has a particular interest for students of Dostoyevsky's creative art, for in several passages he theorizes openly on the whole problem of emotional dualism which plays such a large part in the psychological make-up of some of his greatest characters.

For several years after *A Raw Youth* Dostoyevsky did not undertake another novel. They were quiet years alternating between the pleasures of family life and regretted trips abroad for medical treatment. Not until 1877 do we find him planning a long work of fiction— *The Brothers Karamazov*. Perhaps no novel of his was so slowly and deliberately written, as though he felt that his immortality would rest upon this work alone. The first chapters did not appear until January 1879 and he completed the last part of it only in November 1880.

The Brothers Karamazov is the story of a crime. Dmitri and his father are rivals for the love of Grushenka. Prompted by a second son, Ivan, the illegitimate son Smerdyakov murders the father, and Dmitri is accused and convicted of the crime on circumstantial evidence. Into this sordid tale Dostoyevsky introduces a tremendous struggle of love and hate with all its profound psychological and spiritual implications, and the whole novel is brilliantly illuminated by a persistent, agonizing search for faith—for God.

Though old Karamazov possesses shrewd insights into the deeper motives of human behavior, he is a monster of lust and debauchery, which finally lead him to his death. The young, meek Alyosha is the only one of the three sons who loves life more than the meaning of life. In many respects, the real hero is Dmitri, who loves life, but its meaning continually baffles him. Ivan, the purely rational being and the very mental image of his creator, is perhaps the most remarkable of all Dostoyevsky's split personalities, a man who is more concerned with the meaning of life than with life itself.

The great dramatic scenes are intensely imagined and executed with superb artistry. All of them lead up with impressive inevitability to the fifth and sixth books, "Pro and Contra" and "The Russian Monk," which Dostoyevsky regarded as the culminating point of the novel. For there, in the famous meeting in the tavern with Alyosha and in the scene of the Grand Inquisitor, Ivan offers his crushing rejection of the world of God which permits the suffering of the innocent. The monk Zosima supplies the answer in his doctrine of the spiritualizing role of suffering as a necessary condition to the forgiveness of sin.

Zosima's answer, however, is not convincing, for his philosophy of optimism is essentially one of stagnation. And there is much reason to believe that Dostoyevsky was himself unconvinced by the answer which he put in the mouth of Zosima. In his own search for God his ambivalent nature led him into the same furnace of doubt that consumed Ivan. His mind was identified with the reasoning of Ivan, who denied God's world with all its purposeless suffering and inequality, but his heart was with the precept of Zosima that equality is to be found only in the spiritual dignity of man.

Dostoyevsky planned to return to this subject in a continuation of *The Brothers Karamazov,* but less than three months after finishing his masterpiece he died (January 28, 1881). Shortly before his death, at the unveiling of the Pushkin statue in Moscow, he delivered an impassioned speech, in which, among other things, he proclaimed Russia's mission of regenerating the world through the universal service of its people and the brotherly love of its Orthodox faith. A distinguished audience of enraptured listeners shouted "genius!" "saint!" "prophet!"

January, 1959

Notes from Underground[1]

PART 1

Underground

I

I am a sick man. . . . I am a spiteful man. I am an unattractive man. I believe my liver is diseased. However, I know nothing at all about my disease, and do not know for certain what ails me. I don't consult a doctor for it, and never have, though I have a respect for medicine and doctors. Besides, I am extremely superstitious, sufficiently so to respect medicine, anyway (I am well-educated enough not to be superstitious, but I am superstitious). No, I refuse to consult a doctor from spite. That you probably will not understand. Well, I understand it, though. Of course, I can't explain who it is precisely that I am mortifying in this case by my spite: I am perfectly well aware that I cannot "pay out" the doctors by not consulting them; I know better than any one that by all this I am only injuring myself and no one else. But still, if I don't consult a doctor it is from spite. My liver is bad, well—let it get worse!

I have been going on like that for a long time—twenty years. Now I am forty. I used to be in the government service, but am no longer. I was a spiteful official. I was

---

[1] The author of the diary and the diary itself are, of course, imaginary. Nevertheless it is clear that such persons as the writer of these notes not only may, but positively must, exist in our society, when we consider the circumstances in the midst of which our society is formed. I have tried to expose to the view of the public more distinctly than is commonly done one of the characters of the recent past. He is one of the representatives of a generation still living. In this fragment, entitled "Underground," this person introduces himself and his views, and, as it were, tries to explain the causes owing to which he has made his appearance and was bound to make his appearance in our midst. In the second fragment there are added the actual notes of this person concerning certain events in his life.—AUTHOR'S NOTE

rude and took pleasure in being so. I did not take bribes,
you see, so I was bound to find a recompense in that, at
least. (A poor jest, but I will not scratch it out. I wrote it
thinking it would sound very witty; but now that I have
seen myself that I only wanted to show off in a despicable
way, I will not scratch it out on purpose!)

When petitioners used to come for information to the
table at which I sat, I used to grind my teeth at them, and
felt intense enjoyment when I succeeded in making anybody
unhappy. I almost always did succeed. For the most part
they were all timid people—of course, they were petitioners.
But of the uppish ones there was one officer in particular
I could not endure. He simply would not be humble, and
clanked his sword in a disgusting way. I carried on a feud
with him for eighteen months over that sword. At last I
got the better of him. He left off clanking it. That happened in my youth, though.

But do you know, gentlemen, what was the chief point
about my spite? Why, the whole point, the real sting of it
lay in the fact that continually, even in the moment of the
acutest spleen, I was inwardly conscious with shame that
I was not only not a spiteful but not even an embittered
man, that I was simply scaring sparrows at random and
amusing myself by it. I might foam at the mouth, but bring
me a doll to play with, give me a cup of tea with sugar
in it, and maybe I should be appeased. I might even be
genuinely touched, though probably I should grind my
teeth at myself afterwards and lie awake at night with
shame for months after. That was my way.

I was lying when I said just now that I was a spiteful
official. I was lying from spite. I was simply amusing myself with the petitioners and with the officer, and in reality
I never could become spiteful. I was conscious every moment in myself of many, very many elements absolutely
opposite to that. I felt them positively swarming in me,
these opposite elements. I knew that they had been swarming in me all my life and craving some outlet from me,
but I would not let them, would not let them, purposely
would not let them come out. They tormented me till I

was ashamed: they drove me to convulsions and—sickened me, at last, how they sickened me! Now, are not you fancying, gentlemen, that I am expressing remorse for something now, that I am asking your forgiveness for something? I am sure you are fancying that. . . . However, I assure you I do not care if you are. . . .

It was not only that I could not become spiteful, I did not know how to become anything: neither spiteful nor kind, neither a rascal nor an honest man, neither a hero nor an insect. Now, I am living out my life in my corner, taunting myself with the spiteful and useless consolation that an intelligent man cannot become anything seriously, and it is only the fool who becomes anything. Yes, a man in the nineteenth century must and morally ought to be pre-eminently a characterless creature; a man of character, an active man, is pre-eminently a limited creature. That is my conviction of forty years. I am forty years old now, and you know forty years is a whole lifetime; you know it is extreme old age. To live longer than forty years is bad manners, is vulgar, immoral. Who does live beyond forty? Answer that, sincerely and honestly. I will tell you who do: fools and worthless fellows. I tell all old men that to their face, all these venerable old men, all these silver-haired and reverend seniors! I tell the whole world that to its face. I have a right to say so, for I shall go on living to sixty myself. To seventy! To eighty! . . . Stay, let me take breath. . . .

You imagine no doubt, gentlemen, that I want to amuse you. You are mistaken in that, too. I am by no means such a mirthful person as you imagine, or as you may imagine; however, irritated by all this babble (and I feel that you are irritated) you think fit to ask me who am I—then my answer is, I am a collegiate assessor. I was in the service that I might have something to eat (and solely for that reason), and when last year a distant relation left me six thousand roubles in his will I immediately retired from the service and settled down in my corner. I used to live in this corner before, but now I have settled down in it. My room is a wretched, horrid one in the outskirts of the town. My servant is an old country-woman, ill-natured from stupidity, and, moreover, there is always a nasty smell about her. I am told that the Petersburg climate is bad for me, and that with my small means it is very expensive to live in Petersburg. I know all that better than all these sage and experienced counsellors and monitors. . . . But I am remaining in Petersburg; I am not going away from Petersburg! I am not going away because . . . ech! Why, it is absolutely no matter whether I am going away or not going away.

But what can a decent man speak of with most pleasure? Answer: Of himself.

Well, so I will talk about myself.

II

I want now to tell you, gentlemen, whether you care to hear it or not, why I could not even become an insect. I tell you solemnly, that I have many times tried to become an insect. But I was not equal even to that. I swear, gentlemen, that to be too conscious is an illness—a real thorough-going illness. For man's everyday needs, it would have been quite enough to have the ordinary human consciousness, that is, half or a quarter of the amount which falls to the lot of a cultivated man of our unhappy nineteenth century, especially one who has the fatal ill-luck to inhabit Petersburg, the most theoretical and intentional town on the whole terrestrial globe. (There are intentional and unintentional towns.) It would have been quite enough, for instance, to have the consciousness by which all so-called direct persons and men of action live. I bet you think I am writing all this from affectation, to be witty at the expense of men of action; and what is more, that from ill-bred affectation, I am clanking a sword like my officer. But, gentlemen, whoever can pride himself on his diseases and even swagger over them?

Though, after all, every one does do that; people do pride themselves on their diseases, and I do, may be, more than any one. We will not dispute it; my contention was absurd. But yet I am firmly persuaded that a great deal of consciousness, every sort of consciousness, in fact, is a disease. I stick to that. Let us leave that, too, for a minute. Tell me this: why does it happen that at the very, yes, at the very moments when I am most capable of feeling every refinement of all that is "good and beautiful," as they used to say at one time, it would, as though of design, happen to me not only to feel but to do such ugly things, such that . . . Well, in short, actions that all, perhaps, commit; but which, as though purposely, occurred to me at the very time when I was most conscious that they ought not to be committed. The more conscious I was of goodness and of all that was "good and beautiful," the more deeply I sank into my mire and the more ready I was to sink in it altogether. But the chief point was that all this was, as it were, not accidental in me, but as though it were bound to be so. It was as though it were my most normal condition, and not in the least disease or depravity, so that at last all desire in me to struggle against this depravity passed. It ended by my almost believing (perhaps actually believing) that this was perhaps my normal condition. But at first, in the beginning, what agonies I endured in that struggle! I did not believe it was the same with other people, and all my life I hid this fact about myself as a secret. I was ashamed (even now, perhaps, I am ashamed): I got to the point of feeling a sort of secret abnormal, despicable enjoyment in returning home to my corner on some disgusting Petersburg night, acutely conscious that that day I had committed a loathsome action again, that what was done could never be undone, and secretly, inwardly gnawing, gnawing at myself for it, tearing and consuming myself till at last the bitterness turned into a sort of shameful accursed sweetness, and at last—into positive real enjoyment! Yes, into enjoyment, into enjoyment! I insist upon that. I have spoken of this because I keep wanting to know for a fact whether other people feel such enjoyment. I will explain: the enjoyment was just from the too intense consciousness of one's own degradation; it was from feeling oneself that one had reached the last barrier, that it was horrible, but that it could not be otherwise; that there was no escape for you; that you never could become a different man; that even if time and faith were still left you to change into something different you would most likely not wish to change; or if you did wish to, even then you would do nothing; because perhaps in reality there was nothing for you to change into.

And the worst of it was, and the root of it all, that it was all in accord with the normal fundamental laws of over-acute consciousness, and with the inertia that was the direct result of those laws, and that consequently one was not only unable to change but could do absolutely nothing. Thus it would follow, as the result of acute conscious-ness, that one is not to blame in being a scoundrel; as though that were any consolation to the scoundrel once he has come to realize that he actually is a scoundrel. But enough. . . . Ech, I have talked a lot of nonsense, but what have I explained? How is enjoyment in this to be explained? But I will explain it. I will get to the bottom of it! That is why I have taken up my pen. . . .

I, for instance, have a great deal of *amour propre*. I am as suspicious and prone to take offence as a humpback or a dwarf. But upon my word I sometimes have had mo-ments when if I had happened to be slapped in the face I should, perhaps, have been positively glad of it. I say, in earnest, that I should probably have been able to discover even in that a peculiar sort of enjoyment—the enjoyment, of course, of despair; but in despair there are the most in-tense enjoyments, especially when one is very acutely con-scious of the hopelessness of one's position. And when one is slapped in the face—why then the consciousness of being rubbed into a pulp would positively overwhelm one. The worst of it is, look at it which way one will, it still turns out that I was always the most to blame in everything. And what is most humiliating of all, to blame for no fault of my own but, so to say, through the laws of nature. In the first place, to blame because I am cleverer than any of the people surrounding me. (I have always considered myself

cleverer than any of the people surrounding me, and sometimes, would you believe it, have been positively ashamed
of it. At any rate, I have all my life, as it were, turned my
eyes away and never could look people straight in the face.)
To blame, finally, because even if I had had magnanimity,
I should only have had more suffering from the sense of
its uselessness. I should certainly have never been able to
do anything from being magnanimous—neither to forgive,
for my assailant would perhaps have slapped me from the
laws of nature, and one cannot forgive the laws of nature;
nor to forget, for even if it were owing to the laws of nature, it is insulting all the same. Finally, even if I had
wanted to be anything but magnanimous, had desired on
the contrary to revenge myself on my assailant, I could
not have revenged myself on any one for anything because
I should certainly never have made up my mind to do
anything, even if I had been able to. Why should I not
have made up my mind? About that in particular I want
to say a few words.

III

With people who know how to revenge themselves and to
stand up for themselves in general, how is it done? Why,
when they are possessed, let us suppose, by the feeling of
revenge, then for the time there is nothing else but that
feeling left in their whole being. Such a gentleman simply
dashes straight for his object like an infuriated bull with
its horns down, and nothing but a wall will stop him. (By
the way: facing the wall, such gentlemen—that is, the "direct" persons and men of action—are genuinely nonplussed.
For them a wall is not an evasion, as for us people who
think and consequently do nothing; it is not an excuse for
turning aside, an excuse for which we are always very glad,
though we scarcely believe in it ourselves, as a rule. No,
they are nonplussed in all sincerity. The wall has for them
something tranquillizing, morally soothing, final—maybe
even something mysterious . . . but of the wall later.)

Well, such a direct person I regard as the real normal man, as his tender mother Nature wished to see him when she graciously brought him into being on the earth. I envy such a man till I am green in the face. He is stupid. I am not disputing that, but perhaps the normal man should be stupid, how do you know? Perhaps it is very beautiful, in fact. And I am the more persuaded of that suspicion, if one can call it so, by the fact that if you take, for instance, the antithesis of the normal man, that is, the man of acute consciousness, who has come, of course, not out of the lap of Nature but out of a retort (this is almost mysticism, gentlemen, but I suspect this, too), this retort-made man is sometimes so nonplussed in the presence of his antithesis that with all his exaggerated consciousness he genuinely thinks of himself as a mouse and not a man. It may be an acutely conscious mouse, yet it is a mouse, while the other is a man, and therefore, et caetera, et caetera. And the worst of it is, he himself, his very own self, looks on himself as a mouse; no one asks him to do so; and that is an important point. Now let us look at this mouse in action. Let us suppose, for instance, that it feels insulted, too (and it almost always does feel insulted), and wants to revenge itself, too. There may even be a greater accumulation of spite in it than in *l'homme de la nature et de la vérité*. The base and nasty desire to vent that spite on its assailant rankles perhaps even more nastily in it than in *l'homme de la nature et de la vérité*. For through his innate stupidity the latter looks upon his revenge as justice pure and simple; while in consequence of his acute consciousness the mouse does not believe in the justice of it. To come at last to the deed itself, to the very act of revenge. Apart from the one fundamental nastiness the luckless mouse succeeds in creating around it so many other nastinesses in the form of doubts and questions, adds to the one question so many unsettled questions, that there inevitably works up around it a sort of fatal brew, a stinking mess, made up of its doubts, emotions, and of the contempt spat upon it by the direct men of action who stand solemnly about it as judges and arbitrators, laughing at it till their healthy sides ache. Of course the only thing left for it is to dismiss all that with a wave of its paw, and, with a smile of assumed contempt in which it does not even itself believe, creep ignominiously into its mouse-hole. There in its nasty, stinking, underground home our insulted, crushed and ridiculed mouse promptly becomes absorbed in cold, malignant and, above all, everlasting spite. For forty years together it will remember its injury down to the smallest, most ignominious details, and every time will add, of itself, details still more ignominious, spitefully teasing and tormenting itself with its own imagination. It will itself be ashamed of its imaginings, but yet it will recall it all, it will go over and over every detail, it will invent unheard-of things against itself, pretending that those things might happen, and will forgive nothing. Maybe it will begin to revenge itself, too, but, as it were, piecemeal, in trivial ways, from behind the stove, incognito, without believing either in its own right to vengeance, or in the success of its revenge, knowing that from all its efforts at revenge it will suffer a hundred times more than he on whom it revenges itself, while he, I daresay, will not even scratch himself. On its death-bed it will recall it all over again, with interest accumulated over all the years and . . .

But it is just in that cold, abominable half despair, half belief, in that conscious burying oneself alive for grief in the underworld for forty years, in that acutely recognized and yet partly doubtful hopelessness of one's position, in that hell of unsatisfied desires turned inward, in that fever of oscillations, of resolutions determined for ever and repented of again a minute later—that the savour of that strange enjoyment of which I have spoken lies. It is so subtle, so difficult of analysis, that persons who are a little limited, or even simply persons of strong nerves, will not understand a single atom of it. "Possibly," you will add on your own account with a grin, "people will not understand it either who have never received a slap in the face," and in that way you will politely hint to me that I too, perhaps, have had the experience of a slap in the face in my life, and so I speak as one who knows. I bet that you are thinking that. But set your minds at rest, gentlemen, I have not received a slap in the face, though it is absolutely a matter of indifference to me what you may think about it. Possibly, I even regret myself that I have given so few slaps in the face during my life. But enough . . . not another word on that subject of such extreme interest to you.

I will continue calmly concerning persons with strong nerves who do not understand a certain refinement of enjoyment. Though in certain circumstances these gentlemen bellow their loudest like bulls, though this, let us suppose, does them the greatest credit, yet, as I have said already, confronted with the impossible they subside at once. The impossible means the stone wall! What stone wall? Why, of course, the laws of nature, the deductions of natural science, mathematics. As soon as they prove to you, for instance, that you are descended from a monkey, then it is no use scowling, accept it for a fact. When they prove to you that in reality one drop of your own fat must be dearer to you than a hundred thousand of your fellow creatures, and that this conclusion is the final solution of all so-called virtues and duties and all such prejudices and fancies, then you have just to accept it, there is no help for it, for twice two is a law of mathematics. Just try refuting it.

"Upon my word," they will shout at you, "it is no use protesting: it is a case of twice two makes four! Nature does not ask your permission, she has nothing to do with your wishes, and whether you like her laws or dislike them, you are bound to accept her as she is, and consequently all her conclusions. A wall, you see, is a wall . . . and so on, and so on."

Merciful heavens! but what do I care for the laws of nature and arithmetic, when, for some reason, I dislike those laws and the fact that twice two makes four? Of course I cannot break through the wall by battering my head against it if I really have not the strength to knock it down, but I am not going to be reconciled to it simply because it is a stone wall and I have not the strength.

As though such a stone wall really were a consolation, and really did contain some word of conciliation, simply because it is as true as twice two makes four. Oh, absurdity of absurdities! How much better it is to understand it all, to recognize it all, all the impossibilities and the stone wall; not to be reconciled to one of those impossibilities and stone walls if it disgusts you to be reconciled to it; by the way of the most inevitable, logical combinations, to reach the most revolting conclusions on the everlasting theme, that even for the stone wall you are yourself somehow to blame, though again it is as clear as day you are not to blame in the least, and therefore grinding your teeth in silent impotence to sink into luxurious inertia, brooding on the fact that there is no one even for you to feel vindictive against, that you have not, and perhaps never will have, an object for your spite, that it is a sleight-of-hand, a bit of juggling, a card-sharper's trick, that it is simply a mess, no knowing what and no knowing who, but in spite of all these uncertainties and jugglings, still there is an ache in you, and the more you do not know, the worse the ache.

IV

"Ha, ha, ha! You will be finding enjoyment in toothache next," you cry, with a laugh.

"Well? Even in toothache there is enjoyment," I answer. I had toothache for a whole month and I know there is. In that case, of course, people are not spiteful in silence, but moan; but they are not candid moans, they are malignant moans, and the malignancy is the whole point. The enjoyment of the sufferer finds expression in those moans; if he did not feel enjoyment in them he would not moan. It is a good example, gentlemen, and I will develop it. Those moans express in the first place all the aimlessness of your pain, which is so humiliating to your consciousness; the whole legal system of Nature on which you spit disdainfully, of course, but from which you suffer all the same while she does not. They express the consciousness that you have no enemy to punish, but that you have pain; the consciousness that in spite of all possible Vagenheims you are in complete slavery to your teeth; that if some one wishes it, your teeth will leave off aching, and if he does not, they will go on aching another three months; and that finally if you are still contumacious and still protest, all that is left you for your own gratification is to thrash yourself or beat your wall with your fist as hard as you can, and absolutely nothing more. Well, these mortal insults, these jeers on the part of some one unknown, end at last in an enjoyment which sometimes reaches the highest degree of voluptuousness. I ask you, gentlemen, listen sometimes to the moans of an educated man of the nineteenth century suffering from toothache, on the second or third day of the attack, when he is beginning to moan, not as he moaned on the first day, that is, not simply because he has toothache, not just as any coarse peasant, but as a man affected by progress and European civilization, a man who is "divorced from the soil and the national elements," as they express it nowadays. His moans become nasty, disgustingly malignant, and go on for whole days and nights. And of course he knows himself that he is doing himself no sort of good with his moans; he knows better than any one that he is only lacerating and harassing himself and others for nothing; he knows that even the audience before whom he is making his efforts, and his whole family, listen to him with loathing, do not put a ha'porth of faith in him, and inwardly understand that he might moan differently, more simply, without trills and flourishes, and that he is only amusing himself like that from ill-humour, from malignancy. Well, in all these recognitions and disgraces it is that there lies a voluptuous pleasure. As though he would say: "I am worrying you, I am lacerating your hearts, I am keeping every one in the house awake. Well, stay awake then, you, too, feel every minute that I have toothache. I am not a hero to you now, as I tried to seem before, but simply a nasty person, an impostor. Well, so be it, then! I am very glad that you see through me. It is nasty for you to hear my despicable moans: well, let it be nasty; here I will let you have a nastier flourish in a minute. . . ." You do not understand even now, gentlemen? No, it seems our development and our consciousness must go further to understand all the intricacies of this pleasure. You laugh? Delighted. My jests, gentlemen, are of course in bad taste, jerky, involved, lacking self-confidence. But of course that is because I do not respect myself. Can a man of perception respect himself at all?

V

Come, can a man who attempts to find enjoyment in the very feeling of his own degradation possibly have a spark of respect for himself? I am not saying this now from any mawkish kind of remorse. And, indeed, I could never endure saying, "Forgive me, Papa, I won't do it again," not because I am incapable of saying that—on the contrary, perhaps just because I have been too capable of it, and in what a way, too! As though of design I used to get into trouble in cases when I was not to blame in any way. That was the nastiest part of it. At the same time I was genuinely touched and penitent, I used to shed tears and, of course, deceived myself, though I was not acting in the least and there was a sick feeling in my heart at the time. . . . For that one could not blame even the laws of nature, though the laws of nature have continually all my life offended me more than anything. It is loathsome to remember it all, but it was loathsome even then. Of course, a minute or so later I would realize wrathfully that it was all a lie, a revolting lie, an affected lie, that is, all this penitence, this emotion, these vows of reform. You will ask why did I worry myself with such antics: answer, because it was very dull to sit with one's hands folded, and so one began cutting capers. That is really it. Observe yourselves more carefully, gentlemen, then you will understand that it is so. I invented adventures for myself and made up a life, so as at least to live in some way. How many times it has happened to me—well, for instance, to take offence simply on purpose, for nothing; and one knows oneself, of course, that one is offended at nothing, that one is putting it on, but yet one brings oneself, at last, to the point of being really offended. All my life I have had an impulse to play such pranks, so that in the end I could not control it in myself. Another time, twice, in fact, I tried hard to be in love. I suffered, too, gentlemen, I assure you. In the depth of my heart there was no faith in my suffering, only a faint stir of mockery, but yet I did suffer, and in the real, orthodox way; I was jealous, beside myself . . . and it was all from *ennui,* gentlemen, all from *ennui;* inertia overcame me. You know the direct, legitimate fruit of consciousness is inertia, that is, conscious sitting-with-the-hands-folded. I have referred to this already. I repeat, I repeat with emphasis: all "direct" persons and men of action are active just because they are stupid and limited. How explain that? I will tell you: in consequence of their limitation they take immediate and secondary causes for primary ones, and in that way persuade themselves more quickly and easily than other people do that they have found an infallible foundation for their activity, and their minds are at ease and you know that is the chief thing. To begin to act, you know, you must first have your mind completely at ease and no trace of doubt left in it. Why, how am I, for example, to set my mind at rest? Where are the primary causes on which I am to build? Where are my foundations? Where am I to get them from? I exercise myself in reflection, and consequently with me every primary cause at once draws after itself another still more primary, and so on to infinity. That is just the essence of every sort of consciousness and reflection. It must be a case of the laws of nature again. What is the result of it in the end? Why, just the same. Remember I spoke just now of vengeance. (I am sure you did not take it in.) I said that a man revenges himself because he sees justice in it. Therefore he has found a primary cause, that is, justice. And so he is at rest on all sides, and consequently he carries out his revenge calmly and successfully, being persuaded that he is doing a just and honest thing. But I see no justice in it, I find no sort of virtue in it either, and consequently if I attempt to revenge myself, it is only out of spite. Spite, of course, might overcome everything, all my doubts, and so might serve quite successfully in place of a primary cause, precisely because it is not a cause. But what is to be done if I have not even spite (I began with that just now, you know)? In consequence again of those accursed laws of consciousness, anger in me is subject to chemical disintegration. You look into it, the object flies off into air, your reasons evaporate, the criminal is not to be found, the wrong becomes not a wrong but a phantom, something like the toothache, for which no one is to blame, and consequently there is only the same outlet left again—that is, to beat the wall as hard as you can. So you give it up with a wave of the hand because you have not found a fundamental cause. And try letting yourself be carried away by your feelings, blindly, without reflection, without a primary cause, repelling consciousness at least for a time; hate or love, if only not to sit with your hands folded. The day after to-morrow, at the latest, you will begin despising yourself for having knowingly deceived yourself. Result: a soap-bubble and inertia. Oh, gentlemen, do you know, perhaps I consider myself an intelligent man only because all my life I have been able neither to begin nor to finish anything. Granted I am a babbler, a harmless vexatious babbler, like all of us. But what is to be done if the direct and sole vocation of every intelligent man is babble, that is, the intentional pouring of water through a sieve?

VI

Oh, if I had done nothing simply from laziness! Heavens, how I should have respected myself then. I should have respected myself because I should at least have been capable of being lazy; there would at least have been one quality, as it were, positive in me, in which I could have believed myself. Question: What is he? Answer: A sluggard; how very pleasant it would have been to hear that of oneself! It would mean that I was positively defined, it would mean

that there was something to say about me. "Sluggard"—
why, it is a calling and vocation, it is a career. Do not jest,
it is so. I should then be a member of the best club by
right, and should find my occupation in continually respecting myself. I knew a gentlemen who prided himself all
his life on being a connoisseur of Lafitte. He considered
this as his positive virtue, and never doubted himself. He
died, not simply with a tranquil, but with a triumphant,
conscience, and he was quite right, too. Then I should
have chosen a career for myself, I should have been a sluggard and a glutton, not a simple one, but, for instance, one
with sympathies for everything good and beautiful. How
do you like that? I have long had visions of it. That "good
and beautiful" weighs heavily on my mind at forty. But that
is at forty; then—oh, then it would have been different!
I should have found for myself a form of activity in keeping with it, to be precise, drinking to the health of everything "good and beautiful." I should have snatched at every
opportunity to drop a tear into my glass and then to drain
it to all that is "good and beautiful." I should then have
turned everything into the good and the beautiful; in the
nastiest, unquestionable trash, I should have sought out the
good and the beautiful. I should have exuded tears like a
wet sponge. An artist, for instance, paints a picture worthy
of Gay. At once I drink to the health of the artist who
painted the picture worthy of Gay, because I love all that
is "good and beautiful." An author has written *As you
will:* at once I drink to the health of "any one you will"
because I love all that is "good and beautiful."

I should claim respect for doing so. I should persecute
any one who would not show me respect. I should live at
ease, I should die with dignity, why, it is charming, perfectly charming! And what a good round belly I should
have grown, what a treble chin I should have established,
what a ruby nose I should have coloured for myself, so
that every one would have said, looking at me: "Here is an
asset! Here is something real and solid!" And, say what you
like, it is very agreeable to hear such remarks about oneself in this negative age.

VII

But these are all golden dreams. Oh, tell me, who was it first announced, who was it first proclaimed, that man only does nasty things because he does not know his own interests; and that if he were enlightened, if his eyes were opened to his real normal interests, man would at once cease to do nasty things, would at once become good and noble because, being enlightened and understanding his real advantage, he would see his own advantage in the good and nothing else, and we all know that not one man can, consciously, act against his own interests, consequently, so to say, through necessity, he would begin doing good? Oh, the babe! Oh, the pure, innocent child! Why, in the first place, when in all these thousands of years has there been a time when man has acted only from his own interest? What is to be done with the millions of facts that bear witness that men, *consciously,* that is, fully understanding their real interests, have left them in the background and have rushed headlong on another path, to meet peril and danger, compelled to this course by nobody and by nothing, but, as it were, simply disliking the beaten track, and have obstinately, wilfully, struck out another difficult, absurd way, seeking it almost in the darkness. So, I suppose, this obstinacy and perversity were pleasanter to them than any advantage. . . . Advantage! What is advantage?

And will you take it upon yourself to define with perfect accuracy in what the advantage of man consists? And what if it so happens that a man's advantage, *sometimes,* not only may, but even must, consist in his desiring in certain cases what is harmful to himself and not advantageous. And if so, there can be such a case, the whole principle falls into dust. What do you think—are there such cases? You laugh; laugh away, gentlemen, but only answer me: have man's advantages been reckoned up with perfect certainty? Are there not some which not only have not been included but cannot possibly be included under any classification? You see, you gentlemen have, to the best of my knowledge, taken your whole register of human advantages from the averages of statistical figures and politico-economical formulas. Your advantages are prosperity, wealth, freedom, peace—and so on, and so on. So that the man who should, for instance, go openly and knowingly in opposition to all that list would, to your thinking, and indeed mine too, of course, be an obscurantist or an absolute madman: would not he? But, you know, this is what is surprising: why does it so happen that all these statisticians, sages and lovers of humanity, when they reckon up human advantages invariably leave out one? They don't even take it into their reckoning in the form in which it should be taken and the whole reckoning depends upon that. It would be no great matter, they would simply have to take it, this advantage, and add it to the list. But the trouble is, that this strange advantage does not fall under any classification and is not in place in any list. I have a friend for instance . . . Ech! gentlemen, but of course he is your friend, too; and indeed there is no one, no one, to whom he is not a friend!

When he prepares for any undertaking this gentleman immediately explains to you, elegantly and clearly, exactly how he must act in accordance with the laws of reason and truth. What is more, he will talk to you with excitement and passion of the true normal interests of man; with irony he will upbraid the short-sighted fools who do not understand their own interests, nor the true significance of virtue; and, within a quarter of an hour, without any sudden outside provocation, but simply through something inside him which is stronger than all his interests, he will go off on quite a different tack—that is, act in direct opposition to what he has just been saying about himself, in opposition to the laws of reason, in opposition to his own advantage— in fact, in opposition to everything. . . . I warn you that my friend is a compound personality, and therefore it is difficult to blame him as an individual. The fact is, gentlemen, it seems there must really exist something that is dearer to almost every man than his greatest advantages, or (not to be illogical) there is a most advantageous advantage (the very one omitted of which we spoke just now) which is more important and more advantageous than all other advantages, for the sake of which a man if necessary is ready to act in opposition to all laws; that is, in opposition to reason, honour, peace, prosperity—in fact, in opposition to all those excellent and useful things if only he can attain that fundamental, most advantageous advantage which is dearer to him than all. "Yes, but it's advantage all the same" you will retort. But excuse me, I'll make the point clear, and it is not a case of playing upon words. What matters is, that this advantage is remarkable from the very fact that it breaks down all our classifications, and continually shatters every system constructed by lovers of mankind for the benefit of mankind. In fact, it upsets everything. But before I mention this advantage to you, I want to compromise myself personally, and therefore I boldly declare that all these fine systems—all these theories for explaining to mankind their real normal interests, in order that inevitably striving to pursue these interests they may at once become good and noble—are, in my opinion, so far, mere logical exercises! Yes, logical exercises. Why, to maintain this theory of the regeneration of mankind by means of the pursuit of his own advantage is to my mind almost the same thing as . . . as to affirm, for instance, following Buckle, that through civilization mankind becomes softer, and consequently less bloodthirsty, and less fitted for warfare.

Logically it does seem to follow from his arguments. But man has such a predilection for systems and abstract deductions that he is ready to distort the truth intentionally, he is ready to deny the evidence of his senses only to justify his logic. I take this example because it is the most glaring instance of it. Only look about you: blood is being spilt in streams, and in the merriest way, as though it were champagne. Take the whole of the nineteenth century in which Buckle lived. Take Napoleon—the Great and also the present one. Take North America—the eternal union. Take the farce of Schleswig-Holstein. . . . And what is it that civilization softens in us? The only gain of civilization for mankind is the greater capacity for variety of sensations—and absolutely nothing more. And through the development of this many-sidedness man may come to finding enjoyment in bloodshed. In fact, this has already happened to him. Have you noticed that it is the most civilized gentlemen who have been the subtlest slaughterers, to whom the Attilas and Stenka Razins could not hold a candle, and if they are not so conspicuous as the Attilas and Stenka Razins it is simply because they are so often met with, are so ordinary and have become so familiar to us. In any case civilization has made mankind if not more bloodthirsty, at least more vilely, more loathsomely blood-thirsty. In old days he saw justice in bloodshed and with his conscience at peace exterminated those he thought proper. Now we do think bloodshed abominable and yet we engage in this abomination, and with more energy than ever. Which is worse? Decide that for yourselves.

They say that Cleopatra (excuse an instance from Roman history) was fond of sticking gold pins into her slave-girls' breasts and derived gratification from their screams and writhings. You will say that that was in the comparatively barbarous times; that these are barbarous times too, because also, comparatively speaking, pins are stuck in even now; that though man has now learned to see more clearly than in barbarous ages, he is still far from having learnt to act as reason and science would dictate. But yet you are fully convinced that he will be sure to learn when he gets rid of certain old bad habits, and when common sense and science have completely re-educated human nature and turned it in a normal direction. You are confident that then man will cease from *intentional* error and will, so to say, be compelled not to want to set his will against his normal interests. That is not all; then, you say, science itself will teach man (though to my mind it's a superfluous luxury) that he never has really had any caprice or will of his own, and that he himself is something of the nature of a piano-key or the stop of an organ, and that there are, besides, things called the laws of nature; so that everything he does is not done by his willing it, but is done of itself, by the laws of nature. Consequently we have only to discover these laws of nature, and man will no longer have to answer for his actions and life will become exceedingly easy for him. All human actions will then, of course, be tabulated according to these laws, mathematically, like tables of logarithms up to 108,000, and entered in an index; or, better still, there would be published certain edifying works of the nature of encyclopaedic lexicons, in which everything will be so clearly calculated and explained that there will be no more incidents or adventures in the world.

Then—this is all what you say—new economic relations will be established, all ready-made and worked out with mathematical exactitude, so that every possible question will vanish in the twinkling of an eye, simply because every possible answer to it will be provided. Then the "Palace of Crystal" will be built. Then . . . In fact, those will be halcyon days. Of course there is no guaranteeing (this is my comment) that it will not be, for instance, frightfully dull then (for what will one have to do when everything will be calculated and tabulated?), but on the other hand everything will be extraordinarily rational. Of course boredom may lead you to anything. It is boredom sets one sticking golden pins into people, but all that would not matter. What is bad (this is my comment again) is that I dare say people will be thankful for the gold pins then. Man is stupid, you know, phenomenally stupid; or rather he is not at all stupid, but he is so ungrateful that you could not find another like him in all creation. I, for instance, would not be in the least surprised if all of a sudden, apropos of nothing, in the midst of general prosperity a gentleman with an ignoble, or rather with a reactionary and ironical, countenance were to arise and putting his arms akimbo, say to us all: "I say, gentlemen, hadn't we better kick over the whole show and scatter rationalism to the winds, simply to send these logarithms to the devil, and to enable us to live once more at our own sweet foolish will!" That again would not matter; but what is annoying is that he would be sure to find followers—such is the nature of man. And all that for the most foolish reason, which, one would think, was hardly worth mentioning: that is, that man everywhere and at all times, whoever he may be, has preferred to act as he chose and not in the least as his reason and advantage dictated. And one may choose what is contrary to one's own interests, and sometimes one *positively ought* (that is my idea). One's own free unfettered choice, one's own caprice—however wild it may be, one's own fancy worked up at times to frenzy—is that very "most advantageous advantage" which we have overlooked, which comes under no classification and against which all systems and theories are continually being shattered to atoms. And how do these wiseacres know that man wants a normal, a virtuous choice? What has made them conceive that man must want a rationally advantageous choice? What man wants is simply *independent* choice, whatever that independence may cost and wherever it may lead. And choice, of course, the devil only knows what choice. . . .

VIII

"Ha! ha! ha! But you know there is no such thing as choice in reality, say what you like," you will interpose with a chuckle. "Science has succeeded in so far analyzing man that we know already that choice and what is called freedom of will is nothing else than—"

Stay, gentlemen, I meant to begin with that myself. I confess, I was rather frightened. I was just going to say that the devil only knows what choice depends on, and that perhaps that was a very good thing, but I remembered the teaching of science . . . and pulled myself up. And here you have begun upon it. Indeed, if there really is some day discovered a formula for all our desires and caprices—that is, an explanation of what they depend upon, by what laws they arise, how they develop, what they are aiming at in one case and in another and so on, that is, a real mathematical formula—then, most likely, man will at once cease to feel desire, indeed, he will be certain to. For who would want to choose by rule? Besides, he will at once be transformed from a human being into an organ-stop or something of the sort; for what is a man without desires, without free will and without choice, if not a stop in an organ? What do you think? Let us reckon the chances—can such a thing happen or not?

"H'm!" you decide. "Our choice is usually mistaken from a false view of our advantage. We sometimes choose absolute nonsense because in our foolishness we see in that nonsense the easiest means for attaining a supposed advantage. But when all that is explained and worked out on paper (which is perfectly possible, for it is contemptible and senseless to suppose that some laws of nature man will never understand), then certainly so-called desires will no longer exist. For if a desire should come into conflict with reason we shall then reason and not desire, because it will be impossible retaining our reason to be *senseless* in our desires, and in that way knowingly act against reason and desire to injure ourselves. And as all choice and reasoning can be really calculated—because there will some day be discovered the laws of our so-called free will—so, joking apart, there may one day be something like a table constructed of them, so that we really shall choose in accordance with it. If, for instance, some day they calculate and prove to me that I made a long nose at some one because I could not help making a long nose at him and that I had to do it in that particular way, what *freedom* is left me, especially if I am a learned man and have taken my degree somewhere? Then I should be able to calculate my whole life for thirty years beforehand. In short, if this could be arranged there would be nothing left for us to do; anyway, we should have to understand that. And, in fact, we ought unwearyingly to repeat to ourselves that at such and such a time and in such and such circumstances Nature does not ask our leave; that we have got to take her as she is and not fashion her to suit our fancy, and if we really aspire to formulas and tables of rules, and well, even . . . to the chemical retort, there's no help for it, we must accept the retort too, or else it will be accepted without our consent. . . ."

Yes, but here I come to a stop! Gentlemen, you must excuse me for being over-philosophical; it's the result of forty years underground! Allow me to indulge my fancy. You see, gentlemen, reason is an excellent thing, there's no disputing that, but reason is nothing but reason and satisfies only the rational side of man's nature, while will is a manifestation of the whole life, that is, of the whole human life including reason and all the impulses. And although our life, in this manifestation of it, is often worthless, yet it is life and not simply extracting square roots. Here I, for instance, quite naturally want to live, in order to satisfy all my capacities for life, and not simply my capacity for reasoning, that is, not simply one-twentieth of my capacity for life. What does reason know? Reason only knows what it has succeeded in learning (some things, perhaps, it will never learn; this is a poor comfort, but why not say so frankly?) and human nature acts as a whole, with everything that is in it, consciously or unconsciously, and, even if it goes wrong, it lives. I suspect, gentlemen, that you are looking at me with compassion; you tell me again that an enlightened and developed man, such, in short, as the future man will be, cannot consciously desire anything disadvantageous to himself, that that can be proved mathematically. I thoroughly agree, it can—by mathematics.

But I repeat for the hundredth time, there is one case, one only, when man may consciously, purposely, desire what is injurious to himself, what is stupid, very stupid—simply in order to have the right to desire for himself even what is very stupid and not to be bound by an obligation to desire only what is sensible. Of course, this very stupid thing, this caprice of ours, may be in reality, gentlemen, more advantageous for us than anything else on earth, especially in certain cases. And in particular it may be more advantageous than any advantage even when it does us obvious harm, and contradicts the soundest conclusions of our reason concerning our advantage—for in any circumstances it preserves for us what is most precious and most important—that is, our personality, our individuality. Some, you see, maintain that this really is the most precious thing for mankind; choice can, of course, if it chooses, be in agreement with reason; and especially if this be not abused but kept within bounds. It is profitable and sometimes even praiseworthy. But very often, and even most often, choice is utterly and stubbornly opposed to reason . . . and . . . and . . . do you know that that, too, is profitable, sometimes even praiseworthy? Gentlemen, let us suppose that man is not stupid. (Indeed one cannot refuse to suppose that, if only from the one consideration, that, if man is stupid, then who is wise?) But if he is not stupid, he is monstrously ungrateful! Phenomenally ungrateful. In fact, I believe that the best definition of man is the ungrateful biped. But that is not all, that is not his worst defect; his worst defect is his perpetual moral obliquity, perpetual— from the days of the Flood to the Schleswig-Holstein period.

Moral obliquity and consequently lack of good sense; for it has long been accepted that lack of good sense is due to no other cause than moral obliquity. Put it to the test and cast your eyes upon the history of mankind. What will you see? Is it a grand spectacle? Grand, if you like. Take the Colossus of Rhodes, for instance, that's worth something. With good reason Mr. Anaevsky testifies of it that some say that it is the work of man's hands, while others maintain that it has been created by Nature herself. Is it many-coloured? It may be it is many-coloured, too: if one takes the dress uniforms, military and civilian, of all peoples in all ages—that alone is worth something, and if you take the undress uniforms you will never get to the end of it; no historian would be equal to the job. Is it monotonous? It may be it's monotonous too: it's fighting and fighting; they are fighting now, they fought first and they fought last—you will admit that it is almost too monotonous. In short, one may say anything about the history of the world—anything that might enter the most disordered imagination.

The only thing one can't say is that it's rational. The very word sticks in one's throat. And, indeed, this is the odd thing that is continually happening: there are continually turning up in life moral and rational persons, sages and lovers of humanity, who make it their object to live all their lives as morally and rationally as possible, to be, so to speak, a light to their neighbours simply in order to show them that it is possible to live morally and rationally in this world. And yet we all know that those very people sooner or later have been false to themselves, playing some queer trick, often a most unseemly one. Now I ask you: what can be expected of man since he is a being endowed with such strange qualities? Shower upon him every earthly blessing, drown him in a sea of happiness, so that nothing but bubbles of bliss can be seen on the surface; give him economic prosperity, such that he should have nothing else to do but sleep, eat cakes and busy himself with the continuation of his species, and even then out of sheer ingratitude, sheer spite, man would play you some nasty trick. He would even risk his cakes and would deliberately desire the most fatal rubbish, the most uneconomical absurdity, simply to introduce into all this positive good sense his fatal fantastic element. It is just his fantastic dreams, his vulgar folly, that he will desire to retain, simply in order to prove to himself—as though that were so necessary—that men still are men and not the keys of a piano, which the laws of nature threaten to control so completely that soon one will be able to desire nothing but by the calendar. And that is not all: even if man really were nothing but a piano-key, even if this were proved to him by natural science and mathematics, even then he would not become reasonable, but would purposely do something perverse out of simple ingratitude, simply to gain his point. And if he does not find means he will contrive destruction and chaos, will contrive sufferings of all sorts, only to gain his point! He will launch a curse upon the world, and as only man can curse (it is his privilege, the primary distinction between him and other animals) it may be by his curse alone he will attain his object—that is, convince himself that he is a man and not a piano-key! If you say that all this, too, can be calculated and tabulated—chaos and darkness and curses, so that the mere possibility of calculating it all beforehand would stop it all, and reason would reassert itself—then man would purposely go mad in order to be rid of reason and gain his point! I believe in it, I answer for it, for the whole work of man really seems to consist in nothing but proving to himself every minute that he is a man and not a piano-key! It may be at the cost of his skin, it may be by cannibalism! And this being so, can one help being tempted to rejoice that it has not yet come off, and that desire still depends on something we don't know?

You will scream at me (that is, if you condescend to do so) that no one is touching my free will, that all they are concerned with is that my will should of itself, of its own free will, coincide with my own normal interests, with the laws of nature and arithmetic.

Good heavens, gentlemen, what sort of free will is left when we come to tabulation and arithmetic, when it will all be a case of twice two makes four? Twice two makes four without my will. As if free will meant that!

IX

Gentlemen, I am joking, and I know myself that my jokes are not brilliant, but you know one can't take everything as a joke. I am, perhaps, jesting against the grain. Gentlemen, I am tormented by questions; answer them for me. You, for instance, want to cure men of their old habits and reform their will in accordance with science and good sense. But how do you know, not only that it is possible, but also that it is *desirable*, to reform man in that way? And what leads you to the conclusion that man's inclinations *need* reforming? In short, how do you know that such a reformation will be a benefit to man? And to go to the root of the matter, why are you so positively convinced that not to act against his real normal interests guaranteed by the conclusions of reason and arithmetic is certainly always advantageous for man and must always be a law for mankind? So far, you know, this is only your supposition. It may be the law of logic, but not the law of humanity. You think, gentlemen, perhaps that I am mad? Allow me to defend myself. I agree that man is pre-eminently a creative animal, predestined to strive consciously for an object and to engage in engineering—that is, incessantly and eternally to make new roads, *wherever they may lead.* But the reason why he wants sometimes to go off at a tangent may just be that he is *predestined* to make the road, and perhaps, too, that however stupid the "direct" practical man may be, the thought sometimes will occur to him that the road almost always does lead *somewhere,* and that the destination it leads to is less important than the process of making it, and that the chief thing is to save the well-conducted child from despising engineering, and so giving way to the fatal idleness, which, as we all know, is the mother of all the vices. Man likes to make roads and to create, that is a fact beyond dispute. But why has he such a passionate love for destruction and chaos also? Tell me that! But on that point I want to say a couple of words myself. May it not be that he loves chaos and destruction (there can be no disputing that he does sometimes love it) because he is instinctively afraid of attaining his object and completing the edifice he is constructing? Who knows, perhaps he only loves that edifice from a distance, and is by no means in love with it at close quarters; perhaps he only loves building it and does not want to live in it, but will leave it, when completed, for the use of *les animaux domestiques*—such as the ants, the sheep, and so on. Now the ants have quite a different taste. They have a marvellous edifice of that pattern which endures for ever—the ant-heap.

With the ant-heap the respectable race of ants began and with the ant-heap they will probably end, which does the greatest credit to their perseverance and good sense. But man is a frivolous and incongruous creature, and perhaps, like a chess-player, loves the process of the game, not the end of it. And who knows (there is no saying with certainty), perhaps the only goal on earth to which mankind is striving lies in this incessant process of attaining, in other words, in life itself, and not in the thing to be attained, which must always be expressed as a formula, as positive as twice two makes four, and such positiveness is not life, gentlemen, but is the beginning of death. Anyway, man has always been afraid of this mathematical certainty, and I am afraid of it now. Granted that man does nothing but seek that mathematical certainty, he traverses oceans, sacrifices his life in the quest, but to succeed, really to find it, he dreads, I assure you. He feels that when he has found it there will be nothing for him to look for. When workmen have finished their work they do at least receive their pay, they go to the tavern, then they are taken to the police-station—and there is occupation for a week. But where can man go? Anyway, one can observe a certain awkwardness about him when he has attained such objects. He loves the process of attaining, but does not quite like to have attained, and that, of course, is very absurd. In fact, man is a comical creature; there seems to be a kind of jest in it all. But yet mathematical certainty is, after all, something insufferable. Twice two makes four seems to me simply a piece of insolence. Twice two makes four is a pert coxcomb who stands with arms akimbo barring your path and spitting. I admit that twice two makes four is an excellent thing, but if we are to give everything its due, twice two makes five is sometimes a very charming thing too.

And why are you so firmly, so triumphantly, convinced that only the normal and the positive—in other words, only what is conducive to welfare—is for the advantage of man? Is not reason in error as regards advantage? Does not man, perhaps, love something besides well-being? Perhaps he is just as fond of suffering? Perhaps suffering is just as great a benefit to him as well-being? Man is sometimes extraordinarily, passionately, in love with suffering, and that is a fact. There is no need to appeal to universal history to prove that; only ask yourself, if you are a man and have lived at all. As far as my personal opinion is concerned, to care only for well-being seems to me positively ill-bred. Whether it's good or bad, it is sometimes very pleasant, too, to smash things. I hold no brief for suffering nor for well-being either. I am standing for . . . my caprice, and for its being guaranteed to me when necessary. Suffering would be out of place in vaudevilles, for instance; I know that. In the "Palace of Crystal" it is unthinkable; suffering means doubt, negation, and what would be the good of a "palace of crystal" if there could be any doubt about it? And yet I think man will never renounce real suffering, that is, destruction and chaos. Why, suffering is the sole origin of consciousness. Though I did lay it down at the beginning that consciousness is the greatest misfortune for man, yet I know man prizes it and would not give it up for any satisfaction. Consciousness, for instance, is infinitely superior to twice two makes four. Once you have mathematical certainty there is nothing left to do or to understand. There will be nothing left but to bottle up your five senses and plunge into contemplation. While if you stick to consciousness, even though the same result is attained, you can at least flog yourself at times, and that will, at any rate, liven you up. Reactionary as it is, corporal punishment is better than nothing.

X

You believe in a palace of crystal that can never be destroyed—a palace at which one will not be able to put out one's tongue or make a long nose on the sly. And perhaps that is just why I am afraid of this edifice that it is of crystal and can never be destroyed and that one cannot put one's tongue out at it even on the sly.

You see, if it were not a palace, but a hen-house, I might creep into it to avoid getting wet, and yet I would not call the hen-house a palace out of gratitude to it for keeping me dry. You laugh and say that in such circumstances a hen-house is as good as a mansion. Yes, I answer, if one had to live simply to keep out of the rain.

But what is to be done if I have taken it into my head that that is not the only object in life, and that if one must live one had better live in a mansion. That is my choice, my desire. You will only eradicate it when you have changed my preference. Well, do change it, allure me with something else, give me another ideal. But meanwhile I will not take a hen-house for a mansion. The palace of crystal may be an idle dream, it may be that it is inconsistent with the laws of nature and that I have invented it only through my own stupidity, through the old-fashioned irrational habits of my generation. But what does it matter to me that it is inconsistent? That makes no difference since it exists in my desires, or rather exists as long as my desires exist. Perhaps you are laughing again? Laugh away; I will put up with any mockery rather than pretend that I am satisfied when I am hungry. I know, anyway, that I will not be put off with a compromise, with a recurring zero, simply because it is consistent with the laws of nature and actually exists. I will not accept as the crown of my desires a block of buildings with tenements for the poor on a lease of a thousand years, and perhaps with a sign-board of a dentist hanging out. Destroy my desires, eradicate my ideals, show me something better, and I will follow you. You will say, perhaps, that is not worth your trouble; but in that case I can give you the same answer. We are discussing things seriously; but if you won't deign to give me your attention, I will drop your acquaintance. I can retreat into my underground hole.

But while I am alive and have desires I would rather my hand were withered off than bring one brick to such a building! Don't remind me that I have just rejected the palace of crystal for the sole reason that one cannot put out one's tongue at it. I did not say that because I am so fond of putting my tongue out. Perhaps the thing I resented was, that of all your edifices there has not been one at which one could not put out one's tongue. On the contrary, I would let my tongue be cut off out of gratitude if things could be so arranged that I should lose all desire to put it out. It is not my fault that things cannot be so arranged, and that one must be satisfied with model flats. Then why am I made with such desires? Can I have been constructed simply in order to come to the conclusion that all my construction is a cheat? Can this be my whole purpose? I do not believe it.

But do you know what: I am convinced that we underground folk ought to be kept on a curb. Though we may sit forty years underground without speaking, when we do come out into the light of day and break out we talk and talk and talk. . . .

XI

The long and the short of it is, gentlemen, that it is better to do nothing! Better conscious inertia! And so hurrah for underground! Though I have said that I envy the normal man to the last drop of my bile, yet I should not care to be in his place such as he is now (though I shall not cease envying him). No, no; anyway the underground life is more advantageous. There, at any rate, one can . . . Oh, but even now I am lying! I am lying because I know myself that it is not underground that is better, but something different, quite different, for which I am thirsting, but which I cannot find! Damn underground!

I will tell you another thing that would be better, and that is, if I myself believed in anything of what I have just written. I swear to you, gentlemen, there is not one thing, not one word of what I have written, that I really believe. That is, I believe it, perhaps, but at the same time I feel and suspect that I am lying like a cobbler.

"Then why have you written all this?" you will say to me. me.

"I ought to put you underground for forty years without anything to do and then come to you in your cellar, to find out what stage you have reached! How can a man be left with nothing to do for forty years?

"Isn't that shameful, isn't that humiliating?" you will say, perhaps, wagging your heads contemptuously. "You thirst for life and try to settle the problems of life by a logical tangle. And how persistent, how insolent are your sallies, and at the same time what a scare you are in! You talk nonsense and are pleased with it; you say impudent things and are in continual alarm and apologizing for them. You declare that you are afraid of nothing and at the same time try to ingratiate yourself in our good opinion. You declare that you are gnashing your teeth and at the same time you try to be witty so as to amuse us. You know that your witticisms are not witty, but you are evidently well satisfied with their literary value. You may, perhaps, have really suffered, but you have no respect for your own suffering. You may have sincerity, but you have no modesty; out of the pettiest vanity you expose your sincerity to publicity and ignominy. You doubtlessly mean to say something, but hide your last word through fear, because you have not the resolution to utter it, and only have a cowardly impudence. You boast of consciousness, but you are not sure of your ground, for though your mind works, yet your heart is darkened and corrupt, and you cannot have a full, genuine consciousness without a pure heart. And how intrusive you are, how you insist and grimace! Lies, lies, lies!"

Of course I have myself made up all the things you say. That, too, is from underground. I have been for forty years listening to you through a crack under the floor. I have invented them myself, there was nothing else I could invent. It is no wonder that I have learned it by heart and it has taken a literary form. . . .

But can you really be so credulous as to think that I will print all this and give it to you to read too? And another problem: why do I call you "gentlemen," why do I address you as though you really were my readers? Such confessions as I intend to make are never printed nor given to other people to read. Anyway, I am not strong-minded enough for that, and I don't see why I should be. But you see a fancy has occurred to me and I want to realize it at all costs. Let me explain.

Every man has reminiscences which he would not tell to every one, but only to his friends. He has other matters in his mind which he would not reveal even to his friends, but only to himself, and that in secret. But there are other things which a man is afraid to tell even to himself, and every decent man has a number of such things stored away in his mind. The more decent he is, the greater the number of such things in his mind. Anyway, I have only lately determined to remember some of my early adventures. Till now I have always avoided them, even with a certain uneasiness. Now, when I am not only recalling them, but have actually decided to write an account of them, I want to try the experiment whether one can, even with oneself, be perfectly open and not take fright at the whole truth. I will observe, in parenthesis, that Heine says that a true autobiography is almost an impossibility, and that man is bound to lie about himself. He considers that Rousseau certainly told lies about himself in his confessions, and even intentionally lied, out of vanity. I am convinced that Heine is right; I quite understand how sometimes one may, out of sheer vanity, attribute regular crimes to oneself, and indeed I can very well conceive that kind of vanity. But Heine judged of people who made their confessions to the public. I write only for myself, and I wish to declare once and for all that if I write as though I were addressing readers, that is simply because it is easier for me to write in that form. It is a form, an empty form—I shall never have readers. I have made this plain already. . . .

I don't wish to be hampered by any restrictions in the compilation of my notes. I shall not attempt any system or method. I will jot things down as I remember them.

But here, perhaps, some one will catch at the word and ask me: if you really don't reckon on readers, why do you make such compacts with yourself—and on paper too— that is, that you won't attempt any system or method, that you jot things down as you remember them, and so on, and so on? Why are you explaining? Why do you apologize?

Well, there it is, I answer.

There is a whole psychology in all this, though. Perhaps it is simply that I am a coward. And perhaps that I purposely imagine an audience before me in order that I may be more dignified while I write. There are perhaps thousands of reasons. Again, what is my object precisely in writing? If it is not for the benefit of the public why should I not simply recall these incidents in my own mind without putting them on paper?

Quite so; but yet it is more imposing on paper. There is something more impressive in it; I shall be better able to criticize myself and improve my style. Besides, I shall perhaps obtain actual relief from writing. To-day, for instance, I am particularly oppressed by one memory of a distant past. It came back vividly to my mind a few days ago, and has remained haunting me like an annoying tune that one cannot get rid of. And yet I must get rid of it somehow. I have hundreds of such reminiscences; but at times some one stands out from the hundred and oppresses me. For some reason I believe that if I write it down I should get rid of it. Why not try?

Besides, I am bored, and I never have anything to do. Writing will be a sort of work. They say work makes man kind-hearted and honest. Well, here is a chance for me, anyway.

Snow is falling to-day, yellow and dingy. It fell yesterday, too, and a few days ago. I fancy it is the wet snow that has reminded me of that incident which I cannot shake off now. And so let it be a story apropos of the falling snow.

PART 2

Apropos of the Wet Snow

When from dark error's subjugation
My words of passionate exhortation
    Had wrenched thy fainting spirit free;
And writhing prone in thine affliction
Thou didst recall with malediction
    The vice that had encompassed thee:
And when thy slumbering conscience, fretting
    By recollection's torturing flame,
Thou didst reveal the hideous setting
    Of thy life's current ere I came:
When suddenly I saw thee sicken,
    And weeping, hide thine anguished face,

> Revolted, maddened, horror-stricken,
> At memories of foul disgrace.
>   NEKRASSOV *(translated by Juliet Soskice)*

I

At that time I was only twenty-four. My life was even then gloomy, ill-regulated, and as solitary as that of a savage. I made friends with no one and positively avoided talking, and buried myself more and more in my hole. At work in the office I never looked at any one, and I was perfectly well aware that my companions looked upon me, not only as a queer fellow, but even looked upon me—I always fancied this—with a sort of loathing. I sometimes wondered why it was that nobody except me fancied that he was looked upon with aversion. One of the clerks had a most repulsive, pock-marked face, which looked positively villainous. I believe I should not have dared to look at any one with such an unsightly countenance. Another had such a very dirty old uniform that there was an unpleasant odour in his proximity. Yet not one of these gentlemen showed the slightest self-consciousness—either about their clothes or their countenance or their character in any way. Neither of them ever imagined that they were looked at with repulsion; if they had imagined it they would not have minded—so long as their superiors did not look at them in that way. It is clear to me now that, owing to my unbounded vanity and to the high standard I set for myself, I often looked at myself with furious discontent, which verged on loathing, and so I inwardly attributed the same feeling to every one. I hated my face, for instance: I thought it disgusting, and even suspected that there was something base in my expression, and so every day when I turned up at the office I tried to behave as independently as possible, and to assume a lofty expression, so that I might not be suspected of being abject. "My face may be ugly," I thought, "but let it be lofty, expressive, and, above all, *extremely* intelligent." But I was positively and painfully certain that it was impossible for my countenance ever to express those qualities.

And what was worst of all, I thought it actually stupid-looking, and I would have been quite satisfied if I could have looked intelligent. In fact, I would even have put up with looking base if, at the same time, my face could have been thought strikingly intelligent.

Of course, I hated my fellow-clerks one and all, and I despised them all, yet at the same time I was, as it were, afraid of them. In fact, it happened at times that I thought more highly of them than of myself. It somehow happened quite suddenly that I alternated between despising them and thinking them superior to myself. A cultivated and decent man cannot be vain without setting a fearfully high standard for himself, and without despising and almost hating himself at certain moments. But whether I despised them or thought them superior I dropped my eyes almost every time I met any one. I even made experiments whether I could face So-and-So's looking at me, and I was always the first to drop my eyes. This worried me to distraction. I had a sickly dread, too, of being ridiculous, and so had a slavish passion for the conventional in everything external. I loved to fall into the common rut, and had a whole-hearted terror of any kind of eccentricity in myself. But how could I live up to it? I was morbidly sensitive, as a man of our age should be. They were all stupid, and as like one another as so many sheep. Perhaps I was the only one in the office who fancied that I was a coward and a slave, and I fancied it just because I was more highly developed. But it was not only that I fancied it, it really was so. I was a coward and a slave. I say this without the slightest embarrassment. Every decent man of our age must be a coward and a slave. That is his normal condition. Of that I am firmly persuaded. He is made and constructed to that very end. And not only at the present time owing to some casual circumstances, but always, at all times, a decent man is bound to be a coward and a slave. It is the law of nature for all decent people all over the earth. If any one of them happens to be valiant about something, he need not be comforted nor carried away by that; he would show the white feather just the same before something else. That is how it invariably and inevitably ends. Only donkeys and mules are valiant, and they only till they are pushed up to the wall. It is not worth while to pay attention to them, for they really are of no consequence.

Another circumstance, too, worried me in those days: that there was no one like me and I was unlike any one else. "I am alone and they are *every one*," I thought—and pondered.

From that it is evident that I was still a youngster.

The very opposite sometimes happened. It was loathsome sometimes to go to the office; things reached such a point that I often came home ill. But all at once, apropos of nothing, there would come a phase of skepticism and indifference (everything happened in phases to me), and I would laugh myself at my intolerance and fastidiousness, I would reproach myself with being *romantic*. At one time I was unwilling to speak to any one, while at other times I would not only talk, but go to the length of contemplating making friends with them. All my fastidiousness would suddenly, for no rhyme or reason, vanish. Who knows, perhaps I never had really had it, and it had simply been affected, and got out of books. I have not decided that question even now. Once I quite made friends with them, visited their homes, played preference, drank vodka, talked of promotions. . . . But here let me make a digression.

We Russians, speaking generally, have never had those foolish transcendental "romantics"—German, and still more French—on whom nothing produces any effect; if there were an earthquake, if all France perished at the barricades, they would still be the same, they would not even have the decency to affect a change, but would still go on singing their transcendental songs to the hour of their death, because they are fools. We, in Russia, have no fools; that is well known. That is what distinguishes us from foreign lands. Consequently these transcendental natures are not found amongst us in their pure form. The idea that they are is due to our "realistic" journalists and critics of that day, always on the lookout for Kostanzhoglos and Uncle Pyotr Ivanitches and foolishly accepting them as our ideal; they have slandered our romantics, taking them for the same transcendental sort as in Germany or France. On the contrary, the characteristics of our "romantics" are absolutely and directly opposed to the transcendental European type, and no European standard can be applied to them. (Allow me to make use of this word "romantic"—an old-fashioned and much respected word which has done good service and is familiar to all.) The characteristics of our romantics are to understand everything, *to see everything and to see it often incomparably more clearly than our most realistic minds see it;* to refuse to accept anyone or anything, but at the same time not to despise anything; to give way, to yield, from policy; never to lose sight of a useful practical object (such as rent-free quarters at the government expense, pensions, decorations), to keep their eye on that object through all the enthusiasms and volumes of lyrical poems, and at the same time to preserve "the good and the beautiful" inviolate within them to the hour of their death, and to preserve themselves also, incidentally, like some precious jewel wrapped in cotton wool if only for the benefit of "the good and the beautiful." Our "romantic" is a man of great breadth and the greatest rogue of all our rogues, I assure you. . . . I can assure you from experience, indeed. Of course, that is, if he is intelligent. But what am I saying! The romantic is always intelligent, and I only meant to observe that although we have had foolish romantics they don't count, and they were only so because in the flower of their youth they degenerated into Germans, and to preserve their precious jewel more comfortably, settled somewhere out there—by preference in Weimar or the Black Forest.

I, for instance, genuinely despised my official work and did not openly abuse it simply because I was in it myself and got a salary for it. Anyway, take note, I did not openly abuse it. Our romantic would rather go out of his mind— a thing, however, which very rarely happens—than take to open abuse, unless he had some other career in view; and he is never kicked out. At most, they would take him to the lunatic asylum as "the King of Spain" if he should go very mad. But it is only the thin, fair people who go out of their minds in Russia. Innumerable "romantics" attain later in life to considerable rank in the service. Their many-sidedness is remarkable! And what a faculty they have for the most contradictory sensations! I was comforted by this thought even in those days, and I am of the same opinion now. That is why there are so many "broad natures" among us who never lose their ideal even in the depths of degradation; and though they never stir a finger for their ideal, though they are arrant thieves and knaves, yet they tearfully cherish their first ideal and are extraordinarily honest at heart. Yes, it is only among us that the most incorrigible rogue can be absolutely and loftily honest at heart without in the least ceasing to be a rogue. I repeat, our romantics, frequently, become such accomplished rascals (I use the term "rascals" affectionately), suddenly display such a sense of reality and practical knowledge, that their bewildered superiors and the public generally can only ejaculate in amazement.

Their many-sidedness is really amazing, and goodness knows what it may develop into later on, and what the future has in store for us. It is not a poor material! I do not say this from any foolish or boastful patriotism. But I feel sure that you are again imagining that I am joking. Or perhaps it's just the contrary, and you are convinced that I really think so. Anyway, gentlemen, I shall welcome both views as an honour and a special favour. And do forgive my digression.

I did not, of course, maintain friendly relations with my comrades and soon was at loggerheads with them, and in my youth and inexperience I even gave up bowing to them, as though I had cut off all relations. That, however, only happened to me once. As a rule, I was always alone.

In the first place I spent most of my time at home, reading. I tried to stifle all that was continually seething within me by means of external impressions. And the only external means I had was reading. Reading, of course, was a great help—exciting me, giving me pleasure and pain. But at times it bored me fearfully. One longed for movement in spite of everything, and I plunged all at once into dark, underground, loathsome vice of the pettiest kind. My wretched passions were acute, smarting, from my continual, sickly irritability. I had hysterical impulses, with tears and convulsions. I had no resources except reading—that is, there was nothing in my surroundings which I could respect and which attracted me. I was overwhelmed with depression, too; I had an hysterical craving for incongruity and for contrast, and so I took to vice. I have not said all this to justify myself. . . . But, no! I am lying. I did want to justify myself. I make that little observation for my own benefit, gentlemen. I don't want to lie. I vowed to myself I would not.

And so, furtively, timidly, in solitude, at night, I indulged in filthy vice, with a feeling of shame which never deserted me, even at the most loathsome moments, and which at such moments nearly made me curse. Already even then I had my underground world in my soul. I was fearfully afraid of being seen, of being met, of being recognized. I visited various obscure haunts.

One night as I was passing a tavern I saw through a lighted window some gentlemen fighting with billiard cues, and saw one of them thrown out of the window. At other times I should have felt very much disgusted, but I was in such a mood at the time, that I actually envied the gentleman thrown out of the window—and I envied him so much that I even went into the tavern and into the billiard-room. "Perhaps," I thought, "I'll have a fight, too, and they'll throw me out of the window."

I was not drunk—but what is one to do—depression will drive a man to such a pitch of hysteria? But nothing happened. It seemed that I was not even equal to being thrown out of the window and I went away without having my fight.

An officer put me in my place from the first moment.

I was standing by the billiard-table and in my ignorance blocking up the way, and he wanted to pass; he took me by the shoulders and without a word—without a warning or an explanation—moved me from where I was standing to another spot and passed by as though he had not noticed me.

I could have forgiven blows, but I could not forgive his having moved me without noticing me.

Devil knows what I would have given for a real regular quarrel—a more decent, a more *literary* one, so to speak. I had been treated like a fly. This officer was over six foot, while I was a spindly little fellow. But the quarrel was in my hands. I had only to protest and I certainly would have been thrown out of the window. But I changed my mind and preferred to beat a resentful retreat.

I went out of the tavern straight home, confused and troubled, and the next night I went out again with the same lewd intentions, still more furtively, abjectly and miserably than before, as it were, with tears in my eyes— but still I did go out again. Don't imagine, though, it was cowardice made me slink away from the officer: I never have been a coward at heart, though I have always been a coward in action. Don't be in a hurry to laugh—I assure you I can explain it all.

Oh, if only that officer had been one of the sort who would consent to fight a duel! But no, he was one of those gentlemen (alas, long extinct!) who preferred fighting with cues, or, like Gogol's Lieutenant Pirogov, appealing to the police. They did not fight duels and would have thought a duel with a civilian like me an utterly unseemly procedure in any case—and they looked upon the duel altogether as something impossible, something free-thinking and French. But they were quite ready to bully, especially when they were over six foot.

I did not slink away through cowardice, but through an unbounded vanity. I was afraid not of his six foot, not of getting a sound thrashing and being thrown out of the window; I should have had physical courage enough, I assure you; but I had not the moral courage. What I was afraid of was that every one present, from the insolent marker down to the lowest little stinking, pimply clerk in a greasy collar, would jeer at me and fail to understand when I began to protest and to address them in literary language. For of the point of honour—not of honour, but of the point of honour (*point d'honneur*)—one cannot speak among us except in literary language. You can't allude to the "point of honour" in ordinary language. I was fully convinced (the sense of reality, in spite of all my romanticism!) that they would all simply split their sides with laughter, and that the officer would not simply beat me, that is, without insulting me, but would certainly prod me in the back with his knee, kick me round the billiard-table, and only then perhaps have pity and drop me out of the window.

Of course, this trivial incident could not with me end in that. I often met that officer afterwards in the street and noticed him very carefully. I am not quite sure whether he recognized me, I imagine not; I judge from certain signs. But I—I stared at him with spite and hatred and so it went on . . . for several years! My resentment grew even deeper with years. At first I began making stealthy inquiries about this officer. It was difficult for me to do so, for I knew no one. But one day I heard some one shout his surname in the street as I was following him at a distance, as though I were tied to him—and so I learnt his surname. Another time I followed him to his flat, and for ten kopecks learnt from the porter where he lived, on which storey, whether he lived alone or with others, and so on—in fact, everything one could learn from a porter. One morning, though I had never tried my hand with the pen, it suddenly occurred to me to write a satire on this officer in the form of a novel which would unmask his villainy. I wrote the novel with relish. I did unmask his villainy, I even exaggerated it; at first I so altered his surname that it could easily be recognized, but on second thoughts I changed it, and sent the story to the *Otetchestvenniya Zapiski*. But at that time such attacks were not the fashion and my story was not printed. That was a great vexation to me.

Sometimes I was positively choked with resentment. At last I determined to challenge my enemy to a duel. I composed a splendid, charming letter to him, imploring him to apologize to me, and hinting rather plainly at a duel in case of refusal. The letter was so composed that if the offi-

cer had had the least understanding of the good and the
beautiful he would certainly have flung himself on my
neck and have offered me his friendship. And how fine
that would have been! How we should have got on together!
"He could have shielded me with his higher rank, while
I could have improved his mind with my culture, and, well
. . . my ideas, and all sorts of things might have happened." Only fancy, this was two years after his insult to
me, and my challenge would have been a ridiculous anachronism, in spite of all the ingenuity of my letter in dis-
guising and explaining away the anachronism. But, thank
God (to this day I thank the Almighty with tears in my
eyes) I did not send the letter to him. Cold shivers run
down my back when I think of what might have happened
if I had sent it.

And all at once I revenged myself in the simplest way, by
a stroke of genius! A brilliant thought suddenly dawned
upon me. Sometimes on holidays I used to stroll along the
sunny side of the Nevsky about four o'clock in the afternoon. Though it was hardly a stroll so much as a series
of innumerable miseries, humiliations and resentments;
but no doubt that was just what I wanted. I used to wriggle
along in a most unseemly fashion, like an eel, continually
moving aside to make way for generals, for officers of the
Guards and the Hussars, or for ladies. At such minutes
there used to be a convulsive twinge at my heart, and I
used to feel hot all down my back at the mere thought of
the wretchedness of my attire, of the wretchedness and
abjectness of my little scurrying figure. This was a regular
martyrdom, a continual, intolerable humiliation at the
thought, which passed into an incessant and direct sensation, that I was a mere fly in the eyes of all this world, a
nasty, disgusting fly—more intelligent, more highly developed, more refined in feeling than any of them, of course,
but a fly that was continually making way for every one,
insulted and injured by every one. Why I inflicted this torture upon myself, why I went to the Nevsky, I don't know.
I felt simply drawn there at every possible opportunity.
Already then I began to experience a rush of the enjoy-

ment of which I spoke in the first chapter. After my affair
with the officer I felt even more drawn there than before:
it was on the Nevsky that I met him most frequently, there
I could admire him. He, too, went there chiefly on holidays. He, too, turned out of his path for generals and
persons of high rank, and he, too, wriggled between them
like an eel; but people like me, or even better dressed
than me, he simply walked over; he made straight for them
as though there was nothing but empty space before him,
and never, under any circumstances, turned aside. I gloated
over my resentment watching him and . . . always resentfully made way for him. It exasperated me that even in the
street I could not be on an even footing with him.

"Why must you invariably be the first to move aside?" I
kept asking myself in hysterical rage, waking up sometimes
at three o'clock in the morning. "Why is it you and not he?
There's no regulation about it; there's no written law. Let
the making way be equal as it usually is when refined people meet: he moves half-way and you move half-way; you
pass with mutual respect."

But that never happened, and I always moved aside,
while he did not even notice my making way for him.
And lo and behold a bright idea dawned upon me! "What,"
I thought, "if I meet him and don't move on one side?
What if I don't move aside on purpose, even if I knock
up against him? How would that be?" This audacious idea
took such a hold on me that it gave me no peace. I was
dreaming of it continually, horribly, and I purposely went
more frequently to the Nevsky in order to picture more
vividly how I should do it when I did do it. I was delighted.
This intention seemed to me more and more practical and
possible.

"Of course I shall not really push him," I thought, already more good-natured in my joy. "I will simply not
turn aside, will run up against him, not very violently, but
just shouldering each other—just as much as decency permits. I will push against him just as much as he pushes
against me." At last I made up my mind completely. But
my preparations took a great deal of time. To begin with,

when I carried out my plan I should need to be looking rather more decent, and so I had to think of my get-up. "In case of emergency, if, for instance, there were any sort of public scandal (and the public there is of the most *recherché:* the Countess walks there; Prince D. walks there; all the literary world is there), I must be well dressed; that inspires respect and of itself puts us on an equal footing in the eyes of society."

With this object I asked for some of my salary in advance, and bought at Tchurkin's a pair of black gloves and a decent hat. Black gloves seemed to me both more dignified and *bon ton* than the lemon-coloured ones which I had contemplated at first. "The colour is too gaudy, it looks as though one were trying to be conspicuous," and I did not take the lemon-coloured ones. I had got ready long beforehand a good shirt, with white bone studs; my overcoat was the only thing that held me back. The coat in itself was a very good one, it kept me warm; but it was wadded and it had a raccoon collar which was the height of vulgarity. I had to change the collar at any sacrifice, and to have a beaver one like an officer's. For this purpose I began visiting the Gostiny Dvor and after several attempts I pitched upon a piece of cheap German beaver. Though these German beavers soon grow shabby and look wretched, yet at first they look exceedingly well, and I only needed it for one occasion. I asked the price; even so, it was too expensive. After thinking it over thoroughly I decided to sell my raccoon collar. The rest of the money —a considerable sum for me, I decided to borrow from Anton Antonitch Syetotchkin, my immediate superior, an unassuming person, though grave and judicious. He never lent money to any one, but I had, on entering the service, been specially recommended to him by an important personage who had got me my berth. I was horribly worried. To borrow from Anton Antonitch seemed to me monstrous and shameful. I did not sleep for two or three nights. Indeed, I did not sleep well at that time, I was in a fever; I had a vague sinking at my heart or else a sudden throbbing, throbbing, throbbing! Anton Antonitch was surprised at first, then he frowned, then he reflected, and did after all lend me the money, receiving from me a written authorization to take from my salary a fortnight later the sum that he had lent me.

In this way everything was at last ready. The handsome beaver replaced the mean-looking raccoon, and I began by degrees to get to work. It would never have done to act off-hand, at random; the plan had to be carried out skilfully, by degrees. But I must confess that after many efforts I began to despair: we simply could not run into each other. I made every preparation, I was quite determined—it seemed as though we should run into one another directly—and before I knew what I was doing I had stepped aside for him again and he had passed without noticing me. I even prayed as I approached him that God would grant me determination. One time I had made up my mind thoroughly, but it ended in my stumbling and falling at his feet because at the very last instant when I was six inches from him my courage failed me. He very calmly stepped over me, while I flew on one side like a ball. That night I was ill again, feverish and delirious.

And suddenly it ended most happily. The night before I had made up my mind not to carry out my fatal plan and to abandon it all, and with that object I went to the Nevsky for the last time, just to see how I would abandon it all. Suddenly, three paces from my enemy, I unexpectedly made up my mind—I closed my eyes, and we ran full tilt, shoulder to shoulder, against one another! I did not budge an inch and passed him on a perfectly equal footing! He did not even look round and pretended not to notice it; but he was only pretending, I am convinced of that. I am convinced of that to this day! Of course, I got the worst of it—he was stronger, but that was not the point. The point was that I had attained my object, I had kept up my dignity, I had not yielded a step, and had put myself publicly on an equal social footing with him. I returned home feeling that I was fully avenged for everything. I was delighted. I was triumphant and sang Italian arias. Of course, I will not describe to you what happened to me three days later;

if you have read my first chapter you can guess that for yourself. The officer was afterwards transferred; I have not seen him now for fourteen years. What is the dear fellow doing now? Whom is he walking over?

II

But the period of my dissipation would end and I always felt very sick afterwards. It was followed by remorse—I tried to drive it away: I felt too sick. By degrees, however, I grew used to that too. I grew used to everything, or rather I voluntarily resigned myself to enduring it. But I had a means of escape that reconciled everything—that was to find refuge in "the good and the beautiful," in dreams, of course. I was a terrible dreamer, I would dream for three months on end, tucked away in my corner, and you may believe me that at those moments I had no resemblance to the gentleman who, in the perturbation of his chicken heart, put a collar of German beaver on his greatcoat. I suddenly became a hero. I would not have admitted my six-foot lieutenant even if he had called on me. I could not even picture him before me then. What were my dreams and how I could satisfy myself with them, it is hard to say now, but at the time I was satisfied with them. Though, indeed, even now I am to some extent satisfied with them. Dreams were particularly sweet and vivid after a spell of dissipation; they came with remorse and with tears, with curses and transports. There were moments of such positive intoxication, of such happiness, that there was not the faintest trace of irony within me, on my honour. I had faith, hope, love. I believed blindly at such times that by some miracle, by some external circumstance, all this would suddenly open out, expand; that suddenly a vista of suitable activity—beneficent, good, and, above all, *ready-made* (what sort of activity I had no idea, but the great thing was that it should be all ready for me)—would rise up before me, and I should come out into the light of day, almost riding a white horse and crowned with laurel. Anything but the foremost place I could not conceive for myself, and for that very reason I quite contentedly occupied the lowest in reality. Either to be a hero or to grovel in the mud—there was nothing between. That was my ruin, for when I was in the mud I comforted myself with the thought that at other times I was a hero, and the hero was a cloak for the mud: for an ordinary man it was shameful to defile himself, but a hero was too lofty to be utterly defiled, and so he might defile himself. It is worth noting that these attacks of "the good and the beautiful" visited me even during the period of dissipation and just at the times when I was touching the bottom. They came in separate spurts, as though reminding me of themselves, but did not banish the dissipation by their appearance. On the contrary, they seemed to add a zest to it by contrast, and were only sufficiently present to serve as an appetizing sauce. That sauce was made up of contradictions and sufferings, of agonizing inward analysis, and all these pangs and pinpricks gave a certain piquancy, even a significance to my dissipation—in fact, completely answered the purpose of an appetizing sauce. There was a certain depth of meaning in it. And I could hardly have resigned myself to the simple, vulgar, direct debauchery of a clerk and have endured all the filthiness of it. What could have allured me about it then and have drawn me at night into the street? No, I had a lofty way of getting out of it all.

And what loving-kindness, oh Lord, what loving-kindness I felt at times in those dreams of mine! in those "flights into the good and the beautiful"; though it was fantastic love, though it was never applied to anything human in reality, yet there was so much of this love that one did not feel afterwards even the impulse to apply it in reality; that would have been superfluous. Everything, however, passed satisfactorily by a lazy and fascinating transition into the sphere of art, that is, into the beautiful forms of life, lying ready, largely stolen from the poets and novelists and adapted to all sorts of needs and uses. I, for instance, was triumphant over every one; every one, of course, was in dust and ashes, and was forced spontaneously to recognize my superiority, and I forgave them all. I was a poet and a grand gentleman, I fell in love; I came in for countless millions and immediately devoted them to humanity, and at the same time I confessed before all the people my shameful deeds, which, of course, were not merely shameful, but had in them much that was "good and beautiful," something in the Manfred style. Every one would kiss me and weep (what idiots they would be if they did not), while I should go barefoot and hungry preaching new ideas and fighting a victorious Austerlitz against the obscurantists. Then the band would play a march, an amnesty would be declared, the Pope would agree to retire from Rome to Brazil; then there would be a ball for the whole of Italy at the Villa Borghese on the shores of Lake Como, Lake Como being for that purpose transferred to the neighbourhood of Rome; then would come a scene in the bushes, and so on, and so on—as though you did not know all about it!

You will say that it is vulgar and contemptible to drag all this into public after all the tears and transports which I have myself confessed. But why is it contemptible? Can you imagine that I am ashamed of it all, and that it was stupider than anything in your life, gentlemen? And I can assure you that some of these fancies were by no means badly composed. . . . It did not all happen on the shores of Lake Como. And yet you are right—it really is vulgar and contemptible. And most contemptible of all it is that now I am attempting to justify myself to you. And even more contemptible than that is my making this remark now. But that's enough, or there will be no end to it: each step will be more contemptible than the last. . . .

I could never stand more than three months of dreaming at a time without feeling an irresistible desire to plunge into society. To plunge into society meant to visit my superior at the office, Anton Antonitch Syetotchkin. He was the only permanent acquaintance I have had in my life, and I wonder at the fact myself now. But I only went to see him when that phase came over me, and when my dreams had reached such a point of bliss that it became essential at once to embrace my fellows and all mankind; and for that purpose I needed at least one human being, actually existing. I had to call on Anton Antonitch, however, on Tuesday—his at-home day; so I had always to time my passionate desire to embrace humanity so that it might fall on a Tuesday.

This Anton Antonitch lived on the fourth storey in a house in Five Corners, in four low-pitched rooms, one smaller than the other, of a particularly frugal and sallow appearance. He had two daughters and their aunt, who used to pour out the tea. Of the daughters one was thirteen and another fourteen, they both had snub noses, and I was awfully shy of them because they were always whispering and giggling together. The master of the house usually sat in his study on a leather couch in front of the table with some grey-headed gentleman, usually a colleague from our office or some other department. I never saw more than two or three visitors there, always the same. They talked about the excise duty, about business in the senate, about salaries, about promotions, about His Excellency, and the best means of pleasing him, and so on. I had the patience to sit like a fool beside these people for four hours at a stretch, listening to them without knowing what to say to them or venturing to say a word. I became stupefied, several times I felt myself perspiring, I was overcome by a sort of paralysis; but this was pleasant and good for me. On returning home I deferred for a time my desire to embrace all mankind.

I had, however, one other acquaintance of a sort, Simonov, who was an old schoolfellow. I had a number of schoolfellows indeed in Petersburg, but I did not associate with them and had even given up nodding to them in the street. I believe I had transferred into the department I was in simply to avoid their company and to cut off all connection with my hateful childhood. Curses on that school and all those terrible years of penal servitude! In short, I parted from my schoolfellows as soon as I got out into the world. There were two or three left to whom I nodded in the street. One of them was Simonov, who had been in no way distinguished at school, was of a quiet and equable disposition; but I discovered in him a certain independence of character and even honesty. I don't even suppose that he was particularly stupid. I had at one time spent some rather soulful moments with him, but these had not lasted long and had somehow been suddenly clouded over. He was evidently uncomfortable at these reminiscences, and was, I fancy, always afraid that I might take up the same tone again. I suspected that he had an aversion for me, but still I went on going to see him, not being quite certain of it.

And so on one occasion, unable to endure my solitude and knowing that as it was Thursday Anton Antonitch's door would be closed, I thought of Simonov. Climbing up to his fourth storey I was thinking that the man disliked me and that it was a mistake to go and see him. But as it always happened that such reflections impelled me, as though purposely, to put myself into a false position, I went in. It was almost a year since I had last seen Simonov.

III

I found two of my old schoolfellows with him. They seemed to be discussing an important matter. All of them took scarcely any notice of my entrance, which was strange, for I had not met them for years. Evidently they looked upon me as something on the level of a common fly. I had not been treated like that even at school, though they all hated me. I knew, of course, that they must despise me now for my lack of success in the service, and for my having let myself sink so low, going about badly dressed and so on—which seemed to them a sign of my incapacity and insignificance. But I had not expected such contempt. Simonov was positively surprised at my turning up. Even in the old days he had always seemed surprised at my coming. All this disconcerted me: I sat down, feeling rather miserable, and began listening to what they were saying.

They were engaged in warm and earnest conversation about a farewell dinner which they wanted to arrange for the next day to a comrade of theirs called Zverkov, an officer in the army, who was going away to a distant province. This Zverkov had been all the time at school with me too. I had begun to hate him particularly in the upper forms. In the lower forms he had simply been a pretty, playful boy whom everybody liked. I had hated him, however, even in the lower forms, just because he was a pretty and playful boy. He was always bad at his lessons and got worse and worse as he went on; however, he left with a good certificate, as he had powerful interest. During his last year at school he came in for an estate of two hundred serfs, and as almost all of us were poor he took up a swaggering tone among us. He was vulgar in the extreme, but at the same time he was a good-natured fellow, even in his swaggering. In spite of superficial, fantastic and sham notions of honour and dignity, all but very few of us positively grovelled before Zverkov, and the more so the more he swaggered. And it was not from any interested motive that they grovelled, but simply because he had been favoured by the gifts of nature. Moreover, it was, as it were, an accepted idea among us that Zverkov was a specialist in regard to tact and the social graces. This last fact particularly infuriated me. I hated the abrupt self-confident tone of his voice, his admiration of his own witticisms, which were often frightfully stupid, though he was bold in his language; I hated his handsome but stupid face (for which I would, however, have gladly exchanged my intelligent one), and the free-and-easy military manners in fashion in the "forties." I hated the way in which he used to talk of his future conquests of women (he did not venture to begin his attack upon women until he had the epaulettes of an officer, and was looking forward to them with impatience), and boasted of the duels he would constantly be fighting. I remember how I, invariably so taciturn, suddenly fastened upon Zverkov, when one day talking at a leisure moment with his schoolfellows of his future relations with the fair sex, and growing as sportive as a puppy in the sun, he all at once declared that he would not leave a single village girl on his estate unnoticed, that that was his *droit de sei-*

gneur, and that if the peasants dared to protest he would have them all flogged and double the tax on them, the bearded rascals. Our servile rabble applauded, but I attacked him, not from compassion for the girls and their fathers, but simply because they were applauding such an insect. I got the better of him on that occasion, but though Zverkov was stupid he was lively and impudent, and so laughed it off, and in such a way that my victory was not really complete: the laugh was on his side. He got the better of me on several occasions afterwards, but without malice, jestingly, casually. I remained angrily and contemptuously silent and would not answer him. When we left school he made advances to me; I did not rebuff them, for I was flattered, but we soon parted and quite naturally. Afterwards I heard of his barrack-room success as a lieutenant, and of the fast life he was leading. Then there came other rumours—of his successes in the service. By then he had taken to cutting me in the street, and I suspected that he was afraid of compromising himself by greeting a personage as insignificant as I. I saw him once in the theatre, in the third tier of boxes. By then he was wearing shoulder-straps. He was twisting and twirling about, ingratiating himself with the daughters of an ancient general. In three years he had gone off considerably, though he was still rather handsome and adroit. One could see that by the time he was thirty he would be corpulent. So it was to this Zverkov that my schoolfellows were going to give a dinner on his departure. They had kept up with him for those three years, though privately they did not consider themselves on an equal footing with him, I am convinced of that.

Of Simonov's two visitors, one was Ferfitchkin, a Russianized German—a little fellow with the face of a monkey, a blockhead who was always deriding every one, a very bitter enemy of mine from our days in the lower forms—a vulgar, impudent, swaggering fellow, who affected a most sensitive feeling of personal honour, though, of course, he was a wretched little coward at heart. He

was one of those worshippers of Zverkov who made up
to the latter from interested motives, and often borrowed
money from him. Simonov's other visitor, Trudolyubov,
was a person in no way remarkable—a tall young fellow,
in the army, with a cold face, fairly honest, though he
worshipped success of every sort, and was only capable of
thinking of promotion. He was some sort of distant relation of Zverkov's, and this, foolish as it seems, gave him a
certain importance among us. He always thought me of no
consequence whatever; his behaviour to me, though not
quite courteous, was tolerable.

"Well, with seven roubles each," said Trudolyubov,
"twenty-one roubles between the three of us, we ought to
be able to get a good dinner. Zverkov, of course, won't
pay."

"Of course not, since we are inviting him," Simonov
decided.

"Can you imagine," Ferfitchkin interrupted hotly and
conceitedly, like some insolent flunkey boasting of his
master the general's decorations, "can you imagine that
Zverkov will let us pay alone? He will accept from delicacy, but he will order half a dozen bottles of champagne."

"Do we want half a dozen for the four of us?" observed
Trudolyubov, taking notice only of the half-dozen.

"So the three of us, with Zverkov for the fourth, twenty-
one roubles, at the Hôtel de Paris at five o'clock to-morrow," Simonov, who had been asked to make the arrangements, concluded finally.

"How twenty-one roubles?" I asked in some agitation,
with a show of being offended; "if you count me it will not
be twenty-one, but twenty-eight roubles."

It seemed to me that to invite myself so suddenly and
unexpectedly would be positively graceful, and that they
would all be conquered at once and would look at me with
respect.

"Do you want to join, too?" Simonov observed, with no
appearance of pleasure, seeming to avoid looking at me.
He knew me through and through.

It infuriated me that he knew me so thoroughly.

"Why not? I am an old schoolfellow of his too, I believe, and I must own I feel hurt that you have left me out," I said, boiling over again.

"And where were we to find you?" Ferfitchkin put in roughly.

"You never were on good terms with Zverkov," Trudolyubov added, frowning.

But I had already clutched at the idea and would not give it up.

"It seems to me that no one has a right to form an opinion upon that," I retorted in a shaking voice, as though something tremendous had happened. "Perhaps that is just my reason for wishing it now, that I have not always been on good terms with him."

"Oh, there's no making you out . . . with these refinements," Trudolyubov jeered.

"We'll put your name down," Simonov decided, addressing me. "To-morrow at five o'clock at the Hôtel de Paris."

"What about the money?" Ferfitchkin began in an undertone, indicating me to Simonov, but he broke off, for even Simonov was embarrassed.

"That will do," said Trudolyubov, getting up. "If he wants to come so much, let him."

"But it's a private thing, between us friends," Ferfitchkin said crossly, as he too picked up his hat. "It's not an official gathering."

"We do not want at all, perhaps . . ."

They went away. Ferfitchkin did not greet me in any way as he went out, Trudolyubov barely nodded. Simonov, with whom I was left *tête-à-tête*, was in a state of vexation and perplexity, and looked at me queerly. He did not sit down and did not ask me to.

"H'm . . . yes . . . to-morrow, then. Will you pay your subscription now? I just ask so as to know," he muttered in embarrassment.

I flushed crimson, and as I did so I remembered that I had owed Simonov fifteen roubles for ages—which I had, indeed, never forgotten, though I had not paid it.

"You will understand, Simonov, that I could have no

idea when I came here . . . I am very much vexed that I have forgotten. . . ."

"All right, all right, that doesn't matter. You can pay to-morrow after the dinner. I simply wanted to know. . . . Please don't . . ."

He broke off and began pacing the room still more vexed. As he walked he began to stamp with his heels.

"Am I keeping you?" I asked, after two minutes of silence.

"Oh!" he said, starting, "that is—to be truthful—yes. I have to go and see some one . . . not far from here," he added in an apologetic voice, somewhat abashed.

"My goodness, why didn't you say so?" I cried, seizing my cap with an astonishingly free-and-easy air, which was the last thing I should have expected of myself.

"It's close by . . . not two paces away," Simonov repeated, accompanying me to the front door with a fussy air which did not suit him at all. "So five o'clock, punctually, to-morrow," he called down the stairs after me. He was very glad to get rid of me. I was in a fury.

"What possessed me, what possessed me to force myself upon them?" I wondered, grinding my teeth as I strode along the street. "For a scoundrel, a pig like that Zverkov! Of course, I had better not go; of course, I must just snap my fingers at them. I am not bound in any way. I'll send Simonov a note by to-morrow's post. . . ."

But what made me furious was that I knew for certain that I should go, that I should make a point of going; and the more tactless, the more unseemly my going would be, the more certainly I would go.

And there was a positive obstacle to my going: I had no money. All I had was nine roubles, I had to give seven of that to my servant, Apollon, for his monthly wages. That was all I paid him—he had to keep himself.

Not to pay him was impossible, considering his character. But I will talk about that fellow, about that plague of mine, another time.

However, I knew I should go and should not pay him his wages.

That night I had the most hideous dreams. No wonder; all the evening I had been oppressed by memories of my miserable days at school, and I could not shake them off. I was sent to the school by distant relations, upon whom I was dependent and of whom I have heard nothing since— they sent me there a forlorn, silent boy, already crushed by their reproaches, already troubled by doubt, and looking with savage distrust at every one. My schoolfellows met me with spiteful and merciless jibes because I was not like any of them. But I could not endure their taunts; I could not give in to them with the ignoble readiness with which they gave in to one another. I hated them from the first, and shut myself away from every one in timid, wounded and disproportionate pride. Their coarseness revolted me. They laughed cynically at my face, at my clumsy figure; and yet what stupid faces they had themselves. In our school the boys' faces seemed in a special way to degenerate and grow stupider. How many fine-looking boys came to us! In a few years they became repulsive. Even at sixteen I wondered at them morosely; even when I was struck by the pettiness of their thoughts, the stupidity of their pursuits, their games, their conversations. They had no understanding of such essential things, they took no interest in such striking, impressive subjects, that I could not help considering them inferior to myself. It was not wounded vanity that drove me to it, and for God's sake do not thrust upon me your hackneyed remarks, repeated to nausea, that "I was only a dreamer," while they even then had an understanding of life. They understood nothing, they had no idea of real life, and I swear that that was what made me most indignant with them. On the contrary, the most obvious, striking reality they accepted with fantastic stupidity and even at that time were accustomed to respect success. Everything that was just, but oppressed and looked down upon, they laughed at heartlessly and shamefully. They took rank for intelligence; even at sixteen they were already talking about a snug berth. Of course a great deal of it was due to their stupidity, to the bad examples with which they had always been surrounded in their childhood and boyhood. They were monstrously depraved. Of course a great deal of that, too, was superficial and an assumption of cynicism; of course there were glimpses of youth and freshness even in their depravity; but even that freshness was not attractive, and showed itself in a certain rakishness. I hated them horribly, though perhaps I was worse than any of them. They repaid me in the same way, and did not conceal their aversion for me. But by then I did not desire their affection: on the contrary I continually longed for their humiliation. To escape from their derision I purposely began to make all the progress I could with my studies and forced my way to the very top. This impressed them.

Moreover, they all began by degrees to grasp that I had already read books none of them could read, and understood things (not forming part of our school curriculum) of which they had not even heard. They took a savage and sarcastic view of it, but were morally impressed, especially as the teachers began to notice me on those grounds. The mockery ceased, but the hostility remained, and cold and strained relations became permanent between us. In the end I could not put up with it: with years a craving for society, for friends, developed in me. I attempted to get on friendly terms with some of my schoolfellows; but somehow or other my intimacy with them was always strained and soon ended of itself. Once, indeed, I did have a friend. But I was already a tyrant at heart; I wanted to exercise unbounded sway over him; I tried to instil into him a contempt for his surroundings; I required of him a disdainful and complete break with those surroundings. I frightened him with my passionate affection; I reduced him to tears, to hysterics. He was a simple and devoted soul; but when he devoted himself to me entirely I began to hate him immediately and repulsed him—as though all I needed him for was to win a victory over him, to subjugate him and nothing else. But I could not subjugate all of them; my friend was not at all like them either, he was, in fact, a rare exception. The first thing I did on leaving school was to give up the special job for which I had been des-

tined so as to break all ties, to curse my past and shake the
dust from off my feet. . . . And goodness knows why, after
all that, I should go trudging off to Simonov's!

Early next morning I roused myself and jumped out of
bed with excitement, as though it were all about to happen
at once. But I believed that some radical change in my
life was coming, and would inevitably come that day.
Owing to its rarity, perhaps, any external event, however
trivial, always made me feel as though some radical change
in my life were at hand. I went to the office, however, as
usual, but sneaked away home two hours earlier to get
ready. The great thing, I thought, is not to be the first to
arrive, or they will think I am overjoyed at coming. But
there were thousands of such great points to consider, and
they all agitated and overwhelmed me. I polished my boots
a second time with my own hands; nothing in the world
would have induced Apollon to clean them twice a day, as
he considered that it was more than his duties required of
him. I stole the brushes to clean them from the passage,
being careful he should not detect it, for fear of his contempt. Then I minutely examined my clothes and thought
that everything looked old, worn and threadbare. I had let
myself get too slovenly. My uniform, perhaps, was tidy,
but I could not go out to dinner in my uniform. The worst
of it was that on the knee of my trousers was a big yellow
stain. I had a foreboding that that stain would deprive me
of nine-tenths of my personal dignity. I knew, too, that it
was very poor to think so. "But this is no time for thinking: now I am in for the real thing," I thought, and my
heart sank. I knew, too, perfectly well even then, that I was
monstrously exaggerating the facts. But how could I help
it? I could not control myself and was already shaking
with fever. With despair I pictured to myself how coldly
and disdainfully that "scoundrel" Zverkov would meet me;
with what dull-witted, invincible contempt the blockhead Trudolyubov would look at me; with what impudent
rudeness the insect Ferfitchkin would snigger at me in
order to curry favour with Zverkov; how completely Simonov would take it all in, and how he would despise me

for the abjectness of my vanity and lack of spirit—and, worst of all, how paltry, *unliterary*, commonplace it would all be.

Of course, the best thing would be not to go at all. But that was most impossible of all: if I feel impelled to do anything, I seem to be pitch-forked into it. I should have jeered at myself ever afterwards: "So you funked it, you funked it, you funked the *real thing!*" On the contrary, I passionately longed to show all that "rabble" that I was by no means such a spiritless creature as I seemed to myself. What is more, even in the acutest paroxysm of this cowardly fever, I dreamed of getting the upper hand, of dominating them, carrying them away, making them like me—if only for my "elevation of thought and unmistakable wit." They would abandon Zverkov, he would sit on one side, silent and ashamed, while I should crush him. Then, perhaps, we would be reconciled and drink to our ever-lasting friendship; but what was most bitter and most humiliating for me was that I knew even then, knew fully and for certain, that I needed nothing of all this really, that I did not really want to crush, to subdue, to attract them, and that I did not care a straw really for the result, even if I did achieve it. Oh, how I prayed for the day to pass quickly! In unutterable anguish I went to the window, opened the movable pane and looked out into the troubled darkness of the thickly falling wet snow. At last my wretched little clock hissed out five. I seized my hat and trying not to look at Apollon, who had been all day expecting his month's wages, but in his foolishness was unwilling to be the first to speak about it, I slipt between him and the door and jumping into a high-class sledge, on which I spent my last half-rouble, I drove up in grand style to the Hôtel de Paris.

IV

I had been certain the day before that I should be the first to arrive. But it was not a question of being the first to arrive. Not only were they not there, but I had difficulty in finding our room. The table was not laid even. What did it mean? After a good many questions I elicited from the waiters that the dinner had been ordered not for five, but for six o'clock. This was confirmed at the buffet too. I felt really ashamed to go on questioning them. It was only twenty-five minutes past five. If they changed the dinner hour they ought at least to have let me know—that is what the post is for, and not to have put me in an absurd position in my own eyes and . . . and even before the waiters. I sat down; the servant began laying the table; I felt even more humiliated when he was present. Towards six o'clock they brought in candles, though there were lamps burning in the room. It had not occurred to the waiter, however, to bring them in at once when I arrived. In the next room two gloomy, angry-looking persons were eating their dinners in silence at two different tables. There was a great deal of noise, even shouting, in a room further away; one could hear the laughter of a crowd of people, and nasty little shrieks in French: there were ladies at the dinner. It was sickening, in fact. I rarely passed more unpleasant moments, so much so that when they did arrive all together punctually at six I was overjoyed to see them, as though they were my deliverers, and even forgot that it was incumbent upon me to show resentment.

Zverkov walked in at the head of them; evidently he was the leading spirit. He and all of them were laughing; but, seeing me, Zverkov drew himself up a little, walked up to me deliberately with a slight, rather jaunty bend from the waist. He shook hands with me in a friendly, but not over-friendly, fashion, with a sort of circumspect courtesy like that of a general, as though in giving me his hand he were warding off something. I had imagined, on the contrary, that on coming in he would at once break into his habitual thin, shrill laugh and fall to making his insipid jokes and witticisms. I had been preparing for them ever since the previous day, but I had not expected such condescension, such high-official courtesy. So, then, he felt himself ineffably superior to me in every respect! If he only meant to insult me by that high-official tone, it would not matter, I thought—I could pay him back for it one way or another. But what if, in reality, without the least desire to be offensive, that sheep's-head had a notion in earnest that he was superior to me and could only look at me in a patronizing way? The very supposition made me gasp.

"I was surprised to hear of your desire to join us," he began, lisping and drawling, which was something new. "You and I seem to have seen nothing of one another. You fight shy of us. You shouldn't. We are not such terrible people as you think. Well, anyway, I am glad to renew our acquaintance."

And he turned carelessly to put down his hat on the window sill.

"Have you been waiting long?" Trudolyubov inquired.

"I arrived at five o'clock as you told me yesterday," I answered aloud, with an irritability that threatened an explosion.

"Didn't you let him know that we had changed the hour?" said Trudolyubov to Simonov.

"No, I didn't. I forgot," the latter replied, with no sign of regret, and without even apologizing to me he went off to order the *hors d'œuvres*.

"So you've been here a whole hour? Oh, poor fellow!" Zverkov cried ironically, for to his notions this was bound to be extremely funny. That rascal Ferfitchkin followed with his nasty little snigger like a puppy yapping. My position struck him, too, as exquisitely ludicrous and embarrassing.

"It isn't funny at all!" I cried to Ferfitchkin, more and more irritated. "It wasn't my fault, but other people's. They neglected to let me know. It was . . . it was . . . it was simply absurd."

"It's not only absurd, but something else as well," muttered Trudolyubov, naïvely taking my part. "You are not hard enough upon it. It was simply rudeness—unintentional, of course. And how could Simonov . . . h'm!"

"If a trick like that had been played on me," observed Ferfitchkin, "I should . . ."

"But you should have ordered something for yourself," Zverkov interrupted, "or simply asked for dinner without waiting for us."

"You will allow that I might have done that without your permission," I rapped out. "If I waited, it was . . ."

"Let us sit down, gentlemen," cried Simonov, coming in. "Everything is ready; I can answer for the champagne; it is capitally frozen. . . . You see, I did not know your address, where was I to look for you?" He suddenly turned to me, but again he seemed to avoid looking at me. Evidently he had something against me. It must have been what happened yesterday.

All sat down; I did the same. It was a round table. Trudolyubov was on my left, Simonov on my right. Zverkov was sitting opposite, Ferfitchkin next to him, between him and Trudolyubov.

"Tell me, are you . . . in a government office?" Zverkov went on attending to me. Seeing that I was embarrassed, he seriously thought that he ought to be friendly to me, and, so to speak, cheer me up.

"Does he want me to throw a bottle at his head?" I thought, in a fury. In my novel surroundings I was unnaturally ready to be irritated.

"In the N—— office," I answered jerkily, with my eyes on my plate.

"And ha-ave you a go-od berth? I say, what ma-a-de you leave your original job?"

"What ma-a-de me was that I wanted to leave my original job," I drawled more than he, hardly able to control myself. Ferfitchkin went off into a guffaw. Simonov looked at me ironically. Trudolyubov left off eating and began looking at me with curiosity.

Zverkov winced, but he tried not to notice it.

"And the remuneration?"

"What remuneration?"

"I mean, your sa-a-lary?"

"Why are you cross-examining me?" However, I told him at once what my salary was. I turned horribly red.

"It is not very handsome," Zverkov observed majestically.

"Yes, you can't afford to dine at cafés on that," Ferfitchkin added insolently.

"To my thinking it's very poor," Trudolyubov observed gravely.

"And how thin you have grown! How you have changed!" added Zverkov, with a shade of venom in his voice, scanning me and my attire with a sort of insolent compassion.

"Oh, spare his blushes," cried Ferfitchkin, sniggering.

"My dear sir, allow me to tell you I am not blushing," I broke out at last; "do you hear? I am dining here, at this café, at my own expense, not at other people's—note that, Mr. Ferfitchkin."

"Wha-at? Isn't every one here dining at his own expense? You would seem to be . . ." Ferfitchkin flew out at me, turning as red as a lobster, and looking me in the face with fury.

"Tha-at," I answered, feeling I had gone too far, "and I imagine it would be better to talk of something more intelligent."

"You intend to show off your intelligence, I suppose?"

"Don't disturb yourself, that would be quite out of place here."

"Why are you clacking away like that, my good sir, eh? Have you gone out of your wits in your office?"

"Enough, gentlemen, enough!" Zverkov cried, authoritatively.

"How stupid it is!" muttered Simonov.

"It really is stupid. We have met here, a company of friends, for a farewell dinner to a comrade and you carry on an altercation," said Trudolyubov, rudely addressing himself to me alone. "You invited yourself to join us, so don't disturb the general harmony."

"Enough, enough!" cried Zverkov. "Give over, gentlemen, it's out of place. Better let me tell you how I nearly got married the day before yesterday. . . ."

And then followed a burlesque narrative of how this

gentleman had almost been married two days before. There was not a word about the marriage, however, but the story was adorned with generals, colonels and kammer-junkers, while Zverkov almost took the lead among them. It was greeted with approving laughter; Ferfitchkin positively squealed.

No one paid any attention to me, and I sat crushed and humiliated.

"Good heavens, these are not the people for me!" I thought. "And what a fool I have made of myself before them! I let Ferfitchkin go too far, though. The brutes imagine they are doing me an honour in letting me sit down with them. They don't understand that it's an honour to them and not to me! I've grown thinner! My clothes! Oh, damn my trousers! Zverkov noticed the yellow stain on the knee as soon as he came in. . . . But what's the use! I must get up at once, this very minute, take my hat and simply go without a word . . . with contempt! And to-morrow I can send a challenge. The scoundrels! As though I cared about the seven roubles. They may think . . . Damn it! I don't care about the seven roubles. I'll go this minute!"

Of course I remained. I drank sherry and Lafitte by the glassful in my discomfiture. Being unaccustomed to it, I was quickly affected. My annoyance increased as the wine went to my head. I longed all at once to insult them all in a most flagrant manner and then go away. To seize the moment and show what I could do, so that they would say, "He's clever, though he is absurd," and . . . and . . . in fact, damn them all!

I scanned them all insolently with my drowsy eyes. But they seemed to have forgotten me altogether. They were noisy, vociferous, cheerful. Zverkov was talking all the time. I began listening. Zverkov was talking of some exuberant lady whom he had at last led on to declaring her love (of course, he was lying like a horse), and how he had been helped in this affair by an intimate friend of his, a Prince Kolya, an officer in the Hussars, who had three thousand serfs.

"And yet this Kolya, who has three thousand serfs, has

not put in an appearance here to-night to see you off," I cut in suddenly.

For a minute every one was silent. "You are drunk already." Trudolyubov deigned to notice me at last, glancing contemptuously in my direction. Zverkov, without a word, examined me as though I were an insect. I dropped my eyes. Simonov made haste to fill up the glasses with champagne.

Trudolyubov raised his glass, as did every one else but me.

"Your health and good luck on the journey!" he cried to Zverkov. "To old times, to our future, hurrah!"

They all tossed off their glasses, and crowded round Zverkov to kiss him. I did not move; my full glass stood untouched before me.

"Why, aren't you going to drink it?" roared Trudolyubov, losing patience and turning menacingly to me.

"I want to make a speech separately, on my own account . . . and then I'll drink it, Mr. Trudolyubov."

"Spiteful brute!" muttered Simonov. I drew myself up in my chair and feverishly seized my glass, prepared for something extraordinary, though I did not know myself precisely what I was going to say.

"Silence!" cried Ferfitchkin. "Now for a display of wit!"

Zverkov waited very gravely, knowing what was coming.

"Mr. Lieutenant Zverkov," I began, "let me tell you that I hate phrases, phrasemongers and men in corsets . . . that's the first point, and there is a second one to follow it."

There was a general stir.

"The second point is: I hate ribaldry and ribald talkers. Especially ribald talkers! The third point: I love justice, truth and honesty." I went on almost mechanically, for I was beginning to shiver with horror myself and had no idea how I came to be talking like this. "I love thought, Monsieur Zverkov; I love true comradeship, on an equal footing and not . . . H'm . . . I love . . . But, however, why not? I will drink your health, too, Mr. Zverkov. Seduce the Circassian girls, shoot the enemies of the fatherland and . . . and . . . to your health, Monsieur Zverkov!"

Zverkov got up from his seat, bowed to me and said:

"I am very much obliged to you." He was frightfully offended and turned pale.

"Damn the fellow!" roared Trudolyubov, bringing his fist down on the table.

"Well, he wants a punch in the face for that," squealed Ferfitchkin.

"We ought to turn him out," muttered Simonov.

"Not a word, gentlemen, not a movement!" cried Zverkov solemnly, checking the general indignation. "I thank you all, but I can show him for myself how much value I attach to his words."

"Mr. Ferfitchkin, you will give me satisfaction to-morrow for your words just now!" I said aloud, turning with dignity to Ferfitchkin.

"A duel, you mean? Certainly," he answered. But probably I was so ridiculous as I challenged him and it was so out of keeping with my appearance that everyone, including Ferfitchkin, was prostrate with laughter.

"Yes, let him alone, of course! He is quite drunk," Trudolyubov said with disgust.

"I shall never forgive myself for letting him join us," Simonov muttered again.

"Now is the time to throw a bottle at their heads," I thought to myself. I picked up the bottle . . . and filled my glass. . . . "No, I'd better sit on to the end," I went on thinking; "you would be pleased, my friends, if I went away. Nothing will induce me to go. I'll go on sitting here and drinking to the end, on purpose, as a sign that I don't think you of the slightest consequence. I will go on sitting and drinking, because this is a public-house and I paid my entrance money. I'll sit here and drink, for I look upon you as so many pawns, as inanimate pawns. I'll sit here and drink . . . and sing if I want to, yes, sing, for I have the right to . . . to sing . . . H'm!"

But I did not sing. I simply tried not to look at any of them. I assumed most unconcerned attitudes and waited with impatience for them to speak *first*. But alas, they did not address me! And oh, how I wished, how I wished at that moment to be reconciled to them! It struck eight, at last nine. They moved from the table to the sofa. Zverkov stretched himself on a lounge and put one foot on a round table. Wine was brought there. He did, as a fact, order three bottles on his own account. I, of course, was not invited to join them. They all sat round him on the sofa. They listened to him, almost with reverence. It was evident that they were fond of him. "What for? What for?" I wondered. From time to time they were moved to drunken enthusiasm and kissed each other. They talked of the Caucasus, of the nature of true passion, of snug berths in the service, of the income of an hussar called Podharzhevsky, whom none of them knew personally, and rejoiced in the largeness of it, of the extraordinary grace and beauty of a Princess D., whom none of them had ever seen; then it came to Shakespeare's being immortal.

I smiled contemptuously and walked up and down the other side of the room, opposite the sofa, from the table to the stove and back again. I tried my very utmost to show them that I could do without them, and yet I purposely made a noise with my boots, thumping with my heels. But it was all in vain. They paid no attention. I had the patience to walk up and down in front of them from eight o'clock till eleven, in the same place, from the table to the stove and back again. "I walk up and down to please myself and no one can prevent me." The waiter who came into the room stopped, from time to time, to look at me. I was somewhat giddy from turning round so often; at moments it seemed to me that I was in delirium. During those three hours I was three times soaked with sweat and dry again. At times, with an intense, acute pang I was stabbed to the heart by the thought that ten years, twenty years, forty years would pass, and that even in forty years I would remember with loathing and humiliation those filthiest, most ludicrous, and most awful moments of my life. No one could have gone out of his way to degrade himself more shamelessly, and I fully realized it, fully, and yet I went on pacing up and down from the table to the stove. "Oh, if you only knew what thoughts and feelings I am capable of, how cultured I am!" I thought at moments, mentally addressing the sofa on which my enemies were sitting. But my enemies behaved as though I were not in the room. Once—only once—they turned towards me, just when Zverkov was talking about Shakespeare, and I suddenly gave a contemptuous laugh. I laughed in such an affected and disgusting way that they all at once broke off their conversation, and silently and gravely for two minutes watched me walking up and down from the table to the stove, *taking no notice of them*. But nothing came of it: they said nothing, and two minutes later they ceased to notice me again. It struck eleven.

"Friends," cried Zverkov getting up from the sofa, "let us all be off now, *there!*"

"Of course, of course," the others assented. I turned sharply to Zverkov. I was so harassed, so exhausted, that I would have cut my throat to put an end to it. I was in a fever; my hair, soaked with perspiration, stuck to my forehead and temples.

"Zverkov, I beg your pardon," I said abruptly and resolutely. "Ferfitchkin, yours too, and every one's, every one's: I have insulted you all!"

"Aha! A duel is not in your line, old man," Ferfitchkin hissed venomously.

It sent a sharp pang to my heart.

"No, it's not the duel I am afraid of, Ferfitchkin! I am ready to fight you to-morrow, after we are reconciled. I insist upon it, in fact, and you cannot refuse. I want to show you that I am not afraid of a duel. You shall fire first and I shall fire into the air."

"He is comforting himself," said Simonov.

"He's simply raving," said Trudolyubov.

"But let us pass. Why are you barring our way? What do you want?" Zverkov answered disdainfully.

They were all flushed; their eyes were bright: they had been drinking heavily.

"I ask for your friendship, Zverkov; I insulted you, but . . ."

"Insulted? *You* insulted *me?* Understand, sir, that you never, under any circumstances, could possibly insult *me*."

"And that's enough for you. Out of the way!" concluded Trudolyubov.

"Olympia is mine, friends, that's agreed!" cried Zverkov.

"We won't dispute your right, we won't dispute your right," the others answered, laughing.

I stood as though spat upon. The party went noisily out of the room. Trudolyubov struck up some stupid song. Simonov remained behind for a moment to tip the waiters. I suddenly went up to him.

"Simonov! give me six roubles!" I said, with desperate resolution.

He looked at me in extreme amazement, with vacant eyes. He, too, was drunk.

"You don't mean you are coming with us?"

"Yes."

"I've no money," he snapped out, and with a scornful laugh he went out of the room.

I clutched at his overcoat. It was a nightmare.

"Simonov, I saw you had money. Why do you refuse me? Am I a scoundrel? Beware of refusing me: if you knew, if you knew why I am asking! My whole future, my whole plans depend upon it!"

Simonov pulled out the money and almost flung it at me.

"Take it, if you have no sense of shame!" he pronounced pitilessly, and ran to overtake them.

I was left for a moment alone. Disorder, the remains of dinner, a broken wine-glass on the floor, spilt wine, cigarette ends, fumes of drink and delirium in my brain, an agonizing misery in my heart and finally the waiter, who had seen and heard all and was looking inquisitively into my face.

"I am going there!" I cried. "Either they shall all go down on their knees to beg for my friendship, or I will give Zverkov a slap in the face!"

V

"So this is it, this is it at last—contact with real life," I muttered as I ran headlong downstairs. "This is very different from the Pope's leaving Rome and going to Brazil, very different from the ball on the shores of Lake Como!"

"You are a scoundrel," a thought flashed through my mind, "if you laugh at this now."

"No matter!" I cried, answering myself. "Now everything is lost!"

There was no trace to be seen of them, but that made no difference—I knew where they had gone.

At the steps was standing a solitary night sledge-driver in a rough peasant coat, powdered over with the still falling, wet, and as it were warm, snow. It was hot and steamy. The little shaggy piebald horse was also covered with snow and coughing, I remember that very well. I made a rush for the roughly made sledge; but as soon as I raised my foot to get into it, the recollection of how Simonov had just given me six roubles seemed to double me up and I tumbled into the sledge like a sack.

"No, I must do a great deal to make up for all that," I cried. "But I will make up for it or perish on the spot this very night. Start!"

We set off. There was a perfect whirl in my head.

"They won't go down on their knees to beg for my friendship. That is a mirage, cheap mirage, revolting, romantic and fantastical—that's another ball at Lake Como. And so I am bound to slap Zverkov's face! It is my duty to. And so it is settled; I am flying to give him a slap in the face. Hurry up!"

The driver tugged at the reins.

"As soon as I go in I'll give it him. Ought I before giving him the slap to say a few words by way of preface? No. I'll simply go in and give it him. They will all be sitting in the drawing-room, and he with Olympia on the sofa. That damned Olympia! She laughed at my looks on

one occasion and refused me. I'll pull Olympia's hair, pull
Zverkov's ears! No, better one ear, and pull him by it
round the room. Maybe they will all begin beating me
and will kick me out. That's most likely, indeed. No matter! Anyway, I shall first slap him; the initiative will be
mine; and by the laws of honour that is everything: he will
be branded and cannot wipe off the slap by any blows, by
nothing but a duel. He will be forced to fight. And let
them beat me now. Let them, the ungrateful wretches!
Trudolyubov will beat me hardest, he is so strong; Ferfitchkin will be sure to catch hold sideways and tug at my hair.
But no matter, no matter! That's what I am going for.
The blockheads will be forced at last to see the tragedy of
it all! When they drag me to the door I shall call out to
them that in reality they are not worth my little finger.
Get on, driver, get on!" I cried to the driver. He started
and flicked his whip, I shouted so savagely.

"We shall fight at daybreak, that's a settled thing. I've
done with the office. Ferfitchkin made a joke about it just
now. But where can I get pistols? Nonsense! I'll get my
salary in advance and buy them. And powder, and bullets?
That's the second's business. And how can it all be done
by daybreak? And where am I to get a second? I have
no friends. Nonsense!" I cried, lashing myself up more
and more. "It's of no consequence! the first person I meet
in the street is bound to be my second, just as he would
be bound to pull a drowning man out of water. The most
eccentric things may happen. Even if I were to ask the
Director himself to be my second to-morrow, he would
be bound to consent, if only from a feeling of chivalry,
and to keep the secret! Anton Antonitch. . . ."

The fact is, that at that very minute the disgusting absurdity of my plan and the other side of the question was
clearer and more vivid to my imagination than it could be
to any one on earth. But . . .

"Get on, driver, get on, you rascal, get on!"

"Ugh, sir!" said the son of toil.

Cold shivers suddenly ran down me. Wouldn't it be better . . . to go straight home? My God, my God! Why did

I invite myself to this dinner yesterday? But no, it's impossible. And my walking up and down for three hours from the table to the stove? No, they, they and no one else must pay for my walking up and down! They must wipe out this dishonour! Drive on!

And what if they give me into custody? They won't dare! They'll be afraid of the scandal. And what if Zverkov is so contemptuous that he refuses to fight a duel? He is sure to; but in that case I'll show them . . . I will turn up at the posting station when he is setting off to-morrow, I'll catch him by the leg, I'll pull off his coat when he gets into the carriage. I'll get my teeth into his hand, I'll bite him. "See what lengths you can drive a desperate man to!" He may hit me on the head and they may belabour me from behind. I will shout to the assembled multitude: "Look at this young puppy who is driving off to captivate the Circassian girls after letting me spit in his face!"

Of course, after that everything will be over! The office will have vanished off the face of the earth. I shall be arrested, I shall be tried, I shall be dismissed from the service, thrown in prison, sent to Siberia. Never mind! In fifteen years when they let me out of prison I will trudge off to him, a beggar, in rags. I shall find him in some provincial town. He will be married and happy. He will have a grown-up daughter. . . . I shall say to him: "Look, monster, at my hollow cheeks and my rags! I've lost everything—my career, my happiness, art, science, *the woman I loved*, and all through you. Here are pistols. I have come to discharge my pistol and . . . and I . . . forgive you. Then I shall fire into the air and he will hear nothing more of me. . . ."

I was actually on the point of tears, though I knew perfectly well at that moment that all this was out of Pushkin's *Silvio* and Lermontov's *Masquerade*. And all at once I felt horribly ashamed, so ashamed that I stopped the horse, got out of the sledge, and stood still in the snow in the middle of the street. The driver gazed at me, sighing and astonished.

What was I to do? I could not go on there—it was evidently stupid, and I could not leave things as they were, because that would seem as though . . . Heavens, how could I leave things! And after such insults! "No!" I cried, throwing myself into the sledge again. "It is ordained! It is fate! Drive on, drive on!"

And in my impatience I punched the sledge-driver on the back of the neck.

"What are you up to? What are you hitting me for?" the peasant shouted, but he whipped up his nag so that it began kicking.

The wet snow was falling in big flakes; I unbuttoned myself, regardless of it. I forgot everything else, for I had finally decided on the slap, and felt with horror that it was going to happen *now, at once,* and that *no force could stop it.* The deserted street lamps gleamed sullenly in the snowy darkness like torches at a funeral. The snow drifted under my greatcoat, under my coat, under my cravat, and melted there. I did not wrap myself up—all was lost, anyway.

At last we arrived. I jumped out, almost unconscious, ran up the steps and began knocking and kicking at the door. I felt fearfully weak, particularly in my legs and my knees. The door was opened quickly as though they knew I was coming. As a fact, Simonov had warned them that perhaps another gentleman would arrive, and this was a place in which one had to give notice and to observe certain precautions. It was one of those "millinery establishments" which were abolished by the police a good time ago. By day it really was a shop; but at night, if one had an introduction, one might visit it for other purposes.

I walked rapidly through the dark shop into the familiar drawing-room, where there was only one candle burning, and stood still in amazement: there was no one there. "Where are they?" I asked somebody. But by now, of course, they had separated. Before me was standing a person with a stupid smile, the "madam" herself, who had seen me before. A minute later a door opened and another person came in.

Taking no notice of anything, I strode about the room,

and, I believe, I talked to myself. I felt as though I had been saved from death and was conscious of this, joyfully, all over: I should have given that slap, I should certainly, certainly have given it! But now they were not here and . . . everything had vanished and changed! I looked round. I could not realize my condition yet. I looked mechanically at the girl who had come in: and had a glimpse of a fresh, young, rather pale face, with straight, dark eyebrows, and with grave, as it were wondering, eyes that attracted me at once; I should have hated her if she had been smiling. I began looking at her more intently and, as it were, with effort. I had not fully collected my thoughts. There was something simple and good-natured in her face, but something strangely grave. I am sure that this stood in her way here, and no one of those fools had noticed her. She could not, however, have been called a beauty, though she was tall, strong-looking, and well built. She was very simply dressed. Something loathsome stirred within me. I went straight up to her.

I chanced to look into the glass. My harassed face struck me as revolting in the extreme, pale, angry, abject, with dishevelled hair. "No matter, I am glad of it," I thought; "I am glad that I shall seem repulsive to her; I like that."

VI

. . . Somewhere behind a screen a clock began wheezing, as though oppressed by something, as though some one were strangling it. After an unnaturally prolonged wheezing there followed a shrill, nasty, and as it were unexpectedly rapid, chime—as though some one were suddenly jumping forward. It struck two. I woke up, though I had indeed not been asleep but lying half-conscious.

It was almost completely dark in the narrow, cramped, low-pitched room, cumbered up with an enormous wardrobe and piles of cardboard boxes and all sorts of frippery and litter. The candle end that had been burning on the table was going out and gave a faint flicker from time to time. In a few minutes there would be complete darkness.

I was not long in coming to myself; everything came back to my mind at once, without an effort, as though it had been in ambush to pounce upon me again. And, indeed, even while I was unconscious a point seemed continually to remain in my memory unforgotten, and round it my dreams moved drearily. But strange to say, everything that had happened to me in that day seemed to me now, on waking, to be in the far, far away past, as though I had long, long ago lived all that down.

My head was full of fumes. Something seemed to be hovering over me, rousing me, exciting me, and making me restless. Misery and spite seemed surging up in me again and seeking an outlet. Suddenly I saw beside me two wide-open eyes scrutinizing me curiously and persistently. The look in those eyes was coldly detached, sullen, as it were utterly remote; it weighed upon me.

A grim idea came into my brain and passed all over my body, as a horrible sensation, such as one feels when one goes into a damp and mouldy cellar. There was something unnatural in those two eyes, beginning to look at me only now. I recalled, too, that during those two hours I had not said a single word to this creature, and had, in fact, considered it utterly superfluous; in fact, the silence had for some reason gratified me. Now I suddenly realized vividly the hideous idea—revolting as a spider—of vice, which, without love, grossly and shamelessly begins with that in which true love finds its consummation. For a long time we gazed at each other like that, but she did not drop her eyes before mine and her expression did not change, so that at last I felt uncomfortable.

"What is your name?" I asked abruptly, to put an end to it.

"Liza," she answered almost in a whisper, but somehow far from graciously, and she turned her eyes away.

I was silent.

"What weather! The snow . . . it's disgusting!" I said, almost to myself, putting my arm under my head despondently, and gazing at the ceiling.

She made no answer. This was horrible.

"Have you always lived in Petersburg?" I asked a minute later, almost angrily, turning my head slightly towards her.

"No."

"Where do you come from?"

"From Riga," she answered reluctantly.

"Are you a German?"

"No, Russian."

"Have you been here long?"

"Where?"

"In this house?"

"A fortnight."

She spoke more and more jerkily. The candle went out; I could no longer distinguish her face.

"Have you a father and mother?"

"Yes . . . no . . . I have."

"Where are they?"

"There . . . in Riga."

"What are they?"

"Oh, nothing."

"Nothing? Why, what class are they?"

"Tradespeople."

"Have you always lived with them?"

"Yes."

"How old are you?"

"Twenty."

"Why did you leave them?"

"Oh, for no reason."

That answer meant "Let me alone; I feel sick, sad."

We were silent.

God knows why I did not go away. I felt myself more and more sick and dreary. The images of the previous day began of themselves, apart from my will, flitting through my memory in confusion. I suddenly recalled something I had seen that morning when, full of anxious thoughts, I was hurrying to the office.

"I saw them carrying a coffin out yesterday and they nearly dropped it," I suddenly said aloud, not that I desired to open the conversation, but as it were by accident.

"A coffin?"

"Yes, in the Haymarket; they were bringing it up out of a cellar."

"From a cellar?"

"Not from a cellar, but from a basement. Oh, you know . . . down below . . . from a house of ill-fame. It was filthy all round . . . Eggshells, litter . . . a stench. It was loathsome."

Silence.

"A nasty day to be buried," I began, simply to avoid being silent.

"Nasty, in what way?"

"The snow, the wet." (I yawned.)

"It makes no difference," she said suddenly, after a brief silence.

"No, it's horrid." (I yawned again.) "The grave-diggers must have sworn at getting drenched by the snow. And there must have been water in the grave."

"Why water in the grave?" she asked, with a sort of curiosity, but speaking even more harshly and abruptly than before.

I suddenly began to feel provoked.

"Why, there must have been water at the bottom a foot deep. You can't dig a dry grave in Volkovo Cemetery."

"Why?"

"Why? Why, the place is waterlogged. It's a regular marsh. So they bury them in water. I've seen it myself . . . many times."

(I had never seen it once, indeed I had never been in Volkovo, and had only heard stories of it.)

"Do you mean to say you don't mind how you die?"

"But why should I die?" she answered, as though defending herself.

"Why, some day you will die, and you will die just the same as that dead woman. She was . . . a girl like you. She died of consumption."

"A wench would have died in a hospital. . . ." (She knows all about it already: she said "wench," not "girl.")

"She was in debt to her madam," I retorted, more and more provoked by the discussion; "and went on earning money for her up to the end, though she was in consumption. Some sledge-drivers standing by were talking about her to some soldiers and telling them so. No doubt they knew her. They were laughing. They were going to meet in a pot-house to drink to her memory."

A great deal of this was my invention. Silence followed, profound silence. She did not stir.

"And is it better to die in a hospital?"

"Isn't it just the same? Besides, why should I die?" she added irritably.

"If not now, a little later."

"Why a little later?"

"Why, indeed? Now you are young, pretty, fresh, you fetch a high price. But after another year of this life you will be very different—you will go off."

"In a year?"

"Anyway, in a year you will be worth less," I continued malignantly. "You will go from here to something lower, another house; a year later—to a third, lower and lower, and in seven years you will come to a basement in the Haymarket. That will be if you were lucky. But it would be much worse if you got some disease, consumption, say . . . and caught a chill, or something or other. It's not easy to get over an illness in your way of life. If you catch anything you may not get rid of it. And so you would die."

"Oh, well, then I shall die," she answered, quite vindictively, and she made a quick movement.

"But one is sorry."

"Sorry for whom?"

"Sorry for life."

Silence.

"Have you been engaged to be married? Eh?"

"What's that to you?"

"Oh, I am not cross-examining you. It's nothing to me. Why are you so cross? Of course you may have had your own troubles. What is it to me? It's simply that I felt sorry."

"Sorry for whom?"

"Sorry for you."

"No need," she whispered hardly audibly, and again made a faint movement.

That incensed me at once. What! I was so gentle with her, and she . . .

"Why, do you think that you are on the right path?"

"I don't think anything."

"That's what's wrong, that you don't think. Realize it while there is still time. There still is time. You are still young, good-looking; you might love, be married, be happy. . . ."

"Not all married women are happy," she snapped out in the rude abrupt tone she had used at first.

"Not all, of course, but anyway it is much better than the life here. Infinitely better. Besides, with love one can live even without happiness. Even in sorrow life is sweet; life is sweet, however one lives. But here what is there but . . . foulness. Phew!"

I turned away with disgust; I was no longer reasoning coldly. I began to feel myself what I was saying and warmed to the subject. I was already longing to expound the cherished ideas I had brooded over in my corner. Something suddenly flared up in me. An object had appeared before me.

"Never mind my being here, I am not an example for you. I am, perhaps, worse than you are. I was drunk when I came here, though," I hastened, however, to say in self-defence. "Besides, a man is no example for a woman. It's a different thing. I may degrade and defile myself, but I am not any one's slave. I come and go, and that's an end of it. I shake it off, and I am a different man. But you are a slave from the start. Yes, a slave! You give up everything, your whole freedom. If you want to break your chains afterwards, you won't be able to: you will be more and more fast in the snares. It is an accursed bondage. I know it. I won't speak of anything else, maybe you won't understand, but tell me: no doubt you are in debt to your madam? There, you see," I added, though she made no answer, but only listened in silence, entirely absorbed, "that's a bondage for you! You will never buy your freedom. They will see to that. It's like selling your soul to the Devil. . . . And besides . . . perhaps I, too, am just as unlucky—how do you know—and wallow in the mud on purpose, out of misery? You know, men take to drink from grief; well, maybe I am here from grief. Come, tell me, what is there good here? Here you and I . . . came together . . . just now and did not say one word to one another all the time, and it was only afterwards you began staring at me like a wild creature, and I at you. Is that loving? Is that how one human being should meet another? It's hideous, that's what it is!"

"Yes!" she assented sharply and hurriedly.

I was positively astounded by the promptitude of this "Yes." So the same thought may have been straying through her mind when she was staring at me just before. So she, too, was capable of certain thoughts? "Damn it all, this was interesting, this was a point of likeness!" I thought, almost rubbing my hands. And indeed it's easy to turn a young soul like that!

It was the exercise of my power that attracted me most.

She turned her head nearer to me, and it seemed to me in the darkness that she propped herself on her arm. Perhaps she was scrutinizing me. How I regretted that I could not see her eyes. I heard her deep breathing.

"Why have you come here?" I asked her, with a note of authority already in my voice.

"Oh, I don't know."

"But how nice it would be to be living in your father's house! It's warm and free; you have a home of your own."

"But what if it's worse than this?"

"I must take the right tone," flashed through my mind. "I may not get far with sentimentality." But it was only a momentary thought. I swear she really did interest me. Besides, I was exhausted and moody. And cunning so easily goes hand in hand with feeling.

"Who denies it!" I hastened to answer. "Anything may happen. I am convinced that some one has wronged you, and that you are more sinned against than sinning. Of course, I know nothing of your story, but it's not likely a girl like you has come here of her own inclination. . . ."

"A girl like me?" she whispered, hardly audibly; but I heard it.

Damn it all, I was flattering her. That was horrid. But perhaps it was a good thing. . . . She was silent.

"See, Liza, I will tell you about myself. If I had had a home from childhood, I shouldn't be what I am now. I often think that. However bad it may be at home, anyway they are your father and mother, and not enemies, strangers. Once a year at least, they'll show their love of you. Anyway, you know you are at home. I grew up without a home; and perhaps that's why I've turned so . . . unfeeling."

I waited again. "Perhaps she doesn't understand," I thought, "and, indeed, it is absurd—it's moralizing."

"If I were a father and had a daughter, I believe I should love my daughter more than my sons, really," I began indirectly, as though talking of something else, to distract her attention. I must confess I blushed.

"Why so?" she asked.

Ah! so she was listening!

"I don't know, Liza. I knew a father who was a stern, austere man, but used to go down on his knees to his daughter, used to kiss her hands, her feet, he couldn't make enough of her, really. When she danced at parties he used to stand for five hours at a stretch, gazing at her. He was mad over her: I understand that! She would fall asleep tired at night, and he would wake to kiss her in her sleep and make the sign of the cross over her. He would go about in a dirty old coat, he was stingy to every one else, but would spend his last penny for her, giving her expensive presents, and it was his greatest delight when she was pleased with what he gave her. Fathers always love their daughters more than the mothers do. Some girls live happily at home! And I believe I should never let my daughters marry."

"What next?" she said, with a faint smile.

"I should be jealous, I really should. To think that she should kiss any one else! That she should love a stranger more than her father! It's painful to imagine it. Of course, that's all nonsense, of course every father would be reasonable at last. But I believe before I should let her marry, I should worry myself to death; I should find fault with all her suitors. But I should end by letting her marry whom she herself loved. The one whom the daughter loves always seems the worst to the father, you know. That is always so. So many family troubles come from that."

"Some are glad to sell their daughters, rather than marrying them honourably."

Ah, so that was it!

"Such a thing, Liza, happens in those accursed families in which there is neither love nor God," I retorted warmly, "and where there is no love, there is no sense either. There are such families, it's true, but I am not speaking of them. You must have seen wickedness in your own family, if you talk like that. Truly, you must have been unlucky. H'm! . . . that sort of thing mostly comes about through poverty."

"And is it any better with the gentry? Even among the poor, honest people live happily."

"H'm . . . yes. Perhaps. Another thing, Liza, man is fond of reckoning up his troubles, but does not count his joys. If he counted them up as he ought, he would see that every lot has enough happiness provided for it. And what if all goes well with the family, if the blessing of God is upon it, if the husband is a good one, loves you, cherishes you, never leaves you! There is happiness in such a family! Even sometimes there is happiness in the midst of sorrow; and indeed sorrow is everywhere. If you marry *you will find out for yourself*. But think of the first years of married life with one you love: what happiness, what happiness there sometimes is in it! And indeed it's the ordinary thing. In those early days even quarrels with one's husband end happily. Some women get up quarrels with their husbands just because they love them. Indeed, I knew a woman like that: she seemed to say that because she loved him, she would torment him and make him feel it. You know that you may torment a man on purpose through love. Women are particularly given to that, thinking to themselves 'I will love him so, I will make so much of him afterwards, that it's no sin to torment him a little now.' And all in the house rejoice in the sight of you, and you are happy and gay and peaceful and honourable. . . . Then there are some women who are jealous. If he went off anywhere—I knew one such woman, she couldn't restrain herself, but would jump up at night and run off on the sly to find out where he was, whether he was with some other woman. That's a pity.

"And the woman knows herself it's wrong, and her heart fails her and she suffers, but she loves—it's all through love. And how sweet it is to make it up after quarrels, to own herself in the wrong or to forgive him! And they are both so happy all at once—as though they had met anew, been married over again; as though their love had begun afresh. And no one, no one should know what passes between husband and wife if they love one another. And whatever quarrels there may be between them they ought not to call in their own mothers to judge between them and tell tales of one another. They are their own judges.

"Love is a holy mystery and ought to be hidden from all other eyes, whatever happens. That makes it holier and better. They respect one another more, and much is built on respect. And if once there has been love, if they have been married for love, why should love pass away? Surely one can keep it! It is rare that one cannot keep it. And if the husband is kind and straightforward, why should not love last? The first phase of married love will pass, it is true, but then there will come a love that is better still. Then there will be the union of souls, they will have everything in common, there will be no secrets between them.

"And once they have children, the most difficult times will seem to them happy, so long as there is love and courage. Even toil will be a joy, you may deny yourself bread for your children and even that will be a joy. They will love you for it afterwards; so you are laying by for your future. As the children grow up you feel that you are an example, a support for them; that even after you die your children will always keep your thoughts and feelings, because they have received them from you, they will take on your semblance and likeness. So you see this is a great duty. How can it fail to draw the father and mother nearer? People say it's a trial to have children. Who says that? It is heavenly happiness! Are you fond of little children, Liza? I am awfully fond of them. You know—a little rosy baby boy at your bosom, and what husband's heart is not touched, seeing his wife nursing his child! A plump little rosy baby, sprawling and snuggling, chubby little hands and feet, clean tiny little nails, so tiny that it makes one laugh to look at them; eyes that look as if they understand everything. And while it sucks it clutches at your bosom with its little hand, plays. When its father comes up, the child tears itself away from the bosom, flings itself back, looks at its father, laughs, as though it were fearfully funny, and falls to sucking again. Or it will bite its mother's breast when its little teeth are coming, while it looks sideways at her with its little eyes as though to say, 'Look, I am biting!' Is not all that happiness when they are the three together, husband, wife and child? One can forgive a great deal for the sake of such moments. Yes, Liza, one must first learn to live oneself before one blames others!"

"It's by pictures, pictures like that one must get at you," I thought to myself, though I did speak with real feeling, and all at once I flushed crimson. "What if she were suddenly to burst out laughing, what should I do then?" That idea drove me to fury. Towards the end of my speech I really was excited, and now my vanity was somehow wounded. The silence continued. I almost nudged her.

"Why are you . . ." she began and stopped. But I understood: there was a quiver of something different in her voice, not abrupt, harsh and unyielding as before, but something soft and shamefaced, so shamefaced that I suddenly felt ashamed and guilty.

"What?" I asked, with tender curiosity.

"Why, you . . ."

"What?"

"Why, you . . . speak somehow like a book," she said, and again there was a note of irony in her voice.

That remark sent a pang to my heart. It was not what I was expecting.

I did not understand that she was hiding her feelings under irony, that this is usually the last refuge of modest and chaste-souled people when the privacy of their soul is coarsely and intrusively invaded, and that their pride makes them refuse to surrender till the last moment and shrink from giving expression to their feelings before you. I ought to have guessed the truth from the timidity with which she had repeatedly approached her sarcasm, only bringing herself to utter it at last with an effort. But I did not guess, and an evil feeling took possession of me.

"Wait a bit!" I thought.

VII

"Oh, hush, Liza! How can you talk about being like a book when it makes even me, an outsider, feel sick? Though I don't look at it as an outsider, for, indeed, it touches me to the heart. . . . Is it possible, is it possible that you do not feel sick at being here yourself? Evidently habit does wonders! God knows what habit can do with any one. Can you seriously think that you will never grow old, that you will always be good-looking, and that they will keep you here for ever and ever? I say nothing of the loathsomeness of the life here. . . . Though let me tell you this about it— about your present life, I mean; here though you are young now, attractive, nice, with soul and feeling, yet you know as soon as I came to myself just now I felt at once sick at being here with you! One can only come here when one is drunk. But if you were anywhere else, living as good people live, I should perhaps be more than attracted by you, should fall in love with you, should be glad of a look from you, let alone a word; I should hang about your door, should go down on my knees to you, should look upon you as my betrothed and think it an honour to be allowed to. I should not dare to have an impure thought about you. But here, you see, I know that I have only to whistle and you have to come with me whether you like it or not. I don't consult your wishes, but you mine. The lowest labourer hires himself as a workman but he doesn't make a slave of himself altogether; besides, he knows that he will be free again presently. But when are you free? Only think what you are giving up here! What is it you are making a slave of? It is your soul, together with your body; you are selling your soul which you have no right to dispose of! You give your love to be outraged by every drunkard! Love! But that's everything, you know, it's a priceless diamond, it's a maiden's treasure, love—why, a man would be ready to give his soul, to face death to gain that love. But how much is your love worth now? You are sold, all of you, body and soul, and there is no need to strive for love when you can have everything without love. And you know there is no greater insult to a girl than that, do you understand? To be sure, I have heard that they comfort you, poor fools, they let you have lovers of your own here. But you know that's simply a farce, that's simply a sham, it's just laughing at you, and you are taken in by it!

"Why, do you suppose he really loves you, that lover of yours? I don't believe it. How can he love you when he knows you may be called away from him any minute? He would be a low fellow if he did! Will he have a grain of respect for you? What have you in common with him? He laughs at you and robs you—that is all his love amounts to! You are lucky if he does not beat you. Very likely he does beat you, too. Ask him, if you have got one, whether he will marry you. He will laugh in your face, if he doesn't spit in it or give you a blow—though maybe he is not worth a bad halfpenny himself. And for what have you ruined your life, if you come to think of it? For the coffee they give you to drink and the plentiful meals? But with what object are they feeding you up? An honest girl couldn't swallow the food, for she would know what she was being

fed for. You are in debt here, and, of course, you will always be in debt, and you will go on in debt to the end, till
the visitors here begin to scorn you. And that will soon
happen, don't rely upon your youth—all that flies by express train here, you know. You will be kicked out. And
not simply kicked out; long before that she'll begin nagging at you, scolding you, abusing you, as though you had
not sacrificed your health for her, had not thrown away
your youth and your soul for her benefit, but as though
you had ruined her, beggared her, robbed her. And don't
expect any one to take your part: the others, your companions, will attack you, too, to win her favour, for all are
in slavery here, and have lost all conscience and pity here
long ago. They have become utterly vile, and nothing on
earth is viler, more loathsome, and more insulting than
their abuse.

"And you are laying down everything here, unconditio-
ally, youth and health and beauty and hope, and at twenty-
two you will look like a woman of five-and-thirty, and you
will be lucky if you are not diseased, pray to God for that!
No doubt, you are thinking now that you have a gay time
and no work to do! Yet there is no work harder or more
dreadful in the world or ever has been. One would think
that the heart alone would be worn out with tears. And
you won't dare to say a word, not half a word when they
drive you away from here; you will go away as though
you were to blame. You will change to another house,
then to a third, then somewhere else, till you come down
at last to the Haymarket. There you will be beaten at every
turn; that is good manners there, the visitors don't know
how to be friendly without beating you. You don't believe
that it is so hateful there? Go and look for yourself some
time, you can see with your own eyes. Once, one New
Year's Day, I saw a woman at a door. They had turned
her out as a joke, to give her a taste of the frost because
she had been crying so much, and they shut the door behind her. At nine o'clock in the morning she was already
quite drunk, dishevelled, half-naked, covered with bruises,
her face was powdered, but she had a black eye, blood

was trickling from her nose and her teeth; some cabman had just given her a drubbing. She was sitting on the stone steps, a salt fish of some sort was in her hand; she was crying, wailing something about her luck and beating with the fish on the steps, and cabmen and drunken soldiers were crowding in the doorway taunting her. You don't believe that you will ever be like that? I should be sorry to believe it, too, but how do you know; maybe ten years, eight years ago that very woman with the salt fish came here fresh as a cherub, innocent, pure, knowing no evil, blushing at every word. Perhaps she was like you, proud, ready to take offence, not like the others; perhaps she looked like a queen, and knew what happiness was in store for the man who should love her and whom she should love. Do you see how it ended? And what if at that very minute when she was beating on the filthy steps with that fish, drunken and dishevelled—what if at that very minute she recalled the pure early days in her father's house, when she used to go to school and the neighbour's son watched for her on the way, declaring that he would love her as long as he lived, that he would devote his life to her, and when they vowed to love one another for ever and be married as soon as they were grown up!

"No, Liza, it would be happy for you if you were to die soon of consumption in some corner, in some cellar like that woman just now. In the hospital, do you say? You will be lucky if they take you, but what if you are still of use to the madam here? Consumption is a queer disease, it is not like fever. The patient goes on hoping till the last minute and says he is all right. He deludes himself. And that just suits your madam. Don't doubt it, that's how it is; you have sold your soul, and what is more you owe money, so you daren't say a word. But when you are dying, all will abandon you, all will turn away from you, for then there will be nothing to get from you. What's more, they will reproach you for cumbering the place, for being so long over dying. However you beg you won't get a drink of water without abuse: 'Whenever are you going off, you nasty hussy, you won't let us sleep with your moaning, you make the gentlemen sick.' That's true, I have heard such things said myself. They will thrust you dying into the filthiest corner in the cellar—in the damp and darkness; what will your thoughts be, lying there alone? When you die, strange hands will lay you out, with grumbling and impatience; no one will bless you, no one will sigh for you, they only want to get rid of you as soon as may be; they will buy a coffin, take you to the grave as they did that poor woman to-day, and celebrate your memory at the tavern. In the grave sleet, filth, wet snow—no need to put themselves out for you—'Let her down, Vanuha; it's just like her luck—even here, she is head-foremost, the hussy. Shorten the cord, you rascal.' 'It's all right as it is.' 'All right, is it? Why, she's on her side! She was a fellow-creature, after all! But, never mind, throw the earth on her.' And they won't care to waste much time quarrelling over you. They will scatter the wet blue clay as quick as they can and go off to the tavern . . . and there your memory on earth will end; other women have children to go to their graves, fathers, husbands. While for you neither tear, nor sigh, nor remembrance; no one in the whole world will ever come to you, your name will vanish from the face of the earth—as though you had never existed, never been born at all! Nothing but filth and mud, however you knock at your coffin lid at night, when the dead arise, however you cry: 'Let me out, kind people, to live in the light of day! My life was no life at all; my life has been thrown away like a dishclout; it was drunk away in the tavern at the Haymarket; let me out, kind people, to live in the world again.' "

And I worked myself up to such a pitch that I began to have a lump in my throat myself, and . . . and all at once I stopped, sat up in dismay, and bending over apprehensively, began to listen with a beating heart. I had reason to be troubled.

I had felt for some time that I was turning her soul upside down and rending her heart, and—and the more I was convinced of it, the more eagerly I desired to gain my object as quickly and as effectually as possible. It was the exercise of my skill that carried me away; yet it was not merely sport. . . .

I knew I was speaking stiffly, artificially, even bookishly, in fact, I could not speak except "like a book." But that did not trouble me: I knew, I felt that I should be understood and that this very bookishness might be an assistance. But now, having attained my effect, I was suddenly panic-stricken. Never before had I witnessed such despair! She was lying on her face, thrusting her face into the pillow and clutching it in both hands. Her heart was being torn. Her youthful body was shuddering all over as though in convul-sions. Suppressed sobs rent her bosom and suddenly burst out in weeping and wailing, then she pressed closer into the pillow: she did not want any one here, not a living soul, to know of her anguish and her tears. She bit the pillow, bit her hand till it bled (I saw that afterwards), or, thrusting her fingers into her dishevelled hair, seemed rigid with the effort of restraint, holding her breath and clenching her teeth. I began saying something, begging her to calm herself, but felt that I did not dare; and all at once, in a sort of cold shiver, almost in terror, began fumbling in the dark, trying hurriedly to get dressed to go. It was dark: though I tried my best I could not finish dressing quickly. Suddenly I felt a box of matches and a candlestick with a whole candle in it. As soon as the room was lighted up, Liza sprang up, sat up in bed, and with a contorted face, with a half-insane smile, looked at me almost senselessly. I sat down beside her and took her hands; she came to herself, made an impulsive movement towards me, would have caught hold of me, but did not dare, and slowly bowed her head before me.

"Liza, my dear, I was wrong . . . forgive me, my dear," I began, but she squeezed my hand in her fingers so tightly that I felt I was saying the wrong thing and stopped.

"This is my address, Liza, come to me."

"I will come," she answered resolutely, her head still bowed.

"But now I am going, good-bye . . . till we meet again."

I got up; she, too, stood up and suddenly flushed all over, gave a shudder, snatched up a shawl that was lying on a chair and muffled herself in it to her chin. As she did this she gave another sickly smile, blushed and looked at me strangely. I felt wretched; I was in haste to get away—to disappear.

"Wait a minute," she said suddenly, in the passage just at the doorway, stopping me with her hand on my overcoat. She put down the candle in hot haste and ran off; evidently she had thought of something or wanted to show me something. As she ran away she flushed, her eyes shone, and there was a smile on her lips—what was the meaning of it? Against my will I waited: she came back a minute later with an expression that seemed to ask forgiveness for something. In fact, it was not the same face, not the same look as the evening before: sullen, mistrustful and obstinate. Her eyes now were imploring, soft, and at the same time trustful, caressing, timid. The expression with which children look at people they are very fond of, of whom they are asking a favour. Her eyes were a light hazel, they were lovely eyes, full of life, and capable of expressing love as well as sullen hatred.

Making no explanation, as though I, as a sort of higher being, must understand everything without explanations, she held out a piece of paper to me. Her whole face was positively beaming at that instant with naïve, almost childish, triumph. I unfolded it. It was a letter to her from a medical student or some one of that sort—a very high-flown and flowery, but extremely respectful, love-letter. I don't recall the words now, but I remember well that through the high-flown phrases there was apparent a genuine feeling, which cannot be feigned. When I had finished reading it I met her glowing, questioning, and childishly impatient eyes fixed upon me. She fastened her eyes upon my face and waited impatiently for what I should say. In a few words, hurriedly, but with a sort of joy and pride, she explained to me that she had been to a dance somewhere in a private house, a family of "very nice people, *who knew nothing*, absolutely nothing, for she had only come here so lately and it had all happened . . . and she hadn't made up her mind to stay and was certainly going away as soon as she had paid her debt . . ." and at that party there had been the student who had danced with her all the evening. He had talked to her, and it turned out that he had known her in old days at Riga when he was a child, they had played together, but a very long time ago—and he knew her parents, but *about this* he knew nothing, nothing whatever, and had no suspicion! And the day after the dance (three days ago) he had sent her that letter through the friend with whom she had gone to the party . . . and . . . "well, that was all."

She dropped her shining eyes with a sort of bashfulness as she finished.

The poor girl was keeping that student's letter as a precious treasure, and had run to fetch it, her only treasure, because she did not want me to go away without knowing that she, too, was honestly and genuinely loved; that she, too, was addressed respectfully. No doubt that letter was destined to lie in her box and lead to nothing. But none the less, I am certain that she would keep it all her life as a precious treasure, as her pride and justification, and now at such a minute she had thought of that letter and brought it with naïve pride to raise herself in my eyes that I might see, that I, too, might think well of her. I said nothing, pressed her hand and went out. I so longed to get away. . . . I walked all the way home, in spite of the fact that the melting snow was still falling in heavy flakes. I was exhausted, shattered, in bewilderment. But behind the bewilderment the truth was already gleaming. The loathsome truth.

VIII

It was some time, however, before I consented to recognize that truth. Waking up in the morning after some hours of heavy, leaden sleep, and immediately realizing all that had happened on the previous day, I was positively amazed at my last night's *sentimentality* with Liza, at all those "outcries of horror and pity." "To think of having such an attack of womanish hysteria, pah!" I concluded. And what did I thrust my address upon her for? What if she comes? Let her come, though; it doesn't matter. . . . But *obviously* that was not now the chief and the most important matter: I had to make haste and at all costs save my reputation in the eyes of Zverkov and Simonov as quickly as possible; that was the chief business. And I was so taken up that morning that I actually forgot all about Liza.

First of all I had at once to repay what I had borrowed the day before from Simonov. I resolved on a desperate measure: to borrow fifteen roubles straight off from Anton Antonitch. As luck would have it he was in the best of humours that morning, and gave it to me at once, on the first asking. I was so delighted at this that, as I signed the I O U with a swaggering air, I told him casually that the night before "I had been keeping it up with some friends at the Hôtel de Paris; we were giving a farewell party to a comrade, in fact, I might say a friend of my childhood, and you know—a desperate rake, fearfully spoilt—of course, he belongs to a good family, and has considerable means, a brilliant career; he is witty, charming, a regular Lovelace, you understand; we drank an extra 'half-dozen' and . . ." And it went off all right; all this was uttered very easily, unconstrainedly and complacently.

On reaching home I promptly wrote to Simonov.

To this hour I am lost in admiration when I recall the truly gentlemanly, good-humoured, candid tone of my letter. With tact and good breeding, and, above all, entirely without superfluous words, I blamed myself for all that had happened. I defended myself, "if I really may be allowed to defend myself," by alleging that being utterly unaccustomed to wine, I had been intoxicated with the first glass, which I said I had drunk before they arrived, while I was waiting for them at the Hôtel de Paris between five and six o'clock. I begged Simonov's pardon especially; I asked him to convey my explanations to all the others, especially to Zverkov, whom "I seemed to remember as though in a dream" I had insulted. I added that I would have called upon all of them myself, but my head ached, and besides I had not the face to. I was particularly pleased with a certain lightness, almost carelessness (strictly within the bounds of politeness, however), which was apparent in my style, and better than any possible arguments, gave them at once to understand that I took rather an independent view of "all that unpleasantness last night"; that I was by no means so utterly crushed as you, my friends, probably imagine; but on the contrary, looked upon it as a gentleman serenely respecting himself should look upon it. "On a young hero's past no censure is cast!"

"There is actually an aristocratic playfulness about it!" I thought admiringly, as I read over the letter. "And it's all because I am an intellectual and cultivated man! Another man in my place would not have known how to extricate himself, but here I have got out of it and am as jolly as ever again, and all because I am a cultivated and educated man of our day." And, indeed, perhaps, everything was due to the wine yesterday. H'm! . . . no, it was not the wine. I did not drink anything at all between five and six when I was waiting for them. I had lied to Simonov; I had lied shamelessly; and indeed I wasn't ashamed now. . . . Hang it all, though, the great thing was that I was rid of it.

I put six roubles in the letter, sealed it up, and asked Apollon to take it to Simonov. When he learned that there was money in the letter, Apollon became more respectful and agreed to take it. Towards evening I went out for a walk. My head was still aching and giddy after yesterday. But as evening came on and the twilight grew denser, my impressions and, following them, my thoughts grew more and more different and confused. Something was not dead within me, in the depths of my heart and conscience it would not die, and it showed itself in acute depression. For the most part I jostled my way through the most crowded business streets, along Myeshtchansky Street, along Sadovy Street and in Yusupov Garden. I always liked particularly sauntering along these streets in the dusk, just when there were crowds of working people of all sorts going home from their daily work, with faces looking cross with anxiety. What I liked was just that cheap bustle, that bare prose. On this occasion the jostling of the streets irritated me more than ever. I could not make out what was wrong with me, I could not find the clue, something seemed rising up continually in my soul, painfully, and refusing to be appeased. I returned home completely upset; it was just as though some crime were lying on my conscience.

The thought that Liza was coming worried me continually. It seemed queer to me that of all my recollections of yesterday this tormented me, as it were, especially, as it were, quite separately. Everything else I had quite succeeded in forgetting by the evening; I dismissed it all and was still perfectly satisfied with my letter to Simonov. But on this point I was not satisfied at all. It was as though I were worried only by Liza. "What if she comes," I thought incessantly, "well, it doesn't matter, let her come! H'm! it's horrid that she should see, for instance, how I live. Yesterday I seemed such a hero to her, while now, h'm! It's horrid, though, that I have let myself go so, the room looks like a beggar's. And I brought myself to go out to dinner in such a suit! And my American leather sofa with the stuffing sticking out. And my dressing-gown, which will not cover me, such tatters, and she will see all this and she will see Apollon. That beast is certain to insult her. He will fasten upon her in order to be rude to me. And I, of course, shall be panic-stricken as usual, I shall begin bowing and scraping before her and pulling my dressing-gown round me, I shall begin smiling, telling lies. Oh, the beastliness! And it isn't the beastliness of it that matters most! There is something more important, more loathsome, viler! Yes, viler! And to put on that dishonest lying mask again!" . . .

When I reached that thought I fired up all at once.

"Why dishonest? How dishonest? I was speaking sincerely last night. I remember there was real feeling in me, too. What I wanted was to excite an honourable feeling in her. . . . Her crying was a good thing, it will have a good effect."

Yet I could not feel at ease. All that evening, even when I had come back home, even after nine o'clock, when I calculated that Liza could not possibly come, she still haunted me, and what was worse, she came back to my mind always in the same position. One moment out of all that had happened last night stood vividly before my imagination; the moment when I struck a match and saw her pale, distorted face, with its look of torture. And what a pitiful, what an unnatural, what a distorted smile she had at that moment! But I did not know then that fifteen years later I should still in my imagination see Liza, always with the pitiful, distorted, inappropriate smile which was on her face at that minute.

Next day I was ready again to look upon it all as nonsense, due to over-excited nerves, and, above all, as *exaggerated*. I was always conscious of that weak point of mine, and sometimes very much afraid of it. "I exaggerate everything, that is where I go wrong," I repeated to myself every hour. But, however, "Liza will very likely come all the same" was the refrain with which all my reflections ended. I was so uneasy that I sometimes flew into a fury: "She'll come, she is certain to come!" I cried, running about the room, "if not to-day, she will come to-morrow; she'll find me out! The damnable romanticism of these pure hearts! Oh, the vileness—oh, the silliness—oh, the stupidity of these 'wretched sentimental souls'! Why, how fail to understand? How could one fail to understand?" . . .

But at this point I stopped short, and in great confusion, indeed.

And how few, how few words, I thought, in passing, were needed; how little of the idyllic (and affectedly, bookishly, artificially idyllic too) had sufficed to turn a whole human life at once according to my will. That's virginity, to be sure! Freshness of soil!

At times a thought occurred to me, to go to her, "to tell her all," and beg her not to come to me. But this thought stirred such wrath in me that I believed I should have crushed that "damned" Liza if she had chanced to be near me at the time. I should have insulted her, have spat at her, have turned her out, have struck her!

One day passed, however, another and another; she did not come and I began to grow calmer. I felt particularly

bold and cheerful after nine o'clock, I even sometimes began dreaming, and rather sweetly: I, for instance, became
the salvation of Liza, simply through her coming to me
and my talking to her. . . . I develop her, educate her. Finally, I notice that she loves me, loves me passionately. I
pretend not to understand (I don't know, however, why I
pretend, just for effect, perhaps). At last all confusion,
transfigured, trembling and sobbing, she flings herself at
my feet and says that I am her saviour, and that she loves
me better than anything in the world. I am amazed, but . . .

"Liza," I say, "can you imagine that I have not noticed
your love? I saw it all, I divined it, but I did not dare to
approach you first, because I had an influence over you
and was afraid that you would force yourself, from gratitude, to respond to my love, would try to rouse in your
heart a feeling which was perhaps absent, and I did not wish
that . . . because it would be tyranny . . . it would be indeli-
cate (in short, I launch off at that point into European,
inexplicably lofty subtleties à la George Sand), but now,
now you are mine, you are my creation, you are pure, you
are good, you are my noble wife.

> " 'Into my house come bold and free,
>   Its rightful mistress there to be.' "

Then we begin living together, go abroad and so on, and
so on. In fact, in the end it seemed vulgar to me myself,
and I began putting out my tongue at myself.

Besides, they won't let her out, "the hussy!" I thought.
They don't let them go out very readily, especially in the
evening (for some reason I fancied she would come in the
evening, and at seven o'clock precisely). Though she did
say she was not altogether a slave there yet, and had certain
rights; so, h'm! Damn it all, she will come, she is sure to
come!

It was a good thing, in fact, that Apollon distracted my
attention at that time by his rudeness. He drove me beyond
all patience! He was the bane of my life, the curse laid
upon me by Providence. We had been squabbling continu-

ally for years, and I hated him. My God, how I hated him! I believe I had never hated anyone in my life as I hated him, especially at some moments. He was an elderly, dignified man, who worked part of his time as a tailor. But for some unknown reason he despised me beyond all measure, and looked down upon me insufferably. Though, indeed, he looked down upon every one. Simply to glance at that flaxen, smoothly brushed head, at the tuft of hair he combed upon his forehead and oiled with sunflower oil, at that dignified mouth, compressed into the shape of the letter V, made one feel one was confronting a man who never doubted of himself. He was a pedant, to the most extreme point, the greatest pedant I had met on earth, and with that had a vanity only befitting Alexander of Macedon. He was in love with every button on his coat, every nail on his fingers—absolutely in love with them, and he looked it! In his behaviour to me he was a perfect tyrant, he spoke very little to me, and if he chanced to glance at me he gave me a firm, majestically self-confident and invariably ironical look that drove me sometimes to fury. He did his work with the air of doing me the greatest favour. Though he did scarcely anything for me, and did not, indeed, consider himself bound to do anything. There could be no doubt that he looked upon me as the greatest fool on earth, and that he did not "get rid of me" was simply that he could get wages from me every month. He consented to do nothing for me for seven roubles a month. Many sins should be forgiven me for what I suffered from him. My hatred reached such a point that sometimes his very step almost threw me into convulsions. What I loathed particularly was his lisp. His tongue must have been a little too long or something of that sort, for he continually lisped, and seemed to be very proud of it, imagining that it greatly added to his dignity. He spoke in a slow, measured tone, with his hands behind his back and his eyes fixed on the ground. He maddened me particularly when he read aloud the Psalms to himself behind his partition. Many a battle I waged over that reading! But he was awfully fond of reading aloud in the evenings, in a slow, even, singsong voice, as though over the dead. It

is interesting that that is how he has ended: he hires himself out to read the Psalms over the dead, and at the same
time he kills rats and makes blacking. But at that time I
could not get rid of him, it was as though he were chem-
ically combined with my existence. Besides, nothing would
have induced him to consent to leave me. I could not live
in furnished lodgings: my lodging was my private solitude,
my shell, my cave, in which I concealed myself from all
mankind, and Apollon seemed to me, for some reason, an
integral part of that flat, and for seven years I could not
turn him away.

To be two or three days behind with his wages, for instance, was impossible. He would have made such a fuss, I
should not have known where to hide my head. But I was
so exasperated with every one during those days, that I
made up my mind for some reason and with some object to
punish Apollon and not to pay him for a fortnight the
wages that were owing him. I had for a long time—for
the last two years—been intending to do this, simply in
order to teach him not to give himself airs with me, and to
show him that if I liked I could withhold his wages. I pur-
posed to say nothing to him about it, and was purposely
silent indeed, in order to score off his pride and force him
to be the first to speak of his wages. Then I would take the
seven roubles out of a drawer, show him I have the money
put aside on purpose, but that I won't, I won't, I simply
won't pay him his wages, I won't just because that is "what
I wish," because "I am master, and it is for me to decide,"
because he has been disrespectful, because he has been
rude; but if he were to ask respectfully I might be softened
and give it to him, otherwise he might wait another fortnight, another three weeks, a whole month. . . .

But angry as I was, yet he got the better of me. I could
not hold out for four days. He began as he always did begin in such cases, for there had been such cases already,
there had been attempts (and it may be observed I knew all
this beforehand, I knew his nasty tactics by heart). He
would begin by fixing upon me an exceedingly severe stare,
keeping it up for several minutes at a time, particularly on

meeting me or seeing me out of the house. If I held out and pretended not to notice these stares, he would, still in silence, proceed to further tortures. All at once, apropos of nothing, he would walk softly and smoothly into my room, when I was pacing up and down or reading, stand at the door, one hand behind his back and one foot behind the other, and fix upon me a stare more than severe, utterly contemptuous. If I suddenly asked him what he wanted, he would make me no answer, but continue staring at me persistently for some seconds, then, with a peculiar compression of his lips and a most significant air, deliberately turn round and deliberately go back to his room. Two hours later he would come out again and again present himself before me in the same way. It had happened that in my fury I did not even ask him what he wanted, but simply raised my head sharply and imperiously and began staring back at him. So we stared at one another for two minutes; at last he turned with deliberation and dignity and went back again for two hours.

If I were still not brought to reason by all this, but persisted in my revolt, he would suddenly begin sighing while he looked at me, long, deep sighs as though measuring by them the depths of my moral degradation, and, of course, it ended at last by his triumphing completely: I raged and shouted, but still was forced to do what he wanted.

This time the usual staring manoeuvres had scarcely begun when I lost my temper and flew at him in a fury. I was irritated beyond endurance apart from him.

"Stay," I cried, in a frenzy, as he was slowly and silently turning, with one hand behind his back, to go to his room, "stay! Come back, come back, I tell you!" and I must have bawled so unnaturally, that he turned round and even looked at me with some wonder. However, he persisted in saying nothing, and that infuriated me.

"How dare you come and look at me like that without being sent for? Answer!"

After looking at me calmly for half a minute, he began turning round again.

"Stay!" I roared, running up to him, "don't stir! There. Answer, now: what did you come in to look at?"

"If you have any order to give me it's my duty to carry it out," he answered, after another silent pause, with a slow, measured lisp, raising his eyebrows and calmly twisting his head from one side to another, all this with exasperating composure.

"That's not what I am asking you about, you torturer!" I shouted, turning crimson with anger. "I'll tell you why you came here myself: you see, I don't give you your wages, you are so proud you don't want to bow down and ask for it, and so you come to punish me with your stupid stares, to worry me and you have no sus-pic-ion how stupid it is—stupid, stupid, stupid, stupid!" . . .

He would have turned round again without a word, but I seized him.

"Listen," I shouted to him. "Here's the money, do you see, here it is" (I took it out of the table drawer); "here's the seven roubles complete, but you are not going to have it, you . . . are . . . not . . . going . . . to . . . have it until you come respectfully with bowed head to beg my pardon. Do you hear?"

"That cannot be," he answered, with the most unnatural self-confidence.

"It shall be so," I said, "I give you my word of honour, it shall be!"

"And there's nothing for me to beg your pardon for," he went on, as though he had not noticed my exclamations at all. "Why, besides, you called me a 'torturer,' for which I can summon you at the police-station at any time for insulting behaviour."

"Go, summon me," I roared, "go at once, this very minute, this very second! You are a torturer all the same! a torturer!"

But he merely looked at me, then turned, and regardless of my loud calls to him, he walked to his room with an even step and without looking round.

"If it had not been for Liza nothing of this would have

happened," I decided inwardly. Then, after waiting a minute, I went myself behind his screen with a dignified and solemn air, though my heart was beating slowly and violently.

"Apollon," I said quietly and emphatically, though I was breathless, "go at once without a minute's delay and fetch the police-officer."

He had meanwhile settled himself at his table, put on his spectacles and taken up some sewing. But, hearing my order, he burst into a guffaw.

"At once, go this minute! Go on, or else you can't imagine what will happen."

"You are certainly out of your mind," he observed, without even raising his head, lisping as deliberately as ever and threading his needle. "Whoever heard of a man sending for the police against himself? And as for being frightened— you are upsetting yourself about nothing, for nothing will come of it."

"Go!" I shrieked, clutching him by the shoulder. I felt I should strike him in a minute.

But I did not notice the door from the passage softly and slowly open at that instant and a figure come in, stop short, and begin staring at us in perplexity. I glanced, nearly swooned with shame, and rushed back to my room. There, clutching at my hair with both hands, I leaned my head against the wall and stood motionless in that position.

Two minutes later I heard Apollon's deliberate footsteps. "There is some woman asking for you," he said, looking at me with peculiar severity. Then he stood aside and let in Liza. He would not go away, but stared at us sarcastically.

"Go away, go away," I commanded in desperation. At that moment my clock began whirring and wheezing and struck seven.

IX

> "Into my house come bold and free,
> Its rightful mistress there to be."

I stood before her crushed, crestfallen, revoltingly confused, and I believe I smiled as I did my utmost to wrap myself in the skirts of my ragged wadded dressing-gown—exactly as I had imagined the scene not long before in a fit of depression. After standing over us for a couple of minutes Apollon went away, but that did not make me more at ease. What made it worse was that she, too, was overwhelmed with confusion, more so, in fact, than I should have expected. At the sight of me, of course.

"Sit down," I said mechanically, moving a chair up to the table, and I sat down on the sofa. She obediently sat down at once and gazed at me open-eyed, evidently expecting something from me at once. This naïveté of expectation drove me to fury, but I restrained myself.

She ought to have tried not to notice, as though everything had been as usual, while instead of that, she . . . and I dimly felt that I should make her pay dearly for *all this*.

"You have found me in a strange position, Liza," I began, stammering and knowing that this was the wrong way to begin. "No, no, don't imagine anything," I cried, seeing that she had suddenly flushed. "I am not ashamed of my poverty. . . . On the contrary I look with pride on my poverty. I am poor but honourable. . . . One can be poor and honourable," I muttered. "However . . . would you like tea?" . . .

"No," she was beginning.

"Wait a minute."

I leapt up and ran to Apollon. I had to get out of the room somehow.

"Apollon," I whispered in feverish haste, flinging down before him the seven roubles which had remained all the time in my clenched fist, "here are your wages, you see I give them to you; but for that you must come to my rescue: bring me tea and a dozen rusks from the restaurant. If you won't go, you'll make me a miserable man! You don't know what this woman is. . . . This is—everything! You may be imagining something. . . . But you don't know what that woman is!" . . .

Apollon, who had already sat down to his work and put on his spectacles again, at first glanced askance at the money without speaking or putting down his needle; then, without paying the slightest attention to me or making any answer he went on busying himself with his needle, which he had not yet threaded. I waited before him for three minutes with my arms crossed *à la Napoléon*. My temples were moist with sweat. I was pale, I felt it. But, thank God, he must have been moved to pity, looking at me. Having threaded his needle, he deliberately got up from his seat, deliberately moved back his chair, deliberately took off his spectacles, deliberately counted the money, and finally asking me over his shoulder: "Shall I get a whole portion?" deliberately walked out of the room. As I was going back to Liza, the thought occurred to me on the way: shouldn't I run away just as I was in my dressing-gown, no matter where, and then let happen what would?

I sat down again. She looked at me uneasily. For some minutes we were silent.

"I will kill him," I shouted suddenly, striking the table with my fist so that the ink spurted out of the inkstand.

"What are you saying!" she cried, starting.

"I will kill him! kill him!" I shrieked, suddenly striking the table in absolute frenzy, and at the same time fully understanding how stupid it was to be in such a frenzy. "You don't know, Liza, what that torturer is to me. He is my torturer. . . . He has gone now to fetch some rusks; he . . ."

And suddenly I burst into tears. It was an hysterical attack. How ashamed I felt in the midst of my sobs; but still I could not restrain them.

She was frightened.

"What is the matter? What is wrong?" she cried, fussing about me.

"Water, give me water, over there!" I muttered in a faint voice, though I was inwardly conscious that I could have got on very well without water and without muttering in a faint voice. But I was what is called *putting it on*, to save appearances, though the attack was a genuine one.

She gave me water, looking at me in bewilderment. At that moment Apollon brought in the tea. It suddenly seemed to me that this commonplace, prosaic tea was horribly undignified and paltry after all that had happened, and I blushed crimson. Liza looked at Apollon with positive alarm. He went out without a glance at either of us.

"Liza, do you despise me?" I asked, looking at her fixedly, trembling with impatience to know what she was thinking.

She was confused, and did not know what to answer.

"Drink your tea," I said to her angrily. I was angry with myself, but, of course, it was she who would have to pay for it. A horrible spite against her suddenly surged up in my heart; I believe I could have killed her. To revenge myself on her I swore inwardly not to say a word to her all the time. "She is the cause of it all," I thought.

Our silence lasted for five minutes. The tea stood on the table; we did not touch it. I had got to the point of purposely refraining from beginning in order to embarrass her further; it was awkward for her to begin alone. Several times she glanced at me with mournful perplexity. I was obstinately silent. I was, of course, myself the chief sufferer, because I was fully conscious of the disgusting meanness of my spiteful stupidity, and yet at the same time I could not restrain myself.

"I want to . . . get away . . . from there altogether," she began, to break the silence in some way, but, poor girl, that was just what she ought not to have spoken about at such a stupid moment to a man so stupid as I was. My heart positively ached with pity for her tactless and unnecessary straightforwardness. But something hideous at once stifled all compassion in me; it even provoked me to greater venom. I did not care what happened. Another five minutes passed.

"Perhaps I am in your way," she began timidly, hardly audibly, and was getting up.

But as soon as I saw this first impulse of wounded dignity I positively trembled with spite, and at once burst out.

"Why have you come to me, tell me that, please?" I began, gasping for breath and regardless of logical connection in my words. I longed to have it all out at once, at one burst; I did not even trouble how to begin. "Why have you come? Answer, answer," I cried, hardly knowing what I was doing. "I'll tell you, my good girl, why you have come. You've come because I talked sentimental stuff to you then. So now you are soft as butter and longing for fine sentiments again. So you may as well know that I was laughing at you then. And I am laughing at you now. Why are you shuddering? Yes, I was laughing at you! I had been insulted just before, at dinner, by the fellows who came that evening before me. I came to you, meaning to thrash one of them, an officer; but I didn't succeed, I didn't find him; I had to avenge the insult on some one to get back my own again; you turned up, I vented my spleen on you and laughed at you. I had been humiliated, so I wanted to humiliate; I had been treated like a rag, so I wanted to show my power. . . . That's what it was, and you imagined I had come there on purpose to save you. Yes? You imagined that? You imagined that?"

I knew that she would perhaps be muddled and not take it all in exactly, but I knew, too, that she would grasp the gist of it, very well indeed. And so, indeed, she did. She turned white as a handkerchief, tried to say something, and her lips worked painfully; but she sank on a chair as though she had been felled by an axe. And all the time afterwards she listened to me with her lips parted and her eyes wide-open, shuddering with awful terror. The cynicism, the cynicism of my words overwhelmed her.

"Save you!" I went on, jumping up from my chair and running up and down the room before her. "Save you from what? But perhaps I am worse than you myself. Why didn't you throw it in my teeth when I was giving you that sermon: 'But what did you come here yourself for? Was it to read us a sermon?' Power, power was what I wanted then, sport was what I wanted, I wanted to wring out your tears, your humiliation, your hysteria—that was what I wanted then! Of course, I couldn't keep it up then, because I am a wretched creature, I was frightened, and, the devil knows why, gave you my address in my folly. Afterwards, before I got home, I was cursing and swearing at you because of that address, I hated you already because of the lies I had told you. Because I only like playing with words, only dreaming, but, do you know, what I really want is that you should all go to hell. That is what I want. I want peace; yes, I'd sell the whole world for a farthing, straight off, so long as I was left in peace. Is the world to go to pot, or am I to go without my tea? I say that the world may go to pot for me so long as I always get my tea. Did you know that, or not? Well, anyway, I know that I am a blackguard, a scoundrel, an egoist, a sluggard. Here I have been shuddering for the last three days at the thought of your coming. And do you know what has worried me particularly for these three days? That I posed as such a hero to you, and now you would see me in a wretched torn dressing-gown, beggarly, loathsome. I told you just now that I was not ashamed of my poverty; so you may as well know that I am ashamed of it; I am more ashamed of it than of anything, more afraid of it than of being found out if I were a thief, because I am as vain as though I had been skinned and the very air blowing on me hurt. Surely by now you must realize that I shall never forgive you for having found me in this wretched dressing-gown, just as I was flying at Apollon like a spiteful cur. The saviour, the former hero, was flying like a mangy, unkempt sheep-dog at his lackey, and the lackey was jeering at him! And I shall never forgive you for the tears I could not help shedding before you just now, like some silly woman put to shame! And for what I am confessing to you now, I shall never forgive *you* either! Yes —you must answer for it all because you turned up like this, because I am a blackguard, because I am the nastiest, stupidest, absurdest and most envious of all the worms on earth, who are not a bit better than I am, but, the devil knows why, are never put to confusion; while I shall always be insulted by every louse, that is my doom! And what is it to me that you don't understand a word of this! And what do I care, what do I care about you, and whether you go to ruin there or not? Do you understand? How I shall hate you now after saying this, for having been here and listening. Why, it's not once in a lifetime a man speaks out like this, and then it is in hysterics! . . . What more do you want? Why do you still stand confronting me, after all this? Why are you worrying me? Why don't you go?"

But at this point a strange thing happened: I was so accustomed to think and imagine everything from books, and to picture everything in the world to myself just as I had made it up in my dreams beforehand, that I could not all at once take in this strange circumstance. What happened was this: Liza, insulted and crushed by me, understood a great deal more than I imagined. She understood from all this what a woman understands first of all, if she feels genuine love, that is, that I was myself unhappy.

The frightened and wounded expression on her face was followed first by a look of sorrowful perplexity. When I began calling myself a scoundrel and a blackguard and my tears flowed (the tirade was accompanied throughout by tears) her whole face worked convulsively. She was on the point of getting up and stopping me; when I finished she took no notice of my shouting: "Why are you here, why don't you go away?" but realized only that it must have been very bitter to me to say all this. Besides, she was so crushed, poor girl; she considered herself infinitely beneath me; how could she feel anger or resentment? She suddenly leapt up from her chair with an irresistible impulse and held out her hands, yearning towards me, though still timid and not daring to stir. . . . At this point there was a revulsion in my heart, too. Then she suddenly rushed to me, threw her arms round me and burst into tears. I, too, could not restrain myself, and sobbed as I never had before.

"They won't let me . . . I can't be good!" I managed to articulate; then I went to the sofa, fell on it face downwards, and sobbed on it for a quarter of an hour in genuine hysterics. She came close to me, put her arms round me and stayed motionless in that position. But the trouble was that the hysterics could not go on for ever, and (I am writing the loathsome truth) lying face downwards on the sofa with my face thrust into my nasty leather pillow, I began by degrees to be aware of a far-away, involuntary but irresistible feeling that it would be awkward now for me to raise my head and look Liza straight in the face. Why was I ashamed? I don't know, but I was ashamed. The thought, too, came into my overwrought brain that our parts now were completely changed, that she was now the heroine, while I was just such a crushed and humiliated creature as she had been before me that night—four days before. . . . And all this came into my mind during the minutes I was lying on my face on the sofa.

My God! surely I was not envious of her then.

I don't know, to this day I cannot decide, and at the time, of course, I was still less able to understand what I was feeling than now. I cannot get on without domineering and tyrannizing over some one, but . . . there is no explaining anything by reasoning and so it is useless to reason.

I conquered myself, however, and raised my head; I had to do so sooner or later . . . and I am convinced to this day that it was just because I was ashamed to look at her that another feeling was suddenly kindled and flamed up in my heart . . . a feeling of mastery and possession. My eyes gleamed with passion, and I gripped her hands tightly. How I hated her and how I was drawn to her at that minute! The one feeling intensified the other. It was almost like an act of vengeance. At first there was a look of amazement, even of terror, on her face, but only for one instant. She warmly and rapturously embraced me.

X

A quarter of an hour later I was rushing up and down the room in frenzied impatience, from minute to minute I went up to the screen and peeped through the crack at Liza. She was sitting on the ground with her head leaning against the bed, and must have been crying. But she did not go away, and that irritated me. This time she understood it all. I had insulted her finally, but . . . there's no need to describe it. She realized that my outburst of passion had been simply revenge, a fresh humiliation, and that to my earlier, almost causeless hatred was added now a *personal hatred,* born of envy. . . . Though I do not maintain positively that she understood all this distinctly; but she certainly did fully understand that I was a despicable man, and what was worse, incapable of loving her.

I know I shall be told that this is incredible—but it is incredible to be as spiteful and stupid as I was; it may be added that it was strange I should not love her, or at any rate, appreciate her love. Why is it strange? In the first place, by then I was incapable of love, for, I repeat, with me loving meant tyrannizing and showing my moral superiority. I have never in my life been able to imagine any other sort of love, and have nowadays come to the point of sometimes thinking that love really consists in the right—freely given by the beloved object—to tyrannize over her.

Even in my underground dreams I did not imagine love except as a struggle. I began it always with hatred and ended it with moral subjugation, and afterwards I never knew what to do with the subjugated object. And what is there to wonder at in that, since I had succeeded in so corrupting myself, since I was so out of touch with "real life," as to have actually thought of reproaching her, and putting her to shame for having come to me to hear "fine sentiments"; and did not even guess that she had come not to hear fine sentiments, but to love me, because to a woman all reformation—all salvation from any sort of ruin, and all moral renewal—is included in love and can only show itself in that form.

I did not hate her so much, however, when I was running about the room and peeping through the crack in the screen. I was only insufferably oppressed by her being here. I wanted her to disappear. I wanted "peace," to be left alone in my underground world. Real life oppressed me with its novelty so much that I could hardly breathe.

But several minutes passed and she still remained without stirring, as though she were unconscious. I had the shamelessness to tap softly at the screen as though to remind her. . . . She started, sprang up, and flew to seek her kerchief, her hat, her coat, as though making her escape from me. . . . Two minutes later she came from behind the screen and looked with heavy eyes at me. I gave a spiteful grin, which was forced, however, to *keep up appearances*, and I turned away from her eyes.

"Good-bye," she said, going towards the door.

I ran up to her, seized her hand, opened it, thrust something in it and closed it again. Then I turned at once and dashed away in haste to the other corner of the room to avoid seeing, anyway. . . .

I did mean a moment since to tell a lie—to write that I did this accidentally, not knowing what I was doing through foolishness, through losing my head. But I don't want to lie, and so I will say straight out that I opened her hand and put the money in it . . . from spite. It came into my head to do this while I was running up and down the room and she was sitting behind the screen. But this I can say for certain: though I did that cruel thing purposely, it was not an impulse from the heart, but came from my evil brain. This cruelty was so affected, so purposely made up, so completely a product of the brain, of books, that I could not even keep it up a minute—first I dashed away to avoid seeing her, and then in shame and despair rushed after Liza. I opened the door in the passage and began listening.

"Liza! Liza!" I cried on the stairs, but in a low voice, not boldly.

There was no answer, but I fancied I heard her footsteps, lower down on the stairs.

"Liza!" I cried, more loudly.

No answer. But at that minute I heard the stiff outer glass door open heavily with a creak and slam violently, the sound echoed up the stairs.

She had gone. I went back to my room in hesitation. I felt horribly oppressed.

I stood still at the table beside the chair on which she had sat and looked aimlessly before me. A minute passed, suddenly I started; straight before me on the table I saw. . . . In short, I saw a crumpled blue five-rouble note, the one I had thrust into her hand a minute before. It was the same note; it could be no other, there was no other in the flat. So she had managed to fling it from her hand on the table at the moment when I had dashed into the further corner.

Well! I might have expected that she would do that. Might I have expected it? No, I was such an egoist, I was so lacking in respect for my fellow-creatures that I could not even imagine she would do so. I could not endure it. A minute later I flew like a madman to dress, flinging on what I could at random and ran headlong after her. She could not have got two hundred paces away when I ran out into the street.

It was a still night and the snow was coming down in masses and falling almost perpendicularly, covering the pavement and the empty street as though with a pillow. There was no one in the street, no sound was to be heard. The street lamps gave a disconsolate and useless glimmer. I ran two hundred paces to the cross-roads and stopped short.

Where had she gone? And why was I running after her? Why? To fall down before her, to sob with remorse, to kiss her feet, to entreat her forgiveness! I longed for that, my whole breast was being rent to pieces, and never, never shall I recall that minute with indifference. But—what for? I thought. Should I not begin to hate her, perhaps, even to-morrow, just because I had kissed her feet to-day? Should I give her happiness? Had I not recognized that day, for the hundredth time, what I was worth? Should I not torture her?

I stood in the snow, gazing into the troubled darkness and pondered this.

"And will it not be better?" I mused fantastically, afterwards at home, stifling the living pang of my heart with fantastic dreams. "Will it not be better that she should keep the resentment of the insult for ever? Resentment—why, it is purification; it is a most stinging and painful consciousness! To-morrow I should have defiled her soul and have exhausted her heart, while now the feeling of insult will never die in her heart, and however loathsome the filth awaiting her—the feeling of insult will elevate and purify her . . . by hatred . . . h'm! . . . perhaps too, by forgiveness. . . . Will all that make things easier for her, though? . . ."

And, indeed, I will ask on my own account here an idle question: which is better—cheap happiness or exalted sufferings? Well, which is better?

So I dreamed as I sat at home that evening, almost dead with the pain in my soul. Never had I endured such suffering and remorse, yet could there have been the faintest doubt when I ran out from my lodging that I should turn back half-way? I never met Liza again and I have heard nothing of her. I will add, too, that I remained for a long time afterwards pleased with the phrase about the benefit from resentment and hatred, in spite of the fact that I almost fell ill from misery.

Even now, so many years later, all this is somehow a very evil memory. I have many evil memories now, but . . . hadn't I better end my "Notes" here? I believe I made a mistake in beginning to write them, anyway I have felt ashamed all the time I've been writing this story; so it's hardly literature so much as a corrective punishment. Why, to tell long stories, showing how I have spoiled my life through morally rotting in my corner, through lack of fitting environment, through divorce from real life, and rankling spite in my underground world, would certainly not be interesting; a novel needs a hero, and all the traits for an anti-hero are *expressly* gathered together here, and what matters most, it all produces an unpleasant impression, for we are all divorced from life, we are all cripples, every one of us, more or less. We are so divorced from it that we feel at once a sort of loathing for real life, and so cannot bear to be reminded of it. Why, we have come almost to looking upon real life as an effort, almost as hard work, and we are all privately agreed that it is better in books. And why do we fuss and fume sometimes? Why are we perverse and ask for something else? We don't know what ourselves. It would be the worse for us if our petulant prayers were answered. Come, try, give any one of us, for instance, a little more independence, untie our hands, widen the spheres of our activity, relax the control and we . . . yes, I assure you . . . we should be begging to be under control again at once. I know that you will very likely be angry with me for that, and will begin shouting and stamping. Speak for yourself, you will say, and for your miseries in your underground holes, and don't dare to say all of us—excuse me, gentlemen, I am not justifying myself with that "all of us." As for what concerns me in particular I have only in my life carried to an extreme what you have not dared to carry halfway, and what's more, you have taken your cowardice for good sense, and have found comfort in deceiving yourselves. So that perhaps, after all, there is more life in me than in you. Look into it more carefully! Why, we don't even know what living means now, what it is, and what it is called! Leave us alone without books and we shall be lost and in confusion at once. We shall not know what to join on to, what to cling to, what to love and what to hate, what to respect and what to despise. We are oppressed at being men—men with a real individual body and blood, we are ashamed of it, we think it a disgrace and try to contrive to be some sort of impossible generalized man. We are stillborn, and for generations past have been begotten, not by living fathers, and that suits us better and better. We are developing a taste for it. Soon we shall contrive to be born somehow from an idea. But enough; I don't want to write more from "Underground."

[*The notes of this paradoxalist do not end here, however. He could not refrain from going on with them, but it seems to us that we may stop here.*]

1864

Poor People

A NOVEL

Ah, these story tellers! If only they would write anything useful, pleasant, soothing, but they will unearth all sorts of hidden things! . . . I would prohibit their writing! Why, it is beyond everything; you read . . . and you can't help thinking—and then all sorts of foolishness comes into your head; I would really prohibit their writing; I would simply prohibit it altogether.

PRINCE V. F. ODOEVSKY.

April 8.

MY PRECIOUS VARVARA ALEXYEVNA,

I was happy yesterday, immensely happy, impossibly happy! For once in your life, you obstinate person, you obeyed me. At eight o'clock in the evening I woke up (you know, little mother, that I love a little nap of an hour or two when my work is over). I got out a candle, I got paper ready, was mending a pen when suddenly I chanced to raise my eyes—upon my word it set my heart dancing! So you understood what I wanted, what was my heart's desire! I saw a tiny corner of your window-curtain twitched back and caught against the pot of balsams, just exactly as I hinted that day. Then I fancied I caught a glimpse of your little face at the window, that you were looking at me from your little room, that you were thinking of me. And how vexed I was, my darling, that I could not make out your charming little face distinctly! There was a time when we, too, could see clearly, dearie. It is poor fun being old, my own! Nowadays everything seems sort of spotty before my eyes; if one works a little in the evening, writes something, one's eyes are so red and tearful in the morning that one is really ashamed before strangers. In my imagination, though, your smile was beaming, my little angel, your kind friendly little smile; and I had just the same sensation in my heart as when I kissed you, Varinka, do you remember, little angel? Do you know, my darling, I even fancied that you shook your little finger at me? Did you, you naughty girl? You must be sure to describe all that fully in your letter.

Come, what do you think of our little plan about your curtain, Varinka? It is delightful, isn't it? Whether I am sitting at work, or lying down for a nap, or waking up, I know that you are thinking about me over there, you are remembering me and that you are well and cheerful. You drop the curtain—it means "Good-bye, Makar Alexyevitch, it's bedtime!" You draw it up—"Good morning, Makar Alexyevitch, how have you slept or are you quite well, Makar Alexyevitch? As for me, thank God, I am well and all right!" You see, my darling, what a clever idea; there is no need of letters! It's cunning, isn't it? And you know it was my idea. What do you say to me now, Varvara Alexyevna?

I beg to inform you, Varvara Alexyevna, my dear, that I slept last night excellently, contrary to my expectations, at which I am very much pleased; though in new lodgings, after moving, it is always difficult to sleep; there is always some little thing amiss.

I got up this morning as gay as a lark! What a fine morning it was, my darling! Our window was opened; the sun shone so brightly; the birds were chirping; the air was full of the scents of spring and all nature seemed coming back to life—and everything else was to correspond; everything was right, to fit the spring. I even had rather pleasant dreams to-day, and my dreams were all of you, Varinka. I compared you with a bird of the air created for the delight of men and the adornment of nature. Then I thought, Varinka, that we men, living in care and anxiety, must envy the careless and innocent happiness of the birds of the air— and more of the same sort, like that; that is, I went on making such far-fetched comparisons. I have a book, Varinka, and there is the same thought in it, all very exactly described. I write this, my darling, because one has all sorts of dreams, you know. And now it's spring-time, so one's thoughts are always so pleasant; witty, amusing, and tender dreams visit one; everything is in a rosy light. That is why I have written all this; though, indeed, I took it all out of the book. The author there expresses the same desire in verse and writes:

"Why am I not a bird, a bird of prey!"

And so on, and so on. There are all sorts of thoughts in it, but never mind them now!

Oh, where were you going this morning, Varvara Alexyevna? Before I had begun to get ready for the office, you flew out of your room exactly like a bird of the air and crossed the yard, looking so gay. How glad it made me to look at you! Ah, Varinka, Varinka!—You must not be sad; tears are no help to sorrow; I know that, my dear, I know it from experience. Now you are so comfortable and you are getting a little stronger, too.

Well, how is your Fedora? Ah, what a good-natured woman she is! You must write and tell me, Varinka, how you get on with her now and whether you are satisfied with everything. Fedora is rather a grumbler; but you must not mind that, Varinka. God bless her! She has such a good heart. I have written to you already about Teresa here— she, too, is a good-natured and trustworthy woman. And how uneasy I was about our letters! How were they to be delivered? And behold the Lord sent us Teresa to make us happy. She is a good-natured woman, mild and long-suffering. But our landlady is simply merciless. She squeezes her at work like a rag.

Well, what a hole I have got into, Varvara Alexyevna! It is a lodging! I used to live like a bird in the woods, as you know yourself—it was so quiet and still that if a fly flew across the room you could hear it. Here it is all noise, shouting, uproar! But of course you don't know how it is all arranged here. Imagine a long passage, absolutely dark and very dirty. On the right hand there is a blank wall, and on the left, doors and doors, like the rooms in a hotel, in a long row. Well, these are lodgings and there is one room in each; there are people living by twos and by threes in one room. It is no use expecting order—it is a regular Noah's ark! They seem good sort of people, though, all so well educated and learned. One is in the service, a well-read man (he is somewhere in the literary department): he talks about Homer and Brambeus and authors of all sorts: he talks about everything; a very intelligent man! There are two officers who do nothing but play cards. There is a naval man; and an English teacher.

Wait a bit, I will divert you, my darling; I will describe them satirically in my next letter; that is, I will tell you what they are like in full detail. Our landlady is a very untidy little old woman, she goes about all day long in slippers and a dressing-gown, and all day long she is scolding at Teresa. I live in the kitchen, or rather, to be more accurate, there is a room near the kitchen (and our kitchen, I ought to tell you, is clean, light and very nice), a little room, a modest corner . . . or rather the kitchen is a big room of three windows so I have a partition running along the inside wall, so that it makes as it were another room, an extra lodging; it is roomy and comfortable, and there is a window and all— in fact, every convenience. Well, so that is my little corner. So don't you imagine, my darling, there is anything else about it, any mysterious significance in it; "here he is living in the kitchen!" you'll say. Well, if you like, I really am living in the kitchen, behind the partition, but that is nothing; I am quite private, apart from everyone, quiet and snug. I have put in a bed, a table, a chest of drawers and a couple of chairs, and I have hung up the ikon. It is true there are better lodgings—perhaps there may be much better, but convenience is the great thing; I have arranged it all for my own convenience, you know, and you must not imagine it is for anything else. Your little window is opposite, across the yard; and the yard is narrow, one catches glimpses of you passing—it is more cheerful for a poor, lonely fellow like me, and cheaper, too. The very cheapest room here with board costs thirty-five roubles in paper: beyond my means;

but my lodging costs me seven roubles in paper and my board five in silver—that is, twenty-four and a half, and before I used to pay thirty and make it up by going without a great many things. I did not always have tea, but now I can spare enough for tea and sugar, too. And you know, my dear, one is ashamed as it were not to drink tea; here they are all well-to-do people so one feels ashamed. One drinks it, Varinka, for the sake of the other people, for the look of the thing; for myself I don't care, I am not particular. Think, too, of pocket-money—one must have a certain amount—then some sort of boots and clothes—is there much left? My salary is all I have. I am content and don't repine. It is sufficient. It has been sufficient for several years; there are extras, too.

Well, good-bye, my angel. I have bought a couple of pots of balsam and geranium—quite cheap—but perhaps you love mignonette? Well, there is mignonette, too, you write and tell me; be sure to write me everything as fully as possible, you know. Don't you imagine anything, though, or have any doubts about my having taken such a room, Varinka dear; no, it is my own convenience made me take it, and only the convenience of it tempted me. I am putting by money, you know, my darling, I am saving up: I have quite a lot of money. You must not think I am such a softy that a fly might knock me down with his wing. No, indeed, my own, I am not a fool, and I have as strong a will as a man of resolute and tranquil soul ought to have. Good-bye, my angel! I have scribbled you almost two sheets and I ought to have been at the office long ago. I kiss your fingers, my own, and remain

Your humble and faithful friend
MAKAR DYEVUSHKIN.

P.S.—One thing I beg you: answer me as fully as possible, my angel. I am sending you a pound of sweets with this, Varinka. You eat them up and may they do you good, and for God's sake do not worry about me and make a fuss. Well, good-bye then, my precious.

April 8.

DEAR SIR, MAKAR ALEXYEVITCH,

Do you know I shall have to quarrel with you outright at last. I swear to you, dear Makar Alexyevitch, that it really hurts me to take your presents. I know what they cost you, how you deny yourself, and deprive yourself of what is necessary. How many times have I told you that I need nothing, absolutely nothing; that I shall never be able to repay you for the kindnesses you have showered upon me? And why have you sent me these flowers? Well, the balsams I don't mind, but why the geranium? I have only to drop an incautious word, for instance, about that geranium, and you rush off and buy it. I am sure it must have been expensive? How charming the flowers are! Crimson, in little crosses. Where did you get such a pretty geranium? I have put it in the middle of the window in the most conspicuous place; I am putting a bench on the floor and arranging the rest of the flowers on the bench; you just wait until I get rich myself! Fedora is overjoyed; it's like paradise now, in our room—so clean, so bright!

Now, why those sweets? Upon my word, I guessed at once from your letter that there was something amiss with you—nature and spring and the sweet scents and the birds chirping. "What's this," I thought, "isn't it poetry?" Yes, indeed, your letter ought to have been in verse, that was all that was wanting, Makar Alexyevitch! There are the tender sentiments and dreams in roseate hues—everything in it! As for the curtain, I never thought of it; I suppose it got hitched up of itself when I moved the flower-pots, so there!

Ah, Makar Alexyevitch! Whatever you may say, however you may reckon over your income to deceive me, to prove that your money is all spent on yourself, you won't take me in and you won't hide anything from me. It is clear that you are depriving yourself of necessities for my sake. What possessed you, for instance, to take such a lodging? Why, you will be disturbed and worried; you are cramped for room, uncomfortable. You love solitude, and here, goodness knows what you have all about you! You might live a great deal better, judging from your salary. Fedora says you used to live ever so much better than you do now. Can you have spent all your life like this in solitude, in privation, without pleasure, without a friendly affectionate word, a lodger among strangers? Ah, dear friend, how sorry I am for you! Take care of your health, anyway, Makar Alexyevitch! You say your eyes are weak; so you must not write by candle-light; why write? Your devotion to your work must be known to your superiors without that.

Once more I entreat you not to spend so much money on me. I know that you love me, but you are not well off yourself. . . . I got up this morning feeling gay, too. I was so happy; Fedora had been at work a long time and had got work for me, too. I was so delighted; I only went out to buy silk and then I set to work. The whole morning I felt so lighthearted, I was so gay! But now it is all black thoughts and sadness again; my heart keeps aching.

Ah, what will become of me, what will be my fate! What is painful is that I am in such uncertainty, that I have no future to look forward to, that I cannot even guess what will become of me. It is dreadful to look back, too. There is such sorrow in the past, and my heart is torn in two at the very memory of it. All my life I shall be in suffering, thanks to the wicked people who have ruined me.

It is getting dark. Time for work. I should have liked to have written to you of lots of things but I have not the time, I must get to work. I must make haste. Of course letters are a good thing; they make it more cheerful, anyway. But why do you never come to see us yourself? Why is that, Makar Alexyevitch? Now we are so near, you know, and sometimes you surely can make time. Please do come! I have seen your Teresa. She looks such a sickly creature; I felt sorry for her and gave her twenty kopecks. Yes! I was almost forgetting: you must write to me all about your life and your surroundings as fully as possible. What sort of people are they about you and do you get on with them? I am longing to know all that. Mind you write to me! To-day I will hitch up the curtain on purpose. You should go to

bed earlier; last night I saw your light till midnight. Well,
good-bye. To-day I am miserable and bored and sad! It
seems it is an unlucky day! Good-bye.

Yours,

VARVARA DOBROSELOV.

April 8.

DEAR MADAM, VARVARA ALEXYEVNA,

Yes, dear friend, yes, my own, it seems it was a bad day
for poor luckless me! Yes; you mocked at an old man like
me, Varvara Alexyevna! It was my fault, though, entirely
my fault! I ought not in my old age, with scarcely any hair
on my head, to have launched out into lyrical nonsense and
fine phrases. . . . And I will say more, my dear: man is
sometimes a strange creature, very strange. My goodness!
he begins talking of something and is carried away directly!
And what comes of it, what does it lead to? Why, absolutely
nothing comes of it, and it leads to such nonsense that—
Lord preserve me! I am not angry, Varinka dear, only I
am very much vexed to remember it all, vexed that I wrote
to you in such a foolish, high-flown way. And I went to
the office to-day so cock-a-hoop; there was such radiance in
my heart. For no rhyme or reason there was a regular holiday in my soul; I felt so gay. I took up my papers eagerly
—but what did it all amount to! As soon as I looked about
me, everything was as before, grey and dingy. Still the
same ink-spots, the same tables and papers, and I, too, was
just the same; as I always have been, so I was still—so
what reason was there to mount upon Pegasus? And what
was it all due to? The sun peeping out and the sky growing
blue! Was that it? And how could I talk of the scents of
spring? when you never know what there may be in our
yard under the windows! I suppose I fancied all that in my
foolishness. You know a man does sometimes make such
mistakes in his own feelings and writes nonsense. That is
due to nothing but foolish, excessive warmth of heart.

I did not walk but crawled home. For no particular reason my head had begun to ache; well that, to be sure, was
one thing on the top of another. (I suppose I got a chill to

my spine.) I was so delighted with the spring, like a fool, that I went out in a thin greatcoat. And you were mistaken in my feelings, my dear!

You took my outpouring of them quite in the wrong way. I was inspired by fatherly affection—nothing but a pure fatherly affection, Varvara Alexyevna. For I take the place of a father to you, in your sad fatherless and motherless state; I say this from my soul, from a pure heart, as a relation. After all, though, I am but a distant relation, as the proverb says "only the seventh water on the jelly," still I am a relation and now your nearest relation and protector; seeing that where you had most right to look for protection and support you have met with insult and treachery. As for verses, let me tell you, my love, it would not be seemly for me in my old age to be making verses. Poetry is nonsense! Why, boys are thrashed at school nowadays for making poetry . . . so that is how it is, my dear. . . .

What are you writing to me, Varvara Alexyevna, about comfort, about quiet and all sorts of things? I am not particular, my dear soul, I am not exacting. I have never lived better than I am doing now; so why should I be hard to please in my old age? I am well fed and clothed and shod; and it is not for us to indulge our whims! We are not royalties! My father was not of noble rank and his income was less than mine for his whole family. I have not lived in the lap of luxury! However, if I must tell the truth, everything was a good deal better in my old lodging; it was more roomy and convenient, dear friend. Of course my present lodging is nice, even in some respects more cheerful, and more varied if you like; I have nothing to say against that but yet I regret the old one. We old, that is elderly people, get used to old things as though to something akin to us. The room was a little one, you know; the walls were . . . there, what is the use of talking! . . . the walls were like all other walls, they don't matter, and yet remembering all my past makes me depressed . . . it's a strange thing: it's painful, yet the memories are, as it were, pleasant. Even what was nasty, what I was vexed with at the time, is, as it were, purified from nastiness in my memory and presents itself in an attractive shape to my imagination. We lived peacefully, Varinka, I and my old landlady who is dead. I remember my old landlady with a sad feeling now. She was a good woman and did not charge me much for my lodging. She used to knit all sorts of rugs out of rags on needles a yard long. She used to do nothing else. We used to share light and fuel, so we worked at one table. She had a grand-daughter, Masha—I remember her quite a little thing. Now she must be a girl of thirteen. She was such a mischievous little thing—very merry, always kept us amused, and we lived together, the three of us. Sometimes in the long winter evenings we would sit down to the round table, drink a cup of tea and then set to work. And to keep Masha amused and out of mischief the old lady used to begin to tell tales. And what tales they were! A sensible intelligent man would listen to them with pleasure, let alone a child. Why, I used to light my pipe and be so interested that I forgot my work. And the child, our little mischief, would be so grave, she would lean her rosy cheek on her little hand, open her pretty little mouth and, if the story were the least bit terrible, she would huddle up to the old woman. And we liked to look at her; and did not notice how the candle wanted snuffing nor hear the wind roaring and the storm raging outside.

We had a happy life, Varinka, and we lived together for almost twenty years.

But how I have been prattling on! Perhaps you don't care for such a subject, and it is not very cheering for me to remember it, especially just now in the twilight. Teresa's busy about something, my head aches and my back aches a little, too. And my thoughts are so queer, they seem to be aching as well. I am sad to-day, Varinka!

What's this you write, my dear? How can I come and see you? My darling, what would people say? Why, I should have to cross the yard, our folks would notice it, would begin asking questions—there would be gossip, there would be scandal, they would put a wrong construction on it. No, my angel, I had better see you to-morrow at the evening service, that will be more sensible and more prudent for

both of us. And don't be vexed with me, my precious, for
writing you such a letter; reading it over I see it is all so
incoherent. I am an old man, Varinka, and not well-educated; I had no education in my youth and now I could
get nothing into my head if I began studying over again.
I am aware, Varinka, that I am no hand at writing, and I
know without anyone else pointing it out and laughing at
me that if I were to try to write something more amusing
I should only write nonsense.

I saw you at your window to-day, I saw you let down
your blind. Good-bye, good-bye, God keep you! Good-bye,
Varvara Alexyevna.

Your disinterested friend,
MAKAR DYEVUSHKIN.

P.S.—I can't write satirical accounts of anyone now, my
dear. I am too old, Varvara Alexyevna, to be facetious,
and I should make myself a laughing-stock; as the proverb
has it: "those who live in glass houses should not throw
stones."

April 9.

DEAR SIR, MAKAR ALEXYEVITCH,

Come, are not you ashamed, Makar Alexyevitch, my
friend and benefactor, to be so depressed and naughty?
Surely you are not offended! Oh, I am often too hasty, but
I never thought that you would take my words for a biting
jest. Believe me, I could never dare to jest at your age and
your character. It has all happened through my thoughtlessness, or rather from my being horribly dull, and
dullness may drive one to anything! I thought that you
meant to make fun yourself in your letter. I felt dreadfully
sad when I saw that you were displeased with me. No, my
dear friend and benefactor, you are wrong if you ever
suspect me of being unfriendly and ungrateful. In my heart
I know how to appreciate all you have done for me, defending me from wicked people, from their persecution and
hatred. I shall pray for you always, and if my prayer rises
to God and heaven accepts it you will be happy.

I feel very unwell to-day. I am feverish and shivering

by turns. Fedora is very anxious about me. There is no
need for you to be ashamed to come and see us, Makar
Alexyevitch; what business is it of other people's! We are
acquaintances, and that is all about it. . . .

Good-bye, Makar Alexyevitch. I have nothing more to
write now, and indeed I can't write; I am horribly unwell.
I beg you once more not to be angry with me and to rest
assured of the invariable respect and devotion,

With which I have the honour to remain,

Your most devoted and obedient servant,

VARVARA DOBROSELOV.

April 12.

DEAR MADAM, VARVARA ALEXYEVNA,

Oh, my honey, what is the matter with you! This is how
you frighten me every time. I write to you in every letter
to take care of yourself, to wrap yourself up, not to go
out in bad weather, to be cautious in every way—and, my
angel, you don't heed me. Ah, my darling, you are just
like some child! Why, you are frail, frail as a little straw, I
know that. If there is the least little wind, you fall ill. So
you must be careful, look after yourself, avoid risks and
not reduce your friends to grief and distress.

You express the desire, dear Varinka, to have a full
account of my daily life and all my surroundings. I gladly
hasten to carry out your wish, my dear. I will begin from
the beginning, my love: it will be more orderly.

To begin with, the staircases to the front entrance are
very passable in our house; especially the main staircase—
it is clean, light, wide, all cast-iron and mahogany, but don't
ask about the backstairs: winding like a screw, damp, dirty,
with steps broken and the walls so greasy that your hand
sticks when you lean against them. On every landing there
are boxes, broken chairs and cupboards, rags hung out,
windows broken, tubs stand about full of all sorts of dirt
and litter, eggshells and the refuse of fish; there is a horrid
smell . . . in fact it is not nice.

I have already described the arrangement of the rooms;
it is convenient, there is no denying; that is true, but it is

rather stuffy in them. I don't mean that there is a bad
smell, but, if I may so express it, a rather decaying, acrid,
sweetish smell. At first it makes an unfavourable impression, but this is of no consequence; one has only to be a
couple of minutes among us and it passes off and you
don't notice how it passes off for you begin to smell bad
yourself, your clothes smell, your hands smell and everything smells—well, you get used to it. Siskins simply die
with us. The naval man is just buying the fifth—they can't
live in our air and that is the long and short of it. Our
kitchen is big, roomy and light. In the mornings, it is true,
it is rather stifling when they are cooking fish or meat and
splashing and slopping water everywhere, but in the evening it is paradise. In our kitchen there is always old linen
hanging on a line; and as my room is not far off, that is, is
almost part of the kitchen, the smell of it does worry me a
little; but no matter, in time one gets used to anything.

Very early in the morning the hubbub begins, people
moving about, walking, knocking—everyone who has to
is getting up, some to go to the office, others about their
own business; they all begin drinking tea. The samovars
for the most part belong to the landlady; there are few of
them, so we all use them in turn, and if anyone goes with
his teapot out of his turn, he catches it.

I, for instance, the first time made that mistake, and . . .
but why describe it? I made the acquaintance of everyone at once. The naval man was the first I got to know;
he is such an open fellow, told me everything: about his
father and mother, about his sister married to an assessor
in Tula, and about the town of Kronstadt. He promised
to protect me and at once invited me to tea with him. I
found him in the room where they usually play cards.
There they gave me tea and were very insistent that I
should play a game of chance with them. Whether they
were laughing at me or not I don't know, but they were
losing the whole night and they were still playing when I
went away. Chalk, cards—and the room so full of smoke
that it made my eyes smart. I did not play and they at once
observed that I was talking of philosophy. After that no one

said another word to me the whole time; but to tell the truth I was glad of it. I am not going to see them now; it's gambling with them, pure gambling. The clerk in the literary department has little gatherings in the evening, too. Well, there it is nice, quiet, harmless and delicate; everything is on a refined footing.

Well, Varinka, I will remark in passing that our landlady is a very horrid woman and a regular old hag. You've seen Teresa. You know what she is like, as thin as a plucked, dried-up chicken. There are two of them in the house, Teresa and Faldoni. I don't know whether he has any other name, he always answers to that one and everyone calls him that. He is a red-haired, foul-tongued Finn, with only one eye and a snub nose: he is always swearing at Teresa, they almost fight.

On the whole life here is not exactly perfect at all times. . . .

If only all would go to sleep at once at night and be quiet—that never happens. They are for ever sitting somewhere playing, and sometimes things go on that one would be ashamed to describe. By now I have grown accustomed to it; but I wonder how people with families get along in such a Bedlam. There is a whole family of poor creatures living in one of our landlady's rooms, not in the same row with the other lodgings but on the other side, in a corner apart. They are quiet people! No one hears anything of them. They live in one little room dividing it with a screen. He is a clerk out of work, discharged from the service seven years ago for something. His name is Gorshkov— such a grey little man; he goes about in such greasy, such threadbare clothes that it is sad to see him; ever so much worse than mine. He is a pitiful, decrepit figure (we sometimes meet in the passage); his knees shake, his hands shake, his head shakes, from some illness I suppose, poor fellow. He is timid, afraid of everyone and sidles along edgeways; I am shy at times, but he is a great deal worse. His family consists of a wife and three children. The eldest, a boy, is just like his father, just as frail. The wife was once very good-looking, even now one can see it; she, poor thing, goes about in pitiful tatters. They are in debt to the landlady, I have heard, she is none too gracious to them. I have heard, too, that there is some unpleasant business hanging over Gorshkov in connection with which he lost his place. . . . Whether it is a lawsuit—whether he is to be tried, or prosecuted, or what, I can't tell you for certain. Poor they are, mercy on us! It is always still and quiet in their room as if no one were living there. There is no sound even of the children. And it never happens that the children frolic about and play, and that is a bad sign. One evening I happened to pass their door; it was unusually quiet in the house at the time; I heard a sobbing, then a whisper, then sobbing again as though they were crying but so quietly, so pitifully that it was heart-rending, and the thought of those poor creatures haunted me all night so that I could not get to sleep properly.

Well, good-bye, my precious little friend, Varinka. I have described everything to the best of my abilities. I have been thinking of nothing but you all day. My heart aches over you, my dear. I know, my love, you have no warm cloak. Ah! these Petersburg springs, these winds and rain mixed with snow—they'll be the death of me, Varinka! Such salubrious airs, Lord preserve us!

Don't scorn my description, my love. I have no style, Varinka, no style whatever. I only wish I had. I write just what comes into my head only to cheer you up with something. If only I had had some education it would have been a different matter, but how much education have I had? Not a ha'porth.

> Always your faithful friend,
> MAKAR DYEVUSHKIN.

April 25.

HONOURED SIR, MAKAR ALEXYEVITCH,

I met my cousin Sasha to-day! It is horrible! She will be ruined too, poor thing! I heard, too, from other sources that Anna Fyodorovna is still making inquiries about me. It seems as though she will never leave off persecuting me. She says that she wants to *forgive me*, to forget all the past

and that she must come and see me. She says that you are
no relation to me at all, that she is a nearer relation, that
you have no right to meddle in our family affairs and that
it is shameful and shocking to live on your charity and at
your expense. . . . She says that I have forgotten her hos-
pitality, that she saved mother and me from starving to
death, perhaps, that she gave us food and drink, and for
more than a year and a half was put to expense on our
account, and that besides all that she forgave us a debt.
Even mother she will not spare! and if only poor mother
knew how they have treated me! God sees it! . . . Anna
Fyodorovna says that I was so silly that I did not know
how to take advantage of my luck, that she put me in the
way of good luck, that she is not to blame for anything else,
and that I myself was not able or perhaps was not anxious
to defend my own honour. Who was to blame in that,
great God! She says that Mr. Bykov was perfectly right
and that he would not marry just anybody who . . . but
why write it!

It is cruel to hear such falsehoods, Makar Alexyevitch!
I can't tell you what a state I am in now. I am trembling,
crying, sobbing. I have been two hours over writing this
letter to you. I thought that at least she recognised how
wrongly she had treated me; and you see what she is now!

For God's sake don't be alarmed, my friend, the one
friend who wishes me well! Fedora exaggerates everything,
I am not ill. I only caught cold a little yesterday when I
went to the requiem service for mother at Volkovo. Why
did you not come with me? I begged you so much to do so.
Ah, my poor, poor mother, if she could rise from the grave,
if she could see how they have treated me!   V. D.

May 20.

MY DARLING VARINKA,

I send you a few grapes, my love; I am told they are
good for a convalescent and the doctor recommends them
for quenching the thirst—simply for thirst. You were longing the other day for a few roses, my darling, so I am send-

ing you some now. Have you any appetite, my love?—that is the most important thing.

Thank God, though, that it is all over and done with, and that our troubles, too, will be soon at an end. We must give thanks to heaven!

As for books, I cannot get hold of them anywhere for the moment. I am told there is a good book here written in very fine language; they say it is good. I have not read it myself, but it is very much praised here. I have asked for it and they have promised to lend it me, only will you read it? You are so hard to please in that line; it is difficult to satisfy your taste, I know that already, my darling. No doubt you want poetry, inspiration, lyrics—well, I will get poems too, I will get anything; there is a manuscript book full of extracts here.

I am getting on very well. Please don't be uneasy about me, my dearie. What Fedora told you about me is all nonsense; you tell her that she told a lie, be sure to tell her so, the wicked gossip! . . . I have not sold my new uniform. And why should I . . . judge for yourself, why should I sell it? Here, I am told, I have forty roubles bonus coming to me, so why should I sell it? Don't you worry, my precious; she's suspicious, your Fedora, she's suspicious. We shall get on splendidly, my darling! Only you get well, my angel, for God's sake, get well. Don't grieve your old friend. Who told you I had grown thin? It is slander, slander again! I am well and hearty and getting so fat that I am quite ashamed. I am well fed and well content: the only thing is for you to get strong again!

Come, good-bye, my angel; I kiss your little fingers,
And remain, always,
Your faithful friend,
MAKAR DYEVUSHKIN.

P.S.—Ah, my love, what do you mean by writing like that again? . . . What nonsense you talk! Why, how can I come and see you so often, my precious? I ask you how can I? Perhaps snatching a chance after dark; but there, there's scarcely any night at all now, at this season. As it was, my angel, I scarcely left you at all while you were ill, while you were unconscious; but really I don't know how I managed it all; and afterwards I gave up going to you for people had begun to be inquisitive and to ask questions. There had been gossip going about here, even apart from that. I rely upon Teresa; she is not one to talk; but think for yourself, my darling, what a to-do there will be when they find out everything about us. They will imagine something and what will they say then? So you must keep a brave heart, my darling, and wait until you are quite strong again; and then we will arrange a *rendezvous* somewhere out of doors.

June 1.

My DEAR MAKAR ALEXYEVITCH,

I so long to do something nice that will please you in return for all the care and trouble you have taken about me, and all your love for me, that at last I have overcome my disinclination to rummage in my chest and find my diary, which I am sending to you now. I began it in the happy time of my life. You used often to question me with curiosity about my manner of life in the past, my mother, Pokrovskoe, my time with Anna Fyodorovna and my troubles in the recent past, and you were so impatiently anxious to read the manuscript in which I took the fancy, God knows why, to record some moments of my life that I have no doubt the parcel I am sending will be a pleasure to you. It made me sad to read it over. I feel that I am twice as old as when I wrote the last line in that diary. It was all written at different dates. Good-bye, Makar Alexyevitch! I feel horribly depressed now and often I am troubled with sleeplessness. Convalescence is a very dreary business!   V. D.

I

I was only fourteen when my father died. My childhood was the happiest time of my life. It began not here but far away in a province in the wilds. My father was the steward of Prince P.'s huge estate in the province of T——. We lived in one of the Prince's villages and led a quiet, obscure, happy life. . . . I was a playful little thing; I used to do nothing but run about the fields, the copses and the gardens, and no one troubled about me. My father was constantly busy about his work, my mother looked after the house; no one taught me anything, for which I was very glad. Sometimes at daybreak I would run away either to the pond or to the copse or to the hayfield or to the reapers—and it did not matter that the sun was baking, that I was running, I did not know where, away from the village, that I was scratched by the bushes, that I tore my dress. . . . I should be scolded afterwards at home, but I did not care for that.

And it seems to me that I should have been so happy if it had been my lot to have spent all my life in one place and never to have left the country. But I had to leave my native place while I was still a child. I was only twelve when we moved to Petersburg. Ah, how well I remember our sorrowful preparations! How I cried when I said good-bye to everything that was so dear to me. I remember that I threw myself on father's neck and besought him with tears to remain a little longer in the country. Father scolded me, mother wept; she said that we had to go, that we could not help it. Old Prince P—— was dead. His heirs had discharged father from his post. Father had some money in the hands of private persons in Petersburg. Hoping to improve his position he thought his presence here in person essential. All this I learnt from mother. We settled here on the Petersburg Side and lived in the same spot up to the time of father's death.

How hard it was for me to get used to our new life! We moved to Petersburg in the autumn. When we left the country it was a clear, warm, brilliant day; the work of the fields was over; huge stacks of wheat were piled up on the threshing-floors and flocks of birds were calling about the fields; everything was so bright and gay: here as we came into the town we found rain, damp autumn chilliness, muggy greyness, sleet and a crowd of new, unknown faces, unwelcoming, ill-humoured, angry! We settled in somehow. I remember we were all in such a fuss, so troubled and busy in arranging our new life. Father was never at home, mother had not a quiet minute—I was forgotten altogether. I felt sad getting up in the morning after the first night in our new abode—our windows looked out on a yellow fence. The street was always covered with mud. The passers-by were few and they were all muffled up, they were all so cold. And for whole days together it was terribly miserable and dreary at home. We had scarcely a relation or intimate acquaintance. Father was not on friendly terms with Anna Fyodorovna. (He was in her debt.) People came on business to us pretty often. Usually they quarrelled, shouted and made an uproar. After every visit father was ill-humoured and cross; he would walk up and down the room by the hour together, frowning and not saying a word to anyone. Mother was silent then and did not dare to speak to him. I used to sit in a corner over a book, still and quiet, not daring to stir.

Three months after we came to Petersburg I was sent to boarding-school. How sad I was at first with strangers! Everything was so cold, so unfriendly! The teachers had such loud voices, the girls laughed at me so and I was such a wild creature. It was so stern and exacting! The fixed hours for everything, the meals in common, the tedious teachers—all that at first fretted and harassed me. I could not even sleep there. I used to cry the whole night, the long, dreary, cold night. Sometimes when they were all repeating or learning their lessons in the evening I would sit over my French translation or vocabularies, not daring to move and dreaming all the while of our little home, of father, of mother, of our old nurse, of nurse's stories. . . . Oh, how I used to grieve! The most trifling thing in the house I would recall with pleasure. I would keep dreaming how nice it would be now at home! I should be sitting in our little room by the samovar with my own people; it would be so warm, so nice, so familiar. How, I used to think, I would hug mother now, how tightly, how warmly! One would think and think and begin crying softly from misery, choking back one's tears, and the vocabularies would never get into one's head. I could not learn my lessons for next day; all night I would dream of the teacher, the mistress, the girls; all night I would be repeating my lessons in my sleep and would not know them next day. They would make me kneel down and give me only one dish for dinner. I was so depressed and dejected. At first all the girls laughed at me and teased me and tried to confuse me when I was saying my lessons, pinched me when in rows we walked into dinner or tea, made complaints against me to the teacher for next to nothing. But how heavenly it was when nurse used to come for me on Saturday evening. I used to hug the old darling in a frenzy of joy. She would put on my things, and wrap me up, and could not keep pace with me, while I would chatter and chatter and tell her everything. I would arrive home gay and happy, would hug everyone as though I had been away for ten years. There would be explanations, talks; descriptions would begin. I would greet everyone, laugh, giggle, skip and run about. Then there would be serious conversations with father about our studies, our teachers, French, Lomond's grammar, and we were all so pleased and happy. It makes me happy even now to remember those minutes. I tried my very utmost to learn and please father. I saw he was spending his last farthing on me and God knows what straits he was in. Every day he grew more gloomy, more ill-humoured, more angry. His character was quite changed, his business was unsuccessful, he had a mass of debts. Mother was sometimes afraid to cry, afraid to say a word for fear of making father angry. She was getting quite ill, was getting thinner and thinner and had begun to have a bad cough.

When I came back from school I used to find such sad faces, mother weeping stealthily, father angry. Then there would be scolding and upbraiding. Father would begin saying that I was no joy, no comfort to them; that they were depriving themselves of everything for my sake and I could not speak French yet; in fact all his failures, all his misfortunes were vented on me and mother. And how could he worry poor mother! It was heartrending to look at her; her cheeks were hollow, her eyes were sunken, there was a hectic flush in her face.

I used to come in for more scolding than anyone. It always began with trifles, and goodness knows what it went on to. Often I did not understand what it was about. Everything was a subject of complaint! . . . French and my being a great dunce and that the mistress of our school was a careless, stupid woman; that she paid no attention to our morals, that father was still unable to find a job, that Lomond's was a very poor grammar and that Zapolsky's was very much better, that a lot of money had been thrown away on me, that I was an unfeeling, stony-hearted girl—in fact, though I, poor thing, was striving my utmost, repeating conversations and vocabularies, I was to blame for everything, I was responsible for everything! And this was not because father did not love me; he was devoted to mother and me, but it was just his character.

Anxieties, disappointments, failures worried my poor father to distraction; he became suspicious, bitter; often he was close upon despair, he began to neglect his health, caught cold and all at once fell ill. He did not suffer long, but died so suddenly, so unexpectedly that we were all beside ourselves with the shock for some days. Mother seemed stunned; I actually feared for her reason.

As soon as father was dead creditors seemed to spring up from everywhere and rushed upon us like a torrent. Everything we had we gave them. Our little house on Petersburg Side, which father had bought six months after moving to Petersburg, was sold too. I don't know how they settled the rest, but we were left without refuge, without sustenance. Mother was suffering from a wasting disease, we could not earn our bread, we had nothing to live on, ruin stared us in the face. I was then only just fourteen. It was at this point that Anna Fyodorovna visited us. She always said that she owned landed estates and that she was some sort of relation of ours. Mother said, too, that she was a relation, only a very distant one. While father was

alive she never came to see us. She made her appearance
now with tears in her eyes and said she felt great sympathy
for us; she condoled with us on our loss and our poverty-
stricken condition; added that it was father's own fault;
that he had lived beyond his means, had borrowed right and
left and that he had been too self-confident. She expressed
a desire to be on more friendly terms with us, said we must
let by-gones be by-gones; when mother declared she had
never felt any hostility towards her, she shed tears, took
mother to church and ordered a requiem service for the
"dear man". (That was how she referred to father.) After
that she was solemnly reconciled to mother.

After leading up to the subject in many lengthy pre-
ambles, Anna Fyodorovna first depicted in glaring colours
our poverty-stricken and forlorn position, our helplessness
and hopelessness, and then invited us, as she expressed it,
to take refuge with her. Mother thanked her, but for a
long time could not make up her mind to accept; but seeing
that there was nothing else she could do and no help for
it, she told Anna Fyodorovna at last that we would accept
her offer with gratitude.

I remember as though it were to-day the morning on
which we moved from the Petersburg Side to Vassilyevsky
Ostrov. It was a clear, dry, frosty autumn morning. Mother
was crying. I felt horribly sad; my heart was torn and
ached with a terrible inexplicable misery . . . it was a terrible time. . . .

II

At first till we—that is mother and I—had grown used to
our new home we both felt strange and miserable at Anna
Fyodorovna's. Anna Fyodorovna lived in a house of her
own in Sixth Row. There were only five living-rooms in
the house. In three of them lived Anna Fyodorovna and
my cousin Sasha, a child who was being brought up by
her, an orphan, fatherless and motherless. Then we lived

in one room, and in the last room, next to ours, there was a poor student called Pokrovsky who was lodging in the house.

Anna Fyodorovna lived very well, in a more wealthy style than one could have expected; but her fortune was mysterious and so were her pursuits. She was always in a bustle, was always full of business, she drove out and came back several times a day; but what she was doing, what she was in a fuss about and with what object she was busy I could never make out. She had a large and varied circle of acquaintances. Visitors were always calling upon her, and the queerest people, always on business of some sort and to see her for a minute. Mother always carried me off to my room as soon as the bell rang. Anna Fyodorovna was horribly vexed with mother for this and was continually repeating that we were too proud, that we were proud beyond our means, that we had nothing to be proud about, and she would go on like that for hours together. I did not understand these reproaches at the time and, in fact, it is only now that I have found out, or rather that I guess why mother could not make up her mind to live with Anna Fyodorovna. Anna Fyodorovna was a spiteful woman, she was continually tormenting us. To this day it is a mystery to me why it was she invited us to live with her. At first she was fairly nice to us, but afterwards she began to show her real character as soon as she saw we were utterly helpless and had nowhere else to go. Later on she became very affectionate to me, even rather coarsely affectionate and flattering, but at first I suffered in the same way as mother. Every minute she was upbraiding us, she did nothing but talk of her charitable deeds. She introduced us to outsiders as her poor relations—a helpless widow and orphan to whom in the kindness of her heart, out of Christian charity, she had given a home. At meals she watched every morsel we took, while if we did not eat, there would be a fuss again; she would say we were fastidious, that we should not be over-nice, that we should be thankful for what we had; that she doubted if we had had anything better in our own home. She was continually abusing father, saying that he wanted

to be better than other people and much good that had
done him; that he had left his wife and daughter penniless
and that if they had not had a benevolent relation, a Christian soul with a feeling heart, then, God knows, they might
have been rotting in the street and dying of hunger. What
did she not say! It was not so much painful as disgusting to
hear her.

Mother was continually crying; her health grew worse
from day to day. She was visibly wasting, yet she and I
worked from morning till night, taking in sewing, which
Anna Fyodorovna very much disliked, she was continually
saying that she was not going to have her house turned into
a dressmaker's shop. But we had to have clothes; we had
to lay by for unforeseen expenses; it was absolutely necessary to have money of our own. We saved on the off-
chance, hoping we might be able in time to move elsewhere. But mother lost what little health was left her over
work; she grew weaker every day. The disease sucked the
life out of her like a worm and hurried her to the grave.
I saw it all, I felt it all, I realised it all and suffered; it all
went on before my eyes.

The days passed and each day was like the one before.
We lived as quietly as if we were not in a town. Anna
Fyodorovna calmed down by degrees as she began fully
to recognise her power. Though, indeed, no one ever
thought of contradicting her. We were separated from her
rooms by the corridor, and Pokrovsky's room was, as I
have mentioned before, next to ours. He used to teach
Sasha French and German, history, geography—all the sciences, as Anna Fyodorovna said, and for this he had his
board and lodging from her. Sasha was a very intelligent
child, though playful and mischievous; she was thirteen.
Anna Fyodorovna observed to mother that it would not be
amiss if I were to have lessons, since my education had
not been finished at the boarding-school, and for a whole
year I shared Sasha's lessons with Pokrovsky. Pokrovsky
was poor, very poor. His health had prevented him from
continuing his studies and it was only from habit that he
was called a student. He was so retiring, so quiet and so

still that we heard no sound of him from our room. He was very queer-looking; he walked so awkwardly, bowed so awkwardly and spoke so queerly that at first I could not look at him without laughing. Sasha was continually mocking at him, especially when he was giving us our lessons. He was of an irritable temper, too, was constantly getting cross, was beside himself about every trifle, scolded us, complained of us, and often went off into his own room in anger without finishing the lesson. He used to sit for days together over his books. He had a great many books, and such rare and expensive books. He gave other lessons, too, for which he was paid, and as soon as ever he had money he would go and buy books.

In time I got to know him better and more intimately. He was a very kind and good young man, the best person it has been my lot to meet. Mother had a great respect for him. Afterwards he became the best of my friends—next to mother, of course.

At first, though I was such a big girl, I was as mischievous as Sasha. We used to rack our brains for hours together to find ways to tease him and exhaust his patience. His anger was extremely funny, and we used to find it awfully amusing. (I am ashamed even to think of it now.) Once we teased him almost to the point of tears and I distinctly heard him whisper, "Spiteful children." I was suddenly overcome with confusion; I felt ashamed and miserable and sorry for him. I remember that I blushed up to my ears and almost with tears in my eyes began begging him not to mind and not to be offended at our stupid mischief. But he closed the book and without finishing the lesson went off to his own room. I was torn with penitence all day long. The thought that we children had reduced him to tears by our cruelty was insufferable. So we had waited for his tears. So we had wanted them; so we had succeeded in driving him out of all patience; so we had forced him, a poor unfortunate man, to realise his hard lot.

I could not sleep all night for vexation, sorrow, repentance. They say repentance relieves the soul—on the contrary. There was an element of vanity mixed, I don't know how, with my sadness. I did not want him to look upon me as a child, I was fifteen then.

From that day I began worrying my imagination, creating thousands of plans to make Pokrovsky change his opinion about me. But I had become all of a sudden timid and shy; in my real position I could venture upon nothing and confined myself to dreams (and God knows what dreams!). I left off joining in Sasha's pranks; he left off being angry with us; but for my vanity that was little comfort.

Now I will say a few words about the strangest, most curious and most pathetic figure I have ever chanced to meet. I speak of him now, at this passage in my diary, because until that period I had hardly paid any attention to him. But now everything that concerned Pokrovsky had suddenly become interesting to me.

There used sometimes to come to the house a little old man, grey-headed, grubby, badly-dressed, clumsy, awkward, incredibly queer in fact. At the first glance at him one might imagine that he was, as it were, abashed by something—as it were, ashamed of himself. That is why he always seemed to be shrinking into himself, to be, as it were, cowering; he had such queer tricks and ways that one might almost have concluded he was not in his right mind. He would come to the house and stand at the glass door in the entry without daring to come in. If one of us passed by —Sasha or I or any one of the servants he knew to be rather kind to him—he would begin waving at once, beckoning, making gesticulations, and only when one nodded and called to him—a sign agreed upon that there was no outsider in the house and that he might come in when he liked—only then the old man stealthily opened the door with a smile of glee, and rubbing his hands with satisfaction, walked on tiptoe straight to Pokrovsky's room. This was Pokrovsky's father.

Later on, I learnt the whole story of this poor old man. He had once been in the service, was entirely without ability, and filled the very lowest and most insignificant post. When his first wife (our Pokrovsky's mother) died he took it into his head to marry a second time and married a girl of the working-class. Everything was turned topsy-turvy under the rule of his new wife. She let no one live in peace, she domineered over everyone. Our Pokrovsky was still a child, ten years old. His stepmother hated him, but fate was kind to the boy. A country gentleman called Bykov, who had known the elder Pokrovsky and at one time been his patron, took the child under his protection and sent him to school. He was interested in him because he had known his mother, who had been a protégée of Anna Fyodorovna's and had by her been married to Pokrovsky. Mr. Bykov, a very intimate friend of Anna Fyodorovna's, had generously given the girl a dowry of five thousand roubles on her marriage. Where that money went to I don't know.

That was the story Anna Fyodorovna told me; young Pokrovsky never liked speaking of his family circumstances. They say his mother was very pretty, and it seems strange to me that she should have been so unfortunately married to such an insignificant man. He was quite young when she died four years after their marriage.

From boarding-school young Pokrovsky went on to a high school and then to the university. Mr. Bykov, who very often came to Petersburg, did not confine his protection to that. Owing to the breakdown of his health Pokrovsky could not continue his studies at the university. Mr. Bykov introduced him to Anna Fyodorovna, commended him to her good offices and so young Pokrovsky was taken into the house and was given his board on condition of teaching Sasha everything that was necessary. Old Pokrovsky was driven by grief at his wife's cruelty to the worst of vices and was scarcely ever sober. His wife used to beat him, make him live in the kitchen, and brought things at last to such a pass that he was quite accustomed to being beaten and ill-treated and did not complain of it. He was not a very old man, but his mind had almost given way owing to his bad habits. The one sign he showed of generous and humane feeling was his boundless love for his son. It was said that young Pokrovsky was as like his dead mother as one drop of water is like another. Maybe it was the memory of his first good wife that stirred in the ruined old man's heart this infinite love for his son. The old man could speak of nothing but his son and always visited him twice a week. He did not dare to come oftener, for young Pokrovsky could not endure his father's visits. Of all his failings, undoubtedly the greatest and foremost was his disrespect to his father. The old man certainly was at times the most insufferable creature in the world. In the first place he was horribly inquisitive, secondly, by remarks and questions of the most trivial and senseless kind he interrupted his son's work every minute, and, lastly, he would sometimes come under the influence of drink. The son gradually trained the old man to overcome his vices, his curiosity and incessant chatter, and at last had brought things to such a point that the old man obeyed him in everything like an oracle and did not dare open his mouth without permission.

The poor old man could not sufficiently admire and marvel at his Petinka (as he called his son). When he came to see him he almost always had a timid, careworn air, most likely from uncertainty as to the reception his son would give him. He was usually a long time making up his mind to come in, and if I happened to be there he would spend twenty minutes questioning me: "How was Petinka? Was he quite well? What sort of mood was he in, and was he busy over anything important? What was he doing? Was he writing, or absorbed in reflection?" When I had sufficiently cheered and reassured him, the old man at last ventured to come in, and very, very quietly, very, very cautiously opened the door, first poked in his head, and if his son nodded to him and the old man saw he was not angry, he moved stealthily into the room, took off his overcoat and his hat, which was always crushed, full of holes and with a broken brim, hung them on a hook, did everything quietly, noiselessly; then cautiously sat down on a chair, never taking his eyes off his son, watching every movement and trying to guess what mood his "Petinka" was in. If his son seemed ever so little out of humour and the old man noticed it, he got up from his seat at once and explained, "I just looked in, Petinka, only for a minute. I have been a long walk, I was passing and came in for a rest." And then, dumbly, submissively he would take his coat, his wretched hat, again he would stealthily open the door and go away, keeping a forced smile on his face to check the rush of disappointment in his heart and to hide it from his son.

But when the son made the father welcome, the old man was beside himself with joy. His face, his gestures, his movements all betrayed his pleasure. If his son began talking to him, the old man always rose a little from the chair and answered softly, deferentially, almost with reverence, always trying to use the choicest, that is, the most absurd expressions. But he was not blessed with the gift of words; he was always nervous and confused, so that he did not know what to do with his hands, what to do with himself, and kept whispering the answer to himself long afterwards as though trying to correct himself. If he did succeed in giving a good answer, the old man smoothed himself down, straightened his waistcoat, his tie, his coat and assumed an air of dignity. Sometimes he plucked up so much courage and grew so bold that he stealthily got up from his chair, went up to the bookshelf, took down some book and even began reading something on the spot, whatever the book might be. All this he did with an air of assumed unconcern and coolness, as though he could always do what he liked with his son's books, as though his son's graciousness was nothing out of the way.

But I once happened to see how frightened the poor fellow was when Pokrovsky asked him not to touch the books. He grew nervous and confused, put the book back upside down, then tried to right it, turned it round and put it in with the edges outside; smiled, flushed and did not know how to efface his crime. Pokrovsky by his persuasions did succeed in turning the old man a little from his evil propensities, and whenever the son saw his father sober three times running he would give him twenty-five kopecks, fifty kopecks, or more at parting. Sometimes he would buy his father a pair of boots, a tie or a waistcoat; then the old man was as proud as a cock in his new clothes.

Sometimes he used to come to us. He used to bring Sasha and me gingerbread cocks and apples and always talked to us of Petinka. He used to beg us to be attentive and obedient at lessons, used to tell us that Petinka was a good son, an exemplary son and, what was more, a learned son. Meanwhile he would wink at us so funnily with his left eye and make such amusing grimaces that we could not help smiling, and went into peals of laughter at him. Mother was very fond of him. But the old man hated Anna Fyodorovna, though he was stiller than water, humbler than grass in her presence.

Soon I left off having lessons with Pokrovsky. As before, he looked upon me as a child, a mischievous little girl on a level with Sasha. This hurt me very much, for I was trying my utmost to efface the impression of my behaviour in the past, but I was not noticed. That irritated me more and more. I scarcely ever spoke to Pokrovsky except at our lessons, and indeed I could not speak. I blushed and was confused, and afterwards shed tears of vexation in some corner.

I do not know how all this would have ended if a strange circumstance had not helped to bring us together. One evening when mother was sitting with Anna Fyodorovna I went stealthily into Pokrovsky's room. I knew he was not at home, and I really don't know what put it into my head to go into his room. Until that moment I had never peeped into it, though we had lived next door for over a year. This time my heart throbbed violently, so violently that it seemed it would leap out of my bosom. I looked around with peculiar curiosity. Pokrovsky's room was very poorly furnished: it was untidy. Papers were lying on the table and the chairs. Books and papers! A strange thought came to me, and at the same time an unpleasant feeling of vexation took possession of me. It seemed to me that my affection, my loving heart were little to him. He was learned while I was stupid, and knew nothing, had read

nothing, not a single book . . . at that point I looked enviously at the long shelves which were almost breaking down
under the weight of the books. I was overcome by anger,
misery, a sort of fury. I longed and at once determined
to read his books, every one of them, and as quickly as
possible. I don't know, perhaps I thought that when I
learned all he knew I should be more worthy of his friendship. I rushed to the first shelf; without stopping to think I
seized the first dusty old volume; flushing and turning pale
by turns, trembling with excitement and dread, I carried
off the stolen book, resolved to read it at night—by the
night-light while mother was asleep.

But what was my vexation when, returning to our room,
I hurriedly opened the book and saw it was some old work
in Latin. It was half decayed and worm-eaten. I went back
without loss of time. Just as I was trying to put the book
back in the shelf I heard a noise in the passage and approaching footsteps. I tried with nervous haste to be quick,
but the insufferable book had been so tightly wedged in the
shelf that when I took it out all the others had shifted and
packed closer of themselves, so now there was no room for
their former companion. I had not the strength to force the
book in. I pushed the books with all my might, however.
The rusty nail which supported the shelf, and which seemed
to be waiting for that moment to break, broke. One end
of the shelf fell down. The books dropped noisily on the
floor in all directions. The door opened and Pokrovsky
walked into the room.

I must observe that he could not bear anyone to meddle
in his domain. Woe to anyone who touched his books!
Imagine my horror when the books, little and big, of all
sizes and shapes dashed off the shelf, flew dancing under
the table, under the chairs, all over the room! I would have
run, but it was too late. It is all over, I thought, it is all
over. I am lost, I am done for! I am naughty and mischievous like a child of ten, I am a silly chit of a girl! I am a
great fool!

Pokrovsky was dreadfully angry.

"Well, this is the last straw!" he shouted. "Are not you

ashamed to be so mischievous? . . . Will you ever learn
sense?" and he rushed to collect the books. "Don't, don't!"
he shouted. "You would do better not to come where you
are not invited."

A little softened, however, by my humble movement, he
went on more quietly, in his usual lecturing tone, speaking
as though he were still my teacher:

"Why, when will you learn to behave properly and begin
to be sensible? You should look at yourself. You are not
a little child. You are not a little girl. Why, you are fifteen!"

And at that point, probably to satisfy himself that I
was not a little girl, he glanced at me and blushed up to
his ears. I did not understand. I stood before him staring
in amazement. He got up, came towards me with an embarrassed air, was horribly confused, said something,
seemed to be apologising for something, perhaps for having
only just noticed that I was such a big girl. At last I understood. I don't remember what happened to me then; I was
overcome with confusion, lost my head, blushed even more
crimson than Pokrovsky, hid my face in my hands and
ran out of the room.

I did not know what to do, where to hide myself for
shame. The mere fact that he had found me in his room
was enough! For three whole days I could not look at him:
I blushed until the tears came into my eyes. The most absurd ideas whirled through my brain. One of them—the
maddest—was a plan to go to him, explain myself to him,
confess everything to him, tell him all openly and assure
him I had not behaved like a silly little girl but had acted
with good intentions. I quite resolved to go but, thank God,
my courage failed me. I can imagine what a mess I should
have made of it! Even now I am ashamed to remember it
all.

A few days later mother suddenly became dangerously
ill. After two days in bed, on the third night, she was
feverish and delirious. I did not sleep all one night, looking
after mother, sitting by her bedside, bringing her drink and
giving her medicine at certain hours. The second night I
was utterly exhausted. At times I was overcome with sleep,

my head went round and everything was green before my eyes. I was ready any minute to drop with fatigue, but mother's weak moans roused me, I started up, waked for an instant and then was overwhelmed with drowsiness again. I was in torment. I don't know, I cannot remember, but some horrible dream, some awful apparition haunted my over-wrought brain at the agonising moment of struggling between sleeping and waking. I woke up in terror. The room was dark; the night-light had burned out. Streaks of light suddenly filled the whole room, gleamed over the wall and disappeared. I was frightened, a sort of panic came over me. My imagination had been upset by a horrible dream, my heart was oppressed with misery. . . . I leapt up from my chair and unconsciously shrieked from an agonising, horribly oppressive feeling. At that moment the door opened and Pokrovsky walked into our room.

All I remember is that I came to myself in his arms. He carefully put me in a low chair, gave me a glass of water and showered questions on me. I don't remember what I answered.

"You are ill, you are very ill yourself," he said, taking my hand. "You are feverish, you will kill yourself. You do not think of your health; calm yourself, lie down, go to sleep. I will wake you in two hours time. Rest a little . . . lie down, lie down!" not letting me utter a word in objection. I was too tired to object; my eyes were closing with weakness. I lay down in a low chair, resolved to sleep only half an hour, and slept till morning. Pokrovsky only waked me when the time came to give mother her medicine.

The next evening when, after a brief rest in the daytime, I made ready to sit up by mother's bedside again, firmly resolved not to fall asleep this time, Pokrovsky at eleven o'clock knocked at our door. I opened it.

"It is dull for you, sitting alone," he said to me. "Here is a book; take it, it won't be so dull, anyway."

I took it; I don't remember what the book was like; I hardly glanced into it, though I did not sleep all night. A strange inward excitement would not let me sleep; I could not remain sitting still; several times I got up from the chair and walked about the room. A sort of inward content was suffused through my whole being. I was so glad of Pokrovsky's attention. I was proud of his anxiety and uneasiness about me. I spent the whole night, musing and dreaming. Pokrovsky did not come in again, and I knew he would not come, and I wondered about the following evening.

The next evening, when everyone in the house had gone to bed, Pokrovsky opened his door and began talking to me, standing in the doorway of his room. I do not remember now a single word of what we said to one another; I only remember that I was shy, confused, vexed with myself and looked forward impatiently to the end of the conversation, though I had been desiring it intensely, dreaming of it all day, and making up my questions and answers. . . . The first stage of our friendship began from that evening. All through mother's illness we spent several hours together every night. I got over my shyness by degrees, though after every conversation I found something in it to be vexed with myself about. Yet with secret joy and proud satisfaction I saw that for my sake he was beginning to forget his insufferable books.

By chance the conversation once turned in jest on his books having fallen off the shelf. It was a strange moment. I was, as it were, *too* open and candid. I was carried away by excitement and a strange enthusiasm, and I confessed everything to him. . . . Confessed that I longed to study, to know something, that it vexed me to be considered a little girl. . . . I repeat that I was in a very strange mood; my heart was soft, there were tears in my eyes—I concealed nothing and told him everything—everything—my affection for him, my desire to love him, to live with him, to comfort him, to console him. He looked at me somewhat strangely, with hesitation and perplexity, and did not say one word. I felt all at once horribly sore and miserable. It seemed to me that he did not understand me, that perhaps he was laughing at me. I suddenly burst out crying like a child, I could not restrain myself, and sobbed as though I were in a sort of fit. He took my hands, kissed them and pressed them to his heart; talked to me, comforted me; he was much touched. I do not remember what he said to me, only I kept on crying and laughing and crying again, blushing, and so joyful that I could not utter a word. In spite of my emotion, I noticed, however, that Pokrovsky still showed traces of embarrassment and constraint. It seemed as though he were overwhelmed with wonder at my enthusiasm, my delight, my sudden warm, ardent affection. Perhaps it only seemed strange to him at first; later on his hesitation vanished and he accepted my devotion to him, my friendly words, my attentions, with the same simple, direct feeling that I showed, and responded to it all with the same attentiveness, as affectionately and warmly as a sincere friend, a true brother. My heart felt so warm, so happy. . . . I was not reserved, I concealed nothing from him, he saw it all and grew every day more and more attached to me.

And really I do not remember what we used to talk about in those tormenting, and at the same time happy, hours when we met at night by the flickering light of a little lamp, and almost by my poor mother's bedside. . . . We talked of everything that came into our minds, that broke from our hearts, that craved expression, and we were almost happy. . . . Oh, it was a sad and joyful time, both at once. . . . And it makes me both sad and joyful now to think of him. Memories are always tormenting, whether they are glad or bitter; it is so with me, anyway; but even the torment is sweet. And when the heart grows heavy, sick, weary and sad, then memories refresh and revive it, as the drops of dew on a moist evening after a hot day refresh and revive a poor sickly flower, parched by the midday heat.

Mother began to get better, but I still sat up by her bedside at night. Pokrovsky used to give me books; at first I read them to keep myself awake; then more attentively, and afterwards with eagerness. They opened all at once before me much that was new, unknown and unfamiliar. New thoughts, new impressions rushed in a perfect flood into my heart. And the more emotions, the more perplexity and effort it cost me to assimilate those new impressions, the dearer they were to me and the more sweetly they thrilled my soul. They crowded upon my heart all at once, giving it no rest. A strange chaos began to trouble my whole being. But that spiritual commotion could not upset my balance altogether. I was too dreamy and that saved me.

When mother's illness was over, our long talks and evening interviews were at an end; we succeeded sometimes in exchanging words, often trivial and of little consequence, but I was fond of giving everything its significance, its peculiar underlying value. My life was full, I was happy, calmly, quietly happy. So passed several weeks. . . .

One day old Pokrovsky came to see us. He talked to us for a long time, was exceptionally gay, cheerful and communicative, he laughed, made jokes after his fashion, and at last explained the mystery of his ecstatic condition, and told us that that day week would be Petinka's birthday and that for the occasion he should come and see his son; that he should put on a new waistcoat and that his wife had promised to buy him new boots. In fact, the old man was completely happy and chatted away of everything in his mind. His birthday! That birthday gave me no rest day or night. I made up my mind to give Pokrovsky something as a sign of my affection. But what? At last I thought of giving him books. I knew he wanted to have Pushkin's works in the latest, complete edition, and I decided to buy Pushkin. I had thirty roubles of my own money earned by needlework. The money had been saved up to buy me a dress. I promptly sent old Matrona, our cook, to find out what the whole of Pushkin cost. Alas! The price of the eleven volumes, including the cost of binding, was at least sixty roubles. Where could I get the money? I thought and thought and did not know what to decide upon. I did not want to ask mother. Of course mother would have certainly helped me; but then everyone in the house would have known of our present; besides, the present would have become a token of gratitude in repayment for all that Pokrovsky had done for us during the past year. I wanted to give it alone and no one else to know of it. And for what he had done for me I wanted to be indebted to him for ever without any sort of repayment except my affection.

At last I found a way out of my difficulty.

I knew at the second-hand shops in the Gostiny Dvor one could sometimes, with a little bargaining, buy at half-price a book hardly the worse for wear and almost completely new. I resolved to visit the Gostiny Dvor. As it happened, next day some things had to be bought for us and also for Anna Fyodorovna. Mother was not very well, and Anna Fyodorovna, very luckily, was lazy, so that it fell to me to make these purchases and I set off with Matrona.

I was so fortunate as to find a Pushkin very quickly and one in a very fine binding. I began bargaining. At first they demanded a price higher than that in the bookseller's shops; but in the end, though not without trouble, and walking away several times, I brought the shopman to knocking down the price and asking no more than ten roubles in silver. How I enjoyed bargaining! . . . Poor Matrona could not make out what was the matter with me and what possessed me to buy so many books. But, oh, horror! My whole capital consisted of thirty roubles in paper, and the shopman would not consent to let the books go cheaper. At last I began beseeching him, begged and begged him and at last persuaded him. He gave way but only took off two and a half roubles and swore he only made that concession for my sake because I was such a nice young lady and he would not have done it for anyone else. I still had not enough by two and a half roubles. I was ready to cry with vexation. But the most unexpected circumstance came to my assistance in my distress.

Not far off at another bookstall I saw old Pokrovsky. Four or five second-hand dealers were clustering about him; they were bewildering him completely and he was at his wits' end. Each of them was proffering his wares and there was no end to the books they offered and he longed to buy. The poor old man stood in the midst of them, looking a disconsolate figure and did not know what to

choose from what was offered him. I went up and asked
him what he was doing here. The old man was delighted
to see me; he was extremely fond of me, hardly less than
of his Petinka, perhaps.

"Why, I'm buying books, Varvara Alexyevna," he answered. "I am buying books for Petinka. Here it will soon
be his birthday and he is fond of books, so, you see, I am
going to buy them for him. . . ."

The old man always expressed himself in a very funny
way and now he was in the utmost confusion besides.
Whatever he asked the price of, it was always a silver rouble, or two or three silver roubles; he had by now given
up inquiring about the bigger books and only looked cove-
tously at them, turning over the leaves, weighing them in
his hands and putting them back again in their places.

"No, no, that's dear," he would say in an undertone,
"but maybe there'll be something here."

And then he would begin turning over thin pamphlets,
songbooks, almanacs; these were all very cheap.

"But why do you want to buy those?" I asked him.
"They are all awful rubbish."

"Oh, no," he answered. "No, you only look what good
little books there are here. They are very, very good little
books!"

And the last words he brought out in such a plaintive
sing-song that I fancied he was ready to cry with vexation
at the good books being so dear, and in another moment a
tear would drop from his pale cheeks on his red nose. I
asked him whether he had plenty of money.

"Why, here," the poor fellow pulled out at once all his
money wrapped up in a piece of greasy newspaper. "Here
there's half a rouble, a twenty-kopeck piece and twenty
kopecks in copper."

I carried him off at once to my second-hand bookseller.

"Here, these eleven volumes cost only thirty-two roubles
and a half; I have thirty; put your two and a half to it and
we will buy all these books and give them to him together."

The old man was beside himself with delight, he shook
out all his money, and the bookseller piled all our pur-

chased volumes upon him. The old man stuffed volumes in all his pockets, carried them in both hands and under his arms and bore them all off to his home, giving me his word to bring them all to me in secret next day.

Next day the old man came to see his son, spent about an hour with him as usual, then came in to us and sat down beside me with a very comical mysterious air. Rubbing his hands in proud delight at being in possession of a secret, he began with a smile by telling me that all the books had been conveyed here unnoticed and were standing in a corner in the kitchen under Matrona's protection. Then the conversation naturally passed to the day we were looking forward to; the old man talked at length of how we would give our present, and the more absorbed he became in the subject the more apparent it was to me that he had something in his heart of which he could not, dared not, speak, which, in fact, he was afraid to put into words. I waited and said nothing. The secret joy, the secret satisfaction which I had readily discerned at first in his strange gestures and grimaces and the winking of his left eye, disappeared. Every moment he grew more uneasy and disconsolate; at last he could not contain himself.

"Listen," he began timidly in an undertone.

"Listen, Varvara Alexyevna . . . do you know what, Varvara Alexyevna . . . ?" The old man was in terrible confusion. "When the day of his birthday comes, you know, you take ten books and give them yourself, that is from yourself, on your own account; I'll take only the eleventh, and I, too, will give it from myself, that is, apart, on my own account. So then, do you see—you will have something to give, and I shall have something to give; we shall both have something to give."

At this point the old man was overcome with confusion and relapsed into silence. I glanced at him; he was waiting for my verdict with timid expectation.

"But why do you want us not to give them together, Zahar Petrovitch?"

"Why, you see, Varvara Alexyevna, it's just . . . it's only, you know . . ."

In short, the old man faltered, flushed, got stuck in his sentence and could not proceed.

"You see," he explained at last, "Varvara Alexyevna, I indulge at times . . . that is, I want to tell you that I am almost always indulging, constantly indulging . . . I have a habit which is very bad . . . that is, you know, it's apt to be so cold outdoors and at times there are unpleasantnesses of all sorts, or something makes one sad, or something happens amiss and then I give way at once and begin to indulge and sometimes drink too much. Petrusha dislikes that very much. He gets angry with me, do you see, Varvara Alexyevna, scolds me and gives me lectures, so that I should have liked now to show him by my present that I am reforming and beginning to behave properly, that here I've saved up to buy the book, saved up for ever so long, for I scarcely ever have any money except it may happen Petrusha gives me something. He knows that. So here he will see how I have used my money and will know that I have done all that only for him."

I felt dreadfully sorry for the old man. I thought for a moment. The old man looked at me uneasily.

"Listen, Zahar Petrovitch," I said; "you give him them all."

"How all? Do you mean all the books?"

"Why, yes, all the books."

"And from myself?"

"Yes, from yourself."

"From myself alone? Do you mean on my own account?"

"Why yes, on your own account."

I believe I made my meaning very clear, but it was a long time before the old man could understand me.

"Why yes," he said, after pondering. "Yes! That would be very nice, but how about you, Varvara Alexyevna?"

"Oh, well, I shall give nothing."

"What!" cried the old man, almost alarmed. "So you don't want to give Petinka anything?"

The old man was dismayed; at that moment he was ready, I believe, to give up his project in order that I might be able to give his son something. He was a kind-hearted old fellow! I assured him that I should have been glad to give something, but did not want to deprive him of the pleasure.

"If your son is satisfied and you are glad," I added, "then I shall be glad, for I shall feel secretly in my heart as though I were really giving it myself."

With that the old man was completely satisfied. He spent another two hours with us, but could not sit still in his place and was continually getting up, fussing noisily about, playing with Sasha, stealthily kissing me, pinching my hand and making faces at Anna Fyodorovna on the sly. Anna Fyodorovna turned him out of the house at last. The old man was, in fact, in his delight, more excited than he had perhaps ever been before.

On the festive day he appeared exactly at eleven o'clock, coming straight from mass in a decently mended swallow-tail coat and actually wearing a new waistcoat and new boots. He had a bundle of books in each hand. We were all sitting drinking coffee in Anna Fyodorovna's drawing-room at the time (it was Sunday). The old man began by saying, I believe, that Pushkin was a very fine poet; then, with much hesitation and confusion, he passed suddenly to the necessity of one's behaving oneself properly, and that if a man does not behave properly then he will indulge; that bad habits are the ruin and destruction of a man; he even enumerated several fatal instances of intemperance, and wound up by saying that for some time past he had been completely reformed and his behaviour now was excellent and exemplary; that he had even, in the past, felt the justice of his son's exhortations, that he felt it all long ago and laid it to heart, but now he had begun to control himself in practice, too. In proof of which he presented him with the books bought with money which he had saved up during a long period of time.

I could not help laughing and crying as I listened to the poor old man; so he knew how to lie on occasion! The books were carried into Pokrovsky's room and arranged on the shelves. Pokrovsky at once guessed the truth. The old man was invited to dinner. We were all so merry that day; after dinner we played forfeits and cards; Sasha was in wild spirits and I was hardly less so. Pokrovsky was attentive to me and kept seeking an opportunity to speak to me alone, but I would not let him. It was the happiest day of all those four years of my life.

And now come sad, bitter memories, and I begin the story of my gloomy days. That is why, perhaps, my pen moves more slowly and seems to refuse to write more. That is why, perhaps, I have dwelt in memory with such eagerness and such love on the smallest details of my trivial existence in my happy days. Those days were so brief; they were followed by grief, black grief, and God only knows when it will end.

My troubles began with the illness and death of Pokrovsky.

He fell ill about two months after the last incidents I have described here. He spent those two months in unceasing efforts to secure some means of subsistence, for he still had no settled position. Like all consumptives he clung up to the very last moment to the hope of a very long life. A post as a teacher turned up for him, but he had a great distaste for that calling. He could not take a place in a government office on account of his health. Besides he would have had to wait a long time for the first instalment of his salary. In short, Pokrovsky met with nothing but disappointment on all sides and this tried his temper. His health was suffering, but he paid no attention to it. Autumn was coming on, every day he went out in his thin little overcoat to try and get work, to beg and implore for a place, which was inwardly an agony to him; he used to get his feet wet and to be soaked through with the rain, and at last he took to his bed and never got up from it again. . . . He died in the middle of autumn at the end of October.

I scarcely left his room during the whole time of his illness, I nursed him and looked after him. Often I did not sleep for nights together. He was frequently delirious and rarely quite himself; he talked of goodness knows what, of his post, of his books, of me, of his father . . . and it was then I heard a great deal about his circumstances of which

I had not known or even guessed before. When first he was ill, all of them looked at me somehow strangely; Anna Fyodorovna shook her head. But I looked them all straight in the face and they did not blame me any more for my sympathy for Pokrovsky—at least my mother did not.

Sometimes Pokrovsky knew me, but this was seldom. He was almost all the time unconscious. Sometimes for whole nights together he would carry on long, long conversations with someone in obscure, indistinct words and his hoarse voice resounded with a hollow echo in his narrow room as in a coffin; I used to feel terrified then. Especially on the last night he seemed in a frenzy; he suffered terribly, was in anguish; his moans wrung my heart. Everyone in the house was in alarm. Anna Fyodorovna kept praying that God would take him more quickly. They sent for the doctor. The doctor said that the patient would certainly die by the morning.

Old Pokrovsky spent the whole night in the passage at the door of his son's room; a rug of some sort was put down there for him. He kept coming into the room, it was dreadful to look at him. He was so crushed by sorrow that he seemed utterly senseless and without feeling. His head was shaking with terror. He was trembling all over and kept whispering something, talking about something to himself. It seemed to me he was going out of his mind.

Just before dawn the old man, worn out with mental suffering, fell asleep on his mat and slept like the dead. Between seven and eight his son began to die. I waked the father. Pokrovsky was fully conscious and said good-bye to us all. Strange! I could not cry, but my heart was torn to pieces.

But his last moments distressed and tortured me more than all. He kept asking for something at great length with his halting tongue and I could make out nothing from his words. My heart was lacerated! For a whole hour he was uneasy, kept grieving over something, trying to make some sign with his chill hands and then beginning pitifully to entreat me in his hoarse hollow voice; but his words were disconnected sounds and again I could make nothing of them.

I brought everyone of the household to him, I gave him drink, but still he shook his head mournfully. At last I guessed what he wanted. He was begging me to draw up the window curtain and open the shutters. No doubt he wanted to look for the last time at the day, at God's light, at the sunshine. I drew back the curtain, but the dawning day was sad and melancholy as the poor failing life of the dying man. There was no sun. The clouds covered the sky with a shroud of mist; it was rainy, overcast, mournful. A fine rain was pattering on the window-panes and washing them with little rivulets of cold dirty water; it was dark and dingy. The pale daylight scarcely penetrated into the room and hardly rivalled the flickering flame of the little lamp lighted before the ikon. The dying man glanced at me mournfully, mournfully and shook his head; a minute later he died.

Anna Fyodorovna herself made the arrangements for the funeral. A coffin of the cheapest kind was bought and a carter was hired. To defray these expenses Anna Fyodorovna seized all Pokrovsky's books and other belongings. The old man argued with her, made a noise, took away all the books he could from her, stuffed his pockets full of them, put them in his hat, wherever he could, went about with them all those three days, and did not part with them even when he had to go to church. During those three days he seemed as it were, stupefied, as though he did not know what he was doing, and he kept fussing about the coffin with a strange solicitude; at one moment he set straight the wreath on his dead son and at the next he lighted and took away candles. It was evident that his thoughts could not rest on anything. Neither mother nor Anna Fyodorovna was at the funeral service at the church. Mother was ill; Anna Fyodorovna had got ready to go, but she quarrelled with old Pokrovsky and stayed behind. I went alone with the old man. During the service a terror came upon me—as though a foreboding of the future. I could scarcely stand up in church.

At last the coffin was closed, nailed up, put in the cart and taken away. I followed it only to the end of the street.

The man drove at a trot. The old man ran after him, weeping loudly, his lamentations quivering and broken by his haste. The poor old man lost his hat and did not stop to pick it up. His head was drenched by the rain and the wind was rising; the sleet lashed and stung his face. The old man seemed not to feel the cold and wet and ran wailing from one side of the cart to the other, the skirts of his old coat fluttering in the wind like wings. Books were sticking out from all his pockets; in his hands was a huge volume which he held tightly. The passers-by took off their caps and crossed themselves. Some stopped and stood gazing in wonder at the poor old man. The books kept falling out of his pockets into the mud. People stopped him and pointed to what he had lost, he picked them up and fell to racing after the coffin again. At the corner of the street an old beggar woman joined him to follow the coffin with him. The cart turned the corner at last and disappeared from my sight. I went home. I threw myself on mother's bosom in terrible distress. I pressed her tightly in my arms, I kissed her and burst into floods of tears, huddling up to her fearfully as though trying to keep in my arms my last friend and not to give her up to death . . . but death was already hovering over poor mother. . . .

June 11.

How grateful I am to you for our walk yesterday to the Island, Makar Alexyevitch! How fresh and lovely it is there, how leafy and green! It's so long since I saw green leaves—when I was ill I kept fancying that I had to die and that I certainly should die—judge what must have been my sensations yesterday, how I must have felt . . .

You must not be angry with me for having been so sad yesterday; I was very happy, very content, but in my very best moments I am always for some reason sad. As for my crying, that means nothing. I don't know myself why I am always crying. I feel ill and irritable; my sensations are due to illness. The pale cloudless sky, the sunset, the evening stillness—all that—I don't know—but I was somehow in the mood yesterday to take a dreary and miserable view of everything, so that my heart was too full and needed the relief of tears. But why am I writing all this to you? It is hard to make all that clear to one's own heart and still harder to convey it to another. But you, perhaps, will understand me. Sadness and laughter both at once! How kind you are really, Makar Alexyevitch! You looked into my eyes yesterday as though to read in them what I was feeling and were delighted with my rapture. Whether it was a bush, an avenue, a piece of water—you were there standing before me showing its beauties and peeping into my eyes as though you were displaying your possessions to me. That proves that you have a kind heart, Makar Alexyevitch. It's for that that I love you. Well, good-bye. I'm ill again to-day; I got my feet wet yesterday and have caught cold. Fedora is ailing, too, so now we are both on the sick list. Don't forget me. Come as often as you can.

Your V. D.

June 12.

My darling Varvara Alexyevna,

Well, I had expected, my dear soul, that you would write me a description of our yesterday's expedition in a regular poem, and you have turned out nothing but one simple sheet. I say this because, though you wrote me so little in your sheet, yet you did describe it extraordinarily well and sweetly. The charms of nature, and the various rural scenes and all the rest about your feeling—in short, you described it all very well. Now I have no talent for it. If I smudge a dozen papers there's nothing to show for it; I can't describe anything. I have tried.

You write to me, my own, that I am a kind-hearted, good-natured man, incapable of injuring my neighbour, and able to understand the blessings of the Lord made manifest in nature, and you bestow various praises on me, in fact. All that is true, my darling, all that is perfectly true; I really am all that you say and I know it myself; but when one reads what you write one's heart is touched in spite of oneself and then all sorts of painful reflections come to one. Well, listen to me, Varinka dear, I will tell you something, my own.

I will begin with when I was only seventeen and went into the service, and soon the thirtieth year of my career there will be here. Well, I needn't say I have worn out many a uniform; I grew to manhood and to good sense and saw something of the world; I have lived, I may say, I have lived in the world so that on one occasion they even wanted to send up my name to receive a cross. Maybe you will not believe me, but I am really not lying. But there, my darling, in spite of everything, I have been badly treated by malicious people! I tell you, my own, that though I am an obscure person, a stupid person, perhaps, yet I have my feelings like anyone else. Do you know, Varinka, what a spiteful man did to me? I am ashamed to say what he has done to me; you will ask why did he do it? Why, because I am meek, because I am quiet, because I am good-natured! I did not suit their taste, so that's what brought it upon me. At first it began with, "You are this and that, Makar Alexyevitch," and then it came to saying, "It's no good asking Makar Alexyevitch!" And then it ended by, "Of course, that is Makar Alexyevitch!" You see, my precious, what a pass it came to; always Makar Alexyevitch to blame for everything; they managed to make Makar Alexyevitch a by-word all over the department, and it was not enough that they made me a by-word and almost a term of abuse, they attacked my boots, my uniform, my hair, my figure; nothing was to their taste, everything ought to be different! And all this has been repeated every blessed day from time immemorial. I am used to it, for I grow used to anything, because I am a meek man; but what is it all for? What harm do I do to anyone? Have I stolen promotion from anyone, or what? Have I blackened anyone's reputation with his superiors? Have I asked for anything extra out of turn? Have I got up some intrigue? Why, it's a sin for you to imagine such a thing, my dear soul! As though I could do anything of that sort! You've only to look at me, my own. Have I sufficient ability for intrigue and ambition? Then why have such misfortunes come upon me? God forgive me. Here you consider me a decent man, and you are ever so much better than any of them, my darling. Why, what is the greatest virtue in a citizen? A day or two ago, in private conversation, Yevstafy Ivanovitch said that the most important virtue in a citizen was to earn money. He said in jest (I know it was in jest) that morality consists in not being a burden to anyone. Well, I'm not a burden to anyone. My crust of bread is my own; it is true it is a plain crust of bread, at times a dry one; but there it is, earned by my toil and put to lawful and irreproachable use. Why, what can one do? I know very well, of course, that I don't do much by copying; but all the same I am proud of working and earning my bread in the sweat of my brow. Why, what if I am a copying clerk, after all? What harm is there in copying, after all? "He's a copying clerk," they say, but what is there discreditable in that? My handwriting is good, distinct and pleasant to the eye, and his Excellency is satisfied with it. I have no gift of language, of course, I know myself that I haven't the confounded thing; that's why I have not got on in the service, and why even now, my own, I am writing to you simply, artlessly, just as the thought comes into my heart. . . . I know all that; but there, if everyone became an author, who would do the copying? I ask you that question and I beg you to answer it, Varinka dear. So I see now that I am necessary, that I am indispensable, and that it's no use to worry a man with nonsense. Well, let me be a rat if you like, since they see a resemblance! But the rat is necessary, but the rat is of service, but the rat is depended upon, but the rat is given a reward, so that's the sort of rat he is!

Enough about that subject though, my own! I did not intend to talk about that at all, but I got a little heated. Besides, it's pleasant from time to time to do oneself justice. Good-bye, my own, my darling, my kind comforter! I will come, I will certainly come to see you, my dearie, and meanwhile, don't be dull, I will bring you a book. Well, good-bye, then, Varinka.

> Your devoted well-wisher,
> MAKAR DYEVUSHKIN.

June 20.

DEAR SIR, MAKAR ALEXYEVITCH,

I write a hurried line, I am in haste, I have to finish my work up to time. You see, this is how it is: you can make a good bargain. Fedora says that a friend of hers has a uniform, quite new, underclothes, a waistcoat and cap, and all very cheap, they say; so you ought to buy them. You see, you are not badly off now, you say you have money; you say so yourself. Give over being so stingy, please. You know all those things are necessary. Just look at yourself, what old clothes you go about in. It's a disgrace! You're all in patches. You have no new clothes; I know that, though you declare that you have. God knows how you have managed to dispose of them. So do as I tell you, please buy these things. Do it for my sake; if you love me, do it.

You sent me some linen as a present; but upon my word, Makar Alexyevitch, you are ruining yourself. It's no joke what you've spent on me, it's awful to think how much money! How fond you are of throwing away your money! I don't want it; it's all absolutely unnecessary. I know—I am convinced—that you love me. It is really unnecessary to remind me of it with presents; and it worries me taking them from you; I know what they cost you. Once for all, leave off, do you hear? I beg you, I beseech you. You ask me, Makar Alexyevitch, to send you the continuation of my diary, you want me to finish it. I don't know how what I have written came to be written! But I haven't the strength now to talk of my past; I don't even want to think of it; I feel frightened of those memories. To talk of my poor mother leaving her poor child to those monsters, too, is more painful than anything. My heart throbs at the very thought of it: it is all still so fresh: I have not had time to think things over, still less to regain my calm, though it is all more than a year ago, now. But you know all that.

I've told you what Anna Fyodorovna thinks now; she blames me for ingratitude and repudiates all blame for her association with Mr. Bykov! She invites me to stay with her; she says that I am living on charity, that I am going to the bad. She says that if I go back to her she will undertake to set right everything with Mr. Bykov and compel him to make up for his behaviour to me. She says Mr. Bykov wants to give me a dowry. Bother them! I am happy here with you close by, with my kind Fedora whose devotion reminds me of my old nurse. Though you are only a distant relation you will protect me with your name. I don't know them. I shall forget them if I can. What more do they want of me? Fedora says that it is all talk, that they will leave me alone at last. God grant they may!

V. D.

June 21.

MY DARLING VARINKA,

I want to write, but I don't know how to begin. How strange it is, my precious, how we are living now. I say this because I have never spent my days in such joyfulness. Why, it is as though God had blessed me with a home and family of my own, my child, my pretty! But why are you making such a fuss about the four chemises I sent you? You needed them, you know—I found that out from Fedora. And it's a special happiness for me to satisfy your needs, Varinka, dear; it's my pleasure. You let me alone, my dear soul. Don't interfere with me and don't contradict me. I've never known anything like it, my darling. I've taken to going into society now. In the first place my life is twice as full; because you are living very near me and are a great comfort to me; and secondly, I have been invited to tea to-day by a lodger, a neighbour of mine, that clerk, Ratazyaev, who has the literary evenings. We meet this evening, we are going to read literature. So you see how we are getting on now, Varinka—you see! Well, good-bye. I've written all this for no apparent reason, simply to let you know of the affection I feel for you. You told Teresa to tell me, my love, that you want some silk for coloured embroidery. I will get you it, my darling, I will get the silk, I will get it. To-morrow I shall have the pleasure of satisfying you. I know where to buy it, too. And now I remain,

Your sincere friend,
MAKAR DYEVUSHKIN.

June 22.

DEAR MADAM, VARVARA ALEXYEVNA,

I must tell you, my own, that a very pitiful thing has happened in our flat, truly, truly, deserving of pity! Between four and five this morning Gorshkov's little boy died. I don't know what he died of. It seemed to be a sort of scarlatina, God only knows! I went to see these Gorshkovs. Oh, my dear soul, how poor they are! And what disorder! And no wonder; the whole family lives in one room, only divided by a screen for decency. There was a little coffin standing in the room already—a simple little coffin, but rather pretty; they bought it ready-made; the boy was nine years old, he was a promising boy, they say. But it was pitiful to look at them, Varinka! The mother did not cry, but she was so sad, so poor. And perhaps it will make it easier for them to have got one off their shoulders; but there are still two left, a baby, and a little girl, not much more than six. There's not much comfort really in seeing a child suffer, especially one's own little child, and having no means of helping him! The father was sitting in a greasy old dress suit on a broken chair. The tears were flowing from his eyes, but perhaps not from grief, but just the usual thing—his eyes are inflamed. He's such a strange fellow! He always turns red when you speak to him, gets confused and does not know what to answer. The little girl, their daughter, stood leaning against the coffin, such a poor little, sad, brooding child! And Varinka, my darling, I don't like it when children brood; it's painful to see! A doll made of rags was lying on the floor beside her; she did not play with it, she held her finger on her lips; she stood, without stirring. The landlady gave her a sweetmeat; she took it but did not eat it.

It was sad, Varinka, wasn't it?

MAKAR DYEVUSHKIN.

June 25.

DEAR MAKAR ALEXYEVITCH,

I am sending you back your book. A wretched, worthless little book not fit to touch! Where did you ferret out such a treasure? Joking apart, can you really like such a book, Makar Alexyevitch? I was promised the other day something to read. I will share it with you, if you like. And now good-bye. I really have not time to write more.

V. D.

June 26.

DEAR VARINKA,

The fact is that I really had not read that horrid book, my dear girl. It is true, I looked through it and saw it was nonsense, just written to be funny, to make people laugh; well, I thought, it really is amusing; maybe Varinka will like it, so I sent it you.

Now, Ratazyaev has promised to give me some real literature to read, so you will have some books, my darling. Ratazyaev knows, he's a connoisseur; he writes himself, ough, how he writes! His pen is so bold and he has a wonderful style, that is, there is no end to what there is in every word—in the most foolish ordinary vulgar word such as I might say sometimes to Faldoni or Teresa, even in such he has style. I go to his evenings. We smoke and he reads to us, he reads five hours at a stretch and we listen all the time. It's a perfect feast. Such charm, such flowers, simply flowers, you can gather a bouquet from each page! He is so affable, so kindly and friendly. Why, what am I beside him? What am I? Nothing. He is a man with a reputation, and what am I? I simply don't exist, yet he is cordial even to me. I am copying something for him. Only don't you imagine, Varinka, that there is something amiss in that,

that he is friendly to me just because I am copying for him; don't you believe tittle-tattle, my dear girl, don't you believe worthless tittle-tattle. No, I am doing it of myself, of my own accord for his pleasure. I understand refinement of manners, my love; he is a kind, very kind man, and an incomparable writer.

Literature is a fine thing, Varinka, a very fine thing. I learnt that from them the day before yesterday. A profound thing, strengthening men's hearts, instructing them; there are all sorts of things written about that in their book. Very well written! Literature is a picture, that is, in a certain sense, a picture and a mirror: it's the passions, the expression, the subtlest criticism, edifying instruction and a document. I gathered all that from them. I tell you frankly, my darling, that one sits with them, one listens (one smokes a pipe like them, too, if you please), and when they begin to discuss and dispute about all sorts of matters, then I simply sit dumb; then, my dear soul, you and I can do nothing else but sit dumb. I am simply a blockhead, it seems. I am ashamed of myself, so that I try all the evening how to put in half a word in the general conversation, but there, as ill-luck would have it, I can't find that half word! And one is sorry for oneself, Varinka, that one is not this thing, nor that thing, that, as the saying is, "A man one is grown, but no mind of one's own." Why, what do I do in my free time now? I sleep like a fool! While instead of useless sleep I might have been busy in useful occupation; I might have sat down and written something that would have been of use to oneself and pleasant to others. Why, my dearie, you should only see what they get for it, God forgive them! Take Ratazyaev, for instance, what he gets. What is it for him to write a chapter? Why, sometimes he writes five in a day and he gets three hundred roubles a chapter. Some little anecdote, something curious —five hundred! take it or leave it, give it or be damned! Or another time, we'll put a thousand in our pocket! What do you say to that, Varvara Alexyevna? Why, he's got a little book of poems—such short poems—he's asking seven thousand, my dear girl, he's asking seven thousand; think of it! Why, it's real estate, it's house property! He says that they will give him five thousand, but he won't take it. I reasoned with him. I said, "Take five thousand for them, sir, and don't mind them. Why, five thousand's money!" "No," said he, "they'll give me seven, the swindlers!" He's a cunning fellow, really.

Well, my love, since we are talking of it I will copy a passage from the *Italian Passions* for you. That's the name of his book. Here, read it, Varinka, and judge for yourself. . . .

"Vladimir shuddered and his passion gurgled up furiously within him and his blood boiled. . . .

" 'Countess,' he cried. 'Countess! Do you know how awful is this passion, how boundless this madness? No, my dreams did not deceive me! I love, I love ecstatically, furiously, madly! All your husband's blood would not quench the frantic surging ecstasy of my soul! A trivial obstacle cannot check the all-destroying, hellish fire that harrows my exhausted breast. Oh, Zinaida, Zinaida!' . . .

" 'Vladimir,' whispered the countess, beside herself, leaning on his shoulder. . . .

" 'Zinaida!' cried the enraptured Smyelsky.

"His bosom exhaled a sigh. The fire flamed brightly on the altar of love and consumed the heart of the unhappy victims.

" 'Vladimir,' the countess whispered, intoxicated. Her bosom heaved, her cheeks glowed crimson, her eyes glowed. . . .

"A new, terrible union was accomplished!

.   .   .   .   .

"Half an hour later the old count went into his wife's boudoir.

" 'Well, my love, should we not order the samovar for our welcome guest?' he said, patting his wife on the cheek."

Well, I ask you, my dear soul, what do you think of it after that? It's true, it's a little free, there's no disputing that, but still it is fine. What is fine is fine! And now, if you will allow me, I will copy you another little bit from the novel *Yermak and Zuleika*.

You must imagine, my precious, that the Cossack, Yermak, the fierce and savage conqueror of Siberia, is in love with the daughter of Kutchum, the Tsar of Siberia, the Princess Zuleika, who has been taken captive by him. An episode straight from the times of Ivan the Terrible, as you see. Here is the conversation of Yermak and Zuleika.

" 'You love me, Zuleika! Oh, repeat it, repeat it!' . . .

" 'I love you, Yermak,' whispered Zuleika.

" 'Heaven and earth, I thank you! I am happy! . . . You have given me everything, everything, for which my turbulent soul has striven from my boyhood's years. So it was to this thou hast led me, my guiding star, so it was for this thou hast led me here, beyond the Belt of Stone! I will show to all the world my Zuleika, and men, the frantic monsters, will not dare to blame me! Ah, if they could understand the secret sufferings of her tender soul, if they could see a whole poem in a tear of my Zuleika! Oh, let me dry that tear with kisses, let me drink it up, that heavenly tear . . . unearthly one!"

" 'Yermak,' said Zuleika, 'the world is wicked, men are unjust! They will persecute us, they will condemn us, my sweet Yermak! What is the poor maiden, nurtured amid the snows of Siberia in her father's *yurta* to do in your cold, icy, soulless, selfish world? People will not understand me, my desired one, my beloved one.'

" 'Then will the Cossack's sabre rise up hissing about them.' "

And now, what do you say to Yermak, Varinka, when he finds out that his Zuleika has been murdered? . . . The blind old man, Kutchum, under cover of night steals into Yermak's tent in his absence and slays Zuleika, intending to deal a mortal blow at Yermak, who has robbed him of his sceptre and his crown.

" 'Sweet is it to me to rasp the iron against the stone,' shouted Yermak in wild frenzy, whetting his knife of Damascus steel upon the magic stone; 'I'll have their blood, their blood! I will hack them! hack them! hack them to pieces! ! !'"

And, after all that, Yermak, unable to survive his Zuleika, throws himself into the Irtish, and so it all ends.

And this, for instance, a tiny fragment written in a jocose style, simply to make one laugh.

"Do you know Ivan Prokofyevitch Yellow-paunch? Why, the man who bit Prokofy Ivanovitch's leg. Ivan Prokofyevitch is a man of hasty temper, but, on the other hand, of rare virtues; Prokofy Ivanovitch, on the other hand, is extremely fond of a rarebit on toast. Why, when Pelagea Antonovna used to know him . . . Do you know Pelagea Antonovna? the woman who always wears her petticoat inside out."

That's humour, you know, Varinka, simply humour. He rocked with laughter when he read us that. He *is* a fellow, God forgive him! But though it's rather jocose and very playful, Varinka dear, it is quite innocent, without the slightest trace of free-thinking or liberal ideas. I must observe, my love, that Ratazyaev is a very well-behaved man and so an excellent author, not like other authors.

And, after all, an idea sometimes comes into one's head, you know. . . . What if I were to write something, what would happen then? Suppose that, for instance, apropos of nothing, there came into the world a book with the title—*Poems by Makar Dyevushkin?* What would my little angel say then? How does that strike you? What do you think of it? And I can tell you, my darling, that as soon as my book came out, I certainly should not dare to show myself in the Nevsky Prospect. Why, how should I feel when everyone would be saying, Here comes the author and poet, Dyevushkin? There's Dyevushkin himself, they would say! What should I do with my boots then? They are, I may mention in passing, my dear girl, almost always covered with patches, and the soles too, to tell the truth, sometimes break away in a very unseemly fashion. What should we do when everyone knew that the author Dyevushkin had patches on his boots! Some countess or duchess would hear of it, and what would she say, the darling? Perhaps she would not notice it; for I imagine countesses don't trouble themselves about boots, especially clerks' boots (for you know there are boots and boots), but they would tell her all about it, her friends would give me away. Ratazyaev, for instance, would be the first to give me away; he visits the Countess V.; he says that he goes to all her receptions, and he's quite at home there. He says she is such a darling, such a literary lady, he says. He's a rogue, that Ratazyaev!

But enough of that subject; I write all this for fun, my little angel, to amuse you. Good-bye, my darling, I have scribbled you a lot of nonsense, but that is just because I am in a very good humour to-day. We all dined together to-day at Ratazyaev's (they are rogues, Varinka dear), and brought out such a cordial. . . .

But there, why write to you about that! Only mind you don't imagine anything about me, Varinka. I don't mean anything by it. I will send you the books, I will certainly send them. . . . One of Paul de Kock's novels is being passed round from one to another, but Paul de Kock will not do for you, my precious. . . . No, no! Paul de Kock won't do for you. They say of him, Varinka dear, that he rouses all the Petersburg critics to righteous indignation. I send you a pound of sweetmeats—I bought them on purpose for you. Do you hear, darling? Think of me at every sweetmeat. Only don't nibble up the sugar-candy but only suck it, or you will get toothache. And perhaps you like candied peel?——write and tell me. Well, good-bye, goodbye. Christ be with you, my darling!

I remain ever,
Your most faithful friend,
MAKAR DYEVUSHKIN.

June 27.

DEAR SIR, MAKAR ALEXYEVITCH,

Fedora tells me that, if I like, certain people will be pleased to interest themselves in my position, and will get me a very good position as a governess in a family. What do you think about it, my friend—shall I go, or shall I not?

Of course I should not then be a burden upon you, and the
situation seems a good one; but, on the other hand, I feel
somehow frightened at going into a strange house. They
are people with an estate in the country. When they want
to know all about me, when they begin asking questions,
making inquiries—why, what should I say then?—besides,
I am so shy and unsociable, I like to go on living in the corner I am used to. It's better somehow where one is used
to being; even though one spends half one's time grieving,
still it is better. Besides, it means leaving Petersburg; and
God knows what my duties will be, either; perhaps they
will simply make me look after the children, like a nurse.
And they are such queer people, too; they've had three
governesses already in two years. Do advise me, Makar
Alexyevitch, whether to go or not. And why do you never
come and see me? You hardly ever show your face, we
scarcely ever meet except on Sundays at mass. What an
unsociable person you are! You are as bad as I am! And
you know I am almost a relation. You don't love me,
Makar Alexyevitch, and I am sometimes very sad all alone.
Sometimes, especially when it is getting dark, one sits all
alone. Fedora goes off somewhere, one sits and sits and
thinks—one remembers all the past, joyful and sad alike—it
all passes before one's eyes, it all rises up as though out of a
mist. Familiar faces appear (I am almost beginning to see
them in reality)—I see mother most often of all . . . And
what dreams I have! I feel that I am not at all well, I am
so weak; to-day, for instance, when I got out of bed this
morning, I turned giddy; and I have such a horrid cough,
too! I feel, I know, that I shall soon die. Who will bury
me? Who will follow my coffin! Who will grieve for me!
. . . And perhaps I may have to die in a strange place, in
a strange house! . . . My goodness! how sad life is, Makar
Alexyevitch. Why do you keep feeding me on sweetmeats?
I really don't know where you get so much money from?
Ah, my friend, take care of your money, for God's sake,
take care of it. Fedora is selling the cloth rug I have em-
broidered; she is getting fifty paper roubles for it. That's
very good, I thought it would be less. I shall give Fedora

three silver roubles, and shall get a new dress for myself, a plain one but warm. I shall make you a waistcoat, I shall make it myself, and I shall choose a good material.

Fedora got me a book, *Byelkin's Stories,* which I will send you, if you care to read it. Only don't please keep it, or make it dirty, it belongs to someone else—it's one of Pushkin's works. Two years ago I read these stories with my mother. And it was so sad for me now to read them over again. If you have any books send them to me—only not if you get them from Ratazyaev. He will certainly lend you his books if he has ever published anything. How do you like his works, Makar Alexyevitch? Such nonsense . . . Well, good-bye! How I have been chattering! When I am sad I am glad to chatter about anything. It does me good; at once one feels better, especially if one expresses all that lies in one's heart. Good-bye. Good-bye, my friend!

Your

V. D.

June 28.

My precious Varvara Alexyevna,

Leave off worrying yourself, I wonder you are not ashamed. Come, give over, my angel! How is it such thoughts come into your mind? You are not ill, my love, you are not ill at all; you are blooming, you are really blooming; a little pale, but still blooming. And what do you mean by these dreams, these visions? For shame, my darling, give over; you must simply laugh at them. Why do I sleep well? Why is nothing wrong with me? You should look at me, my dear soul. I get along all right, I sleep quietly, I am as healthy and hearty as can be, a treat to look at. Give over, give over, darling, for shame. You must reform. I know your little ways, my dearie; as soon as any trouble comes, you begin fancying things and worrying about something. For my sake give over, my darling. Go into a family?—Never! No, no, no, and what notion is this of yours? What is this idea that has come over you? And to leave Petersburg too. No, my darling, I won't

allow it. I will use every means in my power to oppose
such a plan. I'll sell my old coat and walk about the street
in my shirt before you shall want for anything. No, Varinka, no, I know you! It's folly, pure folly. And there is no
doubt that it is all Fedora's fault: she's evidently a stupid
woman, she puts all these ideas into your head. Don't you
trust her, my dear girl. You probably don't know everything yet, my love. . . . She's a silly woman, discontented
and nonsensical; she worried her husband out of his life.
Or perhaps she has vexed you in some way? No, no, my
precious, not for anything! And what would become of me
then, what would there be left for me to do? No, Varinka
darling, you put that out of your little head. What is there
wanting in your life with us? We can never rejoice enough
over you, you love us, so do go on living here quietly. Sew
or read, or don't sew if you like—it does not matter—only
go on living with us or, only think yourself, why, what
would it be like without you? . . .

Here, I will get you some books and then maybe we'll
go for a walk somewhere again. Only you must give over,
my dearie, you must give over. Pull yourself together and
don't be foolish over trifles! I'll come and see you and
very soon too. Only accept what I tell you plainly and candidly about it; you are wrong, my darling, very wrong. Of
course, I am an ignorant man and I know myself that I am
ignorant, that I have hardly a ha'porth of education. But
that's not what I am talking about, and I'm not what matters, but I will stand up for Ratazyaev, say what you like.
He writes well, very, very well, and I say it again, he writes
very well. I don't agree with you and I never can agree
with you. It's written in a flowery abrupt style, with figures
of speech. There are ideas of all sorts in it, it is very good!
Perhaps you read it without feeling, Varinka; you were
out of humour when you read it, vexed with Fedora, or
something had gone wrong. No, you read it with feeling;
best when you are pleased and happy and in a pleasant
humour, when, for instance, you have got a sweetmeat in
your mouth, that's when you must read it. I don't dispute
(who denies it?) that there are better writers than Rata-

zyaev, and very much better in fact, but they are good and Ratazyaev is good too. He writes in his own special way, and does very well to write. Well, good-bye, my precious, I can't write more; I must make haste, I have work to do. Mind now, my love, my precious little dearie; calm yourself, and God will be with you, and I remain your faithful friend,

MAKAR DYEVUSHKIN.

P.S.—Thanks for the book, my own; we will read Pushkin too, and this evening I shall be sure to come and see you.

MY DEAR MAKAR ALEXYEVITCH,

No, my friend, no, I ought not to go on living among you. On second thoughts I consider that I am doing very wrong to refuse such a good situation. I shall have at least my daily bread secure; I will do my best, I will win the affection of the strangers, I will even try to overcome my defects, if necessary. Of course it is painful and irksome to live with strangers, to try and win their good-will, to hide one's feelings, and suppress oneself, but God will help me. I mustn't be a recluse all my life. I have had experiences like it before. I remember when I was a little thing and used to go to school. I used to be frolicking and skipping about all Sundays at home; sometimes mother would scold me—but nothing mattered, my heart was light and my soul was full of joy all the while. As evening approached an immense sadness would come over me—at nine o'clock I had to go back to school, and there it was all cold, strange, severe, the teachers were so cross on Mondays, one had such a pain at one's heart, one wanted to cry; one would go into a corner and cry all alone, hiding one's tears—they would say one was lazy; and I wasn't crying in the least because I had to do my lessons.

But, after all, I got used to it, and when I had to leave school I cried also when I said good-bye to my schoolfellows. And I am not doing right to go on being a burden to both of you. That thought is a torment to me. I tell you all this openly because I am accustomed to be open with you. Do you suppose I don't see how early Fedora gets up in the morning, and sets to work at her washing and works till late at night?—and old bones want rest. Do you suppose I don't see how you are ruining yourself over me, and spending every halfpenny? You are not a man of property, my friend! You tell me that you will sell your last rag before I shall want for anything. I believe you, my friend, I trust your kind heart, but you say that now. Now you have money you did not expect, you've received something extra, but later on? You know yourself, I am always ill; and I can't work like you, though I should be heartily glad to, and one does not always get work. What is left for me? To break my heart with grief looking at you two dear ones. In what way can I be of the slightest use to you? And why am I so necessary to you, my friend? What good have I done you? I am only devoted to you with my whole soul, I love you warmly, intensely, with my whole heart, but—my fate is a bitter one! I know how to love and I can love, but I can do nothing to repay you for your kindness. Don't dissuade me any more, think it over and tell me your final opinion. Meanwhile I remain your loving,

V. D.

July 1.

Nonsense, nonsense, Varinka, simply nonsense! Let you alone and there's no knowing what notion you will take into your little head. One thing's not right and another thing's not right. And I see now that it is all nonsense. And what more do you want, my dear girl? just tell me that! We love you, you love us, we're all contented and happy—what more do you want? And what will you do among strangers? I expect you don't know yet what strangers are like . . . You had better ask me and I will tell you what strangers are like. I know them, my darling, I know them very well, I've had to eat their bread. They are spiteful, Varinka, spiteful; so spiteful that you would have no heart left, they would torment it so with reproach, upbraiding and ill looks. You are snug and happy among us as though you were in a little nest; besides, we shall feel as though we had lost our head when you are gone; why, what can we do without you; what is an old man like me to do then? You are no use to us? No good to us? How no good? Come, my love, think yourself how much good you are! You are a great deal of good to me, Varinka. You have such a good influence . . . Here I am thinking about you now and I am happy . . . Sometimes I write you a letter and put all my feelings into it and get a full answer to everything back from you. I bought you a little wardrobe, got you a hat; some commission comes from you; I carry out the commission . . . How can you say, you are no use to me? And what should I be good for in my old age? Perhaps you have not thought of that, Varinka; that's just what you had better think about, 'what will he be good for without me?' I am used to you, my darling. Or else what will come of it? I shall go straight to the Neva, and that will be the end of it. Yes, really, Varinka, that will be the only thing left for me to do when you are gone. Ah, Varinka, my darling. It seems you want me to be taken to Volkovo Cemetery in a common cart; with only an old draggletail beggar-woman to follow me to the grave; you want them to throw the earth upon me and go away and leave me alone. It's too bad, too bad, my dear! It's sinful really, upon my word it's a sin! I send you back your book, Varinka, my darling, and if you ask my opinion about your book, dear, I must say that never in my life have I read such a splendid book. I wonder now, my darling, how I can have lived till now such an ignoramus, God forgive me! What have I been doing? What backwoods have I been brought up in? Why, I know nothing, my dear girl; why, I know absolutely nothing. I know nothing at all. I tell you, Varinka, plainly—I'm a man of no education: I have read little hitherto—very little, scarcely anything: I have read *The Picture of Man,* a clever work; I have read *The boy who played funny tunes on the bells* and *The Cranes of Ibicus;* that's all, and I never read anything else. Now I have read *The Stationmaster* in your book; let me tell you, my darling, it happens that one goes on living, and one does not know that there is a book there at one's side

where one's whole life is set forth, as though it were reckoned
upon one's fingers. And what one never so much as guessed
before, when one begins reading such a book one remembers little by little and guesses and discovers. And this is
another reason why I like your book: one sometimes reads
a book, whatever it may be, and you can't for the life of
you understand it, it's so deep. I, for instance, am stupid,
I'm stupid by nature, so I can't read very serious books;
but I read this as though I had written it myself, as though
I had taken my own heart, just as it is, and turned it inside
out before people and described it in detail, that's what it
is like. And it's a simple subject, my goodness, yet what a
thing it is! Really it is just as I should have described it; why
not describe it? You know I feel exactly the same as in the
book, and I have been at times in exactly the same positions
as, for instance, that Samson Vyrin, poor fellow. And how
many Samson Vyrins are going about amongst us, poor
dears! And how clearly it is all described! Tears almost
started into my eyes when I read that the poor sinner took
to drink, became such a drunkard that he lost his senses
and slept the whole day under a sheepskin coat and
drowned his grief in punch, and wept piteously, wiping his
eyes with the dirty skirt of his coat when he thought of his
lost lamb, his daughter Dunyasha. Yes, it's natural. You
should read it, it's natural. It's living! I've seen it myself;
it's all about me; take Teresa, for instance—but why go
so far? Take our poor clerk, for instance—Why, he is perhaps just a Samson Vyrin, only he has another surname,
Gorshkov. It's the general lot, Varinka dear, it might happen to you or to me. And the count who lives on the Nevsky on the riverside, he would be just the same, it would
only seem different because everything there is done in their
own way, in style, yet he would be just the same, anything
may happen, and the same thing may happen to me. That's
the truth of the matter, my darling, and yet you want to go
away from us; it's a sin, Varinka, it may be the end of me.
You may be the ruin of yourself and me too, my own. Oh,
my little dearie, for God's sake put out of your little head
all these wilful ideas and don't torment me for nothing.

How can you keep yourself, my weak little unfledged bird? How can you save yourself from ruin, protect yourself from villains? Give over, Varinka, think better of it; don't listen to nonsensical advice and persuasion, and read your book again, read it with attention; that will do you good.

I talked of *The Stationmaster* to Ratazyaev. He told me that that was all old-fashioned and that now books with pictures and descriptions have all come in; I really did not quite understand what he said about it. He ended by saying that Pushkin is fine and that he is a glory to holy Russia, and he said a great deal more to me about him. Yes, it's good, Varinka, very good; read it again with attention; follow my advice, and make an old man happy by your obedience. Then God Himself will reward you, my own, He will certainly reward you.

Your sincere friend,
MAKAR DYEVUSHKIN.

DEAR SIR, MAKAR DYEVUSHKIN,

Fedora brought me fifteen silver roubles to-day. How pleased she was, poor thing, when I gave her three! I write to you in haste. I am now cutting you out a waistcoat—it's charming material—yellow with flowers on it. I send you a book: there are all sorts of stories in it; I have read some of them, read the one called *The Cloak*. You persuade me to go to the theatre with you; wouldn't it be expensive? Perhaps we could go to the gallery somewhere. It's a long while since I've been to the theatre, in fact I can't remember when I went. Only I'm afraid whether such a treat would not cost too much? Fedora simply shakes her head. She says that you have begun to live beyond your means and I see how much you spend, on me alone! Mind, my friend, that you don't get into difficulties. Fedora tells me of rumours—that you have had a quarrel with your landlady for not paying your rent; I am very anxious about you. Well, good-bye, I'm in a hurry. It's a trifling matter, I'm altering a ribbon on a hat.

P.S.—You know, if we go to the theatre, I shall wear my new hat and my black mantle. Will that be all right?

July 7.

DEAR MADAM, VARVARA ALEXYEVNA,

   . . . So I keep thinking about yesterday. Yes, my dear girl, even we have had our follies in the past. I fell in love with that actress, I fell head over ears in love with her, but that was nothing. The strangest thing was that I had scarcely seen her at all, and had only been at the theatre once, and yet for all that I fell in love. There lived next door to me five noisy young fellows. I got to know them, I could not help getting to know them, though I always kept at a respectable distance from them. But not to be behind them I agreed with them in everything. They talked to me about this actress. Every evening as soon as the theatre was opened, the whole company—they never had a halfpenny for necessities—the whole party set off to the theatre to the gallery and kept clapping and clapping, and calling, calling for that actress—they were simply frantic! And after that they would not let one sleep; they would talk about her all night without ceasing, everyone called her his Glasha, everyone of them was in love with her, they all had the same canary in their hearts. They worked me up: I was a helpless youngster then. I don't know how I came to go, but one evening I found myself in the fourth gallery with them. As for seeing, I could see nothing more than the corner of the curtain, but I heard everything. The actress certainly had a pretty voice—a musical voice like a nightingale, as sweet as honey; we all clapped our hands and shouted and shouted, we almost got into trouble, one was actually turned out. I went home. I walked along as though I were drunk! I had nothing left in my pocket but one silver rouble, and it was a good ten days before I could get my salary. And what do you think, my love? Next day before going to the office I went to a French perfumer's and spent my whole fortune on perfume and scented soap—I really don't know why I bought all that. And I did not dine at home but spent the whole time walking up and down outside her window. She lived in Nevsky Prospect on the fourth storey. I went home for an hour or so, rested, and out into the Nevsky again, simply to pass by her windows. For six weeks I used to walk to and fro like that and hang about her; I was constantly hiring smart sledges and kept driving about so as to pass her window: I ruined myself completely, ran into debt, and then got over my passion, I got tired of it. So you see, my precious, what an actress can make of a respectable man! I was a youngster though, I was a youngster then! . . .

M. D.

July 8.

DEAR MADAM, VARVARA ALEXYEVNA,

I hasten to return you the book you lent me on the sixth of this month, and therewith I hasten to discuss the matter with you. It's wrong of you, my dear girl, it's wrong of you to put me to the necessity of it. Allow me to tell you, my good friend, every position in the lot of man is ordained by the Almighty. One man is ordained to wear the epaulettes of a general, while it is another's lot to serve as a titular councillor; it is for one to give commands, for another to obey without repining, in fear and humility. It is in accordance with man's capacities; one is fit for one thing and one for another, and their capacities are ordained by God himself. I have been nearly thirty years in the service; my record is irreproachable; I have been sober in my behaviour, and I have never had any irregularity put down to me. As a citizen I look upon myself in my own mind as having my faults, but my virtues, too. I am respected by my superiors, and His Excellency himself is satisfied with me; and though he has not so far shown me any special marks of favour, yet I know that he is satisfied. My handwriting is fairly legible and good, not too big and not too small, rather in the style of italics, but in any case satisfactory; there is no one among us except, perhaps, Ivan Prokofyevitch who writes as well. I am old and my hair is grey; that's the only fault I know of in me. Of course, there is no one without his little failings. We're all sinners, even you are a sinner, my dear! But no serious offence, no impudence has ever been recorded against me, such as anything against the regulations, or any disturbance of public tranquillity; I have never been noticed for anything like that, such a thing has never happened—in fact, I almost got a decoration, but what's the use of talking! You ought to have known all that, my dear, and he ought to have known; if a man undertakes to write he ought to know all about it. No, I did not expect this from you, my dear girl, no, Varinka! You are the last person from whom I should have expected it.

What! So now you can't live quietly in your own little corner—whatever it may be like—not stirring up any mud, as the saying is, interfering with no one, knowing yourself, and fearing God, without people's interfering with you, without their prying into your little den and trying to see what sort of life you lead at home, whether for instance you have a good waistcoat, whether you have all you ought to have in the way of underclothes, whether you have boots and what they are lined with; what you eat, what you drink, what you write? And what even if I do sometimes walk on tiptoe to save my boots where the pavement's bad? Why write of another man that he sometimes goes short, that he has no tea to drink, as though everyone is always bound to drink tea—do I look into another man's mouth to see how he chews his crust, have I ever insulted anyone in that way? No, my dear, why insult people, when they are not interfering with you! Look here, Varvara Alexyevna, this is what it comes to: you work, and work regularly and devotedly; and your superiors respect you (however things may be, they do respect you), and here under your very nose, for no apparent reason, neither with your leave nor by your leave, somebody makes a caricature of you. Of course one does sometimes get something new—and is so pleased that one lies awake thinking about it, one is so pleased, one puts on new boots for instance, with such enjoyment; that is true: I have felt it because it is pleasant to see one's foot in a fine smart boot—that's truly described! But I am really surprised that Fyodor Fyodorovitch should have let such a book pass without notice and without defending himself. It is true that, though he is a high official, he is young and likes at times to make his voice heard. Why shouldn't he make his voice heard, why not give us a scolding if we need it? Scold to keep up the tone of the office, for instance—well, he must, to keep up the tone; you must teach men, you must give them a good talking to; for, between ourselves, Varinka, we clerks do nothing without a good talking to. Everyone is only on the look-out to get off somewhere, so as to say, I was sent here or there, and to avoid work and edge out of it. And as there are various grades in the service and as each grade requires a special sort of reprimand corresponding to the grade, it's natural that the tone of the reprimand should differ in the various grades—that's in the order of things—why, the whole world rests on that, my dear soul, on our all keeping up our authority with one another, on each one of us scolding the other. Without that precaution, the world could not go on and there would be no sort of order. I am really surprised that Fyodor Fyodorovitch let such an insult pass without attention. And why write such things? And what's the use of it? Why, will someone who reads it order me a cloak because of it; will he buy me new boots? No, Varinka, he will read it and ask for a contribution. One hides oneself sometimes, one hides oneself, one tries to conceal one's weak points, one's afraid to show one's nose at times anywhere because one is afraid of tittle-tattle, because they can work up a tale against you about anything in the world—anything. And here now all one's private and public life is being dragged into literature, it is all printed, read, laughed and gossiped about! Why, it will be impossible to show oneself in the street. It's all so plainly told, you know, that one might be recognised in one's walk. To be sure, it's as well that he does make up for it a little at the end, that he does soften it a bit, that after that passage when they throw the papers at his head, it does put in, for instance, that for all that he was a conscientious man, a good citizen, that he did not deserve such treatment from his fellow-clerks, that he respected his elders (his example might be followed, perhaps, in that), had no ill-will against anyone, believed in God and died (if he will have it that he died) regretted. But it would have been better not to let him die, poor fellow, but to make the coat be found, to make Fyodor Fyodorovitch—what am I saying? I mean, make that general, finding out his good qualities, question him in his office, promote him in his office, and give him a good increase in his salary, for then, you see, wickedness would have been punished, and virtue would have been triumphant, and his fellow-clerks would have got nothing by it. I should have done that, for instance, but as it is, what is there special about it, what is there good in it? It's just an insignificant example from vulgar, everyday life. And what induced you to send me such a book, my own? Why, it's a book of an evil tendency, Varinka, it's untrue to life, for there cannot have been such a clerk. No, I must make a complaint, Varinka. I must make a formal complaint.

> Your very humble servant,
> MAKAR DYEVUSHKIN.

July 27.

DEAR SIR, MAKAR ALEXYEVITCH,

Your latest doings and letters have frightened, shocked, and amazed me, and what Fedora tells me has explained it all. But what reason had you to be so desperate and to sink to such a depth as you have sunk to, Makar Alexyevitch? Your explanation has not satisfied me at all. Isn't it clear that I was right in trying to insist on taking the situation that was offered me? Besides, my last adventure has thoroughly frightened me. You say that it's your love for me that makes you keep in hiding from me. I saw that I was deeply indebted to you while you persuaded me that you were only spending your savings on me, which you said you had lying by in the bank in case of need. Now, when I learn that you had no such money at all, but, hearing by chance of my straitened position, and touched by it, you actually spent your salary, getting it in advance, and even sold your clothes when I was ill—now that I have discovered all this I am put in such an agonising position that I still don't know how to take it, and what to think about it. Oh, Makar Alexyevitch! You ought to have confined yourself to that first kind help inspired by sympathy and the feeling of kinship and not have wasted money afterwards on luxuries. You have been false to our friendship, Makar

Alexyevitch, for you weren't open with me. And now, when I see that you were spending your last penny on finery, on sweetmeats, on excursions, on the theatre and on books—now I am paying dearly for all that in regret for my frivolity (for I took it all from you without troubling myself about you); and everything with which you tried to give me pleasure is now turned to grief for me, and has left nothing but useless regret. I have noticed your depression of late, and, although I was nervously apprehensive of some trouble, what has happened never entered my head. What! Could you lose heart so completely, Makar Alexyevitch! Why, what am I to think of you now, what will everyone who knows you say of you now? You, whom I always respected for your good heart, your discretion, and your good sense. You have suddenly given way to such a revolting vice, of which one saw no sign in you before. What were my feelings when Fedora told me you were found in the street in a state of inebriety, and were brought home to your lodgings by the police! I was petrified with amazement, though I did expect something extraordinary, as there had been no sign of you for four days. Have you thought, Makar Alexyevitch, what your chiefs at the office will say when they learn the true cause of your absence? You say that everyone laughs at you, that they all know of our friendship, and that your neighbours speak of me in their jokes, too. Don't pay any attention to that, Makar Alexyevitch, and for goodness' sake, calm yourself. I am alarmed about your affair with those officers, too; I have heard a vague account of it. Do explain what it all means. You write that you were afraid to tell me, that you were afraid to lose my affection by your confession, that you were in despair, not knowing how to help me in my illness, that you sold everything to keep me and prevent my going to hospital, that you got into debt as far as you possibly could, and have unpleasant scenes every day with your landlady— but you made a mistake in concealing all this from me. Now I know it all, however. You were reluctant to make me realise that I was the cause of your unhappy position, and now you have caused me twice as much grief by your behaviour. All this has shocked me, Makar Alexyevitch. Oh, my dear friend! misfortune is an infectious disease, the poor and unfortunate ought to avoid one another, for fear of making each other worse. I have brought you trouble such as you knew nothing of in your old humble and solitary existence. All this is distressing and killing me.

Write me now openly all that happened to you and how you came to behave like that. Set my mind at rest if possible. It isn't selfishness makes me write to you about my peace of mind, but my affection and love for you, which nothing will ever efface from my heart. Good-bye. I await your answer with impatience. You had a very poor idea of me, Makar Alexyevitch.

Your loving
VARVARA DOBROSELOV.

July 28.

MY PRECIOUS VARVARA ALEXYEVNA—

Well, as now everything is over and, little by little, things are beginning to be as they used to be, again let me tell you one thing, my good friend: you are worried by what people will think about me, to which I hasten to assure you, Varvara Alexyevna, that my reputation is dearer to me than anything. For which reason and with reference to my misfortunes and all those disorderly proceedings I beg to inform you that no one of the authorities at the office knows anything about it or will know anything about it. So that they will all feel the same respect for me as before. The one thing I'm afraid of is gossip. At home our landlady did nothing but shout, and now that with the help of your ten roubles I have paid part of what I owe her she does nothing more than grumble; as for other people, they don't matter, one mustn't borrow money of them, that's all, and to conclude my explanations I tell you, Varvara Alexyevna, that your respect for me I esteem more highly than anything on earth, and I am comforted by it now in my temporary troubles. Thank God that the first blow and the first shock are over and that you have taken it as you have, and don't look on me as a false friend, or an egoist for keeping you here and deceiving you because I love you as my angel and could not bring myself to part from you. I've set to work again assiduously and have begun performing my duties well. Yevstafy Ivanovitch did just say a word when I passed him by yesterday. I will not conceal from you, Varinka, that I am overwhelmed by my debts and the awful condition of my wardrobe, but that again does not matter, and about that too, I entreat you, do not despair, my dear. Send me another half rouble. Varinka, that half rouble rends my heart too. So that's what it has come to now, that is how it is, old fool that I am; it's not I helping you, my angel, but you, my poor little orphan, helping me. Fedora did well to get the money. For the time I have no hopes of getting any, but if there should be any prospects I will write to you fully about it all. But gossip, gossip is what I am most uneasy about. I kiss your little hand and implore you to get well. I don't write more fully because I am in haste to get to the office. For I want by industry and assiduity to atone for all my shortcomings in the way of negligence in the office; a further account of all that happened and my adventures with the officers I put off till this evening.

Your respectful and loving
MAKAR DYEVUSHKIN.

July 28.

MY PRECIOUS VARINKA—

Ach, Varinka, Varinka! This time the sin is on your side and your conscience. You completely upset and perplexed me by your letter, and only now, when at my leisure I looked into the inmost recesses of my heart, I saw that I was right, perfectly right. I am not talking of my drinking (that's enough of it, my dear soul, that's enough) but about my loving you and that I was not at all unreasonable in loving you, not at all unreasonable. You know nothing about it, my darling; why, if only you knew why it all was, why I was bound to love you, you wouldn't talk like that. All your reasoning about it is only talk, and I am sure that in your heart you feel quite differently.

My precious, I don't even know myself and don't remem-

ber what happened between me and the officers. I must tell
you, my angel, that up to that time I was in the most terrible perturbation. Only imagine! for a whole month I had
been clinging to one thread, so to say. My position was most
awful. I was concealing it from you, and concealing it at
home too. But my landlady made a fuss and a clamour. I
should not have minded that. The wretched woman might
have clamoured but, for one thing, it was the disgrace and,
for another, she had found out about our friendship—God
knows how—and was making such talk about it all over
the house that I was numb with horror and put wool in my
ears, but the worst of it is that other people did not put
wool in theirs, but pricked them up, on the contrary. Even
now I don't know where to hide myself. . . .

Well, my angel, all this accumulation of misfortunes of
all sorts overwhelmed me utterly. Suddenly I heard a
strange thing from Fedora: that a worthless profligate had
called upon you and had insulted you by dishonourable
proposals; that he did insult you, insult you deeply, I can
judge from myself, my darling, for I was deeply insulted
myself. That crushed me, my angel, that overwhelmed me
and made me lose my head completely. I ran out, Varinka
dear, in unutterable fury. I wanted to go straight to him,
the reprobate. I did not know what I meant to do. I won't
have you insulted, my angel! Well, I was sad! And at that
time it was raining, sleet was falling, it was horribly
wretched! . . . I meant to turn back. . . . Then came my
downfall. I met Emelyan Ilyitch—he is a clerk, that is,
was a clerk, but he is not a clerk now because he was
turned out of our office. I don't know what he does now, he
just hangs about there. Well, I went with him. Then—but
there, Varinka, will it amuse you to read about your friend's
misfortunes, his troubles, and the story of the trials he has
endured? Three days later that Emelyan egged me on and
I went to see him, that officer. I got his address from our
porter. Since we are talking about it, my dear, I noticed
that young gallant long ago: I kept an eye upon him when
he lodged in our buildings. I see now that what I did was
unseemly, because I was not myself when I was shown up

to him. Truly, Varinka, I don't remember anything about it, all I remember is that there were a great many officers with him, else I was seeing double—goodness knows. I don't remember what I said either, I only know that I said a great deal in my honest indignation. But then they turned me out, then they threw me downstairs—that is, not really threw me down stairs, but turned me out. You know already, Varinka, how I returned: that's the whole story. Of course I lowered myself and my reputation has suffered, but, after all, no one knows of it but you, no outsider knows of it, and so it is all as though it had never happened. Perhaps that is so, Varinka, what do you think? The only thing is, I know for a fact that last year Aksenty Osipovitch in the same way assaulted Pyotr Petrovitch but in secret, he did it in secret. He called him into the porter's room—I saw it all through the crack in the door—and there he settled the matter, as was fitting, but in a gentlemanly way, for no one saw it except me, and I did not matter—that is, I did not tell anyone. Well, after that Pyotr Petrovitch and Aksenty Osipovitch were all right together. Pyotr Petrovitch, you know, is a man with self-respect, so he told no one, so that now they even bow and shake hands. I don't dispute, Varinka, I don't venture to dispute with you that I have degraded myself terribly, and, what is worst of all, I have lowered myself in my own opinion, but no doubt it was destined from my birth, no doubt it was my fate, and there's no escaping one's fate, you know.

Well, that is an exact account of my troubles and misfortunes, Varinka, all of them, things such that reading of them is unprofitable. I am very far from well, Varinka, and have lost all the playfulness of my feelings. Herewith I beg to testify to my devotion, love and respect. I remain, dear madam, Varvara Alexyevna,

Your humble servant,
MAKAR DYEVUSHKIN.

July 29.

MY DEAR MAKAR ALEXYEVITCH!
I have read your two letters, and positively groaned!

Listen, my dear; you are either concealing something from me and have written to me only part of all your troubles, or . . . really, Makar Alexyevitch, there is a touch of incoherency about your letters still. . . . Come and see me, for goodness' sake, come to-day; and listen, come straight to dinner, you know I don't know how you are living, or how you have managed about your landlady. You write nothing about all that, and your silence seems intentional. So, good-bye, my friend; be sure and come to us to-day; and you would do better to come to us for dinner every day. Fedora cooks very nicely. Good-bye.

Your
VARVARA DOBROSELOV.

August 1.

MY DEAR VARVARA ALEXYEVNA—

You are glad, my dear girl, that God has sent you a chance to do one good turn for another and show your gratitude to me. I believe that, Varinka, and I believe in the goodness of your angelic heart, and I am not saying it to reproach you—only do not upbraid me for being a spendthrift in my old age. Well, if I have done wrong, there's no help for it; only to hear it from you, my dearie, is very bitter! Don't be angry with me for saying so, my heart's all one ache. Poor people are touchy—that's in the nature of things. I felt that even in the past. The poor man is exacting; he takes a different view of God's world, and looks askance at every passer-by and turns a troubled gaze about him and looks to every word, wondering whether people are not talking about him, whether they are saying that he is so ugly, speculating about what he would feel exactly, what he would be on this side and what he would be on that side, and everyone knows, Varinka, that a poor man is worse than a rag and can get no respect from anyone; whatever they may write, those scribblers, it will always be the same with the poor man as it has been. And why will it always be as it has been? Because to their thinking the poor man must be turned inside out, he must have no privacy, no pride whatever! Emelyan told me the other day that they got up a subscription for him and made a sort of official inspection over every sixpence; they thought that they were giving him his sixpences for nothing, but they were not; they were paid for them by showing him he was a poor man. Nowadays, my dear soul, benevolence is practised in a very queer way . . . and perhaps it always has been so, who knows! Either people don't know how to do it or they are first-rate hands at it—one of the two. Perhaps you did not know it, so there it is for you. On anything else we can say nothing, but on this subject we are authorities! And how is it a poor man knows all this and thinks of it all like this? Why?—from experience! Because he knows for instance, that there is a gentleman at his side, who is going somewhere to a restaurant and saying to himself, "What's this beggarly clerk going to eat to-day? I'm going to eat *sauté papillotte* while he is going to eat porridge without butter, maybe." And what business is it to him that I am going to eat porridge without butter? There are men, Varinka, there are men who think of nothing else. And they go about, the indecent caricaturists, and look whether one puts one's whole foot down on the pavement or walks on tiptoe; they notice that such a clerk, of such a department, a titular councillor, has his bare toes sticking out of his boot, that he has holes in his elbow—and then they sit down at home and describe it all and publish such rubbish . . . and what business is it of yours, sir, if my elbows are in holes? Yes, if you will excuse me the coarse expression, Varinka, I will tell you that the poor man has the same sort of modesty on that score as you, for instance, have maidenly modesty. Why, you wouldn't divest yourself of your clothing before everyone—forgive my coarse comparison. So, in the same way, the poor man does not like people to peep into his poor hole and wonder about his domestic arrangements. So what need was there to join in insulting me, Varinka, with the enemies who are attacking an honest man's honour and reputation?

And in the office to-day I sat like a hen, like a plucked sparrow, so that I almost turned with shame at myself. I was ashamed, Varinka! And one is naturally timid, when one's elbows are seeing daylight through one's sleeves, and one's buttons are hanging on threads. And, as ill-luck would have it, all my things were in such disorder! You can't help losing heart. Why! . . . Stepan Karlovitch himself began speaking to me about my work to-day, he talked and talked away and added, as though unawares, "Well, really, Makar Alexyevitch!" and did not say what was in his mind, only I understood what it was for myself, and blushed so that even the bald patch on my head was crimson. It was really only a trifle, but still it made me uneasy, and aroused bitter reflections. If only they have heard nothing! Ah, God forbid that they should hear about anything! I confess I do suspect one man. I suspect him very much. Why, these villains stick at nothing, they will betray me, they will give away one's whole private life for a halfpenny—nothing is sacred to them.

I know now whose doing it is; it is Ratazyaev's doing. He knows someone in our office, and most likely in the course of conversation has told them the whole story with additions; or maybe he has told the story in his own office, and it has crept out and crept into our office. In our lodging, they all know it down to the lowest, and point at your window; I know that they do point. And when I went to dinner with you yesterday, they all poked their heads out of the window and the landlady said: "Look," said she, "the devil has made friends with the baby." And then she called you an unseemly name. But all that's nothing beside Ratazyaev's disgusting design to put you and me into his writing and to describe us in a cunning satire; he spoke of this himself, and friendly fellow-lodgers have repeated it to me. I can think of nothing else, my darling, and don't know what to decide to do. There is no concealing the fact, we have provoked the wrath of God, little angel. You meant to send me a book, my good friend, to relieve my dullness; what is the use of a book, my love, what's the good of it? It's arrant nonsense! The story is nonsense and it is written as nonsense, just for idle people to read; trust me, my dear soul, trust the experience of my age. And what if they talk to you of some Shakespeare, saying, "You see that Shake-

speare wrote literature," well, then, Shakespeare is nonsense; it's all arrant nonsense and only written to jeer at
folk!

Yours,
MAKAR DYEVUSHKIN.

August 2.

DEAR MAKAR ALEXYEVITCH!

Don't worry about anything; please God it will all be set
right. Fedora has got a lot of work both for herself and for
me, and we have set to work very happily; perhaps we shall
save the situation. She suspects that Anna Fyodorovna had
some hand in this last unpleasant business; but now I don't
care. I feel somehow particularly cheerful to-day. You want
to borrow money—God forbid! You'll get into trouble afterwards when you need to pay it back. We had much better
live more frugally; come to us more often, and don't take
any notice of your landlady. As for your other enemies
and ill-wishers, I am sure you are worrying yourself with
needless suspicions, Makar Alexyevitch! Mind, I told you
last time that your language was very exaggerated. Well,
good-bye till we meet. I expect you without fail.

Your
V. D.

August 3.

MY ANGEL, VARVARA ALEXYEVNA,

I hasten to tell you, my little life, I have fresh hopes of
something. But excuse me, my little daughter, you write, my
angel, that I am not to borrow money. My darling, it is impossible to avoid it; here I am in a bad way, and what if
anything were suddenly amiss with you! You are frail, you
know; so that's why I say we must borrow. Well, so I will
continue.

I beg to inform you, Varvara Alexyevna, that in the
office I am sitting next to Emelyan Ivanovitch. That's not
the Emelyan Ilyitch whom you know. He is, like me, a
titular councillor, and he and I are almost the oldest vet-
erans in the office. He is a good-natured soul, an unworldly

soul; he's not given to talking and always sits like a regular bear. But he is a good clerk and has a good English hand-writing and, to tell the whole truth, he writes as well as I do —he's a worthy man! I never was very intimate with him, but only just say good-morning and good-evening; or if I wanted the pen-knife, I would say, "Give me the pen-knife, Emelyan Ivanovitch"; in short, our intercourse was confined to our common necessities. Well, so he says to me to-day, "Makar Alexyevitch, why are you so thoughtful?" I see the man wishes me kindly, so I told him—I said, "This is how it is, Emelyan Ivanovitch"—that is, I did not tell him everything, and indeed, God forbid! I never will tell the story because I haven't the heart to, but just told him something, that I was in straits for money, and so on. "You should borrow, my good soul," said Emelyan Ivanovitch: "you should borrow; from Pyotr Petrovitch you might borrow, he lends money at interest; I have borrowed and he asks a decent rate of interest, not exorbitant." Well, Varinka, my heart gave a leap. I thought and thought maybe the Lord will put it into the heart of Pyotr Petrovitch and in his benevolence he will lend me the money. Already I was reckoning to myself that I could pay the landlady and help you, and clear myself all round. Whereas now it is such a disgrace, one is afraid to be in one's own place, let alone the jeers of our grinning jackanapes. Bother them! And besides, his Excellency sometimes passes by our table: why, God forbid! he may cast a glance in my direction and notice I'm not decently dressed! And he makes a great point of neatness and tidiness. Maybe he would say nothing, but I should die of shame—that's how it would be. In consequence I screwed myself up and, putting my pride in my ragged pocket, I went up to Pyotr Petrovitch full of hope and at the same time more dead than alive with suspense. But, after all, Varinka, it all ended in foolishness! He was busy with something, talking with Fedosey Ivanovitch. I went up to him sideways and pulled him by the sleeve, saying, "Pyotr Petrovitch, I say, Pyotr Petrovitch!" He looked round, and I went on: saying, "this is how it is, thirty roubles," and so on. At first he did not understand me, and when I explained it all to him, he laughed, and said nothing. I said the same thing again. And he said to me, "Have you got a pledge?" And he buried himself in his writing and did not even glance at me. I was a little flustered. "No," I said, "Pyotr Petrovitch, I've no pledge," and I explained to him that when I got my salary I would pay him, would be sure to pay him, I should consider it my first duty. Then somebody called him. I waited for him, he came back and began mending a pen and did not seem to notice me, and I kept on with "Pyotr Petrovitch, can't you manage it somehow?" He said nothing and seemed not to hear me. I kept on standing there. Well, I thought I would try for the last time, and pulled him by the sleeve. He just muttered something, cleaned his pen, and began writing. I walked away. You see, my dear girl, they may be excellent people, but proud, very proud—but I don't mind! We are not fit company for them, Varinka! That is why I have written all this to you. Emelyan Ivanovitch laughed, too, and shook his head, but he cheered me up, the dear fellow—Emelyan Ivanovitch is a worthy man. He promised to introduce me to a man who lives in the Vybord Side, Varinka, and lends money at interest too; he is some sort of clerk of the fourteenth class. Emelyan Ivanovitch says he will be sure to lend it. Shall I go to him to-morrow, my angel, eh? What do you think? It is awful if I don't. My landlady is almost turning me out and won't consent to give me my dinner; besides, my boots are in a dreadful state, my dear; I've no buttons either and nothing else besides. And what if anyone in authority at the office notices such unseemliness; it will be awful, Varinka, simply awful!

MAKAR DYEVUSHKIN.

August 4.

DEAR MAKAR ALEXYEVITCH,

For God's sake, Makar Alexyevitch, borrow some money as soon as possible! I would not for anything have asked you for help as things are at present, but if you only knew what a position I am in. It's utterly impossible for us to

remain in this lodging. A horribly unpleasant thing has
happened here, and if only you knew how upset and agitated I am! Only imagine, my friend; this morning a stranger came into our lodging, an elderly, almost old man,
wearing orders. I was amazed, not knowing what he wanted
with us. Fedora had gone out to a shop at the time. He began asking me how I lived and what I did, and without
waiting for an answer, told me that he was the uncle of that
officer; that he was very angry with his nephew for his disgraceful behaviour, and for having given us a bad name all
over the buildings; said that his nephew was a feather-
headed scamp, and that he was ready to take me under his
protection; advised me not to listen to young men, added
that he sympathised with me like a father, that he felt a
father's feeling for me and was ready to help me in any
way. I blushed all over, not knowing what to think, but was
in no haste to thank him. He took my hand by force,
patted me on the cheek, told me I was very pretty and that
he was delighted to find I had dimples in my cheeks (goodness knows what he said!) and at last tried to kiss me, saying that he was an old man (he was so loathsome). At that
point Fedora came in. He was a little disconcerted and began saying again that he felt respect for me, for my discretion and good principles, and that he was very anxious that
I should not treat him as a stranger. Then he drew Fedora
aside and on some strange pretext wanted to give her a lot
of money. Fedora, of course, would not take it. At last he
got up to go, he repeated once more all his assurances, said
that he would come and see me again and bring me some
ear-rings (I believe he, too, was very much embarrassed);
he advised me to change my lodgings and recommended
me a very nice lodging which he had his eye on, and which
would cost me nothing; he said that he liked me very much
for being an honest and sensible girl, advised me to beware
of profligate men, and finally told us that he knew Anna
Fyodorovna and that Anna Fyodorovna had commissioned
him to tell me that she would come and see me herself.
Then I understood it all. I don't know what came over me;

it was the first time in my life I had had such an experience; I flew into a fury, I put him to shame completely. Fedora helped me, and we almost turned him out of the flat. We've come to the conclusion that it is all Anna Fyodorovna's doing; how else could he have heard of us?

Now I appeal to you, Makar Alexyevitch, and entreat you to help us. For God's sake, don't desert me in this awful position. Please borrow, get hold of some money anyway; we've no money to move with and we mustn't stay here any longer; that's Fedora's advice. We need at least thirty-five roubles; I'll pay you back the money; I'll earn it. Fedora will get me some more work in a day or two, so that if they ask a high interest, never mind it, but agree to anything. I'll pay it all back, only for God's sake, don't abandon me. I can't bear worrying you now when you are in such circumstances . . . Good-bye, Makar Alexyevitch; think of me, and God grant you are successful.

Yours,
V. D.

August 4.

My darling Varvara Alexyevna!

All these unexpected blows positively shatter me! Such terrible calamities destroy my spirit! These scoundrelly libertines and rascally old men will not only bring you, my angel, to a bed of sickness, they mean to be the death of me, too. And they will be, too, I swear they will. You know I am ready to die sooner than not help you! If I don't help you it will be the death of me, Varinka, the actual literal death of me, and if I do help you, you'll fly away from me like a bird out of its nest, to escape these owls, these birds of prey that were trying to peck her. That's what tortures me, my precious. And you too, Varinka, you are so cruel! How can you do it? You are tormented, you are insulted, you, my little bird, are in distress, and then you regret that you must worry me and promise to repay the debt, which means, to tell the truth, that with your delicate health you will kill yourself, in order to get the money for me in time. Why, only think, Varinka, what you are talking about. Why should you sew? Why should you work, worry your poor little head with anxiety, spoil your pretty eyes and destroy your health? Ah, Varinka, Varinka! You see, my darling, I am good for nothing, I know myself that I am good for nothing, but I'll manage to be good for something! I will overcome all obstacles. I will get outside work, I will copy all sorts of manuscripts for all sorts of literary men. I will go to them, I won't wait to be asked, I'll force them to give me work, for you know, my darling, they are on the look-out for good copyists, I know they look out for them, but I won't let you wear yourself out; I won't let you carry out such a disastrous intention. I will certainly borrow it, my angel, I'd sooner die than not borrow it. You write, my darling, that I am not to be afraid of a high rate of interest—and I won't be afraid of it, my dear soul, I won't be frightened. I won't be frightened of anything now. I will ask for forty roubles in paper, my dear; that's not much, you know, Varinka, what do you think? Will they trust me with forty roubles at the first word? That is, I mean to say, do you consider me capable of inspiring trust and confidence at first sight. Can they form a favourable impression of me from my physiognomy at first sight? Recall my appearance, my angel; am I capable of inspiring confidence? What do you think yourself? You know I feel such terror; it makes me quite ill, to tell the truth, quite ill. Of the forty roubles I set aside twenty-five for you, Varinka, two silver roubles will be for the landlady, and the rest I design for my own expenses. You see I ought to give the landlady more, I must, in fact; but if you think it all over, my dear girl, and reckon out all I need, then you'll see that it is impossible to give her more, consequently there's no use talking about it and no need to refer to it. For a silver rouble I shall buy a pair of boots—I really don't know whether I shall be able to appear at the office in the old ones; a new necktie would have been necessary, too, for I have had the old one a year, but since you've promised to make me, not only a tie, but a shirtfront cut out of your old apron, I shall think no more of a tie. So there we have boots and a tie. Now for buttons, my dear. You will agree, my darling, that I can't go on without buttons and almost half have dropped off. I tremble when I think that his Excellency may notice such untidiness and say something, and what he would say! I shouldn't hear what he would say, my darling, for I should die, die, die on the spot, simply go and die of shame at the very thought!—Ah, Varinka!—Well, after all these necessities, there will be three roubles left, so that would do to live on and get half a pound of tobacco, for I can't live without tobacco, my little angel, and this is the ninth day since I had my pipe in my mouth. To tell the truth, I should have bought it and said nothing to you, but I was ashamed. You are there in trouble depriving yourself of everything, and here am I enjoying luxuries of all sorts; so that's why I tell you about it to escape the stings of conscience. I frankly confess, Varinka, I am now in an extremely straitened position, that is, nothing like it has ever happened before. My landlady despises me, I get no sort of respect from anyone; my terrible lapses, my debts; and at the office, where I had anything but a good time, in the old days, at the hands of my fellow clerks—now, Varinka, it is beyond words. I hide everything, I carefully hide everything from everyone, and I edge into the office sideways, I hold aloof from all. It's only to you that I have the heart to confess it. . . . And what if they won't give me the money! No, we had better not think about that, Varinka, not depress our spirits beforehand with such thoughts. That's why I am writing this, to warn you not to think about it, and not to worry yourself with evil imaginations. Ah! my God! what will happen to you then! It's true that then you will not move from that lodging and I shall be with you then. But, no, I should not come back then, I should simply perish somewhere and be lost. Here I have been writing away to you and I ought to have been shaving; it makes one more presentable, and to be presentable always counts for something. Well, God help us, I will say my prayers, and then set off.

M. DYEVUSHKIN.

August 5.

MY DEAR MAKAR ALEXYEVITCH,

You really mustn't give way to despair. There's trouble enough without that.

I send you thirty kopecks in silver, I cannot manage more. Buy yourself what you need most, so as to get along somehow, until to-morrow. We have scarcely anything left ourselves, and I don't know what will happen to-morrow. It's sad, Makar Alexyevitch! Don't be sad, though, if you've not succeeded, there's no help for it. Fedora says that there is no harm done so far, that we can stay for the time in this lodging, that if we did move we shouldn't gain much by it, and that they can find us anywhere if they want to. Though I don't feel comfortable at staying here now. If it were not so sad I would have written you an account of something.

What a strange character you have, Makar Alexyevitch; you take everything too much to heart and so you will be always a very unhappy man. I read all your letters attentively and I see in every letter you are anxious and worried about me as you never are about yourself. Everyone says, of course, that you have a good heart, but I say that it is too good. I will give you some friendly advice, Makar Alexyevitch. I am grateful to you, very grateful for all that you have done for me, I feel it very much; so judge what it must be for me to see that even now, after all your misfortunes of which I have been the unconscious cause—that even now you are only living in my life, my joys, my sorrows, my feelings! If one takes all another person's troubles so to heart and sympathises so intensely with everything it is bound to make one very unhappy. To-day, when you came in to see me from the office I was frightened at the sight of you. You were so pale, so despairing, so frightened-looking; you did not look like yourself—and all because you were afraid to tell me of your failure, afraid of disappointing me, of frightening me, and when you saw I nearly laughed your heart was almost at ease. Makar Alexyevitch, don't grieve, don't despair, be more sensible, I beg you, I implore you. Come, you will see that everything will be all right. Everything will take a better turn: why, life will be a misery to you, for ever grieving and being miserable over other people's troubles. Good-bye, my dear friend. I beseech you not to think too much about it.

V. D.

August 5.

My darling Varinka,

Very well, my angel, very well! You have made up your mind that it is no harm so far that I have not got the money. Well, very good, I feel reassured, I am happy as regards you. I am delighted, in fact, that you are not going to leave me in my old age but are going to stay in your lodging. In fact, to tell you everything, my heart was brimming over with joy when I saw that you wrote so nicely about me in your letter and gave due credit to my feelings. I don't say this from pride, but because I see how you love me when you are so anxious about my heart. Well, what's the use of talking about my heart! The heart goes its own way, but you hint, my precious, that I mustn't be downhearted. Yes, my angel, maybe, and I say myself it is of no use being downhearted! but for all that, you tell me, my dear girl, what boots I am to go to the office in to-morrow! That's the trouble, Varinka; and you know such a thought destroys a man, destroys him utterly. And the worst of it is, my own, that it is not for myself I am troubled, it is not for myself I am distressed; as far as I am concerned I don't mind going about without an overcoat and without boots in the hardest frost; I don't care: I can stand anything, and put up with anything. I am a humble man of no importance,—but what will people say? My enemies with their spiteful tongues, what will they say, when one goes about without an overcoat? You know it is for the sake of other people one wears an overcoat, yes, and boots, too, you put on, perhaps, on their account. Boots, in such cases, Varinka darling, are necessary to keep up one's dignity and good name: in boots with holes in them, both dignity and good name are lost; trust the experience of my years, my dear child, listen to an old man like me who

knows the world and what people are, and not to any scur-
rilous scribblers and satirists.

I have not yet told you in detail, my darling, how it all
happened to-day. I suffered so much, I endured in one
morning more mental anguish than many a man endures in
a year. This is how it was: first, I set off very early in the
morning, so as to find him and be in time for the office afterwards. There was such a rain, such a sleet falling this
morning! I wrapped myself up in my overcoat, my little
dearie. I walked on and on and I kept thinking: "Oh, Lord,
forgive my transgressions and grant the fulfilment of my desires!" Passing St. X's Church, I crossed myself, repented
of all my sins, and thought that it was wrong of me to bargain with the Almighty. I was lost in my thoughts and did
not feel like looking at anything; so I walked without picking my way. The streets were empty, and the few I met all
seemed anxious and preoccupied, and no wonder: who
would go out at such an early hour and in such weather! A
gang of workmen, grinning all over, met me, the rough fellows shoved against me! A feeling of dread came over me,
I felt panic-stricken, to tell the truth I didn't like even to
think about the money—I felt I must just take my chance!
Just at Voskressensky Bridge the sole came off my boot, so
I really don't know what I walked upon. And then I met
our office attendant, Yermolaev. He drew himself up at
attention and stood looking after me as though he would
ask for a drink. "Ech, a drink, brother," I thought; "not
much chance of a drink!" I was awfully tired. I stood still,
rested a bit and pushed on farther; I looked about on purpose for something to fasten my attention on, to distract
my mind, to cheer me up, but no, I couldn't fix one thought
on anything and, besides, I was so muddy that I felt
ashamed of myself. At last I saw in the distance a yellow
wooden house with an upper storey in the style of a belve-
dere. "Well," thought I, "so that's it, that's how Emelyan
Ivanovitch described it—Markov's house." (It is this Markov himself, Varinka, who lends money.) I scarcely knew
what I was doing, and I knew, of course, that it was Markov's house, but I asked a policeman. "Whose house is

that, brother?" said I. The policeman was a surly fellow, seemed loth to speak and cross with someone; he filtered his words through his teeth, but he did say it was Markov's house. These policemen are always so unfeeling, but what did the policeman matter?—well, it all made a bad and unpleasant impression, in short, there was one thing on the top of another; one finds in everything something akin to one's own position, and it is always so. I took three turns past the house, along the street, and the further I went, the worse I felt. "No," I thought, "he won't give it me, nothing will induce him to give it me. I am a stranger and it's a ticklish business, and I am not an attractive figure. Well," I thought, "leave it to Fate, if only I do not regret it afterwards; they won't devour me for making the attempt," and I softly opened the gate, and then another misfortune happened. A wretched, stupid yard dog fastened upon me. It was beside itself and barked its loudest!—and it's just such wretched, trivial incidents that always madden a man, Varinka, and make him nervous and destroy all the determination he has been fortifying himself with beforehand; so that I went into the house more dead than alive and walked straight into trouble again. Without seeing what was below me straight in the doorway. I went in, stumbled over a woman who was busy straining some milk from a pail into a jug, and spilt all the milk. The silly woman shrieked and made an outcry, saying, "Where are you shoving to, my man?" and made a deuce of a row. I may say, Varinka, it is always like this with me in such cases; it seems it is my fate, I always get mixed up in something. An old hag, the Finnish landlady, poked her head out at the noise. I went straight up to her. "Does Markov live here?" said I. "No," said she. She stood still and took a good look at me. "And what do you want with him?" I explained to her that Emelyan had told me this and that, and all the rest of it—said it was a matter of business. The old woman called her daughter, a barelegged girl in her teens. "Call your father; he's upstairs at the lodger's, most likely."

I went in. The room was all right, there were pictures on

the wall—all portraits of generals, a sofa, round table, mignonette, and balsam—I wondered whether I had not better clear out and take myself off for good and all. And, oh dear, I did want to run away, Varinka. "I had better come to-morrow," I thought, "and the weather will be better and I will wait a little—to-day the milk's been spilt and the generals look so cross . . ." I was already at the door— but he came in—a greyheaded man with thievish eyes, in a greasy dressing-gown with a cord round his waist. He enquired how and why, and I told him that Emelyan Ivanovitch had told me this and that—"Forty roubles," I said, "is what I've come about"—and I couldn't finish. I saw from his eyes that the game was lost. "No," says he; "the fact is, I've no money; and have you brought anything to pledge as security?"

I began explaining that I had brought nothing to pledge, but that Emelyan Ivanovitch—I explained in fact, what was wanted. He heard it all. "No," said he; "what is Emelyan Ivanovitch! I've no money."

Well, I thought, "There it is, I knew—I had a foreboding of it." Well, Varinka, it would have been better really if the earth had opened under me. I felt chill all over, my feet went numb and a shiver ran down my back. I looked at him and he looked at me and almost said, Come, run along, brother, it is no use your staying here—so that if such a thing had happened in other circumstances, I should have been quite ashamed. "And what do you want money for?" —(do you know, he asked that, Varinka). I opened my mouth, if only not to stand there doing nothing, but he wouldn't listen. "No," he said, "I have no money, I would have lent it with pleasure," said he. Then I pressed him, telling him I only wanted a little, saying I would pay him back on the day fixed, that I would pay him back before the day fixed, that he could ask any interest he liked and that, by God! I would pay him back. At that instant, my darling, I thought of you, I thought of all your troubles and privations, I thought of your poor little half-rouble. "But no," says he, "the interest is no matter; if there had been a pledge now! Besides, I have no money. I have none, by God! or I'd oblige you with pleasure,"—he took God's name, too, the villain!

Well, I don't remember, my own, how I went out, how I walked along Vyborgsky Street; how I got to Voskressensky Bridge. I was fearfully tired, shivering, wet through, and only succeeded in reaching the office at ten o'clock. I wanted to brush the mud off, but Snyegirev, the porter, said I mustn't, I should spoil the brush, and "the brush is government property," said he. That's how they all go on now, my dear, these gentry treat me no better than a rag to wipe their boots on. Do you know what is killing me, Varinka? it's not the money that's killing me, but all these little daily cares, these whispers, smiles and jokes. His Excellency may by chance have to refer to me. Oh, my darling, my golden days are over. I read over all your letters to-day; it's sad, Varinka! Good-bye, my own! The Lord keep you.

M. DYEVUSHKIN.

P.S.—I meant to describe my troubles half in joke, Varinka, only it seems that it does not come off with me, joking. I wanted to satisfy you. I am coming to see you, my dear girl, I will be sure to come.

August 11.

VARVARA ALEXYEVNA, MY DARLING,

I am lost, we are both lost, both together irretrievably lost. My reputation, my dignity—all is destroyed! I am ruined and you are ruined, my darling. You are hopelessly ruined with me! It's my doing, I have brought you to ruin! I am persecuted, Varinka, I am despised, turned into a laughing-stock, and the landlady has simply begun to abuse me; she shouted and shouted at me, to-day; she rated and rated at me and treated me as though I were dirt. And in the evening, at Ratazyaev's, one of them began reading aloud the rough copy of a letter to you which I had accidentally dropped out of my pocket. My precious, what a joke they made of it! They called us all sorts of flattering names and roared with laughter, the traitors! I went to them

and taxed Ratazyaev with his perfidy, told him he was a
traitor! And Ratazyaev answered that I was a traitor myself,
that I amused myself with making conquests among the fair
sex. He said, "You take good care to keep it from us; you're
a Lovelace," he said; and now they all call me Lovelace and
I have no other name! Do you hear, my little angel, do you
hear?—they know it all now, they know all about it, and
they know about you, my own, and whatever you have, they
know about it all! And that's not all. Even Faldoni is in it,
he's following their lead; I sent him to-day to the sausage-
shop to get me something; he wouldn't go. "I am busy,"
that was all he said! "But you know it's your duty," I said.
"No, indeed," he said, "it's not my duty. Here, you don't pay
my mistress her money, so I have no duty to you." I could
not stand this insult from him, an illiterate peasant, and I
said, "You fool," and he answered back, "Fool yourself."
I thought he must have had a drop too much to be so rude,
and I said: "You are drunk, you peasant!" and he answered: "Well, not at your expense, anyway, you've nothing to get drunk on yourself; you are begging for twenty
kopecks from somebody yourself," and he even added:
"Ugh! and a gentleman too!" There, my dear girl, that's
what it has come to! One's ashamed to be alive, Varinka!
As though one were some sort of outcast, worse than a
tramp without a passport. An awful calamity! I am ruined,
simply ruined! I am irretrievably ruined!

M. D.

August 13.

MY DEAR MAKAR ALEXYEVITCH,

It's nothing but one trouble after another upon us. I don't
know myself what to do! What will happen to you now?—
and I have very little to hope for either; I burnt my left
hand this morning with an iron; I dropped it accidentally
and bruised myself and burnt my hand at the same time. I
can't work at all, and Fedora has been poorly for the last
three days. I am in painful anxiety. I send you thirty kopecks in silver; it is almost all we have left, and God knows
how I should have liked to help you in your need. I am so

vexed I could cry. Good-bye, my friend! You would comfort me very much if you would come and see us to-day.

V. D.

August 14.

MAKAR ALEXYEVITCH

What is the matter with you? It seems you have no fear of God! You are simply driving me out of my mind. Aren't you ashamed? You will be your own ruin; you should at least think of your good name! You're a man of honour, of gentlemanly feelings, of self-respect; well, when everyone finds out about you! Why, you will simply die of shame! Have you no pity for your grey hairs? Have you no fear of God? Fedora says she won't help you again, and I won't give you money either. What have you brought me to, Makar Alexyevitch? I suppose you think that it is nothing to me, your behaving so badly? You don't know what I have to put up with on your account! I can't even go down our staircase; everyone looks at me and points at me, and says such awful things; they say plainly that I have *taken up with a drunkard*. Think what it is to hear that! When you are brought in all the lodgers point at you with contempt: "Look," they say, "they've brought that clerk in." And I'm ready to faint with shame over you. I swear I shall move from here. I shall go somewhere as a housemaid or a laundrymaid, I shan't stay here. I wrote to you to come and see me here but you did not come. So are my tears and entreaties nothing to you, Makar Alexyevitch? And where do you get the money? For God's sake, do be careful. Why, you are ruining yourself, ruining yourself for nothing! And it's a shame and a disgrace! The landlady would not let you in last night, you spent the night on the porch. I know all about it. If only you knew how miserable I was when I knew all about it. Come to see me; you will be happy with us; we will read together, we will recall the past. Fedora will tell us about her wanderings as a pilgrim. For my sake, don't destroy yourself and me. Why, I only live for you, for your sake I am staying with you. And this is how you are behaving now! Be a fine man, steadfast in misfortune, remember that poverty is not a vice. And why despair? It is all temporary! Please God, it will all be set right, only you must restrain yourself now. I send you twenty kopecks. Buy yourself tobacco or anything you want, only for God's sake don't spend it on what's harmful. Come and see us, be sure to come. Perhaps you will be ashamed as you were before, but don't be ashamed; it's false shame. If only you would show genuine penitence. Trust in God. He will do all things for the best.

V. D.

August 19.

VARVARA ALEXYEVNA, DARLING,

I am ashamed, little dearie, Varvara Alexyevna; I am quite ashamed. But, after all, what is there so particular about it, my dear? Why not rejoice the heart a little? Then I don't think about my sole, for one's sole is nonsense, and will always remain a simply, nasty, muddy sole. Yes, and boots are nonsense, too! The Greek sages used to go about without boots, so why should people like us pamper ourselves with such unworthy objects? Oh! my dearie, my dearie, you have found something to write about! You tell Fedora that she is a nonsensical, fidgety, fussy woman, and, what's more, she's a silly one, too, unutterably silly! As for my grey hairs, you are quite mistaken about that, my own, for I am by no means so old as you think. Emelyan sends you his regards. You write that you have been breaking your heart and crying; and I write to you that I am breaking my heart, too, and crying. In conclusion I wish you the best of health and prosperity, and as for me I am in the best of health and prosperity, too, and I remain, my angel, your friend,

MAKAR DYEVUSHKIN.

August 21.

HONOURED MADAM AND DEAR FRIEND,
VARVARA ALEXYEVNA,

I feel that I am to blame, I feel that I have wronged you, and to my mind there's no benefit at all, dear friend, in my feeling it, whatever you may say. I felt all that even before my misconduct, but I lost heart and fell, knowing I was doing wrong. My dear, I am not a bad man and not cruel-hearted, and to torture your little heart, my little darling, one must be, more or less, like a bloodthirsty tiger. Well, I have the heart of a lamb and, as you know, have no inclination towards bloodthirstiness; consequently, my angel, I am not altogether to blame in my misconduct, since neither my feelings nor my thoughts were to blame; and in fact, I don't know what was to blame; it's all so incomprehensible, my darling! you sent me thirty kopecks in silver, and then you sent me twenty kopecks. My heart ached looking at your poor little coins. You had burnt your hand, you would soon be going hungry yourself, and you write that I am to buy tobacco. Well, how could I behave in such a position? Was I without a pang of conscience to begin plundering you, poor little orphan, like a robber! Then I lost heart altogether, my darling—that is, at first I could not help feeling that I was good for nothing and that I was hardly better than the sole of my boot. And so I felt it was unseemly to consider myself of any consequence, and began to look upon myself as something unseemly and somewhat indecent. Well, and when I lost my self-respect and denied my good qualities and my dignity, then it was all up with me, it meant degradation, inevitable degradation! That is ordained by destiny and I'm not to blame for it.

I went out at first to get a little air, then it was one thing after another; nature was so tearful, the weather was cold and it was raining. Well, Emelyan turned up. He had pawned everything he had, Varinka, everything he had is gone: and when I met him he had not put a drop of the rosy to his lips for two whole days and nights, so that he was ready to pawn what you can't pawn, because such things are never taken in pawn. Well, Varinka, I gave way more from a feeling of humanity than my own inclination, that's how the sin came to pass, my dear! How we wept together! We spoke of you. He's very good-natured, he's a very good-natured fellow and a very feeling man. I feel all that myself, my dear girl, that is just why it all happens to

me, that I feel it all very much. I know how much I owe
to you, my darling. Getting to know you, I came first to
know myself better and to love you; and before I knew
you, my angel, I was solitary and as it were asleep, and
scarcely alive. They said, the spiteful creatures, that even
my appearance was unseemly and they were disgusted with
me, and so I began to be disgusted with myself; they said I
was stupid and I really thought that I was stupid. When
you came to me, you lighted up my dark life, so that my
heart and my soul were filled with light and I gained peace
at heart, and knew that I was no worse than others; that the
only thing is that I am not brilliant in any way, that I have
no polish or style about me, but I am still a man, in heart
and mind a man. Well now, feeling that I was persecuted
and humiliated by destiny, I lost all faith in my own good
qualities, and, shattered by calamities, I lost all heart. And
now since you know all about it, my dear, I beg you with
tears not to question me further about that matter, for my
heart is breaking and it is very bitter for me and hard to bear.

Assuring you of my respect, I remain, your faithful

MAKAR DYEVUSHKIN.

September 3.

I did not finish my last letter, Makar Alexyevitch, because it was difficult for me to write. Sometimes I have moments when I am glad to be alone, to mourn, with none to
share my grief, and such moments are becoming more and
more frequent with me. In my recollections there is something inexplicable to me, which attacks me unaccountably
and so intensely that for hours at a stretch I am insensible
to all surrounding me and I forget everything—all the present. And there is no impression of my present life, whether
pleasant or painful and sad, which would not remind me
of something similar in my past, and most often in my
childhood, my golden childhood! But I always feel oppressed after such moments. I am somehow weakened by
them; my dreaminess exhausts me, and apart from that my
health grows worse and worse. But to-day the fresh bright
sunny morning, such as are rare in autumn here, revived

me and I welcomed it joyfully. And so autumn is with us already! How I used to love the autumn in the country! I was a child then, but I had already felt a great deal. I loved the autumn evening better than the morning. I remember that there was a lake at the bottom of the hill a few yards from our house. That lake—I feel as though I could see it now—that lake was so broad, so smooth, as bright and clear as crystal! At times, if it were a still evening, the lake was calm; not a leaf would stir on the trees that grew on the bank, and the water would be as motionless as a mirror. It was so fresh, so cool! The dew would be falling on the grass, the lights begin twinkling in the cottages on the bank, and they would be driving the cattle home. Then I could creep out to look at my lake, and I would forget everything, looking at it. At the water's edge, the fishermen would have a faggot burning and the light would be reflected far, far, over the water. The sky was so cold and blue, with streaks of fiery red along the horizon, and the streaks kept growing paler and paler; the moon would rise; the air so resonant that if a frightened bird fluttered, or a reed stirred in the faint breeze, or a fish splashed in the water, everything could be heard. A white steam, thin and transparent, rises up over the blue water: the distance darkens; everything seems drowned in the mist, while close by it all stands out so sharply, as though cut by a chisel, the boat, the banks, the islands; the tub thrown away and forgotten floats in the water close to the bank, the willow branch hangs with its yellow leaves tangled in the reeds, a belated gull flies up, then dives into the cold water, flies up again and is lost in the mist—while I gaze and listen. How lovely, how marvellous it was to me! and I was a child, almost a baby. . . .

I was so fond of the autumn, the late autumn when they were carrying the harvest, finishing all the labours of the year, when the peasants began gathering together in their cottages in the evening, when they were all expecting winter. Then it kept growing darker. The yellow leaves strewed the paths at the edges of the bare forest while the forest grew bluer and darker—especially at evening when a damp mist fell and the trees glimmered in the mist like giants, like terrible misshapen phantoms. If one were late out for a walk, dropped behind the others, how one hurried on alone—it was dreadful! One trembled like a leaf and kept thinking that in another minute someone terrible would peep out from behind that hollow tree; meanwhile the wind would rush through the woods, roaring and whistling, howling so plaintively, tearing a crowd of leaves from a withered twig, whirling them in the air, and with wild, shrill cries the birds would fly after them in a great, noisy flock, so that the sky would be all covered and darkened with them. One feels frightened, and then, just as though one heard someone speaking—some voice—as though someone whispered: "Run, run, child, don't be late; it will be dreadful here soon; run, child!"—with a thrill of horror at one's heart one would run till one was out of breath. One would reach home, breathless; there it was all noise and gaiety; all of us children had some work given to us to do, shelling peas or shaking out poppy seeds. The damp wood crackles in the stove. Cheerfully mother looks after our cheerful work; our old nurse, Ulyana, tells us stories about old times or terrible tales of wizards and dead bodies. We children squeeze up to one another with smiles on our lips. Then suddenly we are all silent . . . Oh! a noise as though someone were knocking—it was nothing; it was old Frolovna's spindle; how we laughed! Then at night we would lie awake for hours, we had such fearful dreams. One would wake and not dare to stir, and lie shivering under the quilt till daybreak. In the morning one would get up, fresh as a flower. One would look out of the window; all the country would be covered with frost, the thin hoarfrost of autumn would be hanging on the bare boughs, the lake would be covered with ice, thin as a leaf, a white mist would be rising over it, the birds would be calling merrily, the sun would light up everything with its brilliant rays and break the thin ice like glass. It was so bright, so shining, so gay, the fire would be crackling in the stove again, we would sit down round the samovar while our black dog, Polkan, numb with cold from the night, would peep in at the window with a friendly wag of his tail. A peasant would ride by the window on his good horse to fetch wood from the forest. Everyone was so gay, so happy! . . . There were masses and masses of corn stored up in the threshing-barns; the huge, huge stacks covered with straw shone golden in the sun, a comforting sight! And all are calm and joyful. God has blessed us all with the harvest; they all know they will have bread for the winter; the peasant knows that his wife and children will have food to eat; and so there is no end to the singing of the girls and their dances and games in the evening, and on the Saints' days! All pray in the house of God with grateful tears! Oh! what a golden, golden age was my childhood! . . .

Here I am crying like a child, carried away by my reminiscences. I remembered it all so vividly, so vividly, all the past stood out so brightly before me, and the present is so dim, so dark! . . . How will it end, how will it all end? Do you know I have a sort of conviction, a feeling of certainty, that I shall die this autumn. I am very, very ill. I often think about dying, but still I don't want to die like this, to lie in the earth here. Perhaps I shall be laid up as I was in the spring; I've not fully recovered from that illness yet. I am feeling very dreary just now. Fedora has gone off somewhere for the whole day and I am sitting alone. And for some time now I've been afraid of being left alone; I always feel as though there were someone else in the room, that someone is talking to me; especially when I begin dreaming about something and suddenly wake up from my brooding, then I feel frightened. That is why I've written you such a long letter; it goes off when I write. Good-bye; I finish my letter because I have neither time nor paper for more. Of the money from pawning my dress and my hat I have only one rouble in silver left. You have given the landlady two roubles in silver; that's very good. She will keep quiet now for a time.

You must improve your clothes somehow. Good-bye, I'm so tired; I don't know why I am growing so feeble. The least work exhausts me. If I do get work, how am I to work? It is that thought that's killing me.

V. D.

September 5.

MY DARLING VARINKA,

I have received a great number of impressions this morning, my angel. To begin with I had a headache all day. To freshen myself up a bit I went for a walk along Fontanka. It was such a damp, dark evening. By six o'clock it was getting dusk—that is what we are coming to now. It was not raining but there was mist equal to a good rain. There were broad, long stretches of storm-cloud across the sky. There were masses of people walking along the canal bank, and, as ill-luck would have it, the people had such horrible depressing faces, drunken peasants, snub-nosed Finnish women, in high boots with nothing on their heads, workmen, cab-drivers, people like me out on some errand, boys, a carpenter's apprentice in a striped dressing-gown, thin and wasted-looking, with his face bathed in smutty oil, and a lock in his hand; a discharged soldier seven feet high waiting for somebody to buy a pen-knife or a bronze ring from him. That was the sort of crowd. It seems it was an hour when no other sort of people could be about. Fontanka is a canal for traffic! Such a mass of barges that one wonders how there can be room for them all! On the bridges there are women sitting with wet gingerbread and rotten apples, and they all of them looked so muddy, so drenched. It's dreary walking along Fontanka! The wet granite under one's feet, with tall black, sooty houses on both sides. Fog underfoot and fog overhead. How dark and melancholy it was this evening!

When I went back to Gorohovoy Street it was already getting dark and they had begun lighting the gas. I have not been in Gorohovoy Street for quite a long while, I haven't happened to go there. It's a noisy street! What shops, what magnificent establishments; everything is simply shining and resplendent; materials, flowers under glass, hats of all sorts with ribbons. One would fancy they were all displayed as a show—but no: you know there are people who buy all those things and present them to their wives. It's a wealthy street! There are a great many German bakers in Gorohovoy Street, so they must be a very prosperous set of people, too. What numbers of carriages roll by every minute; I wonder the paving is not worn out! Such gorgeous equipages, windows shining like mirrors, silk and velvet inside, and aristocratic footmen wearing epaulettes and carrying a sword; I glanced into all the carriages, there were always ladies in them dressed up to the nines, perhaps countesses and princesses. No doubt it was the hour when they were all hastening to balls and assemblies. It would be interesting to get a closer view of princesses and ladies of rank in general; it must be very nice; I have never seen them; except just as to-day, a passing glance at their carriages. I thought of you then. Ah, my darling, my own! When I think of you my heart begins aching! Why are you so unlucky, my Varinka? You are every bit as good as any of them. You are good, lovely, well-educated—why has such a cruel fortune fallen to your lot? Why does it happen that a good man is left forlorn and forsaken, while happiness seems thrust upon another? I know, I know, my dear, that it's wrong to think that, that it is free-thinking; but to speak honestly, to speak the whole truth, why is it fate, like a raven, croaks good fortune for one still unborn, while another begins life in the orphan asylum? And you know it often happens that Ivan the fool is favoured by fortune. "You, Ivan the fool, rummage in the family money bags, eat, drink and be merry, while you, So-and-so, can lick your lips. That's all you are fit for, you, brother So-and-so!" It's a sin, my darling, it's a sin to think like that, but sometimes one cannot help sin creeping into one's heart. You ought to be driving in such a carriage, my own little dearie. Generals should be craving the favour of a glance from you—not the likes of us; you ought to be dressed in silk and gold, instead of a little old linen gown. You would not be a thin, delicate little thing, as you are now, but like a little sugar figure, fresh, plump and rosy. And then, I should be happy simply to look in at you from the street through the brightly lighted windows; simply to see your shadow. The thought that you were happy and gay, my pretty little bird, would be enough to make me gay, too. But as it is, it is not enough that spiteful people have ruined you, a worthless profligate wretch goes and insults you. Because his coat hangs smartly on him, because he stares at you from a golden eye-glass, the shameless fellow, he can do what he likes, and one must listen to what he says indulgently, however unseemly it is! Wait a bit—is it really so, my pretty gentlemen? And why is all this? Because you are an orphan, because you are defenceless, because you have no powerful friend to help and protect you. And what can one call people who are ready to insult an orphan? They are worthless beasts, not men; simply trash. They are mere ciphers and have no real existence, of that I am convinced. That's what they are like, these people! And to my thinking, my own, the hurdy-gurdy man I met to-day in Gorohovoy Street is more worthy of respect than they are. He goes about the whole day long, hoping to get some wretched spare farthing for food, but he is his own master, he does earn his own living. He won't ask for charity; but he works like a machine wound up to give pleasure. "Here," he says, "I do what I can to give pleasure." He's a beggar, he's a beggar, it is true, he's a beggar all the same, but he's an honourable beggar; he is cold and weary, but still he works; though it's in his own way, still he works. And there are many honest men, my darling, who, though they earn very little in proportion to the amount and usefulness of their work, yet they bow down to no one and buy their bread of no one. Here I am just like that hurdy-gurdy man—that is, not at all like him. But in my own sense, in an honourable and aristocratic sense, just as he does, to the best of my abilities, I work as I can. That's enough about me, it's neither here nor there.

I speak of that hurdy-gurdy, my darling, because it has happened that I have felt my poverty twice as much to-day. I stopped to look at the hurdy-gurdy man. I was in such a mood that I stopped to distract my thoughts. I was standing there, and also two cab-drivers, a woman of some sort, and a little girl, such a grubby little thing. The hurdy-gurdy man stopped before the windows of a house. I noticed a little boy about ten years old; he would have been pretty, but he looked so ill, so frail, with hardly anything but his shirt on and almost barefoot, with his mouth open; he was listening to the music—like a child! He watched the German's dolls dancing, while his own hands and feet were numb with cold; he shivered and nibbled the edge of his sleeve. I noticed that he had a bit of paper of some sort in his hands. A gentleman passed and flung the hurdy-gurdy man some small coin, which fell straight into the box in a little garden in which the toy Frenchman was dancing with the ladies. At the clink of the coin the boy started, looked round and evidently thought that I had given the money. He ran up to me, his little hands trembling, his little voice trembling, he held the paper out to me and said, "A letter." I opened the letter; well, it was the usual thing, saying: "Kind gentleman, a mother's dying with three children hungry, so help us now, and as I am dying I will pray for you, my benefactor, in the next world for not forgetting my babes now." Well, what of it?—one could see what it meant, an everyday matter, but what could I give him? Well, I gave him nothing, and how sorry I was! The boy was poor, blue with cold, perhaps hungry, too, and not lying, surely he was not lying, I know that for certain. But what is wrong is that these horrid mothers don't take care of their children and send them out half naked in the cold to beg. Maybe she's a weak-willed, silly woman; and there's no one, maybe, to do anything for her, so she simply sits with her legs tucked under her, maybe she's really ill. Well, anyway, she should apply in the proper quarter. Though, maybe, she's a cheat and sends a hungry, delicate child out on purpose to deceive people, and makes him ill. And what sort of training is it for a poor boy? It simply hardens his heart, he runs about begging, people pass and have no time for him. Their hearts are stony, their words are cruel. "Get away, go along, you are naughty!" that is what he hears from everyone, and the child's heart grows hard, and in vain the poor little frightened boy shivers with cold like a fledgling fallen out of a broken nest. His hands and feet are frozen, he gasps for breath. The next thing he is coughing, before long disease, like an unclean reptile, creeps into his bosom and death is standing over him in some dark corner, no help, no escape, and that's his life! That is what life is like sometimes! Oh, Varinka, it's wretched to hear "for Christ's sake," and to pass by and give nothing, telling him "God will provide." Sometimes "for Christ's sake" is all right (it's not always the same, you know, Varinka), sometimes it's a long, drawling, habitual, practised, regular beggar's whine; it's not so painful to refuse one like that; he's an old hand, a beggar by profession. He's accustomed to it, one thinks; he can cope with it and knows how to cope with it. Sometimes "for Christ's sake" sounds unaccustomed, rude, terrible—as to-day, when I was taking the letter from the boy, a man standing close to the fence, not begging from everyone, said to me: "Give us a halfpenny, sir, for Christ's sake," and in such a harsh, jerky voice that I started with a horrible feeling and did not give him a halfpenny, I hadn't one. Rich people don't like the poor to complain aloud of their harsh lot, they say they disturb them, they are troublesome! Yes, indeed, poverty is always troublesome; maybe their hungry groans hinder the rich from sleeping!

To make a confession, my own, I began to describe all this to you partly to relieve my heart but chiefly to give you an example of the fine style of my composition, for you have no doubt noticed yourself, my dear girl, that of late my style has been forming, but such a depression came over me that I began to pity my feelings to the depth of my soul, and though I know, my dear, that one gets no good by self-pity, yet one must do oneself justice in some way, and often, my own, for no reason whatever, one literally annihilates oneself, makes oneself of no account, and not worth a straw. And perhaps that is why it happens that I am panic-stricken and persecuted like that poor boy who asked me for alms. Now I will tell you, by way of instance and illustration, Varinka; listen: hurrying to the office early in the morning, my own, I sometimes look at the town, how it wakes, gets up, begins smoking, hurrying with life, re-sounding—sometimes you feel so small before such a sight that it is as though someone had given you a flip on your intrusive nose and you creep along your way noiseless as water, and humble as grass, and hold your peace! Now just look into it and see what is going on in those great, black, smutty buildings. Get to the bottom of that and then judge whether one was right to abuse oneself for no reason and to be reduced to undignified mortification. Note, Varinka, that I am speaking figuratively, not in a literal sense. But let us look what is going on in those houses. There, in some smoky corner, in some damp hole, which, through poverty, passes as a lodging, some workman wakes up from his sleep; and all night he has been dreaming of boots, for in-stance, which he had accidentally slit the day before, as though a man ought to dream of such nonsense! But he's an artisan, he's a shoemaker; it's excusable for him to think of nothing but his own subject. His children are crying and his wife is hungry; and it's not only shoemakers who get up in the morning like that, my own—that would not matter, and would not be worth writing about, but this is the point, Varinka: close by in the same house, in a storey higher or lower, a wealthy man in his gilded apartments dreams at night, it may be, of those same boots, that is, boots in a different manner, in a different sense, but still boots, for in the sense I am using the word, Varinka, every-one of us is a bit of a shoemaker, my darling; and that would not matter, only it's a pity there is no one at that wealthy person's side, no man who could whisper in his ear: "Come, give over thinking of such things, thinking of nothing but yourself, living for nothing but yourself; your children are healthy, your wife is not begging for food. Look about you, can't you see some object more noble to worry about than your boots?" That's what I wanted to say to you in a figurative way, Varinka. Perhaps it's too free a thought, my own, but sometimes one has that thought, sometimes it comes to one and one cannot help its bursting out from one's heart in warm language. And so it seems there was no reason to make oneself so cheap, and to be scared by mere noise and uproar. I will conclude by saying, Varinka, that perhaps you think what I am saying is unjust, or that I'm suffering from a fit of the spleen, or that I have copied this out of some book. No, my dear girl, you must dismiss that idea, it is not that; I abominate injustice, I am not suffering from spleen, and I've not copied anything out of a book—so there.

I went home in a melancholy frame of mind; I sat down to the table and heated my teapot to have a glass or two of tea. Suddenly I saw coming towards me Gorshkov, our poor lodger. I had noticed in the morning that he kept hanging about round the other lodgers, and trying to approach me. And I may say, in passing, Varinka, that they live ever so much worse than I do. Yes, indeed, he has a wife and children! So that if I were in his place I don't know what I should do. Well, my Gorshkov comes up to me, bows to me, a running tear as always on his eyelashes, he scrapes with his foot and can't utter a word. I made him sit down on a chair—it was a broken one, it is true, but there was no other. I offered him some tea. He refused from politeness, refused for a long time, but at last he took a glass. He would have drunk it without sugar, began apologising again, when I tried to persuade him that he must have sugar; he argued for a long time, kept refusing, but at last put the very smallest lump of sugar in his glass, and began declaring that his tea was extremely sweet. Oh, to what degradation poverty does reduce people! "Well, my good friend, what is it?" I said. "Well, it is like this, Makar Alexyevitch, my benefactor," he said, "show the mercy of the Lord, come to the help of my unhappy family; my wife and children have nothing to eat; think what it is for me, their father," said he. I tried to speak, but he interrupted me. "I am afraid of everyone here, Makar Alexyevitch—that is, not exactly afraid but as it were ashamed with them; they are all proud and haughty people. I would not have troubled you, my benefactor, I know that you have been in difficulties yourself, I know you can't give me

much, but do lend me a trifle, and I make bold to ask you,"
said he, "because I know your kind heart. I know that
you are in need yourself, that you know what trouble is
now, and so your heart feels compassion." He ended by
saying, "Forgive my boldness and unmannerliness, Makar
Alexyevitch." I answered him that I should be heartily
glad, but that I had nothing, absolutely nothing. "Makar
Alexyevitch, sir," said he, "I am not asking for much,
but you see it is like this—(then he flushed crimson)—
my wife, my children, hungry—if only a ten-kopeck piece."
Well, it sent a twinge to my heart. Why, I thought, they
are worse off than I, even. Twenty kopecks was all I had
left, and I was reckoning on it. I meant to spend it next
day on my most pressing needs.

"No, my dear fellow, I can't, it is like this," I said.

"Makar Alexyevitch, my dear soul, what you like," he
said, "if it is only ten kopecks."

Well, I took my twenty kopecks out of my box, Varinka,
and gave it him; it's a good deed anyway! Ah! poverty! I
had a good talk with him: "Why, how is it, my good
soul," I said, "that you are in such want and yet you rent
a room for five silver roubles?" He explained to me that
he had taken it six months before and paid for it six months
in advance; and since then circumstances had been such
that the poor fellow does not know which way to turn. He
expected his case would be over by this time. It's an unpleasant business. You see, Varinka, he has to answer
for something before the court, he is mixed up in a case
with a merchant who swindled the government over a con-
tract; the cheat was discovered and the merchant was arrested and he's managed to implicate Gorshkov, who had
something to do with it, too. But in reality Gorshkov was
only guilty of negligence, of injudiciousness and unpardonable disregard of the interests of government. The case has
been going on for some years. Gorshkov has had to face
all sorts of difficulties.

"I'm not guilty, not in the least guilty of the dishonesty
attributed to me," said Gorshkov; "I am not guilty of swin-
dling and robbery."

This case has thrown a slur on his character; he has been turned out of the service, and though he has not been found guilty of any legal crime, yet, till he has completely cleared himself he cannot recover from the merchant a considerable sum of money due to him which is now the subject of dispute before the courts. I believe him, but the court won't take his word for it; the case is all in such a coil and a tangle that it would take a hundred years to unravel it. As soon as they untie one knot the merchant brings forward another and then another. I feel the deepest sympathy for Gorshkov, my own, I am very sorry for him. The man's out of work, he won't be taken anywhere without a character; all they had saved has been spent on food, the case is complicated and, meanwhile, they have had to live, and meanwhile, apropos of nothing and most inappropriately, a baby has been born, and that is an expense; his son fell ill—expense; died—expense; his wife is ill; he's afflicted with some disease of long standing—in fact, he has suffered, he has suffered to the utmost; he says, however, that he is expecting a favourable conclusion to his business in a day or two and that there is no doubt of it now. I am sorry for him. I am sorry for him; I am very sorry for him, Varinka. I was kind to him, he's a poor lost, scared creature; he needs a friend so I was kind to him. Well, good-bye, my dear one, Christ be with you, keep well. My darling! when I think of you it's like laying a salve on my sore heart. And though I suffer for you, yet it eases my heart to suffer for you.

Your true friend,
MAKAR DYEVUSHKIN.

September 9.

MY DARLING, VARVARA ALEXYEVNA,

I am writing to you almost beside myself. I have been thoroughly upset by a terrible incident. My head is going round. Ah, my own, what a thing I have to tell you now! This we did not foresee. No, I don't believe that I did not foresee it; I did foresee it all. I had a presentiment of it in my heart. I even dreamed of something of the kind a day or two ago.

This is what happened! I will write to you regardless of style, just as God puts it into my heart. I went to the office to-day. I went in, I sat down, I began writing. And you must know, Varinka, that I was writing yesterday too. Well, this is how it was: Timofey Ivanovitch came up to me and was pleased to explain to me in person, "The document is wanted in a hurry," said he. "Copy it very clearly as quickly as possible and carefully, Makar Alexyevitch," he said; "it goes to be signed to-day." I must observe, my angel, that I was not myself yesterday, I could not bear the sight of anything; such a mood of sadness and depression had come over me! It was cold in my heart and dark in my soul, you were in my mind all the while, my little dearie. But I set to work to copy it; I copied it clearly, legibly, only—I really don't know how to explain it— whether the devil himself muddled me, or whether it was ordained by some secret decree of destiny, or simply it had to be—but I left out a whole line, goodness knows what sense it made, it simply made none at all. They were late with the document yesterday and only took it to his Excellency to be signed to-day. I turned up this morning at the usual hour as though nothing had happened and settled myself beside Emelyan Ivanovitch. I must observe, my own, that of late I have been more abashed and ill at ease than ever. Of late I have given up looking at anyone. If I hear so much as a chair creak I feel more dead than alive. That is just how it was to-day, I sat down like a hedgehog crouched up and shrinking into myself, so that Efim Akimovitch (there never was such a fellow for teasing) said in the hearing of all: "Why are you sitting like a picture of misery, Makar Alexyevitch?" And he made such a grimace that everyone sitting near him and me went off into roars of laughter, and at my expense of course. And they went on and on. I put my hands over my ears, and screwed up my eyes, I sat without stirring. That's what I always do; they leave off the sooner. Suddenly I heard a noise, a fuss and a bustle; I heard—did not my ears deceive me?—

they were mentioning me, asking for me, calling Dyevushkin. My heart began shuddering within me, and I don't know myself why I was so frightened; I only know I was panic-stricken as I had never been before in my life. I sat rooted to my chair—as though there were nothing the matter, as though it were not I. But they began getting nearer and nearer. And at last, close to my ear, they were calling, "Dyevushkin, Dyevushkin! Where is Dyevushkin?" I raised my eyes: Yevstafy Ivanovitch stood before me; he said: "Makar Alexyevitch, make haste to his Excellency! You've made a mistake in that document!" That was all he said, but it was enough; enough had been said, hadn't it, Varinka? Half dead, frozen with terror, not knowing what I was doing, I went—why, I was more dead than alive. I was led through one room, through a second, through a third, to his Excellency's study. I was in his presence! I can give you no exact account of what my thoughts were then. I saw his Excellency standing up, they were all standing round him. I believe I did not bow, I forgot. I was so flustered that my lips were trembling, my legs were trembling. And I had reason to be, my dear girl! To begin with, I was ashamed; I glanced into the looking-glass on the right hand and what I saw there was enough to send one out of one's mind. And in the second place, I had always tried to behave as if there was no such person in the world. So that his Excellency could hardly have been aware of my existence. Perhaps he may have heard casually that there was a clerk called Dyevushkin in the office, but he had never gone into the matter more closely.

He began, angrily: "What were you about, sir? Where were your eyes? The copy was wanted; it was wanted in a hurry, and you spoil it."

At this point, his Excellency turned to Yevstafy Ivanovitch. I could only catch a word here and there: "Negligence! Carelessness! You will get us into difficulties!" I would have opened my mouth to say something. I wanted to beg for forgiveness, but I could not; I wanted to run away, but dared not attempt it, and then . . . then, Varinka, something happened so awful that I can hardly hold my pen, for shame, even now. A button—the devil take the button—which was hanging by a thread on my uniform—suddenly flew off, bounced on the floor (I must have caught hold of it accidentally) with a jingle, the damned thing, and rolled straight to his Excellency's feet, and that in the midst of a profound silence! And that was my only justification, my sole apology, my only answer, all that I had to say to his Excellency! What followed was awful. His Excellency's attention was at once turned to my appearance and my attire. I remembered what I had seen in the looking-glass; I flew to catch the button! Some idiocy possessed me! I bent down, I tried to pick up the button—it twirled and rolled, I couldn't pick it up—in fact, I distinguished myself by my agility. Then I felt that my last faculties were deserting me, that everything, everything was lost, my whole reputation was lost, my dignity as a man was lost, and then, apropos of nothing, I had the voices of Teresa and Faldoni ringing in my ears. At last I picked up the button, stood up and drew myself erect, and if I were a fool I might at least have stood quietly with my hands at my sides! But not a bit of it. I began fitting the button to the torn threads as though it might hang on, and I actually smiled, actually smiled. His Excellency turned away at first, then he glanced at me again—I heard him say to Yevstafy Ivanovitch: "How is this? . . . Look at him! . . . What is he? . . . What sort of man? . . ." Ah, my own, think of that! "What is he?" and, "what sort of man?" I had distinguished myself! I heard Yevstafy Ivanovitch say: "No note against him, no note against him for anything, behaviour excellent, salary in accordance with his grade . . ." "Well, assist him in some way, let him have something in advance," says his Excellency. . . . "But he has had an advance," he said; "he has had his salary in advance for such and such a time. He is apparently in difficulties, but his conduct is good, and there is no note, there never has been a note against him."

My angel, I was burning, burning in the fires of hell! I was dying. . . .

"Well," said his Excellency, "make haste and copy it

again; Dyevushkin, come here, copy it over again without a mistake; and listen . . ." Here his Excellency turned to the others, gave them various instructions and they all went away. As soon as they had gone, his Excellency hurriedly took out his notebook and from it took a hundred-rouble note. "Here," said he, "take it as you like, so far as I can help you, take it . . ." and he thrust it into my hand. I trembled, my angel, my whole soul was quivering; I don't know what happened to me, I tried to seize his hand to kiss it, but he flushed crimson, my darling, and—here I am not departing one hair's breadth from the truth, my own—he took my unworthy hand and shook it, just took it and shook it, as though I had been his equal, as though I had been just such a General as himself. "You can go," he said; "whatever I can do for you . . . don't make mistakes, but there, no great harm done this time."

Now, Varinka, this is what I have decided. I beg you and Fedora, and if I had any children I should bid them, to pray every day and all our lives for his Excellency as they would not pray for their own father! I will say more, my dear, and I say it solemnly—pay attention, Varinka—I swear that however cast down I was and afflicted in the bitterest days of our misfortunes, looking at you, at your poverty, and at myself, my degradation and my uselessness, in spite of all that, I swear that the hundred roubles is not as much to me as that his Excellency deigned to shake hands with me, a straw, a worthless drunkard! By that he has restored me to myself, by that action he has lifted up my spirit, has made my life sweeter for ever, and I am firmly persuaded that, however sinful I may be before the Almighty, yet my prayers for the happiness and prosperity of his Excellency will reach His Throne! . . .

My darling! I am dreadfully upset, dreadfully excited now, my heart is beating as though it would burst out of my breast, and I feel, as it were, weak all over.

I am sending you forty-five roubles; I am giving the landlady twenty and leaving thirty-five for myself. For twenty I can put my wardrobe in order, and I shall have fifteen left to go on with. But just now all the impressions of the morning have shaken my whole being, I am going to lie down. I am at peace, quite at peace, though; only there is an ache in my heart and deep down within me I feel my soul quivering, trembling, stirring.

I am coming to see you: but now I am simply drunk with all these sensations. . . . God sees all, my Varinka, my priceless darling!

Your worthy friend,
MAKAR DYEVUSHKIN.

September 10.

MY DEAR MAKAR ALEXYEVITCH,

I am unutterably delighted at your happiness and fully appreciate the goodness of your chief, my friend. So now you will have a little respite from trouble! But, for God's sake, don't waste your money again. Live quietly and as frugally as possible, and from to-day begin to put by a little that misfortune may not find you unprepared again. For goodness' sake don't worry about us. Fedora and I will get along somehow. Why have you sent us so much money, Makar Alexyevitch? We don't need it at all. We are satisfied with what we have. It is true we shall soon want money for moving from this lodging, but Fedora is hoping to be repaid an old debt that has been owing for years. I will keep twenty roubles, however, in case of extreme necessity. The rest I send you back. Please take care of your money, Makar Alexyevitch. Good-bye. Be at peace now, keep well and happy. I would write more to you, but I feel dreadfully tired; yesterday I did not get up all day. You do well to promise to come. Do come and see me, please, Makar Alexyevitch.

V. D.

September 11.

MY DEAR VARVARA ALEXYEVNA,

I beseech you, my own, not to part from me now, now when I am quite happy and contented with everything. My darling! Don't listen to Fedora and I will do anything you like; I shall behave well if only from respect to his Excellency. I will behave well and carefully; we will write to

each other happy letters again, we will confide in each
other our thoughts, our joys, our cares, if we have any
cares; we will live together in happiness and concord. We'll
study literature . . . My angel! My whole fate has changed
and everything has changed for the better. The landlady
has become more amenable. Teresa is more sensible, even
Faldoni has become prompter. I have made it up with Ratazyaev. In my joy I went to him of myself. He's really a
good fellow, Varinka, and all the harm that was said of him
was nonsense. I have discovered that it was all an abominable slander. He had no idea whatever of describing us. He
read me a new work of his. And as for his calling me a
Lovelace, that was not an insulting or abusive name; he
explained it to me. The word is taken straight from a foreign source and means *a clever fellow*, and to express it
more elegantly, in a literary fashion, it means a young man
you must be on the lookout with, you see, and nothing of
that sort. It was an innocent jest, my angel! I'm an ignoramus and in my foolishness I was offended. In fact, it is I
who apologised to him now. . . . And the weather is so
wonderful to-day, Varinka, so fine. It is true there was a
slight frost this morning, as though it had been sifted
through a sieve. It was nothing. It only made the air a little
fresher. I went to buy some boots, and I bought some wonderful boots. I walked along the Nevsky. I read the *Bee*.
Why! I am forgetting to tell you the principal thing.

It was this, do you see.

This morning I talked to Emelyan Ivanovitch and to
Axentey Mihalovitch about his Excellency. Yes, Varinka,
I'm not the only one he has treated so graciously. I am not
the only one he has befriended, and he is known to all
the world for the goodness of his heart. His praises are
sung in very many quarters, and tears of gratitude are shed.
An orphan girl was brought up in his house. He gave her
a dowry and married her to a man in a good position, to
a clerk on special commissions, who was in attendance on
his Excellency. He installed a son of a widow in some office, and has done a great many other acts of kindness. I
thought it my duty at that point to add my mite and de-

scribed his Excellency's action in the hearing of all; I told
them all and concealed nothing. I put my pride in my
pocket, as though pride or dignity mattered in a case like
that. So I told it aloud—to do glory to the good deeds of
his Excellency! I spoke enthusiastically, I spoke with
warmth, I did not blush, on the contrary, I was proud that
I had such a story to tell. I told them about everything
(only I was judiciously silent about you, Varinka), about
my landlady, about Faldoni, about Ratazyaev, about my
boots and about Markov—I told them everything. Some
of them laughed a little, in fact, they all laughed a little.
Probably they found something funny in my appearance,
or it may have been about my boots—yes, it must have
been about my boots. They could not have done it with any
bad intention. It was nothing, just youthfulness, or perhaps because they are well-to-do people, but they could
not jeer at what I said with any bad, evil intention. That is,
what I said about his Excellency—that they could not do.
Could they, Varinka?

I still can't get over it, my darling. The whole incident
has so overwhelmed me! Have you got any firewood? Don't
catch cold, Varinka; you can so easily catch cold. Ah, my
own precious, you crush me with your sad thoughts. I
pray to God, how I pray to Him for you, my dearie! For
instance, have you got woollen stockings, and other warm
underclothing? Mind, my darling, if you need anything, for
God's sake don't wound your old friend, come straight to
me. Now our bad times are over. Don't be anxious about
me. Everything is so bright, so happy in the future!

It was a sad time, Varinka! But there, no matter, it's
past! Years will pass and we shall sigh for that time. I remember my young days. Why, I often hadn't a farthing! I
was cold and hungry, but light-hearted, that was all. In the
morning I would walk along the Nevsky, see a pretty little
face and be happy all day. It was a splendid, splendid time,
my darling! It is nice to be alive, Varinka! Especially in
Petersburg. I repented with tears in my eyes yesterday, and
prayed to the Lord God to forgive me all my sins in that
sad time: my repining, my liberal ideas, my drinking and

despair. I remembered you with emotion in my prayers. You were my only support, Varinka, you were my only comfort, you cheered me on my way with counsel and good advice. I can never forget that, dear one. I have kissed all your letters to-day, my darling! Well, good-bye, my precious. They say that somewhere near here there is a sale of clothing. So I will make inquiries a little. Good-bye, my angel. Good-bye!

Your deeply devoted,
MAKAR DYEVUSHKIN.

September 15.

DEAR MAKAR ALEXYEVITCH,

I feel dreadfully upset. Listen what has happened here. I foresee something momentous. Judge yourself, my precious friend; Mr. Bykov is in Petersburg, Fedora met him. He was driving, he ordered the cab to stop, went up to Fedora himself and began asking where she was living. At first she would not tell him. Then he said, laughing, that he knew who was living with her. (Evidently Anna Fyodorovna had told him all about it.) Then Fedora could not contain herself and began upbraiding him on the spot, in the street, reproaching him, telling him he was an immoral man and the cause of all my troubles. He answered, that one who has not a halfpenny is bound to have misfortunes. Fedora answered that I might have been able to earn my own living, that I might have been married or else have had some situation, but that now my happiness was wrecked for ever and that I was ill besides, and would not live long. To this he answered that I was still young, that I had still a lot of nonsense in my head and that my virtues were getting a little tarnished (his words). Fedora and I thought he did not know our lodging when suddenly, yesterday, just after I had gone out to buy some things in the Gostiny Dvor he walked into our room. I believe he did not want to find me at home. He questioned Fedora at length concerning our manner of life, examined everything we had; he looked at my work; at last asked, "Who is this clerk you have made friends with?" At that moment you walked across the yard; Fedora pointed to you; he glanced and laughed; Fedora begged him to go away, told him that I was unwell, as it was, from grieving, and that to see him in our room would be very distasteful to me. He was silent for a while; said that he had just looked in with no object and tried to give Fedora twenty-five roubles; she, of course, did not take it.

What can it mean? What has he come to see us for? I cannot understand where he has found out all about us! I am lost in conjecture. Fedora says that Axinya, her sister-in-law, who comes to see us, is friendly with Nastasya the laundress, and Nastasya's cousin is a porter in the office in which a friend of Anna Fyodorovna's nephew is serving. So has not, perhaps, some ill-natured gossip crept round? But it is very possible that Fedora is mistaken; we don't know what to think. Is it possible he will come to us again! The mere thought of it terrifies me! When Fedora told me all about it yesterday, I was so frightened that I almost fainted with terror! What more does he want? I don't want to know him now! What does he want with me, poor me? Oh! I am in such terror now, I keep expecting Bykov to walk in every minute. What will happen to me, what more has fate in store for me? For Christ's sake, come and see me now, Makar Alexyevitch. Do come, for God's sake, come.

September 18.

MY DARLING VARVARA ALEXYEVNA!

To-day an unutterably sad, quite unaccountable and unexpected event has occurred here. Our poor Gorshkov (I must tell you, Varinka) has had his character completely cleared. The case was concluded some time ago and to-day he went to hear the final judgment. The case ended very happily for him. He was fully exonerated of any blame for negligence and carelessness. The merchant was condemned to pay him a considerable sum of money, so that his financial position was vastly improved and no stain left on his honour and things were better all round—in fact, he won everything he could have desired.

He came home at three o'clock this afternoon. He did not look like himself, his face was white as a sheet, his lips quivered and he kept smiling—he embraced his wife and children. We all flocked to congratulate him. He was greatly touched by our action, he bowed in all directions, shook hands with all of us several times. It even seemed to me as though he were taller and more erect, and no longer had that running tear in his eye. He was in such excitement, poor fellow. He could not stand still for two minutes: he picked up anything he came across, then dropped it again; and kept continually smiling and bowing, sitting down, getting up and sitting down again. Goodness knows what he said: "My honour, my honour, my good name, my children," and that was how he kept talking! He even shed tears. Most of us were moved to tears, too; Ratazyaev clearly wanted to cheer him up, and said, "What is honour, old man, when one has nothing to eat? The money, the money's the thing, old man, thank God for that!" and thereupon he slapped him on the shoulder. It seemed to me that Gorshkov was offended—not that he openly showed dissatisfaction, but he looked rather strangely at Ratazyaev and took his hand off his shoulder. And that had never happened before, Varinka! But characters differ. Now I, for instance, should not have stood on my dignity, at a time of such joy; why, my own, sometimes one is too liberal with one's bows and almost cringing from nothing but excess of good-nature and soft-heartedness. . . . However, no matter about me!

"Yes," he said, "the money is a good thing too, thank God, thank God!" And then all the time we were with him he kept repeating, "Thank God, thank God."

His wife ordered a rather nicer and more ample dinner. Our landlady cooked for them herself. Our landlady is a good-natured woman in a way. And until dinner-time Gorshkov could not sit still in his seat. He went into the lodgers' rooms, without waiting to be invited. He just went in, smiled, sat down on the edge of a chair, said a word or two, or even said nothing, and went away again. At the naval man's he even took a hand at cards; they made up a game with him as fourth. He played a little, made a muddle of it, played three or four rounds and threw down the cards. "No," he said, "you see, I just looked in, I just looked in," and he went away from them. He met me in the passage, took both my hands, looked me straight in the face, but so strangely; then shook hands with me and walked away, and kept smiling, but with a strange, painful smile like a dead man. His wife was crying with joy; everything was cheerful as though it were a holiday. They soon had dinner. After dinner he said to his wife: "I tell you what, my love, I'll lie down a little," and he went to his bed. He called his little girl, put his hand on her head, and for a long time he was stroking the child's head. Then he turned to his wife again, "And what of Petinka? our Petya!" he said. "Petinka?" . . . His wife crossed herself and answered that he was dead. "Yes, yes, I know all about it. Petinka is now in the Kingdom of Heaven." His wife saw that he was not himself, that what had happened had completely upset him, and she said to him, "You ought to have a nap, my love." "Yes, very well, I will directly . . . just a little," then he turned away, lay still for a bit, then turned round, tried to say something. His wife could not make out what he said, and asked him, "What is it, my dear?" and he did not answer. She waited a little, "Well, he's asleep," she thought, and went into the landlady's for an hour. An hour later she came back, she saw her husband had not woken up and was not stirring. She thought he was asleep, and she sat down and began working at something. She said that for half an hour she was so lost in musing that she did not know what she was thinking about, all she can say is that she did not think of her husband. But suddenly she was roused by the feeling of uneasiness, and what struck her first of all was the death-like silence in the room. . . . She looked at the bed and saw that her husband was lying in the same position. She went up to him, pulled down the quilt and looked at him—and he was already cold —he was dead, my darling. Gorshkov was dead, he had died suddenly, as though he had been killed by a thunderbolt. And why he died, God only knows. It was such a shock to me, Varinka, that I can't get over it now. One can't believe that a man could die so easily. He was such a poor, unlucky fellow, that Gorshkov! And what a fate, what a fate! His wife was in tears and panic-stricken. The little girl crept away into a corner. There is such a hubbub going on, they will hold a post-mortem and inquest . . . I can't tell you just what. But the pity of it, oh, the pity of it! It's sad to think that in reality one does not know the day or the hour . . . One dies so easily for no reason. . . .

Your
MAKAR DYEVUSHKIN.

September 19.

DEAR VARVARA ALEXYEVNA,

I hasten to inform you, my dear, that Ratazyaev has found me work with a writer. Someone came to him, and brought him such a fat manuscript—thank God, a lot of work. But it's so illegibly written that I don't know how to set to work on it: they want it in a hurry. It's all written in such a way that one does not understand it. . . . They have agreed to pay forty kopecks the sixteen pages. I write you all this, my own, because now I shall have extra money. And now, good-bye, my darling, I have come straight from work.

Your faithful friend,
MAKAR DYEVUSHKIN.

September 23.

MY DEAR FRIEND, MAKAR ALEXYEVITCH,

For three days I have not written you a word, and I have had a great many anxieties and worries.

The day before yesterday Bykov was here. I was alone, Fedora had gone off somewhere. I opened the door to him, and was so frightened when I saw him that I could not move. I felt that I turned pale. He walked in as he always does, with a loud laugh, took a chair and sat down. For a long while I could not recover myself. At last I sat down in the corner to my work. He even left off laughing. I believe my appearance impressed him. I have grown so thin of late, my eyes and my cheeks are hollow, I was as white as a sheet . . . it would really be hard for anyone to recognise me who had known me a year ago. He looked long and intently at me; then at last he began to be lively again, said something or other; I don't know what I answered, and he laughed again. He stayed a whole hour with me; talked to me a long time; asked me some questions. At last just before leaving, he took me by the hand and said (I write you it word for word): "Varvara Alexyevitch, between ourselves, be it said, your relation and my intimate friend, Anna Fyodorovna, is a very nasty woman" (then he used an unseemly word about her). "She led your cousin astray, and ruined you. I behaved like a rascal in that case, too; but after all, it's a thing that happens every day." Then he laughed heartily. Then he observed that he was not great at fine speeches, and that most of what he had to explain, about which the obligations of gentlemanly feeling forebade him to be silent, he had told me already, and that in brief words he would come to the rest. Then he told me he was asking my hand in marriage, that he thought it his duty to restore my good name, that he was rich, that after the wedding he would take me away to his estates in the steppes, that he wanted to go coursing hares there; that he would never come back to Petersburg again, because it was horrid in Petersburg; that he had here in Petersburg—as he expressed it—a good-for-nothing nephew whom he had sworn to deprive of the estate, and it was just for that reason in the hope of having legitimate heirs that he sought my hand, that it was the chief cause of his courtship. Then he observed that I was living in a very poor way: and it was no wonder I was ill living in such a slum; predicted that I should certainly die if I stayed there another month; said that lodgings in Petersburg were horrid, and finally asked me if I wanted anything.

I was so overcome at his offer that, I don't know why, I began crying. He took my tears for gratitude and told me he had always been sure I was a good, feeling, and educated girl, but that he had not been able to make up his mind to take this step till he had found out about my present behaviour in full detail. Then he asked me about you, said that he had heard all about it, that you were a man of good principles, that he did not want to be indebted to you and asked whether five hundred roubles would be enough for all that you had done for me. When I explained to him that what you had done for me no money could repay, he said that it was all nonsense, that that was all romantic stuff out of novels, that I was young and read poetry, that novels were the ruin of young girls, that books were destructive of morality and that he could not bear books of any sort, he advised me to wait till I was his age and then talk about people. "Then," he added, "you will know what men are like." Then he said I was to think over his offer thoroughly, that he would very much dislike it if I were to take such an important step thoughtlessly; he added that thoughtlessness and impulsiveness were the ruin of inexperienced youth, but that he quite hoped for a favourable answer from me, but that in the opposite event, he should be forced to marry some Moscow shopkeeper's daughter, "because," he said, "I have sworn that good-for-nothing nephew shall not have the estate."

He forced five hundred roubles into my hands, as he said, "to buy sweetmeats." He said that in the country I should grow as round as a bun, that with him I should be living on the fat of the land, that he had a terrible number of things to see to now, that he was dragging about all day on business, and that he had just slipped in to see me between his engagements. Then he went away.

I thought for a long time, I pondered many things, I wore myself out thinking, my friend; at last I made up my mind. My friend, I shall marry him. I ought to accept his offer. If anyone can rescue me from my shame, restore my good name, and ward off poverty, privation and misfortune from me in the future, it is he and no one else. What more can one expect from the future, what more can one expect from fate? Fedora says I must not throw away my good fortune; she says, if this isn't good fortune, what is? Anyway, I can find no other course for me, my precious friend. What am I to do? I have ruined my health with work as it is; I can't go on working continually. Go into a family? I should pine away with depression, besides I should be of no use to anyone. I am of a sickly constitution, and so I shall always be a burden on other people. Of course I am not going into a paradise, but what am I to do, my friend, what am I to do? What choice have I?

I have not asked your advice. I wanted to think it over alone. The decision you have just read is unalterable, and I shall immediately inform Bykov of it, he is pressing me to answer quickly. He said that his business would not wait, that he must be off, and that he couldn't put it off for nonsense. God knows whether I shall be happy, my fate is in His holy, inscrutable power, but I have made up my mind. They say Bykov is a kind-hearted man: he will respect me; perhaps I, too, shall respect him. What more can one expect from such a marriage?

I will let you know about everything, Makar Alexyevitch. I am sure you will understand all my wretchedness. Do not try to dissuade me from my intention. Your efforts will be in vain. Weigh in your own mind all that has forced me to this step. I was very much distressed at first, but now I am calmer. What is before me, I don't know. What will be, will be; as God wills! . . .

Bykov has come, I leave this letter unfinished. I wanted to tell you a great deal more. Bykov is here already!

September 23.

My darling Varvara Alexyevna,

I hasten to answer you, my dear; I hasten to tell you, my precious, that I am dumbfounded. It all seems so . . . Yesterday we buried Gorshkov. Yes, that is so, Varinka, that is so; Bykov has behaved honourably; only, you see, my own . . . so you have consented. Of course, everything is according to God's will; that is so, that certainly must be so—that is, it certainly must be God's will in this; and the providence of the Heavenly Creator is blessed, of course, and inscrutable, and it is fate too, and they are the same. Fedora sympathises with you too. Of course you will be happy now, my precious, you will live in comfort, my darling, my little dearie, little angel and light of my eyes—

only Varinka, how can it be so soon? . . . Yes, business.
. . . Mr. Bykov has business—of course, everyone has
business, and he may have it too. . . . I saw him as he
came out from you. He's a good-looking man, good-looking; a very good-looking man, in fact. Only there is something queer about it, the point is not whether he is a good-
looking man. Indeed, I am not myself at all. Why, how are
we to go on writing to one another? I . . . I shall be left
alone. I am weighing everything, my angel, I am weighing
everything as you write to me, I am weighing it all in my
heart, the reasons. I had just finished copying the twentieth
quire, and meanwhile these events have come upon us!
Here you are going a journey, my darling, you will have
to buy all sorts of things, shoes of all kinds, a dress, and
I know just the shop in Gorohovoy Street; do you remember how I described it to you, Varinka? what are you about?
Varinka? what are you about? You can't go away now, it's
quite impossible, utterly impossible. Why, you will have
to buy a great many things and get a carriage. Besides,
the weather is so awful now; look, the rain is coming down
in bucketfuls, and such soaking rain, too, and what's more
. . . what's more, you will be cold, my angel; your little
heart will be cold! Why, you are afraid of anyone strange,
and yet you go. And to whom am I left, all alone here?
Yes! Here, Fedora says that there is great happiness in
store for you . . . but you know she's a headstrong woman,
she wants to be the death of me. Are you going to the
evening service to-night, Varinka? I would go to have a
look at you. It's true, perfectly true, my darling, that you
are a well-educated, virtuous and feeling girl, only he had
much better marry the shopkeeper's daughter! Don't you
think so, my precious? He had better marry the shopkeeper's daughter! I will come to see you, Varinka, as soon as
it gets dark, I shall just run in for an hour. It will get dark
early to-day, then I shall run in. I shall certainly come to
you for an hour this evening, my darling. Now you are
expecting Bykov, but when he goes, then . . . Wait a bit,
Varinka, I shall run across . . .

MAKAR DYEVUSHKIN.

September 27.

MY DEAR FRIEND, MAKAR ALEXYEVITCH,

Mr. Bykov says I must have three dozen linen chemises. So I must make haste and find seamstresses to make two dozen, and we have very little time. Mr. Bykov is angry and says there is a great deal of bother over these rags. Our wedding is to be in five days, and we are to set off the day after the wedding. Mr. Bykov is in a hurry, he says we must not waste much time over nonsense. I am worn out with all this fuss and can hardly stand on my feet. There is a terrible lot to do, and perhaps it would have been better if all this had not happened. Another thing: we have not enough net or lace, so we ought to buy some more, for Mr. Bykov says he does not want his wife to go about like a cook, and that I simply must "wipe all the country ladies' noses for them". That was his own expression. So, Makar Alexyevitch, please apply to Madame Chiffon in Gorohovoy Street, and ask her first to send us some seamstresses, and secondly, to be so good as to come herself. I am ill to-day. It's so cold in our new lodging and the disorder is terrible. Mr. Bykov's aunt can scarcely breathe, she is so old. I am afraid she may die before we set off, but Mr. Bykov says that it is nothing, she'll wake up. Everything in the house is in the most awful confusion. Mr. Bykov is not living with us, so the servants are racing about in all directions, goodness knows where. Sometimes Fedora is the only one to wait on us, and Mr. Bykov's valet, who looks after everything, has disappeared no one knows where for the last three days. Mr. Bykov comes to see us every morning, and yesterday he beat the superintendent of the house, for which he got into trouble with the police. I have not even had anyone to take my letters to you. I am writing by post. Yes! I had almost forgotten the most important point. Tell Madame Chiffon to be sure and change the net, matching it with the pattern she had yesterday, and to come to me herself to show the new, and tell her, too, that I have changed my mind about the embroidery, that it must be done in crochet; and another thing, that the letters for the monogram on the handkerchiefs must be done in tambour stitch, do you hear? Tambour stitch and not satin stitch. Mind you don't forget that it is to be tambour stitch! Something else I had almost forgotten! For God's sake tell her also that the leaves on the pelerine are to be raised and that the tendrils and thorns are to be in appliqué; and, then, the collar is to be edged with lace, or a deep frill. Please tell her, Makar Alexyevitch.

Your

V. D.

P.S.—I am so ashamed of worrying you with all my errands. The day before yesterday you were running about all the morning. But what can I do! There's no sort of order in the house here, and I am not well. So don't be vexed with me, Makar Alexyevitch. I'm so miserable. Oh, how will it end, my friend, my dear, my kind Makar Alexyevitch? I'm afraid to look into my future. I have a presentiment of something and am living in a sort of delirium.

P.P.S.—For God's sake, my friend, don't forget anything of what I have told you. I am so afraid you will make a mistake. Remember tambour, not satin stitch.

V. D.

September 27.

DEAR VARVARA ALEXYEVNA,

I have carried out all your commissions carefully. Madame Chiffon says that she had thought herself of doing them in tambour stitch; that it is more correct, or something, I don't know, I didn't take it in properly. And you wrote about a frill, too, and she talked about the frill. Only I have forgotten, my darling, what she told me about the frill. All I remember is, that she said a great deal; such a horrid woman! What on earth was it? But she will tell you about it herself. I have become quite dissipated, Varinka, I have not even been to the office to-day. But there's no need for you to be in despair about that, my own. I am ready to go the round of all the shops for your peace of mind. You say you are afraid to look into the future. But at seven o'clock this evening you will know all about it.

Madame Chiffon is coming to see you herself. So don't be in despair; you must hope for the best, everything will turn out for the best—so there. Well, now, I keep thinking about that cursed frill—ugh! bother that frill! I should have run round to you, my angel, I should have looked in, I should certainly have looked in; I have been to the gates of your house, once or twice. But Bykov—that is, I mean, Mr. Bykov—is always so cross, you see it doesn't . . . Well, what of it!

MAKAR DYEVUSHKIN.

September 28.

MY DEAR MAKAR ALEXYEVITCH,

For God's sake, run at once to the jeweller's: tell him that he must not make the pearl and emerald ear-rings. Mr. Bykov says that it is too gorgeous, that it's too expensive. He is angry; he says, that as it is, it is costing him a pretty penny, and we are robbing him, and yesterday he said that if he had known beforehand and had any notion of the expense he would not have bound himself. He says that as soon as we are married we will set off at once, that we shall have no visitors and that I needn't hope for dancing and flirtation, and that the holidays are a long way off. That's how he talks. And, God knows, I don't want anything of that sort! Mr. Bykov ordered everything himself. I don't dare to answer him: he is so hasty. What will become of me?

V. D.

September 28.

MY DARLING VARVARA ALEXYEVNA,

I—that is, the jeweller said—very good; and I meant to say at first that I have been taken ill and cannot get up. Here now, at such an urgent, busy time I have caught a cold, the devil take it! I must tell you, to complete my misfortunes, his Excellency was pleased to be stern and was very angry with Emelyan Ivanovitch and scolded him, and he was quite worn out at last, poor man. You see, I tell you about everything. I wanted to write to you about something else, but I am afraid to trouble you. You see, I am a foolish, simple man, Varinka, I just write what comes, so that, maybe, you may—— But there, never mind!

Your

MAKAR DYEVUSHKIN.

September 29.

VARVARA ALEXYEVITCH, MY OWN,

I saw Fedora to-day, my darling, she says that you are to be married to-morrow, and that the day after you are setting off, and that Mr. Bykov is engaging horses already. I have told you about his Excellency already, my darling. Another thing—I have checked the bills from the shop in Gorohovoy; it is all correct, only the things are very dear. But why is Mr. Bykov angry with you? Well, may you be happy, Varinka! I am glad, yes, I shall be glad if you are happy. I should come to the church, my dear, but I've got lumbago. So I keep on about our letters; who will carry them for us, my precious? Yes! You have been a good friend to Fedora, my own! You have done a good deed, my dear, you have done quite right. It's a good deed! And God will bless you for every good deed. Good deeds never go unrewarded, and virtue will sooner or later be rewarded by the eternal justice of God. Varinka! I wanted to write to you a great deal; I could go on writing and writing every minute, every hour! I have one of your books still, *Byelkin's Stories*. I tell you what, Varinka, don't take it away, make me a present of it, my darling. It is not so much that I want to read it. But you know yourself, my darling, winter is coming on: the evenings will be long; it will be sad, and then I could read. I shall move from my lodgings, Varinka, into your old room and lodge with Fedora. I would not part from that honest woman for anything now; besides, she is such a hard-working woman. I looked at your empty room carefully yesterday. Your embroidery frame has remained untouched, just as it was with embroidery on it. I examined your needlework; there were all sorts of little scraps left there, you had begun winding thread on one of my letters. On the little table I found a piece of paper with the words "Dear Makar Alexyevitch, I hasten—" and that was all. Someone must have interrupted you at the most interesting place. In the corner behind the screen stands your little bed. . . . Oh, my darling! ! ! Well, good-bye, good-bye, send me some answer to this letter quickly.

MAKAR DYEVUSHKIN.

September 30.

MY PRECIOUS FRIEND, MAKAR ALEXYEVITCH,

Everything is over! My lot is cast; I don't know what it will be, but I am resigned to God's will. To-morrow we set off. I say good-bye to you for the last time, my precious one, my friend, my benefactor, my own! Don't grieve for me, live happily, think of me, and may God's blessing descend on us! I shall often remember you in my thoughts, in my prayers. So this time is over! I bring to my new life little consolation from the memories of the past; the more precious will be my memory of you, the more precious will your memory be to my heart. You are my one friend; you are the only one there who loved me. You know I have seen it all, I know how you love me! You were happy in a smile from me and a few words from my pen. Now you will have to get used to being without me. How will you do, left alone here? To whom am I leaving you my kind, precious, only friend! I leave you the book, the embroidery frame, the unfinished letter; when you look at those first words, you must read in your thoughts all that you would like to hear or read from me, all that I should have written to you; and what I could not write now! Think of your poor Varinka who loves you so truly. All your letters are at Fedora's in the top drawer of a chest. You write that you are ill and Mr. Bykov will not let me go out anywhere to-day. I will write to you, my friend, I promise; but, God alone knows what may happen. And so we are saying good-bye now for ever, my friend, my darling, my own, for ever. . . . Oh, if only I could embrace you now! Good-bye, my dear; good-bye, good-bye. Live happily, keep well.

My prayers will be always for you. Oh! how sad I am, how weighed down in my heart. Mr. Bykov is calling me.

Your ever loving

V.

P.S.—My soul is so full, so full of tears now . . . tears are choking me, rending my heart. Good-bye. Oh, God, how sad I am!

Remember me, remember your poor Varinka.

VARINKA, MY DARLING, MY PRECIOUS,

You are being carried off, you are going. They had better have torn the heart out of my breast than take you from me! How could you do it? Here you are weeping and going away! Here I have just had a letter from you, all smudged with tears. So you don't want to go; so you are being taken away by force; so you are sorry for me; so you love me! And with whom will you be now? Your little heart will be sad, sick and cold out there. It will be sapped by misery, torn by grief. You will die out there, they will put you in the damp earth; there will be no one to weep for you there! Mr. Bykov will be always coursing hares. Oh, my darling, my darling! What have you brought yourself to? How could you make up your mind to such a step? What have you done, what have you done, what have you done to yourself? They'll drive you to your grave out there; they will be the death of you, my angel. You know you are as weak as a little feather, my own! And where was I, old fool, where were my eyes! I saw the child did not know what she was doing, the child was simply in a fever! I ought simply—— But no, fool, fool, I thought nothing and saw nothing, as though that were the right thing, as though it had nothing to do with me; and went running after frills and flounces too. . . . No, Varinka, I shall get up; tomorrow, maybe, I shall be better and then I shall get up! . . . I'll throw myself under the wheels, my precious, I won't let you go away! Oh, no, how can it be? By what right is all this done? I will go with you; I will run after your carriage if you won't take me, and will run my hardest as long as there is a breath left in my body. And do you know what it is like where you are going, my darling? Maybe you don't know—if so, ask me! There it is, the steppe, my own, the steppe, the bare steppe; why, it is as bare as my hand; there, there are hard-hearted peasant women and uneducated drunken peasants. There the leaves are falling off the trees now, there it is cold and rainy—and you are going there! Well, Mr. Bykov has something to do there: he will be with his hares; but what about you? Do you want to be a grand country lady, Varinka? But, my little cherub! you should just look at yourself. Do you look like a grand country lady? . . . Why, how can such a thing be, Varinka? To whom am I going to write letters, my darling? Yes! You must take that into consideration, my darling—you must ask yourself, to whom is he going to write letters? Whom am I to call my darling; whom am I to call by that loving name, where am I to find you afterwards, my angel? I shall die, Varinka, I shall certainly die; my heart will never survive such a calamity! I loved you like God's sunshine, I loved you like my own daughter, I loved everything in you, my darling, my own! And I lived only for you! I worked and copied papers, and walked and went about and put my thought down on paper, in friendly letters, all because you, my precious, were living here opposite, close by; perhaps you did not know it, but that was how it was. Yes, listen, Varinka; you only think, my sweet darling, how is it possible that you should go away from us? You can't go away, my own, it is impossible; it's simply utterly impossible! Why, it's raining, you are delicate, you will catch cold. Your carriage will be wet through; it will certainly get wet through. It won't get beyond the city gates before it will break down; it will break down on purpose. They make these carriages in Petersburg so badly; I know all those carriage makers; they are only fit to turn out a little model, a plaything, not anything solid. I'll take my oath they won't build it solid. I'll throw myself on my knees before Mr. Bykov: I will explain to him, I will explain everything, and you, my precious, explain to him, make him see reason! Tell him that you will stay and that you cannot go away!

. . . Ah, why didn't he marry a shopkeeper's daughter in Moscow? He might just as well have married her! The shopkeeper's daughter would have suited him much better, she would have suited him much better. I know why! And I should have kept you here. What is he to you, my darling, what is Bykov? How has he suddenly become so dear to you? Perhaps it's because he is always buying you frills and flounces. But what are frills and flounces? What good are frills and flounces? Why, it is nonsense, Varinka! Here it is a question of a man's life: and you know a frill's a rag; it's a rag, Varinka, a frill is; why, I shall buy you frills myself, that's all the reward I get; I shall buy them for you, my darling, I know a shop, that's all the reward you let me hope for, my cherub, Varinka. Oh Lord! Lord! So, you are really going to the steppes with Mr. Bykov, going away never to return! Ah, my darling! . . . No, you must write to me again, you must write another letter about everything, and when you go away you must write to me from there, or else, my heavenly angel, this will be the last letter and you know that this cannot be, this cannot be the last letter! Why, how can it be, so suddenly, actually the last? Oh no, I shall write and you will write. . . . Besides, I am acquiring a literary style. . . . Oh, my own, what does style matter, now? I don't know, now, what I am writing, I don't know at all, I don't know and I don't read it over and I don't improve the style. I write only to write, only to go on writing to you . . . my darling, my own, my Varinka. . . .

1846

The Friend of the Family

PART 1

Introduction

I

When my uncle, Colonel Yegor Ilyitch Rostanev, left the army, he settled down in Stepantchikovo, which came to him by inheritance, and went on steadily living in it, as though he had been all his life a regular country gentleman who had never left his estates. There are natures that are perfectly satisfied with every one and can get used to everything; such was precisely the disposition of the retired colonel. It is hard to imagine a man more peaceable and ready to agree to anything. If by some caprice he had been gravely asked to carry some one for a couple of miles on his shoulders he would perhaps have done so. He was so good-natured that he was sometimes ready to give away everything at the first asking, and to share almost his last shirt with any one who coveted it. He was of heroic proportions; tall and well made, with ruddy cheeks, with teeth white as ivory, with a long brown moustache, with a loud ringing voice, and with a frank hearty laugh; he spoke rapidly and jerkily. He was at the time of my story about forty, and had spent his life almost from his sixteenth year in the Hussars. He had married very young and was passionately fond of his wife; but she died, leaving in his heart a noble memory that nothing could efface.

When he inherited Stepantchikovo, which increased his fortune to six hundred serfs, he left the army, and, as I have said already, settled in the country together with his children, Ilyusha a boy of eight, whose birth had cost his mother her life, and Sashenka a girl of fifteen, who had been brought up at a boarding-school in Moscow. But my uncle's house soon became a regular Noah's Ark. This was how it happened.

Just at the time when he came into the property and retired from the army, his mother, who had, sixteen years before, married a certain General Krahotkin, was left a widow. At the time of her second marriage my uncle was only a cornet, and yet he, too, was thinking of getting married. His mother had for a long time refused her blessing, had shed bitter tears, had reproached him with egoism, with ingratitude, with disrespect. She had proved to him that his estates amounting to only two hundred and fifty serfs, were, as it was, barely sufficient for the maintenance of his family (that is, for the maintenance of his mamma, with all her retinue of toadies, pug-dogs, Pomeranians, Chinese cats and so on). And, in the midst of these reproaches, protests and shrill upbraidings, she all at once quite unexpectedly got married herself before her son, though she was forty-two years of age. Even in this, however, she found an excuse for blaming my poor uncle, declaring that she was getting married solely to secure in her old age the refuge denied her by the undutiful egoist, her son, who was contemplating the unpardonable insolence of making a home of his own.

I never could find out what really induced a man apparently so reasonable as the deceased General Krahotkin to marry a widow of forty-two. It must be supposed that he suspected she had money. Other people thought that he only wanted a nurse, as he had already had a foretaste of the swarm of diseases which assailed him in his old age. One thing is certain, the general never had the faintest respect for his wife at any time during his married life, and he ridiculed her sarcastically at every favourable opportunity. He was a strange person. Half educated and extremely shrewd, he had a lively contempt for all and every one; he had no principles of any sort; laughed at everything and everybody, and in his old age, through the infirmities that were the consequence of his irregular and immoral life, he became spiteful, irritable and merciless.

He had been a successful officer; yet he had been forced, through "an unpleasant incident," to resign his commission, losing his pension and only just escaping prosecution. This had completely soured his temper. Left almost without means, with no fortune but a hundred ruined serfs, he folded his hands and never during the remaining twelve years of his life troubled himself to inquire what he was living on and who was supporting him. At the same time he insisted on having all the comforts of life, kept his carriage and refused to curtail his expenses. Soon after his marriage he lost the use of his legs and spent the last ten years of his life in an invalid-chair wheeled about by two seven-foot flunkeys, who never heard anything from him but abuse of the most varied kind. The carriage, the flunkeys and the invalid-chair were paid for by the undutiful son, who sent his mother his last farthing, mortgaged and re-mortgaged his estate, denied himself necessaries, and incurred debts almost impossible for him to pay in his circumstances at the time; and yet the charge of being an egoist and an undutiful son was persistently laid at his door. But my uncle's character was such that at last he quite believed himself that he was an egoist, and therefore to punish himself and to avoid being an egoist, he kept sending them more and more money. His mother stood in awe of her husband; but what pleased her most was that he was a general, and that through him she was "Madame la Générale."

She had her own apartments in the house, where, during the whole period of her husband's semi-existence, she queened it in a society made up of toadies, lapdogs, and the gossips of the town. She was an important person in her little town. Gossip, invitations to stand god-mother at christenings and to give the bride away at weddings, a halfpenny rubber, and the respect shown her in all sorts of ways as the wife of a general, fully made up to her for the drawbacks of her home life. All the magpies of the town came to her with their reports, the first place everywhere was always hers—in fact, she got out of her position all she could get out of it. The general did not meddle in all that; but before people he laughed mercilessly at his wife, asked himself, for instance, such questions as why he had married "such a dowdy," and nobody dared contradict him. Little by little all his acquaintances left him, and at the same time society was essential to him; he loved chatting, arguing; he liked to have a listener always sitting beside him. He was a free-thinker and atheist of the old school, and so liked to hold forth on lofty subjects.

But the listeners of the town of N—— had no partiality for lofty subjects, and they became fewer and fewer. They tried to get up a game of whist in the household; but as a rule the game ended in outbreaks on the part of the general, which so terrified his wife and her companions that they put up candles before the ikons, had a service sung, divined the future with beans and with cards, distributed rolls among the prisoners, and looked forward in a tremor to the after-dinner hour when they would have to take a hand at whist again and at every mistake to endure shouts, screams, oaths and almost blows. The general did not stand on ceremony with anybody when something was not to his taste; he screamed like a peasant woman, swore like a coachman, sometimes tore up the cards, threw them about the floor, drove away his partners, and even shed tears of anger and vexation—and for no more than a knave's having been played instead of a nine. At last, as his eyesight was failing, they had to get him a reader; it was then that Foma Fomitch Opiskin appeared upon the scene.

I must confess I announce this new personage with a certain solemnity. There is no denying that he is one of the principal characters in my story. How far he has a claim on the attention of the reader I will not explain; the reader can answer that question more suitably and more readily himself.

Foma Fomitch entered General Krahotkin's household as a paid companion—neither more nor less. Where he turned up from is shrouded in the mists of obscurity. I have, however, made special researches and have found out something of the past circumstances of this remarkable man. He was said in the first place to have been sometime and somewhere in the government service, and somewhere

or other to have suffered, I need hardly say, "for a good
cause." It was said, too, that at some time he had been
engaged in literary pursuits in Moscow. There is nothing
surprising in that; Foma Fomitch's crass ignorance would,
of course, be no hindrance to him in a literary career. But
all that is known for certain is that he did not succeed in
anything, and that at last he was forced to enter the general's service in the capacity of reader and martyr. There
was no ignominy which he had not to endure in return
for eating the general's bread. It is true that in later years,
when on the general's death he found himself a person of
importance and consequence, he more than once assured us
all that his consenting to be treated as a buffoon was an
act of magnanimous self-sacrifice on the altar of friendship; that the general had been his benefactor; that the deceased had been a great man misunderstood, who only to
him, Foma, had actually at the general's urgent desire
played the part of various wild beasts and posed in gro-
tesque attitudes, this had been solely in order to entertain
and distract a suffering friend shattered by disease. But
Foma Fomitch's assurances and explanations on this score
can only be accepted with considerable hesitation; and yet
this same Foma Fomitch, even at the time when he was a
buffoon, was playing a very different part in the ladies'
apartments of the general's house. How he managed this,
it is difficult for any one not a specialist in such matters
to conceive. The general's lady cherished a sort of mysterious reverence for him—why? There is no telling. By
degrees he acquired over the whole feminine half of the
general's household a marvellous influence, to some extent comparable to the influence exercised by the Ivan
Yakovlevitches and such-like seers and prophets, who are
visited in madhouses by certain ladies, who devote themselves to the study of their ravings. He read aloud to them
works of spiritual edification; held forth with eloquent
tears on the Christian virtues; told stories of his life and
his heroic doings; went to mass, and even to matins; at
times foretold the future; had a peculiar faculty for inter-
preting dreams, and was a great hand at throwing blame on

his neighbours. The general had a notion of what was going on in the back rooms, and tyrannized over his dependent more mercilessly than ever. But Foma's martyrdom only increased his prestige in the eyes of Madame la Générale and the other females of the household.

At last everything was transformed. The general died. His death was rather original. The former free-thinker and atheist became terror-stricken beyond all belief. He shed tears, repented, had ikons put up, sent for priests. Services were sung, and extreme unction was administered. The poor fellow screamed that he did not want to die, and even asked Foma Fomitch's forgiveness with tears. This latter circumstance was an asset of some value to Foma Fomitch later on. Just before the parting of the general's soul from the general's body, however, the following incident took place. The daughter of Madame la Générale by her first marriage, my maiden aunt, Praskovya Ilyinitchna, who always lived in the general's house, and was one of his favourite victims, quite indispensable to him during the ten years that he was bedridden, always at his beck and call, and with her meek and simple-hearted mildness the one person who could satisfy him, went up to his bedside shedding bitter tears, and would have smoothed the pillow under the head of the sufferer; but the sufferer still had strength to clutch at her hair and pull it violently three times, almost foaming at the mouth with spite. Ten minutes later he died. They had sent word to the colonel, though Madame la Générale had declared that she did not want to see him and would sooner die than set eyes on him at such a moment. There was a magnificent funeral at the expense, of course, of the undutiful son on whom the widowed mother did not wish to set her eyes.

In the ruined property of Knyazevka, which belonged to several different owners and in which the general had his hundred serfs, there stands a mausoleum of white marble, diversified with laudatory inscriptions to the glory of the intellect, talents, nobility of soul, orders of merit and rank of the deceased. Foma Fomitch took a prominent part in the composition of these eulogies. Madame la Générale

persisted for a long time in keeping up her dignity and refusing to forgive her disobedient son. Sobbing and making
a great outcry, surrounded by her crowd of toadies and
pug-dogs, she kept declaring that she would sooner live on
dry bread and I need hardly say "soak it in her tears," that
she would sooner go stick in hand to beg alms under the
windows than yield to the request of her "disobedient" son
that she should come and live with him at Stepantchikovo,
and that she would never, never set foot within his house!
As a rule the word foot in this connection is uttered with
peculiar effect by ladies. Madame la Générale's utterance
of the word was masterly, artistic. . . . In short, the amount
of eloquence that was expended was incredible. It must be
observed that at the very time of these shrill protests, they
were by degrees packing up to move to Stepantchikovo.
The colonel knocked up all his horses driving almost every
day thirty miles from Stepantchikovo to the town, and it
was not till a fortnight after the general's funeral that he
received permission to appear before the eyes of his aggrieved parent. Foma Fomitch was employed as go-be-
tween. During the whole of that fortnight he was reproaching the disobedient son and putting him to shame for his
"inhuman" conduct, reducing him to genuine tears, almost
to despair. It is from this time that the incomprehensible,
inhumanly despotic domination of Foma Fomitch over my
poor uncle dates. Foma perceived the kind of man he had
to deal with, and felt at once that his days of playing the
buffoon were over, and that in the wilds even Foma might
pass for a nobleman. And he certainly made up for lost
time.

"What will you feel like," said Foma, "if your own
mother, the authoress, so to speak, of your days, should
take a stick and leaning on it with trembling hands wasted
with hunger, should actually begin to beg for alms under
people's windows? Would it not be monstrous, considering
her rank as a general's lady and the virtues of her character? What would you feel like if she should suddenly come,
by mistake, of course—but you know it might happen—
and should stretch out her hand under your windows, while

you, her own son, are perhaps at that very moment nestling in a feather-bed, and . . . in fact, in luxury? It's awful, it's awful! But what is most awful of all—allow me to speak candidly, Colonel—what is most awful of all is the fact that you are standing before me now like an unfeeling post, with your mouth open and your eyes blinking, so that it is a positive disgrace, while you ought to be ready at the mere thought of such a thing to tear your hair out by the roots and to shed streams—what am I saying?—rivers, lakes, seas, oceans of tears. . . ."

In short, Foma in his excessive warmth grew almost incoherent. But such was the invariable outcome of his eloquence. It ended of course, in Madame la Générale together with her female dependents and lapdogs, with Foma Fomitch and with Mademoiselle Perepelitsyn, her chief favourite, at last honouring Stepantchikovo by her presence. She said that she would merely make the *experiment* of living at her son's till she had tested his dutifulness. You can imagine the colonel's position while his dutifulness was being tested! At first, as a widow recently bereaved, Madame la Générale thought it her duty two or three times a week to be overcome by despair at the thought of her general, never to return; and punctually on each occasion the colonel for some unknown reason came in for a wigging. Sometimes, especially if visitors were present, Madame la Générale would send for her grandchildren, little Ilyusha and fifteen-year-old Sashenka, and making them sit down beside her would fix upon them a prolonged, melancholy, anguished gaze, as upon children, ruined in the hands of *such a father;* she would heave deep, painful sighs, and finally melt into mute mysterious tears, for at least a full hour. Woe betide the colonel if he failed to grasp the significance of those tears! And, poor fellow, he hardly ever succeeded in grasping their significance, and in the simplicity of his heart almost always put in an appearance at such tearful moments, and whether he liked it or not came in for a severe heckling. But his filial respect in no way decreased and reached at last an extreme limit. In short, both Madame la Générale and Foma Fomitch were fully conscious that the storm which had for so many years menaced them in the presence of General Krahotkin had passed away and would never return. Madame la Générale used at times to fall on her sofa in a swoon. A great fuss and commotion arose. The colonel was crushed, and trembled like a leaf.

"Cruel son!" Madame la Générale would shriek as she came to. "You have lacerated my inmost being . . . *mes entrailles, mes entrailles!*"

"But how have I lacerated your inmost being, Mamma?" the colonel would protest timidly.

"You have lacerated it, lacerated it! He justifies himself, too. He is rude. Cruel son! I am dying! . . ."

The colonel was, of course, annihilated. But it somehow happened that Madame la Générale always revived again. Half an hour later he would be taking some one by the button-hole and saying—

"Oh, well, my dear fellow, you see she is a *grande dame*, the wife of a general. She is the kindest-hearted old lady; she is accustomed to all this refined . . . She is on a different level from a blockhead like me! Now she is angry with me. No doubt I am to blame. My dear fellow, I don't know yet what I've done, but no doubt it's my fault. . . ."

It would happen that Mademoiselle Perepelitsyn, an old maid in a shawl, with no eyebrows, with little rapacious eyes, with lips thin as a thread, with hands washed in cucumber water, and with a spite against the whole universe, would feel it her duty to read the colonel a lecture.

"It's all through your being undutiful, sir; it's all through your being an egoist, sir; through your wounding your mamma, sir—she's not used to such treatment. She's a general's lady, and you are only a colonel, sir."

"That is Mademoiselle Perepelitsyn, my dear fellow," the colonel would observe to his listener; "an excellent lady, she stands up for my mother like a rock! A very rare person! You mustn't imagine that she is in a menial position; she is the daughter of a major herself! Yes, indeed."

But, of course, this was only the prelude. The great lady who could carry out such a variety of performances in her turn trembled like a mouse in the presence of her

former dependent. Foma Fomitch had completely bewitched her. She could not make enough of him and she
saw with his eyes and heard with his ears. A cousin of mine,
also a retired hussar, a man still young, though he had
been an incredible spendthrift, told me bluntly and simply
that it was his firm conviction, after staying for a time at
my uncle's, that Madame la Générale was on terms of improper intimacy with Foma Fomitch. I need hardly say
that at the time I rejected this supposition with indignation
as too coarse and simple. No, it was something different,
and that something different I cannot explain without first
explaining to the reader the character of Foma Fomitch
as I understood it later.

Imagine the most insignificant, the most cowardly creature, an outcast from society, of no service to any one,
utterly useless, utterly disgusting, but incredibly vain,
though entirely destitute of any talent by which he might
have justified his morbidly sensitive vanity. I hasten to
add that Foma Fomitch was the incarnation of unbounded
vanity, but that at the same time it was a special kind of
vanity—that is, the vanity found in a complete nonentity,
and, as is usual in such cases, a vanity mortified and oppressed by grievous failures in the past; a vanity that has
begun rankling long, long ago, and ever since has given
off envy and venom, at every encounter, at every success
of any one else. I need hardly say that all this was seasoned
with the most unseemly touchiness, the most insane suspi-
ciousness. It may be asked, how is one to account for such
vanity? How does it arise, in spite of complete insignificance, in pitiful creatures who are forced by their social position to know their place? How answer such a question?
Who knows, perhaps, there are exceptions, of whom my
hero is one? He certainly is an exception to the rule, as
will be explained later. But allow me to ask: are you certain that those who are completely resigned to be your buffoons, your parasites and your toadies, and consider it an
honour and a happiness to be so, are you certain that they
are quite devoid of vanity and envy? What of the slander
and backbiting and tale-bearing and mysterious whisper-

ings in back corners, somewhere aside and at your table? Who knows, perhaps, in some of these degraded victims of fate, your fools and buffoons, vanity far from being dispelled by humiliation is even aggravated by that very humiliation, by being a fool and buffoon, by eating the bread of dependence and being for ever forced to submission and self-suppression. Who knows, maybe, this ugly exaggerated vanity is only a false fundamentally depraved sense of personal dignity, first outraged, perhaps, in childhood by oppression, poverty, filth, spat upon, perhaps, in the person of the future outcast's parents before his eyes. But I have said that Foma Fomitch was also an exception to the general rule; that is true. He had at one time been a literary man slighted and unrecognized, and literature is capable of ruining men very different from Foma Fomitch—I mean, of course, when it is not crowned with success. I don't know, but it may be assumed that Foma Fomitch had been unsuccessful before entering on a literary career; possibly in some other calling, too, he had received more kicks than halfpence, or possibly something worse. About that, however, I cannot say; but I made inquiries later on, and I know for certain that Foma Fomitch composed, at some time in Moscow, a romance very much like those that were published every year by dozens in the 'thirties, after the style of *The Deliverance of Moscow, The Chieftains of the Tempest, Sons of Love, or the Russions in 1104*—novels which in their day afforded an agreeable butt for the wit of Baron Brambeus. That was, of course, long ago; but the serpent of literary vanity sometimes leaves a deep and incurable sting, especially in insignificant and dull-witted persons. Foma Fomitch had been disappointed from his first step in a literary career, and it was then that he was finally enrolled in the vast army of the disappointed, from which all the crazy saints, hermits and wandering pilgrims come later on. I think that his monstrous boastfulness, his thirst for praise and distinction, for admiration and homage, dates from the same period. Even when he was a buffoon he got together a group of idiots to do homage to him. Somewhere and somehow to stand first, to be an oracle, to swagger and give himself airs—that was his most urgent craving! As others did not praise him he began to praise himself. I have myself in my uncle's house at Stepantchikovo heard Foma's sayings after he had become the absolute monarch and oracle of the household. "I am not in my proper place among you," he would say sometimes with mysterious impressiveness. "I am not in my proper place here. I will look round, I will settle you all, I will show you, I will direct you, and then good-bye; to Moscow to edit a review! Thirty thousand people will assemble every month to hear my lectures. My name will be famous at last, and then—woe to my enemies."

But while waiting to become famous the genius insisted upon immediate recognition in substantial form. It is always pleasant to receive payment in advance, and in this case it was particularly so. I know that he seriously assured my uncle that some great work lay before him, Foma, in the future—a work for which he had been summoned into the world, and to the accomplishment of this work he was urged by some sort of person with wings, who visited him at night, or something of that kind. This great work was to write a book full of profound wisdom in the soul-saving line, which would set the whole world agog and stagger all Russia. And when all Russia was staggered, he, Foma, disdaining glory, would retire into a monastery, and in the catacombs of Kiev would pray day and night for the happiness of the Fatherland. All this imposed upon my uncle.

Well, now imagine what this Foma, who had been all his life oppressed and crushed, perhaps actually beaten too, was vain and secretly lascivious, who had been disappointed in his literary ambitions, who had played the buffoon for a crust of bread, who was at heart a despot in spite of all his previous abjectness and impotence, who was a braggart, and insolent when successful, might become when he suddenly found himself in the haven he had reached after so many ups and downs, honoured and glorified, humoured and flattered, thanks to a patroness who was an idiot and a patron who was imposed upon and ready to agree to anything. I must, of course, explain my uncle's character more fully, or Foma Fomitch's success cannot be understood. But for the moment I will say that Foma was a complete illustration of the saying, "Let him sit down to the table and he will put his feet on it." He paid us out for his past! A base soul escaping from oppression becomes an oppressor. Foma had been oppressed, and he had at once a craving to oppress others; he had been the victim of whims and caprices and now he imposed his own whims and caprices on others. He had been the butt of others, and now he surrounded himself with creatures whom he could turn into derision. His boasting was ridiculous; the airs he gave himself were incredible; nothing was good enough for him; his tyranny was beyond all bounds, and it reached such a pitch that simple-hearted people who had not witnessed his manoeuvres, but only heard queer stories about him, looked upon all this as a miracle, as the work of the devil, crossed themselves and spat.

I was speaking of my uncle. Without explaining his remarkable character (I repeat) it is, of course, impossible to understand Foma Fomitch's insolent domination in another man's house; it is impossible to understand the metamorphosis of the cringing dependent into the great man. Besides being kind-hearted in the extreme, my uncle was a man of the most refined delicacy in spite of a somewhat rough exterior, of the greatest generosity and of proved courage. I boldly say of "courage"; nothing could have prevented him from fulfilling an obligation, from doing his duty—in such cases no obstacle would have dismayed him. His soul was as pure as a child's. He was a perfect child at forty, open-hearted in the extreme, always good-humoured, imagining everybody an angel, blaming himself for other people's shortcomings, and exaggerating the good qualities of others, even pre-supposing them where they could not possibly exist. He was one of those very generous and pure-hearted men who are positively ashamed to assume any harm of another, are always in haste to endow their neighbours with every virtue, rejoice at other people's success, and in that way always live in an ideal world, and when anything goes wrong always blame themselves

first. To sacrifice themselves in the interests of others is
their natural vocation. Some people would have called
him cowardly, weak-willed and feeble. Of course he was
weak, and indeed he was of too soft a disposition; but it
was not from lack of will, but from the fear of wounding,
of behaving cruelly, from excess of respect for others and
for mankind in general. He was, however, weak-willed and
cowardly only when nothing was at stake but his own interests, which he completely disregarded, and for this he
was continually an object of derision, and often with the
very people for whom he was sacrificing his own advantage.
He never believed, however, that he had enemies; he had
them, indeed, but he somehow failed to observe them. He
dreaded fuss and disturbance in the house like fire, and
immediately gave way to any one and submitted to anything. He gave in through a sort of shy good nature, from
a sort of shy delicacy. "So be it," he would say, quickly
brushing aside all reproaches for his indulgence and weakness; "so be it . . . that every one may be happy and contented!" I need hardly say that he was ready to submit to
every honourable influence. What is more, an adroit rogue
might have gained complete control over him, and even
have lured him on to do wrong, of course misrepresenting
the wrong action as a right one. My uncle very readily put
faith in other people, and was often far from right in doing
so. When, after many sufferings, he brought himself at last
to believe that the man who deceived him was dishonest, he
always blamed himself first—and sometimes blamed himself
only. Now, imagine, suddenly queening it in his quiet home,
a capricious, doting, idiot woman—inseparable from another idiot, her idol—a woman who had only feared her
general, and was now afraid of nothing, and impelled by a
craving to make up to herself for what she had suffered in
the past; and this idiot woman my uncle thought it his duty
to revere, simply because she was his mother. They began
with proving to my uncle at once that he was coarse, impatient, ignorant and selfish to the utmost degree. The remarkable thing is that the idiotic old lady herself believed
in what she professed. And I believe that Foma Fomitch

did also, at least to some extent. They persuaded my uncle, too, that Foma had been sent from heaven by Divine Providence for the salvation of his soul and the subduing of his unbridled passions; that he was haughty, proud of his wealth, and quite capable of reproaching Foma Fomitch for eating his bread. My poor uncle was very soon convinced of the depth of his degradation, was ready to tear his hair and to beg forgiveness. . . .

"It's all my own fault, brother," he would say sometimes to one of the people he used to talk to. "It's all my fault! One ought to be doubly delicate with a man who is under obligations to one. . . . I mean that I . . . Under obligations, indeed! I am talking nonsense again! He is not under obligations to me at all: on the contrary, it is I who am under an obligation to him for living with me! And here I have reproached him for eating my bread! . . . Not that I did reproach him, but it seems I made some slip of the tongue—I often do make such slips. . . . And, after all, the man has suffered, he has done great things; for ten years in spite of insulting treatment he was tending his sick friend! And then his learning. . . . He's a writer! A highly educated man! A very lofty character; in short . . ." short . . ."

The conception of the highly educated and unfortunate Foma ignominiously treated by the cruel and capricious general rent my uncle's heart with compassion and indignation. All Foma's peculiarities, all his ignoble doings my uncle at once ascribed to his sufferings, the humiliations he had endured in the past, and the bitterness left by them. . . . He at once decided in his soft and generous heart that one could not be so exacting with a man who had suffered as with an ordinary person; that one must not only forgive him, but more than that, one must, by gentle treatment, heal his wounds, restore him and reconcile him with humanity. Setting this object before him he was completely fired by it, and lost all power of perceiving that his new friend was a lascivious and capricious animal, an egoist, a sluggard, a lazy drone—and nothing more. He put implicit faith in Foma's genius and learning. I forgot to mention that my uncle had the most naïve and disinterested reverence for the words "learning" and "literature," though he had himself never studied anything. This was one of his chief and most guileless peculiarities.

"He is writing," he would whisper, walking on tiptoe, though he was two rooms away from Foma's study. "I don't know precisely what he is writing," he added, with a proud and mysterious air. "but no doubt he is brewing something, brother. . . . I mean in the best sense, of course; it would be clear to some people, but to you and me, brother, it would be just a jumble that . . . I fancy he is writing of productive forces of some sort—he said so himself. I suppose that has something to do with politics. Yes, his name will be famous! Then we shall be famous through him. He told me that himself, brother. . . ."

I know for a fact that my uncle was forced by Foma's orders to shave off his beautiful fair whiskers. Foma considered that these whiskers made my uncle look like a Frenchman, and that wearing them showed a lack of patriotism. Little by little Foma began meddling in the management of the estate, and giving sage counsels on the subject. These sage counsels were terrible. The peasants soon saw the position and understood who was their real master, and scratched their heads uneasily. Later on I overheard Foma talking to the peasants; I must confess I listened. Foma had told us before that he was fond of talking to intelligent Russian peasants. So one day he went to the threshing floor: after talking to the peasants about the farm-work, though he could not tell oats from wheat, after sweetly dwelling on the sacred obligations of the peasant to his master, after touching lightly on electricity and the division of labour, subjects of which I need hardly say he knew nothing, after explaining to his listeners how the earth went round the sun, and being at last quite touched by his own eloquence—he began talking about the ministers. I understood. Pushkin used to tell a story of a father who impressed upon his little boy of four that he, his papa, was so brave "that the Czar loves Papa. . . ." So evidently this papa needed this listener of four years old! And the peasants always listened to Foma Fomitch with cringing respect.

"And did you get a large salary from royalty, little father?" a grey-headed old man called Arhip Korotky asked suddenly from the crowd of peasants, with the evident intention of being flattering; but the question struck Foma Fomitch as familiar, and he could not endure familiarity.

"And what business is that of yours, you lout?" he answered, looking contemptuously at the poor peasant. "Why are you thrusting forward your pug-face? Do you want me to spit in it?"

Foma Fomitch always talked in that tone to the "intelligent Russian peasant."

"You are our father," another peasant interposed; "you know we are ignorant people. You may be a major or a colonel or even your Excellency, we don't know how we ought to speak to you."

"You lout!" repeated Foma Fomitch, mollified however. "There are salaries and salaries, you blockhead! One will get nothing, though he is a general—because he does nothing to deserve it, he is of no service to the Czar. But I got twenty thousand when I was serving in the Ministry, and I did not take it, I served for the honour of it. I had plenty of money of my own. I gave my salary to the cause of public enlightenment, and to aid those whose homes had been burnt in Kazan."

"I say! So it was you who rebuilt Kazan, little father?" the amazed peasant went on.

The peasants wondered at Foma Fomitch as a rule.

"Oh, well, I had my share in it," Foma answered, with a show of reluctance, as though vexed with himself for deigning to converse on *such* a subject with *such* a person.

His conversations with my uncle were of a different stamp.

"What were you in the past?" Foma would say, for instance, lolling after an ample dinner in an easy-chair, while a servant stood behind him brandishing a fresh lime branch to keep off the flies. "What were you like before I came? But now I have dropped into your soul a spark of that heavenly fire which is glowing there now. Did I drop a spark of heavenly fire into your soul or not? Answer. Did I drop a spark or did I not?"

Foma Fomitch, indeed, could not himself have said why he asked such a question. But my uncle's silence and confusion at once spurred him on. He who had been so patient and down-trodden in the past now exploded like gunpowder at the slightest provocation. My uncle's silence seemed to him insulting, and he now insisted on an answer.

"Answer: is the spark glowing in you or not?"

My uncle hesitated, shrank into himself, and did not know what line to take.

"Allow me to observe that I am waiting," said Foma in an aggrieved voice.

"*Mais, répondez donc,* Yegorushka," put in Madame la Générale, shrugging her shoulders.

"I am asking you, is that spark burning within you or not?" Foma repeated condescendingly, taking a sweetmeat out of a bonbon box, which always stood on a table before him by Madame la Générale's orders.

"I really don't know, Foma," my uncle answered at last with despair in his eyes. "Something of the sort, no doubt. . . . You really had better not ask or I am sure to say something wrong. . . ."

"Oh, very well! So you look upon me as so insignificant as not to deserve an answer—that's what you meant to say. But so be it; let me be a nonentity."

"Oh, no, Foma, God bless you! Why, when did I imply that?"

"Yes, that's just what you did mean to say."

"I swear I didn't."

"Oh, very well, then, I lie. So then you charge me with trying to pick a quarrel on purpose; it's another insult added to all the past, but I will put up with this too. . . ."

"*Mais, mon fils!*" cried Madame la Générale in alarm.

"Foma Fomitch! Mamma!" exclaimed my uncle in despair. "Upon my word it's not my fault. Perhaps I may have let slip such a thing without knowing it. . . . You mustn't mind me, Foma; I am stupid, you know; I feel I am stupid myself; I feel there is something amiss with me. . . . I know, Foma, I know! You need not say anything," he went on, waving his hand. "I have lived forty years, and until now, until I knew you, I thought I was all right . . . like every one else. And I didn't notice before that I was as sinful as a goat, an egoist of the worst description, and I've done such a lot of mischief that it is a wonder the world puts up with me."

"Yes, you certainly are an egoist," observed Foma, with conviction.

"Well, I realize myself that I am an egoist now! Yes, that's the end of it! I'll correct myself and be better!"

"God grant you may!" concluded Foma Fomitch, and sighing piously he got up from his arm-chair to go to his room for an after-dinner nap. Foma Fomitch always dozed after dinner.

To conclude this chapter, may I be allowed to say something about my personal relations with my uncle, and to explain how I came to be face to face with Foma Fomitch, and with no thought or suspicion suddenly found myself in a vortex of the most important incidents that had ever happened in the blessed village of Stepantchikovo? With this I intend to conclude my introduction and to proceed straight with my story.

In my childhood, when I was left an orphan and alone in the world, my uncle took the place of a father to me; educated me at his expense, and did for me more than many a father does for his own child. From the first day he took me into his house I grew warmly attached to him. I was ten years old at the time, and I remember that we got on capitally, and thoroughly understood each other. We spun tops together, and together stole her cap from a very disagreeable old lady, who was a relation of both of us. I promptly tied the cap to the tail of a paper kite and sent it flying to the clouds. Many years afterwards I saw something of my uncle for a short time in Petersburg, where I was finishing my studies at his expense. During that time I became attached to him with all the warmth of youth:

something generous, mild, truthful, light-hearted and naïve
to the utmost degree struck me in his character and attracted every one. When I left the university I spent some
time in Petersburg with nothing to do for the time, and, as
is often the case with callow youths, was convinced that in
a very short time I should do much that was very interesting and even great. I did not want to leave Petersburg. I
wrote to my uncle at rather rare intervals and only when
I wanted money, which he never refused me. Meanwhile,
I heard from a house serf of my uncle's, who came to Petersburg on some business or other, that marvellous things were
taking place at Stepantchikovo. These first rumours interested and surprised me. I began writing to my uncle more
regularly. He always answered me somewhat obscurely and
strangely, and in every letter seemed trying to talk of nothing but learned subjects, expressing great expectations of
me in the future in a literary and scientific line, and pride
in my future achievements. At last, after a rather long silence, I received a surprising letter from him, utterly unlike
all his previous letters. It was full of such strange hints, such
rambling and contradictory statements, that at first I could
make nothing of it. All that one could see was that the
writer was in great perturbation. One thing was clear in
the letter: my uncle gravely, earnestly, almost imploringly
urged me as soon as possible to marry his former ward, the
daughter of a very poor provincial government clerk, called
Yezhevikin. This girl had received an excellent education at
a school in Moscow at my uncle's expense, and was now
the governess of his children. He wrote that she was unhappy, that I might make her happy, that I should, in fact,
be doing a noble action. He appealed to the generosity of
my heart, and promised to give her a dowry. Of the dowry,
however, he spoke somewhat mysteriously, timidly, and he
concluded the letter by beseeching me to keep all this a
dead secret. This letter made such an impression on me that
my head began to go round. And, indeed, what raw young
man would not have been affected by such a proposition, if
only on its romantic side? Besides, I had heard that this

young governess was extremely pretty. Yet I did not know what to decide, though I wrote to my uncle that I would set off for Stepantchikovo immediately. My uncle had sent me the money for the journey with the letter. Nevertheless, I lingered another three weeks in Petersburg, hesitating and somewhat uneasy.

All at once I happened to meet an old comrade of my uncle's, who had stayed at Stepantchikovo on his way back from the Caucasus to Petersburg. He was an elderly and judicious person, an inveterate bachelor. He told me with indignation about Foma Fomitch, and thereupon informed me of one circumstance of which I had no idea till then: namely, that Foma Fomitch and Madame la Générale had taken up a notion, and were set upon the idea of marrying my uncle to a very strange lady, not in her first youth and scarcely more than half-witted, with an extraordinary history, and almost half a million of dowry; that Madame la Générale had nearly succeeded in convincing this lady that they were relations, and so alluring her into the house; that my uncle, of course, was in despair, but would probably end by marrying the half-million of dowry; and that, finally, these two wiseacres, Madame la Générale and Foma Fomitch, were making a terrible onslaught on the poor defenceless governess, and were doing their utmost to turn her out of the house, apparently afraid that my uncle might fall in love with her, or perhaps knowing that he was already in love with her. These last words impressed me. However, to all my further questions as to whether my uncle really was or was not in love with her, my informant either could not or would not give me an exact answer, and indeed he told his whole story briefly, as it were reluctantly, and noticeably avoided detailed explanations. I thought it over; the news was so strangely contradictory of my uncle's letter and his proposition! . . . But it was useless to delay. I decided to go to Stepantchikovo, hoping not only to comfort my uncle and bring him to reason, but even to save him; that is, if possible, to turn Foma out, to prevent the hateful marriage with the old maid, and finally

—as I had come to the conclusion that my uncle's love was only a spiteful invention of Foma's—to rejoice the unhappy but of course interesting young lady by the offer of my hand, and so on and so on. By degrees I so worked myself up that, being young and having nothing to do, I passed from hesitation to the opposite extreme; I began burning with the desire to perform all sorts of great and wonderful deeds as quickly as possible. I even fancied that I was displaying extraordinary generosity by nobly sacrificing myself to secure the happiness of a charming and innocent creature; in fact, I remember that I was exceedingly well satisfied with myself during the whole of my journey. It was July, the sun was shining brightly, all around me stretched a vast expanse of fields full of unripe corn. . . . I had so long sat bottled up in Petersburg, that I felt as though I were only now looking at God's world!

Mr. Bahtcheyev

II

I was approaching my destination. Driving through the little town of B——, from which I had only eight miles further to Stepantchikovo, I was obliged to stop at the blacksmith's near the town gate, as the tyre of the front wheel of my chaise broke. To repair it in some way well enough to stand the remaining eight miles was a job that should not take very long, and so I made up my mind not to go elsewhere, but to remain at the blacksmith's while he set it right. As I got out of the chaise I saw a stout gentleman who, like me, had been compelled to stop to have his carriage repaired. He had been standing a whole hour in the insufferable heat, shouting and swearing, and with fretful impatience urging on the blacksmiths who were busy about his fine carriage. At first sight this angry gentleman struck me as extremely peevish. He was about five-and-forty, of middle height, very stout, and pock-marked; his stoutness, his double chin and his puffy, pendant cheeks testified to the blissful existence of a landowner. There was something feminine about his whole figure which at once caught the eye. He was dressed in loose, comfortable, neat clothes which were, however, quite unfashionable.

I cannot imagine why he was annoyed with me, since he saw me for the first time in his life, and had not yet spoken a single word to me. I noticed the fact from the extraordinarily furious looks he turned upon me as soon as I got out of the carriage. Yet I felt a great inclination to make his acquaintance. From the chatter of his servants, I gathered that he had just come from Stepantchikovo, from my uncle's, and so it was an opportunity for making full inquiries about many things. I was just taking off my cap and trying as agreeably as possible to observe how unpleasant these delays on the road sometimes were; but the fat gentleman, as it were reluctantly, scanned me from head to boots with a displeased and ill-humoured stare, muttered something to himself and turned heavily his full back view to me. This aspect of his person, however interesting to the observer, held out no hopes of agreeable conversation.

"Grishka! Don't grumble to yourself! I'll thrash you! . . ." he shouted suddenly to his valet, as though he had not heard what I said about delays on the journey.

This Grishka was a grey-headed, old-fashioned servant dressed in a long-skirted coat and wearing very long grey whiskers. Judging from certain signs, he too was in a very bad humour, and was grumbling morosely to himself. An explanation immediately followed between the master and the servant.

"You'll thrash me! Bawl a little louder!" muttered Grishka, as though to himself, but so loudly that everybody heard it; and with indignation he turned away to adjust something in the carriage.

"What? What did you say? 'Bawl a little louder.' . . . So you are pleased to be impudent!" shouted the fat man, turning purple.

"What on earth are you nagging at me for? One can't say a word!"

"Why nag at you? Do you hear that? He grumbles at me and I am not to nag at him!"

"Why, what should I grumble at?"

"What should you grumble at . . . you're grumbling, right enough! I know what you are grumbling about; my having come away from the dinner—that's what it is."

"What's that to me! You can have no dinner at all for all I care. I am not grumbling at you; I simply said a word to the blacksmiths."

"The blacksmiths. . . . Why grumble at the blacksmiths?"

"I did not grumble at them, I grumbled at the carriage."

"And why grumble at the carriage?"

"What did it break down for? It mustn't do it again."

"The carriage. . . . No, you are grumbling at me, and not at the carriage. It's his own fault and he swears at other people!"

"Why on earth do you keep on at me, sir? Leave off, please!"

"Why have you been sitting like an owl all the way, not saying a word to me, eh? You are ready enough to talk at other times!"

"A fly was buzzing round my mouth, that's why I didn't talk and sat like an owl. Why, am I to tell you fairy tales, or what? Take Malanya the storyteller with you if you are fond of fairy tales."

The fat man opened his mouth to reply, but apparently could think of nothing and held his peace. The servant, proud of his skill in argument and his influence over his master displayed before witnesses, turned to the workmen with redoubled dignity and began showing them something.

My efforts to make acquaintance were fruitless, and my own awkwardness did not help matters. I was assisted, however, by an unexpected incident. A sleepy, unwashed and unkempt countenance suddenly peeped out of the window of a closed carriage which had stood from time immemorial without wheels in the blacksmith's yard, daily though vainly expecting to be repaired. At the appearance of this countenance there was a general outburst of laughter from the workmen. The joke was that the man peeping out of the dismantled carriage was locked in and could not get out. Having fallen asleep in it drunk, he was now vainly begging for freedom; at last he began begging some one to run for his tool. All this immensely entertained the spectators.

There are persons who derive peculiar delight and entertainment from strange things. The antics of a drunken peasant, a man stumbling and falling down in the street, a wrangle between two women and other such incidents arouse at times in some people the most good-humoured and unaccountable delight. The fat gentleman belonged precisely to that class. Little by little his countenance from being sullen and menacing began to look pleased and good-humoured, and at last brightened up completely.

"Why, that's Vassilyev, isn't it?" he asked with interest. "How did he get here?"

"Yes, it is Vassilyev, sir!" was shouted on all sides.

"He's been on the spree, sir," added one of the workmen, a tall, lean, elderly man with a pedantically severe expression of face, who seemed disposed to take the lead; "he's been on the spree, sir. It's three days since he left his master, and he's lying hidden here; he's come and planted himself upon us! Here he is asking for a chisel. Why, what do you want a chisel for now, you addlepate? He wants to pawn his last tool."

"Ech, Arhipushka! Money's like a bird, it flies up and flies away again! Let me out, for God's sake," Vassilyev entreated in a thin cracked voice, poking his head out of the carriage.

"You stay where you are, you idol; you are lucky to be there!" Arhip answered sternly. "You have been drunk since the day before yesterday; you were hauled out of the street at daybreak this morning. You must thank God we hid you, we told Matvey Ilyitch that you were ill, that you had a convenient attack of colic."

There was a second burst of laughter.

"But where is the chisel?"

"Why, our Zuey has got it! How he keeps on about it! A drinking man, if ever there was one, Stepan Alexyevitch."

"He-he-he! Ah, the scoundrel! So that's how you work in the town; you pawn your tools!" wheezed the fat man, spluttering with glee, quite pleased and suddenly becoming extraordinarily good-humoured. "And yet it would be hard to find such a carpenter even in Moscow, but this is how he always recommends himself, the ruffian," he added, quite unexpectedly turning to me. "Let him out, Arhip, perhaps he wants something."

The gentleman was obeyed. The nail with which they had fastened up the carriage door, chiefly in order to amuse themselves at Vassilyev's expense when he should wake up, was taken out, and Vassilyev made his appearance in the light of day, muddy, dishevelled and ragged. He blinked at the sunshine, sneezed and gave a lurch; and then putting up his hand to screen his eyes, he looked round.

"What a lot of people, what a lot of people!" he said, shaking his head, "and all, seemingly, so . . . ober," he drawled, with a sort of mournful pensiveness as though reproaching himself: "Well, good-morning, brothers, good-day."

Again there was a burst of laughter.

"Good-morning! Why, see how much of the day is gone, you heedless fellow!"

"Go it, old man!"

"As we say, have your fling, if it don't last long."

"He-he-he! he has a ready tongue!" cried the fat man, rolling with laughter and again glancing genially at me. "Aren't you ashamed, Vassilyev?"

"It's sorrow drives me to it! Stepan Alexyevitch, sir, it's sorrow," Vassilyev answered gravely, with a wave of his hand, evidently glad of another opportunity to mention his sorrow.

"What sorrow, you booby?"

"A trouble such as was never heard of before. We are being made over to Foma Fomitch."

"Whom? When?" cried the fat man, all of a flutter.

I, too, took a step forward; quite unexpectedly, the question concerned me too.

"Why, all the people of Kapitonovko. Our master, the colonel—God give him health—wants to give up all our Kapitonovko, his property, to Foma Fomitch. Some seventy souls he is handing over to him. 'It's for you, Foma,' says he. 'Here, now, you've nothing of your own, one may say; you are not much of a landowner; all you have to keep you are two smelts in Lake Ladoga—that's all the serfs your father left you. For your parent,' " Vassilyev went on, with a sort of spiteful satisfaction, putting touches of venom into his story in all that related to Foma Fomitch— " 'for your parent was a gentleman of ancient lineage, though from no one knows where, and no one knows who he was; he too, like you, lived with the gentry, was allowed to be in the kitchen as a charity. But now when I make over Kapitonovko to you, you will be a landowner too, and a gentleman of ancient lineage, and will have serfs of your own. You can lie on the stove and be idle as a gentleman. . . .' "

But Stepan Alexyevitch was no longer listening. The effect produced on him by Vassilyev's half-drunken story was extraordinary. The fat man was so angry that he turned positively purple; his double chin was quivering, his little eyes grew bloodshot. I thought he would have a stroke on the spot.

"That's the last straw!" he said, gasping. "That low brute Foma, the parasite, a landowner! Tfoo! Go to perdition! Damn it all! Hey, you make haste and finish! Home!"

"Allow me to ask you," I had said, stepping forward uncertainly, "you were pleased to mention the name of Foma Fomitch just now; I believe his surname, if I am not mistaken, is Opiskin. Well, you see, I should like . . . in short, I have a special reason for being interested in that personage, and I should be very glad to know on my own account, how far one may believe the words of this good man that his master, Yegor Ilyitch Rostanev, means to make Foma Fomitch a present of one of his villages. That interests me extremely, and I . . ."

"Allow me to ask you," the fat man broke in, "on what grounds are you interested in that personage, as you style him; though to my mind 'that damned low brute' is what he ought to be called, and not a personage. A fine sort of personage, the scurvy knave! He's a simple disgrace, not a personage!"

I explained that so far I was in complete ignorance in regard to this person, but that Yegor Ilyitch Rostanev was my uncle, and that I myself was Sergey Alexandrovitch So-and-so.

"The learned gentleman? My dear fellow! they are expecting you impatiently," cried the fat man, genuinely delighted. "Why, I have just come from them myself, from Stepantchikovo; I went away from dinner, I got up from the pudding, I couldn't sit it out with Foma! I quarrelled with them all there on account of that damned Foma. . . . Here's a meeting! You must excuse me, my dear fellow. I am Stepan Alexyevitch Bahtcheyev, and I remember you that high. . . . Well, who would have thought it! . . . But allow me."

And the fat man advanced to kiss me.

After the first minutes of excitement, I at once proceeded to question him: the opportunity was an excellent one.

"But who is this Foma?" I asked. "How is it he has gained the upper hand of the whole house? Why don't they kick him out of the yard? I must confess . . ."

"Kick him out? You must be mad. Why, Yegor Ilyitch tiptoes before him! Why, once Foma laid it down that Thursday was Wednesday, and so every one in the house counted Thursday Wednesday. 'I won't have it Thursday, let it be Wednesday! So there were two Wednesdays in one week. Do you suppose I am making it up? I am not exaggerating the least little bit. Why, my dear fellow, it's simply beyond all belief."

"I have heard that, but I must confess . . ."

"I confess and I confess! The way the man keeps on! What is there to confess? No, you had better ask me what sort of jungle I have come out of. The mother of Yegor Ilyitch, I mean of the colonel, though a very worthy lady and a general's widow too, in my opinion is in her dotage; why, that damned Foma is the very apple of her eye. She is the cause of it all; it was she brought him into the house. He has talked her silly, she hasn't a word to say for herself now, though she is called her Excellency—she skipped into marriage with General Krahotkin at fifty! As for Yegor Ilyitch's sister, Praskovya Ilyinitchna, who is an old maid of forty, I don't care to speak of her. It's oh dear, and oh my, and cackling like a hen. I am sick of her—bless her! The only thing about her is that she is of the female sex; and so I must respect her for no cause or reason, simply because she is of the female sex! Tfoo! It's not the thing for me to speak of her, she's your aunt. Alexandra Yegorovna, the colonel's daughter, though she is only a little girl—just in her sixteenth year—to my thinking is the cleverest of the lot; she doesn't respect Foma; it was fun to see her. A sweet young lady, and that's the fact! And why should she respect him? Why, Foma was a buffoon waiting on the late General Krahotkin. Why, he used to imitate all sorts of beasts to entertain the general! And it seems that in old days Jack was the man; but nowadays Jack is the master, and now the colonel, your uncle, treats this retired buffoon as though he were his own father. He has set him up in a frame, the rascal, and bows down at the feet of the man who is sponging upon him. Tfoo!"

"Poverty is not a vice, however . . . and I must confess . . . allow me to ask you, is he handsome, clever?"

"Foma? A perfect picture!" answered Bahtcheyev, with an extraordinary quiver of spite in his voice. (My questions seemed to irritate him, and he began to look at me suspiciously.) "A perfect picture! Do you hear, good people: he makes him out a beauty! Why, he is like a lot of brute beasts in one, if you want to know the whole truth, my good man. Though that wouldn't matter if he had wit; if only he had wit, the rogue—why, then I would be ready to do violence to my feelings and agree, maybe, for the sake of wit; but, you see, there's no trace of wit about him whatever! He has cast a spell on them; he is a regular alchemist! Tfoo! I am tired of talking. One ought to curse them and say no more about it. You have upset me with your talk, my good sir! Hey, you! Are you ready or not?"

"Raven still wants shoeing," Grishka answered gloomily.

"Raven. I'll let you have a raven! . . . Yes, sir, I could tell you a story that would simply make you gape with wonder, so that you would stay with your mouth open till the Second Coming. Why, I used to feel a respect for him myself. Would you believe it? I confess it with shame, I frankly confess it, I was a fool. Why, he took me in too. He's a know-all. He knows the ins and outs of everything, he's studied all the sciences. He gave me some drops; you see, my good sir, I am a sick man, a poor creature. You may not believe it, but I am an invalid. And those drops of his almost turned me inside out. You just keep quiet and listen; go yourself and you will be amazed. Why, he will make the colonel shed tears of blood; the colonel will shed tears of blood through him, but then it will be too late. You know, the whole neighbourhood all around has dropped his acquaintance owing to this accursed Foma. No one can come to the place without being insulted by him. I don't count; even officials of high rank he doesn't spare. He lectures every one. He sets up for a teacher of morality, the scoundrel. 'I am a wise man,' says he; 'I am cleverer than all of you, you must listen to no one but me, I am a learned man.' Well, what of it? Because he is learned, must he persecute people who are not? . . . And when he begins in his learned language, he goes hammering on ta-ta-ta! Ta-ta-ta! I'll tell you his tongue is such a one to wag, that if you cut it off and throw it on the dungheap it will go on wagging there till a crow picks it up. He is as conceited and puffed out as a mouse in a sack of grain. He is trying to climb so high that he will overreach himself. Why, here, for instance, he has taken it into his head to teach the house serfs French. You can believe it or not, as you like. It will be a benefit to him, he says. To a lout, to a servant! Tfoo! A shameless fellow, damn him, that is what he is. What does a clodhopper want with French, I ask you? And indeed what do the likes of us want with French? For gallivanting with young ladies in the mazurka or dancing attendance on other men's wives? Profligacy, that's what it is, I tell you! But to my thinking, when one has drunk a bottle of vodka one can talk in any language. So that is all the respect I have for your French language! I dare say you can chatter away in French: Ta-ta-ta, the tabby has married the tom," Bahtche-yev said, looking at me in scornful indignation. "Are you a learned man, my good sir—eh? Have you gone in for some learned line?"

"Well . . . I am somewhat interested . . ."

"I suppose you have studied all the sciences, too?"

"Quite so, that is, no . . . I must own I am more interested now in observing . . . I have been staying in Petersburg, but now I am hurrying to my uncle's."

"And who is the attraction at your uncle's? You had better have stayed where you were, since you had somewhere to stay. No, my good sir, I can tell you, you won't make much way by being learned, and no uncle will be of any use to you; you'll get caught in a trap! Why, I got quite thin, staying twenty-four hours with them. Would you believe that I got thin, staying with them? No, I see you don't believe it. Oh, well, you needn't believe it if you don't want to, bless you."

"No, really I quite believe it, only I still don't understand," I answered, more and more bewildered.

"I believe it, but I don't believe you! You learned gentlemen are all fond of cutting capers! All you care about is hopping about on one leg and showing off! I am not fond of learned people, my good sir; they give me the spleen! I have come across your Petersburgers—a worthless lot! They are all Freemasons; they spread infidelity in all directions; they are afraid of a drop of vodka, as though it would bite them—Tfoo! You have put me out of temper, sir, and I don't want to tell you anything! After all, I have not been engaged to tell you stories, and I am tired of talking. One doesn't pitch into everybody, sir, and indeed it's a sin to do it. . . . Only your learned gentleman at your uncle's has driven the footman Vidoplyasov almost out of his wits. Vidoplyasov has gone crazy all through Foma Fomitch. . . ."

"As for that fellow Vidoplyasov," put in Grishka, who had till then been following the conversation with severe decorum, "I'd give him a flogging. If I came across him, I'd thrash the German nonsense out of him. I'd give him more than you could get into two hundred."

"Be quiet!" shouted his master. "Hold your tongue; no one's talking to you."

"Vidoplyasov," I said, utterly nonplussed and not knowing what to say. "Vidoplyasov, what a queer name!"

"Why is it queer? There you are again. Ugh, you learned gentlemen, you learned gentlemen!"

I lost patience.

"Excuse me," I said, "but why are you so cross with me? What have I done? I must own I have been listening to you for half an hour, and I still don't know what it is all about. . . ."

"What are you offended about, sir?" answered the fat man. "There is no need for you to take offence! I am speaking to you for your good. You mustn't mind my being such a grumbler and shouting at my servant just now. Though he is the most natural rascal, my Grishka, I like him for it, the scoundrel. A feeling heart has been the ruin of me—I tell you frankly; and Foma is to blame for it all. He'll be the ruin of me, I'll take my oath of that. Here, thanks to him, I have been baking in the sun for two hours. I should have liked to have gone to the priest's while these fools were dawdling about over their job. The priest here is a very nice fellow. But he has so upset me, Foma has, that it has even put me off seeing the priest. What a set they all are! There isn't a decent tavern here. I tell you they are all scoundrels, every one of them. And it would be a different thing if he were some great man in the service," Bahtcheyev went on, going back again to Foma Fomitch, whom he seemed unable to shake off, "it would be pardonable perhaps for a man of rank; but as it is he has no rank at all; I know for a fact that he hasn't. He says he has suffered in the cause of justice in the year forty something that never was, so we have to bow down to him for that! If the least thing is not to his liking—up he jumps and begins squealing: 'They are insulting me, they are insulting my poverty, they have no respect for me.' You daren't sit down to table without Foma, and yet he keeps them waiting. 'I have been slighted,' he'd say; 'I am a poor wanderer, black bread is good enough for me.' As soon as they sit down he turns up, our fiddle strikes up again, 'Why did you sit down to table without me? So no respect is shown me in anything.' In fact, your soul is not your own. I held my peace for a long time, sir, he imagined that I was going to fawn upon him, like a lapdog on its hind legs begging; 'Here, boy, here's a bit, eat it up.' No, my lad, you run in the shafts, while I sit in the cart. I served in the same regiment with Yegor Ilyitch, you know; I took my discharge with the rank of a Junker, while he came to his estate last year, a retired colonel. I said to him, '*Aïe*, you will be your own undoing, don't be too soft with Foma! You'll regret it.' 'No,' he would say, 'he is a most excellent person' (meaning Foma), 'he is a friend to me; he is teaching me a higher standard of life.' Well, thought I, there is no fighting against a higher standard; if he has set out to teach a higher standard of life, then it is all up. What do you suppose he made a to-do about to-day? To-morrow is the day of Elijah the Prophet" (Mr. Bahtcheyev crossed himself), "the patron saint of your uncle's son Ilyusha. I was thinking to spend the day with them and to dine there, and had ordered a plaything from Petersburg, a German on springs, kissing the hand of his betrothed, while she wiped away a tear with her handkerchief—a magnificent thing! (I shan't give it now, no thank you; it's lying there in my carriage and the German's nose is smashed off; I am taking it back.) Yegor Ilyitch himself would not have been disinclined to enjoy himself and be festive on such a day, but Foma won't have it. As much as to say: 'Why are you beginning to make such a fuss over Ilyusha? So now you are taking no notice of me.' Eh? What do you say to a goose like that? He is jealous of a boy of eight over his nameday! 'Look here,' he says, 'it is my nameday too.' But you know it will be St. Ilya's, not St. Foma's. 'No,' he says, 'that is my nameday too!' I looked on and put up with it. And what do you think? Now they are walking about on tiptoe, whispering, uncertain what to do—to reckon Ilya's day as the nameday or not, to congratulate him or not. If they don't congratulate him he may be offended, if they do he may take it for scoffing. Tfoo, what a plague! We sat down to dinner. . . . But are you listening, my good sir?"

"Most certainly I am; I am listening with peculiar gratification, in fact, because through you I have now learned . . . and . . . I must say . . ."

"To be sure, with peculiar gratification! I know your peculiar gratification. . . . You are not jeering at me, talking about your gratification?"

"Upon my word, how could I be jeering? On the contrary. And indeed you express yourself with such originality that I am tempted to note down your words."

"What's that, sir, noting down?" asked Mr. Bahtcheyev, looking at me with suspicion and speaking with some alarm.

"Though perhaps I shall not note them down. . . . I didn't mean anything."

"No doubt you are trying to flatter me?"

"Flatter you, what do you mean?" I asked wth surprise.

"Why, yes. Here you are flattering me now; I am telling you everything like a fool, and later on you will go and write a sketch of me somewhere."

I made haste at once to assure Mr. Bahtcheyev that I was not that sort of person, but he still looked at me suspiciously.

"Not that sort of person! Who can tell what you are? Perhaps better still, Foma there threatened to write an account of me and to send it to be published."

"Allow me to ask," I interrupted, partly from a desire to change the conversation. "Is it true that my uncle wants to get married?"

"What if he does? That would not matter. Get married if you have a mind to, that's no harm; but something else is. . . ." added Mr. Bahtcheyev meditatively. "H'm! that question, my good sir, I cannot answer fully. There are a lot of females mixed up in the business now, like flies in jam; and you know there is no making out which wants to be married. And as a friend I don't mind telling you, sir, I don't like woman! It's only talk that she is a human being, but in reality she is simply a disgrace and a danger to the soul's salvation. But that your uncle is in love like a Siberian cat, that I can tell you for a fact. I'll say no more about that now, sir, you will see for yourself; but what's bad is that the business drags on. If you are going to get married, get married; but he is afraid to tell Foma and afraid to tell the old lady, she will be squealing all over the place and begin kicking up a rumpus. She takes Foma's part: 'Foma Fomitch will be hurt,' she'd say, 'if a new mistress comes into the house, for then he won't be able to stay two hours in it.' The bride will chuck him out by the scruff of his neck, if she is not a fool, and in one way or another will make such an upset that he won't be able to find a place anywhere in the neighbourhood. So now he is at his pranks, and he and the mamma are trying to foist a queer sort of bride on him. . . . But why did you interrupt me, sir? I wanted to tell you what was most important, and you interrupted me! I am older than you are, and it is not the right thing to interrupt an old man."

I apologized.

"You needn't apologize! I wanted to put before you as a learned man, how he insulted me to-day. Come, tell me what you think of it, if you are a good-hearted man. We sat down to dinner; well, he fairly bit my head off at dinner, I can tell you! I saw from the very beginning; he sat there as cross as two sticks, as though nothing were to his liking. He'd have been glad to drown me in a spoonful of water, the viper! He is a man of such vanity that his skin's not big enough for him. So he took it into his head to pick a quarrel with me, to teach me a higher standard. Asked me to tell him why I was so fat! The man kept pestering me, why was I fat and not thin? What do you think of that question? Tell me, my good sir. Do you see anything witty in it? I answered him very reasonably: 'That's as God has ordained, Foma Fomitch. One man's fat and one man's thin; and no mortal can go against the decrees of Divine Providence.' That was sensible, wasn't it? What do you say? 'No,' said he; 'you have five hundred serfs, you live at your ease and do nothing for your country; you ought to be in the service, but you sit at home and play your concertina'—and it is true when I am depressed I am fond of playing on the concertina. I answered very reasonably again: 'How should I go into the service, Foma Fomitch? What uniform could I pinch my corpulence into? If I pinched myself in and put on a uniform, and sneezed unwarily—all the buttons would fly off, and what's more, maybe before my superiors, and, God forbid! they might take it for a practical joke, and what then?' Well, tell me, what was there funny in that? But there, there was such a roar at my expense, such a ha-ha-ha and he-he-he. . . . The fact is he has no sense of decency, I tell you, and he even thought fit to slander me in the French dialect: '*cochon*,' he called me. Well, I know what *cochon* means. 'Ah, you damned philosopher,' I thought. 'Do you suppose I'm going to give in to you?' I bore it as long as I could, but I couldn't stand it. I got up from the table, and before all the honourable company I blurted out in his face: 'I have done you an injustice, Foma Fomitch, my kind benefactor.' I said, 'I thought that you were a well-bred man, and you turn out to be just as great a hog as any one of us.' I said that and I left the table, left the pudding—they were just handing the pudding round. 'Bother you and your pudding!' I thought. . . ."

"Excuse me," I said, listening to Mr. Bahtcheyev's whole story; "I am ready, of course, to agree with you completely. The point is, that so far I know nothing positive. . . . But I have got ideas of my own on the subject, you see."

"What ideas, my good sir?" Mr. Bahtcheyev asked mistrustfully.

"You see," I began, hesitating a little, "it is perhaps not the moment, but I am ready to tell it. This is what I think: perhaps we are both mistaken about Foma Fomitch, perhaps under these oddities lies hidden a peculiar, perhaps a gifted nature, who knows? Perhaps it is a nature that has been wounded, crushed by sufferings, avenging itself, so to speak, on all humanity. I have heard that in the past he was something like a buffoon; perhaps that humiliated him,

mortified him, overwhelmed him. . . . Do you understand:
a man of noble nature . . . perception . . . and to play the
part of a buffoon! . . . And so he has become mistrustful
of all mankind and . . . and perhaps if he could be reconciled to humanity . . . that is, to his fellows, perhaps he
would turn out a rare nature, perhaps even a very remarkable one and . . . and . . . you know there must be something in the man. There is a reason, of course, for every
one doing homage to him."

I was conscious myself that I was maundering horribly.
I might have been forgiven in consideration of my youth.
But Mr. Bahtcheyev did not forgive me. He looked gravely
and sternly into my face and suddenly turned crimson as a
turkey cock.

"Do you mean that Foma's a remarkable man?" he
asked abruptly.

"Listen, I scarcely myself believe a word of what I said
just now. It was merely by way of a guess. . . ."

"Allow me, sir, to be so inquisitive as to ask: have you
studied philosophy?"

"In what sense?" I asked in perplexity.

"No, in no particular sense; you answer me straight out,
apart from any sense, sir: have you studied philosophy or
not?"

"I must own I am intending to study it, but . . ."

"There it is!" shouted Mr. Bahtcheyev, giving full rein
to his indignation. "Before you opened your mouth, sir, I
guessed that you were a philosopher! There is no deceiving
me! No, thank you! I can scent out a philosopher two
miles off! You can go and kiss your Foma Fomitch. A remarkable man, indeed! Tfoo! confound it all! I thought you
were a man of good intentions too, while you . . . Here!" he
shouted to the coachman, who had already clambered on
the box of the carriage which by now had been put in
order. "Home!"

With difficulty I succeeded somehow in soothing him;
somehow or other he was mollified at last; but it was a long
time before he could bring himself to lay aside his wrath

and look on me with favour. Meantime he got into the carriage, assisted by Grishka and Arhip, the man who had reproved Vassilyev.

"Allow me to ask you," I said, going up to the carriage. "Are you never coming again to my uncle's?"

"To your uncle's? Curse the fellow who has told you that! Do you think that I am a consistent man, that I shall keep it up? That's just my trouble, that I am not a man, but a rag. Before a week's past, I shall fly round there again. And why? There it is, I don't know myself why, but I shall go; I shall fight with Foma again. That's just my trouble, sir! The Lord has sent that Foma to chastise me for my sins. I have as much will as an old woman, there is no consistency in me, I am a first-class coward, my good sir. . . ."

We parted friends, however; he even invited me to dine with him.

"You come, sir, you come, we will dine together; I have got some vodka brought on foot from Kiev, and my cook has been in Paris. He serves such fricassees, he makes such pasties, that you can only lick your fingers and bow down to him, the rascal. A man of culture! Only it is a long time since I thrashed him, he is getting spoilt with me. . . . It is a good thing you reminded me. . . . Do come. I'd invite you to come to-day, only somehow I am out of sorts, down in the mouth—in fact, quite knocked up. I am a sick man, you know, a poor creature. Maybe you won't believe it. . . . Well, good-bye, sir, it is time for me to set sail. And your little trap yonder is ready. And tell Foma he had better not come across me; I should give him such a sentimental greeting that he . . ."

But his last words were out of hearing; the carriage, drawn by four strong horses, vanished in clouds of dust. My chaise too was ready; I got into it and we at once drove through the little town. "Of course this gentleman is exaggerating," I thought; "he is too angry and cannot be impartial. But, again, all that he said about uncle was very remarkable. So that makes two people in the same story, that uncle is in love with that young lady. . . . H'm! Shall I get married or not?" This time I meditated in earnest.

My Uncle

III

I must own I was actually a little daunted. My romantic dreams suddenly seemed to me extremely queer, even rather stupid, as soon as I reached Stepantchikovo. That was about five o'clock in the afternoon. The road ran by the manor house. I saw again after long absence the immense garden in which some happy days of my childhood had been passed, and which I had often seen afterwards in my dreams, in the dormitories of the various schools which undertook my education. I jumped out of the carriage and walked across the garden to the house. I very much wanted to arrive unannounced, to inquire for my uncle, to fetch him out and to talk to him first of all. And so I did. Passing down the avenue of lime-trees hundreds of years old, I went up on to the verandah, from which one passed by a glass door into the inner rooms. The verandah was surrounded by flower-beds and adorned with pots of expensive flowers. Here I met one of the natives, old Gavrila, who had at one time looked after me and was now the honoured valet of my uncle. The old fellow was wearing spectacles, and was holding in his hand a manuscript book which he was reading with great attention. I had seen him three years before in Petersburg, where he had come with my uncle, and so he recognized me at once. With exclamations of joy he fell to kissing my hand, and as he did so the spectacles fell off his nose on to the floor. Such devotion on the part of the old man touched me very much. But disturbed by my recent conversation with Mr. Bahtcheyev, I looked first at the suspicious manuscript book which had been in Gavrila's hands.

"What's this, Gavrila? Surely they have not begun teaching you French too?" I asked the old man.

"They are teaching me in my old age, like a starling, sir," Gavrila answered mournfully.

"Does Foma himself teach you?"

"Yes, sir; a very clever man he must be."

"Not a doubt that he is clever! Does he teach you by conversations?"

"By a copy book, sir."

"Is that what you have in your hands? Ah! French words in Russian letters, a sharp dodge! You give in to such a blockhead, such an arrant fool, aren't you ashamed, Gavrila?" I cried, instantly forgetting my lofty theories about Foma Fomitch for which I had caught it so hotly from Mr. Bahtcheyev.

"How can he be a fool, sir," answered the old man, "if he manages our betters as he does?"

"H'm, perhaps you are right, Gavrila," I muttered, pulled up by this remark. "Take me to my uncle."

"My falcon! But I can't show myself, I dare not, I have begun to be afraid even of him. I sit here in my misery and step behind the flower-beds when he is pleased to come out."

"But why are you afraid?"

"I didn't know my lesson this morning. Foma Fomitch made me go down on my knees, but I didn't stay on my knees. I am too old, Sergey Alexandrovitch, for them to play such tricks with me. The master was pleased to be vexed at my disobeying Foma Fomitch, 'he takes trouble about your education, old grey-beard,' said he; 'he wants to teach you the pronunciation.' So here I am walking to and fro repeating the vocabulary. Foma Fomitch promised to examine me again this evening."

It seemed to me that there was something obscure about this.

"There must be something connected with French," I thought, "which the old man cannot explain."

"One question, Gavrila: what sort of man is he? Good-looking, tall?"

"Foma Fomitch? No, sir, he's an ugly little scrub of a man."

"H'm! Wait a bit, Gavrila, perhaps it can be all set right; in fact, I can promise you it certainly will be set right. But . . . where is my uncle?"

"He is behind the stables seeing some peasants. The old men have come from Kapitonovko to pay their respects to him. They had heard that they were being made over to Foma Fomitch. They want to beg not to be."

"But why behind the stables?"

"They are frightened, sir. . . ."

I did, in fact, find my uncle behind the stables. There he was, standing before a group of peasants who were bowing down to the ground and earnestly entreating him. Uncle was explaining something to them with warmth. I went up and called to him. He turned round and we rushed into each other's arms.

He was extremely glad to see me; his delight was almost ecstatic. He hugged me, pressed my hands, as though his own son had returned to him after escaping some mortal danger, as though by my arrival I had rescued him from some mortal danger and brought with me the solution of all his perplexities, as well as joy and lifelong happiness for him and all whom he loved. Uncle would not have consented to be happy alone. After the first outburst of delight, he got into such a fuss that at last he was quite flustered and bewildered. He showered questions upon me, wanted to take me at once to see his family. We were just going, but my uncle turned back, wishing to present me first to the peasants of Kapitonovko. Then, I remember, he suddenly began talking, apropos of I don't know what, of some Mr. Korovkin, a remarkable man whom he had met three days before, on the high road, and whom he was very impatiently expecting to pay him a visit. Then he dropped Mr. Korovkin too and spoke of something else. I looked at him with enjoyment. Answering his hurried questions, I told him that I did not want to go into the service, but to continue my studies. As soon as the subject of study was broached, my uncle at once knitted his brows and assumed an extraordinarily solemn air. Learning that of late I had been engaged on mineralogy, he raised his head and looked about him proudly, as though he had himself, alone and unaided, discovered the whole of that science and written all that was published about it. I have mentioned already that he cherished the most disinterested reverence for the word "science," the more disinterested that he himself had no scientific knowledge whatever.

"Ah, my boy, there are people in the world who know everything," he said to me once, his eyes sparkling with enthusiasm. "One sits among them, listens, and one knows one understands nothing of it all, and yet one loves it. And why? Because it is in the cause of reform, of enlightenment, of the general welfare! That I do understand. Here I now travel by train, and my Ilyusha, perhaps, may fly through the air. . . . And then trade, manufactures—those channels, so to say . . . that is, I mean, turn it which way you will, it's of service. . . . It is of service, isn't it?"

But to return to our meeting.

"But wait a bit, wait a bit, my dear," he began speaking rapidly and rubbing his hands, "you will see a man! A rare man, I tell you, a learned man, a man of science; 'he will survive his century.' It's a good saying, isn't it, 'will survive his century'? Foma explained it to me. . . . Wait a little, I will introduce you to him."

"Are you speaking of Foma Fomitch, uncle?"

"No, no, my dear, I was speaking of Korovkin, though Foma too, he too . . . but I am simply talking of Korovkin just now," he added, for some unknown reason turning crimson, and seeming embarrassed as soon as Foma's name was mentioned.

"What sciences is he studying, uncle?"

"Science, my boy, science, science in general. I can't tell you which exactly, I only know that it is science. How he speaks about railways! And you know," my uncle added in a half-whisper, screwing up his right eye significantly, "just a little of the free-thinker. I noticed it, especially when he was speaking of marriage and the family . . . it's a pity I did not understand much of it myself (there was no time), I would have told you all about it in detail. And he is a man of the noblest qualities, too! I have invited him to visit me, I am expecting him from hour to hour."

Meanwhile the peasants were gazing at me with round eyes and open mouths as though at some marvel.

"Listen, uncle," I interrupted him; "I believe I am hindering the peasants. No doubt they have come about something urgent. What do they want? I must own I suspect something, and I should be very glad to hear . . ."

Uncle suddenly seemed nervous and flustered.

"Oh, yes! I had forgotten. Here, you see . . . what is one to do with them? They have got a notion—and I should very much like to know who first started it—they have got a notion, that I am giving them away together with the whole of Kapitonovko—do you remember Kapitonovko? We used to drive out there in the evenings with dear Katya —the whole of Kapitonovko with the sixty-eight souls in it to Foma Fomitch. 'We don't want to leave you,' they say, and that is all about it."

"So it is not true, uncle, you are not giving him Kapitonovko," I cried, almost rapturously.

"I never thought of it, it never entered my head! And from whom did you hear it? Once one drops a word, it is all over the place. And why do they so dislike Foma? Wait a little, Sergey, I will introduce you to him," he added, glancing at me timidly, as though he were aware in me, too, of hostility towards Foma Fomitch. "He is a wonderful man, my boy."

"We want no one but you, no one!" the peasants suddenly wailed in chorus. "You are our father, we are your children!"

"Listen, uncle," I said. "I have not seen Foma Fomitch yet, but . . . you see . . . I have heard something. I must confess that I met Mr. Bahtcheyev to-day. However, I have my own idea on that subject. Anyway, uncle, finish with the peasants and let them go, and let us talk by ourselves without witnesses. I must own, that's what I have come for. . . ."

"To be sure, to be sure," my uncle assented; "to be sure.

We'll dismiss the peasants and then we can have a talk, you know, a friendly, affectionate, thorough talk. Come," he went on, speaking rapidly and addressing the peasants, "you can go now, my friends. And for the future come to me whenever there is need; straight to me, and come at any time."

"You are our father, we are your children! Do not give us to Foma Fomitch for our undoing! All we, poor people, are beseeching you!" the peasants shouted once more.

"See what fools! But I am not giving you away, I tell you."

"Or he'll never leave off teaching us, your honour. He does nothing but teach the fellows here, so they say."

"Why, you don't mean to say he is teaching you French?" I cried, almost in alarm.

"No, sir, so far God has had mercy on us!" answered one of the peasants, probably a great talker, a red-haired man with a huge bald patch on the back of his head, with a long, scanty, wedge-shaped beard, which moved as he talked as though it were a separate individual. "No, sir, so far God has had mercy on us."

"But what does he teach you?"

"Well, your honour, what he teaches us, in a manner of speaking, is buying a gold casket to keep a brass farthing in."

"How do you mean, a brass farthing?"

"Seryozha, you are mistaken, it's a slander!" cried my uncle, turning crimson and looking terribly embarrassed. "The fools have misunderstood what was said to them. He merely . . . there was nothing about a brass farthing. There is no need for you to understand everything, and shout at the top of your voice," my uncle continued, addressing the peasant reproachfully. "One wants to do you good and you don't understand, and make an uproar!"

"Upon my word, uncle, teaching them French?"

"That's for the sake of pronunciation, Seryozha, simply for the pronunciation," said my uncle in an imploring voice. "He said himself that it was for the sake of the pronunciation. . . . Besides, something special happened in connection with this, which you know nothing about and so you cannot judge. You must investigate first and then blame. . . . It is easy to find fault!"

"But what are you about?" I shouted, turning impetuously to the peasants again. "You ought to speak straight out. You should say, 'This won't do, Foma Fomitch, this is how it ought to be!' You have got a tongue, haven't you?"

"Where is the mouse who will bell the cat, your honour? 'I am teaching you, clodhoppers, cleanliness and order,' he says. 'Why is your shirt not clean?' Why, one is always in a sweat, that's why it isn't clean! One can't change every day. Cleanliness won't save you and dirt won't kill you."

"And look here, the other day he came to the threshing floor," began another peasant, a tall, lean fellow all in patches and wearing wretched bark shoes, apparently one of those men who are always discontented about something and always have some vicious venomous word ready in reserve. Till then he had been hidden behind the backs of the other peasants, had been listening in gloomy silence, and had kept all the time on his face an ambiguous, bitterly subtle smile. "He came to the threshing floor. 'Do you know,' he said, 'how many miles it is to the sun?' 'Why, who can tell? Such learning is not for us but for the gentry.' 'No,' says he; 'you are a fool, a lout, you don't understand what is good for you; but I,' said he, 'am an astronomer! I know all God's planets.'"

"Well, and did he tell you how many miles it is to the sun?" my uncle put in, suddenly reviving and winking gaily to me, as though to say, "See what's coming!"

"Yes, he did tell us how many," the peasant answered reluctantly, not expecting such a question.

"Well, how many did he say, how many exactly?"

"Your honour must know best, we live in darkness."

"Oh, I know, my boy, but do you remember?"

"Why, he said it would be so many hundreds or thousands, it was a big number, he said. More than you could carry in three cartloads."

"Try and remember, brother! I dare say you thought it would be about a mile, that you could reach up to it with your hand. No, my boy; you see, the earth is like a round ball, do you understand?" my uncle went on, describing a sphere in the air with his hands.

The peasant smiled bitterly.

"Yes, like a ball, it hangs in the air of itself and moves round the sun. And the sun stands still, it only seems to you that it moves. There's a queer thing! And the man who discovered this was Captain Cook, a navigator . . . devil only knows who did discover it," he added in a half-whisper, turning to me. "I know nothing about it myself, my boy. . . . Do you know how far it is to the sun?"

"I do, uncle," I answered, looking with surprise at all this scene. "But this is what I think: of course ignorance means slovenliness; but on the other hand . . . to teach peasants astronomy . . ."

"Just so, just so, slovenliness," my uncle assented, delighted with my expression, which struck him as extremely apt. "A noble thought! Slovenliness precisely! That is what I have always said . . . that is, I never said so, but I felt it. Do you hear?" he cried to the peasants. "Ignorance is as bad as slovenliness, it's as bad as dirt. That's why Foma wanted to teach you. He wanted to teach you something good—that was all right. That's as good as serving one's country—it's as good as an official rank. So you see what science is! Well, that's enough, that's enough, my friends. Go, in God's name; and I am glad, glad. . . . Don't worry yourselves, I won't forsake you."

"Protect us, father!"

"Let us breathe freely!"

And the peasants plumped down at his feet.

"Come, come, that's nonsense. Bow down to God and your Czar, and not to me. . . . Come, go along, behave well, be deserving . . . and all that. You know," he said, turning suddenly to me as soon as the peasants had gone away, and beaming with pleasure, "the peasant loves a kind word, and a little present would do no harm. Shall I give them something, eh? What do you think? In honour of your arrival. . . . Shall I or not?"

"But you are a kind of Frol Silin, uncle, a benevolent person, I see."

"Oh, one can't help it, my boy, one can't help it; that's nothing. I have been meaning to give them a present for a long time," he said, as though excusing himself. "And as for your thinking it funny of me to give the peasants a lesson in science, I simply did that, my boy, in delight at seeing you, Seryozha. I simply wanted the peasants to hear how many miles it was to the sun and gape in wonder. It's amusing to see them gape, my dear. . . . One seems to rejoice over them. Only, my boy, don't speak in the drawing-room of my having had an interview with the peasants, you know. I met them behind the stables on purpose that we should not be seen. It was impossible to have it there, my boy: it is a delicate business, and indeed they came in secret themselves. I did it more for their sake. . . ."

"Well, here I have come, uncle," I began, changing the conversation and anxious to get to the chief point as quickly as possible. "I must own your letter so surprised me that I . . ."

"My dear, not a word of that," my uncle interrupted, as though in alarm, positively dropping his voice. "Afterwards, afterwards, all that shall be explained. I have, perhaps, acted wrongly towards you, very wrongly, perhaps. . . ."

"Acted wrongly towards me, uncle?"

"Afterwards, afterwards, my dear, afterwards! It shall all be explained. But what a fine fellow you have grown! My dear boy! How eager I have been to see you! I wanted to pour out my heart, so to speak . . . you are clever, you are my only hope . . . you and Korovkin. I must mention to you that they are all angry with you here. Mind, be careful, don't be rash."

"Angry with me?" I asked, looking at uncle in wonder, unable to understand how I could have angered people with whom I was as yet unacquainted. "Angry with me?"

"Yes, with you, my boy. It can't be helped! Foma Fomitch is a little . . . and . . . well . . . mother following his example. Be careful, respectful, don't contradict. The great thing is to be respectful. . . ."

"To Foma Fomitch, do you mean, uncle?"

"It can't be helped, my dear; you see, I don't defend him. Certainly he has his faults, perhaps, and especially just now, at this particular moment. . . . Ah, Seryozha dear, how it all worries me. And if only it could be settled comfortably, if only we could all be satisfied and happy! . . . But who has not faults? We are not perfect ourselves, are we?"

"Upon my word, uncle! Consider what he is doing. . . ."

"Oh, my dear! It's all trivial nonsense, nothing more! Here, for instance, let me tell you, he is angry with me, and what for, do you suppose? . . . Though perhaps it's my own fault. . . . I'd better tell you afterwards. . . ."

"But do you know, uncle, I have formed an idea of my own about it," I interrupted, in haste to give expression to my theory. Indeed, we both seemed nervous and hurried. "In the first place, he has been a buffoon; that has mortified him, rankled, outraged his ideal; and that has made his character embittered, morbid, resentful, so to say, against all humanity. . . . But if one could reconcile him with mankind, if one could bring him back to himself . . ."

"Just so, just so," cried my uncle, delighted; "that's just it. A generous idea! And in fact it would be shameful, ungenerous of us to blame him! Just so! . . . Oh, my dear, you understand me; you have brought me comfort! If only things could be set straight, somehow! Do you know, I am afraid to show myself. Here you have come, and I shall certainly catch it from them!"

"Uncle, if that's how it is . . ." I began, disconcerted by this confession.

"No-no-no! For nothing in the world," he cried, clutching my hands. "You are my guest and I wish it!"

"Uncle, tell me at once," I began insistently, "why did you send for me? What do you expect of me, and, above all, in what way have you been to blame towards me?"

"My dear, don't ask. Afterwards, afterwards; all that shall be explained afterwards. I have been very much to blame, perhaps, but I wanted to act like an honest man, and . . . and . . . you shall marry her! You will marry her, if there is one grain of gentlemanly feeling in you," he added, flushing all over with some sudden feeling and warmly and enthusiastically pressing my hand. "But enough, not another word, you will soon see for yourself. It will depend on you. . . . The great thing is that you should be liked, that you should make a good impression. Above all —don't be nervous."

"Come, listen, uncle. Whom have you got there? I must own I have been so little in society, that . . ."

"That you are rather frightened," put in my uncle, smiling. "Oh, that's no matter. Cheer up, they are all our own people! The great thing is to be bold and not afraid. I keep feeling anxious about you. Whom have we got there, you ask? Yes, who is there? . . . In the first place, my mother," he began hurriedly. "Do you remember mamma or not? The most kind-hearted, generous woman, no airs about her— that one can say; a little of the old school, perhaps, but that's all to the good. To be sure she sometimes takes fancies into her head, you know, will say one thing and another; she is vexed with me now, but it is my own fault, I know it is my own fault. And the fact is—you know she is what is called a *grande dame*, a general's lady . . . her husband was a most excellent man. To begin with, he was a general, a most cultivated man; he left no property, but he was covered with wounds—he was deserving of respect, in fact. Then there's Miss Perepelitsyn; well, she . . . I don't know . . . of late she has been rather . . . her character is so . . . but one mustn't find fault with every one. There, never mind her . . . you mustn't imagine she is in a menial position, she's a major's daughter herself, my boy, she is mother's confidante and favourite, my dear! Then there is my sister Praskovya Ilyinitchna. Well, there is no need to say much about her, she is simple and good-natured, a bit fussy, but what a heart! The heart is the great thing. Though she is middle-aged, yet, do you know, I really believe that queer fellow Bahtcheyev is making up to her. He wants to make a match of it. But, mind you don't say a word, it is a secret! Well, and who else is there? I won't tell you about the children, you will see for yourself. It's Ilyusha's nameday to-morrow. . . . Why there, I was almost forgetting, we have had staying with us for the last month Ivan Ivanitch Mizintchikov, your second cousin, I believe; yes, of course, he is your second cousin! He has lately given up his commission; he was a lieutenant in the Hussars; still a young man. A noble soul! But, you know, he has got through his money. I really can't think how he managed to get rid of it. Though indeed he had next to nothing, but anyway he got through it and ran into debt. . . . Now he is staying with me. I didn't know him at all till lately; he came and introduced himself. He is a dear fellow, good-humoured, quiet and respectful. No one gets a word out of him. He is always silent. Foma calls him in jest the 'silent stranger'— he doesn't mind; he isn't vexed. Foma's satisfied, he says Ivan's not very bright. And Ivan never contradicts him, but always falls in with everything he says. H'm! he seems so crushed . . . but there, God bless him, you will see for yourself. There are guests from the town, Pavel Semyonitch Obnoskin and his mother; he's young but a man of superior mind, something mature, steadfast, you know . . . only I don't know how to express it; and what's more, of the highest principles; strict morals. And lastly there is staying with us, you know, a lady called Tatyana Ivanovna; she, too, may be a distant relation. You don't know her. She is not quite young, that one must own, but . . . she is not without attractions: she is rich enough to buy Stepantchikovo twice over, she has only lately come into her money, and has had a wretched time of it till now. Please, Seryozha, my boy, be careful; she is such a nervous invalid . . . something phantasmagorial in her character, you know. Well, you are a gentleman, you will understand; she has had troubles, you know, one has to be doubly careful with a person who has had troubles! But you mustn't imagine anything, you know. Of course she has her weaknesses; sometimes she is in such a hurry, she speaks so fast, that she says the wrong thing. Not that she lies, don't imagine that . . . it all comes, my boy, from a pure and noble heart, so to say. I mean, even if she does say something false, it's simply from excess of noble-heartedness, so to say—do you understand?"

I fancied that my uncle was horribly confused.

"Listen, uncle," I began, "I am so fond of you . . . forgive the direct question: are you going to marry some one here or not?"

"Why, from whom did you hear that?" he answered, blushing like a child. "You see, my dear . . . I'll tell you all about it; in the first place, I am not going to get married. Mamma, my sister to some extent, and most of all Foma Fomitch, whom mamma worships—and with good reason, he has done a great deal for her—they all want me to marry that same Tatyana Ivanovna, as a sensible step for the benefit of all. Of course they desire nothing but my good— I understand that, of course; but nothing will induce me to marry—I have made up my mind about that. In spite of that I have not succeeded in giving them a decided answer, I have not said yes, or no. It always happens like that with me, my boy. They thought that I had consented and are insisting that to-morrow, in honour of the festive occasion, I should declare myself . . . and so there is such a flutter in preparation for to-morrow that I really don't know what line to take! And besides, Foma Fomitch, I don't know why, is vexed with me, and mamma is too. I must say, my boy, I have simply been reckoning on you and on Korovkin. . . . I wanted to pour out my troubles, so to say. . . ."

"But how can Korovkin be of any use in this matter, uncle?"

"He will help, he will help, my dear—he is a wonderful man; in short, a man of learning! I build upon him as on a rock; a man who would conquer anything! How he speaks of domestic happiness! I must own I have been reckoning on you too; I thought you might bring them to reason. Consider and judge . . . granted that I have been to blame, really to blame—I understand all that—I am not without feeling. But all the same I might be forgiven some day! Then how well we should get on together! Oh, my boy, how my Sashenka has grown up, she'll be thinking of getting married directly! What a fine boy my Ilyusha has become! To-morrow is his nameday. But I am afraid for my Sashenka— that's the trouble."

"Uncle! Where is my portmanteau? I will change my things and make my appearance in a minute, and then . . ."

"In the upper room, my boy, in the upper room. I gave orders beforehand that as soon as you arrived you should be taken straight up there, so that no one should see you. Yes, yes, change your things! That's capital, capital, first rate. And meanwhile I will prepare them all a little. Well, good luck to us! You know, my boy, we must be diplomatic. One is forced to become a Talleyrand. But there, never mind. They are drinking tea there now. We have tea early. Foma Fomitch likes to have his tea as soon as he wakes up; it is better, you know. Well, I'll go in, then, and you make haste and follow me, don't leave me alone; it will be awkward for me, my boy, alone. . . . But, stay! I have another favour to ask of you: don't cry out at me in there as you did out here just now—will you? If you want to make some criticism you can make it afterwards here when we are alone; till then hold yourself in and wait! You see, I have put my foot in it already with them. They are annoyed with me. . . ."

"I say, uncle, from all that I have seen and heard it seems to me that you . . ."

"That I am as soft as butter, eh? Don't mind speaking out!" he interrupted me quite unexpectedly. "There is no help for it, my boy. I know it myself. Well, so you will come? Come as quick as you can, please!"

Going upstairs, I hurriedly opened my portmanteau, remembering my uncle's instructions to come down as soon as possible. As I was dressing, I realized that I had so far learned scarcely anything I wanted to know, though I had been talking to my uncle for a full hour. That struck me. Only one thing was pretty clear to me: my uncle was still set upon my getting married; consequently, all rumours to the opposite, that is, that my uncle was in love with the same lady himself, were wide of the mark. I remember that I was much agitated. Among other things the thought occurred to me that by my coming, and by my silence, I had almost made a promise, given my word, bound myself for ever. "It is easy," I thought, "it is easy to say a word which

will bind one, hand and foot, for ever. And I have not yet
seen my proposed bride!" And again: why this antagonism
towards me on the part of the whole family? Why were
they bound to take a hostile attitude to my coming, as my
uncle said they did? And what a strange part my uncle was
playing here in his own house? What was the cause of his
secretiveness? Why these worries and alarms? I must own
that it all struck me suddenly as something quite senseless;
and my romantic and heroic dreams took flight completely
at the first contact with reality. Only now after my conversation with my uncle, I suddenly realized all the incongruity
and eccentricity of his proposition, and felt that no one but
my uncle would have been capable of making such a proposal and in such circumstances. I realized, too, that I was
something not unlike a fool for galloping here full speed at
his first word, in high delight at his suggestion. I was dressing hurriedly, absorbed in my agitating doubts, so that I did
not at first notice the man who was waiting on me.

"Will your honour wear the Adelaïda coloured tie or the
one with the little checks on it?" the man asked suddenly,
addressing me with exceptionally mawkish obsequiousness.

I glanced at him, and it seemed to me that he, too, was
worthy of attention. He was a man still young, for a flunkey
well dressed, quite as well as many a provincial dandy. The
brown coat, the white breeches, the straw-coloured waistcoat, the patent-leather boots and the pink tie had evidently
been selected with intention. All this was bound at once to
attract attention to the young dandy's refined taste. The
watch-chain was undoubtedly displayed with the same object. He was pale, even greenish in face, and had a long
hooked nose, thin and remarkably white, as though it were
made of china. The smile on his thin lips expressed melancholy, a refined melancholy, however. His large prominent
eyes, which looked as though made of glass, had an extraordinarily stupid expression, and yet there was a gleam of refinement in them. His thin soft ears were stuffed up with
cotton wool—also a refinement. His long, scanty, flaxen hair
was curled and pomaded. His hands were white, clean, and
might have been washed in rosewater; his fingers ended in

extremely long dandified pink nails. All this indicated a
spoilt and idle fop. He lisped and mispronounced the letter
"r" in fashionable style, raised and dropped his eyes, sighed
and gave himself incredibly affected airs. He smelt of scent.
He was short, feeble and flabby-looking, and moved about
with knees and haunches bent, probably thinking this the
height of refinement—in fact, he was saturated with refinement, subtlety and an extraordinary sense of his own dignity. This last characteristic displeased me, I don't know
why, and moved me to wrath.

"So that tie is Adelaïda colour?" I asked, looking severely at the young valet.

"Yes, Adelaïda," he answered, with undisturbed refinement.

"And is there an Agrafena colour?"

"No, sir, there cannot be such a colour."

"Why not?"

"Agrafena is not a polite name, sir."

"Not polite! Why not?"

"Why, Adelaïda, we all know, is a foreign name anyway,
a ladylike name, but any low peasant woman can be called
Agrafena."

"Are you out of your mind?"

"No, sir, I am in my right mind, sir. Of course you are
free to call me any sort of name, but many generals and
even some counts in Moscow and Petersburg have been
pleased with my conversation, sir."

"And what's your name?"

"Vidoplyasov."

"Ah, so you are Vidoplyasov?"

"Just so, sir."

"Well, wait a bit, my lad, and I will make your acquaintance."

"It is something like Bedlam here," I thought to myself
as I went downstairs.

At Tea

IV

Tea was being served in the room that gave on to the verandah where I had that afternoon met Gavrila. I was much perturbed by my uncle's mysterious warnings in regard to the reception awaiting me. Youth is sometimes excessively vain, and youthful vanity is almost always cowardly. And so it was extremely unpleasant for me when immediately going in at the door and seeing the whole party round the tea-table, I stumbled over a rug, staggered, and recovering my balance, flew unexpectedly into the middle of the room. As overwhelmed with confusion as though I had at one stroke lost my career, my honour and my good name, I stood without moving, turning as red as a crab and looking with a senseless stare at the company. I mention this incident, in itself so trivial, only because of the effect it had on my state of mind during the whole of that day, and consequently my attitude to some of the personages of my story. I tried to bow, did not fully succeed, turned redder than ever, flew up to my uncle and clutched at his hand.

"How do you do, uncle?" I gasped out breathlessly, intending to say something quite different and much cleverer, but to my own surprise I said nothing but "How do you do?"

"Glad to see you, glad to see you, my boy," answered my uncle, distressed on my account. "You know, we have met already. Don't be nervous, please," he added in a whisper, "it's a thing that may happen to any one, and worse still, one sometimes falls flat! . . . And now, mother, let me introduce to you: this is our young man; he is a little overcome at the moment, but I am sure you will like him. My nephew, Sergey Alexandrovitch," he added, addressing the company.

But before going on with my story, allow me, gentle reader, to introduce to you by name the company in which I suddenly found myself. This is essential to the orderly sequence of my narrative.

The party consisted of several ladies and two men besides my uncle and me. Foma Fomitch, whom I was so eager to see, and who—even then I felt it—was absolute monarch in the house, was not there; he was conspicuous by his absence, and seemed to have taken with him all brightness from the room. They all looked gloomy and worried. One could not help noticing it from the first glance; embarrassed and upset as I was at the moment, I yet discerned that my uncle, for instance, was almost as upset as I was, though he was doing his utmost to conceal his anxiety under a show of ease. Something was lying like a heavy weight on his heart. One of the two gentlemen in the room was a young man about five-and-twenty, who turned out to be the Obnoskin my uncle had spoken of that afternoon, praising his intelligence and high principles. I did not take to this gentleman at all, everything about him savoured of vulgar *chic;* his dress, in spite of its *chic,* was shabby and common; his face looked, somehow, shabby too. His thin flaxen moustaches like a beetle's whiskers, and his unsuccessful wisps of beard, were evidently intended to show that he was a man of independent character and perhaps advanced ideas. He was continually screwing up his eyes, smiling with an affectation of malice; he threw himself into attitudes on his chair, and repeatedly stared at me through his eyeglass; but when I turned to him, he immediately dropped his eyeglass and seemed overcome with alarm. The other gentleman was young too, being about twenty-eight. He was my cousin, Mizintchikov. He certainly was extremely silent. He did not utter a single word at tea, and did not laugh when every one else laughed; but I saw in him no sign of that "crushed" condition my uncle had detected; on the contrary, the look in his light brown eyes expressed resoluteness and a certain decision of character. Mizintchikov was dark and rather good-looking, with black hair; he was very correctly dressed—at my uncle's expense, as I learned

later. Of the ladies the one I noticed first of all from her
spiteful anaemic face was Miss Perepelitsyn. She was sitting near Madame la Générale—of whom I will give a special account later—not beside her, but deferentially a little
behind; she was continually bending down and whispering
something into the ear of her patroness. Two or three elderly lady companions were sitting absolutely mute in a row
by the window, gazing open-eyed at Madame la Générale
and waiting respectfully for their tea. My attention was attracted also by a fat, absolutely redundant lady, of about
fifty, dressed very tastelessly and gaudily, wearing rouge,
I believe, though she had hardly any teeth except blackened and broken stumps; this fact did not, however, prevent
her from mincing, screwing up her eyes, dressing in the
height of fashion and almost making eyes. She was hung
round with chains, and like Monsieur Obnoskin was continually turning her lorgnette on me. This was his mother.
Praskovya Ilyinitchna, my meek aunt, was pouring out the
tea. She obviously would have liked to embrace me after
our long separation, and of course to have shed a few tears
on the occasion, but she did not dare. Everything here was,
it seemed, under rigorous control. Near her was sitting a
very pretty black-eyed girl of fifteen, who looked at me
intently with childish curiosity—my cousin Sashenka.
Finally, and perhaps most conspicuous of all, was a very
strange lady, dressed richly and extremely youthfully,
though she was far from being in her first youth and must
have been at least five-and-thirty. Her face was very thin,
pale, and withered, but extremely animated; a bright colour
was constantly appearing in her pale cheeks, almost at every
movement, at every flicker of feeling; she was in continual
excitement, twisting and turning in her chair, and seemed
unable to sit still for a minute. She kept looking at me with
a kind of greedy curiosity, and was continually bending
down to whisper something into the ear of Sashenka, or of
her neighbour on the other side, and immediately afterwards laughing in the most childish and simple-hearted way.
But to my surprise her eccentricities seemed to pass unnoticed by the others, as though they had all agreed to pay

no attention to them. I guessed that this was Tatyana Ivanovna, the lady in whom, to use my uncle's expression, "there was something phantasmagorial," whom they were trying to force upon him as a bride, and whose favour almost every one in the house was trying to court for the sake of her money. But I liked her eyes, blue and mild; and though there were already crow's-feet round the eyes, their expression was so simple-hearted, so merry and good-humoured, that it was particularly pleasant to meet them. Of Tatyana Ivanovna, one of the real "heroines" of my story, I shall speak more in detail later; her history was very remarkable. Five minutes after my entrance, a very pretty boy, my cousin Ilyusha, ran in from the garden, with his pockets full of knuckle-bones and a top in his hand. He was followed by a graceful young girl, rather pale and weary-looking, but very pretty. She scanned the company with a searching, mistrustful, and even timid glance, looking intently at me, and sat down by Tatyana Ivanovna. I remember that I could not suppress a throb at my heart; I guessed that this was the governess. . . . I remember, too, that on her entrance my uncle stole a swift glance at me and flushed crimson, then he bent down, caught up Ilyusha in his arms, and brought him up to me to be kissed. I noticed, too, that Madame Obnoskin first stared at my uncle and then with a sarcastic smile turned her lorgnette on the governess. My uncle was very much confused, and not knowing what to do, was on the point of calling to Sashenka to introduce her to me; but the girl merely rose from her seat and in silence, with grave dignity, dropped me a curtsey. I liked her doing this, however, for it suited her. At the same instant my kindly aunt, Praskovya Ilyinitchna, could hold out no longer, and abandoning the tea-tray, dashed up to embrace me; but before I had time to say a couple of words to her I heard the shrill voice of Miss Perepelitsyn hissing out that Praskovya Ilyinitchna seemed to have forgotten Madame la Générale. "That Madame has asked for her tea, and you do not pour it out, and she is waiting." And Praskovya Ilyinitchna, leaving me, flew back in all haste to her duties. Madame la Générale, the most important person of the party, in whose presence all the others were on their best behaviour, was a lean, spiteful old woman, dressed in mourning—spiteful, however, chiefly from old age and from the loss of her mental faculties (which had never been over-brilliant); even in the past, she had been a nonsensical creature. Her rank as a general's wife had made her even stupider and more arrogant. When she was in a bad humour the house became a perfect hell. She had two ways of displaying her ill-humour. The first was a silent method, when the old lady would not open her lips for days together, but maintained an obstinate silence and pushed away or even sometimes flung on the floor everything that was put before her. The other method was the exact opposite—garrulous. This would begin, as a rule, by my grandmother's—for she was my grandmother, of course—being plunged into a state of extreme despondency, and expecting the end of the world and the failure of all her undertakings, foreseeing poverty and every possible trouble in the future, being carried away by her own presentiments, reckoning on her fingers the calamities that were coming, and reaching a climax of enthusiasm and intense excitement over the enumeration. It always appeared, of course, that she had foreseen all this long before, and had said nothing only because she was forced to be silent "in this house." But if only she had been treated with respect, if only they had cared to listen to her earlier, then, etc., etc. In all this, the flock of lady companions and Miss Perepelitsyn promptly followed suit, and finally it was solemnly ratified by Foma Fomitch. At the minute when I was presented to her she was in a horrible rage, and apparently it was taking the silent form, the most terrible. Every one was watching her with apprehension. Only Tatyana Ivanovna, who was completely unconscious of it all, was in the best of spirits. My uncle purposely with a certain solemnity led me up to my grandmother; but the latter, making a wry face, pushed away her cup ill-humouredly.

"Is this that *vol-ti-geur?*" she drawled through her teeth, addressing Miss Perepelitsyn.

This foolish question completely disconcerted me. I

don't understand why she called me a *voltigeur*. But such questions were easy enough to her. Miss Perepelitsyn bent down and whispered something in her ear, but the old lady waved her off angrily. I remained standing with my mouth open and looked inquiringly at my uncle. They all looked at one another and Obnoskin even grinned, which I did not like at all.

"She sometimes talks at random, my boy," my uncle, a little disconcerted himself, whispered in my ear; "but it means nothing, it's just her goodness of heart. The heart is what one must look at."

"Yes, the heart, the heart," Tatyana Ivanovna's bell-like voice rang out. She had not taken her eyes off me all this time, and seemed as though she could not sit still in her chair. I suppose the word "heart," uttered in a whisper, had reached her ear.

But she did not go on, though she was evidently longing to express herself. Whether she was overcome with confusion or some other feeling, she suddenly subsided into silence, flushed extremely red, turned quickly to the governess and whispered something in her ear, and suddenly putting her handkerchief before her mouth and sinking back in her chair, began giggling as though she were in hysterics. I looked at them all in extreme amazement; but to my surprise, every one was particularly grave and looked as though nothing exceptional had happened. I realized, of course, the kind of person Tatyana Ivanovna was. At last I was handed tea, and I recovered myself a little. I don't know why, but I suddenly felt that it was my duty to begin a polite conversation with the ladies.

"It was true what you told me, uncle," I began, "when you warned me that I might be a little abashed. I openly confess—why conceal it?" I went on, addressing Madame Obnoskin with a deprecating smile, "that I have hitherto had hardly any experience of ladies' society. And just now when I made my entry so unsuccessfully, it seemed to me that my position in the middle of the room was very ridiculous and made me look rather a simpleton, didn't it? Have you read *The Simpleton*?" I added, feeling more and more lost, blushing at my ingratiating candour, and glaring at Monsieur Obnoskin, who was still looking me up and down with a grin on his face.

"Just so, just so, just so!" my uncle cried suddenly with extreme animation, genuinely delighted that the conversation had been set going somehow and that I had recovered myself. "That's no great matter, my boy, your talking of the likelihood of your being abashed. Well, you have been, and that's the end of it. But when I first made my début, I actually told a lie, my boy, would you believe that? Yes, really, Anfisa Petrovna, I assure you, it's worth hearing. Just after I had become a Junker, I went to Moscow, and presented myself to a very important lady with a letter of introduction; that is, she was a very haughty woman, but in reality, very good-natured, in spite of what they said. I went in—I was shown up. The drawing-room was full of people, chiefly swells. I made my bow and sat down. At the second word, she asked me: 'Have you estates in the country?' And I hadn't got as much as a hen—what was I to answer? I felt crushed to the earth. Every one was looking at me (I was only a young Junker!). Why not say: no, I have nothing; and that would have been the right thing because it was the truth. But I couldn't face it! 'Yes,' I said, 'a hundred and seventeen serfs.' And why did I stick on that seventeen? If one must tell a lie, it is better to tell it with a round number, isn't it? A minute later, through my letter of introduction, it appeared that I was as poor as a church mouse, and I had told a lie into the bargain! . . . Well, there was no help for it. I took myself off as fast as I could, and never set foot in the place again. In those days I had nothing, you know. All I have got now is three hundred serfs from Uncle Afanasy Matveyitch, and two hundred serfs with Kapitonovko which came to me earlier from my grandmother Akulina Panfilovna, a total of more than five hundred serfs. That's capital! But from that day I gave up lying and don't tell lies now."

"Well, I shouldn't have given it up, if I were you. There is no knowing what may happen," observed Obnoskin, smiling ironically.

"To be sure, that's true! Goodness knows what may happen," my uncle assented good-naturedly.

Obnoskin burst into loud laughter, throwing himself back in his chair; his mother smiled; Miss Perepelitsyn sniggered in a particularly disgusting way; Tatyana Ivanovna giggled too, without knowing why, and even clapped her hands; in fact, I saw distinctly that my uncle counted for nothing in his own house. Sashenka's eyes flashed angrily, and she looked steadily at Obnoskin. The governess flushed and looked down. My uncle was surprised.

"What is it? What's happened?" he repeated, looking round at us all in perplexity.

All this time my cousin Mizintchikov was sitting a little way off, saying nothing and not even smiling when every one laughed. He drank tea zealously, gazed philosophically at the whole company, and several times as though in an access of unbearable boredom broke into whistling, probably a habit of his, but pulled himself up in time. Obnoskin, who had jeered at my uncle and had attempted to attack me, seemed not to dare to glance at Mizintchikov; I noticed that. I noticed, too, that my silent cousin looked frequently at me and with evident curiosity, as though he was trying to make up his mind what sort of person I was.

"I am certain," Madame Obnoskin minced suddenly, "I am perfectly certain Monsieur Serge—that is your name I believe?—that at home, in Petersburg, you were not greatly devoted to the ladies. I know that there are many, a great many young men nowadays in Petersburg who shun the society of ladies altogether. But in my opinion they are all free-thinkers. Nothing would induce me to regard it as anything but unpardonable free-thinking. And I must say it surprises me, young man, it surprises me, simply surprises me! . . ."

"I have not been into society at all," I answered with extraordinary animation. "But that . . . I imagine at least . . . is of no consequence. I have lived, that is I have generally had lodgings . . . but that is no matter, I assure you. I shall be known one day; but hitherto I have always stayed at home. . . ."

"He is engaged in learned pursuits," observed my uncle, drawing himself up with dignity.

"Oh, uncle, still talking of your learned pursuits! . . . Only fancy," I went on with an extraordinarily free and easy air, smirking affably, and again addressing Madame Obnoskin, "my beloved uncle is so devoted to learning that he has unearthed somewhere on the high road a marvellous practical philosopher, a Mr. Korovkin; and his first word to me after all these years of separation was, that he was expecting this phenomenal prodigy with the most acute, one may say, impatience . . . from love of learning, of course. . . ."

And I sniggered, hoping to provoke a general laugh at my facetiousness.

"Who is that? Of whom is he talking?" Madame la Générale jerked out sharply, addressing Miss Perepelitsyn.

"Yegor Ilyitch has been inviting visitors, learned gentlemen; he drives along the highroads collecting them," the lady hissed out.

My uncle was completely dumbfounded.

"Oh, yes! I had forgotten," he cried, turning upon me a glance that expressed reproach. "I am expecting Korovkin. A man of learning, a man who will survive his century. . . ."

He broke off and relapsed into silence. Madame la Générale waved her arm, and this time so successfully that she knocked over a cup, which flew off the table and was smashed. General excitement followed.

"She always does that when she is angry; she throws things on the floor," my uncle whispered in confusion. "But she only does it when she is angry. . . . Don't stare, my boy, don't take any notice, look the other way. . . . What made you speak of Korovkin? . . ."

But I was looking away already; at that moment I met the eyes of the governess, and it seemed to me that in their expression there was something reproachful, even contemptuous; a flush of indignation glowed upon her pale cheeks. I understood the look in her face, and guessed that by my mean and disgusting desire to make my uncle ridiculous in order to make myself a little less so, I had not gained much in that young lady's estimation. I cannot express how ashamed I felt!

"I must go on about Petersburg with you," Anfisa Petrovna gushed again, when the commotion caused by the breaking of the cup had subsided. "I recall with such enjoyment, I may say, our life in that charming city. . . . We were very intimately acquainted with a family—do you remember, Pavel, General Polovitsin. . . . Oh, what a fascinating, fas-ci-na-ting creature his wife was! You know that aristocratic distinction, *beau monde!* . . . Tell me, you have most likely met her? . . . I must own I have been looking forward to your being here with impatience; I have been hoping to hear a great deal, a very great deal about our friends in Petersburg. . . ."

"I am very sorry that I cannot . . . excuse me. . . . As I have said already, I have rarely been into society, and I don't know General Polovitsin; I have never even heard of him," I answered impatiently, my affability being suddenly succeeded by a mood of extreme annoyance and irritability.

"He is studying mineralogy," my incorrigible uncle put in with pride. "Is that investigating all sorts of stones, mineralogy, my boy?"

"Yes, uncle, stones. . . ."

"H'm. . . . There are a great many sciences and they are all of use! And do you know, my boy, to tell you the truth, I did not know what mineralogy meant! It's all Greek to me. In other things I am so-so, but at learned subjects I am stupid—I frankly confess it!"

"You frankly confess!" Obnoskin caught him up with a snigger.

"Papa!" cried Sashenka, looking reproachfully at her father.

"What is it, darling? Oh, dear, I keep interrupting you, Anfisa Petrovna," my uncle caught himself up suddenly, not understanding Sashenka's exclamation. "Please forgive me."

"Oh, don't distress yourself," Anfisa Petrovna answered

with a sour smile. "Though I have said everything already to your nephew, and will finish perhaps, Monsieur Serge— that is right, isn't it?—by telling you that you really must reform. I believe that the sciences, the arts . . . sculpture, for instance . . . all those lofty ideas, in fact, have their fas-ci-na-ting side, but they do not take the place of ladies! . . . Women, women would form you, young man, and so to do without them is impossible, young man, impos- sible, im-poss-ible!"

"Impossible, impossible," Tatyana Ivanovna's rather shrill voice rang out again. "Listen," she began, speaking with a sort of childish haste and flushing crimson, of course, "listen, I want to ask you something. . . ."

"Pray do," I answered, looking at her attentively.

"I wanted to ask you whether you have come to stay long or not?"

"I really don't know, that's as my affairs . . ."

"Affairs! What sort of affairs can he have? Oh, the mad fellow! . . ."

And Tatyana Ivanovna, blushing perfectly crimson and hiding behind her fan, bent down to the governess and at once began whispering something to her. Then she sud- denly laughed and clapped her hands.

"Stay! stay!" she cried, breaking away from her con- fidante and again addressing me in a great hurry as though afraid I were going away. "Listen, do you know what I am going to tell you? You are awfully, awfully like a young man, a fas-ci-na-ting young man! Sashenka, Nas- tenka, do you remember? He is awfully like that madman —do you remember, Sashenka? We were out driving when we met him . . . on horseback in a white waistcoat . . . he put up his eyeglass at me, too, the shameless fellow! Do you remember, I hid myself in my veil, too, but I couldn't resist putting my head out of the carriage window and shouting to him: 'You shameless fellow!' and then I threw my bunch of flowers on the road? . . . Do you remember, Nastenka?"

And the lady, half-crazy over eligible young men, hid her face in her hands, all excitement; then suddenly leaped up from her seat, darted to the window, snatched a rose from a bowl, threw it on the floor near me and ran out of the room. She was gone in a flash! This time a certain embarrassment was apparent, though Madame la Générale was again completely unmoved. Anfisa Petrovna, for instance, showed no surprise, but seemed suddenly a little troubled and looked with anxiety at her son; the young ladies blushed, while Pavel Obnoskin, with a look of vexation which at the time I did not understand, got up from his chair and went to the window. My uncle was beginning to make signs to me, but at that instant another person walked into the room and drew the attention of all.

"Ah, here is Yevgraf Larionitch! Talk of angels!" cried my uncle, genuinely delighted. "Well, brother, have you come from the town?"

"Queer set of creatures! They seem to have been collected here on purpose!" I thought to myself, not yet understanding fully what was passing before my eyes, and not suspecting either that I was probably adding another to the collection of queer creatures by appearing among them.

Yezhevikin

V

There walked or rather squeezed himself into the room (though the doors were very wide ones) a little figure which even in the doorway began wriggling, bowing and smirking, looking with extraordinary curiosity at all the persons present. It was a little pock-marked old man with quick and furtive eyes, with a bald patch at the top of his head and another at the back, with a look of undefined subtle mockery on his rather thick lips. He was wearing a very shabby dress-coat which looked as though it were second-hand. One button was hanging by a thread; two or three were completely missing. His high boots full of holes, and his greasy cap, were in keeping with his pitiful attire; he had a very dirty check pocket-handkerchief in his hand, with which he wiped the sweat from his brow and temples. I noticed that the governess blushed slightly and looked rapidly at me. I fancied, too, that there was something proud and challenging in this glance.

"Straight from the town, benefactor! Straight from there, my kind protector! I will tell you everything, only first let me pay my respects," said the old man. And he made straight for Madame la Générale, but stopped half-way and again addressed my uncle.

"You know my leading characteristic, benefactor—a sly rogue, a regular sly rogue! You know that as soon as I walk in I make for the chief person of the house, I turn my toes in her direction first of all, so as from the first step to win favour and protection. A sly rogue, my good sir, a sly rogue, benefactor. Allow me, my dear lady, allow me, your Excellency, to kiss your dress, or I might sully with my lips your hand of gold, of general's rank."

Madame la Générale to my surprise gave him her hand to kiss rather graciously.

"And my respects to you, our beauty," he went on, "Miss Perepelitsyn. There is no help for it, madame, I am a sly rogue. As long ago as 1841 it was settled that I was a rogue, when I was dismissed from the service just at the time when Valentin Ignatyevitch Tihontsev became 'your honour.' He was made an assessor; he was made an assessor and I was made a rogue. And, you know, I am so open by nature that I make no secret of it. It can't be helped. I have tried living honestly, I have tried it, but now I must try something else. Alexandra Yegorovna, our little apple in syrup," he went on, going round the table and making his way up to Sashenka, "let me kiss your dress; there is a smell of apples and all sorts of nice things about you, young lady. Our respects to the hero of the day; I have brought you a bow and arrow, my little sir. I was a whole morning making it, my lads helped me; we will shoot with it presently. And when you grow up you will be an officer and cut off a Turk's head. Tatyana Ivanovna . . . but oh,

she is not here, my benefactress! Or I would have kissed
her dress too. Praskovya Ilyinitchna, my kindest friend, I
can't get near you or I would kiss your foot as well as your
hand, so there! Anfisa Petrovna, I protest my profound respect for you. I prayed for you only to-day, benefactress,
on my knees with tears I prayed for you and for your son
also that God might send him honours of all sorts—and
talents too, talents especially! And by the way, our hum-
blest duty to Ivan Ivanitch Mizintchikov. May God send
you all that you desire for yourself, for you will never
make out, sir, what you do want for yourself: such a silent
gentleman. . . . Good-day, Nastya! All my small fry send
their love to you, they talk of you every day. And now a
deep bow to my host. I come from the town, your honour,
straight off from the town. And this, no doubt, is your
nephew who is being trained in a learned faculty? My humble duty, sir; let me have your hand."

There was laughter. One could see that the old man
played the part of an amateur clown. His arrival livened
the party up. Many did not even understand his sarcasms,
and yet he had made slight digs at them all. Only the governess, whom to my surprise he called simply Nastya,
blushed and frowned. I was pulling back my hand, but
I believe that was just what the horrid old man wanted.

"But I only asked to shake it, sir, if you will allow me;
not to kiss it. And you thought I meant to kiss it? No, my
dear sir, for the time being I will only shake it. I suppose
you took me for the clown of the establishment, kind sir?"
he said, looking at me mockingly.

"N-no, really, I . . ."

"To be sure, sir! If I am a fool, then some one else here
is one too. Treat me with respect; I am not such a rogue
yet as you imagine. Though maybe I am a clown too. I am
a slave, my wife is a slave, and so there is nothing for it but
flattery. That's how it is! You get something by it anyway,
if only to make sop for the children. Sugar, scatter as much
sugar as you can in everything, that will make things more
wholesome for you. I tell you this in secret, sir; maybe you

will have need of it. Fortune has been hard on me, that is why I am a clown."

"He-he-he! The old man is a comical fellow! He always makes us laugh!" piped Anfisa Petrovna.

"My dear madame and benefactress, a fool has a better time of it in this world! If I had only known that, I would have enlisted among the fools in early childhood, and I dare say by now I might have been a wise man. But as it is, I wanted to be a clever man at first, so now I am a fool in my old age."

"Tell me, please," interposed Obnoskin (he probably was not pleased by the remark about *talents*), lolling in a particularly free and easy way in his arm-chair and staring at the old man through his eyeglass as though at an insect, "tell me, please . . . I always forget your surname . . . what the deuce is it? . . ."

"Oh, my dear sir! Why, my surname, if it please you, is Yezhevikin; but what does that matter? Here I have been sitting without a job these nine years, I just go on living in accordance with the laws of nature. And my children, my children are simply a family of Holmskys. As the proverb goes, 'The rich man has calves, the poor man has kids.' "

"Oh, yes . . . calves . . . but that's beside the point. Come, listen, I have been wanting to ask you a long time: why is it that when you come in, you look back at once? It's very funny."

"Why do I look back? Why, I am always fancying, sir, that someone behind me wants to slap me on the back and squash me like a fly. That is why I look round. I have become a monomaniac, sir."

Again there was laughter. The governess got up from her seat as though she would go away, but sank back in her chair again. There was a look of pain and suffering on her face in spite of the colour that flooded her cheeks.

"You know who it is, my boy?" my uncle whispered. "It's *her* father, you know!"

I stared at my uncle open-eyed. The name of Yezhevikin

had completely slipped out of my mind. I had been playing the hero, had been dreaming all the journey of my proposed bride, had been building magnificent plans for her
benefit, and had utterly forgotten her name, or rather had
taken no notice of it from the first.

"What, her father?" I answered, also in a whisper. "Why,
I thought she was an orphan."

"It's her father, my boy, her father. And do you know,
a most honest, a most honourable man and he does not
even drink, but only plays at being a fool; fearfully poor,
my boy, eight children! They live on Nastya's salary. He
was turned out of the service through his tongue. He comes
here every week. He is such a proud fellow—nothing will
induce him to take help. I have offered it, many times I
have offered it—he won't take it. An embittered man."

"Well, Yevgraf Larionitch, what news have you?" uncle
asked, and slapped him warmly on the shoulder, noticing
that the suspicious old man was already listening to our
conversation.

"What news, benefactor? Valentin Ignatyitch made a
statement about Trishin's case yesterday. The flour under
his charge turned out to be short weight. It is that Trishin,
madame, who looks at you and puffs like a samovar. Perhaps you graciously remember him? So Valentin Ignatyitch
writes of Trishin: 'If,' said he, 'the often-mentioned Trishin
could not guard his own niece's honour'—she eloped with
an officer last year—'how,' said he, 'should he take care
of government property?' He stuck that into his report, by
God, I am not lying."

"Fie! What stories you tell!" cried Anfisa Petrovna.

"Just so, just so, just so! You've overshot the mark,
friend Yevgraf," my uncle chimed in. "*Aïe!* your tongue
will be your ruin. You are a straightforward man, honourable and upright, I can say that, but you have a venomous tongue! And I can't understand how it is you can't
get on with them. They seem good-natured people, simple . . ."

"Kind friend and benefactor! But it's just the simple

man that I am afraid of," cried the old man with peculiar fervour.

I liked the answer. I went rapidly up to Yezhevikin and warmly pressed his hand. The truth is, I wanted in some way to protest against the general tone and to show my sympathy for the old man openly. And perhaps, who knows? perhaps I wanted to raise myself in the opinion of Nastasya Yevgrafovna! But my movement led to no good.

"Allow me to ask you," I said, blushing and flustered as usual, "have you heard of the Jesuits?"

"No, my good sir, I haven't; well, maybe something . . . though how should we! But why?"

"Oh . . . I meant to tell you something apropos. . . . But remind me some other time. But now let me assure you, I understand you and . . . know how to appreciate . . ."

And utterly confused, I gripped his hand again.

"Certainly, I will remind you, sir, certainly. I will write it in golden letters. If you will allow me, I'll tie a knot in my handkerchief."

And he actually looked for a dry corner in his dirty, snuffy handkerchief, and tied a knot in it.

"Yevgraf Larionitch, take your tea," said Praskovya Ilyinitchna.

"Immediately, my beautiful lady; immediately, my princess, I mean, not my lady! That's in return for your tea. I met Stepan Alexyevitch Bahtcheyev on the road, madame. He was so festive, that I didn't know what to make of it! I began to wonder whether he wasn't going to get married. Flatter away, flatter away!" he said in a half-whisper, winking at me and screwing up his eyes as he carried his cup by me. "And how is it that my benefactor, my chief one, Foma Fomitch, is not to be seen? Isn't he coming to tea?"

My uncle started as though he had been stung, and glanced timidly at his mother.

"I really don't know," he answered uncertainly, with a strange perturbation. "We sent for him, but he . . . I don't know really, perhaps he is indisposed. I have already sent Vidoplyasov and . . . Perhaps I ought to go myself, though?"

"I went in to him myself just now," Yezhevikin brought out mysteriously.

"Is it possible!" cried out my uncle in alarm. "Well, how was it?"

"I went in to him, first of all, I paid him my respects. His honour said he should drink his tea in solitude, and then added that a crust of dry bread would be enough for him, yes."

These words seemed to strike absolute terror into my uncle.

"But you should have explained to him, Yevgraf Larionitch; you should have told him" . . . my uncle said at last, looking at the old man with distress and reproach.

"I did, I did."

"Well?"

"For a long time he did not deign to answer me. He was sitting over some mathematical problem, he was working out something; one could see it was a brain-racking problem. He drew the breeches of Pythagoras, while I was there, I saw him myself. I repeated it three times, only at the fourth he raised his head and seemed to see me for the first time. 'I am not coming,' he said; 'a *learned* gentleman has arrived here now, so I should be out of place beside a luminary like that!' He made use of that expression 'beside a luminary.' "

And the horrid old man stole a sly glance at me.

"That is just what I expected," cried my uncle, clasping his hands. "That's how I thought it would be. He says that about you, Sergey, that you are a 'learned gentleman.' Well, what's to be done now?"

"I must confess, uncle," I answered with dignity, shrugging my shoulders, "it seems to me such an absurd refusal that it is not worth noticing, and I really wonder at your being troubled by it. . . ."

"Oh, my boy, you know nothing about it!" he cried, with a vigorous wave of his hand.

"It's no use grieving now, sir," Miss Perepelitsyn put in suddenly, "since all the wicked causes of it have come from you in the first place, Yegor Ilyitch. If you take off your head you don't weep for your hair. You should have listened to your mamma, sir, and you would have had no cause for tears now."

"Why, how am I to blame, Anna Nilovna? Have some fear of God!" said my uncle in an imploring voice, as though begging for an explanation.

"I do fear God, Yegor Ilyitch; but it all comes from your being an egoist, sir, and not loving your mother," Miss Perepelitsyn answered with dignity. "Why didn't you respect her wishes in the first place? She is your mother, sir. And I am not likely to tell you a lie, sir. I am a major's daughter myself, and not just anybody, sir."

It seemed to me that Miss Perepelitsyn had intervened in the conversation with the sole object of informing us all, and me in particular as a newcomer, that she was a major's daughter and not just anybody.

"It's because he ill-treats his own mother," Madame la Générale herself brought out at last in a menacing voice.

"Mamma, have mercy on us! How am I ill-treating you?"

"It is because you are a black-hearted egoist, Yegorushka," Madame la Générale went on, growing more and more animated.

"Mamma, mamma! in what way am I a black-hearted egoist?" cried my uncle, almost in despair. "For five days, for five whole days you have been angry with me and will not speak to me. And what for? what for? Let them judge me, let the whole world judge me! But let them hear my defence too. I have long kept silent, mamma, you would not hear me; let these people hear me now. Anfisa Petrovna! Pavel Semyonitch, generous Pavel Semyonitch! Sergey, my dear! You are an outsider, you are, so to speak, a spectator. You can judge impartially. . . ."

"Calm yourself, Yegor Ilyitch, calm yourself," cried Anfisa Petrovna, "don't kill your mamma."

"I am not killing my mamma, Anfisa Petrovna; but here I lay bare my heart, you can strike at it!" my uncle went on, worked up to the utmost pitch as people of weak character sometimes are when they are driven out of all patience, though their heat is like the fire of burning straws. "I want to say, Anfisa Petrovna, that I am not ill-treating any one. I start with saying that Foma Fomitch is the noblest and the most honourable of men, and a man of superior qualities too, but . . . but he has been unjust to me in this case."

"H'm!" grunted Obnoskin, as though he wanted to irritate my uncle still more.

"Pavel Semyonitch, noble-hearted Pavel Semyonitch! Can you really think that I am, so to speak, an unfeeling stone? Why, I see, I understand—with tears in my heart, I may say I understand—that all this misunderstanding comes from the excess of *his* affection for me. But, say what you like, he really is unjust in this case. I will tell you all about it. I want to tell the whole story, Anfisa Petrovna, clearly and in full detail, that you may see from what the thing started, and whether mamma is right in being angry with me for not satisfying Foma Fomitch. And you listen too, Seryozha," he added, addressing me, which he did, indeed, during the rest of his story, as though he were afraid of his other listeners and doubtful of their sympathy; "you, too, listen and decide whether I am right or wrong. You will see what the whole business arose from. A week ago—yes, not more than a week—my old chief, General Rusapetov, was passing through our town with his wife and stepdaughter, and broke the journey there. I was overwhelmed. I hastened to seize the opportunity, I flew over, presented myself and invited them to dinner. He promised to come if it were possible. He is a very fine man, I assure you; he is conspicuous for his virtues and is a man of the highest rank into the bargain! He has been a benefactor to his stepdaughter; he married an orphan girl to an admirable young man (now a lawyer at Malinova; still a young man, but with, one may say, an all-round education); in short, he is a general of generals. Well, of course there was a tremendous fuss and bustle in the house—cooks, fricassees—I sent for an orchestra. I was delighted, of course, and looked festive; Foma Fomitch did not like my being delighted and looking festive! He sat down to the table—I remember, too, he was handed his favourite jelly and cream—he sat on and on without saying a word, then all at once jumped up. 'I am being insulted, insulted!' 'But why, in what way are you being insulted, Foma Fomitch?' 'You despise me now,' he said; 'you are taken up with generals now, you think more of generals now than of me.' Well, of course I am making a long story short, so to say, I am only giving you the pith of it; but if only you knew what he said besides . . . in a word, he stirred me to my inmost depths. What was I to do? I was depressed by it, of course; it was a blow to me, I may say. I went about like a cock drenched with rain. The festive day arrived. The general sent to say he couldn't come, he apologized—so he was not coming. I went to Foma. 'Come, Foma,' I said, 'set your mind at rest, he is not coming.' And would you believe it, he wouldn't forgive me, and that was the end of it. 'I have been insulted,' he said, 'and that is all about it!' I said this and that. 'No,' he said. 'You can go to your generals; you think more of generals than of me, you have broken our bonds of friendship,' he said. Of course, my dear, I understand what he was angry over, I am not a block, I am not a sheep, I am not a perfect post. It was, of course, from the excess of his affection for me, from jealousy—he says that himself—he is jealous of the general on my account, he is afraid of losing my affection, he is testing me, he wants to see how much I am ready to sacrifice for him. 'No,' he said, 'I am just as good as the general for you, I am myself "your Excellency" for you! I will be reconciled to you when you prove your respect for me.' 'In what way am I to prove my respect for you, Foma Fomitch?' 'Call me for a whole day "your Excellency,"' says he, 'then you will prove your respect.' I felt as though I were dropping from the clouds; you can picture my amazement. 'That will serve you,' said he, 'as a lesson not to be in ecstasies at the sight of generals when there are other people, perhaps, superior to all your generals.' Well, at that point I lost patience, I confess it! I confess it openly. 'Foma Fomitch,' I said, 'is such a thing possible? Can I take it upon myself to do it? Can I, have I the right to promote you to be a general? Think who it is bestows the rank of a general! How can I address you as, "your Excellency"? Why, it is infringing the decrees of Providence! Why, the general is an honour to his country; the general has faced the enemy, he has shed his blood on the field of honour. How am I to call you, your "Excellency"?' He would not give way, there was no doing anything. "Whatever you want, Foma,' I said, 'I will do anything for you. Here you told me to shave off my whiskers because they were not patriotic enough—I shaved them off; I frowned, but I did shave them. What is more, I will do anything you like, only do give up the rank of a general!' 'No,' said he, 'I won't be reconciled till you call me "your Excellency"; that,' said he, 'will be good for your moral character, it will humble your spirit!' said he. And so now for a week, a whole week, he won't speak to me; he is cross to every one that comes; he heard about you, that you were learned—that was my fault; I got warm and said too much—so he said he would not set foot in the house if you came into it. 'So I am not learned enough for you now,' said he. So there will be trouble when he hears now about Korovkin! Come now, please, tell me in what way have I been to blame? Was I to take on myself to call him 'your Excellency'? Why, it is impossible to live in such a position! What did he drive poor Bahtcheyev away from the table to-day for? Supposing Bahtcheyev is not a great astronomer, why, I am not a great astronomer, and you are not a great astronomer. . . . Why is it? Why is it?"

"Because you are envious, Yegorushka," mumbled Madame la Générale again.

"Mamma," cried my uncle in despair, "you will drive me out of my mind! . . . Those are not your words, you are repeating what others say, mamma! I am, in fact, made out a stone, a block, a lamp-post and not your son."

"I heard, uncle," I interposed, utterly amazed by his story—"I heard from Bahtcheyev, I don't know whether it was true or not—that Foma Fomitch was jealous of Ilyusha's nameday, and declares that to-morrow is his nameday too. I must own that this characteristic touch so astounded me that I . . ."

"His birthday, my dear, his birthday!" my uncle interrupted me, speaking rapidly. "He only made a mistake in the word, but he is right; to-morrow is his birthday. Truth, my boy, before everything. . . ."

"It's not his birthday at all!" cried Sashenka.

"Not his birthday!" cried my uncle, in a fluster.

"It's not his birthday, papa. You simply say what isn't true to deceive yourself and to satisfy Foma Fomitch. His birthday was in March. Don't you remember, too, we went on a pilgrimage to the monastery just before, and he wouldn't let any one sit in peace in the carriage? He kept crying out that the cushion was *crushing* his side, and pinching us; he pinched auntie twice in his ill-humour. 'I am fond of camellias,' he said, 'for I have the taste of the most refined society, and you grudge picking me any from the conservatory.' And all day long he sulked and grizzled and would not talk to us. . . ."

I fancy that if a bomb had fallen in the middle of the room it would not have astounded and alarmed them all as much as this open mutiny—and of whom?—of a little girl who was not even permitted to speak aloud in her grandmother's presence. Madame la Générale, dumb with amazement and fury, rose from her seat, stood erect and stared at her insolent grandchild, unable to believe her eyes. My uncle was paralyzed with horror.

"She is allowed to do just as she likes, she wants to be the death of her grandmother!" cried Miss Perepelitsyn.

"Sasha, Sasha, think what you are saying! What's the matter with you, Sasha?" cried my uncle, rushing from one to the other, from his mother to Sashenka to stop her.

"I won't hold my tongue, papa!" cried Sashenka, leaping up from her chair with flashing eyes and stamping with her feet. "I won't hold my tongue! We have all suffered too long from Foma Fomitch, from your nasty, horrid Foma Fomitch! Foma Fomitch will be the ruin of us all, for people keep on telling him that he is so clever, generous, noble, learned, a mix-up of all the virtues, a sort of potpourri, and like an idiot Foma Fomitch believes it all. So many nice things are offered to him that any one else would be ashamed; but Foma Fomitch gobbles up all that is put before him and asks for more. You'll see, he will be the ruin of us all, and it's all papa's fault! Horrid, horrid Foma Fomitch! I speak straight out, I am not afraid of any one! He is stupid, ill-tempered, dirty, ungentlemanly, cruel-hearted, a bully, a mischief-maker, a liar. . . . Oh, I'd turn him out of the house this minute, I would, but papa adores him, papa is crazy over him!"

"Oh!" shrieked her grandmother, and she fell in a swoon on the sofa.

"Agafya Timofyevna, my angel," cried Anfisa Petrovna, "take my smelling-salts! Water, make haste, water!"

"Water, water!" shouted my uncle. "Mamma, mamma, calm yourself! I beg you on my knees to calm yourself! . . ."

"You ought to be kept on bread and water and shut up in a dark room . . . you're a murderess!" Miss Perepelitsyn, shaking with spite, hissed at Sashenka.

"I will be kept on bread and water, I am not afraid of anything!" cried Sashenka, moved to frenzy in her turn. "I will defend papa because he can't defend himself. Who is he, who is your Foma Fomitch compared with papa? He eats papa's bread and insults papa, the ungrateful creature. I would tear him to pieces, your Foma Fomitch! I'd challenge him to a duel and shoot him on the spot with two pistols! . . ."

"Sasha, Sasha," cried my uncle in despair. "Another word and I am ruined, hopelessly ruined."

"Papa," cried Sashenka, flinging herself headlong at her father, dissolving into tears and hugging him in her arms, "papa, how can you ruin yourself like this, you so kind, and good, and merry and clever? How can you give in to that horrid ungrateful man, be his plaything and let him turn you into ridicule? Papa, my precious papa! . . ."

She burst into sobs, covered her face with her hands and ran out of the room.

A fearful hubbub followed. Madame la Générale lay in a swoon. My uncle was kneeling beside her kissing her hands. Miss Perepelitsyn was wriggling about them and casting spiteful but triumphant glances at us. Anfisa Petrovna was moistening the old lady's temples and applying her smelling-salts. Praskovya Ilyinitchna was shedding tears and trembling, Yezhevikin was looking for a corner to seek refuge in, while the governess stood pale and completely overwhelmed with terror. Mizintchikov was the only one who remained unchanged. He got up, went to the window and began looking out of it, resolutely declining to pay attention to the scene around him.

All at once Madame la Générale sat up, drew herself up and scanned me with a menacing eye.

"Go away!" she shouted, stamping her foot at me.

I must confess that this I had not in the least expected.

"Go away! Go out of the house! What has he come for? Don't let me see a trace of him!"

"Mamma, mamma, what do you mean? Why, this is Seryozha," my uncle muttered, shaking all over with terror. "Why, he has come to pay us a visit, mamma."

"What Seryozha? Nonsense. I won't hear a word. Go away! It's Korovkin. I am convinced it is Korovkin. My presentiments never deceive me. He has come to turn Foma Fomitch out; he has been sent for with that very object. I have a presentiment in my heart. . . . Go away, you scoundrel!"

"Uncle, if this is how it is," I said, spluttering with honest indignation, "then excuse me, I'll . . ." And I reached after my hat.

"Sergey, Sergey, what are you about? . . . Well, this really is . . . Mamma, this is Seryozha! . . . Sergey, upon my word!" he cried, racing after me and trying to take away my hat. "You are my visitor; you'll stay, I wish it! She doesn't mean it," he went on in a whisper; "she only goes on like this when she is angry. . . . You only keep out of her sight just at first . . . keep out of the way and it will all pass over. She will forgive you, I assure you! She is good-natured, only she works herself up. You hear she takes you for Korovkin, but afterwards she will forgive you, I assure you. . . . What do you want?" he cried to Gavrila, who came into the room trembling with fear.

Gavrila came in not alone; with him was a very pretty

peasant boy of sixteen who had been taken as a house serf, on account of his good looks as I heard afterwards. His name was Falaley. He was wearing a peculiar costume, a red silk shirt with embroidery at the neck and a belt of gold braid, full black velveteen breeches, and goatskin boots turned over with red. This costume was designed by Madame la Générale herself. The boy was sobbing bitterly, and tears rolled one after another from his big blue eyes.

"What's this now?" cried my uncle. "What has happened? Speak, you ruffian!"

"Foma Fomitch told us to come here; he is coming after us himself," answered the despondent Gavrila. "Me for an examination, while he . . ."

"He?"

"He has been dancing, sir," answered Gavrila in a tearful voice.

"Dancing!" cried my uncle in horror.

"Dancing," blubbered Falaley with a sob.

"The Komarinsky!"

"Yes, the Kom-a-rin-sky."

"And Foma Fomitch found him?"

"Ye-es, he found me."

"You'll be the death of me!" cried my uncle. "I am done for!" And he clutched his head in both hands.

"Foma Fomitch!" Vidoplyasov announced, entering the room.

The door opened, and Foma Fomitch in his own person stood facing the perplexed company.

Of the White Bull and the Komarinsky Peasant

VI

Before I have the honour of presenting the reader with Foma Fomitch in person, I think it is absolutely essential to say a few words about Falaley and to explain what there was terrible in the fact of his dancing the Komarinsky and Foma Fomitch's finding him engaged in that light-hearted diversion. Falaley was a house serf boy, an orphan from the cradle, and a godson of my uncle's late wife. My uncle was very fond of him. That fact alone was quite sufficient to make Foma Fomitch, after he had settled at Stepantchikovo and gained complete domination over my uncle, take a dislike to the latter's favourite, Falaley. But Madame la Générale took a particular fancy to the boy, who, in spite of Foma Fomitch's wrath, remained upstairs in attendance on the family. Madame la Générale herself insisted upon it, and Foma gave way, storing up the injury —he looked on everything as an injury—in his heart and revenging it on every favourable occasion on my uncle, who was in no way responsible. Falaley was wonderfully good-looking. He had a girlish face, the face of a beautiful peasant girl. Madame la Générale petted and spoiled him, prized him as though he were a rare and pretty toy, and there was no saying which she loved best, her little curly black dog Ami or Falaley. We have already referred to his costume, which was her idea. The young ladies gave him pomatum, and it was the duty of the barber Kuzma to curl his hair on holidays. This boy was a strange creature. He could not be called a perfect idiot or imbecile, but he was so naïve, so truthful and simple-hearted, that he might sometimes be certainly taken for a fool. If he had a dream,

he would go at once to tell it to his master or mistress. He
joined in the conversation of the gentlefolk without car-
ing whether he was interrupting them. He would tell them
things quite impossible to tell gentlefolks. He would dissolve into the most genuine tears when his mistress fell into
a swoon or when his master was too severely scolded. He
sympathized with every sort of distress. He would sometimes go up to Madame la Générale, kiss her hands, and
beg her not to be cross—and the old lady would magnani-
mously forgive him these audacities. He was sensitive in the
extreme, kind-hearted, as free from malice as a lamb and
as gay as a happy child. They gave him dainties from the
dinner-table.

He always stood behind Madame la Générale's chair and
was awfully fond of sugar. When he was given a lump of
sugar he would nibble at it with his strong milk-white
teeth, and a gleam of indescribable pleasure shone in his
merry blue eyes and all over his pretty little face.

For a long time Foma Fomitch raged; but reflecting at
last that he would get nothing by anger, he suddenly made
up his mind to be Falaley's benefactor. After first pitching
into my uncle for doing nothing for the education of his
house serfs, he determined at once to set about training
the poor boy in morals, good manners and French.

"What!" he would say in defence of his absurd idea (an
idea not confined to Foma Fomitch, as the writer of these
lines can testify), "what! he is always upstairs waiting on
his mistress; one day, forgetting that he does not know
French, she will say to him, for instance: 'Donnay mooah
mon mooshooar'—he ought to be equal to the occasion
and able to do his duty even then!"

But it appeared not only that it was impossible to teach
Falaley French, but that the cook Andron, the boy's uncle, who had disinterestedly tried to teach him to read
Russian, had long ago given it up in despair and put the
alphabet away on the shelf. Falaley was so dull at book-
learning that he could understand absolutely nothing. Moreover, this led to further trouble. The house serfs began
calling Falaley, in derision, a Frenchman, and old Gavrila,

my uncle's valet, openly ventured to deny the usefulness of learning French. This reached Foma Fomitch's ears, and bursting with wrath, he made his opponent, Gavrila, himself learn French as a punishment. This was the origin of the whole business of teaching the servants French which so exasperated Mr. Bahtcheyev. It was still worse in regard to manners. Foma was absolutely unable to train Falaley to suit his ideas, and in spite of his prohibition, the boy would go in to tell him his dreams in the morning, which Foma Fomitch considered extremely ill-mannered and familiar. But Falaley obstinately remained Falaley. My uncle was, of course, the first to suffer for all this.

"Do you know, do you know what he has done to-day?" Foma would exclaim, selecting a moment when all were gathered together in order to produce a greater sensation. "Do you know what your systematic spoiling is coming to? To-day he gobbled up a piece of pie given him at the table; and do you know what he said of it? Come here, come here, silly fool; come here, idiot; come here, red face. . . ."

Falaley would come up weeping and rubbing his eyes with both hands.

"What did you say when you greedily ate up your pie? Repeat it before every one!"

Falaley would dissolve in bitter tears and make no answer.

"Then I'll speak for you, if that's how it is. You said, slapping yourself on your stuffed and vulgar stomach: 'I've gobbled up the pie as Martin did the soap!' Upon my word, Colonel, can expressions like that be used in educated society, still more in aristocratic society? Did you say it or not? Speak!"

"I di-id . . ." Falaley would assent, sobbing.

"Well, then, tell me now, does Martin eat soap? Where have you seen a Martin who eats soap? Tell me, give me an idea of this phenomenal Martin!"

Silence.

"I am asking you," Foma would persist, "who is this Martin? I want to see him, I want to make his acquaintance. Well, what is he? A registry clerk, an astronomer, a provincial, a poet, an army captain, a serving man—he must have been something. Answer!"

"A ser-er-ving ma-an," Falaley would answer at last, still weeping.

"Whose? Who is his master?"

But Falaley was utterly unable to say who was his master. It would end, of course, in Foma Fomitch's rushing out of the room in a passion, crying out that he had been insulted; Madame la Générale would show symptoms of an attack, while my uncle would curse the hour of his birth, beg everybody's pardon, and for the rest of the day walk about on tiptoe in his own rooms.

As ill-luck would have it, on the day after the trouble over Martin and the soap, Falaley, who had succeeded in completely forgetting about Martin and all his woes of the previous day, informed Foma Fomitch as he took in his tea in the morning, that he had had a dream about a white bull. This was the last straw! Foma Fomitch was moved to indescribable indignation, he promptly summoned my uncle and began upbraiding him for the vulgarity of the dream dreamed by his Falaley. This time severe steps were taken: Falaley was punished, he had to kneel down in the corner. He was sternly forbidden to dream of such coarse rustic subjects.

"What I am angry at," said Foma, "apart from the fact that he really ought not to dare to think of blurting out his dreams to me, especially a dream of a white bull—apart from that—you must agree, Colonel—what is the white bull but a proof of coarseness, ignorance and loutishness in your unkempt Falaley? As the thoughts are, so will the dreams be. Did I not tell you before that you would never make anything of him, and that he ought not to remain upstairs waiting upon the family? You will never, never develop that senseless peasant soul into anything lofty or poetical. Can't you manage," he went on, addressing Falaley, "can't you manage to dream of something elegant, refined, genteel, some scene from good society, such as gentlemen playing cards or ladies walking in a lovely garden?"

Falaley promised he would be sure to dream next night of gentlemen or ladies walking in a lovely garden.

As he went to bed, Falaley prayed tearfully on the subject and wondered for a long time what he could do so as not to dream of the accursed white bull. But deceitful are the hopes of man. On waking up next morning, he remembered with horror that he had again been dreaming all night of the hateful white bull, and had not dreamed of even one lady walking in a lovely garden. This time the consequences were singular. Foma Fomitch positively declared that he did not believe in the possibility of such a coincidence, the possibility of such a repetition of a dream, and that Falaley was prompted to say this by some one of the household, perhaps even by the colonel himself on purpose to annoy Foma Fomitch. There was no end of an uproar, tears and reproaches. Madame la Générale was taken ill towards the evening, the whole household wore a dejected air. There was still a faint hope that the following, that is, the third night, Falaley would be sure to have some dream of refined society. What was the universal indignation when for a whole week, every blessed night, Falaley went on dreaming of the white bull and nothing but the white bull. It was no use even to think of refined society.

But the most interesting point was that Falaley was utterly incapable of thinking of lying, of simply saying that he had dreamed not of the white bull, but of a carriage, for instance, full of ladies and Foma Fomitch. This was all the more strange since lying indeed would not have been so very sinful in so extreme a case. But Falaley was so truthful that he positively could not tell a lie even if he wanted to. It was, indeed, not even suggested to him by any one. They all knew that he would betray himself at the first moment, and Foma Fomitch would immediately detect him in lying. What was to be done? My uncle's position was becoming intolerable. Falaley was absolutely incorrigible. The poor boy was positively growing thinner from worry.

The housekeeper Malanya declared that he was bewitched, and sprinkled him with magic water. She was assisted in this compassionate and salutary operation by the tender-hearted Praskovya Ilyinitchna, but even that was no use. Nothing was of use!

"The deuce take the damned thing!" Falaley said. "The same dream every night! Every evening I pray, 'Don't let me dream of the white bull, don't let me dream of the white bull!' and there it is, there it is, the damned beast facing me, huge, with horns and such thick lips, oo-oo-oo!"

My uncle was in despair, but luckily Foma Fomitch seemed all at once to have forgotten about the white bull. Of course no one believed that Foma Fomitch could forget a circumstance so important. Every one assumed with terror that he was keeping the white bull in reserve, and would bring it out on the first suitable occasion. It appeared later on that Foma Fomitch had no thoughts to spare for the white bull at that moment. He had other business in hand, other cares. Other plans were maturing in his beneficent and fertile brain. That is why he let Falaley breathe in peace, and every one else too had a respite. The boy grew gay again, and even began to forget what had happened; even the white bull began to visit him less and less frequently, though it still at times reminded him of its fantastic existence. In fact, everything would have gone well if there had been no such thing as the Komarinsky.

It must be noted that Falaley was an excellent dancer. Dancing was his chief accomplishment, even something like his vocation. He danced with vigour, with inexhaustible gaiety, and he was particularly fond of dancing the Komarinsky Peasant. Not that he was so much attracted by the frivolous and in any case inexplicable steps of that volatile peasant—no, he liked dancing the Komarinsky solely because to hear the Komarinsky and not dance to the tune was utterly beyond him. Sometimes in the evenings two or three of the footmen, the coachmen, the gardener who played the fiddle, and even some of the ladies of the servants' hall would gather together in a circle in some back yard as far away as possible from Foma Fomitch. Music and dances would begin, and finally the Komarinsky would triumphantly come into its own. The orchestra consisted of two balalaikas, a guitar, a fiddle, and a tambourine, with which the postillion Mityushka was a capital hand. Falaley's condition was worth watching at such times: he would dance to complete oblivion of himself, to utter exhaustion, encouraged by the shouts and laughter of his audience. He would squeal, shout, laugh, clap his hands. He danced as though carried away by some intangible outside force with which he could not cope, and he struggled persistently to keep up with the continually increasing pace of the reckless tune as he tapped on the ground with his heels. These were minutes of real delight to him; and everything would have gone happily and merrily if rumours of the Komarinsky had not at last reached Foma Fomitch.

Foma Fomitch was petrified, and sent at once for the colonel.

"There is only one thing I wish to learn from you," Foma began, "have you positively sworn to be the ruin of that luckless idiot or not? In the first case I will stand aside at once; if not, then I . . ."

"But what is the matter? What has happened?" cried my uncle, alarmed.

"You ask what has happened? Do you know that he is dancing the Komarinsky?"

"Well . . . well, what of it?"

"Well, what of it!" shrieked Foma. "And you say that— you, their master, standing in a sense in the place of their father! But have you then a true idea of what the Komarinsky is? Do you know that that song describes a debauched peasant, attempting in a state of drunkenness the most immoral action? Do you know what sacrilege it is that vicious little Russian is committing? He is trampling upon the most precious bonds and, so to say, stamping them under his big loutish boots, accustomed to tread only the floor of the village inn. And do you realize that you have wounded my moral feelings by your answer? Do you realize that you have insulted me personally by your answer? Do you understand that or not?"

"But, Foma; why, it's only a song, Foma. . . ."

"You say only a song! And you are not ashamed that you own to me that you know that song—you, a member of honourable society, the father of honourable, innocent children and a colonel into the bargain! Only a song! But I am certain that the song is drawn from real life. Only a song! But what decent man can without a blush of shame admit that he knows that song, that he has ever heard that song? What man could?"

"Well, but, you see, you know it yourself, Foma, since you ask about it," my disconcerted uncle answered in the simplicity of his heart.

"What, I know it, I . . . I? You have insulted me," Foma Fomitch cried at once, leaping up from his chair and spluttering with fury.

He had never expected such a crushing answer.

I will not undertake to describe the wrath of Foma Fomitch. The colonel was ignominiously driven from the presence of the guardian of morality for the ill manners and tactlessness of his reply. But from that hour Foma Fomitch vowed to catch Falaley in the act of dancing the Komarinsky. In the evening, when every one supposed he was busy at work, he stole out into the garden, went the round of the kitchen garden, and threaded his way into the hemp patch, from which there was a view in the distance of the back yard in which the dances took place. He stalked poor Falaley as a sportsman stalks a bird, picturing with relish the wigging he would, if he succeeded, give the whole household and the colonel in particular. His unwearying efforts were at last crowned with success. He had come upon the Komarinsky! It will be understood now why my uncle tore his hair when he saw Falaley weeping and heard Vidoplyasov announce Foma Fomitch, who so unexpectedly and at such a moment of perturbation was standing before us in person.

Foma Fomitch

VII

I scrutinized this gentleman with intense curiosity. Gavrila had been right in saying that he was an ugly little man. Foma was short, with light eyebrows and eyelashes and grizzled hair, with a hooked nose, and with little wrinkles all over his face. On his chin there was a big wart. He was about fifty. He came in softly with measured steps, with his eyes cast down. But yet the most insolent self-confidence was expressed in his face, and in the whole of his pedantic figure. To my astonishment, he made his appearance in a dressing-gown—of a foreign cut it is true, but still a dressing-gown—and he wore slippers too. The collar of his shirt unadorned by any cravat was a lay-down one *à l'enfant;* this gave Foma Fomitch an extremely foolish look. He went up to an empty arm-chair, moved it to the table, and sat down in it without saying a word to any one. All the hubbub, all the excitement that had been raging a minute before, vanished instantaneously. There was such a hush that one could have heard a pin drop. Madame la Générale became as meek as a lamb. The cringing infatuation of this poor imbecile for Foma Fomitch was apparent now. She fixed her eyes upon her idol as though gloating over the sight of him. Miss Perepelitsyn rubbed her hands with a simper, and poor Praskovya Ilyinitchna was visibly trembling with alarm. My uncle began bustling about at once.

"Tea, tea, sister! Only plenty of sugar in it, sister; Foma Fomitch likes plenty of sugar in his tea after his nap. You do like plenty of sugar, don't you, Foma?"

"I don't care for any tea just now!" Foma pronounced deliberately and with dignity, waving him off with a careworn air. "You always keep on about plenty of sugar."

These words and Foma's entrance, so incredibly ludi-

crous in its pedantic dignity, interested me extremely. I
was curious to find out to what point, to what disregard
of decency, the insolence of this upstart little gentleman
would go.

"Foma," cried my uncle. "Let me introduce my nephew
Sergey Alexandrovitch! He has just arrived."

Foma Fomitch looked him up and down.

"I am surprised that you always seem to take pleasure in
systematically interrupting me, Colonel," he said after a
significant silence, taking absolutely no notice of me. "One
talks to you of something serious, and you . . . *discourse*
. . . of goodness knows what. . . . Have you seen Falaley?"

"I have, Foma. . . ."

"Ah, you have seen him. Well, I will show you him
again though you have seen him; you can admire your handiwork . . . in a moral sense. Come here, you idiot! come
here, you Dutch-faced fool! Well, come along! Don't be
afraid!"

Falaley went up to him with his mouth open, sobbing
and gulping back his tears. Foma Fomitch looked at him
with relish.

"I called him a Dutch-faced fool with intention, Pavel
Semyonitch," he observed, lolling at his ease in his low
chair and turning slightly towards Obnoskin, who was sitting next him. "And speaking generally, you know, I see
no necessity for softening my expressions in any case. The
truth should be the truth. And however you cover up filth
it will still remain filth. Why trouble to soften it? It's deceiving oneself and others. Only a silly worldly numskull
can feel the need of such senseless conventions. Tell me—
I submit it to your judgment—do you find anything lovely
in that face? I mean, of course, anything noble, lovely, exalted, not just vulgar red cheeks."

Foma Fomitch spoke quietly, evenly, and with a kind of
majestic nonchalance.

"Anything lovely in him?" answered Obnoskin, with insolent carelessness. "I think that he is simply a good piece
of roast beef—and nothing else."

"Went up to the looking-glass and looked into it to-day,"

Foma continued, pompously omitting the pronoun *I*. "I am far from considering myself a beauty, but I could not help coming to the conclusion that there is something in these grey eyes which distinguished me from any Falaley. There is thought, there is life, there is intelligence in these eyes. It is not myself I am praising. I am speaking generally of our class. Now what do you think, can there be a scrap, a grain, of soul in that living beefsteak? Yes, indeed, take note, Pavel Semyonitch, how these people, utterly devoid of thought and ideal, and living by meat alone, always have revoltingly fresh complexions, coarsely and stupidly fresh! Would you like to know the level of his intellectual faculties? Hey, you image! Come nearer, let us admire you. Why are you gaping? Do you want to swallow a whale? Are you handsome? Answer, are you handsome?"

"I am!" answered Falaley, with smothered sobs.

Obnoskin roared with laughter. I felt that I was beginning to tremble with anger.

"Do you hear?" Foma went on, turning to Obnoskin in triumph. "Would you like to hear something more? I have come to put him through an examination. You see, Pavel Semyonitch, there are people who are desirous of corrupting and ruining this poor idiot. Perhaps I am too severe in my judgment, perhaps I am mistaken; but I speak from love of humanity. He was just now dancing the most improper of dances. That is of no concern to any one here. But now hear for yourself. . . . Answer: what were you doing just now? Answer, answer immediately—do you hear?"

"I was da-ancing," said Falaley, mastering his sobs.

"What were you dancing? What dance? Speak!"

"The Komarinsky."

"The Komarinsky! And who was that Komarinsky? What was the Komarinsky? Do you suppose I can understand anything from that answer? Come, give us an idea. Who was your Komarinsky?"

"A pea-easant. . . ."

"A peasant, only a peasant! I am surprised! A remarkable peasant, then! Then was it some celebrated peasant, if poems and dances are made about him? Come, answer!"

Foma could not exist without tormenting people, he played with his victim like a cat with a mouse; but Falaley remained mute, whimpering and unable to understand the question.

"Answer," Foma persisted. "You are asked what sort of peasant was it? Speak! . . . Was he a seignorial peasant, a crown peasant, free, bond, industrial? There are ever so many sorts of peasants. . . ."

"In-dus-tri-al. . . ."

"Ah, industrial! Do you hear, Pavel Semyonitch? A new historical fact: the Komarinsky peasant was industrial. H'm. . . . Well, what did that industrial peasant do? For what exploits is he celebrated in song . . . and dance?"

The question was a delicate one, and since it was put to Falaley, a risky one too.

"Come . . . Though . . ." Obnoskin began, glancing towards his mamma, who was beginning to wriggle on the sofa in a peculiar way.

But what was to be done? Foma Fomitch's whims were respected as law.

"Upon my word, uncle, if you don't suppress that fool he'll . . . you see what he is working up to—Falaley will blurt out some nonsense, I assure you," I whispered to my uncle, who was utterly distracted and did not know what line to take.

"You had really better, Foma . . ." he began. "Here, I want to introduce to you, Foma, my nephew, a young man who is studying mineralogy."

"I beg you, Colonel, not to interrupt me with your mineralogy, a subject of which, as far as I am aware, you know nothing, and *others* perhaps little more. I am not a baby. He will answer me that this peasant, instead of working for the welfare of his family, has been drinking till he is tipsy, has sold his coat for drink, and is running about the street in an inebriated condition. That is, as is well known, the subject of the poem that sings the praises of drink. Don't be uneasy, he knows *now* what he has to answer. Come, answer: what did that peasant do? Come, I have prompted you, I have put the words into your mouth. What I want is to hear it from you yourself, what he did, for what he was famous, how he gained the immortal glory of being sung by the troubadours. Well?"

The luckless Falaley looked round him in misery, and not knowing what to say, opened and shut his mouth like a carp, hauled out of the water on to the sand.

"I am ashamed to sa-ay!" he bellowed at last in utter despair.

"Ah, ashamed to say!" bellowed Foma in triumph. "See, that's the answer I have wrung out of him, Colonel! Ashamed to say, but not ashamed to do. That's the morality which you have sown, which has sprung up and which you are now . . . watering; but it is useless to waste words! Go to the kitchen now, Falaley. I'll say nothing to you now, out of regard for my audience, but to-day, to-day you will be severely and rigorously punished. If not, if this time they put you before me, you may stay here and entertain your betters with the Komarinsky while I will leave this house to-day! That's enough. I have spoken, you can go!"

"Come, I think you really are severe . . ." mumbled Obnoskin.

"Just so, just so, just so," my uncle began crying out, but he broke off and subsided. Foma looked gloomily askance at him.

"I wonder, Pavel Semyonitch," he went on, "what all our contemporary writers, poets, learned men and thinkers are about? How is it they pay no attention to what songs are being sung by the Russian people and to what songs they are dancing? What have the Pushkins, the Lermontovs, the Borozdins been about all this time? I wonder at them. The people dance the Komarinsky, the apotheosis of drunkenness, while they sing of forget-me-nots! Why don't they write poems of a more moral tone for popular use, why don't they fling aside their forget-me-nots? It's a social question. Let them depict a peasant, but a peasant made genteel, so to say, a villager and not a peasant; let them paint me the village sage in his simplicity, maybe even in his bark shoes—I don't object even to that—but brim-

ming over with the virtues which—I make bold to say—
some over-lauded Alexander of Macedon may envy. I
know Russia and Russia knows me, that is why I say this.
Let them portray that peasant, weighed down maybe with
a family and grey hair, in a stuffy hut, hungry, too, maybe,
but contented; not repining, but blessing his poverty, and
indifferent to the rich man's gold. Let the rich man at last
with softened heart bring him his gold; let, indeed, in this
the virtues of the peasant be united with the virtues of his
master, perhaps a grand gentleman. The villager and the
grand gentleman so widely separated in social grade are
made one at last in virtue—that is an exalted thought! But
what do we see? On one side forget-me-nots, and on the
other the peasant dashing out of the pothouse and running
about the street in a dishevelled condition! What is there
poetic in that? Tell me, pray, what is there to admire in
that? Where is the wit? Where is the grace? Where is the
morality? I am amazed at it!"

"I am ready to pay you a hundred roubles for such
words," said Yezhevikin, with an enthusiastic air. "And
you know the bald devil will try and get it out of me," he
whispered on the sly. "Flatter away, flatter away!"

"H'm, yes . . . you've put that very well," Obnoskin pronounced.

"Exactly so, exactly so," cried my uncle, who had been
listening with the deepest attention and looking at me with
triumph. "What a subject has come up!" he whispered, rubbing his hands. "A topic of many aspects, dash it all!
Foma Fomitch, here is my nephew," he added, in the over-
flow of his feelings. "He is engaged in literary pursuits too,
let me introduce him."

As before, Foma Fomitch paid not the slightest attention to my uncle's introduction.

"For God's sake, don't introduce me any more! I entreat you in earnest," I whispered to my uncle, with a resolute air.

"Ivan Ivanitch!" Foma began, suddenly addressing Mizintchikov and looking intently at him, "we have just been
talking. What is your opinion?"

"Mine? You are asking me?" Mizintchikov responded in surprise, looking as though he had only just woken up.

"Yes, you. I am asking you because I value the opinion of really clever people, and not the problematic wiseacres who are only clever because they are being continually introduced as clever people, as learned people, and are sometimes sent for expressly to be made a show of or something of the sort."

This thrust was aimed directly at me. And yet there was no doubt that though Foma Fomitch took no notice whatever of me, he had begun this whole conversation concerning literature entirely for my benefit, to dazzle, to annihilate, to crush at the first step the clever and learned young man from Petersburg. I at any rate had no doubt of it.

"If you want to know my opinion, I . . . I agree with your opinion," answered Mizintchikov listlessly and reluctantly.

"You always agree with me! It's positively wearisome," replied Foma. "I tell you frankly, Pavel Semyonitch," he went on, after a brief silence again addressing Obnoskin, "if I respect the immortal Karamzin it is not for his history, not for *Marfa Posadnitsa,* not for *Old and New Russia,* but just for having written *Frol Silin;* it is a noble epic! It is a purely national product, and will live for ages and ages! a most lofty epic!"

"Just so, just so! a lofty *epoch!* Frol Silin, a benevolent man! I remember, I have read it. He bought the freedom of two girls, too, and then looked towards heaven and wept. A very lofty trait," my uncle chimed in, beaming with satisfaction.

My poor uncle! he never could resist taking part in an *intellectual* conversation. Foma gave a malicious smile, but he remained silent.

"They write very interestingly, though, even now," Anfisa Petrovna intervened discreetly. *"The Mysteries of Brussels,* for instance."

"I should not say so," observed Foma, as it were regretfully. "I was lately reading one of the poems . . . not up to much! 'Forget-me-nots.' Of contemporary writers, if you will, the one I like best of all is 'Scribbler,' a light pen!"

" 'Scribbler!' " cried Anfisa Petrovna. "Is that the man who writes letters in the magazine? Ah, how enchanting it is, what playing with words!"

"Precisely, playing with words; he, so to speak, plays with his pen. An extraordinary lightness of style."

"Yes, but he is a pedant!" Obnoskin observed carelessly.

"Yes, a pedant he is, I don't dispute it; but a charming pedant, a graceful pedant! Of course, not one of his ideas would stand serious criticism, but one is carried away by his lightness! A babbler, I agree, but a charming babbler, a graceful babbler. Do you remember, for instance, in one of his articles, he mentions that he has his own estates?"

"Estates!" my uncle caught up. "That's good! In what province?"

Foma stopped, looked fixedly at my uncle, and went on in the same tone—

"Tell me in the name of common sense, of what interest is it to me, the reader, to know that he has his own estates? If he has—I congratulate him on it! But how charmingly, how jestingly, it is described! He sparkles with wit, he splashes with wit, he boils over! He is a Narzan of wit! Yes, that is the way to write! I fancy I should write just like that, if I were to consent to write for magazines. . . ."

"Perhaps you would do even better," Yezhevikin observed respectfully.

"There is positively something musical in the language," my uncle put in.

Foma Fomitch lost patience at last.

"Colonel," he said, "is it not possible to ask you—with all conceivable delicacy of course—not to interfere with us, but to allow us to finish our conversation in peace. You cannot offer an opinion in our conversation! You cannot. Don't disturb our agreeable literary chat. Look after your land, drink your tea, but . . . leave literature alone. It will lose nothing by it, I assure you—I assure you!"

This was surpassing the utmost limit of impudence! I did not know what to think.

"Why, you yourself, Foma, said it was musical," my uncle brought out in confusion and distress.

"Quite so, but I spoke with a knowledge of the subject, I spoke appropriately; while you . . ."

"To be sure, but we spoke with intellect," put in Yezhevikin, wriggling round Foma Fomitch. "We have just a little intelligence, though we may have to borrow some; just enough to run a couple of government departments and we might manage a third, if need be—that's all we can boast of!"

"So it seems I have been talking nonsense again," said my uncle in conclusion, and he smiled his good-natured smile.

"You admit it, anyway," observed Foma.

"It's all right, it's all right, Foma, I am not angry. I know that you pull me up like a friend, like a relation, like a brother. I have myself allowed you to do it, begged you to, indeed. It's a good thing. It's for my benefit. I thank you for it and will profit by it."

My patience was exhausted. All that I had hitherto heard about Foma Fomitch had seemed to me somewhat exaggerated. Now when I saw it all for myself, my astonishment was beyond all bounds. I could not believe my senses; I could not understand such impudence, such insolent domineering on one side and such voluntary slavery, such credulous good-nature on the other. Though indeed, my uncle himself was confused by such impudence. That was evident. . . . I was burning with desire to come to grips with Foma, to do battle with him, to be rude to him in some way, in as startling a fashion as possible—and then let come what may! This idea excited me. I looked for an opportunity, and completely ruined the brim of my hat while I waited for it. But the opportunity did not present itself. Foma absolutely refused to notice me.

"You are right, perfectly right, Foma," my uncle went on, doing his utmost to recover himself, and to smooth over the unpleasantness of what had been said before. "What you say is true, Foma. I thank you for it. One must know the subject before one discusses it. I am sorry! It is not the first time I have been in the same predicament. Only fancy, Sergey, on one occasion I was an examiner . . . you laugh! But there it is! I really was an examiner, and that was all about it. I was invited to an institution, to be present at an examination, and they set me down together with the examiners, as a sign of respect, there was an empty seat. So, I will own to you, I was frightened, I was positively alarmed, I do not know a single science. What was I to do? I thought that in another minute they would drag me myself to the blackboard! Well, what then? Nothing happened, it went off all right, I even asked questions myself; who was Noah? On the whole they answered splendidly; then we had lunch and toasted enlightenment in champagne. It was a fine school!"

Foma Fomitch and Obnoskin burst into roars of laughter.

"Indeed, I laughed myself afterwards," cried my uncle, laughing in a most good-natured way and delighted that general cheerfulness was restored. "Yes, Foma, here goes! I will amuse you all telling you how I put my foot in it once. . . . Only fancy, Sergey, we were staying at Krasnogorsk . . ."

"Allow me to inquire, Colonel, will you be long in telling your story?" Foma interposed.

"Oh, Foma! Why, it is the most delightful story, enough to make one split with laughter; you only listen, it is good, it really is good. I'll tell you how I put my foot in it."

"I always listen with pleasure to your stories when they are of that sort," Obnoskin pronounced, yawning.

"There is no help for it, we must listen," Foma decided.

"But upon my word it is good, Foma, it really is. I want to tell you how I put my foot into it on one occasion, Anfisa Petrovna. You listen too, Sergey, it is an edifying story indeed. We were staying at Krasnogorsk," my uncle began, beaming with pleasure, talking with nervous haste, and falling into innumerable parentheses as he always did when he was beginning to tell some story for the pleasure of his audience. "As soon as we arrived, the same evening we went to the theatre. There was a first-rate actress, Kuropatkina; she afterwards ran away with the cavalry captain

Zvyerkov and did not finish the play she was acting: so they let down the curtain. . . . This Zvyerkov was a beast, both for drinking and playing cards, and not that he was a drunkard, but simply ready to join his comrades at festive moments. But when he did get really drunk then he forgot everything, where he lived, in what country, and what his name was. Absolutely everything, in fact—but he was a very fine fellow really. . . . Well, I was sitting in the theatre. In the interval I got up, and I ran across a comrade called Kornouhov. . . . A unique fellow, I assure you. We had not seen each other for six years, it is true. Well, he had stayed in the company and was covered with crosses. I have heard lately—he's an actual civil councillor; he transferred to the civil service and worked his way up to a high grade. . . . Well, of course, we were delighted. One thing and another. In the box next to us were three ladies; the one on the left was the ugliest woman in the world. . . . Afterwards I found out that she was a splendid woman, the mother of a family, and the happiness of her husband. . . . Well, so I like a fool blurt out to Kornouhov: 'I say, old man, can you tell me who that scarecrow is?' 'Who do you mean?' 'Why, that one.' 'That's my cousin.' Tfoo, the devil! judge of my position! To put myself right: 'Not that one,' I said. 'What eyes you've got! I mean the one who is sitting there, who is that?' 'That's my sister.' Tfoo, plague take it all! And his sister, as luck would have it, was a regular rosebud, a sweet little thing; dressed up like anything —brooches, gloves, bracelets; in fact, a perfect cherub. Afterwards she married a very fine fellow called Pyhtin; she eloped with him, it was a runaway match; but now it is all right, and they are very well off; their parents are only too delighted! Well, so I cried out, 'Oh, no!' not knowing how to get out of it, 'not that one, the one in the middle, who is she?' 'In the middle? Well, my boy, that's my wife.' . . . And she, between ourselves, was a perfect sugarplum. I felt that I could have eaten her up at one mouthful, I was so delighted with her. . . . 'Well,' I said, 'have you ever seen a fool? Here is one facing you, and here's his head; cut it off, don't spare it!' He laughed. Afterwards he introduced them to me and must have told them, the rascal. They were in fits of laughter over something! And I must say I never spent an evening more merrily. So you see, Foma, old man, how one can put one's foot in it! Ha-ha-ha-ha!"

But it was no use my poor uncle laughing; in vain he looked round the company with his kind and good-humoured eyes; a dead silence was the response that greeted his light-hearted story. Foma Fomitch sat in gloomy dumbness and all the others followed his example; only Obnoskin gave a faint smile, foreseeing the baiting my uncle would get. My uncle was embarrassed and flushed crimson. This was what Foma desired.

"Have you finished?" he asked at last, turning with dignity to the embarrassed storyteller.

"Yes, Foma."

"And are you satisfied?"

"How do you mean, satisfied?" asked my poor uncle miserably.

"Are you happier now? Are you pleased at having broken up the pleasant literary conversation of your friends by interrupting them and so satisfying your petty vanity?"

"Oh, come, Foma, I wanted to amuse you all, and you . . ."

"Amuse!" cried Foma, suddenly becoming extraordinarily heated; "but you are only able to depress us, not amuse us. Amuse! but do know that your story was almost immoral. I say nothing of its impropriety, that is self-evident. . . . You informed us just now with rare coarseness of feeling that you laughed at innocence, at an honourable lady, simply because she had not the honour to please you, and you wanted to make us, *us* laugh, that is, applaud you, that is, applaud a coarse and improper action, and all because you are the master of this house! You can do as you like, Colonel, you can seek out toadies, flatterers, sycophants, you can even send for them from distant parts and so increase your retinue to the detriment of straightforwardness and frank nobility of soul, but never will Foma Opiskin be your toady, your flatterer, your sycophant! I can assure you of that, if of anything. . . ."

"Oh, Foma! You misunderstand me, Foma."

"No, Colonel; I have seen through you for a long time, I know you through and through. You are devoured by boundless vanity. You have pretensions to an incomparable keenness of wit, and forget that wit is blunted by pretension. You . . ."

"Oh, stop, Foma, for God's sake! Have some shame, if only before people!"

"It's sad, you know, to see all this, Colonel, and it's impossible to be silent when one sees it. I am poor, I am living at the expense of your mother. It may be expected, perhaps, that I should flatter you by my silence, and I don't care for any milksop to take me for your toady! Possibly when I came into this room just now I intentionally accentuated my truthful candour, was forced to be intentionally rude, just because you yourself put me into such a position. You are too haughty with me, Colonel, I may be taken for your slave, your toady. Your pleasure is to humiliate me before *strangers,* while I am really your equal—your equal in every respect. Perhaps *I* am doing you a favour in living with you, and not *you* doing me one. I am insulted, so I am forced to sing my own praises—that's natural! I cannot help speaking, I must speak, I am bound at once to protest, and that is why I tell you straight out that you are phenomenally envious. You see, for instance, some one in a simple friendly conversation unconsciously reveals his knowledge, his reading, his taste, and so you are annoyed, you can't sit still. 'Let me display my knowledge and my taste,' you think! And what taste have you, if you will allow me to ask? You know as much about art—if you will excuse my saying so, Colonel—as a bull about beef! That's harsh and rude, I admit; anyway it is straightforward and just. You won't hear that from your flatterers, Colonel."

"Oh, Foma! . . ."

"It is 'Oh, Foma,' to be sure. The truth is not a feather-bed, it seems. Very well, then, we will speak later about this, but now let me entertain the company a little. You can't be the only one to distinguish yourself all the time. Pavel Semyonitch, have you seen this sea monster in human form? I have been observing him for a long time. Look well at him; why, he would like to devour me whole, at one gulp."

He was speaking of Gavrila. The old servant was standing at the door, and certainly was looking on with distress at the scolding of his master.

"I want to entertain you, too, with a performance, Pavel Semyonitch. Come here, you scarecrow, come here. Condescend to approach us a little nearer, Gavrila Ignatitch! Here you see, Pavel Semyonitch, is Gavrila; as a punishment for rudeness he is studying the French dialect. Like Orpheus, I soften the manners of these parts not only with songs but with the French dialect. Come, Mossoo Frenchy —he can't bear to be called Mossoo—do you know your lesson?"

"I have learnt it," said Gavrila, hanging his head.

"Well, Parlay—voo—fransay?"

"Vee, moossyu, zhe—le—parl—on—peu. . . ."

I don't know whether it was Gavril's mournful face as he uttered the French phrase, or whether they were all aware of Foma's desire that they should laugh, but anyway they all burst into a roar of laughter as soon as Gavrila opened his lips. Even Madame la Générale deigned to be amused. Anfisa Petrovna, sinking back on the sofa, shrieked, hiding her face behind her fan. What seemed most ludicrous was that Gavrila, seeing what his examination was being turned into, could not restrain himself from spitting and commenting reproachfully: "To think of having lived to such a disgrace in my old age!"

Foma Fomitch was startled.

"What? What did you say? So you think fit to be rude?"

"No, Foma Fomitch," Gavrila replied with dignity. "My words were no rudeness, and it's not for me, a serf, to be rude to you, a gentleman born. But every man bears the image of God upon him, His image and semblance. I am sixty-three years old. My father remembers Pugatchev, the monster, and my grandfather helped his master, Matvey Nigititch—God grant him the kingdom of heaven!—to hang Pugatchev on an aspen tree, for which my father was honoured beyond all others by our late master, Afanasy Matveyitch: he was his valet, and ended his life as butler. As for me, Foma Fomitch, sir, though I am my master's bondman, I have never known such a shame done me from my birth upward till now."

And at the last word Gavrila spread out his hands and hung his head. My uncle was watching him uneasily.

"Come, that's enough, Gavrila," he cried. "No need to say more, that's enough!"

"Never mind, never mind," said Foma, turning a little pale and giving a forced smile. "Let him speak, these are the fruits of your . . ."

"I will tell you everything," said Gavrila with extraordinary fervour, "I will conceal nothing! You may bind the hands, but there is no binding the tongue. Though I may seem beside you, Foma Fomitch, a low man, in fact, a slave, yet I can feel insulted! Service and obedience I am always bound to give you, because I am born a slave and must do my duty in fear and trembling. You sit writing a book, it's my duty not to let you be interrupted—that is my real duty. Any service that is needed I am pleased to do. But in my old age to bleat in some outlandish way and be put to shame before folk! Why, I can't go into the servants' room now: 'You are a Frenchy!' they say, 'a Frenchy!' No. Foma Fomitch, sir, it's not only a fool like me, but all good folks have begun to say the same: that you have become now a wicked man and that our master is nothing but a little child before you, that though you are a gentleman by birth and a general's son, and yourself may be near being a general too, yet you are as wicked as a real fury must be."

Gavrila had finished. I was beside myself with delight. Foma Fomitch sat pale with rage in the midst of the general discomfiture and seemed unable to recover from Gavrila's sudden attack upon him; he seemed at that moment to be deliberating how far his wrath should carry him. At last the outburst followed.

"What, he dares be rude to me—me! but this is mutiny!" shrieked Foma, and he leapt up from his chair.

Madame la Générale followed his example, clasping her hands. There was a general commotion, my uncle rushed to turn the culprit out.

"Put him in fetters, put him in fetters!" cried Madame la Générale. "Take him to the town at once and send him for a soldier, Yegorushka, or you shall not have any blessing. Fix the fetters on him at once, and send him for a soldier."

"What!" cried Foma. "Slave! Lout! Hamlet! He dares to be rude to me! He, he, a rag to wipe my boots! He dares to call me a fury!"

I slipped forward with unusual determination.

"I must confess that in this affair I am completely of Gavrila's opinion," I said, looking Foma Fomitch straight in the face and trembling with excitement.

He was so taken aback by this onslaught that for the first minute he seemed unable to believe his ears.

"What's this, now?" he cried out at last, pouncing upon me in a frenzy, and fixing his little bloodshot eyes upon me. "Why, who are you?"

"Foma Fomitch . . ." my uncle, utterly distracted, began, "this is Seryozha, my nephew. . . ."

"The learned gentleman!" yelled Foma. "So he's the learned gentleman! *Liberté—égalité—fraternité. Journal des Débats!* No, my friend, you won't take me in! I am not such a fool. This isn't Petersburg, you won't impose upon us. And I spit on your *des Débats.* You have your *des Débats,* but to us that's all fiddlesticks, young man! Learned. You know as much as I have forgotten seven times over. So much for your learning!"

If they had not held him back I believe he would have fallen upon me with his fists.

"Why, he is drunk," I said, looking about me in bewilderment.

"Who, I?" cried Foma, in a voice unlike his own.

"Yes, you!"

"Drunk?"

"Yes, drunk."

This was more than Foma could endure. He uttered a screech as though he were being murdered and rushed out of the room. Madame la Générale seemed desirous of falling into a swoon, but reflected that it would be better to run after Foma Fomitch. She was followed by all the others, and last of all by my uncle. When I recovered myself and looked round I saw in the room no one but Yezhevikin. He was smiling and rubbing his hands.

"You promised just now to tell me about the Jesuits," he said in an insinuating voice.

"What?" I asked, not understanding what he was talking about.

"About the Jesuits, you promised just now to tell me . . . some little anecdote. . . ."

I ran out into the verandah and from there into the garden. My head was going round. . . .

A Declaration of Love

VIII

I wandered about the garden for about a quarter of an hour, feeling irritated and extremely dissatisfied with myself, and deliberating what I should do now. The sun was setting. Suddenly at a turning into a dark avenue I met Nastenka face to face. She had tears in her eyes, in her hand a handkerchief with which she was wiping them.

"I was looking for you," she said.

"And I for you," I answered. "Tell me, am I in a madhouse?"

"Certainly not in a madhouse," she answered resentfully, with an intent glance at me.

"Well, if that's so, what's the meaning of it all? For Christ's sake give me some advice. Where has my uncle gone now? Can I go to him? I am very glad that I have met you; perhaps you will be able to suggest what I ought to do."

"No, better not go to him. I have just come away from them."

"Why, where are they?"

"Who knows? Perhaps by now they have run into the kitchen garden again," she said irritably.

"Into the kitchen garden!"

"Why, last week, Foma Fomitch began shouting that he wouldn't stay in the house, and all at once he ran into the kitchen garden, found a spade in the shed and began digging the beds. We were all amazed, and wondered whether he hadn't gone out of his mind. 'That I may not be reproached for doing nothing for my keep,' said he, 'here I will dig and pay for the bread I have eaten, and then I will go away. That's what you have driven me to.' And then they all began crying and almost falling on their knees before him; they took the spade away from him; but he would go on digging; he·dug up all the turnips, that was all he did. They humoured him once, he may do it again. That would be just like him."

"And you . . . you tell that with such coolness!" I cried out, with intense indignation.

She looked at me with flashing eyes.

"Forgive me, I really don't know what I am saying! Listen! do you know what I've come here for?"

"N-no," she answered, flushing crimson, and some painful feeling was reflected in her charming face.

"You must excuse me," I went on. "I am upset, I feel that this is not how I ought to have begun speaking of this . . . especially with you. . . . But never mind! To my thinking, openness in such matters is best. I confess . . . that is, I meant to say . . . you know my uncle's design? He has told me to ask for your hand. . . ."

"Oh, what nonsense! don't speak of it, please," she said hurriedly interrupting me and flushing crimson.

I was disconcerted.

"How nonsense? But he wrote to me, you see."

"So he wrote to you?" she asked eagerly. "Oh, what a

man! How he promised that he would not write! What nonsense! Good heavens, what nonsense!"

"Forgive me," I muttered, not knowing what to say. "Perhaps I have acted incautiously, crudely . . . but, you see, it's such a moment! Only think, goodness knows what's going on around us. . . ."

"Oh, for God's sake don't apologize! Believe me that it is painful for me to hear this apart from that, and yet, do you know, I wanted to speak to you myself, to find out something. . . . Oh, how vexatious! So he really wrote to you? That's what I was most afraid of! My God, what a man he is! And you believed him and galloped here full speed? Well, that's the last straw!"

She did not conceal her annoyance. My position was not an attractive one.

"I must confess I did not expect . . ." I blurted out in the utmost confusion, "such a turn . . . I expected, on the contrary . . ."

"Ah, so that's what you expected? . . ." she brought out with light irony, biting her lip. "And do you know, you must show me the letter he wrote."

"Very good."

"And please don't be angry with me, don't be offended; I have trouble enough without that!" she said in an imploring voice, though a mocking smile faintly gleamed on her pretty lips.

"Oh, please don't take me for a fool," I cried hotly. "But perhaps you are prejudiced against me, perhaps some one has spoken against me? Perhaps you say this because I put my foot in it just now? But that is nothing, I assure you. I know what a fool I must look to you now. Don't laugh at me, please! I don't know what I am saying, and it is all because I am twenty-two, damn it."

"Oh, mercy on us, why?"

"You ask why? Any one who is twenty-two, you know, has it written in his face; as I had, for instance, when I bounced out just now in the middle of the room, or as when I stand before you now. . . . It's a damnable age!"

"Oh, no, no!" answered Nastenka, hardly able to restrain her laughter. "I am sure that you are kind and nice and clever, and I say that sincerely, I do really! But . . . you are only very vain. You may get over that in time."

"I fancy I am only as vain as I ought to be."

"Oh, no. Think how embarrassed you were just now, and what for? Because you stumbled as you came in! . . . What right had you to turn into ridicule your good generous uncle who has done you so much kindness? Why did you try to turn the laugh against him when you were laughable yourself? That was horrid, shameful! It does not do you credit, and I must own I disliked you very much at that minute, so there!"

"That's true! I was a blockhead! more than that—I did a mean thing! You noticed it, and that is my punishment. Abuse me, laugh at me, but listen; perhaps you will change your opinion of me in the end," I added, carried away by a strange feeling. "You know so little of me as yet; afterwards when you know more of me, then . . . perhaps . . ."

"For God's sake let us stop this conversation!" cried Nastenka, with visible impatience.

"Very well, very well, let us stop! But . . . where can I see you?"

"Where can you see me?"

"Why, you know, this cannot be the last word we have to say to each other, Nastasya Yevgrafovna! For God's sake, let me meet you again to-day, for instance. But it's already getting dark. So if it is anyhow possible let it be to-morrow early; I will ask to be called earlier on purpose. You know there's an arbour over there by the pond. You see, I remember it, I know the way. I used to stay here when I was little."

"Meet you! What for? Why, we are talking now."

"But I know nothing yet, Nastasya Yevgrafovna, I will first find out everything from my uncle. Why, he is bound to tell me everything now. And then, perhaps, I shall have something very important to tell you. . . ."

"No, no! You mustn't!" cried Nastenka. "Let us end it all at once now, so that we may never think of it again. And don't go to that arbour for nothing; I assure you I shall not go. And please put all this nonsense out of your head—I beg you in earnest. . . ."

"So then uncle has behaved like a madman to me!" I cried, in an excess of insufferable vexation. "Why did he send for me? But listen, what is that noise?"

We were close to the house; from the open windows came the sounds of shrieking and extraordinary outcries.

"My God!" she said, turning pale, "again! I foresaw it would be so!"

"You foresaw it? Nastasya Yevgrafovna, one more question. Of course I have not the least right to do so, but I venture to put this last question to you for the good of us all. Tell me—and I will keep it secret to the grave—tell me frankly: is my uncle in love with you or not?"

"Oh! Please, please put that nonsense out of your head once for all," she cried, flushing crimson with anger. "And you, too! If he were in love with me, he wouldn't have wanted to have married me to you," she added with a bitter smile. "And what put that idea into your head? Don't you know what the trouble's about? Do you hear those shouts?"

"But . . . It's Foma Fomitch. . . ."

"Yes, of course it is Foma Fomitch; but now the trouble is over me because they are saying the same thing as you, the same senseless thing; they, too, suspect that he is in love with me. And as I am poor and of no consequence, and as it costs nothing to throw dirt on me and they want to marry him to someone else, they are insisting that he should send me home to my father to make things sure. And when they talk to him of that he flies into a rage at once; he's ready to tear Foma Fomitch to pieces even. They are quarrelling about that now; I feel that it is about that."

"So that's the truth! So he really is going to marry that silly fool Tatyana, then."

"Not a silly fool at all! She is good; you have no right to talk like that! She has a noble heart, nobler than many other people. It's not her fault that she is unfortunate."

"Forgive me. Supposing you are quite right about that,

yet aren't you mistaken about the chief point? Tell me, how is it, then, that they make your father welcome, as I noticed? Why, if they were so set against you as you say and were turning you out, they would be angry with him too, and would give him a cold welcome."

"Why, don't you see what my father is doing for my sake? He is playing the fool before them! He is received just because he has succeeded in ingratiating himself with Foma Fomitch; and as Foma Fomitch was a buffoon himself, you see it flatters him to have buffoons about him now. For whose sake do you suppose my father does it? He does it for me, only for me. He wants nothing; he wouldn't bow down to any one for himself. He may be very absurd in some people's eyes, but he is a noble man, the noblest of men! He thinks—goodness knows why, and certainly not because I get a good salary here, I assure you—he thinks that it is best for me to stay here in this house; but now I have quite brought him round. I wrote to him firmly. He has come on purpose to take me; and if it comes to extremes, to-morrow. For things have got beyond everything; they are ready to tear me to pieces, and I am certain that they are quarrelling about me now. They are at *him*, on my account, they will be the death of *him!* And he is like a father to me—do you hear? more even than my own father. I won't stay to see it. I know more than other people. To-morrow, to-morrow I am going! Who knows: perhaps that will make them put off, if only for a time, his marriage to Tatyana Ivanovna. . . . Here I have told you all about it now. Tell him this, because I can't speak to him now; we are watched, especially by that Perepelitsyn woman. Tell him not to worry about me, tell him I would rather eat black bread and live in my father's hut than be the cause of his sufferings here. I am a poor girl, and I ought to live like a poor girl. But, my God, what an uproar! What shouting! What is happening? Yes, come what may I shall go in! I will tell them all this straight to their faces myself, whatever happens! I ought to do it! Good-bye."

She ran away. I remained standing on the same spot, fully conscious of the absurdity of the part it had just been my lot to play, and completely puzzled to think how it would all be settled. I was sorry for the poor girl, and I was afraid for my uncle. All at once I found Gavrila at my side; he was still holding the exercise book in his hand.

"Please come to your uncle," he said in a dejected voice.

I pulled myself together.

"To my uncle? Where is he? What's happening to him now?"

"In the tea-room. Where your honour had tea this afternoon."

"Who is with him?"

"His honour's alone. He is waiting."

"For whom? For me?"

"He has sent for Foma Fomitch. Happy days have come for us," he added, with a deep sigh.

"Foma Fomitch? H'm! Where are the others? Where's your mistress?"

"In her own apartments. Her honour's fallen into a swoon, and now she is lying unconscious and crying."

Conversing in this way, we reached the verandah. It was almost completely dark outside. My uncle really was alone in the very room in which my encounter with Foma Fomitch had taken place, and he was striding up and down it. There were lighted candles on the tables. Seeing me, he rushed up to me and warmly pressed my hands. He was pale and breathing hard; his hands were trembling, and from time to time a nervous shudder ran over his whole frame.

Your Excellency

IX

"My dear boy, it's all over, it's all settled," he pronounced in a tragic half-whisper.

"Uncle," I said, "I heard shouts and uproar."

"Yes, my boy, shouts there were; shouts of all sorts! Mamma is in a swoon, and everything is upside down now. But I have made up my mind, and shall insist on my own way. I am afraid of no one now, Seryozha. I want to show them that I, too, have a will of my own, and I will show them! And so I have sent for you on purpose that you may help me show them. . . . My heart is broken, Seryozha . . . but I ought, I am bound to act with severity. Justice is inexorable."

"But whatever has happened, uncle?"

"I am parting with Foma," my uncle pronounced in a resolute voice.

"Uncle," I cried, delighted, "you could have thought of nothing better! And if I can assist in any way to carry out your decision . . . make use of me now and always."

"Thank you, my boy, thank you! But now it is all settled. I am waiting for Foma, I have already sent for him. Either he or I! We must part. Either Foma leaves this house to-morrow or I swear I'll throw up everything and go into the Hussars again. They will take me and give me a division. Away with all this bobbery! A fresh start in every way now. What have you got that French exercise book for?" he cried furiously, addressing Gavrila. "Away with it! Burn it, stamp on it, tear it to pieces! *I* am your master, and *I* order you not to learn French. You can't disobey me, you dare not, for *I* am your master, and not Foma Fomitch!"

"I thank Thee, O Lord!" Gavrila muttered to himself.

Evidently things had got beyond a joke.

"My dear," my uncle went on, with deep feeling, "they are asking me the impossible. You shall decide; you stand between me and them now as an impartial judge. You don't know what they have insisted on my doing, you don't know, and at last they have formally demanded it, they have spoken out. But it's repugnant of humanity, to decent feeling, to honour. . . . I will tell you all about it, but first . . ."

"I know about it already, uncle!" I cried, interrupting him. "I can guess . . . I have just been talking to Nastasya Yevgrafovna."

"My dear, not a word, not a word of that now!" he interrupted me hurriedly, as though he were frightened. "I will explain about it later on, but meanwhile. . . . Well?" he cried to Vidoplyasov, who walked in. "Where is Foma Fomitch?"

Vidoplyasov entered with the information "that Foma Fomitch did not wish to come, and considered that the insistence on his doing so was rude to the point of impertinence, so that his honour, Foma Fomitch, was greatly offended by it."

"Bring him! Drag him! Fetch him here! Drag him here by force!" cried my uncle, stamping.

Vidoplyasov, who had never seen his master in such a rage, retreated in alarm. I was surprised.

"Something very important must have happened," I thought, "if a man of his character is capable of being moved to such wrath and such determination."

For some moments my uncle walked up and down the room as though struggling with himself.

"Don't tear up your exercise book though," he said to Gavrila at last. "Wait a little and stay here. You may perhaps be wanted. My dear," he went on, turning to me, "I think I was too noisy just now. Everything must be done with dignity and manliness, but without shouting and insulting people. Do you know what, Seryozha; wouldn't it be better if you were to go out? It will be just the same to you. I will tell you all about it later on—eh? What do you think? Do that for my sake, please."

"Are you frightened, uncle? Are you repenting?" I said, looking at him intently.

"No, no, my dear boy, I am not repenting," cried my uncle, with redoubled earnestness. "I am afraid of nothing now. I have taken decisive steps, the most decisive! You don't know, you can't imagine what they have demanded of me! Ought I to consent? No, I will show them. I have made a stand against them and I will show them. I was bound to show them sooner or later! But you know, my dear boy, I am sorry I sent for you; it will be very hard, perhaps, for Foma if you are here, so to say, the witness of his humiliation. You see, I want to turn him out of the house in a gentlemanly way, without humiliating him at all. Though, indeed, it is only a form of words to say, without humiliation. The position is such, my boy, that however honeyed one's speech is it will still be insulting. I am coarse, uneducated perhaps, I may do something in my foolishness that I may regret later. Anyway he has done a great deal for me. . . . Go away, my dear. . . . Here, they are bringing him! Seryozha, I entreat you, go away; I will tell you all about it afterwards. For Christ's sake go away!"

And uncle led me out on to the verandah at the very moment when Foma walked into the room. But I must confess I did not go away; I made up my mind to stay on the verandah where it was very dark, and so it was difficult to see me from within. I made up my mind to play the eavesdropper! I do not justify my action, but I can boldly say that I consider I performed an heroic feat in standing that whole half-hour on the verandah without losing patience.

From my position I could not only hear well, but could even see well; the doors were of glass. I now beg the reader to imagine Foma Fomitch after he had been *commanded* to come, and threatened with force if he refused.

"Can my ears have heard that threat aright, Colonel?" cried Foma, entering the room. "Was that your message?"

"Yes, Foma, yes; calm yourself," my uncle answered valiantly. "Sit down; we must have a little serious friendly talk like brothers. Sit down, Foma."

Foma Fomitch majestically sat down on a low chair. My uncle walked about the room with rapid and uneven steps, evidently puzzled how to begin.

"Like brothers, precisely," he repeated. "You understand me, Foma; you are not a boy, I am not a boy either—in fact, we are both getting on. . . . H'm! You see, Foma, we don't get on together on certain points . . . yes, on certain points precisely, and so, Foma, would it not be better to part? I am convinced that you are a generous man, that you wish me well, and so . . . But why prolong the discussion? Foma, I am your friend now and always, and I swear that by all the saints! Here are fifteen thousand roubles in

silver; it's all I have to bless myself with. I have scraped together every farthing, I have robbed my own children. Take
it boldly! I ought—it is my duty—to secure your future. It's
almost all in banknotes and very little in cash. Take it boldly;
you owe me nothing, for I shall never be able to repay you
for all you have done for me. Yes, yes, precisely, I feel that,
though now we are in disagreement over the most important
point. To-morrow or the day after, or when you like, let us
part. Drive to our little town, Foma, it is not eight miles
away; there behind the church in the first side street there
is a little house with green shutters, a charming little house
belonging to the widow of a priest, that looks as though it
had been built for you. She is selling it, and I will buy it for
you in addition to this money. Settle there near us. Work at
literature, study science, you will win fame. . . . The officials there are gentlemanly, agreeable, disinterested men;
the head priest is learned. You shall come and stay with us
for the holidays—and we shall all live as in paradise. Will
you?"

"So these are the terms on which Foma is to be kicked
out!" I thought. "Uncle did not say a word to me about
money."

For a long time a profound silence reigned. Foma sat in
his easy-chair as though struck dumb, gazing fixedly at my
uncle, who was evidently becoming uncomfortable from
that silence and that stare.

"The money!" Foma articulated at last in an affectedly
faint voice. "Where is it? Where is that money? Give it me,
give it here at once!"

"Here it is, Foma, everything I have to the last farthing,
just fifteen thousand. Here are notes and securities; you can
see for yourself . . . here!"

"Gavrila, take that money," Foma said mildly, "it may
be of use to you, old man. But no!" he cried all at once,
raising his voice to an extraordinary squeal and leaping up
from his chair; "no, give me that money first, Gavrila!
Give it me. Give it me. Give me those millions that I may
trample them under foot; give them to me that I may tear
them to pieces, spit on them, fling them away, spurn them,

scorn them! . . . They offer money to me—to me! They
try to buy me to leave this house! Have I heard that? Have
I lived to see this last ignominy? Here they are, here are
your millions! Look! there, there, there, there. That is how
Foma Opiskin behaves if you did not know it before,
Colonel!"

And Foma threw the whole roll of notes about the room.
It was noticeable that he did not tear or spit on one of the
notes as he had boasted of doing; he only crumpled them
a little, and even that rather carefully. Gavrila flew to pick
up the notes from the floor, and later on, after Foma's departure, he carefully restored them to his master.

Foma's action produced an overwhelming impression
upon my uncle. In his turn, he now stood facing him, im-
movably, senselessly, open-mouthed. Foma meanwhile had
replaced himself in his arm-chair and was panting as
though from unutterable agitation.

"You are a man of lofty feelings, Foma!" my uncle
cried out at last, recovering himself. "You are the noblest
of men!"

"I know it," Foma answered in a faint voice, but with
ineffable dignity.

"Foma, forgive me! I have been a mean wretch to you,
Foma!"

"Yes, to me," Foma assented.

"Foma, it is not your disinterestedness that I marvel at,"
my uncle went on enthusiastically, "but that I could have
been so coarse, blind and mean as to offer you money in
such circumstances. But, Foma, you are mistaken about
one thing; I was not bribing you, I was not paying you for
leaving this house, but just simply I wanted you to have
money that you might not be in straits when you leave me.
I swear that! On my knees, on my knees I am ready to beg
your forgiveness, Foma; and if you like, I am ready to go
down on my knees before you this moment . . . if you wish
me to. . . ."

"I don't want your kneeling, Colonel."

"But, my God! Foma, consider: you know I was carried away, overwhelmed, I was not myself. . . . But do tell

me, do say in what way I can, in what way I may be able
to efface this insult! Instruct me, admonish me. . . ."

"In no way, in no way, Colonel! And rest assured that
to-morrow morning I shall shake the dust from off my
boots on the threshold of this house."

And Foma began to get up from his chair. My uncle
rushed in horror to make him sit down again.

"No, Foma, you will not go away, I assure you!" cried
my uncle. "It is no use talking about dust and boots, Foma!
You are not going away, or I will follow you to the utmost
ends of the earth, and I will follow you till such time as
you forgive me. . . . I swear it, Foma, and I will do it!"

"Forgive you? You are to blame?" said Foma. "But do
you yet understand the wrong you have done me? Do you
understand that even the fact that you have given me a
piece of bread here has become a wrong to me now? Do
you understand that now in one minute you have poisoned
every morsel I have tasted in your house? You reproached
me just now with those morsels, with every mouthful of
the bread I have eaten; you have shown me now that I
have been living like a slave in your house, like a flunkey,
like a rag to wipe your polished boots! And yet I, in the
purity of my heart, imagined up to now that I was residing
in your house as a friend and a brother! Did you not, did
you not yourself in your snake-like speeches assure me a
thousand times of that brotherly relation? Why did you
mysteriously weave for me the snare, in which I have been
caught like a fool? Why have you dug in the darkness this
wolf-pit into which you have yourself thrust me now? Why
did you not strike me down with one blow before? Why did
you not wring my neck at the very beginning like a cock,
because he . . . well, for instance, simply because he doesn't
lay eggs? Yes, that's just it! I stick to that comparison, Colonel, though it is taken from rustic life and recalls the trivial
tone of modern literature; I stick to it, because one sees in
it all the senselessness of your accusation; for I am as much
in fault as this supposititious cock who displeases his frivolous owner by not laying eggs! Upon my word, Colonel!
Does one pay a friend, a brother, with money—and what

for? That's the point, what for? 'Here, my beloved brother, I am indebted to you; you have even saved my life; here are a few of Judas's silver pieces for you, only get away out of my sight!' How naïve! How crudely you have behaved to me! You thought that I was thirsting for your gold, while I was cherishing only the heavenly feeling of securing your welfare. Oh, how you have broken my heart! You have played with my finest feelings like some wretched boy with a ninepin! Long, long ago, Colonel, I foresaw all this—that is why I have long choked over your bread, I have been suffocated by your bread! That is why your feather-beds have stifled me, they have stifled me instead of lulling me to slumber! That is why your sugar, your sweetmeats have been cayenne pepper to me and not sweetmeats! No, Colonel! live alone, prosper alone, and let Foma go his sorrowful way with a wallet on his back. So it shall be, Colonel!"

"No, Foma, no! It shall not be so, it cannot be so!" moaned my uncle, utterly crushed.

"Yes, Colonel, yes! So it shall be, for so it must be. Tomorrow I shall depart from you. Scatter your millions, strew all my way, all the high road to Moscow with your banknotes—and I will walk proudly and scornfully over your notes; this very foot, Colonel, will trample your notes into the mud and crush them; for Foma Opiskin the nobility of his own soul will be enough! I have said it and I have shown it! Farewell, Colonel, fa-re-we-ell!"

And Foma began again getting up from his chair.

"Forgive me, forgive me, Foma; forget it! . . ." repeated my uncle, in an imploring voice.

"Forgive you! Why, what use will my forgiveness be to you? Why, supposing I do forgive you: I am a Christian; I cannot refuse to forgive; I have almost forgiven you already. But consider yourself: is it in the least consistent with common sense and gentlemanly feeling for me to stay one minute longer in your house? Why, you have turned me out of it!"

"It is consistent, it is consistent, Foma! I assure you that it is consistent!"

"It is? But are we equals now? Don't you understand that

I have, so to speak, crushed you by my generosity, and you have crushed yourself by your degrading action? You are crushed and I am uplifted. Where is the equality? Is friendship possible without equality? I say this, uttering a cry of lamentation from my heart, and not triumphing, not exalting myself over you, as you perhaps imagine."

"But I am uttering a cry of lamentation from my heart too, Foma, I assure you."

"And this is the man," Foma went on, changing his severe tone for a sanctimonious one, "this is the man for whom I so often kept vigil at night! How many times on my sleepless nights have I arisen from my bed, have lighted a candle and said to myself, 'Now he is sleeping peacefully, trusting in you. Do not you, Foma, sleep, be valiant for him; maybe you will think of something more for the welfare of that man.' That is what Foma thought on his sleepless nights, Colonel! And this is how that colonel has repaid him! But I will deserve, enough . . ."

"But I will deserve your friendship again, Foma; I will deserve it, I swear to you."

"You will deserve it? Where is the guarantee? As a Christian I will forgive you, and even love you; but as a man and a gentleman I shall not be able to help despising you. I must, I am bound to, in the name of morality, because—I repeat it—you have disgraced yourself, while my action has been most high-minded. Why, who out of *your* set would perform such an action? Would any one of them refuse an immense sum of money which poor destitute Foma, despised by all, has refused from devotion to true greatness? No, Colonel; to be on a level with me you must perform now a regular series of heroic deeds. And what are you capable of when you cannot even address me as your equal, but call me Foma like a servant. . . ."

"Foma! but I call you so from affection!" wailed my uncle. "I did not know you disliked it. My God! if I had only known! . . ."

"You," Foma pursued, "you who could not, or rather, would not, grant the most insignificant, the most trivial re-

quest when I asked you to address me like a general as
'your Excellency' . . ."

"But, Foma, you know that is really, so to say, high
treason, Foma."

"High treason! You have learnt some phrase out of a
book and repeat it like a parrot! But, do you know, you put
me to shame, covered me with ignominy by your refusal
to call me 'your Excellency'; you covered me with ignominy
because without understanding my reasons you made me
look a capricious fool worthy of a madhouse. Why, do you
suppose I don't understand that I should have been ridiculous if I had wanted to be styled 'Excellency'——I who despise all these ranks and earthly grandeurs, insignificant in
themselves if they are not lighted up by virtue? For a million I would not accept your rank of general, without virtue. And meanwhile you looked upon me as a madman! It
was for your benefit I sacrificed my pride and allowed you,
you to be able to look upon me as a madman, you and your
learned gentlemen! It was solely in order to enlighten your
mind, to develop your morals, and to shed upon you the
light of new ideas that I made up my mind to demand from
you a general's title. I wanted you for the future not to regard generals as the highest luminaries on this earthly
sphere; I wanted to show you that rank is nothing without
greatness of soul, and that there is no need to rejoice at the
arrival of your general when there are, perhaps, standing at
your side, people made illustrious by virtue! But you have
so constantly prided yourself before me on your rank of
colonel that it was hard for you to say to me: 'your Excellency.' That was the root of it! That was where one must
look for the reason, and not in any breach of the decrees of
Providence! The whole reason is, that you are a colonel
and I am simply Foma. . . ."

"No, Foma; no, I assure you that it is not so. You are a
learned man . . . you are not simply Foma. . . . I respect
you. . . ."

"You respect me! Good! Then tell me, since you respect
me, what is your opinion, am I worthy of the rank of a
general or am I not? Answer at once and straightforwardly,

am I or not? I want to see your intelligence, your development."

"For honesty, for disinterestedness, for intelligence, for lofty nobility of soul you are worthy of it," my uncle brought out with pride.

"Well, if I am worthy of it, why will you not say 'your Excellency' to me?"

"Foma, I will, perhaps."

"But, I insist! And I insist now, Colonel, I require it and insist. I see how hard it is for you, that is why I insist. That sacrifice on your side will be the first step in your moral victory, for—don't forget it—you will have to gain a series of moral victories to be on a level with me; you must conquer yourself, and only then I shall feel certain of your sincerity. . . ."

"Tomorrow, then, I will call you 'your Excellency,' Foma."

"No, not to-morrow, Colonel, to-morrow can take care of itself. I insist that you now at once address me as 'your Excellency.' "

"Certainly, Foma, I am ready; only what do you mean by 'at once,' Foma?"

"Why not at once, or are you ashamed? That's an insult to me if you are ashamed."

"Oh, well, if you like, Foma. I am ready . . . I am proud to do so, indeed; only it's queer, Foma, apropos of nothing, 'Good-day, your Excellency.' You see, one can't."

"No, not 'Good-day, your Excellency.' That's an offensive tone, it is like a joke, a farce. I do not permit such jokes with me. You forget yourself, Colonel, you forget yourself. Change your tone!"

"And you are not joking, Foma?"

"In the first place, I am not Foma, Yegor Ilyitch, and don't you forget it. I am Foma Fomitch."

"Oh, Foma Fomitch, I am delighted, really, I am altogether delighted, only what am I to say?"

"You are puzzled what to add to the phrase 'your Excellency.' That I understand. You should have explained yourself long ago. It is excusable indeed, especially if a man is not a *literary character,* to put it politely. Well, I will help you, since you are not a literary character. Repeat after me, 'Your Excellency!' . . ."

"Well, your Excellency . . ."

"No, not 'Well, your Excellency,' but simply 'your Excellency!' I tell you, Colonel, you must change your tone. I hope, too, that you will not be offended if I suggest that you should make a slight bow. And at the same time bend forward, expressing in that way respectfulness and readiness, so to say, to fly on his errands. I have been in the society of generals myself, and I know all that, so then 'your Excellency.' "

"Your Excellency . . ."

"How inexpressibly delighted I am that I have at last an opportunity of asking your forgiveness for not having recognized from the first moment your Excellency's soul. I make bold to assure you that I will not for the future spare my poor efforts for the public welfare. . . . Well, that's enough!"

Poor uncle! He had to repeat all this rigmarole phrase by phrase, word by word. I stood and blushed as though I were guilty. I was choking with rage.

"Well, don't you feel now," the torturer went on, "that your heart is suddenly lighter, as though an angel had flown into your soul? . . . Do you feel the presence of that angel? Answer."

"Yes, Foma, I certainly feel more at ease," answered my uncle.

"As though after you have conquered yourself your heart were, so to say, steeped in holy oil?"

"Yes, Foma; certainly it all seems as it were in butter."

"As it were in butter? H'm I wasn't talking of butter, though. . . . Well, never mind! You see, Colonel, the value of a duty performed! Conquer yourself. You are vain, immensely vain!"

"I see I am, Foma," my uncle answered, with a sigh.

"You are an egoist, and indeed a gloomy egoist. . . ."

"An egoist I am, it is true, Foma, and I see it; ever since I have come to know you, I have learned to know that too."

"I am speaking to you now like a father, like a tender

mother. . . . You repel people and forget that a friendly calf sucks two mothers."

"That is true too, Foma!"

"You are coarse. You jar so coarsely upon the human heart, you so egoistically insist upon attention, that a decent man is ready to run from you to the utmost ends of the earth."

My uncle heaved another deep sigh.

"Be softer, more attentive, more loving to others; forget yourself for the sake of others, then they will think of you. Live and let others live—that is my rule! Suffer, labour, pray and hope—those are the truths which I would like to instil into all mankind at once! Model yourself on them and then I shall be the first to open my heart to you, I shall weep on your bosom . . . if need be. . . . As it is, it is always 'I' and 'I' and 'my gracious self' with you. But, you know, one may get sick at last of your gracious self, if you will allow me to say so."

"A sweet-tongued gentleman," Gavrila brought out, awe-struck.

"That's true, Foma, I feel all that," my uncle assented, deeply touched. "But I am not altogether to blame, Foma. I've been brought up like this, I have lived with soldiers; but I swear, Foma, I have not been without feeling. When I said good-bye to the regiment, all the hussars, all my division, simply shed tears and said they would never get another like me. I thought at the time that I too was not altogether a lost soul."

"Again a piece of egoism! Again I catch you in vanity. You are boasting and at the same time reproaching me with the hussars' tears. Why don't I boast of any one's tears? And yet there may have been grounds, there may have been grounds for doing so."

"I meant nothing, Foma, it was a slip of the tongue. I couldn't help remembering those old happy times."

"Happy times do not fall from heaven, we make them ourselves; it lies in our hearts, Yegor Ilyitch. That is why I am always happy and, in spite of my sufferings, contented, tranquil in spirit, and am not a burden to any one unless it

is to fools, upstarts and *learned gentlemen,* on whom I have
no mercy and don't care to have. I don't like fools! And
what are these learned gentlemen? 'A man of learning'; and
his learning turns out to be nothing but a hoaxing trick, and
not learning. Why, what did *he* say just now? Let him come
here! Let all these men of learning come here! I can refute
them all; I can refute all their propositions! I say nothing
of greatness of soul . . ."

"Of course, Foma. Who doubts it?"

"This afternoon, for instance, I showed intelligence, talent, colossal erudition, knowledge of the human heart,
knowledge of contemporary literature; I showed and displayed in a brilliant fashion how some wretched Komarinsky may furnish a lofty topic of conversation for a man of
talent. And did any one of them appreciate me as I deserved? No, they turned away! Why, I am certain he has
told you already that I know nothing, and yet perhaps
Macchiavelli himself or some Mercadante was sitting before
him and only to blame for being poor and in obscurity. . . .
That does not penetrate to them! . . . I hear of Korovkin
too. What sort of queer fish is he?"

"He is a clever man, Foma, a man of learning. . . . I am
expecting him. He will certainly be a nice man, Foma."

"H'm, I doubt it. Most likely some modern ass laden
with books; there is no soul in them, Colonel, no heart in
them! And what is learning without virtue?"

"No, Foma, no. How he talked of family happiness! The
heart feels it of itself, Foma."

"H'm! We will have a look at him; we will examine
Korovkin too. But enough," Foma concluded, getting up
from his easy-chair. "I cannot altogether forgive you yet,
Colonel; the insult was too deadly; but I will pray, and perhaps God will shed peace on the wounded heart. We will
speak further of this to-morrow, but now permit me to
withdraw. I am tired and exhausted. . . ."

"Oh, Foma!" cried my uncle in a fluster, "why, of course
you are tired! I say, won't you have something to support
you, a snack of something? I will order something at once."

"A snack! Ha-ha-ha!" answered Foma, with a contemptuous laugh. "First they offer you a drink of poison, and then they ask you if you won't have a snack of something. They want to heal the wounds of the heart with stewed mushrooms or pickled apples! What a pitiful materialist you are, Colonel!"

"Oh, Foma, I spoke in all simplicity . . ."

"Oh, very well. Enough of that. I will withdraw, and you go at once to your mother; fall on your knees, sob, weep, but beg for her forgiveness, that is your duty, that is a moral obligation."

"Oh, Foma, I have been thinking of nothing but that all the time; even now while I have been talking to you I have been thinking of it. I am ready to implore her on my knees till dawn. But only think, Foma, what they are expecting of me. Why, you know it's unjust, Foma, it's cruel. Be entirely magnanimous, make me completely happy, think a little, decide, and then . . . then . . . I swear! . . ."

"No, Yegor Ilyitch, no, it's no business of mine," answered Foma. "You know that I do not meddle in the slightest degree in all that; you may be persuaded that I am at the bottom of it all, but I assure you that from the very beginning I have held entirely aloof from this affair. It is solely the desire of your mother, and she, of course, wishes for nothing but your good. . . . Go to her, make haste, fly and rectify the position by your obedience . . . and let not the sun go down upon your wrath; while I . . . I shall be all night long praying for you. I have known no sleep for many a night, Yegor Ilyitch. Good-night! I forgive you too, old man," he said, turning to Gavrila. "I know you did not do it of yourself. You forgive me too if I have offended you. . . . Good-night, good-night all, and may the Lord bless you."

Foma went out. I rushed at once into the room.

"You've been listening!" cried my uncle.

"Yes, uncle, I have been listening! And you, you could call him 'your Excellency'?"

"What could I do, brother? Indeed, I am proud of it. . . . That was no great act of sacrifice. But what a noble, what a disinterested, what a great man! Sergey, why, you

heard yourself . . . and how I could, how I could thrust
that money on him, I simply don't understand! My dear, I
was carried away, I was in a rage. I did not understand
him; I suspected him, I accused him. . . . But no, he could
not be antagonistic to me—I see that now . . . and do you
remember what a noble expression there was on his face
when he was refusing the money?"

"Very well, uncle, you can be as proud as you like, but
I am going; my patience is at an end. For the last time I
say it, tell me what you want of me? Why did you send for
me, and what do you expect? And if it is all over and I am
of no use to you, then I am going. I can't endure such exhi-
bitions! I am going this very day."

"My dear!" My uncle was in a fluster as usual. "Only
wait two minutes; I am going now, dear boy, to mamma, to
settle there . . . a grave, important, immense question! . . .
And you meanwhile go to your room. Here, Gavrila will
take you to the summer lodge. You know the summer
lodge, it is in the garden. I have given orders, and your
trunk has been taken there; and I am going in to beg forgiveness and settle one question—I know now what to do—
and then I will be with you in a flash, and then I'll tell you
everything, I'll open my whole soul to you and . . . and . . .
happy days will come for us too, some time! Two minutes,
only two minutes, Sergey!"

He pressed my hand and hurriedly went out. There was
nothing to be done, I had to go off with Gavrila again.

Mizintchikov

X

The lodge to which Gavrila conducted me was called "the
new lodge" only from old habit, because it was built long
ago in the time of the former owners. It was a pretty little
wooden house, standing in the garden a few paces from the

old house. It was surrounded on three sides by tall old lime-trees which touched the roof with their branches. All the four rooms of this little house were kept ready for visitors, and were not badly furnished. Going into the room assigned me, to which my portmanteau had been already taken, I saw on a little table before the bedstead a sheet of note-paper, covered with magnificent handwriting in various styles framed in garlands and flourishes. The capital letters and the garlands were illuminated in various colours. The whole made a very pretty specimen of calligraphy. From the first words I read I saw that it was a begging letter addressed to me, and that in it I was styled "Enlightened benefactor." It was headed "The Plaints of Vidoplyasov." Though I tried with strained attention to make out something of what was written, my efforts were all in vain; it was the most inflated nonsense, written in a high-flown flunkey lingo. I could only surmise that Vidoplyasov was in trouble of some sort, was begging for my assistance, was building great hopes upon me, "by reason of my enlightenment," and in conclusion begged me to interest myself on his behalf with my uncle and to work upon him with "my machinery," as he expressed it at the end of this epistle. I was still reading it when the door opened and Mizintchikov walked in.

"I hope you will allow me to make your acquaintance," he said in a free and easy way, though with extreme courtesy, offering me his hand. "I could not say two words to you this afternoon, and yet from the first glance I felt a desire to know you better."

I answered at once that I was delighted and so on, though I was, in fact, in an extremely bad temper. We sat down.

"What have you got here?" he said, glancing at the sheet of paper which I was still holding in my hand. "Not 'The Plaints of Vidoplyasov'? That's what it is. I was certain that Vidoplyasov was attacking you too. He presented me with just such a document with the same complaints; and he has been expecting you a long time and most likely got ready beforehand. You need not be surprised: there's a great deal that's queer here, and really there is plenty to laugh at."

"Only to laugh at?"

"Oh, well, surely not to cry over. If you like I will give you Vidoplyasov's history, and I am certain that you will laugh."

"I confess I am not interested in Vidoplyasov just now," I answered with vexation.

It was evident to me that Mr. Mizintchikov's friendliness and his polite conversation were all assumed by him with some object, and that he was simply trying to get something out of me. He had sat scowling and serious in the afternoon; now he was good-humoured, smiling, and ready to tell me long stories. It was evident from the first glance that the man was perfectly self-possessed, and he seemed to understand human nature.

"That cursed Foma!" I said, banging my fist on the table with fury. "I am positive that he is at the bottom of every sort of mischief here and mixed up in it all! Cursed brute!"

"I think your anger is excessive," Mizintchikov observed.

"My anger excessive," I cried, instantly firing up. "I let myself go too far this afternoon, of course, and so gave every one a right to blame me. I know very well that I plunged in and put my foot in it on every point, and I think there is no need to tell me that! . . . I know, too, that that's not the way to behave in decent society; but how could I help letting myself go? tell me that. Why, this is a madhouse, if you care to know! And . . . and . . . in fact . . . I am simply going away, so there."

"Do you smoke?" Mizintchikov asked calmly.

"Yes."

"Then you will probably allow me to smoke? They won't let me in there, and I am wretched without it. I agree," he went on, as he lighted a cigarette, "that all this is like a madhouse; but believe me, I do not venture to criticize you, just because in your place I should perhaps be three times as excited and violent as you."

"And why were you not violent if you really were angry too? I remember you very cool, on the contrary, and, I confess, I even thought it strange that you did not stand up for my poor uncle, who is ready to befriend . . . all and every one!"

"You are right: he has befriended many people; but I consider it perfectly useless to stand up for him: in the first place it would be useless and even derogatory for him in a way; and in the second I should be kicked out to-morrow. And I tell you frankly my circumstances are such that to be a guest here is a great advantage for me."

"But I do not make the slightest claim on your frankness in regard to your circumstances. . . . I should, however, have liked to ask, since you have been here a month . . ."

"Please, do, ask anything: I am at your service," Mizintchikov answered, hurriedly moving up a chair.

"Well, explain this, for instance: Foma Fomitch has just refused fifteen thousand roubles which were in his hands—I saw it with my own eyes."

"What? Impossible!" cried Mizintchikov. "Tell me, please."

I told him, saying nothing about "your Excellency." Mizintchikov listened with greedy curiosity. He positively changed countenance when the fifteen thousand were mentioned.

"That's smart!" he said, when he heard my story. "I really did not expect it of Foma."

"He did refuse the money, though! How do you explain that? Surely not by the nobility of his soul?"

"He refused fifteen thousand to take thirty later. Though, do you know," he added after a moment's thought, "I doubt whether Foma had any mercenary design in it. He is not a practical man; he is a sort of a poet, too, in his own way. Fifteen thousand . . . h'm. He would have taken the money, do you see, but he couldn't resist the temptation to strike an attitude and give himself airs. I tell you he's a sentimental mush, and the sloppiest old sniveller and all that, with the most unbounded vanity!"

Mizintchikov was positively roused to anger. It was evident that he was very much annoyed and even envious. I looked at him with curiosity.

"H'm! We may expect great changes," he added, musing. "Now Yegor Ilyitch is ready to worship Foma. I shouldn't wonder if he does get married now that his heart is softened," he muttered through his teeth.

"So you think that this abominable, unnatural marriage with that crazy fool really will come off?"

Mizintchikov looked at me searchingly.

"The scoundrels!" I cried emphatically.

"There is a fairly sound idea at the back of it, though. They maintain that he ought to do something for his family."

"As though he hadn't done enough for them," I cried indignantly. "And you, you talk of there being a sound idea in marrying a vulgar fool!"

"Of course I agree with you that she is a fool. . . . H'm! It's a good thing that you are so fond of your uncle; I sympathize with him myself . . . though he could round off his estate finely with her fortune! They have other reasons, though; they are afraid that Yegor Ilyitch may marry that governess . . . do you remember, an attractive girl?"

"But is that likely to be true? . . ." I asked in agitation. "It seems to me that it's spiteful gossip. Tell me, for goodness' sake, it interests me extremely. . . ."

"Oh, he is head over ears in love with her! Only, of course, he conceals it."

"He conceals it? You think that he is concealing it? And she? Does she love him?"

"It is very likely she does. It is all to her advantage to marry him, though; she is very poor."

"But what grounds have you for your supposition that they love each other?"

"Oh, you know, you can't help seeing it; besides, I believe they meet in secret. They do say that she has illicit relations with him, in fact. Only, please, don't repeat that. I tell you as a secret."

"Is it possible to believe that?" I cried. "And you, you acknowledge that you believe it?"

"Of course I do not fully believe it. I wasn't there. But it's very possible, though."

"Very possible? Think of my uncle's sense of honour, his noble character."

"I agree; but one may be carried away, with a conviction that one is going to make it right with matrimony afterwards. People often are. But, I repeat, I don't insist on the absolute certainty of the facts, especially as they have blackened her character in all sorts of ways here; they even say that she had an intrigue with Vidoplyasov."

"There, you see," I cried, "with Vidoplyasov. Why, as though it were possible! Isn't it revolting even to listen to such a thing? Surely you can't believe it?"

"I tell you that I do not quite believe it," answered Mizintchikov calmly, "but it might happen. Anything may happen in this world. I was not there, and besides, I consider it not my business. But as I see you take great interest in all this, I feel I ought to add that I really don't put much faith in the story about Vidoplyasov. It's all the invention of Anna Nilovna, that Miss Perepelitsyn; it's she who has set those rumours going here out of envy because she dreamed in the past of marrying Yegor Ilyitch herself—yes, by Jove, on the ground that she is a major's daughter. Now she is disappointed and awfully furious. But I believe I have told you all about that business now, and I confess I greatly dislike gossip, especially as we are losing precious time. I have come to ask you a trifling favour, you see."

"A favour? Certainly; any way in which I can be of use to you."

"I understand, and indeed I hope to interest you, for I see you love your uncle and take great interest in his fate in the matrimonial line; but before I ask you that favour I will ask you another, a preliminary one."

"What is that?"

"I'll tell you; perhaps you will consent to grant my chief request, and perhaps not; but in any case, before telling it you I will humbly ask you to grant one great favour, to give me your word of honour as a nobleman and a gentleman that all you hear from me shall remain a dead secret, and that you will not betray the secret in any case or for the sake of any person, and will not take advantage for your own benefit of the idea which I now find it necessary to communicate to you. Do you agree or not?"

It was a solemn introduction. I gave my assent.

"Well?" . . . I said.

"It is really a very simple matter," Mizintchikov began. "I want to elope with Tatyana Ivanovna and to marry her; in short, there is to be something in the Gretna Green style, do you understand?"

I stared Mizintchikov straight in the face, and for some time I could not utter a word.

"I confess I don't understand at all," I brought out at last; "and what's more," I went on, "expecting that I had to do with a sensible man, I did not in the least expect . . ."

"Expecting you did not expect," interrupted Mizintchikov; "which may be translated, that I and my project are stupid—that's so, isn't it?"

"Oh, not at all . . . but . . ."

"Oh, please, don't mind speaking plainly! Don't be uneasy; you will do me a great pleasure by plain speaking, in fact, for so we shall get nearer our object. I agree with you, though, that all this must seem somewhat strange at the first glance. But I venture to assure you that so far from being foolish, my project is extremely sensible; and if you will be so good as to listen to all the circumstances . . ."

"Oh, certainly! I am listening eagerly."

"There is scarcely anything to tell, though. You see, I am in debt and haven't a farthing. I have, besides, a sister, a girl of nineteen, fatherless and motherless, living in a family and entirely without means, you know. For that I am partly to blame. We inherited a property of forty serfs. Just at that time I was promoted to be a cornet. Well, at first, of course, I mortgaged, and then I squandered our money in other ways too. I lived like a fool, set the fashion, gave myself airs, gambled, drank—it was idiotic, in fact, and I am ashamed to remember it. Now I have come to my senses and want to change my manner of life completely. But to do so it is absolutely essential to have a hundred thousand roubles. As I shall never get anything in the service, since I am not qualified for anything and have scarcely

any education, there are, of course, only two resources left
me: to steal or to marry a rich wife. I came here almost
without boots to my feet, I walked, I could not drive. My
sister gave me her last three roubles when I set off from
Moscow. Here I saw Tatyana Ivanovna, and at once the
idea dawned upon me. I immediately resolved to sacrifice
myself and marry her. You will agree that all that is nothing but good sense. Besides, I am doing it more for my
sister's sake . . . though, of course, for my own too."

"But allow me to ask, do you mean to make a formal
proposal to Tatyana Ivanovna? . . ."

"God forbid, they would kick me out at once; but if I
suggest an elopement, a runaway match, she will marry me
at once. That's the whole point, that there should be something romantic and sensational about it. Of course it would
all immediately end in legal matrimony. If only I can allure
her away from here!"

"But why are you so sure that she will elope with you?"

"Oh, don't trouble about that! I am perfectly sure of
that. The whole plan rests on the idea that Tatyana Ivanovna is ready to carry on an intrigue with any one she
meets, with any one, in fact, to whom it occurs to respond
to her. That is why I first asked you to give me your word
of honour that you would not take advantage of the idea.
You will understand, of course, that it would be positively
wicked of me not to take advantage of such an opportunity,
especially in my circumstances."

"So then she is quite mad. . . . Oh, I beg your pardon," I
added, catching myself up. "Since you now have intentions . . ."

"Please don't mind speaking out, as I have asked you
already. You ask, is she quite mad? What shall I tell you?
Of course she is not mad, since she is not yet in a madhouse; besides, I really don't see anything particularly mad
in this mania for love affairs. She is a respectable girl in
spite of everything. You see, till a year ago she was horribly
poor, and from her birth up has lived in bondage to the
ladies who befriended her. Her heart is exceptionally susceptible; no one has asked her in marriage. . . . Well, you

understand: dreams, desires, hopes, the fervour of feelings which she has always had to conceal, perpetual agonies at the hands of the ladies who befriended her—all that of course might well drive a sensitive character to derangement. And all at once she comes in for a fortune; you'll allow that is enough to upset any one. Well, now of course people make up to her and hang about her, and all her hopes have risen up. She told us this afternoon about a dandy in a white waistcoat; that's a fact which happened literally as she described. From that fact you can judge of the rest. With sighs, notes, verses you can inveigle her at once; and if with all that you hint at a silken rope ladder, a Spanish serenade and all that nonsense, you can do what you like with her. I have put it to the test, and at once obtained a secret interview. But meanwhile I have put it off till the right moment. But I must carry her off within four days. The evening before I shall begin to make tender speeches, to sigh: I can sing and play the guitar pretty well. At night there will be a meeting in the arbour, and at dawn the coach will be in readiness; I shall entice her away, we shall get into the coach and drive off. You understand that there is no risk about it whatever; she is of age, and what's more, completely her own mistress. And if once she ran away with me she would, of course, be bound to me. I should take her to a poor but respectable family, thirty miles away, who would look after her, and not let any one come near her till the wedding; and meanwhile I shan't lose time, we'll get married within three days—it can be done. Of course, first of all, money is needed; but I have reckoned that I shall not need more than five hundred roubles for the whole business, and for that I rely on Yegor Ilyitch. He will give it, of course, without knowing what is up. Do you understand now?"

"I do," I answered, taking it all in fully. "But tell me, in what way can I be of use to you?"

"Oh, in a great deal, I assure you, or I would not have asked you. I told you that I had in view a poor but very respectable family. You can help me both here and there, and as a witness. I must own that without your help I should be at a loss."

"Another question, why have you done me the honour to select me to receive your confidence, though you know nothing of me, since I have only been here a few hours?"

"Your question," Mizintchikov answered with the most polite smile, "your question, I frankly confess, gives me great satisfaction, because it affords me an opportunity of expressing my special regard for you."

"Oh, you do me too much honour!"

"No; you see, I have been studying you a little this afternoon. Admitting you are both hasty and . . . and . . . well, young, I tell you what I am thoroughly certain of: when you have given me your word that you will tell no one you will certainly keep it. You are not Obnoskin—that's the first point. Secondly, you are honest and will not take advantage of my idea—for yourself, of course, I mean—unless you would like to enter into a friendly compact with me. In that case I will perhaps agree to yield to you my idea—that is, Tatyana Ivanovna—and be ready to help you zealously in the elopement, only on condition of receiving from you a month after your marriage fifty thousand roubles, for which you would of course give me security beforehand in the shape of an I O U."

"What!" I cried out. "So now you are offering her to me?"

"Naturally, I can give it up to you if on reflection you wish it. I should of course be a loser, but . . . the idea belongs to me, and you know one is paid for one's ideas. Thirdly and lastly I asked you because I had no choice. And taking into consideration the position here, it was impossible to delay long; besides which it will soon be the fast of the Assumption, and they won't celebrate weddings. I hope you fully understand me now?"

"Perfectly. And once more I feel bound to keep your secret quite sacred; but I cannot be your accomplice in the business, and I think it my duty to tell you so at once."

"Why so?"

"You ask, why so?" I cried, giving the rein to my pent-up

feelings at last. "Why, surely you must understand that such an act is positively dishonourable. Supposing you were quite correct in your calculations, reckoning on the lady's weakness of mind and unhappy mania, why, it's that very thing which ought to restrain you as an honourable man! You say yourself that she is worthy of respect in spite of being ridiculous, and you are taking advantage of her misfortune to rob her of a hundred thousand. You will not, of course, be a real husband to her, carrying out your obligations: you will certainly leave her . . . it's so dishonourable that, excuse me, I can't even understand how you could bring yourself to ask me to assist you."

"Ough! my goodness! how romantic!" cried Mizintchikov, looking at me with unfeigned surprise. "Though, indeed, it's not that it's romantic, but simply I believe that you don't understand the position. You say that it's dishonourable, and yet all the advantages are not on my side, but hers . . . only consider . . ."

"Of course, if one looks at it from your point of view I dare say it will appear that you will be doing something most magnanimous in marrying Tatyana Ivanovna," I answered, with a sarcastic smile.

"Well, what else? Just so, it is something most magnanimous," cried Mizintchikov, growing hot in his turn. "Only consider: in the first place, I am sacrificing myself in consenting to be her husband. Is not that some sacrifice? In the second place, although she has certainly a hundred thousand in silver roubles I shall only take a hundred thousand in paper, and I have sworn that I won't take another farthing from her all my life, though I could; that's some sacrifice again. Lastly, look into it more deeply. Could she anyway lead a peaceful life? For her to live in peace one would have to take her money from her and put her in a madhouse, for one may expect any minute that some worthless fellow, some scheming rogue, some adventurer, will turn up with a moustache and an imperial, with a guitar and serenades, some one in the style of Obnoskin, who will inveigle her, marry her and strip her completely, and then turn her out into the gutter. This, for instance, is a most respectable household, and yet they are only keeping her here because they are speculating on her fortune. From such risks she must be saved, rescued. Well, you see, as soon as she marries me such risks are over, it will be my duty to see that no trouble comes near her. In the first place, I shall settle her at once in Moscow, in a poor but honourable family—not the one I have spoken of to you, but another; my sister will be constantly with her; they will look after her and pay her every attention. She will have two hundred and fifty thousand, possibly three hundred, in paper left, one can do well on that, you know! Every pleasure will be provided for her, all sorts of entertainment, balls, masquerades and concerts. She may even dream of love affairs, only of course I shall look after that. She may dream as much as she likes, but not so in reality! Now, for instance, any one can ill-treat her, but no one will be able to then; she will be my wife, she will be a Mizintchikov, and I won't allow my name to be insulted! That alone is worth something, isn't it? Naturally I am not going to live with her. She will live in Moscow, and I shall live somewhere in Petersburg. I admit that, because I am doing things straightforwardly with you. But what if we do live apart? Look at her character and just consider, is she fit to be a wife and live with a husband? Is it possible to go on living with her continually? Why, she is the most light-headed creature in the world. She must have incessant change; she is capable next day of forgetting that she was married yesterday and made a lawful wife. Why, I should make her wretched in the end if I were to live with her and insist on her strictly performing her duties. Naturally I shall go and see her once a year or oftener, and not to get money, I assure you. I have told you that I am not going to take more than a hundred thousand in paper from her, and I shan't either! On the money side I shall treat her in the most honourable way. If I come to see her for two or three days, my visit will actually be a pleasure to her and not a bore; I shall laugh with her, tell her stories, take her to a ball, make love to her, give her little souvenirs, sings songs to her, make her a present of a lapdog, have a romantic parting from her, and keep up an exchange of love letters. Why, she will be in ecstasies over such a romantic, devoted, and amusing husband. To my thinking, that is the rational way to proceed; that's how all husbands ought to behave. Husbands are only precious to their wives when they are absent, and following my system, I shall engage Tatyana Ivanovna's heart in the most honeyed way for the whole of her life. What more can she want? tell me that. Why, it is paradise, not life!"

I listened in silence and with wonder; I realized that it was impossible to turn Mr. Mizintchikov from his plan. He was fanatically persuaded of the rectitude and even the greatness of his project, and spoke of it with the enthusiasm of an inventor. But there was still one rather delicate question which was essential to clear up.

"Have you reflected," I said, "that she is almost betrothed to my uncle? It will be a great insult to him if you elope with her; you will be carrying her off almost on the eve of her wedding, and what's more, will borrow from him to carry out your exploit."

"That is just where I have you!" Mizintchikov cried out with heat. "You needn't trouble, I foresaw your objection. But first and foremost, your uncle has not yet made her an offer, consequently there is no need for me to know that they are intending her for a match for him; moreover, I beg you to note that I thought of this enterprise three weeks ago, when I knew nothing of their intentions, so I am perfectly justified from the moral point of view as regards them. And in fact, strictly speaking, it is rather he who is carrying off my betrothed than I his, whom, take note, I have already met in secret at night in the arbour. And lastly, allow me to ask, were not you yourself in a perfect frenzy at your uncle's being forced to marry Tatyana Ivanovna? And now you are all at once standing up for the marriage, and talking of honour, of some insult to the family! Why, on the contrary, I am doing your uncle the greatest service, I am saving him—you ought to understand that. He looks on the match with aversion, and what's more, is in love with another young lady! Why, what sort of wife would Tatyana Ivanovna be to him? And she would be wretched with him too because, say what you like, she would then have to be restrained from throwing roses at young men. And you know if I elope with her in the night, then no Madame la Générale, no Foma Fomitch, will be able to do anything. To bring back a bride who has run away from the wedding would be too discreditable. Isn't that a service, isn't it a benefit to Yegor Ilyitch?"

I must own this last argument had a great effect on me.

"But what if he makes her an offer to-morrow?" I said. "You see, it would be rather too late then; she will be formally betrothed to him."

"To be sure it will be, but that is just why we must work to prevent it. What am I asking you to help me for? It's hard for me alone, but the two of us together can arrange things and prevent Yegor Ilyitch from making a proposal. We must do everything we can to prevent it, even if it comes to thrashing Foma Fomitch and so distracting the general attention from all thoughts of the match. Of course that is only in the last extremity, I only give that for the sake of example. This is what I am relying on you for."

"One more last question: have you told no one but me of your scheme?"

Mizintchikov scratched the back of his head and made a very wry face.

"I must confess that question is worse than the bitterest pill for me. That's just the trouble, that I have given away the idea . . . in fact, I have been the most awful fool! And to whom, do you suppose? To Obnoskin! I can scarcely believe it myself. I don't know how it happened! He is always about the place, I did not know him so well, and when this inspiration dawned upon me I was, of course, greatly excited; and as I realized even then that I should need some one to help me, I appealed to Obnoskin . . . it was unpardonable, unpardonable!"

"Well, and what did Obnoskin say?"

"He agreed with enthusiasm, but next day early in the morning he disappeared. Three days later he turned up again with his mamma. He doesn't say a word to me, and in fact avoids me as though he were afraid of me. I saw at once what was up. And his mother is a regular shark, she's been in tight places before now. I used to know her in the past. Of course he has told her all about it. I am waiting and keeping quiet; they are spying on me, and things are in rather a strained position . . . that's why I am in a hurry."

"What is it exactly you fear from them?"

"They can't do a great deal, of course, but that they will do something nasty—that is certain. They will insist on having money for keeping quiet and helping, that I expect. . . . Only I can't give them a great deal, and I am not going to. I have made up my mind about that. I can't give more than three thousand paper roubles. Judge for yourself: three thousand to them, five hundred in silver for the wedding, for I must pay your uncle back in full; then my old debts; then at least something for my sister, something at least. There won't be much left out of a hundred thousand, will there? Why, it will be ruin! . . . The Obnoskins have gone away, though."

"Gone away?" I asked with curiosity.

"Just after tea, damn them! but they will turn up again to-morrow, you will see. Well, how is it to be, then? Do you agree?"

"I must own," I answered, shrugging, "I really don't know what to say. It's a delicate matter. . . . Of course I will keep it all secret, I am not Obnoskin; but . . . I think it's no use your building hopes on me."

"I see," said Mizintchikov, getting up from his chair, "that you are not yet sick of Foma Fomitch and your grandmother; and though you do care for your kind and generous uncle, you have not yet sufficiently realized how he is being tormented. You are new to the place. . . . But patience! You will be here to-morrow, look about you, and by evening you'll consent. Your uncle is lost if you don't, do you understand? They will certainly force him to marry her. Don't forget that to-morrow he may perhaps make her an offer. It will be too late, we must settle things to-day."

"Really, I wish you every success, but as for helping you . . . I don't know in what way."

"We know! But let us wait till to-morrow," said Mizintchikov, smiling ironically. *"La nuit porte conseil.* Good-bye for the present. I will come to you early in the morning, and you think things over. . . ."

He turned and went out whistling.

I almost followed him out, to get a breath of fresh air. The moon had not yet risen; it was a dark night, warm and stifling. The leaves on the trees did not stir. In spite of being terribly tired, I wanted to walk to distract my mind, collect my thoughts; but I had not gone above ten paces when I suddenly heard my uncle's voice. He was mounting the steps of the lodge in company with some one, and speaking with great animation. I turned back and called to him. My uncle was with Vidoplyasov.

The Extreme of Perplexity

XI

"Uncle," I said, "at last I have got you."

"My dear boy, I was rushing to you myself. Here, I will just finish with Vidoplyasov, and then we can talk to our hearts' content. I have a great deal to tell you."

"What, Vidoplyasov now! Oh, get rid of him, uncle."

"Only another five or ten minutes, Sergey, and I shall be entirely at your disposal. You see, it's important."

"Oh, no doubt, it is his foolishness," I said, with vexation.

"What can I say to you, my dear? The man has certainly found a time to worry me with his nonsense! Yes, my good Grigory, couldn't you find some other time for your complaints? Why, what can I do for you? You might have compassion even on me, my good boy. Why, I am, so to say, worn out by you all, devoured alive, body and soul! They are too much for me, Sergey!" And my uncle made a gesture of the profoundest misery with both hands.

"But what business can be so important that you can't leave it? And, uncle, I do so want . . ."

"Oh, my dear boy, as it is they keep crying out that I take no trouble over my servants' morals! Very likely he will complain of me to-morrow that I wouldn't listen to him, and then . . ." and my uncle waved his hand in despair again.

"Well, then make haste and finish with him! Perhaps I can help you; let us go up the steps. What is it? What does he want?" I said as we went into the room.

"Well, you see, my dear, he doesn't like his own surname, and asks leave to change it. What do you think of that?"

"His surname! What do you mean? . . . Well, uncle, before I hear what he has to say himself, allow me to remark that it is only in your household such queer things can happen," I said, flinging up my hands in amazement.

"Oh, my dear boy, I might fling up my hands like you, but that's no good," my uncle said with vexation. "Come, talk to him yourself, you have a try. He has been worrying me for two months past. . . ."

"It's not a respectable surname," Vidoplyasov observed.

"But why is it not respectable?" I asked him in surprise.

"Oh, because it suggests all sorts of abomination."

"But why abomination? And how can you change it? Does any one change his surname?"

"Well, really, sir, do other people have such surnames?"

"I agree that your surname is a somewhat strange one," I went on, in complete bewilderment; "but there is no help for it now, you know. Your father had the same surname, I suppose, didn't he?"

"That is precisely so, that through my parent I have in that way had to suffer all my life, inasmuch as I am destined by my name to accept many jeers and to endure many sorrows," answered Vidoplyasov.

"I bet, uncle, that Foma Fomitch has a hand in this!" I cried with vexation.

"Oh no, my boy; oh no, you are mistaken. Foma certainly has befriended him. He has taken him to be his secretary, that's the whole of his duty. Well, of course he has developed him, has filled him with noble sentiments, so that he is even in some ways cultivated. . . . You see, I will tell you all about it. . . ."

"That is true," Vidoplyasov interrupted, "that Foma Fomitch is my true benefactor, and being a true benefactor to me, he has brought me to understand my insignificance, what a worm I am upon the earth, so that through his honour I have for the first time learned to comprehend my destiny."

"There you see, Seryozha, there you see what it all means," my uncle went on, growing flustered as he always did. "He lived at first in Moscow, almost from childhood, in the service of a teacher of calligraphy. You should see how he has learned to write from him, and he illuminates in colours and gold with cupids round, you know—in fact, he is an artist, you know. Ilyusha has lessons from him; I pay him a rouble and a half a lesson. Foma himself fixed on a rouble and a half. He goes to three gentlemen's houses in the neighbourhood; they pay him too. You see how he is dressed! What's more, he writes poetry."

"Poetry! That's the last straw!"

"Poetry, my dear boy, poetry. And don't imagine I am joking; real poetry, so to say, versifications, and so well composed, you know, on all sorts of subjects. He'll describe any subject you like in a poem. It's a real talent! On mamma's nameday he concocted such a harangue that we listened with our mouths open; there was something from mythology in it, and the Muses flying about, so that indeed, you know, one could see the . . . what do you call it? . . . polish of form—in fact, it was perfectly in rhyme. Foma corrected it. Well, I have nothing against that, and indeed I am quite pleased. Let him compose, as long as he doesn't get into mischief. You see, Grigory, my boy, I speak to you like a father. Foma heard of it, looked at his poetry, encouraged him, and chose him as his reader and copyist—in fact, he has educated him. It is true, as he says, that Foma has been a benefactor to him. Well, and so, you know, he has begun to have gentlemanly and romantic sentiments, and a feeling of independence—Foma explained it all to me, but I have really forgotten; only I must own that I wanted, apart from Foma, to give him his freedom. I feel somehow ashamed, you know! . . . but Foma opposes that and says that he finds him useful, that he likes him; and. what's more he says: 'It's a great honour to me, as his master, to have poets among my own servants; that that's how some barons somewhere used to live, and that it is living *en grand*.' Well, *en grand* so be it, then! I have begun to respect him, my boy—you understand. . . . Only goodness knows how he is behaving! The worst of it is that since he has taken to poetry he has become so stuck-up with the rest of the servants that he won't speak to them. Don't you take offence, Grigory, I am speaking to you like a father. Last winter, he promised to marry a serf girl here, Matryona, and a very nice girl she is, honest, hard-working and merry. But now it is 'No, I won't.' That's all about it, he has given her up. Whether it is that he has grown conceited, or has planned first to make a name and then to seek a match in some other place."

"More through the advice of Foma Fomitch," observed Vidoplyasov, "seeing that his honour is my true well-wisher."

"Oh, of course Foma Fomitch has a hand in everything," I could not help exclaiming.

"Ough, my dear boy, that's not it!" my uncle interrupted me hurriedly. "Only, you see, now he has no peace. She's a bold, quarrelsome girl, she has set them all against him, they mimic him, bait him, even the serf boys look upon him as a buffoon. . . ."

"It's chiefly owing to Matryona," observed Vidoplyasov; "for Matryona's a real fool, and being a real fool, she's a woman of unbridled character. Through her I have come in this manner to endure such prolonged sufferings."

"Ough, Grigory, my boy, I have talked to you already," my uncle went on, looking reproachfully at Vidoplyasov. "You see, Sergey, they have made up some horrid rhyme on his surname. He comes to me and complains, asks whether he cannot somehow change his surname, says that he has long been upset at its ugly sound. . . ."

"It's an undignified name," Vidoplyasov put in.

"Come, you be quiet, Grigory! Foma approved of it too . . . that is, he did not approve exactly, but, you see, this was his idea; that in case he were to publish his poems—and Foma has a project of his doing so—such a surname perhaps might be a drawback, mightn't it?"

"So he wants to publish his verses, uncle?"

"Yes, my boy. It's settled already—at my expense, and on the title-page will be put, 'the serf of so-and-so,' and in the preface, the author's thanks to Foma for his education. It's dedicated to Foma. Foma is writing the preface himself. Well, so just fancy if on the title-page there stands, 'The Poems of Vidoplyasov.' "

"The Plaints of Vidoplyasov," Vidoplyasov corrected.

"There, you see, plaints too! Well, Vidoplyasov is no use for a surname, it positively revolts the delicacy of one's feelings, so Foma says. And all these critics, they say, are such fellows for picking holes and jeering; Brambeus, for instance. . . . They don't stick at anything, you know! They will make a laughingstock of him for his surname alone; they'll tickle your sides for you till you can do nothing but scratch them, won't they? What I say is, put any surname you like on your poems—a pseudonym it's called, isn't it? I don't remember; some word ending in *nym*. 'But no,' he says; 'give the order to the whole servants' hall to call me by a new name hereafter, for ever, so that I may have a genteel surname to suit my talent.' "

"I bet that you consented, uncle. . . ."

"I did, Seryozha, my boy, to avoid quarrelling with them; let them do as they like. You see, at that time there was a misunderstanding between Foma and me. So since then it has come to a new surname every week, and he keeps choosing such dainty ones as Oleandrov, Tulipov. . . . Only think, Grigory, at first you asked to be called 'Vyerny' (*i. e.* true, faithful)—'Grigory Vyerny'; afterwards you didn't like the name yourself because some simpleton found a rhyme to it, 'skverny' (*i. e.* nasty, horrid). You complained, and the fellow was punished. You were a fortnight thinking of a new name—what a selection you had!—at last you made up your mind and came to be asked to be called 'Ulanov.' Come, tell me, my boy, could anything be sillier than 'Ulanov'? I agreed to that too, and gave instructions a second time about changing your surname to Ulanov. It was simply to get rid of him," added my uncle, turning to me. "You spoilt all the walls, all the window-sills in the arbour, scribbling 'Ulanov' in pencil; they have had to paint it since. You wasted a whole quire of good paper on signing your name 'Ulanov.' At last that was a failure too, they found a rhyme for you: 'Bolvanov' (*i. e.* fool, blockhead). He didn't want to be a blockhead, so the name must be changed again! What did you choose next? I have forgotten."

"Tantsev," answered Vidoplyasov. "If I am destined through my surname to be connected with dancing, it would be more dignified in the foreign form: 'Tantsev.' "

"Oh, yes; 'Tantsev.' I agreed to that too, Sergey. Only they found a rhyme to that which I don't like to repeat. To-day he comes forward again, he has thought of something new. I bet he has got some new surname. Have you, Grigory? Confess!"

"I have truly been meaning for a long time to lay at your feet a new name, a genteel one."

"What is it?"

"Essbouquetov."

"Aren't you ashamed, really ashamed, Grigory? A surname off a pomatum pot! And you call yourself a clever man. How many days he must have been thinking about it! Why, that's what is written on scent-bottles."

"Upon my word, uncle," I said in a half-whisper, "why, he is simply a fool, a perfect fool."

"It can't be helped," my uncle answered, also in a whisper. "They declare all round that he is clever, and that all this is due to the working of noble qualities. . . ."

"But for goodness' sake, get rid of him!"

"Listen, Grigory! I have really no time, my boy," my uncle began in something of an imploring tone, as though he were afraid even of Vidoplyasov. "Come, judge for yourself, how can I attend to your complaints now? You say that they have insulted you in some way again. Come, I give you my word that to-morrow I will go into it all; and now go, and God be with you. . . . Stay! What is Foma Fomitch doing?"

"He has lain down to rest. He told me that if I was asked about him, I was to say, that he is at prayer, that he intends to be praying a long time to-night."

"H'm! Well, you can go, you can go, my boy! You see, Seryozha, he is always with Foma, so that I am actually afraid of him. And that's why the servants don't like him, because he is always telling tales to Foma. Now he has gone away, and very likely to-morrow he will have spun some fine yarn about something! I've made it all right, my boy, and feel at peace now. . . . I was in haste to get to you. Now at last I am with you again," he brought out with feeling, pressing my hand. "And you know I thought, my dear, that you were desperately angry with me, and would be sure to slip off. I sent them to keep an eye on you. But now, thank God! And this afternoon, Gavrila, what a to-do; and Falaley, and you, and one thing after another! Well, thank God! thank God! At last we can talk to our hearts' content. I will open my heart to you. You mustn't go away, Seryozha; you are all I have, you and Korovkin. . . ."

"But excuse me, uncle, how have you put things right, and what have I to expect here after what has happened? I must own my head's going round."

"And do you suppose that mine isn't? It has been waltzing round for the last six months, my head has, my boy! But, thank God, everything is settled now. In the first place, they have forgiven me, completely forgiven me, on certain conditions of course; but now I am scarcely afraid of anything. Sashenka has been forgiven too. Ah, Sasha, Sasha, this afternoon . . . a passionate little heart! She went a little too far, but she has a heart of gold! I am proud of that girl, Seryozha. May the blessing of God be with her for ever. You too have been forgiven, and even—do you know —you can do just what you like; you can go all over the house and into the garden, and even among the guests. In fact, you can do just as you like; but only on one condition, that you will say nothing to-morrow in the presence of mamma or Foma—that's an absolute condition, that is, literally not half a word, I have promised for you already—but will only listen to what your elders . . . that is, I mean what others may say. They say that you are young. Don't you be offended, Seryozha; you know you really are young. . . . That's what Anna Nilovna says. . . ."

Of course I was very young, and showed it at once by boiling over with indignation at such insulting conditions.

"Listen, uncle," I cried, almost breathless. "Tell me one thing and set my mind at rest: am I really in a madhouse or not?"

"There you are, my boy, criticizing at once! You can't be patient," my uncle answered, in distress. "It's not a madhouse at all, it's nothing but over-hastiness on both sides. But you must consider, my boy, how you have behaved yourself. You remember what a sousing you gave him—a man, so to say, of venerable years?"

"Such men have no venerable years, uncle."

"Oh, there, my boy, you go too far! That's really free-thinking. I have nothing against rational free-thinking myself, my boy, but really that is beyond the mark; you really surprise me, Sergey."

"Don't be angry, uncle. I beg pardon, but I only beg your pardon. As for your Foma Fomitch . . ."

"There, now it is *your!* Oh, Sergey, my boy, don't judge him too harshly; he is a misanthropical man and nothing more, morbid! You mustn't judge him too severely. But he is a high-minded man; in fact, he is simply the most high-minded of men! Why, you saw it yourself just now; he was simply glorious. And as far as for the tricks he plays sometimes, it is no use noticing it. Why, it happens to every one."

"On the contrary, uncle, it happens to nobody."

"Ough, he keeps on at the same thing! There is not much good nature in you, Seryozha; you don't know how to forgive."

"Oh, all right, uncle, all right! Let us leave that. Tell me, have you seen Nastasya Yevgrafovna?"

"Oh, my dear, the whole bother has been about her. I tell you what, Seryozha, and first, what is most important: we've all decided to congratulate him to-morrow on his birthday—Foma, I mean—for to-morrow really is his birthday. Sashenka is a good girl, but she is mistaken; so we will go, the whole tribe of us, rather early, before mass. Ilyusha will recite some verses to him which will be like oil on his heart—in fact, it will flatter him. Oh, if only you, Seryozha, would congratulate him with us! He would perhaps forgive you altogether. How splendid it would be if you were reconciled! Forget your wrongs, Seryozha; you insulted him too, you know . . . he is a most worthy man. . . ."

"Uncle! uncle!" I cried, losing all patience, "I want to talk of what is important, and you . . . Do you know, I say again, what is happening to Nastasya Yevgrafovna?"

"Why, what is the matter, my boy? Why are you shouting? All the trouble has arisen over her, though indeed it arose some time ago. I did not want to tell you about it before, so as not to frighten you, for they wanted simply to turn her out, and they insisted on my sending her away too. You can imagine my position. . . . Oh, well, thank God, all that is set right now. They thought, you see—I will confess it all to you—that I was in love with her myself, and wanted to marry her; that I was, in short, rushing to ruin, for that really would be rushing to my ruin, they have explained it so to me. And so, to save me, they meant to turn her out. It was mamma's doing, and most of all Anna Nilovna's. Foma says nothing so far. But now I have convinced them all that they are wrong; and must confess I have told them already, that you are making Nastenka a formal proposal and that is what you have come for. Well, that has pacified them to some extent, and now she will remain, though not altogether; that is, so far only on probation. Still, she will remain. And indeed you have risen in general esteem since I told them you were courting her. Anyway, mamma seems pacified. Only Anna Nilovna goes on grumbling! I really don't know what to think of to satisfy her. And what is it she really wants, Anna Nilovna?"

"Uncle, you are greatly in error! Why, do you know

that Nastasya Yevgrafovna is going away to-morrow if she has not gone away already? Do you know that her father came to-day on purpose to take her away? That it's all a settled thing, that she told me of it to-day herself, and in conclusion asked me to give you her greetings? Do you know that or not?"

My uncle stood blankly facing me with his mouth open. I fancied that he shuddered, and a moan broke from his lips.

Without loss of time I hastened to describe to him all my conversation with Nastenka; my attempt to pay her my addresses, her resolute refusal, her anger with my uncle for having summoned me. I explained that she was hoping by her departure to save him from marrying Tatyana Ivanovna. In fact, I concealed nothing from him; indeed, I purposely exaggerated everything that was unpleasant in my story. I wanted to impress my uncle so as to wring some resolute step out of him, and I really did impress him. He cried out and clutched at his head.

"Where is she, don't you know? Where is she now?" he brought out at last, turning pale with alarm. "And I, like a fool, came here quite easy in my mind, I thought everything had been set right," he added in despair.

"I don't know where she is now; only when the uproar was beginning she went to you: she meant to proclaim all this aloud, before them all. Most likely they would not let her go in."

"No, indeed! What might she not have done! Ah, the hot-headed proud little thing! And what is she going to? What is she going to? And you, you are a pretty fellow. Why, what did she refuse you for? It's nonsense! You ought to have made her like you. Why doesn't she like you? For God's sake, answer, why are you standing there?"

"Have mercy on me, uncle! How can you ask such questions?"

"But you know this is impossible! You must marry her, you must. What did I bring you from Petersburg for? You must make her happy! Now they will drive her away, but when she is your wife, my own niece, they won't drive her away. If not, what has she to go to? What will become of her? To be a governess. Why, that is simply senseless nonsense, being a governess. While she is looking for a place, what is she going to live upon at home? Her old father has got nine to keep; they go hungry themselves. She won't take a farthing from me, you know, if she goes away through this disgusting gossip; she won't, nor will her father. And to go away like this—it is awful! It will cause a scandal—I know. And her salary has been paid for a long time in advance for necessities at home; you know she is their breadwinner. Why, supposing I do recommend her as a governess, and find an honest and honourable family . . . But where the devil is one to find them, honourable, really honourable people? Well, granting that there are many—indeed it's blasphemy to doubt it, but, my dear boy, you see it's risky—can one rely on people? Besides, any one poor is suspicious, and apt to fancy he is being forced to pay for food and kindness with humiliation! They will insult her; she is proud, and then . . . and what then? And what if some scoundrelly seducer turns up? She would spurn him, I know she would, but yet he would insult her, the scoundrel! And some discredit, some slur, some suspicion may be cast upon her all the same, and then . . . My head is going round! Ah, my God!"

"Uncle, forgive me for one question," I said solemnly. "Don't be angry with me; understand that your answer to this question may decide much. Indeed, I have a right in a way to demand an answer from you, uncle!"

"What, what is it? What question?"

"Tell me as in God's presence, openly and directly; don't you feel that you are a little in love with Nastasya Yevgrafovna yourself and would like to marry her? Just think; that is why she is being turned away from here."

My uncle made a vigorous gesture of the most violent impatience.

"I? In love? With her? Why, they have all gone off their heads, or are in a conspiracy against me. And why did I write to you to come if not to prove to them that they were all off their heads? Why am I making a match for her with you? I? In love? With her? They are all crazy, that's all about it!"

"But if it is so, uncle, do allow me to speak freely. I declare to you solemnly that I see absolutely nothing against the suggestion. On the contrary, you would make her happy, if only you love her and—and—God grant it may be so! And God give you love and good counsel!"

"But upon my word, what are you talking about?" cried my uncle, almost with horror. "I wonder how you can say such a thing coolly . . . and . . . you are altogether, my boy, in too great a hurry, I notice that characteristic in you! Why, aren't you talking nonsense? How, pray, am I to marry her when I look upon her as a daughter and nothing else? It would be shameful for me, indeed, to look upon her in any other light; it would be a sin, in fact! I am an old man, while she is a flower! Indeed, Foma made that clear to me in those very words. My heart glows with a father's love for her, and here you talk of marriage! Maybe out of gratitude she would not refuse me, but you know she would despise me afterwards for taking advantage of her gratitude. I should spoil her life, I should lose her affection! And I would give my soul for her, she is my beloved child! I love her just as I do Sasha, even more, I must own. Sasha is my daughter by right, by law, but this one I have made my daughter by love. I took her out of poverty, I have brought her up. Katya, my lost angel, loved her; she left her to me as a daughter. I have given her a good education: she speaks French and plays the piano, she has read books and everything. . . . Such a sweet smile she has! Have you noticed it, Seryozha? As though she were laughing at one, but yet she is not laughing, but on the contrary, loving one. . . . You see I thought that you would come and make her an offer; they would be convinced that I had no intentions in regard to her, and would give over spreading these disgusting stories. She would remain with us then in peace, in comfort, and how happy we should be! You are both my children, both almost orphans, you have both grown up under my guardianship . . . I should have loved you so! I would have devoted my life to you; I would not part from you; I would follow you anywhere! Oh, how happy we might have been! And why are these people always so cross, always so angry, why do they hate each other? If only I could explain it all to them! If only I could make them see the whole truth! Ah, my God!"

"Yes, uncle, yes, that is all so; but, you see, she has refused me."

"Refused you! H'm. . . . Do you know, I had a sort of presentiment that she would refuse you," he said, musing. "But no!" he cried. "I don't believe it. It's impossible. In that case, all our plans are upset! But you must have begun injudiciously somehow, even offended her perhaps. Perhaps you tried your hand at paying compliments. . . . Tell me how it was again, Sergey."

I repeated the whole story in full detail again. When I came to Nastenka's hoping by her departure to save my uncle from Tatyana Ivanovna, he gave a bitter smile.

"Save me!" he said. "Save me till to-morrow morning. . . ."

"But you don't mean to say that you are going to marry Tatyana Ivanovna!" I cried in alarm.

"How else could I have paid for Nastasya's not being sent away to-morrow? To-morrow I make the offer—the formal proposal."

"And you have made up your mind to it, uncle?"

"What could I do, my boy, what could I do? It rends my heart, but I have made up my mind to it. The proposal will be to-morrow; they suggest that the wedding should be a quiet one, at home; it would certainly be better at home. You will perhaps be best man. I have already dropped a hint about you, so they won't drive you away before then. There is no help for it, my boy. They say, 'It's a fortune for your children!' Of course one would do anything for one's children. One would turn head over heels, especially as really, perhaps, what they say is right. You know I really ought to do something for my family. One can't sit an idle drone for ever!"

"But, uncle, she is mad, you know!" I cried, forgetting myself, and there was a sickly pang at my heart.

"Oh, mad, is she now? She is not mad at all; it's only, you know, that she has had trouble. . . . There is no help for it, my boy. Of course I should have been glad of one with sense. . . . Though, after all, some who have sense are no better! If only you knew what a kind-hearted creature she is, noble-hearted!"

"But, my God! he is resigning himself to the thought of it already," I said in despair.

"And what else is there to do? You know they are doing their utmost for my benefit, and, indeed, I felt beforehand that sooner or later they would force me to marry, that there is no getting out of it. So better now than make more quarrelling about it, I am telling you everything quite openly, Seryozha. In a way I am actually glad. I have made up my mind, anyway, and it's a load off my back—I am more at ease, somehow. Why, I came here with my mind almost at ease. It seems, it's my fate. And the great thing to make up for it was that Nastenka would stay on. You know I agreed on that condition. And now she wants to run away of herself! But that shall not be!" my uncle cried, stamping. "Listen, Sergey," he added with a determined air; "wait for me here, don't go away. I will come back to you in an instant."

"Where are you off to, uncle?"

"Perhaps I shall see her, Sergey; it will all be cleared up, believe me that it will all be cleared up, and . . . and . . . you shall marry her I give you my word of honour!"

My uncle went quickly out of the room, and turned not towards the house, but into the garden. I watched him from the window.

The Catastrophe

XII

I was left alone. My position was insufferable; I had been rejected, and my uncle meant to marry me off almost by force. I was perplexed and lost in a tangle of ideas. Mizin-tchikov and his proposition were not absent from my mind for an instant. At all costs uncle must be saved! I even thought of going to look for Mizintchikov and telling him all about it. But where had my uncle gone, though? He had said himself that he was going to look for Nastenka, but had turned in the direction of the garden. The thought of secret meetings flashed through my mind, and a very un-pleasant feeling clutched at my heart. I remembered what Mizintchikov had said of a secret liaison. After a moment's thought I rejected my suspicions with indignation. My un-cle was incapable of deceit: that was obvious. My uneasiness grew greater every moment. Unconsciously I went out on to the steps, and walked into the garden down the very ave-nue into which my uncle had disappeared. The moon was beginning to rise. I knew that garden through and through, and was not afraid of losing myself. As I drew near the old arbour which stood in solitude on the bank of the neglected scum-covered pond, I suddenly stood rooted to the spot; I heard voices in the arbour. I cannot describe the strange feeling of annoyance that took possession of me. I felt con-vinced that my uncle and Nastenka were there, and went on going nearer, appeasing my conscience by thinking that I was walking at the same pace as before and not trying to approach stealthily. Suddenly there was the distinct sound of a kiss, then stifled exclamations, and immediately afterwards a shrill feminine shriek. At that instant a woman in a white dress ran out of the arbour and flashed by me like a swal-low. It even seemed to me that she hid her face in her hands that she might not be recognized: probably I had been noticed from the arbour. But what was my amazement when in the swain who emerged after the flying lady I recognized—Obnoskin, Obnoskin, who, according to Mizin-tchikov's words, had gone away some hours before. Obnos-kin on his side was greatly confused when he saw me; all his impudence vanished instantly.

"Excuse me, but . . . I did not in the least expect to meet you," he brought out, smiling and hesitating.

"Nor I you," I answered ironically, "especially as I heard you had already gone away."

"No. . . . It was just . . . I went a little on the way with my mother. But may I appeal to you as an absolutely honourable man?"

"What about?"

"There are cases—and you will agree yourself that it is so—when a truly honourable man is forced to appeal to the highest sense of honour of another truly honourable man. . . . I hope you understand me. . . ."

"Do not hope, I understand absolutely nothing. . . ."

"You saw the lady who was here with me in the arbour?"

"I saw her, but I did not recognize her."

"Ah, you did not recognize her. . . . That lady I shall shortly call my wife."

"I congratulate you. But in what way can I be of use to you?"

"Only in one way, by keeping it a dead secret that you have seen me with that lady."

Who can she be? I wondered. Surely not . . .

"I really don't know," I answered Obnoskin. "I hope that you will excuse me for not being able to promise."

"Yes, please, for God's sake," Obnoskin besought me. "Understand my position, it's a secret. You may be betrothed too: then I . . ."

"Sh! some one is coming!"

"Where?" We did indeed catch a glimpse thirty paces away of the shadow of some one passing.

"It . . . it must be Foma Fomitch!" Obnoskin whispered, trembling all over. "I know him from his walk. My God! And steps again from the other direction! Do you hear? . . . Good-bye! I thank you . . . and I entreat you . . ."

Obnoskin vanished. A minute later, as though he had sprung out of the earth, my uncle was before me.

"Is it you?" he greeted me. "It is all over, Seryozha, it is all over!"

I noticed, too, that he was trembling from head to foot.

"What is all over, uncle?"

"Come along!" he said, gasping for breath, and clutching my hand tightly, he drew me after him. He did not utter a word all the way to the lodge, nor did he let me speak. I was expecting something monstrous, and my expectations were almost realized.

When we went indoors he was overcome with giddiness, he was deathly pale. I promptly sprinkled him with water. "Something very awful must have happened," I thought, "for a man like this to faint."

"Uncle, what is the matter with you?" I asked him at last.

"All is over, Seryozha! Foma found me in the garden with Nastenka, at the very moment when I was kissing her."

"Kissing her! In the garden!" I cried, looking at my uncle in amazement.

"In the garden, my boy. The Lord confounded me! I went there to be sure of seeing her. I wanted to speak openly to her to make her see reason—about you, I mean. And she had been waiting for me a whole hour, on the broken seat, beyond the pond. . . . She often goes there when she wants to speak to me."

"Often, uncle?"

"Yes, often, my boy! Of late we have been meeting almost every night. Only they must have watched us—in fact, I know that they watched us and that it was Anna Nilovna's doing. We gave it up for a time. The last four days we have not met; but to-day it was necessary again. You saw yourself how necessary it was; how else could I have said anything to her? I went in the hope of finding her, and she had been sitting there a whole hour, waiting for me: she, too, wanted to tell me something. . . ."

"Good heavens, how incautious! Why, you knew that you were being watched!"

"But, you see, it was a critical matter, Seryozha; there was a great deal we had to discuss together. I don't dare to look at her in the daytime. She looks in one corner and I look in another, as though she did not exist. But towards night we meet and have a talk. . . ."

"Well, what happened, uncle?"

"Before I could utter a couple of words, you know, my heart began throbbing and the tears gushed from my eyes. I began trying to persuade her to marry you, and she answered me: 'You certainly don't love me—you must be blind.' And all of a sudden she flings herself on my neck, throws her arms round me, and begins crying and sobbing! 'I love no one but you,' she said, 'and won't marry any one. I have loved you for ever so long, but I will never marry you. And to-morrow I am going away and going into a nunnery.' "

"My goodness! Did she really say that? Well, what then, uncle, what then?"

"I looked up and there was Foma facing us! And where had he sprung from? Could he have been sitting behind a bush, and waiting for some such lapse?"

"The scoundrel!"

"I was petrified, Nastenka ran away, while Foma Fomitch passed by without a word and held up his finger at me. Sergey, do you understand what a hubbub there will be to-morrow?"

"I should think I do!"

"Do you understand?" he cried in despair, leaping up from his seat. "Do you understand that they will try to ruin her, to disgrace her, to dishonour her; they are looking for a pretext to accuse her of something disgraceful, and now the pretext is found. You know they will say that she is carrying on an abominable intrigue with me! You know, the scoundrels made out that she had an intrigue with Vidoplyasov! It's all Anna Nilovna's tales. What will happen now? What will happen to-morrow? Will Foma really tell them?"

"He'll certainly tell them, uncle."

"If he does, if he really does tell . . ." he brought out, biting his lips and clenching his fists. "But no, I don't believe it! He won't tell, he will understand . . . he is a man of the loftiest character! He will spare her. . . ."

"Whether he spares her or whether he doesn't," I answered resolutely, "it is your duty in any case to make Nastasya Yevgrafovna an offer to-morrow."

My uncle looked fixedly at me.

"Do you understand, uncle, that you have ruined the girl's reputation if this story gets about? Do you understand that you ought to prevent that calamity as quickly as possible; that you ought to look them all in the face boldly and proudly, ought to offer her your hand publicly, to spurn their arguments and pound Foma to a jelly if he hints a word against her?"

"My dear boy," cried my uncle, "I thought of that as I came along here!"

"And did you make up your mind?"

"Yes, and finally! I had made up my mind before I began speaking to you."

"Bravo, uncle!" And I rushed to embrace him.

We talked for a long time. I put before him all the arguments, all the absolute necessity for marrying Nastenka, which, indeed, he understood far better than I did. But my eloquence was aroused. I was delighted on my uncle's account. He was impelled by a sense of duty or he would never have taken a stand. He had the deepest reverence for duty, for obligation. But in spite of that I was quite unable to imagine how things would be settled. I knew and blindly believed that nothing would induce my uncle to fall short of what he had once recognized as his duty; but yet I could not believe that he would have the strength to stand out against his household. And so I did my utmost to incite him and urge him on, and set to work with all the fervour of youth.

"The more so," I said, "as now everything is settled and your last doubts have vanished! What you did not expect, though in reality every one else saw it, and every one noticed it before you did, has happened; Nastasya Yevgrafovna loves you! Surely," I cried, "you will not let that pure love be turned into shame and disgrace for her?"

"Never! But, my dear boy, can I really be going to be so happy?" cried my uncle, throwing himself on my neck. "And how is it she loves me, and what for? What for? It seems to me there is nothing in me likely to . . . I am an old man compared to her; I certainly did not expect it! My

angel, my angel! . . . Listen, Seryozha! you asked me this evening whether I were not in love with her: had you any idea?"

"All I saw, uncle, was that you love her as much as
any one can love: you love her and at the same time you
don't know it yourself. Upon my word! You invite me,
you want to marry me to her solely in order that she may
become your niece, and so you may have her always with
you. . . ."

"But you . . . you do forgive me, Sergey?"

"Oh, uncle. . . ."

And he embraced me again.

"Mind, uncle, they will all be against you: you must
stand up for yourself and resist them, and no later than to-
morrow!"

"Yes . . . yes, to-morrow . . ." he repeated somewhat
pensively. "And you know we must attack the business
with manliness, with true nobility of soul, with strength
of will. . . . Yes, with strength of will!"

"Don't be frightened, uncle."

"I am not frightened, Seryozha! There's one thing, I
don't know how to begin, how to proceed."

"Don't think about it, uncle. To-morrow will settle
everything. Set your mind at rest for to-day. The more you
think the worse it will be. And if Foma begins—kick him
out of the house at once and pound him to a jelly."

"And can't we avoid kicking him out? What I have decided, my boy, is this. To-morrow I shall go to him early,
at dawn, I shall tell him all about it, just as I have told you
here. Surely he cannot but understand me, he is a high-
minded man, the most high-minded of men. But I tell you
what does worry me: what if mamma speaks to Tatyana
Ivanovna to-day of the offer to be made to her to-morrow?
That would be unlucky, won't it?"

"Don't worry yourself about Tatyana Ivanovna, uncle."

And I told him about the scene in the arbour with Obnoskin. My uncle was extremely surprised. I did not say a
word about Mizintchikov.

"A fantastical person. A really fantastical person!" he
cried. "Poor thing! They ingratiate themselves with her

and try to take advantage of her simplicity. Was it really Obnoskin? But you know he has gone away. . . . Strange, awfully strange! I am astonished, Seryozha. . . . We must look into it to-morrow and take steps. . . . But are you perfectly certain that it was Tatyana Ivanovna?"

I answered that I had not seen her face, but for certain reasons I was positive that it was Tatyana Ivanovna.

"H'm. Wasn't it a little intrigue with one of the servant girls and you fancied it was Tatyana Ivanovna? Wasn't it Dasha, the gardener's daughter? A sly hussy! She has been remarked upon, that's why I say so. Anna Nilovna caught her! . . . But it wasn't she, though! He said he meant to marry her. Strange, strange!"

At last we parted. I embraced my uncle and gave him my blessing.

"To-morrow, to-morrow," he repeated, "it will all be settled; before you are up it will be settled. I shall go to Foma and take a chivalrous line, I will speak frankly as I would to my own brother, I will lay bare the inmost recesses of my heart. Good-bye, Seryozha. You go to bed, you are tired; but I am sure I shan't shut my eyes all night."

He went away. I went to bed at once, tired out and utterly exhausted. It had been a hard day. My nerves were overwrought, and before I fell really asleep, I kept starting and waking up again. But strange as my impressions were on going off to sleep, the strangeness of them was as nothing beside the queerness of my awakening next morning.

PART 2

The Pursuit

I

I slept soundly without dreaming. Suddenly I felt as though a load of some hundredweights was lying on my feet. I cried out and woke up. It was daylight; the sun was peeping brightly into the room. On my bed, or rather on my feet, was sitting Mr. Bahtcheyev.

It was impossible to doubt that it was he. Managing somehow to release my legs, I sat up in bed and looked at him with the blank amazement of a man just awake.

"And now he is looking about him," cried the fat man. "Why are you staring at me? Get up, sir, get up. I have been waking you for the last half-hour; rub away at your eyes!"

"Why, what has happened? What's the time?"

"It's still early by the clock, but our Fevronya did not wait for dawn, but has given us the slip. Get up, we are going in pursuit!"

"What Fevronya?"

"Why, our young lady, the crazy one! She has given us the slip! She was off before dawn. I came to you, sir, only for a minute, to wake you, and here I have been busy with you a couple of hours. Get up, your uncle's waiting for you. They waited for the festive day!" he added, with a malignant quiver in his voice.

"But whom and what are you talking about?" I asked impatiently, though I was beginning to guess. "Surely not Tatyana Ivanovna?"

"To be sure. She it is. I said so, I foretold it; they wouldn't listen to me. A nice treat she has given us for the festive day now! She is mad on *amour*, and has *amour* on the brain. Tfoo! And that fellow, what do you say to that fellow? With his little beard, eh?"

"Can you mean Mizintchikov?"

"Tfoo, plague take it! Why, my dear sir, you had better rub your eyes and pull yourself together—if only for the great holy festive day. You must have had a great deal too much at supper last night, if you are still hazy this morning! With Mizintchikov! It's with Obnoskin, not Mizintchikov. Ivan Ivanovitch Mizintchikov is a moral young man and he is coming with us in pursuit."

"What are you saying?" I cried, jumping up in bed. "Is it really with Obnoskin?"

"Tfoo, you annoying person!" answered the fat man, leaping up from his seat. "I come to him as to a man of culture to inform him of what has happened, and he still doubts it. Well, sir, if you want to come with us, get up, shoot into your breeches. It's no good my spending more words on you; I've wasted golden time on you as it is."

And he went out in extreme indignation.

Amazed by the news, I jumped out of bed, hurriedly dressed, and ran downstairs. Thinking to find my uncle in the house, where every one still seemed asleep and knowing nothing of what had happened, I cautiously mounted the front steps, and in the hall I met Nastenka. She seemed to have dressed hurriedly in some sort of *peignoir* or *schlafrock*. Her hair was in disorder; it was evident that she had only just jumped out of bed, and she seemed to be waiting for some one in the hall.

"Tell me, is it true that Tatyana Ivanovna has run away with Obnoskin?" she asked hurriedly in a breaking voice, looking pale and frightened.

"I am told it is true. I am looking for my uncle, we want to go after them."

"Oh, bring her back, make haste and bring her back. She will be ruined if you don't fetch her back."

"But where is uncle?"

"Most likely in the stable; they are getting the carriage out. I have been waiting for him here. Listen: tell him from me that I must go home to-day; I have quite made up my mind. My father will take me; I shall go at once if I can. Everything is hopeless now. All is lost!"

Saying this, she looked at me as though she were utterly lost, and suddenly dissolved into tears. I think she began to be hysterical.

"Calm yourself," I besought her. "Why, it's all for the best—you will see. What is the matter with you, Nastasya Yevgrafovna?"

"I . . . I don't know . . . what is the matter with me," she said, sighing and unconsciously squeezing my hands. "Tell him . . ."

At that instant there was a sound from the other side of the door on the right.

She let go of my hand and, panic-stricken, ran away upstairs without finishing her sentence.

I found the whole party—that is, my uncle, Bahtcheyev, and Mizintchikov—in the back yard by the stable. Fresh horses had been harnessed in Bahtcheyev's carriage. Everything was ready for setting off; they were only waiting for me.

"Here he is!" cried my uncle on my appearance. "Have you heard, my boy?" he asked, with a peculiar expression on his face.

Alarm, perplexity, and at the same time, hope were expressed in his looks, in his voice and in his movements. He was conscious that a momentous crisis had come in his life.

I was immediately initiated into all the details of the case. Mr. Bahtcheyev, who had spent a very bad night, left his house at dawn to reach the monastery five miles away in time for early mass. Just at the turning from the high road to the monastery he suddenly saw a chaise dashing along at full trot, and in the chaise Tatyana Ivanovna and Obnoskin. Tatyana Ivanovna with a tear-stained, and as it seemed frightened face, uttered a shriek and stretched out her hands to Mr. Bahtcheyev as though imploring his protection—so at least it appeared from his story; "while he, the scoundrel, with the little beard," he went on, "sits more dead than alive and tries to hide himself. But you are wrong there, my fine fellow, you can't hide yourself." Without stopping, Stepan Alexyevitch turned back to the road and galloped to Stepantchikovo and woke my uncle, Mizintchikov, and finally me. They decided to set off at once in pursuit.

"Obnoskin, Obnoskin," said my uncle, looking intently at me, looking at me as though he would like to say something else as well. "Who would have thought it!"

"Any dirty trick might have been expected of that low fellow!" cried Mizintchikov with the most vigorous indignation, and at once turned away to avoid my eye.

"What are we going to do, go or not? Or are we going

to stand here till night babbling!" interposed Mr. Bah-tcheyev as he clambered into the carriage.

"We are going, we are going," cried my uncle.

"It's all for the best, uncle," I whispered to him. "You see how splendidly it has all turned out?"

"Hush, my boy, don't be sinful. . . . Ah, my dear! They will simply drive *her* away now, to punish her for their fail-ure, you understand. It's fearful, the prospect I see before me!"

"Well, Yegor Ilyitch, are you going on whispering or starting?" Mr. Bahtcheyev cried out a second time. "Or shall we unharness the horses and have a snack of some-thing? What do you say; shall we have a drink of vodka?"

These words were uttered with such furious sarcasm that it was impossible not to satisfy Bahtcheyev at once. We all promptly got into the carriage, and the horses set off at a gallop.

For some time we were all silent. My uncle kept looking at me significantly, but did not care to speak to me before the others. He often sank into thought; then as though waking up, started and looked about him in agitation, Mizintchikov was apparently calm, he smoked a cigar, and his looks expressed the indignation of an unjustly treated man. But Bahtcheyev had excitement enough for all of us. He grumbled to himself, looked at every one and everything with absolute indignation, flushed crimson, fumed, continually spat aside, and could not recover him-self.

"Are you sure, Stepan Alexyevitch, that they have gone to Mishino?" my uncle asked suddenly. "It's fifteen miles from here, my boy," he added, addressing me. "It's a little village of thirty souls, lately purchased from the former owners by a provincial official. The most pettifogging fel-low in the world. So at least they say about him, perhaps, mistakenly. Stepan Alexyevitch declares that that is where Obnoskin has gone, and that that official will be helping him now."

"To be sure," cried Bahtcheyev, starting. "I tell you, it is Mishino. Only by now maybe there is no trace of him left at Mishino. I should think not, we have wasted three hours chattering in the yard!"

"Don't be uneasy," observed Mizintchikov. "We shall find them."

"Find them, indeed! I dare say he will wait for you. The treasure is in his hands. You may be sure we have seen the last of him!"

"Calm yourself, Stepan Alexyevitch, calm yourself, we shall overtake them," said my uncle. "They have not had time to take any steps yet, you will see that is so."

"Not had time!" Mr. Bahtcheyev brought out angrily. "She's had time for any mischief, for all she's such a quiet one! 'She's a quiet one,' they say, 'a quiet one,' he added in a mincing voice, as though he were mimicking some one. 'She has had troubles.' Well, now, she has shown us her heels, for all her troubles. Now you have to chase after her along the high roads with your tongue out before you can see where you are going! They won't let a man go to church for the holy saint's day. Tfoo!"

"But she is not under age," I observed; "she is not under guardianship. We can't bring her back if she doesn't want to come. What are we going to do?"

"Of course," answered my uncle; "but she will want to— I assure you. What she is doing now means nothing. As soon as she sees us she will want to come back—I'll answer for it. We can't leave her like this, my boy, at the mercy of fate, to be sacrificed; it's a duty, so to say. . . ."

"She's not under guardianship!" cried Bahtcheyev, pouncing on me at once. "She is a fool, my dear sir, a perfect fool—it's not a case of her being under guardianship. I didn't care to talk to you about her yesterday, but the other day I went by mistake into her room and what did I see, there she was before the looking-glass with her arms akimbo dancing a schottische! And dressed up to the nines: a fashion-plate, a regular fashion-plate! I simply spat in disgust and walked away. Then I foresaw all this, as clear as though it were written in a book!"

"Why abuse her so?" I observed with some timidity. "We know that Tatyana Ivanovna . . . is not in perfect health

. . . or rather she has a mania. . . . It seems to me that Obnoskin is the one to blame, not she."

"Not in perfect health! Come, you get along," put in the fat man, turning crimson with wrath. "Why, he has taken an oath to drive a man to fury! Since yesterday he has taken an oath to! She is a fool, my dear sir, I tell you, an absolute fool. It's not that she's not in perfect health; from early youth she has been mad on Cupid. And now Cupid has brought her to this pass. As for that fellow with the beard, it's no use talking about him. I dare say by now he is racing off double quick with the money in his pocket and a grin on his face."

"Do you really think, then, that he'll cast her off at once?"

"What else should he do? Is he going to drag such a treasure about with him? And what good is she to him? He'll fleece her of everything and then sit her down somewhere under a bush on the highroad—and make off. While she can sit there under the bush and sniff the flowers."

"Well, you are too hasty there, Stepan, it won't be like that!" cried my uncle. "But why are you so cross? I wonder at you, Stepan. What's the matter with you?"

"Why, am I a man or not? It does make one cross, though it's no busines of mine. Why, I am saying it perhaps in kindness to her. . . . Ech, damnation take it all! Why, what have I come here for? Why, what did I turn back for? What is it to do with me? What is it to do with me?"

So grumbled Mr. Bahtcheyev, but I left off listening to him and mused on the woman whom we were now in pursuit of—Tatyana Ivanovna. Here is a brief biography of her which I gathered later on from the most trustworthy sources, and which is essential to the explanation of her adventures.

A poor orphan child who grew up in a strange unfriendly house, then a poor girl, then a poor young woman, and at last a poor old maid, Tatyana Ivanovna in the course of her poor life had drained the overfull cup of sorrow, friendlessness, humiliation and reproach, and had tasted to the full the bitterness of the bread of others. Naturally of a gay, highly susceptible and frivolous temperament, she had at first endured her bitter lot in one way or another and had even been capable at times of the gayest careless laughter; but with years destiny at last got the upper hand of her. Little by little Tatyana Ivanovna grew thin and sallow, became irritable and morbidly susceptible, and sank into the most unrestrained, unbounded dreaminess, often interrupted by hysterical tears and convulsive sobbing. The fewer earthly blessings real life left to her lot, the more she comforted and deluded herself in imagination. The more certainly, the more irretrievably her last hopes in real life were passing and at last were lost, the more seductive grew her dreams, never to be realized. Fabulous wealth, unheard-of beauty, rich, elegant, distinguished suitors, always princes and sons of generals, who for her sake had kept their hearts in virginal purity and were dying at her feet from infinite love; and finally, *he*—*he*, the ideal of beauty combining in himself every possible perfection, passionate and loving, an artist, a poet, the son of a general —all at once or all by turns—began to appear to her not only in her dreams but almost in reality. Her reason was already beginning to fail, unable to stand the strain of this opiate of secret incessant dreaming. . . . And all at once destiny played a last fatal jest at her expense. Living in the last extreme of humiliation, in melancholy surroundings that crushed the heart, a companion to a toothless old lady, the most peevish in the world, scolded for everything, reproached for every crust she ate, for every threadbare rag she wore, insulted with impunity by any one, protected by no one, worn out by her miserable existence and secretly plunged in the luxury of the maddest and most fervid dreams—she suddenly heard the news of the death of a distant relation, all of whose family had died long before (though she in her frivolous way had never taken the trouble to ascertain the fact); he was a strange man, a phrenologist and a money-lender, who led a solitary, morose, unnoticed life, in seclusion somewhere very remote in the wilds. And now all at once immense wealth fell as

though by miracle from heaven and scattered gold at Tatyana Ivanovna's feet; she turned out to be the sole legitimate heiress of the dead money-lender. A hundred thousand silver roubles came to her at once. This jest of destiny
was the last straw. Indeed, how could a mind already tot-
tering doubt the truth of dreams when they were actually
beginning to come true? And so the poor thing took leave
of her last remaining grain of common-sense. Swooning
with bliss, she soared away beyond recall into her enchanted
world of impossible imagination and seductive fancies.
Away with all reflection, all doubt, all the checks of real
life, all its laws clear and inevitable as twice two make
four. Thirty-five years and dreams of dazzling beauty, the
sad chill of autumn and the luxuriance of the infinite bliss
of love—all blended in her without discord. Her dreams
had once already been realized in life; why should not all
the rest come true? Why should not *he* appear? Tatyana
Ivanovna did not reason, but she had faith. But while waiting for *him,* the ideal—suitors and knights of various orders and simple gentlemen, officers and civilians, infantry
men and cavalry men, grand noblemen and simply poets
who had been in Paris or had been only in Moscow, with
beards and without beards, with imperials and without imperials, Spaniards and not Spaniards (but Spaniards, by
preference), began appearing before her day and night in
horrifying numbers that awakened grave apprehensions in
onlookers; she was but a step from the madhouse. All these
lovely phantoms thronged about her in a dazzling, infatu-
ated procession. In reality, in actual life, everything went
the same fantastic way: any one she looked at was in love
with her; any one who passed by was a Spaniard; if any one
died it must be for love of her. As ill-luck would have it,
all this was confirmed in her eyes by the fact that men such
as Obnoskin, Mizintchikov, and dozens of others with the
same motives began running after her. Every one began
suddenly trying to please her, spoiling her, flattering her.
Poor Tatyana Ivanovna refused to suspect that all this was
for the sake of her money. She was fully convinced that,
as though at some signal, people had suddenly reformed,

and all, every one of them, grown gay and kind, friendly and good. *He* had not appeared himself in person; but though there could be no doubt that *he* would appear, her daily life as it was was so agreeable, so alluring, so full of all sorts of distractions and diversions, that she could wait. Tatyana Ivanovna ate sweetmeats, culled the flowers of pleasure, and read novels. The novels heated her imagination and were usually flung aside at the second page; she could not read longer, but was carried to dreamland by the very first lines, by the most trivial hint at love, sometimes simply by the description of scenery, of a room, of a toilette. New finery, lace, hats, hair ornaments, ribbons, samples, paper patterns, designs, sweetmeats, flowers, lapdogs were being continually sent her. Three girls spent whole days sewing for her in the maid's room, while their lady was trying on bodices and flounces, and twisting and turning before the looking-glass from morning to night, and even in the night. She actually seemed younger and prettier on coming into her fortune. To this day I don't know what was her relationship to the late General Krahotkin. I have always been persuaded that it was the invention of Madame la Générale, who wanted to get possession of Tatyana Ivanovna and at all costs to marry her to my uncle for her money. Mr. Bahtcheyev was right when he spoke of its being Cupid that had brought Tatyana Ivanovna to the last point; and my uncle's idea on hearing of her elopement with Obnoskin—to run after her and bring her back even by force—was the most rational one. The poor creature was not fit to live without a guardian, and would have come to grief at once if she had fallen into evil hands.

It was past nine when we reached Mishino. It was a poor little village, lying in a hole two miles from the high road. Six or seven peasants' huts, begrimed with smoke, slanting on one side and barely covered with blackened thatch, looked dejectedly and inhospitably at the traveller. There was not a garden, not a bush, to be seen for a quarter of a mile round. Only an old willow hung drowsily over the greenish pool that passed for a pond. Such a new abode could hardly make a cheering impression on Tatyana Ivanovna. The manor house consisted of a new long, narrow, wooden building with six windows in a row, and had been roughly thatched. The owner, the official, had only lately taken possession. The yard was not even fenced, and only on one side a new hurdle had been begun from which the dry leaves of the nut branches had not yet dropped. Obnoskin's chaise was standing by the hurdle. We had fallen on the fugitives like snow on the head. From an open window came the sound of cries and weeping.

The barefoot boy who met us dashed away at breakneck speed. In the first room Tatyana Ivanovna with a tear-stained face was seated on a long chintz-covered sofa without a back. On seeing us she uttered a shriek and hid her face in her hands. Beside her stood Obnoskin, frightened and pitifully confused. He was so distraught that he flew to shake hands with us, as though overjoyed at our arrival. From the door that opened into the other room we had a peep of some lady's dress; some one was listening and looking through a crack imperceptible to us. The people of the house did not put in an appearance; it seemed as though they were not in the house; they were all in hiding somewhere.

"Here she is, the traveller! Hiding her face in her hands too!" cried Mr. Bahtcheyev, lumbering after us into the room.

"Restrain your transports, Stepan Alexyevitch! They are quite unseemly. No one has a right to speak now but Yegor Ilyitch; we have nothing to do here!" Mizintchikov observed sharply.

My uncle, casting a stern glance at Mr. Bahtcheyev, and seeming not to observe the existence of Obnoskin, who had rushed to shake hands with him, went up to Tatyana Ivanovna, whose face was still hidden in her hands, and in the softest voice, with the most unaffected sympathy, said to her—

"Tatyana Ivanovna, we all so love and respect you, that we have come ourselves to learn your intentions. Would you care to drive back with us to Stepantchikovo? It is Ilyusha's nameday, mamma is expecting you impatiently, while Sasha and Nastenka have no doubt been crying over you all the morning. . . ."

Tatyana Ivanovna raised her head timidly, looked at him through her fingers, and suddenly bursting into tears, flung herself on his neck.

"Oh, take me away, make haste and take me away from here!" she said, sobbing. "Make haste, as much haste as you can!"

"She's gone off on the spree and made an ass of herself!" hissed Mr. Bahtcheyev, nudging my arm.

"Everything is at an end, then," said my uncle, turning drily to Obnoskin and scarcely looking at him. "Tatyana Ivanovna, please give me your arm. Let us go!"

There was a rustle the other side of the door; the door creaked and opened wider.

"If you look at it from another point of view though," Obnoskin observed uneasily, looking at the open door, "you will see yourself, Yegor Ilyitch . . . your action in my house . . . and in fact I was bowing to you, and you would not even bow to me, Yegor Ilyitch. . . ."

"Your action in *my* house, sir, was a low action," said my uncle, looking sternly at Obnoskin, "and this house is not yours. You have heard: Tatyana Ivanovna does not wish to remain here a minute. What more do you want? Not a word—do you hear? not another word, I beg! I am extremely desirous of avoiding further explanations, and indeed it would be more to your interest to do so."

But at this point Obnoskin was so utterly crestfallen that he began uttering the most unexpected drivel.

"Don't despise me, Yegor Ilyitch," he began in a half-whisper, almost crying with shame and continually glancing towards the door, probably from fear of being overheard. "It's not my doing, but my mother's. I didn't do it from mercenary motives, Yegor Ilyitch; I didn't mean anything; I did, of course, do it from interested motives, Yegor Ilyitch . . . but I did it with a noble object, Yegor Ilyitch. I should have used the money usefully . . . I should have helped the poor. I wanted to support the movement for enlightenment, too, and even dreamed of endowing a university scholarship. . . . That was what I wanted to turn my wealth to, Yegor Ilyitch; and not to use it just for anything, Yegor Ilyitch."

We all felt horribly ashamed. Even Mizintchikov reddened and turned away, and my uncle was so confused that he did not know what to say.

"Come, come, that's enough," he said at last. "Calm yourself, Pavel Semyonitch. It can't be helped! It might happen to any one. . . . If you like, come to dinner . . . and I shall be delighted."

But Mr. Bahtcheyev behaved quite differently.

"Endow a scholarship!" he bawled furiously. "You are not the sort to endow a scholarship! I bet you'd be ready to fleece any one you come across. . . . Not a pair of breeches of his own, and here he is bragging of scholarships! Oh, you rag-and-bone man! So you've made a conquest of a soft heart, have you? And where is she, the parent? Hiding, is she? I bet she is sitting somewhere behind a screen, or has crept under the bed in a fright. . . ."

"Stepan, Stepan!" cried my uncle.

Obnoskin flushed and was on the point of protesting; but before he had time to open his mouth the door was flung open and Anfisa Petrovna herself, violently irritated, with flashing eyes, crimson with wrath, flew into the room.

"What's this?" she shouted. "What's this going on here? You break into a respectable house with your rabble, Yegor Ilyitch, frighten ladies, give orders! . . . What's the meaning of it? I have not taken leave of my senses yet, Yegor Ilyitch! And you, you booby," she went on yelling, pouncing upon her son, "you are snivelling before them already. Your mother is insulted in her own house, and you stand gaping. Do you call yourself a gentlemanly young man after that? You are a rag, and not a young man, after that."

Not a trace of the mincing airs and fashionable graces of the day before, not a trace of the lorgnette even was to be seen about Anfisa Petrovna now. She was a regular fury, a fury without a mask.

As soon as my uncle saw her he made haste to take Tatyana Ivanovna on his arm, and would have rushed out of the room, but Anfisa Petrovna at once barred the way.

"You are not going away like that, Yegor Ilyitch," she clamoured again. "By what right are you taking Tatyana Ivanovna away by force? You are annoyed that she has escaped the abominable snares you had caught her in, you and your mamma and your imbecile Foma Fomitch; you would have liked to marry her yourself for the sake of filthy lucre. I beg your pardon, but our ideas here are not so low! Tatyana Ivanovna, seeing that you were plotting against her, that you were bringing her to ruin, confided in Pavlusha of herself. She herself begged him to save her from your snares, so to say; she was forced to run away from you by night—that's a pretty thing! That's what you have driven her to, isn't it, Tatyana Ivanovna? And since that's so, how dare you burst, a whole gang of you, into a respectable gentleman's house and carry off a young lady by force in spite of her tears and protests? I will not permit it! I will not permit it! I have not taken leave of my senses! Tatyana Ivanovna will remain because she wishes it! Come, Tatyana Ivanovna, it is useless to listen to them, they are your enemies, not your friends! Come along, don't be frightened! I'll see them all out directly! . . ."

"No, no!" cried Tatyana Ivanovna, terrified. "I don't want to, I don't want to! He is no husband for me. I don't want to marry your son! He's no husband for me!"

"You don't want to!" shouted Anfisa Petrovna, breathless with rage. "You don't want to! You have come and you don't want to! Then how dared you deceive us like this? Then how dared you give him your promise? You ran away with him by night, you forced yourself upon him, and have led us into embarrassment and expense. My son has perhaps lost an excellent match through you! He may have lost a dowry of ten thousand through you! . . . No! you must pay for it, you ought to pay for it; we have proofs; you ran away at night. . . ."

But we did not hear this tirade to the end. All at once, grouping ourselves round my uncle, we moved forward straight upon Anfisa Petrovna and went out on to the steps. The carriage was at hand at once.

"None but dishonourable people, none but scoundrels, behave like that," cried Anfisa Petrovna from the steps, in an absolute frenzy. "I will lodge a petition, you shall pay for it . . . you are going to a disreputable house, Tatyana Ivanovna. You cannot marry Yegor Ilyitch; under your very nose he is keeping his governess as his mistress."

My uncle shuddered, turned pale, bit his lip and rushed to assist Tatyana Ivanovna into the carriage. I went round to the other side of the carriage, and was waiting for my turn to get in, when I suddenly found Obnoskin by my side, clutching at my hand.

"Allow me at least to seek your friendship!" he said warmly, squeezing my hand, with an expression of despair on his face.

"What's that, friendship?" I said, lifting my foot to the carriage step.

"Yes! I recognized in you yesterday a man of culture; do not condemn me. . . . My mother led me on, I had nothing to do with it. My inclinations are rather for literature—I assure you; this was all my mother. . . ."

"I believe you, I believe you," I said. "Good-bye!"

We got in and the horses set off at a gallop. The shouts and curses of Anfisa Petrovna resounded for a long way after us, and unknown faces suddenly poked out of all the windows of the house and stared after us with wild curiosity.

There were five of us now in the carriage, but Mizintchikov got on to the box, giving up his former seat to Mr. Bahtcheyev, who had now to sit directly facing Tatyana Ivanovna. The latter was greatly relieved that we had taken her away, but she was still crying. My uncle consoled her as best he could. He was himself sad and brooding; it was evident that Anfisa Petrovna's frantic words about Nastenka were echoing painfully and bitterly in his heart. Our return journey would, however, have ended without any disturbance if only Mr. Bahtcheyev had not been with us.

Sitting opposite Tatyana Ivanovna, he seemed not himself, he could not look indifferent, he shifted in his seat, turned as red as a crab, and rolled his eyes fearfully, particularly when my uncle began trying to console Tatyana Ivanovna. The fat man was absolutely beside himself, and grumbled like a bulldog when it is teased. My uncle looked at him apprehensively. At last Tatyana Ivanovna, noticing the extraordinary state of mind of her *vis-à-vis*, began watching him intently; then she looked at us, smiled, and all at once picking up her parasol, gracefully gave Mr. Bahtcheyev a light tap on the shoulder.

"Crazy fellow!" she said with a most enchanting playfulness, and at once hid her face in her fan.

This sally was the last straw.

"Wha-a-at?" roared the fat man. "What's that, madame? So you are after me now!"

"Crazy fellow! crazy fellow!" repeated Tatyana Ivanovna, and she suddenly burst out laughing and clapped her hands.

"Stop!" cried Bahtcheyev to the coachman, "stop!"

We stopped. Bahtcheyev opened the door, and hurriedly began clambering out of the carriage.

"Why, what is the matter, Stepan Alexyevitch? Where are you off to?" cried my uncle in astonishment.

"No, I have had enough of it," answered the fat man, trembling with indignation. "Deuce take it all! I am too old, madame, to be besieged with amours. I would rather die on the highroad! Good-bye, madame. *Comment vous portez-vous?*"

And he actually began walking on foot. The carriage followed him at a walking pace.

"Stepan Alexyevitch!" cried my uncle, losing all patience at last. "Don't play the fool, come, get in! Why, it's time we were home."

"Bother you!" Stepan Alexyevitch brought out, breathless with walking, for owing to his corpulence he had quite lost the habit of exercise.

"Drive on full speed," Mizintchikov shouted to the coachman.

"What are you doing? Stop!" my uncle cried out as the carriage dashed on.

Mizintchikov was not out in his reckoning, the desired result followed at once.

"Stop! Stop!" we heard a despairing wail behind us. "Stop, you ruffian! Stop, you cut-throat. . . ."

The fat man came into sight at last, half-dead with exhaustion, with drops of sweat on his brow, untying his cravat and taking off his cap. Silently and gloomily he got into the carriage, and this time I gave him my seat; he was not anyway sitting directly opposite Tatyana Ivanovna, who all through this scene had been gushing with laughter and clapping her hands. She could not look gravely at Stepan Alexyevitch all the rest of the journey. He for his part sat without uttering a single word all the way home, staring intently at the hind wheel of the carriage.

It was midday when we got back to Stepantchikovo. I went straight to my lodge, where Gavrila immediately made his appearance with tea. I flew to question the old man, but my uncle walked in almost on his heels and promptly sent him away.

New Developments

II

"I have come to you for a minute, dear boy," he began, "I was in haste to tell you. . . . I have heard all about everything. None of them have even been to mass to-day, except Ilyusha, Sasha and Nastenka. They tell me mamma has been in convulsions. They have been rubbing her, it was all they could do to bring her to by rubbing. Now it has been settled for us all to go together to Foma, and I have been summoned. Only I don't know whether to congratulate Foma on the nameday or not—it's an important point! And in fact how are they going to take this whole episode? It's awful, Seryozha, I foresee it. . . ."

"On the contrary, uncle," I hastened in my return to reply, "everything is settling itself splendidly. You see you can't marry Tatyana Ivanovna now—that's a great deal in itself. I wanted to make that clear to you on our way."

"Oh, yes, my dear boy. But that's not the point; there is the hand of Providence in it no doubt, as you say, but I wasn't thinking of that. . . . Poor Tatyana Ivanovna! What adventures happen to her, though! . . . Obnoskin's a scoundrel, a scoundrel! Though why do I call him 'a scoundrel'? Shouldn't I have been doing the same if I married her? . . . But that, again, is not what I have come about. . . . Did you hear what that wretch Anfisa Petrovna shouted about Nastenka this morning?"

"Yes, uncle. Haven't you realized now that you must make haste?"

"Certainly, at all costs!" answered my uncle. "It is a solemn moment. Only there is one thing, dear boy, which we did not think of, but I was thinking of it afterwards all night. Will she marry me, that's the point?"

"Mercy on us, uncle! After she told you herself that she loves you . . ."

"But, my dear boy, you know she also said at once that nothing would induce her to marry me."

"Oh, uncle, that's only words; besides, circumstances are different to-day."

"Do you think so? No, Sergey, my boy, it's a delicate business, dreadfully delicate! H'm. . . . But do you know, though I was worrying, yet my heart was somehow aching with happiness all night. Well, good-bye, I must fly. They are waiting for me; I am late as it is. I only ran in to have a word with you. Oh, my God!" he cried, coming back, "I have forgotten what is most important! Do you know what? I have written to him, to Foma!"

"When?"

"In the night, and in the morning, at daybreak, I sent the letter by Vidoplyasov. I put it all before him on two sheets of paper, I told him everything truthfully and frankly, in short that I ought, that is, absolutely must— do you understand?—make Nastenka an offer. I besought him not to say a word about our meeting in the garden, and I have appealed to all the generosity of his heart to help me with mamma. I wrote a poor letter, of course, my boy, but I wrote it from my heart, and so to say, watered it with my tears. . . ."

"Well? No answer?"

"So far no; only this morning when we were getting ready to set off, I met him in the hall in night attire, in slippers and nightcap—he sleeps in a nightcap—he had come out of his room. He didn't say a word, he didn't even glance at me. I peeped up into his face, not a sign."

"Uncle, don't rely on him; he'll play you some dirty trick."

"No, no, my boy, don't say so!" cried my uncle, gesticulating. "I am sure of him. Besides, you know, it's my last hope. He will understand, he'll appreciate it. He's peevish, he's capricious, I don't deny it; but when it comes to a question of true nobility, then he shines out like a pearl. . . . Yes, like a pearl. You think all that, Sergey, because you have never seen him yet, when he is most noble . . . but my God! if he really does spread abroad my secret of yesterday, then . . . I don't know what will happen then, Sergey! What will be left me in the world that I can believe in? But no, he cannot be such a scoundrel. I am not worth the sole of his shoe. Don't shake your head, my boy; it's true—I am not."

"Yegor Ilyitch! Your mamma is anxious about you." We heard from below the unpleasant voice of Miss Perepelitsyn, who had probably succeeded in hearing the whole of our conversation from the open window. "They are looking for you all over the house, and cannot find you."

"Oh, dear, I am late! How dreadful," cried my uncle in a fluster. "My dear boy, for goodness' sake dress and come too. Why, it was just for that I ran in, so that we might go together. . . . I fly, I fly! Anna Nilovna, I fly!"

When I was left alone, I recalled my meeting with Nastenka that morning and was very glad I had not told my uncle of it; I should have upset him even more. I foresaw a great storm, and could not imagine how my uncle would arrange his plans and make an offer to Nastenka. I repeat: in spite of my faith in his honour, I could not help feeling doubtful of his success.

However, I had to make haste. I considered myself bound to assist him, and at once began dressing; but as I wanted to be as well dressed as possible, I was not very quick in spite of my haste. Mizintchikov walked in.

"I have come for you," he said. "Yegor Ilyitch begs you to come at once."

"Let us go!"

I was quite ready, we set off.

"What news there?" I asked on the way.

"They are all in Foma's room, the whole party," answered Mizintchikov. "Foma is not in bad humour, but he is somewhat pensive and doesn't say much, just mutters through his teeth. He even kissed Ilyusha, which of course delighted Yegor Ilyitch. He announced beforehand through Miss Perepelitsyn that they were not to congratulate him on the nameday, and that he had only wanted to test them. . . . Though the old lady keeps sniffing her smelling-salts, she is calm because Foma is calm. Of our adventure no one drops a hint, it is as though it had never happened; they hold their tongues because Foma holds his. He hasn't let any one in all the morning, though. While we were away the old lady implored him by all the saints to come that she might consult him, and indeed she hobbled down to the door herself; but he locked himself in and answered that he was praying for the human race, or something of the sort. He has got something up his sleeve, one can see that from his face. But as Yegor Ilyitch is incapable of seeing anything from any one's face, he is highly delighted now with Foma's mildness; he is a regular baby! Ilyusha has prepared some verses, and they have sent me to fetch you."

"And Tatyana Ivanovna?"

"What about Tatyana Ivanovna?"

"Is she there? With them?"

"No; she is in her own room," Mizintchikov answered drily. "She is resting and crying. Perhaps she is ashamed too. I believe that . . . governess is with her now. I say! surely it is not a storm coming on? Look at the sky!"

"I believe it is a storm," I answered, glancing at a storm-cloud that looked black on the horizon.

At that moment we went up to the terrace.

"Tell me, what do you think of Obnoskin, eh?" I went on, not able to refrain from probing Mizintchikov on that point.

"Don't speak to me of him! Don't remind me of that blackguard," he cried, suddenly stopping, flushing red and stamping. "The fool! the fool! to ruin such a splendid plan, such a brilliant idea! Listen: I am an ass, of course, for not having detected what a rogue he is!—I admit that solemnly, and perhaps that admission is just what you want. But I swear if he had known how to carry it through properly, I should perhaps have forgiven him. The fool! the fool! And how can such people be allowed in society, how can they be endured! How is it they are not sent to Siberia, into exile, into prison! But that's all nonsense, they won't get over me! Now I have experience anyway, and we shall see who gets the best of it. I am thinking over a new idea now. . . . You must admit one can't lose one's object simply because some outside fool has stolen one's idea and not known how to set about it. Why, it's unjust! And, in fact, this Tatyana will inevitably be married, that's her predestined fate. And if no one has put her into a madhouse up to now, it was just because it is still possible to marry her. I will tell you my new idea. . . ."

"But afterwards, I suppose," I interrupted him, "for here we are."

"Very well, very well, afterwards," Mizintchikov answered, twisting his lips into a spasmodic smile. "And now . . . But where are you going? I tell you, straight to Foma Fomitch's room! Follow me; you have not been there yet. You will see another farce. . . . For it has really come to a farce."

Ilyusha's Nameday

III

Foma occupied two large and excellent rooms; they were
even better decorated than any other of the rooms in the
house. The great man was surrounded by perfect comfort.
The fresh and handsome wall-paper, the particoloured silk
curtains on the windows, the rugs, the pier-glass, the fire-
place, the softly upholstered elegant furniture—all testified
to the tender solicitude of the family for Foma's comfort.
Pots of flowers stood in the windows and on little marble
tables in front of the windows. In the middle of the study
stood a large table covered with a red cloth and littered
with books and manuscripts. A handsome bronze inkstand
and a bunch of pens which Vidoplyasov had to look after—
all this was to testify to the severe intellectual labours of
Foma Fomitch. I will mention here by the way that though
Foma had sat at that table for nearly eight years, he had
composed absolutely nothing that was any good. Later on,
when he had departed to a better world, we went through
his manuscripts; they all turned out to be extraordinary
trash. We found, for instance, the beginning of an historical novel, the scene of which was laid in Novgorod, in the
seventh century; then a monstrous poem, "An Anchorite
in the Churchyard," written in blank verse; then a meaning-
less meditation on the significance and characteristics of
the Russian peasant, and how he should be treated; and
finally "The Countess Vlonsky," a novel of aristocratic life,
also unfinished. There was nothing else. And yet Foma
Fomitch had made my uncle spend large sums every year
on books and journals. But many of them were actually
found uncut. Later on, I caught Foma Fomitch more than
once reading Paul de Kock, but he always slipped the book
out of sight when people came in. In the further wall of

the study there was a glass door which led to the courtyard of the house.

They were waiting for us. Foma Fomitch was sitting in a comfortable arm-chair, wearing some sort of long coat that reached to his heels, but yet he wore no cravat. He certainly was silent and thoughtful. When we went in he raised his eyebrows slightly and bent a searching glance on me. I bowed; he responded with a slight bow, a fairly polite one, however. Grandmother, seeing that Foma Fomitch was behaving graciously to me, gave me a nod and a smile. The poor woman had not expected in the morning that her paragon would take the news of Tatyana Ivanovna's "escapade" so calmly, and so she was now in the best of spirits, though she really had been in convulsions and fainting fits earlier in the day. Behind her chair, as usual, stood Miss Perepelitsyn, compressing her lips till they looked like a thread, smiling sourly and spitefully and rubbing her bony hands one against the other. Two always mute lady companions were installed beside Madame la Générale. There was also a nun of sorts who had strayed in that morning, and an elderly lady, a neighbour who had come in after mass to congratulate Madame la Générale on the nameday and who also sat mute. Aunt Praskovya Ilyinitchna was keeping in the background somewhere in a corner, and was looking with anxiety at Foma Fomitch and her mother. My uncle was sitting in an easy-chair, and his face was beaming with a look of exceptional joy. Facing him stood Ilyusha in his red holiday shirt, with his hair in curls, looking like a little angel. Sasha and Nastenka had in secret from every one taught him some verses to rejoice his father on this auspicious day by his progress in learning. My uncle was almost weeping with delight. Foma's unexpected mildness, Madame la Générale's good humour, Ilyusha's nameday, the verses, all moved him to real enthusiasm, and with a solemnity worthy of the occasion he had asked them to send for me that I might hasten to share the general happiness and listen to the verses. Sasha and Nastenka, who had come in just after us, were standing near Ilyusha. Sasha was continually laugh-

ing, and at that moment was as happy as a little child.
Nastenka, looking at her, also began smiling, though she
had come into the room a moment before pale and depressed. She alone had welcomed Tatyana Ivanovna on
her return from her excursion, and until then had been
sitting upstairs with her. The rogue Ilyusha seemed, too,
as though he could not keep from laughing as he looked
at his instructresses. It seemed as though the three of them
had prepared a very amusing joke which they meant to play
now. . . . I had forgotten Bahtcheyev. He was sitting on a
chair at a little distance, still cross and red in the face;
holding his tongue, sulking, blowing his nose and altogether
playing a very gloomy part at the family festivity. Near
him Yezhevikin was fidgeting about; he was fidgeting about
everywhere, however, kissing the hands of Madame la Générale and of the visitors, whispering something to Miss
Perepelitsyn, showing attention to Foma Fomitch, in fact
he was all over the place. He, too, was awaiting Ilyusha's
verses with great interest, and at my entrance flew to greet
me with bows as a mark of the deepest respect and devotion. Altogether there was nothing to show that he had
come to protect his daughter, and to take her from Stepantchikovo for ever.

"Here he is!" cried my uncle gleefully on seeing me. "Ilyusha has got a poem for us, that's something unexpected,
a real surprise! I am overpowered, my boy, and sent for
you on purpose, and have put off the verses till you came.
. . . Sit down beside me! Let us listen. Foma Fomitch, confess now, it must have been you who put them all up to it
to please an old fellow like me. I'll wager that is how it is!"

Since my uncle was talking in such a tone and voice in
Foma's room one would have thought that all must be
well. But unluckily my uncle was, as Mizintchikov expressed it, incapable of reading any man's face. Glancing
at Foma's face, I could not help admitting that Mizintchikov
was right and that something was certainly going to happen. . . .

"Don't trouble about me, Colonel," Foma answered in

a faint voice, the voice of a man forgiving his enemies. "I approve of the surprise, of course; it shows the sensibility and good principles of your children. . . . Poetry is of use, too, even for the pronunciation. . . . But I have not been busy over verses this morning, Yegor Ilyitch; I have been praying . . . you know that. . . . I am ready to listen to the verses, however."

Meanwhile I had congratulated Ilyusha and kissed him.

"Quite so, Foma, I beg your pardon. I had forgotten . . . though I am sure of your affection, Foma! Kiss him once more, Seryozha! Look what a fine big boy! Come, begin, Ilyusha! What is it about? I suppose it is something solemn from Lomonosov?"

And my uncle drew himself up with a dignified air. He could scarcely sit still in his seat for impatience and delight.

"No, papa, not from Lomonosov," said Sashenka, hardly able to suppress her laughter; "but as you have been a soldier and fought the enemy, Ilyusha has learnt a poem about warfare. . . . The siege of Pamba, papa!"

"The siege of Pampa! I don't remember it. . . . What is this Pamba, do you know, Ilyusha? Something heroic, I suppose."

And my uncle drew himself up again.

"Begin, Ilyusha!" Sasha gave the word of command.

Ilyusha began in a little, clear, even voice, without stops or commas, as small children generally recite verses they have learned by heart—

> "Nine long years Don Pedro Gomez
> Has besieged the fort of Pamba,
> On a diet of milk supported.
> And Don Pedro's gallant warriors,
> Brave Castilians, full nine thousand,
> All to keep the vow they've taken
> Taste no bread nor other victuals,
> Milk they drink and milk alone."

"What? What's that about milk?" cried my uncle, looking at me in perplexity.

"Go on reciting, Ilyusha!" cried Sashenka.

> "Every day Don Pedro Gomez,
> In his Spanish cloak enveloped,
> Bitterly his lot bewails.
> Lo, the tenth year is approaching;
> Still the fierce Moors are triumphant;
> And of all Don Pedro's army
> Only nineteen men are left. . . ."

"Why, it's a regular string of nonsense!" cried my uncle uneasily. "Come, that's impossible. Only nineteen men left out of a whole army, when there was a very considerable corps before? What is the meaning of it, my boy?"

But at that point Sasha could not contain herself, and went off into the most open and childish laughter; and though there was nothing very funny, it was impossible not to laugh too as one looked at her.

"They are funny verses, papa," she cried, highly delighted with her childish prank. "The author made them like that on purpose to amuse everybody."

"Oh! Funny!" cried my uncle, with a beaming face. "Comic, you mean! That's just what I thought. . . . Just so, just so, funny! And very amusing, extremely amusing: he starved all his army on milk owing to some vow. What possessed them to take such a vow? Very witty, isn't it, Foma? You see, mamma, these are jesting verses, such as authors sometimes do write, don't they, Sergey? Extremely amusing. Well, well, Ilyusha, what next?"

> "Only nineteen men are left!
> Them Don Pedro doth assemble
> And says to them: 'Noble Nineteen!
> Let us raise aloft our standards!
> Let us blow on our loud trumpets!
> And with clashing of our cymbals
> Let us from Pamba retreat!

Though the fort we have not taken,
Yet with honour still untarnished
We can swear on faith and conscience
That our vow we have not broken;
Nine long years we have not eaten,
Not a morsel have we eaten,
Milk we've drunk and milk alone!' "

"What a noodle! What comfort was it for him that he
had drunk milk for nine years?" my uncle broke in again.
"What is there virtuous in it? He would have done better
to have eaten a whole sheep, and not have been the death
of people! Excellent! capital! I see, I see now: it is a satire
on . . . what do they call it? an allegory, isn't it? And
perhaps aimed at some foreign general," my uncle added,
addressing me, knitting his brows significantly, and screwing up his eyes, "eh? What do you think? But of course a
harmless, good, refined satire that injures nobody! Excellent! excellent! and what matters most, it is refined. Well,
Ilyusha, go on. Ah, you rogues, you rogues!" he added
with feeling, looking at Sasha and stealthily also at Nastenka, who blushed and smiled.

"And emboldened by that saying,
Those nineteen Castilian warriors,
Each one swaying in his saddle,
Feebly shouted all together:
'Sant' Iago Compostello!
Fame and glory to Don Pedro!
Glory to the Lion of Castile!'
And his chaplain, one Diego,
Through his teeth was heard to mutter:
'But if I had been commander,
I'd have vowed to eat meat only,
Drinking good red wine alone.' "

"There! Didn't I tell you so?" cried my uncle, extremely
delighted. "Only one sensible man was found in the whole
army, and he was some sort of a chaplain. And what is that,

Sergey: a captain among them, or what?"

"A monk, an ecclesiastical person, uncle."

"Oh, yes, yes. Chaplain? I know, I remember. I have read of it in Radcliffe's novels. They have all sorts of orders, don't they. . . . Benedictines, I believe? . . . There are Benedictines, aren't there?"

"Yes, uncle."

"H'm! . . . I thought so. Well, Ilyusha, what next? Excellent! capital!"

> "And Don Pedro overhearing,
> With loud laughter gave the order:
> 'Fetch a sheep and give it to him!
> He has jested gallantly!'"

"What a time to laugh! What a fool! Even he saw it was funny at last! A sheep! So they had sheep; why did he not eat some himself! Well, Ilyusha, go on. Excellent! capital! Extraordinarily cutting!"

"But that's the end, papa!"

"Oh, the end. Indeed there wasn't much left to be done—was there, Sergey? Capital, Ilyusha! Wonderfully nice. Kiss me, darling. Ah, my precious! Who was it thought of it: you, Sasha?"

"No, it was Nastenka. We read it the other day. She read it and said: 'What ridiculous verses! It will soon be Ilyusha's nameday, let us make him learn them and recite them. It will make them laugh!'"

"Oh, it was Nastenka? Well, thank you, thank you," my uncle muttered, suddenly flushing like a child. "Kiss me again, Ilyusha. You kiss me too, you rogue," he said, embracing Sashenka and looking into her face with feeling. "You wait a bit, Sashenka, it will be your nameday soon," he added, as though he did not know what to say to express his pleasure.

I turned to Nastenka and asked whose verses they were.

"Yes, yes, whose are the verses?" my uncle hurriedly chimed in. "It must have been a clever poet who wrote them, mustn't it, Foma?"

"H'm . . ." Foma grunted to himself.

A biting sarcastic smile had not left his face during the whole time of the recitation of the verses.

"I have really forgotten," said Nastenka, looking timidly at Foma Fomitch.

"It's Mr. Kuzma Prutkov wrote it, papa; it was published in the *Contemporary*," Sashenka broke in.

"Kuzma Prutkov! I don't know his name," said my uncle. "Pushkin I know! . . . But one can see he is a gifted poet—isn't he, Sergey? And what's more, a man of refined qualities, that's as clear as twice two! Perhaps, indeed, he is an officer. . . . I approve of him. And the *Contemporary* is a first-rate magazine. We certainly must take it in if poets like that are among the contributors. . . . I like poets! They are fine fellows! They picture everything in verse. Do you know, Sergey, I met a literary man at your rooms in Petersburg. He had rather a peculiar nose, too . . . really! . . . What did you say, Foma?"

Foma Fomitch, who was getting more and more worked up, gave a loud snigger.

"No, I said nothing . . ." he said, as though hardly able to suppress his laughter. "Go on, Yegor Ilyitch, go on! I will say my word later. . . . Stepan Alexyevitch is delighted to hear how you made the acquaintance of literary men in Petersburg."

Stepan Alexyevitch, who had been sitting apart all the time lost in thought, suddenly raised his head, reddened, and turned in his chair with exasperation.

"Don't you provoke me, Foma, but leave me in peace," he said, looking wrathfully at Foma with his little bloodshot eyes. "What is your literature to me? May God only give me good health," he muttered to himself, "and plague take them all . . . and their authors too. . . . Voltairians, that's what they are!"

"Authors are Voltairians?" said Yezhevikin immediately at his side. "Perfectly true what you have been pleased to remark, Stepan Alexyevitch. Valentin Ignatyitch was pleased to express the same sentiments the other day. He actually called me a Voltairian, upon my soul he did! And

yet, as you all know, I have written very little so far. . . .
If a bowl of milk goes sour—it's all Voltaire's fault! That's
how it is with everything here."

"Well, no," observed my uncle with dignity, "that's an
error, you know! Voltaire was nothing but a witty writer;
he laughed at superstitions; and he never was a Voltairian! It was his enemies spread that rumour about him. Why
were they all against him, really, poor fellow? . . ."

Again the malignant snigger of Foma Fomitch was audi-
ble. My uncle looked at him uneasily and was perceptibly
embarrassed.

"Yes, Foma, I am thinking about the magazine, you see,"
he said in confusion, trying to put himself right somehow.
"You were perfectly right, my dear Foma, when you said
the other day that we ought to subscribe to one. I think we
ought to, myself. H'm . . . after all, they do assist in the
diffusion of enlightenment; one would be a very poor
patriot if one did not support them. Wouldn't one, Sergey?
H'm. . . . Yes. . . . The *Contemporary*, for instance. But,
do you know, Seryozha, the most instruction, to my thinking, is to be found in that thick magazine—what's it's
name?—in a yellow cover . . ."

"Notes of the Fatherland, papa."

"Oh, yes, *Notes of the Fatherland*, and a capital title,
Sergey, isn't it? It is, so to say, the whole Fatherland sitting writing notes. . . . A very fine object. A most edifying
magazine. And what a thick one! What a job to publish
such an omnibus! And the information in it almost makes
one's eyes start out of one's head. I came in the other day,
the volume was lying here, I took it up and from curiosity
opened it and reeled off three pages at a go. It made me
simply gape, my dear! And, you know, there is information
about everything; what is meant, for instance, by a broom,
a spade, a ladle, an ovenrake. To my thinking, a broom
is a broom and an ovenrake an ovenrake! No, my boy, wait
a bit. According to the learned, an ovenrake turns out not
an ovenrake, but an emblem or something mythological; I
don't remember exactly, but something of the sort. . . . So
that's how it is! They have gone into everything!"

I don't know what precisely Foma was preparing to do after this fresh outburst from my uncle, but at that moment Gavrila appeared and stood with bowed head in the doorway.

Foma Fomitch glanced at him significantly.

"Ready, Gavrila?" he asked in a faint but resolute voice.

"Yes, sir," Gavrila answered mournfully, and heaved a sigh.

"And have you put my bundle on the cart?"

"Yes, sir."

"Well, then, I am ready too!" said Foma, and he deliberately got up from his easy-chair. My uncle looked at him in amazement. Madame la Générale jumped up from her seat and looked about her uneasily.

"Allow me, Colonel," Foma began with dignity, "to ask you to leave for a moment the interesting subject of literary overrakes; you can continue it after I am gone. As I am *taking leave of you for ever,* I should like to say a few last words to you. . . ."

Every listener was spellbound with alarm and amazement.

"Foma! Foma! but what is the matter with you? Where are you going?" my uncle cried at last.

"I am about to leave your house, Colonel," Foma brought out in a perfectly composed voice. "I have made up my mind to go where fortune takes me, and so I have hired at my own expense a humble peasant's cart. My bundle is lying in it already, it is of no great dimensions: a few favourite books, two changes of linen—that is all! I am a poor man, Yegor Ilyitch, but nothing in the world would induce me now to take your gold, which I refused even yesterday!"

"But for God's sake, Foma, what is the meaning of it?" cried my uncle, turning as white as a sheet.

Madame la Générale uttered a shriek and looked in despair at Foma Fomitch, stretching out her hands to him. Miss Perepelitsyn flew to support her. The lady companions sat petrified in their chairs. Mr. Bahtcheyev got up heavily from his seat.

"Well, here's a pretty to-do!" Mizintchikov whispered beside me.

At that moment a distant rumble of thunder was heard; a storm was coming on.

The Expulsion

IV

"You ask me, I believe, Colonel, what is the meaning of this?" Foma brought out with solemn dignity, as though enjoying the general consternation. "I am surprised at the question! Will you on your side explain how it is *you* can bring yourself to look me in the face now? Explain to me this last psychological problem in human shamelessness, and then I shall depart, the richer for new knowledge of the depravity of the human race."

But my uncle was not equal to answering him. With open mouth and staring eyes he gazed at Foma, alarmed and annihilated.

"Merciful heavens! What passions!" hissed Miss Perepelitsyn.

"Do you understand, Colonel," Foma went on, "that you had better let me go now, simply without asking questions? In your house even I, a man of years and understanding, begin to feel the purity of my morals gravely endangered. Believe me, that your questions can lead to nothing but putting you to shame."

"Foma! Foma!" cried my uncle, and a cold perspiration came out on his forehead.

"And so allow me without further explanation to say a few farewell words at parting, my last words in your house, Yegor Ilyitch. The thing is done and there is no undoing it! I hope that you understand to what I am referring. But I implore you on my knees: if one spark of moral feeling is left in your heart, curb your unbridled passions! And if the noxious poison has not yet caught the whole edifice, then, as far as possible, extinguish the fire!"

"Foma, I assure you that you are in error!" cried my uncle, recovering himself little by little and foreseeing with horror the climax.

"Moderate your passions," Foma continued in the same solemn voice, as though he had not heard my uncle's exclamation, "conquer yourself. 'If thou would'st conquer all the world—conquer thyself.' That is my invariable rule. You are a landowner; you ought to shine like a diamond in your estate, and what a vile example of unbridled passion you set your inferiors! I have been praying for you the whole night, and trembled as I sought for your happiness. I did not find it, for happiness lies in virtue. . . ."

"But this is impossible, Foma!" my uncle interrupted him again. "You have misunderstood and what you say is quite wrong."

"And so remember you are a landowner," Foma went on, still regardless of my uncle's exclamations. "Do not imagine that repose and sensuality are the destined vocation of the landowning class. Fatal thought! Not repose, but zealous work, zealous towards God, towards your sovereign, and towards your country! Hard work, hard work is the duty of the landowner, he should work as hard as the poorest of his peasants!"

"What, am I to plough for the peasant, or what?" growled Bahtcheyev. "Why, I am a landowner, too. . . ."

"I turn to you now, servants of the house," Foma went on, addressing Gavrila and Falaley, who had appeared in the doorway. "Love your master and his family, and obey them humbly and meekly, and they will reward you with their love. And you, Colonel, be just and compassionate to them. A fellow-man—the image of God—like a child of tender years, so to say, is entrusted to you by your sovereign and your country. Great is the duty, but great also is the merit."

"Foma Fomitch, my dear man, what notion is this?" cried Madame la Générale in despair, almost swooning with horror.

"Well, that is enough, I think," Foma concluded, paying no attention even to Madame la Générale. "Now to lesser things; they may be small, but they are essential, Yegor Ilyitch. Your hay on the Harinsky waste has not been cut yet. Do not be too late with it: mow it and mow it quickly. That is my advice. . . ."

"But, Foma . . ."

"You meant to cut down the Zyryanovsky copse, I know; don't cut it—that's a second piece of advice. Preserve forest land, for trees retain humidity on the surface of the earth. It is a pity that you have sown the spring corn so late; it's amazing how late you have been in sowing the spring corn! . . ."

"But, Foma . . ."

"But enough! One cannot convey everything, and indeed there is not time. I will send you written instructions in a special book. Well, good-bye, good-bye all, God be with you, and the Lord bless you. I bless you too, my child," he went on, turning to Ilyusha; "and may God keep you from the noxious poison of your passions. I bless you too, Falaley; forget the Komarinsky! . . . And all of you. . . . Remember Foma. . . . Well, let us go, Gavrila! Come and help me in, old man."

And Foma turned towards the door. Madame la Générale gave a piercing shriek and flew after him.

"No, Foma, I will not let you go like this," cried my uncle, and overtaking him, he seized him by the hand.

"So you mean to have resort to force?" Foma asked haughtily.

"Yes, Foma . . . even to force," answered my uncle, quivering with emotion. "You have said too much, and must explain your words! You have misunderstood my letter, Foma! . . ."

"Your letter!" squealed Foma, instantly flaring up as though he had been awaiting that minute for an explosion; "your letter! Here it is, your letter! Here it is. I tear this letter, I spit upon it! I trample your letter under my foot, and in doing so fulfil the most sacred duty of humanity. That is what I will do if you compel me by force to an explanation! Look! Look! Look! . . ."

And scraps of paper flew about the room.

"I repeat, Foma, you have misunderstood it," cried my uncle, turning paler and paler. "I am making an offer of marriage, Foma, I am seeking my happiness."

"Marriage! You have seduced this young girl, and are trying to deceive me by offering her marriage, for I saw you with her last night in the garden, under the bushes."

Madame la Générale uttered a scream and fell fainting into an armchair. A fearful hubbub arose. Poor Nastenka sat deathly pale. Sasha, frightened, clutched Ilyusha and trembled as though she were in a fever.

"Foma!" cried my uncle in a frenzy, "if you divulge that secret you are guilty of the meanest action on earth!"

"I do divulge that secret," squealed Foma, "and I am performing the most honourable action! I am sent by God Himself to unmask your villainies to all the world. I am ready to clamber on some peasant's thatched roof and from there to proclaim your vile conduct to all the gentlemen of the neighbourhood and all the passers-by. . . . Yes, let me tell you all, all of you, that yesterday in the night I found him in the garden, under the bushes with this young girl whose appearance is so innocent. . . ."

"Oh, what a disgrace!" piped Miss Perepelitsyn.

"Foma! Don't be your own destruction!" cried my uncle, with clenched fists and flashing eyes.

"He," squealed Foma, "he, alarmed at my having seen him, had the audacity to try with a lying letter to persuade me into conniving at his crime—yes, crime! . . . for you have turned a hitherto innocent young girl into a . . ."

"Another word insulting to her and I will kill you, Foma, I swear! . . ."

"I say that word, since you have succeeded in turning the most innocent young girl into a most depraved girl."

Foma had hardly uttered this last word when my uncle seized him by the shoulder, turned him round like a straw, and flung him violently at the glass door, which led from the study into the courtyard. The shock was so violent that the closed door burst open, and Foma, flying head over heels down the stone steps, fell full length in the yard. Bits of broken glass were scattered tinkling about the steps.

"Gavrila, pick him up!" cried my uncle, as pale as a corpse. "Put him in the cart, and within two minutes let there be no trace of him in Stepantchikovo!"

Whatever Foma's design may have been, he certainly had not expected such a climax.

I will not undertake to describe what happened for the first minutes after this episode. The heart-rending wail of Madame la Générale as she rolled from side to side in an arm-chair; the stupefaction of Miss Perepelitsyn at this unexpected behaviour of my hitherto submissive uncle; the sighs and groans of the lady companions; Nastenka almost fainting with fright while her father hovered over her; Sashenka terror-stricken; my uncle in indescribable excitement pacing up and down the room waiting for his mother to come to herself; and lastly, the loud weeping of Falaley in lamentation over the troubles of his betters—all this made up an indescribable picture. I must add, too, that at this moment a violent storm broke over us; peals of thunder were more and more frequent, and big drops of rain began pattering on the window.

"Here's a nice holiday!" muttered Mr. Bahtcheyev, bowing his head and flinging wide his arms.

"It's a bad business," I whispered to him, beside myself with excitement too. "But anyway they have turned Foma out, and he won't come back again."

"Mamma! Are you conscious? Are you better? Can you listen to me at last?" asked my uncle, stopping before the old lady's arm-chair.

She raised her head, clasped her hands, and looked with imploring eyes at her son, whom she had never in her life before seen moved to such wrath.

"Mamma," he went on, "it was the last straw, you have seen for yourself. It was not like this that I meant to approach this subject, but the hour has come, and it is useless to put it off. You have heard the calumny, hear my defence. Mamma, I love this noble and high-minded girl, I have loved her a long while, and I shall never cease to love her. She will make the happiness of my children, and will be a dutiful daughter to you. And so now, before you, and in the presence of my friends and my family, I solemnly plead at her feet, and beseech her to do me infinite honour by consenting to be my wife."

Nastenka started, then flushed crimson all over and got up from her seat. Madame la Générale stared some time at her son as though she did not understand what he was saying to her, and all at once with a piercing wail flung herself on her knees.

"Yegorushka, my darling, bring Foma Fomitch back," she cried. "Bring him back at once, or without him I shall die before night."

My uncle was petrified at the sight of his self-willed and capricious old mother kneeling before him. His painful distress was reflected in his face. At last, recovering himself, he flew to raise her up and put her back in her chair.

"Bring Foma Fomitch back, Yegorushka," the old lady went on wailing. "Bring him back, darling! I cannot live without him!"

"Mamma," my uncle cried sorrowfully, "have you heard nothing of what I have just said to you? I cannot bring Foma back—understand that. I cannot and I have not the right to after his low and scoundrelly slander on this angel of honour and virtue. Do you understand, mamma, that it is my duty, that my honour compels me now to defend virtue? You have heard: I am asking this young lady to be my wife, and I beg you to bless our union."

Madame la Générale got up from her seat again and fell on her knees before Nastenka.

"My dear girl!" she wailed, "do not marry him. Do not marry him, but entreat him, my dear, to fetch back Foma Fomitch. Nastasya Yevgrafovna, darling! I will give up everything, I will sacrifice everything if only you will not marry him. Old as I am, I have not spent everything, I had a little left me when my poor husband died. It's all yours, my dear, I will give you everything, and Yegorushka will give you something too, but do not lay me living in my grave, beg him to bring back Foma Fomitch."

And the old woman would have gone on wailing and
drivelling if Miss Perepelitsyn and all the lady companions
had not, with shrieks and moans, rushed to lift her up,
indignant that she should be on her knees before a hired
governess. Nastenka was so frightened that she could hardly
stand, while Miss Perepelitsyn positively shed tears of fury.

"You will be the death of your mamma," she screamed
at my uncle. "You will be the death of her. And you, Nastasya Yevgrafovna, ought not to make dissension between
mother and son; the Lord has forbidden it. . . ."

"Anna Nilovna, hold your tongue!" cried my uncle. "I
have put up with enough!"

"Yes, and I have had enough to put up with from you
too. Why do you reproach me with my friendless position? It is easy to insult the friendless. I am not your slave
yet. I am the daughter of a major myself. You won't see
me long in your house, this very day . . . I shall be
gone. . . ."

But my uncle did not hear; he went up to Nastenka and
with reverence took her by the hand.

"Nastasya Yevgrafovna! You have heard my offer?" he
said, looking at her with anguish, almost with despair.

"No, Yegor Ilyitch, no! We had better give it up," said
Nastenka, utterly dejected too. "It is all nonsense," she
said, pressing his hand and bursting into tears. "You only
say this because of yesterday . . . but it cannot be. You
see that yourself. We have made a mistake, Yegor Ilyitch.
. . . But I shall always think of you as my benefactor and
. . . I shall pray for you, always, always! . . ."

At this point tears choked her. My poor uncle had evidently foreseen this answer; he did not even think of protesting, of insisting. He listened, bending down to her, still
holding her hand, crushed and speechless. There were tears
in his eyes.

"I told you yesterday," Nastya went on, "that I could
not be your wife. You see that I am not wanted here . . .
and I foresaw all this long ago; your mamma will not give
you her blessing . . . *others* too. Though you would not

regret it afterwards, because you are the most generous of men, yet you would be made miserable through me . . . with your soft-heartedness . . ."

"Just because of your *soft-heartedness!* Just because you are so *soft-hearted!* That's it, Nastenka, that's it!" chimed in her old father, who was standing on the other side of her chair "That's just it, that's just the right word."

"I don't want to bring dissension into your house on my account," Nastenka went on. "And don't be uneasy about me, Yegor Ilyitch; no one will interfere with me, no one will insult me . . . I am going to my father's . . . this very day. . . . We had better say good-bye, Yegor Ilyitch. . . ."

And poor Nastenka dissolved into tears again.

"Nastasya Yevgrafovna! Surely this is not your final answer?" said my uncle, looking at her in unutterable despair. "Say only one word and I will sacrifice everything for you! . . ."

"It is final, it is final, Yegor Ilyitch . . ." Yezhevikin put in again, "and she has explained it all very well to you, as I must own I did not expect her to. You are a very soft-hearted man, Yegor Ilyitch, yes, very soft-hearted, and you have graciously done us a great honour! A great honour, a great honour! . . . But all the same we are not a match for you, Yegor Ilyitch. You ought to have a bride, Yegor Ilyitch, who would be wealthy and of high rank, and a great beauty and with a voice too, who would walk about your rooms all in diamonds and ostrich feathers. . . . Then perhaps Foma Fomitch would make a little concession and give his blessing! And you will bring Foma Fomitch back! It was no use, no use your insulting him. It was from virtue, you know, from excess of fervour that he said too much, you know. You will say yourself that it was through his virtue—you will see! A most worthy man. And here he is getting wet through now. It would be better to fetch him back now. . . . For you will have to fetch him back, you know. . . ."

"Fetch him back, fetch him back!" shrieked Madame la Générale. "What he says is right, my dear! . . ."

"Yes," Yezhevikin went on. "Here your illustrious parent has upset herself about nothing. . . . Fetch him back! And Nastya and I meanwhile will be on the march. . . ."

"Wait a minute, Yevgraf Larionitch!" cried my uncle, "I entreat you. There is one thing more must be said, Yevgraf, one thing only. . . ."

Saying this, he walked away, sat down in an arm-chair in the corner, bowed his head, and put his hands over his eyes as though he were thinking over something.

At that moment a violent clap of thunder sounded almost directly over the house. The whole building shook. Madame la Générale gave a scream, Miss Perepelitsyn did the same, the lady companions, and with them Mr. Bahtcheyev, all stupefied with terror, crossed themselves.

"Holy saint, Elijah the prophet!" five or six voices murmured at once.

The thunder was followed by such a downpour that it seemed as though a whole lake were suddenly being emptied upon Stepantchikovo.

"And Foma Fomitch, what will become of him now out in the fields?" piped Miss Perepelitsyn.

"Yegorushka, fetch him back!" Madame la Générale cried in a voice of despair, and she rushed to the door as though crazy. Her attendant ladies held her back; they surrounded her, comforted her, whimpered, squealed. It was a perfect Bedlam!

"He went off with nothing over his coat. If he had only taken an overcoat with him!" Miss Perepelitsyn went on. "He did not take an umbrella either. He will be struck by lightning! . . ."

"He will certainly be struck!" Bahtcheyev chimed in. "And he will be soaked with rain afterwards, too."

"You might hold your tongue!" I whispered to him.

"Why, he is a man, I suppose, or isn't he?" Bahtcheyev answered wrathfully. "He is not a dog. I bet you wouldn't go out of doors yourself. Come, go and have a bath for your *plaisir.*"

Foreseeing how it might end and dreading the possibility, I went up to my uncle, who sat as though chained to his chair.

"Uncle," I said, bending down to his ear, "surely you won't consent to bring Foma Fomitch back? Do understand that that would be the height of unseemliness, at any rate as long as Nastasya Yevgrafovna is here."

"My dear," answered my uncle, raising his head and looking at me resolutely, "I have been judging myself at this moment and I know what I ought to do. Don't be uneasy, there shall be no offence to Nastenka, I will see to that. . . ."

He got up from his seat and went to his mother.

"Mamma," he said, "don't worry yourself, I will bring Foma Fomitch back, I will overtake him; he cannot have gone far yet. But I swear he shall come back only on one condition, that here publicly in the presence of all who were witnesses of the insult he should acknowledge how wrong he has been, and solemnly beg the forgiveness of this noble young lady. I will secure that, I will make him do it! He shall not cross the threshold of this house without it! I swear, too, mamma, solemnly, that if he consents to this of his own free will, I shall be ready to fall at his feet, and will give him anything, anything I can, without injustice to my children. I myself will renounce everything from this very day. The star of my happiness has set. I shall leave Stepantchikovo. You must all live here calmly and happily. I am going back to my regiment, and in the turmoil of war, on the field of battle, I will end my despairing days. . . . Enough! I am going!"

At that moment the door opened, and Gavrila, soaked through and incredibly muddy, stood facing the agitated company.

"What's the matter? Where have you come from? Where is Foma?" cried my uncle, rushing up to Gavrila.

Every one followed him, and with eager curiosity crowded round the old man, from whom dirty water was literally trickling in streams. Shrieks, sighs, exclamations accompanied every word Gavrila uttered.

"I left him at the birch copse, a mile away," he began in a tearful voice. "The horse took fright at the lightning and bolted into the ditch."

"Well? . . ." cried my uncle.

"The cart was upset. . . ."

"Well? . . . and Foma?"

"He fell into the ditch."

"And then? Tell us, you tantalizing old man!"

"He bruised his side and began crying. I unharnessed the horse, got on him and rode here to tell you."

"And Foma remained there?"

"He got up and went on with his stick," Gavrila concluded; then he heaved a sigh and bowed his head.

The tears and sobs of the tender sex were indescribable.

"Polkan!" cried my uncle, and he flew out of the room. Polkan was brought, my uncle leapt on him barebacked, and a minute later the thud of the horse's hoofs told us that the pursuit of Foma Fomitch had begun. My uncle had actually galloped off without his cap.

The ladies ran to the windows. Among the sighs and groans were heard words of advice. There was talk of a hot bath, of Foma Fomitch being rubbed with spirits, of some soothing drink, of the fact that Foma Fomitch "had not had a crumb of bread between his lips all day and that he is wet through on an emptly stomach." Miss Perepelitsyn found his forgotten spectacles in their case, and the find produced an extraordinary effect: Madame la Générale pounced on them with tears and lamentations, and still keeping them in her hand, pressed up to the window again to watch the road. The suspense reached the utmost pitch of intensity at last. In another corner Sashenka was trying to comfort Nastya; they were weeping in each other's arms. Nastenka was holding Ilyusha's hand and kissing him from time to time. Ilyusha was in floods of tears, though he did not yet know why. Yezhevikin and Mizintchikov were talking of something aside. I fancied that Bahtcheyev was looking at the girls as though he were ready to blubber himself. I went up to him.

"No, my good sir," he said to me, "Foma Fomitch may leave here one day perhaps, but the time for that has not yet come; they haven't got gold-horned bulls for his chariot yet. Don't worry yourself, sir, he'll drive the owners out of the house and stay there himself!"

The storm was over, and Mr. Bahtcheyev had evidently changed his views.

All at once there was an outcry: "They are bringing him, they are bringing him," and the ladies ran shrieking to the door. Hardly ten minutes had passed since my uncle set off; one would have thought it would have been impossible to bring Foma Fomitch back so quickly; but the enigma was very simply explained later on. When Foma Fomitch had let Gavrila go he really had "set off walking with his stick," but finding himself in complete solitude in the midst of the storm, the thunder, and the pouring rain, he was ignominiously panic-stricken, turned back towards Stepantchikovo and ran after Gavrila. He was already in the village when my uncle came upon him. A passing cart was stopped at once; some peasants ran up and put the unresisting Foma Fomitch into it. So they conveyed him straight to the open arms of Madame la Générale, who was almost beside herself with horror when she saw the condition he was in. He was even muddier and wetter than Gavrila. There was a terrific flurry and bustle, they wanted at once to drag him upstairs to change his linen; there was an outcry for elder-flower tea and other invigorating beverages, they scurried in all directions without doing anything sensible; they all talked at once. . . . But Foma seemed to notice nobody and nothing. He was led in, supported under the arms. On reaching his easy-chair, he sank heavily into it and closed his eyes. Some one cried out that he was dying; a terrible howl was raised, and Falaley was the loudest of all, trying to squeeze through the crowd of ladies up to Foma Fomitch to kiss his hand at once. . . .

Foma Fomitch
Makes Every One Happy

V

"Where have they brought me?" Foma articulated at last, in the voice of a man dying in a righteous cause.

"Damnable humbug!" Mizintchikov whispered beside me. "As though he didn't see where he had been brought! Now he will give us a fine exhibition!"

"You are among us, Foma, you are in your own circle!" cried my uncle. "Don't give way, calm yourself! And really, Foma, you had better change your things, or you will be ill. . . . And won't you take something to restore you, eh? Just something . . . a little glass of something to warm you. . . ."

"I could drink a little Malaga," Foma moaned, closing his eyes again.

"Malaga? I am not sure there is any," my uncle said, anxiously looking towards Praskovya Ilyinitchna.

"To be sure there is!" the latter answered. "There are four whole bottles left." And jingling her keys she ran to fetch the Malaga, followed by exclamations of the ladies, who were clinging to Foma like flies round jam. On the other hand, Mr. Bahtcheyev was indignant in the extreme.

"He wants Malaga!" he grumbled almost aloud. "And who asks for a wine that no one drinks. Who drinks Malaga nowadays but rascals like him? Tfoo, you confounded fellow! What am I standing here for? What am I waiting for?"

"Foma," my uncle began, stumbling over every word, "you see now . . . when you are rested and are with us again . . . that is, I meant to say, Foma, that I understand how accusing, so to say, the most innocent of beings . . ."

"Where is it, my innocence, where?" Foma interrupted, as though he were feverish and in delirium. "Where are my

golden days? Where art thou, my golden childhood, when
innocent and lovely I ran about the fields chasing the spring
butterflies? Where are those days? Give me back my innocence, give it me back! . . ."

And Foma, flinging wide his arms, turned to each one
of us in succession as though his innocence were in somebody's pocket. Bahtcheyev was ready to explode with wrath.

"Ech, so that's what he wants!" he muttered in a fury.
"Give him his innocence! Does he want to kiss it, or what?
Most likely he was as great a villain when he was a boy as
he is now! I'll take my oath he was."

"Foma!" . . . my uncle was beginning again.

"Where, where are they, those days when I still had faith
in love and loved mankind?" cried Foma; "when I embraced man and wept upon his bosom? But now where am
I? Where am I?"

"You are with us, Foma, calm yourself," cried my uncle.
"This is what I wanted to say to you, Foma. . . ."

"You might at least keep silent now," hissed Miss Perepelitsyn, with a spiteful gleam in her viperish eyes.

"Where am I?" Foma went on. "Who are about me?
They are bulls and buffaloes turning their horns against
me. Life, what art thou? If one lives one is dishonoured,
disgraced, humbled, crushed; and when the earth is scattered
on one's coffin, only then men will remember one and pile a
monument on one's poor bones!"

"Holy saints, he is talking about monuments!" whispered
Yezhevikin, clasping his hands.

"Oh, do not put up a monument to me," cried Foma,
"do not! I don't need monuments. Raise up a monument
to me in your hearts, I want nothing more, nothing, nothing more!"

"Foma," my uncle interposed, "enough, calm yourself!
There is no need to talk about monuments. Only listen.
You see, Foma, I understand that you were perhaps, so to
say, inspired with righteous fervour when you reproached
me, but you were carried away, Foma, beyond the limit of
righteousness—I assure you you were mistaken, Foma. . . ."

"Oh, will you give over?" hissed Miss Perepelitsyn again. "Do you want to murder the poor man because he is in your hands? . . ."

After Miss Perepelitsyn, Madame la Générale made a stir, and all her suite followed her example; they all waved their hands at my uncle to stop him.

"Anna Nilovna, be silent yourself, I know what I am saying!" my uncle answered firmly. "This is a sacred matter! A question of honour and justice. Foma! you are a sensible man, you must at once ask the forgiveness of the virtuous young lady whom you have insulted."

"What young lady? What young lady have I insulted?" Foma articulated in amazement, staring round at every one as though he had entirely forgotten everything that had happened, and did not know what was the matter.

"Yes, Foma; and if now of your own accord you frankly acknowledge you have done wrong, I swear, Foma, I will fall at your feet and then . . ."

"Whom have I insulted?" wailed Foma. "What young lady? Where is she? Where is the young lady? Recall to me something about the young lady! . . ."

At that instant, Nastenka, confused and frightened, went up to Yegor Ilyitch and pulled him by his sleeve.

"No, Yegor Ilyitch, leave him alone, there is no need of an apology. What is the object of it all?" she said in an imploring voice. "Give it up!"

"Ah, now I begin to remember," cried Foma. "My God, I understand. Oh, help me, help me to remember!" he implored, apparently in great excitement. "Tell me, is it true that I was turned out of this house, like the mangiest of curs? Is it true that I was struck by lightning? Is it true that I was kicked down the steps? Is it true? Is it true?"

The weeping and wailing of the fair sex were the most eloquent reply to Foma Fomitch.

"Yes, yes," he repeated, "I remember . . . I remember now that after the lightning and my fall I was running here, pursued by the thunder, to do my duty and then vanish for ever! Raise me up! Weak as I may be now, I must do my duty."

He was at once helped up from his chair. Foma stood in the attitude of an orator and stretched out his hands.

"Colonel," he cried, "now I have quite recovered. The thunder has not extinguished my intellectual capacities; it has left, it is true, a deafness in my right ear, due perhaps not so much to the thunder as to my fall down the steps, but what of that? And what does any one care about Foma's right ear!"

Foma threw such a wealth of mournful irony into these last words, and accompanied them with such a pathetic smile, that the groans of the deeply moved ladies resounded again. They all looked with reproach, and some also with fury, at my uncle, who was beginning to be crushed by so unanimous an expression of public opinion. Mizintchikov, with a curse, walked away to the window. Bahtcheyev kept prodding me more and more violently with his elbow; he could hardly stand still.

"Now listen to my whole confession!" yelled Foma, turning upon all a proud and determined gaze, "and at the same time decide the fate of poor Opiskin! Yegor Ilyitch, for a long time past I have been watching over you, watching over you with a tremor at my heart, and I have seen everything, everything, while you were not suspecting that I was watching over you. Colonel! Perhaps I was mistaken, but I knew your egoism, your boundless vanity, your phenomenal sensuality, and who would blame me for trembling for the honour of an innocent young person?"

"Foma, Foma! . . . you need not enlarge on it, Foma," cried my uncle, looking uneasily at Nastenka's suffering face.

"What troubled me was not so much the innocence and trustfulness of the person in question as her inexperience," Foma went on, as though he had not heard my uncle's warning. "I saw that a tender feeling was blossoming in her heart, like a rose in spring and I could not help recalling Petrarch's saying, 'Innocence is often but a hair's breadth from ruin.' I sighed, I groaned, and though I was ready to shed the last drop of my blood to safeguard that pure pearl of maidenhood, who could answer to me for you, Yegor

Ilyitch? I know the unbridled violence of your passions, and knowing that you are ready to sacrifice everything for their momentary gratification, I was plunged in the depths of alarm and apprehension for the fate of the noblest of girls. . . ."

"Foma! Could you really imagine such a thing?" cried my uncle.

"With a shudder at my heart I watched over you. And if you want to know what I have been suffering, go to Shakespeare: in his *Hamlet* he describes the state of my soul. I became suspicious and terrible. In my anxiety, in indignation, I saw everything in the blackest colour and that not the 'black colour' sung of in the well-known song—I can assure you. That was the cause of the desire you saw in me to remove *her* far away from this house: I wanted to save her; that was why you have seen me of late irritable and bitter against the whole human race. Oh! who will reconcile me with humanity? I feel that I was perhaps over-exacting and unjust to your guests, to your nephew, to Mr. Bahtcheyev, when I expected from him a knowledge of astronomy; but who will blame me for my state of mind at the time? Going to Shakespeare again, I may say that the future looked to my imagination like a gloomy gulf of unfathomed depth with a crocodile lying at the bottom. I felt that it was my duty to prevent disaster, that I was destined, appointed for that purpose—and what happened? You did not understand the generous impulse of my heart, and have been repaying me all this time with anger, with ingratitude, with jeers, with slights . . ."

"Foma! If that is so . . . of course I feel . . ." cried my uncle, in extreme agitation.

"If you really do feel it, Colonel, be so kind as to listen and not interrupt me. I will continue. My whole fault lay in the fact, therefore, that I was too much troubled over the fate and the happiness of this child; for compared with you she is a child. It was the truest love for humanity that turned me all this time into a fiend of wrath and suspicion. I was ready to fall on people and tear them to pieces. And you know, Yegor Ilyitch, all your actions as though of design, made me more suspicious every hour, and confirmed my fears. You know, Yegor Ilyitch, when you showered your gold upon me yesterday to drive me from you, I thought: 'He's driving away in my person his conscience, so as more easily to perpetrate this wickedness. . . .'"

"Foma, Foma, can you have thought that yesterday?" my uncle cried out with horror. "Merciful heavens! and I hadn't the faintest suspicion . . ."

"Heaven itself inspired those suspicions," Foma went on. "And judge for yourself: what could I suppose when chance led me that very evening to that fatal seat in the garden? What were my feelings at that moment—oh, my God!— when I saw with my own eyes that all my suspicions were justified in the most flagrant manner? But I had still one hope left, a faint one indeed, but still it was a hope, and— this morning you shattered it into dust and ashes! You sent me your letter, you alleged your intention to marry; you besought me not to make it public. . . . 'But why?' I wondered. 'Why did he write now after I have found him out and not before? Why did he not run to me before, happy and comely—for love adorns the countenance—why did he not fly to my embrace, why did he not weep upon my bosom tears of infinite bliss and tell me all about it, all about it?' Or am I a crocodile who would have devoured you instead of giving you good advice? Or am I some loathsome beetle who would only have bitten you and not assisted your happiness? 'Am I his friend or the most repulsive of insects?' that was the question I asked myself this morning. 'With what object,' I asked myself, 'with what object did he invite his nephew from Petersburg and try to betroth him to this girl, if not to deceive us and his *frivolous* nephew, and meanwhile in secret to persist in his criminal designs?' Yes, Colonel, if any one confirmed in me the thought that your mutual love was criminal, it was you yourself and you only! What is more, you have behaved like a criminal to this young girl; for through your tactlessness and selfish mistrustfulness you have exposed her, a modest and high-principled girl, to slander and odious suspicions."

My uncle stood silent with bowed head, Foma's eloquence was evidently getting the better of his convictions, and he was beginning to regard himself as a complete criminal. Madame la Générale and her followers were listening to Foma in awestruck silence, while Miss Perepelitsyn looked with spiteful triumph at poor Nastenka.

"Overwhelmed, nervously exhausted and shattered," Foma went on, "I locked myself in this morning and prayed, and the Lord showed me the right path. At last I decided: for the last time and publicly to put you to the test. I may have gone about it with too much fervour, I may have given way too much to my indignation; but for my well-meaning effort, you flung me out of the window! As I fell out of the window I thought to myself: 'This is how virtue is rewarded all the world over.' Then I struck the earth, and I scarcely remember what happened to me afterwards."

Shrieks and groans interrupted Foma Fomitch at this tragic recollection. Madame la Générale made a dash at him with a bottle of Malaga in her hand, which she had just snatched from Praskovya Ilyinitchna, but Foma majestically waved aside the hand and the Malaga and Madame la Générale herself.

"Let me alone," he shouted; "I must finish. What happened after my fall—I don't know. I know one thing only, that now, wet through and on the verge of fever, I am standing here to secure your mutual happiness. Colonel! From many signs which I do not wish now to particularize, I am convinced at last that your love was pure and even exalted, though at the same time criminally distrustful. Beaten, humiliated, suspected of insulting a young lady in defence of whose honour I am ready like a mediaeval knight to shed the last drop of my blood I have made up my mind to show you how Foma Opiskin revenges an injury. Give me your hand, Colonel!"

"With pleasure, Foma!" cried my uncle. "And since you have now fully cleared the honour of this young lady from every aspersion, why . . . of course . . . here is my hand, Foma, together with my regrets. . . ."

And my uncle gave him his hand warmly, not yet suspecting what was to come of it.

"Give me your hand too," went on Foma in a faint voice, parting the crowd of ladies who were pressing round him and appealing to Nastenka.

Nastenka was taken aback and confused, she looked timidly at Foma.

"Approach, approach, my sweet child! It is essential for your happiness," Foma added caressingly, still holding my uncle's hand in his.

"What's he up to now?" said Mizintchikov.

Nastenka, frightened and trembling, went slowly up to Foma and timidly held out her hand.

Foma took her hand and put it in my uncle's.

"I join your hands and bless you," he pronounced in the most solemn voice. "And if the blessing of a poor sorrow-stricken sufferer may avail you, be happy. This is how Foma Opiskin takes his revenge! Hurrah!"

The amazement of every one was immense. The conclusion was so unexpected that every one was struck dumb. Madame la Générale stood rooted to the spot, with her mouth open and the bottle of Malaga in her hand. Miss Perepelitsyn turned pale and trembled with fury. The lady companions clasped their hands and sat petrified in their seats. My uncle trembled and tried to say something, but could not. Nastya turned deathly pale and timidly murmured that "it could not be" . . . but it was too late. Bahtcheyev was the first—we must do him that credit—to second Foma's hurrah. I followed suit, and after me Sashenka shouted at the top of her ringing voice as she flew to embrace her father; then Ilyusha joined in, then Yezhevikin, and last of all Mizintchikov.

"Hurrah!" Foma cried once more; "hurrah! And on your knees, children of my heart, on your knees before the tenderest of mothers! Ask her blessing, and if need be I will kneel before her by your side. . . ."

My uncle and Nastya, not looking at each other, and seeming not to understand what was being done to them, fell on their knees before Madame la Générale, the whole company flocked round them; but the old lady seemed to be stupefied, not knowing what to do. Foma came to the rescue at this juncture too; he plumped down himself before his patroness. This at once dispelled all her hesitation. Dissolving into tears, she said at last that she consented. My uncle jumped up and clasped Foma in his arms.

"Foma, Foma! . . ." he began, but his voice broke and he could not go on.

"Champagne!" bawled Mr. Bahtcheyev. "Hurrah!"

"No, sir, not champagne," Miss Perepelitsyn caught him up. She had by now recovered herself, and realized the position and at the same time its consequences. "Put up a candle to God, pray to the holy image and bless with the holy image, as is done by all godly people. . . ."

At once all flew to carry out the sage suggestion; a fearful bustle followed. They had to light the candle. Mr. Bahtcheyev drew up a chair and got up on it to put the candle before the holy image, but immediately broke the chair and came down heavily on the floor—still on his feet, however. Not in the least irritated by this, he at once respectfully made way for Miss Perepelitsyn. The slender Miss Perepelitsyn had done the job in a flash: the candle was lighted. The nun and the lady companions began crossing themselves and bowing down to the ground. They took down the image of the Saviour and carried it to Madame la Générale. My uncle and Nastya went down on their knees again and the ceremony was carried out under the pious instructions of Miss Perepelitsyn, who was saying every minute: "Bow down to her feet, kiss the image, kiss your mamma's hand." Mr. Bahtcheyev thought himself bound to kiss the image after the betrothed couple, and at the same time he kissed the hand of Madame la Générale.

"Hurrah!" he shouted again. "Come, now, we will have some champagne."

Every one, however, was delighted. Madame la Générale was weeping, but it was now with tears of joy. Foma's blessing had at once made the union sanctified and suitable, and what mattered most to her was that Foma Fomitch had distinguished himself and that now he would remain with her for ever. All the lady companions, in appearance at least, shared the general satisfaction. My uncle at one moment was on his knees kissing his mother's hands, at the next was flying to embrace me, Bahtcheyev, Mizintchikov and Yezhevikin. Ilyusha he almost smothered in his embraces. Sasha ran to hug and kiss Nastenka. Praskovya Ilyinitchna dissolved into tears. Bahtcheyev, noticing this, went up to kiss her hand. Poor old Yezhevikin was completely overcome, he was weeping in a corner and was wiping his eyes with the same check handkerchief. In another corner Gavrila was whimpering and gazing reverently at Foma Fomitch, and Falaley was sobbing loudly and going up to each of the company in turn, kissing his hand. All were overwhelmed with feeling; no one yet had begun to talk, or explain things; it seemed as though everything had been said; nothing was heard but joyful exclamations. No one understood yet how all this had been so quickly arranged. They knew one thing only, that it had all been arranged by Foma Fomitch, and that this was a solid fact which could not be changed.

But not five minutes had passed after the general rejoicing when suddenly Tatyana Ivanovna made her appearance among us. In what way, by what intuition, could she, sitting in her own room upstairs, have so quickly divined love and marriage below? She fluttered in with a radiant face, with tears of joy in her eyes, in a fascinating and elegant get-up (she had had time to change her dress before coming down), and flew straight to embrace Nastenka with loud exclamations.

"Nastenka, Nastenka! You loved him and I did not know!" she cried. "Goodness! They loved each other, they suffered in silence! They have been persecuted. What a romance! Nastya, darling, tell me the whole truth: do you really love this crazy fellow?"

By way of reply Nastya hugged and kissed her.

"My goodness, what a fascinating romance!" And Tatyana Ivanovna clapped her hands in delight. "Nastya, listen, my angel: all these men, all, every one, are ungrateful wretches, monsters, and not worthy of our love. But perhaps he is the best of them. Come to me, you crazy fellow!" she cried, addressing my uncle and clutching him by the arm. "Are you really in love? Are you really capable of loving? Look at me, I want to look into your eyes, I want to see whether those eyes are lying or not? No, no, they are not lying; there is the light of love in them. Oh, how happy I am! Nastenka, my dear, you are not rich—I shall make you a present of thirty thousand roubles. Take it, for God's sake. I don't want it, I don't want it; I shall have plenty left. No, no, no," she cried, waving her hand as she saw Nastenka was meaning to refuse. "Don't you speak, Yegor Ilyitch, it is not your affair. No, Nastya, I had made up my mind already to give you the money; I have been wanting to make you a present for a long time, and was only waiting for you to be in love. . . . I shall see your happiness. You will wound me if you don't take it; I shall cry, Nastya. No, no, no and no!"

Tatyana Ivanovna was so overjoyed that for the moment at least it was impossible, it would have been a pity indeed, to cross her. They could not bring themselves to do it, but put it off. She flew to kiss Madame la Générale, Miss Perepelitsyn and all of us. Mr. Bahtcheyev squeezed his way up to her very respectfully and asked to kiss her hand.

"My dear, good girl! Forgive an old fool like me for what happened this morning. I didn't know what a heart of gold you had."

"Crazy fellow! I know you," Tatyana Ivanovna lisped with gleeful playfulness. She gave Mr. Bahtcheyev a flick on the nose with her glove, and swishing against him with her gorgeous skirts, fluttered away like a zephyr.

The fat man stepped aside respectfully.

"A very worthy young lady!" he said with feeling. "They have stuck a nose on to the German! You know!" he whispered to me confidentially, looking at me joyfully.

"What nose? What German?" I asked in surprise.

"Why, the one I ordered, the German kissing his lady's hand while she is wiping away a tear with her handkerchief. Only yesterday my Yevdokem mended it; and when we came back from our expedition this morning I sent a man on horseback to fetch it. . . . They will soon be bringing it. A superb thing."

"Foma!" cried my uncle in a frenzy of delight. "It is you who have made our happiness. How can I reward you?"

"Nohow, Colonel," replied Foma, with a sanctimonious air. *"Continue to pay no attention to me* and be happy without Foma."

He was evidently piqued; in the general rejoicing he seemed, as it were, forgotten.

"It is all due to our joy, Foma," cried my uncle. "I don't know whether I am on my head or my feet. Listen, Foma, I have insulted you. My whole blood is not enough to atone for my wrong to you, and that is why I say nothing and do not even beg your pardon. But if ever you have need of my head, my life, if you ever want some one to throw himself over a precipice for your sake, call upon me, and you shall see. . . . I will say nothing more, Foma."

And my uncle waved his hand, fully recognizing the impossibility of adding anything that could more strongly express his feeling. He only gazed at Foma with grateful eyes full of tears.

"See what an angel he is!" Miss Perepelitsyn piped in her turn in adulation of Foma.

"Yes, yes," Sashenka put in, "I did not know you were such a good man, Foma Fomitch, and I was disrespectful to you. But forgive me, Foma Fomitch, and you may be sure I will love you with all my heart. If you knew how much I respect you now!"

"Yes, Foma," Bahtcheyev chimed in. "Forgive an old fool like me too. I didn't know you, I didn't know you. You are not merely a learned man, Foma, but also—simply a hero. My whole house is at your service. But there, the best of all would be, if you would come to me the day after to-morrow, old man, with Madame la Générale too, and the betrothed couple—the whole company, in fact. And we will have a dinner, I tell you. I won't praise it beforehand, but one thing I can say, you will find everything you want unless it is bird's milk. I give you my word of honour."

In the midst of these demonstrations, Nastenka, too, went up to Foma Fomitch and without further words warmly embraced him and kissed him.

"Foma Fomitch," she said, "you have been a true friend to us, you have done so much for us, that I don't know how to repay you for it all; but I only know that I will be for you a most tender and respectful sister. . . ."

She could say no more, she was choked by tears. Foma kissed her on the head and grew tearful.

"My children, the children of my heart," he said. "Live and prosper, and in moments of happiness think sometimes of the poor exile. For myself, I will only say that misfortune is perhaps the mother of virtue. That, I believe, is said by Gogol, a frivolous writer; but from whom one may sometimes glean fruitful thoughts. Exile is a misfortune. I shall wander like a pilgrim with my staff over the face of the earth, and who knows?—perchance my troubles will make me more righteous yet! That thought is the one consolation left me!"

"But . . . where are you going, Foma?" my uncle asked in alarm.

All were startled, and pressed round Foma.

"Why, do you suppose I can remain in your house after your behaviour this morning?" Foma inquired with extraordinary dignity.

But he was not allowed to finish, outcries from all the company smothered his voice. They made him sit down in an easy-chair, they besought him, they shed tears over him, and I don't know what they didn't do. Of course he hadn't the faintest intention of leaving "this house," just as he had not earlier that morning, nor the day before, nor on the occasion when he had taken to digging in the garden. He knew now that they would reverently detain him, would clutch at him, especially since he had made them all happy, since they all had faith in him again and were ready to carry him on their shoulders and to consider it an honour and a happiness to do so. But most likely his cowardly return, when he was frightened by the storm, was rankling in his mind and egging him on to play the hero in some way. And above all, there was such a temptation to give himself airs; the opportunity of talking, of using fine phrases and laying it on thick, of blowing his own trumpet, was too good for any possibility of resisting the temptation. He did not resist it; he tore himself out of the grasp of those who held him. He asked for his staff, besought them to let him have his freedom, to let him wander out into the wide, wide world, declared that in *that house* he had been dishonoured, beaten, that he had only come back to make every one happy, and, he asked, could he remain in this "house of ingratitude and eat soup, sustaining, perhaps, but seasoned with blows"? At last he left off struggling. He was reseated in his chair, but his eloquence was not arrested.

"Have I not been insulted here?" he cried. "Have I not been taunted? Haven't you, you yourself, Colonel, have you not every hour pointed the finger of scorn and made the long nose of derision at me, like the ignorant children of the working-class in the streets of the town? Yes, Colonel, I insist on that comparison, because if you have not done so physically it has yet been a moral long nose, and in some cases a moral long nose is more insulting than a physical one. I say nothing of blows. . . ."

"Foma, Foma," cried my uncle, "do not crush me with these recollections. I have told you already that all my blood is not enough to wash out the insults. Be magnanimous! Forgive, forget, and remain to contemplate our happiness! Your work, Foma . . ."

"I want to love my fellow-man, to love him," cried Foma, "and they won't give me him, they forbid me to love him, they take him from me. Give me, give me my fellow-man that I may love him! Where is that fellow-man? Where is he hidden? Like Diogenes with his candle, I have been looking for him all my life and cannot find him; and I can love no one, to this day I cannot find the man. Woe to him who has made me a hater of mankind! I cry: Give me my fellow-man that I may love him, and they thrust Falaley upon me! Am I to love Falaley? Do I want to love Falaley? Could I love Falaley, even if I wanted to? No. Why not? Because he is Falaley. Why do I not love humanity? Because all on earth are Falaleys or like Falaley. I don't want Falaley, I hate Falaley, I spit on Falaley, I trample Falaley under my feet. And if I had to choose I would rather love Asmodeus than Falaley. Come here, come here, my everlasting torment, come here," he cried, suddenly addressing Falaley, who was in the most innocent way standing on tiptoe, looking over the crowd that was surrounding Foma Fomitch.

"Come here. I will show you, Colonel," cried Foma, drawing towards him Falaley, who was almost unconscious with terror, "I will show you the truth of my words about the everlasting long nose and finger of scorn! Tell me, Falaley, and tell the truth: what did you dream about last night? Come, Colonel, you will see your handiwork! Come, Falaley, tell us!"

The poor boy, shaking with terror, turned despairing eyes about him, looking for some one to rescue him; but every one was in a tremor waiting for his answer.

"Come, Falaley, I am waiting."

Instead of answering, Falaley screwed up his face, opened his mouth wide, and began bellowing like a calf.

"Colonel! Do you see this stubbornness? Do you mean to tell me it's natural? For the last time I ask you, Falaley, tell me: what did you dream of last night?"

"O-of . . ."

"Say you dreamed of me," said Bahtcheyev.

"Of your virtue, sir," Yezhevikin prompted in his other ear.

Falaley merely looked about him.

"O-of . . . of your vir . . . of a white bu-ull," he roared at last, and burst into scalding tears.

Every one groaned. But Foma Fomitch was in a paroxysm of extraordinary magnanimity.

"Anyway, I see your sincerity, Falaley," he said. "A sincerity I do not observe in others. God bless you! If you are purposely mocking at me with that dream at the instigation of others, God will repay you and those others. If not, I respect your truthfulness; for even in the lowest of creatures like you it is my habit to discern the image and semblance of God. . . . I forgive you, Falaley. Embrace me, my children. I will remain with you."

"He will remain!" they all cried in delight.

"I will remain and I will forgive. Colonel, reward Falaley with some sugar, do not let him cry on such a day of happiness for all."

I need hardly say that such magnanimity was thought astounding. To take *so much* thought at *such* a moment and for whom? For Falaley. My uncle flew to carry out his instruction in regard to the sugar. Immediately a silver sugar-basin—I don't know where it came from—appeared in the hands of Praskovya Ilyinitchna. My uncle was about to take out two pieces with a trembling hand, then three, then he dropped them, at last, seeing he was incapable of doing anything from excitement.

"Ah!" he cried, "for a day like this! Hold out your coat, Falaley," and he poured into his coat all the contents of the sugar-basin. "That's for your truthfulness," he said, by way of edification.

"Mr. Korovkin!" Vidoplyasov announced, suddenly appearing in the doorway.

A slight flutter of consternation followed—Korovkin's visit was obviously ill-timed. They all looked inquiringly at my uncle.

"Korovkin!" cried my uncle, in some embarrassment. "Of course I am delighted . . ." he added, glancing timidly towards Foma; "but really I don't know whether to ask him in at such a moment. What do you think, Foma?"

"Oh, yes, why not," said Foma amicably. "Invite Korovkin too; let him, too, share in the general rejoicing."

In short, Foma Fomitch was in an angelic frame of mind.

"I most respectfully make bold to inform you," observed Vidoplyasov, "that the gentleman is not quite himself."

"Not quite himself? How? What nonsense are you talking?" cried my uncle.

"It is so, indeed; he is not quite in a sober condition."

But before my uncle had time to open his mouth, flush red, and show his alarm and extreme embarrassment, the mystery was explained. Korovkin appeared in the doorway, pushed Vidoplyasov aside and confronted the astonished company. He was a short, thickset gentleman of forty, with dark hair touched with grey and closely cropped, with a round purple face and little bloodshot eyes, wearing a high horsehair cravat, fastened at the back with a buckle, an extraordinarily threadbare swallow-tail coat covered with fluff and hay and disclosing a bad rent under the arm, and unspeakable trousers, and carrying an incredibly greasy cap which he was holding out at arm's length. This gentleman was completely drunk. Advancing into the middle of the room, he stood still, staggering, nodding his head as though he were pecking at something with his nose in drunken hesitation; then he slowly grinned from ear to ear.

"Excuse me, ladies and gentlemen," he began, "I . . . er . . ." (here he gave a tug at his collar) "got 'em!"

Madame la Générale immediately assumed an air of offended dignity. Foma, sitting in his easy-chair, ironically looked the eccentric visitor up and down. Bahtcheyev stared at him in perplexity, through which some sympathy was, however, apparent. My uncle's embarrassment was incredible; he was deeply distressed on Korovkin's account.

"Korovkin," he began. "Listen."

"Attendez!" Korovkin interrupted him. "Let me introduce myself: a child of nature. . . . But what do I see? There are ladies here. . . . Why didn't you tell me, you rascal, that you had ladies here?" he added with a roguish smile. "Never mind! Don't be shy. Let us be presented to the fair sex. Charming ladies," he began, articulating with difficulty and stumbling over every word, "you see a luckless mortal . . . who . . . and so on. . . . The rest must remain unsaid. . . . Musicians! A polka!"

"Wouldn't you like a nap?" asked Mizintchikov, quietly going up to Korovkin.

"A nap? You say that to insult me?"

"Not at all. You know a little sleep is a good thing after a journey. . . ."

"Never!" Korovkin answered with indignation. "Do you

think I am drunk?—not a bit. But where do they sleep here?"

"Come along, I'll take you at once."

"Where? In the coach-house? No, my lad, you won't take me in! I have spent a night there already. . . . Lead the way, though. Why not go along with a good fellow. . . . I don't want a pillow. A military man does not want a pillow. . . . But you produce a sofa for me, old man . . . a sofa. And, I say," he added, stopping, "I see you are a jolly fellow; produce something else for me . . . you know? A bit of the rummy, enough to drown a fly in, only enough for that, only one little glass, I mean."

"Very well, very well!" answered Mizintchikov.

"Very well. But you wait a bit, I must say good-bye. *Adieu, mesdames* and *mesdemoiselles*. You have, so to speak, smitten . . . But there, never mind! We will talk about that afterwards . . . only do wake me when it begins . . . or even five minutes before it begins . . . don't begin without me! Do you hear. Don't begin! . . ."

And the merry gentleman vanished behind Mizintchikov.

Every one was silent. The company had not got over their astonishment. At last Foma without a word began noiselessly chuckling, his laughter grew into a guffaw. Seeing that, Madame la Générale, too, was amused, though the expression of insulted dignity still remained on her face. Irrepressible laughter arose on all sides. My uncle stood as though paralyzed, flushing almost to tears, and was for some time incapable of uttering a word.

"Merciful heavens!" he brought out at last. "Who could have known this? But you know . . . you know it might happen to any one. Foma, I assure you that he is a most straightforward, honourable man, and an extremely well-read man too, Foma . . . you will see! . . ."

"I do see, I do see," cried Foma, shaking with laughter; "extraordinarily well-read. Well-read is just the word."

"How he can talk about railways!" Yezhevikin observed in an undertone.

"Foma," my uncle was beginning, but the laughter of all

the company drowned his words. Foma Fomitch was simply
in fits, and looking at him, my uncle began laughing too.

"Well, what does it matter?" he said enthusiastically.
"You are magnanimous, Foma, you have a great heart; you
have made me happy . . . you forgive Korovkin too."

Nastenka was the only one who did not laugh. She
looked with eyes full of love at her future husband, and
looked as though she would say—

"How splendid, how kind you are, the most generous of
men, and how I love you!"

Conclusion

VI

Foma's triumph was complete and beyond attack. Certainly
without him nothing would have been settled, and the accomplished fact stifled all doubts and objections. The gratitude of those he had made happy was beyond all bounds.
My uncle and Nastya waved me off when I attempted to
drop a faint hint at the process by which Foma's consent to
their marriage had been obtained. Sashenka cried: "Good,
kind Foma Fomitch; I will embroider him a cushion in
wool-work!" and even reproached me for my hard-heartedness. I believe that Bahtcheyev in the fervour of his conver-
sion would have strangled me if I had ventured to say
anything disrespectful about Foma Fomitch. He followed
Foma about like a little dog, gazed at him with devout reverence, and at every word the latter uttered he would exclaim: "You are a noble man, Foma. You are a learned
man, Foma." As for Yezhevikin, he was highly delighted.
The old man had for a long time past seen that Nastenka
had turned Yegor Ilyitch's head, and from that time forward his one dream, waking and sleeping, was to bring
about this marriage. He had clung to the idea to the last,
and had only given it up when it had been impossible not

to do so. Foma had changed the aspect of the affair. I need hardly say that in spite of his delight the old man saw through Foma; in short, it was clear that Foma Fomitch would be supreme in that household for ever, and that there would be no limit to his despotism. We all know that even the most unpleasant and ill-humoured people are softened, if only for a time, when their desires are gratified. Foma Fomitch, on the contrary, seemed to grow stupider when he was successful, and held his nose higher in the air than ever. Just before dinner, having changed all his clothes, he settled down in an arm-chair, summoned my uncle, and in the presence of the whole family began giving him another lecture.

"Colonel," he began, "you are about to enter upon holy matrimony. Do you realize the obligation . . ."

And so on and so on. Imagine ten pages of the size of the *Journal des Débats,* of the smallest print, filled with the wildest nonsense, in which there was absolutely nothing dealing with the duties of marriage, but only the most shameful eulogies of the intellect, mildness, magnanimity, manliness and disinterestedness of himself, Foma Fomitch. Every one was hungry, they all wanted their dinners; but in spite of that no one dared to protest, and every one heard the twaddle reverently to the end. Even Bahtcheyev, in spite of his ravenous appetite, sat without stirring, absolutely respectful. Gratified by his own eloquence, Foma Fomitch grew livelier, and even drank rather heavily at dinner, proposing the most extraordinary toasts. He proceeded to display his wit by being jocose, at the expense of the happy pair, of course. Everybody laughed and applauded. But some of the jokes were so gross and suggestive that even Bahtcheyev was embarrassed by them. At last Nastenka jumped up from the table and ran away, to the indescribable delight of Foma Fomitch, but he immediately pulled himself up. Briefly but in strong terms he dwelt upon Nastenka's virtues, and proposed a toast to the health of the absent one. My uncle, who a minute before had been embarrassed and unhappy, was ready to hug Foma Fomitch again. Altogether the betrothed pair seemed somewhat ashamed of each other and their happiness—and I noticed that they had not said one word to each other from the time of the blessing, they even seemed to avoid looking at one another. When they got up from dinner, my uncle vanished, I don't know where. I strolled out on to the terrace to look for him. There I found Foma sitting in an easy-chair, drinking coffee and holding forth, extremely exhila-rated. Only Yezhevikin, Bahtcheyev and Mizintchikov were by him. I stopped to listen.

"Why," asked Foma, "am I ready at this moment to go through fire for my convictions? And why is it that none of you are capable of going through fire? Why is it? Why is it?"

"Well, but it's unnecessary, Foma Fomitch, to go through fire," Yezhevikin said banteringly. "Why, what's the sense of it? In the first place it would hurt, and in the second it would burn—what would be left?"

"What would be left? Noble ashes would be left. But how should you understand, how should you appreciate me? To you, no great men exist but perhaps some Caesar or Alexander of Macedon. And what did your Caesars do? Whom did they make happy? What did your vaunted Alex-ander of Macedon do? He conquered the whole earth? But give me such a phalanx and I could be a conqueror too, and so could you, and so could he. . . . On the other hand, he killed the virtuous Clitus, but I have not killed the virtu-ous Clitus. . . . A puppy, a scoundrel! He ought to have had a thrashing, and not to have been glorified in universal history . . . and Caesar with him!"

"You might spare Caesar, anyway, Foma Fomitch!"

"I won't spare the fool!" cried Foma.

"No, don't spare him!" Bahtcheyev, who had also been drinking, backed him up. "There is no need to spare them, they are all flighty fellows, they care for nothing but pirou-etting on one leg! Sausage-eaters! Here, one of them was wanting to found a scholarship just now—and what is a scholarship? The devil only knows what it means! I bet it's some new villainy! And here is another who in honourable society is staggering about and asking for rum. I have no objection to drinking. But one should drink and drink and then take a rest, and afterwards, maybe, drink again. It's no good sparing them! They are all scoundrels. You are the only enlightened one among them, Foma!"

If Bahtcheyev surrendered to any one he surrendered unconditionally and absolutely without criticism.

I looked for my uncle in the garden, by the pond in the most secluded spot. He was with Nastenka. Seeing me, Nastenka shot into the bushes as though she were in fault. My uncle came to meet me with a beaming face; there were tears of happiness in his eyes. He took both my hands and warmly pressed them.

"My dear," he said, "I still cannot believe in my happiness. . . . Nastya feels the same. We only marvel and glorify the Almighty. She was crying just now. Would you believe it, I hardly know what I am doing yet, I am still utterly beside myself, and don't know whether to believe it or not! And why has this come to me? Why? What have I done? How have I deserved it?"

"If any one deserves anything, it is you, uncle," I said with conviction. "I have never seen such an honest, such a fine, such a kind-hearted man as you."

"No, Seryozha, no, it is too much," he answered, as it were with regret. "What is bad, is that we are kind (I am talking only about myself really) when we are happy; but when we are unhappy it is best not to come near us! Nastenka and I were only just talking of that. Though I was dazzled by Foma, up to this very day perhaps, would you believe it, I did not quite believe in him, though I did assure you of his perfection; even yesterday I did not believe in him when he refused such a present! To my shame I say it. My heart shudders at the memory of this morning, but I could not control myself. . . . When he spoke of Nastya something seemed to stab me to the very heart. I did not understand and behaved like a tiger. . . ."

"Well, uncle, perhaps that was only natural."

My uncle waved away the idea.

"No, no, my boy, don't say so. The fact of it is all this comes from the depravity of my nature, from my being a gloomy and sensual egoist and abandoning myself to my passions without restraint. That's what Foma says." (What could one answer to that?) "You don't know, Seryozha," he went on with deep feeling, "how often I have been irritable, unfeeling, unjust, haughty, and not only to Foma. Now it has all come back to my mind, and I feel ashamed that I have done nothing hitherto to deserve such happiness. Nastya has just said the same thing, though I really don't know what sins she has, as she is an angel, not a human being! She has just been saying that we owe a terrible debt of gratitude to God; that we must try now to be better and always be doing good deeds. . . . And if only you had heard how fervently, how beautifully she said all that! My God, what a wonderful girl!"

He stopped in agitation. A minute later he went on.

"We resolved, my dear boy, to cherish Foma in particular, mamma and Tatyana Ivanovna. Tatyana Ivanovna! What a generous-hearted creature! Oh, how much I have been to blame towards all of them! I have behaved badly to you too. . . . But if any one should dare to insult Tatyana Ivanovna now, oh! then . . . Oh, well, never mind! . . . We must do something for Mizintchikov too."

"Yes, uncle, I have changed my opinion of Tatyana Ivanovna now. One cannot help respecting her and feeling for her."

"Just so, just so," my uncle assented warmly. "One can't help respecting her! Now Korovkin, for instance, no doubt you laugh at him," he added, glancing at me timidly, "and we all laughed at him this afternoon. And yet, you know, that was perhaps unpardonable. . . . You know, he may be an excellent, good-hearted man, but fate . . . he has had misfortunes. . . . You don't believe it, but perhaps it really is so."

"No, uncle, why shouldn't I believe it?"

And I began fervently declaring that even in the creature who has fallen lowest there may still survive the finest human feelings; that the depths of the human soul are unfathomable; that we must not despise the fallen, but on the contrary ought to seek them out and raise them up; that the commonly accepted standard of goodness and morality was not infallible, and so on, and so on; in fact, I warmed up to the subject, and even began talking about the realist school. In conclusion I even repeated the verses: 'When from dark error's subjugation.' . . ."

My uncle was extraordinarily delighted.

"My dear, my dear," he said, much touched, "you understand me fully, and have said much better than I could what I wanted to express. Yes, yes! Good heavens! Why is it man is wicked? Why is it I am so often wicked when it is so splendid, so fine to be good? Nastya was saying the same thing just now. . . . But look, though, what a glorious place this is," he added, looking round him. "What scenery! What a picture! What a tree! Look: you could hardly get your arms round it. What sap! What foliage! What sunshine! How gay everything is, washed clean after the storm! . . . One would think that even the trees understand something, have feeling and enjoyment of life. . . . Is that out of the question—eh? What do you think?"

"It's very likely they do, uncle, in their own way, of course. . . ."

"Oh, yes, in their own way, of course. . . . Marvellous, marvellous is the Creator! You must remember all this garden very well, Seryozha; how you used to race about and play in it when you were little! I remember, you know, when you were little," he added, looking at me with an indescribable expression of love and happiness. "You were not allowed to go to the pond alone. But do you remember one evening dear Katya called you to her and began fondling you. . . . You had been running in the garden just before, and were flushed; your hair was so fair and curly. . . . She kept playing with it, and said: 'It is a good thing that you have taken the little orphan to live with us!' Do you remember?"

"Faintly, uncle."

"It was evening, and you were both bathed in the glow of sunset, I was sitting in a corner smoking a pipe and watching you. . . . I drive in to the town every month to her grave . . ." he added, dropping his voice, which quivered with suppressed tears. "I was just speaking to Nastya about it; she said we would go together. . . ."

My uncle paused, trying to control his emotion. At that instant Vidoplyasov came up to us.

"Vidoplyasov!" said my uncle, starting. "Have you come from Foma Fomitch?"

"No, I have come more on my own affairs."

"Oh, well, that's capital. Now we shall hear about Korovkin. I wanted to inquire. . . . I told him to look after him— Korovkin, I mean. What's the matter, Vidoplyasov?"

"I make bold to remind you," said Vidoplyasov, "that yesterday you were graciously pleased to refer to my petition and to promise me your noble protection from the daily insults I receive."

"Surely you are not harping on your surname again?" cried my uncle in alarm.

"What can I do? Hourly insults . . ."

"Oh, Vidoplyasov, Vidoplyasov! What am I to do with you?" said my uncle in distress. "Why, what insults can you have to put up with? You will simply go out of your mind. You will end your days in a madhouse!"

"I believe I am in my right mind . . ." Vidoplyasov was beginning.

"Oh, of course, of course," my uncle interposed. " I did not say that to offend you, my boy, but for your good. Why, what sort of insults do you complain of? I am ready to bet that it is only some nonsense."

"They won't let me pass."

"Who interferes with you?"

"They all do, and chiefly owing to Matryona. My life is a misery through her. It is well known that all discriminating people who have seen me from my childhood up have said that I am exactly like a foreigner, especially in the features of the face. Well, sir, now they won't let me pass on account of it. As soon as I go by, they all shout all sorts of bad words after me; even the little children, who ought to be whipped, shout after me. . . . As I came along here now they shouted. . . . I can't stand it. Defend me, sir, with your protection!"

"Oh, Vidoplyasov! Well, what did they shout? No doubt it was some foolishness, that you ought not to notice."

"It would not be proper to repeat."

"Why, what was it?"

"It's a disgusting thing to say."

"Well, say it!"

"Grishka the dandy has eaten the candy."

"Tfoo, what a man! I thought it was something serious! You should spit, and pass by."

"I did spit, they shouted all the more."

"But listen, uncle," I said. "You see he complains that he can't get on in this house, send him to Moscow for a time, to that calligrapher. You told me that he was trained by a calligrapher."

"Well, my dear, that man, too, came to a tragic end."

"Why, what happened to him?"

"He had the misfortune," Vidoplyasov replied, "to appropriate the property of another, for which in spite of his talent he was put in prison, where he is ruined irrevocably."

"Very well, Vidoplyasov, calm yourself now, and I will go into it all and set it right," said my uncle, "I promise! Well, what news of Korovkin? Is he asleep?"

"No, sir, his honour has just gone away. I came to tell you."

"What? Gone away! What do you mean? How could you let him go?" cried my uncle.

"Through the kindness of my heart, sir, it was pitiful to see him, sir. When he came to himself and remembered all the proceedings, he struck himself on the forehead and shouted at the top of his voice. . . ."

"At the top of his voice! . . ."

"It would be more respectful to express it, he gave utterance to many varied lamentations. He cried out: how could he present himself now to the fair sex? And then added: 'I am unworthy to be a man!' and he kept talking so pitifully in choice language."

"A man of refined feeling! I told you, Sergey. . . . But how could you let him go, Vidoplyasov, when I told you particularly to look after him? Oh, dear! oh, dear!"

"It was through the pity of my heart. He begged me not to tell you. His cabman fed the horses and harnessed them. And for the sum lent him three days ago, he begged me to thank you most respectfully and say that he would send the money by one of the first posts."

"What money is that, uncle?"

"He mentioned twenty-five silver roubles," answered Vidoplyasov.

"I lent it him at the station, my dear; he hadn't enough with him. Of course he will send it by the first post. . . . Oh, dear, how sorry I am! Shouldn't we send some one to overtake him, Seryozha?"

"No, uncle, better not send."

"I think so too. You see, Seryozha, I am not a philosopher of course, but I believe there is much more good in every man than appears on the surface. Korovkin now; he couldn't face the shame of it. . . . But let us go to Foma! We have lingered here a long time; he may be wounded by our ingratitude, and neglect. . . . Let us go. Oh, Korovkin, Korovkin!"

My story is ended. The lovers were united, and their good genius in the form of Foma Fomitch held undisputed sway. I might at this point make very many befitting observations; but in reality all such observations are now completely superfluous. Such, anyway, is my opinion. I will instead say a few words about the subsequent fortunes of all the heroes of my tale. As is well known, no story is finished without this, and indeed it is prescribed by the rules.

The wedding of the couple who had been so graciously "made happy" took place six weeks after the events I have described. It was a quiet family affair, without much display or superfluous guests. I was Nastenka's best man, Mizintchikov was my uncle's. There were some visitors, however. But the foremost, the leading figure, was of course Foma Fomitch. He was made much of; he was carried on their shoulders. But it somehow happened that on this one occasion he was overcome by champagne. A scene followed, with all the accompaniment of reproaches, lamentations and outcries. Foma ran off to his room, locked himself in, cried that he was held in contempt, that now "new people had come into the family and that he was therefore nothing, not more than a bit of rubbish that must be thrown away." My uncle was in despair; Nastenka wept; Madame la Générale, as usual, had an attack of hysterics. . . . The wedding festival was like a funeral. And seven years of living like that with their benefactor, Foma Fomitch, fell to the lot of my poor uncle and poor Nastenka. Up to the time of his death (Foma Fomitch died a year ago), he was sulky, gave himself airs, was ill-humoured and quarrelsome; but the reverence for him of the couple he had "made happy," far from diminishing, actually increased every day with his caprices. Yegor Ilyitch and Nastenka were so happy with each other that they were actually afraid of their happiness, and thought that God had given them too much; that they were not worthy of such blessings and were inclined to expect that their latter days would be spent in hardship and suffering to atone for them. It will be readily understood that in this meek household, Foma Fomitch could do anything that took his fancy. And what did he not do in those seven years! One could never imagine to what unbridled absurdities his pampered, idle soul led him in inventing the most perverse, morally Sybaritic caprices. My grandmother died three years after my uncle's marriage. Foma was stricken with despair at his bereavement. His condition at the time is described with horror in my uncle's household to this day. When they were throwing earth into the grave, he leapt into it, shouting that he would be buried in it too. For a whole month they would not give him a knife or fork; and on one occasion four of them forced open his mouth and took out of it a pin which he was trying to swallow. An outsider who witnessed the conflict, observed that Foma Fomitch might have swallowed the pin a thousand times over during the struggle, but did not, however, do so. But every one heard this criticism with positive indignation, and at once charged the critic with hard-heartedness and bad manners. Only Nastenka held her peace and gave a faint smile, while my uncle looked at her with some uneasiness.

It must be observed that though Foma gave himself airs, and indulged his whims in my uncle's house as before, yet the insolent and despotic presumption with which he used to rail at my uncle was now a thing of the past. Foma complained, wept, blamed, reproached, cried shame, but did not scold as he had done—there was never another scene like the one concerned with "your Excellency," and this, I think, was due to Nastenka. Almost imperceptibly she compelled Foma to yield some points and to recognize some limits. She would not see her husband humiliated, and insisted on her wishes being respected. Foma perceived clearly that she almost understood him. I say *almost*, for Nastenka, too, humoured Foma and even seconded her husband whenever he sang the praises of his mentor. She tried to make other people, too, respect everything in her husband, and so publicly justified his devotion to Foma Fomitch. But I am sure that Nastenka's pure heart had forgiven all the insults of the past; she forgave Foma everything when he brought about her marriage. And what is more, I believe she seriously with all her heart entered into my uncle's idea that too much must not be expected from a "victim" who had once been a buffoon, but on the contrary, balm must be poured on his wounded heart. Poor Nastenka had herself been one of the *humiliated*, she had suffered and she remembered it. A month after the death of his old patroness, Foma became quieter, even mild and friendly; but on the other hand, he began to have quite sudden attacks of a different sort—he would fall into a sort of magnetic trance, which alarmed every one extremely. Suddenly, for instance, the sufferer, while saying something, or even laughing, would in one instant become unconscious and rigid, and rigid in the very position he happened to be in a moment before the attack. If, for instance, he was laughing, he would remain with a smile on his lips; if he were holding something, a fork for instance, the fork would remain in his raised hand. Later on, of course, the hand would drop, but Foma Fomitch felt nothing and knew nothing of its dropping. He would sit, stare, even blink, but would say nothing, hear nothing, and understand nothing. This would last sometimes for a whole hour. Of course every one in the house nearly died of fright, held their breath, walked about on tiptoe and shed tears. At last Foma would wake up feeling terribly exhausted, and would declare that he had seen and heard absolutely nothing all that time. The man must have been so perverse, so eager to show off, that he endured whole hours of voluntary agony, solely in order to say afterwards: "Look at me, I even feel more intensely than you." Finally Foma cursed my uncle for the "hourly slights and insults" he received from him, and went to stay with Mr. Bahtcheyev. The latter, who had quarrelled with Foma Fomitch many times since my uncle's marriage, but always ended by begging his pardon, on this occasion took the matter up with extraordinary warmth; he welcomed Foma with enthusiasm, stuffed him with good things, and at once resolved on a formal breach with my uncle, and even on lodging a complaint against him. There was a bit of land in dispute between them, though they never disputed about it, for my uncle had yielded all claim to it and had freely given it to Mr. Bahtcheyev. Without saying a word to any one, Mr. Bahtcheyev ordered out his carriage, drove off to the town, there scribbled off a petition and handed it in, appealing to the court to adjudge him the land formally with compensation for loss and damage and so to punish contumacy and robbery. Meanwhile next day Foma Fomitch, getting bored at Mr. Bahtcheyev's, forgave my uncle, who came to apologize, and went back to Stepantchikovo. The wrath of Mr. Bahtcheyev when he returned from the town and did not find Foma was terrible; but three days later, he turned up at Stepantchikovo to apologize, begged my uncle's pardon with tears in his eyes, and quashed his petition. My uncle made the peace between him and Foma Fomitch the same day, and Bahtcheyev followed Foma Fomitch about like a little dog, and again said at every word: "You are a clever fellow, Foma! You are a learned man, Foma!"

Foma Fomitch is now lying in his grave near his old patroness; over him stands an expensive monument of white marble covered with lamentations and eulogistic inscriptions. Yegor Ilyitch and Nastenka sometimes go for a walk to the cemetery to pay reverent homage to his memory. They cannot even now speak of him without great feeling; they recall all his sayings, what he ate, what he liked. His things have been preserved as priceless treasures. Feeling so bereaved, my uncle and Nastya grew even more attached to each other. God has not granted them children; they grieve over this, but dare not repine. Sashenka has long been married to an excellent young man. Ilyusha is studying in Moscow. And so my uncle and Nastya are alone together, and are devoted to each other. Their anxiety over each other is almost morbid. Nastya prays unceasingly. If one of them dies first, I think the other will not survive a week. But God grant them long life. They receive every one with a most cordial welcome, and are ready to share all they have with any one who is unfortunate. Nastenka is fond of reading the lives of the saints, and says with compunction that to do ordinary good work is not enough, that one ought to give everything to the poor and be happy in poverty. But for his concern for Ilyusha and Sashenka, my uncle would have done this long ago, for he always agrees with his wife in everything. Praskovya Ilyinitchna lives with them, and enjoys looking after their comfort; she superintends the management of the place. Mr. Bahtcheyev made her an offer of marriage very soon after my uncle's wedding, but she refused him point-blank. It was concluded from that that she would go into a nunnery, but that did not come off either. There is one striking peculiarity about Praskovya Ilyinitchna's character: the craving to obliterate herself completely for the sake of those she loves, to efface herself continually for them, to watch for their every inclination, to humour all their caprices, to wait upon them and serve them. Now, on the death of her mother, she considers it her duty not to leave her brother, and to take care of Nastenka in every way. Old Yezhevikin is still living, and has taken to visiting his daughter more and more frequently of late. At first he drove my uncle to despair by absenting himself from Stepantchikovo almost entirely and also keeping away his "small fry" (as he called his children). All my uncle's invitations were in vain; he was not so much proud as sensitive and touchy. His over-sensitive amour-propre sometimes approached morbidity. The idea that he, a poor man, should be entertained in a wealthy house from kindness, that he might be regarded as an intrusive and unwelcome guest, was too much for him; he sometimes even declined Nastenka's help, and only accepted what was absolutely essential. From my uncle he would take absolutely nothing. Nastenka was quite mistaken when she told me that time in the garden that her father played the fool for *her sake*. It was true that he was extremely eager at that time to marry Nastenka to Yegor Ilyitch; but he acted as he did simply through an inner craving to give vent to his accumulated malice. The impulse to jeer and mock was in his blood. He posed as the most abject, grovelling flatterer, but at the same time made it perfectly clear that he was only doing this for show; and the more cringing his flattery, the more malignantly and openly apparent was the mockery behind it. It was his way. All his children were successfully placed in the best scholastic establishments in Moscow and Petersburg. But this was only after Nastenka had made it perfectly clear to him that it was being paid for out of her own pocket, that is, out of the thirty thousand given her by Tatyana Ivanovna. That thirty thousand she had actually never taken from Tatyana Ivanovna; but not to grieve and mortify her, they appeased her by promising to appeal to her at any sudden emergency. What they did was this: to satisfy her, considerable sums were borrowed from her on two occasions. But Tatyana Ivanovna died three years ago, and Nastya received her thirty thousand all the same. The death of poor Tatyana Ivanovna was sudden. The whole family were getting ready for a ball given by a neighbour, and she had hardly decked herself out in her ball-dress and put on a fascinating wreath of white roses, when she suddenly felt giddy, sat down in an easy-chair and died. They buried her in the wreath. Nastya was in despair. Tatyana Ivanovna had been cherished and looked after like a little child in the house. She astonished every one by the good sense of her will. Apart from Nastenka's thirty thousand,

her whole fortune of three hundred thousand was devoted
to the education of poor orphan girls and the provision of
a sum of money for each on leaving the institution. In the
year that she died Miss Perpelitsyn was married; on the
death of Madame la Générale she had remained in the family in the hope of ingratiating herself with Tatyana Ivanovna. Meanwhile the petty official who had bought Mishino,
the little village in which our scene with Obnoskin and his
mother over Tatyana Ivanovna took place, was left a
widower. This individual was terribly fond of going to law,
and had six children. Supposing that Miss Perepelitsyn had
money, he began making proposals to her through a third
person and she promptly accepted them. But Miss Perepelitsyn was as poor as a hen, her whole fortune was three
hundred silver roubles, and that was given her by Nastenka
on her wedding day. Now the husband and wife are quarrelling from morning till night. She pulls his children's hair,
and boxes their ears; as for him, she scratches his face (so
people say), and is constantly throwing her superior station as a major's daughter in his face. Mizintchikov has
also established himself. He very sensibly gave up all his
hopes of Tatyana Ivanovna, and began little by little to learn
farming. My uncle recommended him to a wealthy count,
who had an estate of three thousand serfs, sixty miles from
Stepantchikovo, and who occasionally visited his property.
Observing Mizintchikov's abilities, and influenced by my
uncle's recommendation of him, the count offered him the
post of steward on his estate, dismissed his former German
steward, who in spite of the vaunted German honesty
stripped his master like a lime-tree. Five years later the
estate was unrecognizable: the peasants were prosperous;
the farming was developed in ways previously impossible;
the returns were almost doubled; in fact, the new steward
distinguished himself, and was talked of for his abilities as
a farmer all over the province. Great was the amazement
and chagrin of the count when at the end of five years
Mizintchikov insisted on giving up his situation in spite of
all protests and offers of increased salary! The count imagined that he had been lured away by a rival landowner in

his own neighbourhood or in another province. And every one was astonished when, two months after giving up his post, Mizintchikov acquired an excellent estate of a hundred serfs, about thirty miles from the count's, purchased from a hussar, a friend of his who had squandered all his fortune! The hundred serfs he promptly mortgaged, and a year later he had acquired another property of sixty serfs in the neighbourhood. Now he is a landowner, and the management of his estate is unequalled. Every one wonders how he came by the money all at once. Some people shake their heads. But Mizintchikov is perfectly self-possessed, and feels that he is absolutely right. He has sent for his sister from Moscow, the sister who gave him her last three roubles to buy boots when he was setting off for Stepantchikovo—a very sweet girl, no longer in her first youth, gentle and loving, well educated, but extremely timid. She had been all the time dragging out a miserable existence somewhere in Moscow as a companion to some charitable lady. Now she worships her brother, and keeps house for him; she regards his will as law and thinks herself happy. Her brother does not spoil her, he makes her work rather hard, but she does not notice it. She has become a great favourite at Stepantchikovo, and I am told that M. Bahtcheyev is not indifferent to her. He would make her an offer, but is afraid of being refused. We hope, however, to give a fuller account of Mr. Bahtcheyev's doings in another story.

Well, I think I have dealt with all the characters of Stepantchikovo . . . Oh! I had forgotten: Gavrila has greatly aged and completely forgotten his French; Falaley has made a very decent coachman; while poor Vidoplyasov was for many years in a madhouse and, I believe, died there. In a few days I am going to Stepantchikovo, and will certainly inquire about him from my uncle.

1859